PLANET TERRY
Writer: **LENNIE HERMAN** • Penciler: **WARREN KREMER**
Inkers: **JON D'AGOSTINO & VINCE COLLETTA** • Letterer: **GRACE KREMER**
Coloritst: **PETER KREMER**

ROYAL ROY
Writers: **STAN KAY & ANGELO DECESARE** • Penciler: **WARREN KREMER**
Inker: **JACQUELINE ROETTCHER & WARREN KREMER**
Letterer: **GRACE KREMER** • Colorist: **GEORGE ROUSSOS**

TOP DOG
Writer: **LENNIE HERMAN** • Penciler: **WARREN KREMER**
Inker: **JACQUELINE ROETTCHER & WARREN KREMER**
Letterer: **GRACE KREMER** • Colorists: **GEORGE ROUSSOS & PETER KREMER**

WALLY THE WIZARD
Writer/Artist: **BOB BOLLING** • Inker: **JON D'AGOSTINO**
Letterers: **JOE ROSEN & JIM NOVAK** • Colorist: **GEORGE ROUSSOS**

Editor: **SID JACOBSON** • Cover Artist: **WARREN KREMER**
Cover Colorist: **TOM SMITH**

Collection Editor: **MARK D. BEAZLEY** • Assistant Editors: **JOHN DENNING & ALEX STARBUCK**
Editor, Special Projects: **JENNIFER GRÜNWALD** • Senior Editor, Special Projects: **JEFF YOUNGQUIST**
Production: **COLORTEK** • Book Designer: **SPRING HOTELING**
Senior Vice President of Sales: **DAVID GABRIEL**

Editor in Chief: **JOE QUESADA** • Publisher: **DAN BUCKLEY**
Executive Producer: **ALAN FINE**

SPECIAL THANKS TO JASON SMITH

COMICS: ALL-STAR COLLECTION VOL. 2. Contains material originally published in magazine form as PLANET TERRY #3-4, TOP DOG #4-6, WALLY THE WIZARD #3-4 and ROYAL ROY. First printing 2010. ISBN# 978-0-7851-4292-8. Published by MARVEL PUBLISHING, INC., a subsidiary of MARVEL ENTERTAINMENT, INC. OFFICE OF PUBLICATION: 417 5th Avenue, York, NY 10016. Copyright © 1985 and 2010 Marvel Characters, Inc. All rights reserved. $19.99 per copy in the U.S. (GST #R127032852); Canadian Agreement #40668537. All ...cters featured in this issue and the distinctive names and likenesses thereof, and all related indicia are trademarks of Marvel Characters, Inc. No similarity between any of the names, ...cters, persons, and/or institutions in this magazine with those of any living or dead person or institution is intended, and any such similarity which may exist is purely coincidental. ...d in the U.S.A. ALAN FINE, EVP - Office Of The Chief Executive Officer Marvel Entertainment, Inc. & CMO Marvel Characters B.V.; DAN BUCKLEY, Chief Executive Officer and Publisher - Print, ...tion & Digital Media; JIM SOKOLOWSKI, Chief Operating Officer; DAVID GABRIEL, SVP of Publishing Sales & Circulation; DAVID BOGART, SVP of Business Affairs & Talent Management; ...AEL PASCIULLO, VP Merchandising & Communications; JIM O'KEEFE, VP of Operations & Logistics; DAN CARR, Executive Director of Publishing Technology; JUSTIN F. GABRIE, ...tor of Publishing & Editorial Operations; SUSAN CRESPI, Editorial Operations Manager; ALEX MORALES, Publishing Operations Manager; STAN LEE, Chairman Emeritus. For information ...ding advertising in Marvel Comics or on Marvel.com, please contact Ron Stern, VP of Business Development, at rstern@marvel.com. For Marvel subscription inquiries, please call ...17-9158. Manufactured between 12/18/09 and 1/13/10 by R.R. DONNELLEY, INC. (CRAWFORD), CRAWFORDSVILLE, IN, USA.

8 7 6 5 4 3 2 1

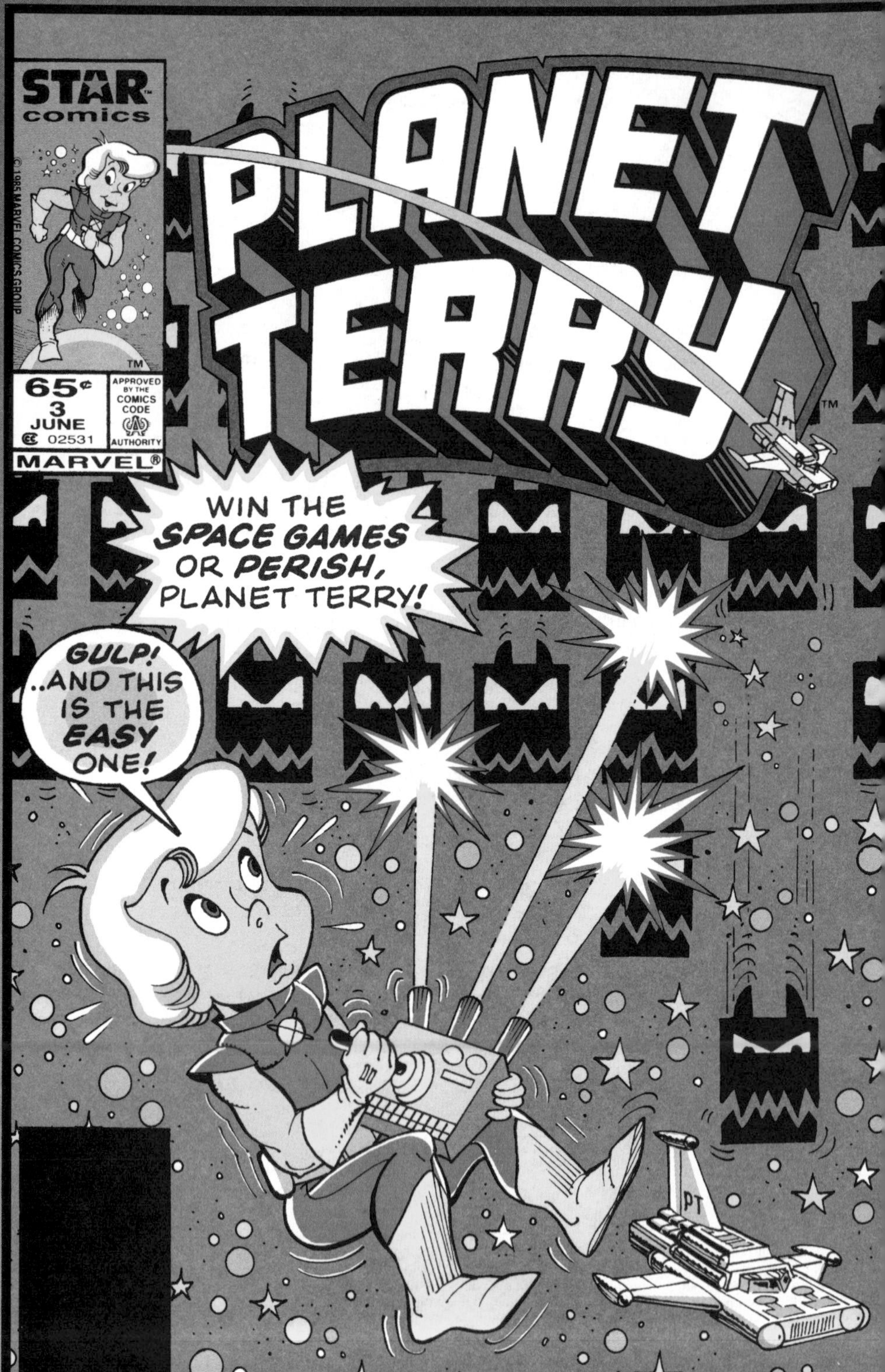
STAR comics
© 1985 MARVEL COMICS GROUP
PLANET TERRY
65¢
3
JUNE
02531
APPROVED BY THE COMICS CODE AUTHORITY
MARVEL®
WIN THE SPACE GAMES OR PERISH, PLANET TERRY!
GULP! ..AND THIS IS THE EASY ONE!
PT

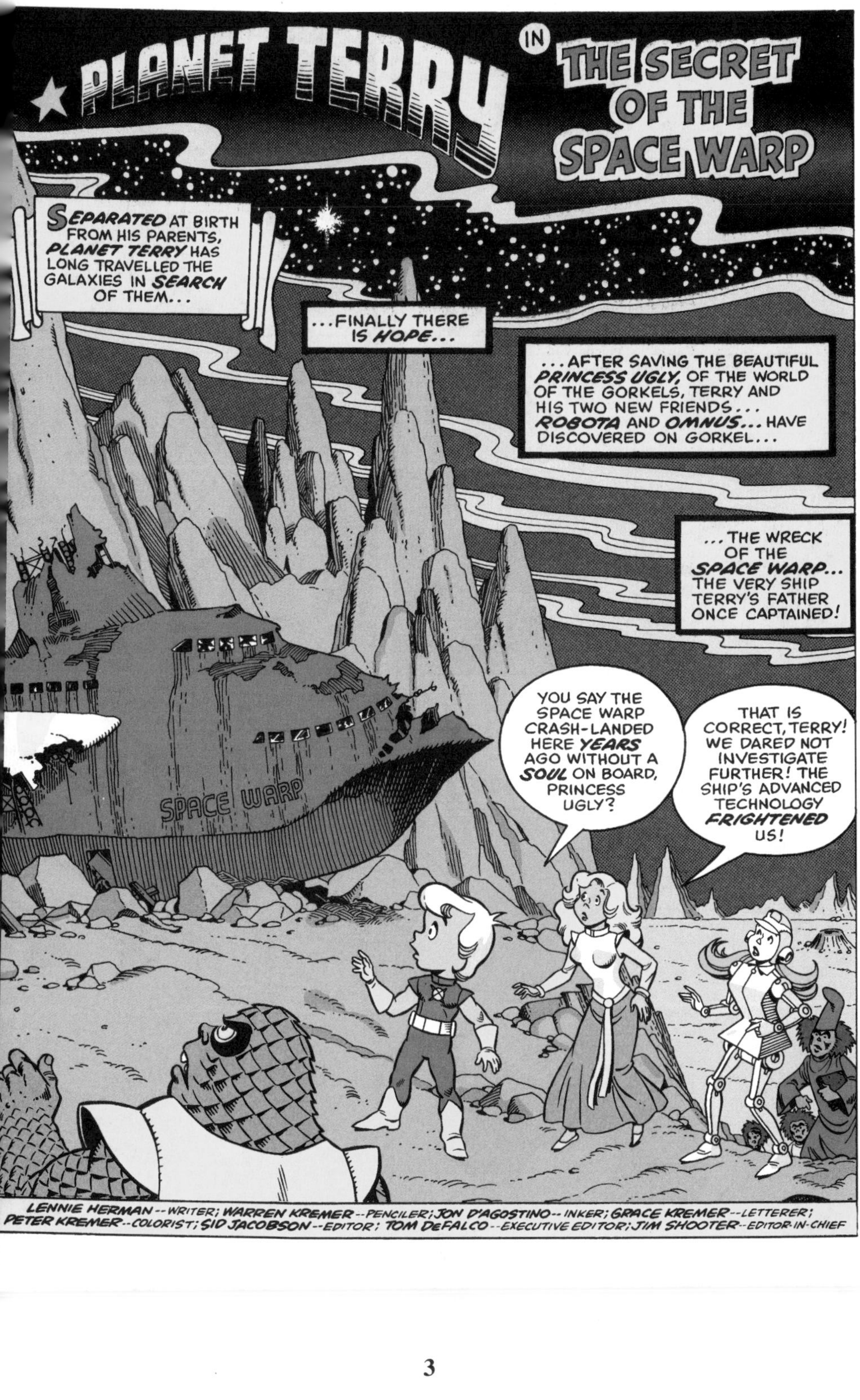
PLANET TERRY IN THE SECRET OF THE SPACE WARP
SEPARATED AT BIRTH FROM HIS PARENTS, PLANET TERRY HAS LONG TRAVELLED THE GALAXIES IN SEARCH OF THEM...
...FINALLY THERE IS HOPE...
...AFTER SAVING THE BEAUTIFUL PRINCESS UGLY, OF THE WORLD OF THE GORKELS, TERRY AND HIS TWO NEW FRIENDS... ROBOTA AND OMNUS... HAVE DISCOVERED ON GORKEL...
...THE WRECK OF THE SPACE WARP... THE VERY SHIP TERRY'S FATHER ONCE CAPTAINED!
SPACE WARP
YOU SAY THE SPACE WARP CRASH-LANDED HERE YEARS AGO WITHOUT A SOUL ON BOARD, PRINCESS UGLY?
THAT IS CORRECT, TERRY! WE DARED NOT INVESTIGATE FURTHER! THE SHIP'S ADVANCED TECHNOLOGY FRIGHTENED US!
LENNIE HERMAN--WRITER; WARREN KREMER--PENCILER; JON D'AGOSTINO--INKER; GRACE KREMER--LETTERER; PETER KREMER--COLORIST; SID JACOBSON--EDITOR; TOM DEFALCO--EXECUTIVE EDITOR; JIM SHOOTER--EDITOR-IN-CHIEF

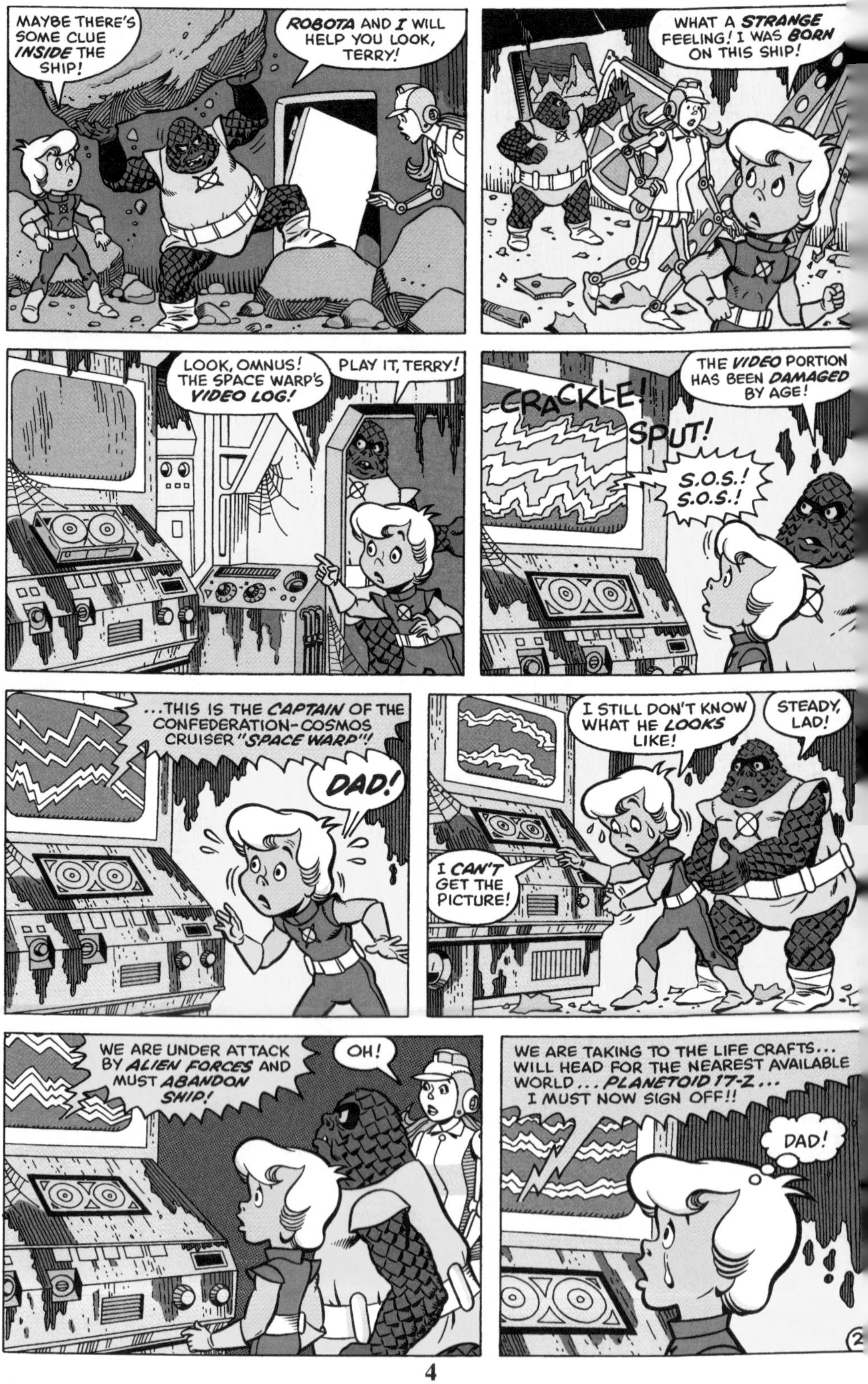
MAYBE THERE'S SOME CLUE INSIDE THE SHIP!
ROBOTA AND I WILL HELP YOU LOOK, TERRY!
WHAT A STRANGE FEELING! I WAS BORN ON THIS SHIP!
LOOK, OMNUS! THE SPACE WARP'S VIDEO LOG!
PLAY IT, TERRY!
THE VIDEO PORTION HAS BEEN DAMAGED BY AGE!
CRACKLE!
SPUT!
S.O.S.! S.O.S.!
...THIS IS THE CAPTAIN OF THE CONFEDERATION-COSMOS CRUISER "SPACE WARP"!
DAD!
I STILL DON'T KNOW WHAT HE LOOKS LIKE!
STEADY, LAD!
I CAN'T GET THE PICTURE!
WE ARE UNDER ATTACK BY ALIEN FORCES AND MUST ABANDON SHIP!
OH!
WE ARE TAKING TO THE LIFE CRAFTS... WILL HEAD FOR THE NEAREST AVAILABLE WORLD... PLANETOID 17-Z... I MUST NOW SIGN OFF!!
DAD!
2

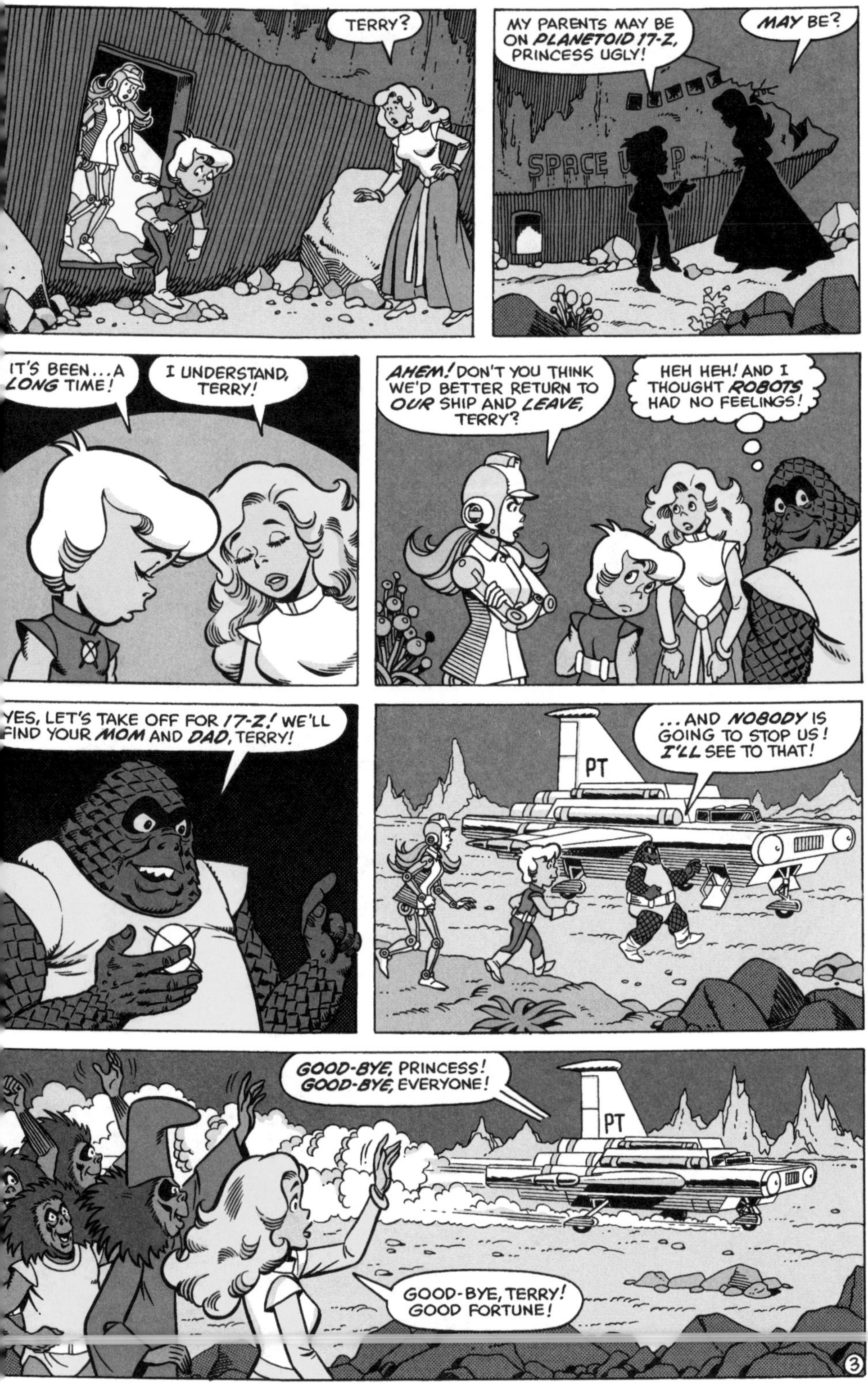
TERRY?
MY PARENTS MAY BE ON PLANETOID 17-Z, PRINCESS UGLY!
MAY BE?
SPACE U P
IT'S BEEN... A LONG TIME!
I UNDERSTAND, TERRY!
AHEM! DON'T YOU THINK WE'D BETTER RETURN TO OUR SHIP AND LEAVE, TERRY?
HEH HEH! AND I THOUGHT ROBOTS HAD NO FEELINGS!
YES, LET'S TAKE OFF FOR 17-Z! WE'LL FIND YOUR MOM AND DAD, TERRY!
PT
...AND NOBODY IS GOING TO STOP US! I'LL SEE TO THAT!
GOOD-BYE, PRINCESS! GOOD-BYE, EVERYONE!
PT
GOOD-BYE, TERRY! GOOD FORTUNE!
3

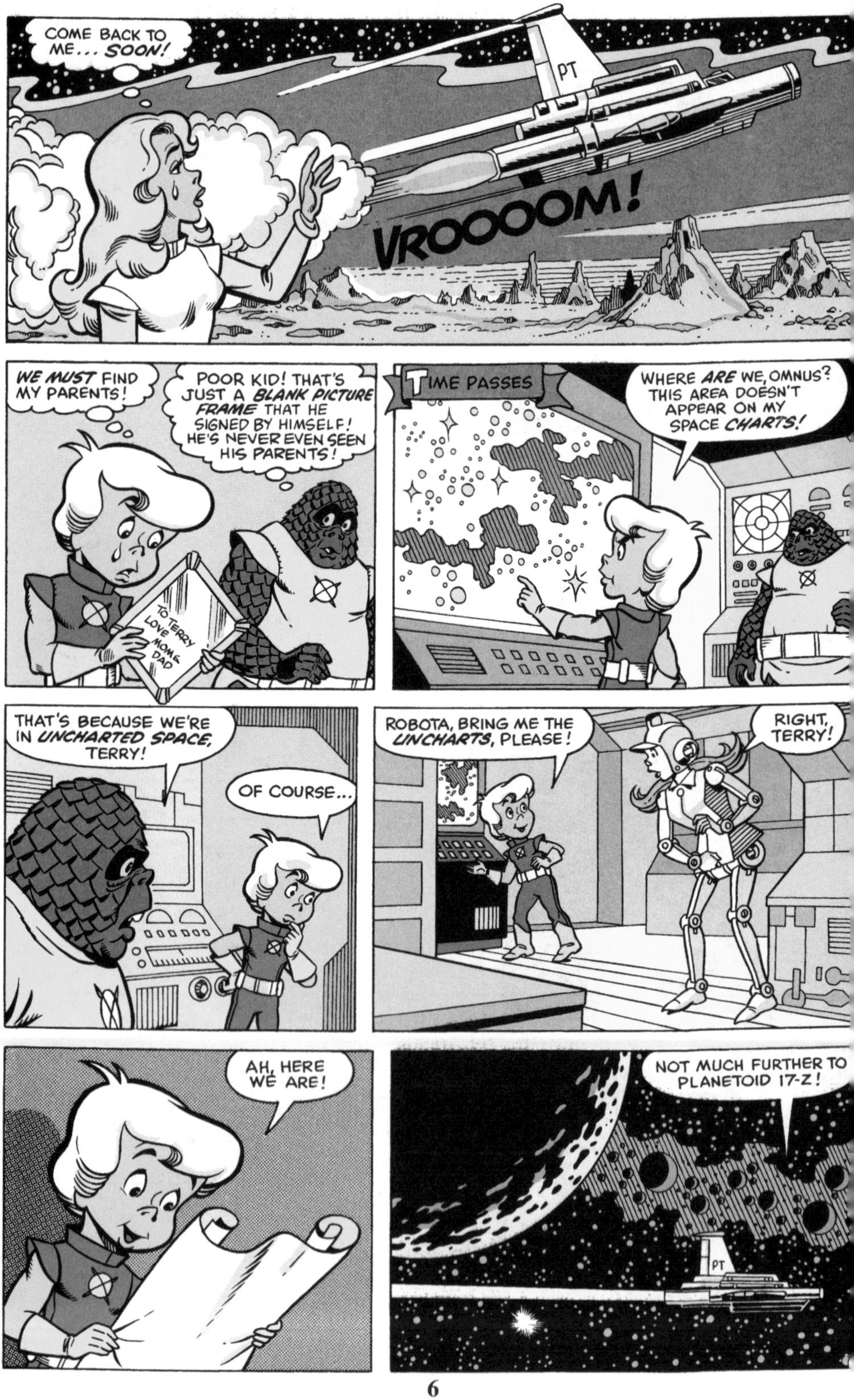

COME BACK TO ME... SOON!
VROOOOM!
PT
WE MUST FIND MY PARENTS!
POOR KID! THAT'S JUST A BLANK PICTURE FRAME THAT HE SIGNED BY HIMSELF! HE'S NEVER EVEN SEEN HIS PARENTS!
TO TERRY LOVE MOM & DAD
TIME PASSES
WHERE ARE WE, OMNUS? THIS AREA DOESN'T APPEAR ON MY SPACE CHARTS!
THAT'S BECAUSE WE'RE IN UNCHARTED SPACE, TERRY!
OF COURSE...
ROBOTA, BRING ME THE UNCHARTS, PLEASE!
RIGHT, TERRY!
AH, HERE WE ARE!
NOT MUCH FURTHER TO PLANETOID 17-Z!
PT

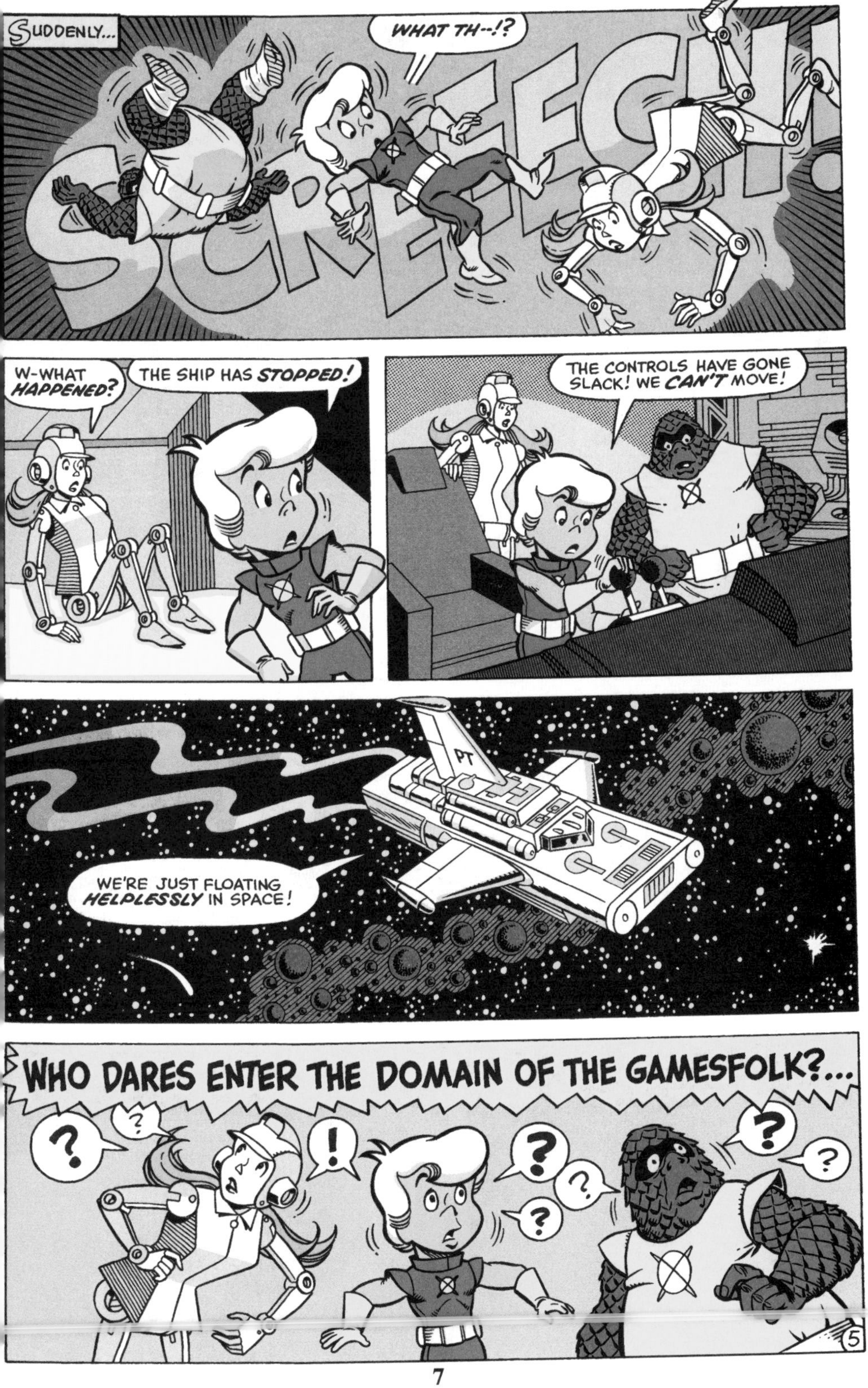
SUDDENLY...
WHAT TH--!?
SCREECH!
W-WHAT HAPPENED?
THE SHIP HAS STOPPED!
THE CONTROLS HAVE GONE SLACK! WE CAN'T MOVE!
PT
WE'RE JUST FLOATING HELPLESSLY IN SPACE!
WHO DARES ENTER THE DOMAIN OF THE GAMESFOLK?...
?
?
!
?
?
?
?
?
5

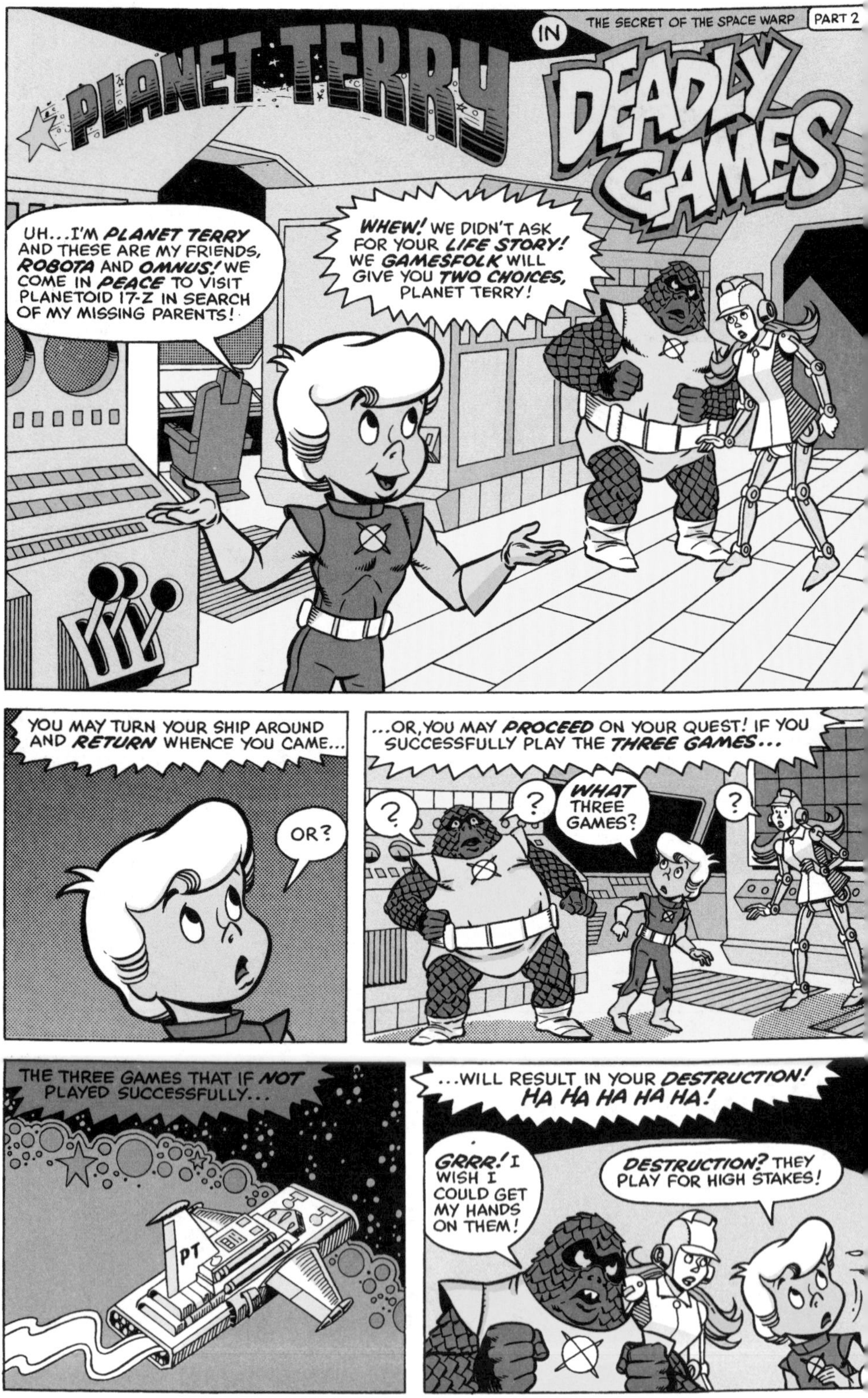
THE SECRET OF THE SPACE WARP
PART 2
PLANET TERRY
IN
DEADLY GAMES
UH...I'M PLANET TERRY AND THESE ARE MY FRIENDS, ROBOTA AND OMNUS! WE COME IN PEACE TO VISIT PLANETOID 17-Z IN SEARCH OF MY MISSING PARENTS!
WHEW! WE DIDN'T ASK FOR YOUR LIFE STORY! WE GAMESFOLK WILL GIVE YOU TWO CHOICES, PLANET TERRY!
YOU MAY TURN YOUR SHIP AROUND AND RETURN WHENCE YOU CAME...
OR?
...OR, YOU MAY PROCEED ON YOUR QUEST! IF YOU SUCCESSFULLY PLAY THE THREE GAMES...
?
?
WHAT THREE GAMES?
?
THE THREE GAMES THAT IF NOT PLAYED SUCCESSFULLY...
PT
...WILL RESULT IN YOUR DESTRUCTION! HA HA HA HA HA!
GRRR! I WISH I COULD GET MY HANDS ON THEM!
DESTRUCTION? THEY PLAY FOR HIGH STAKES!

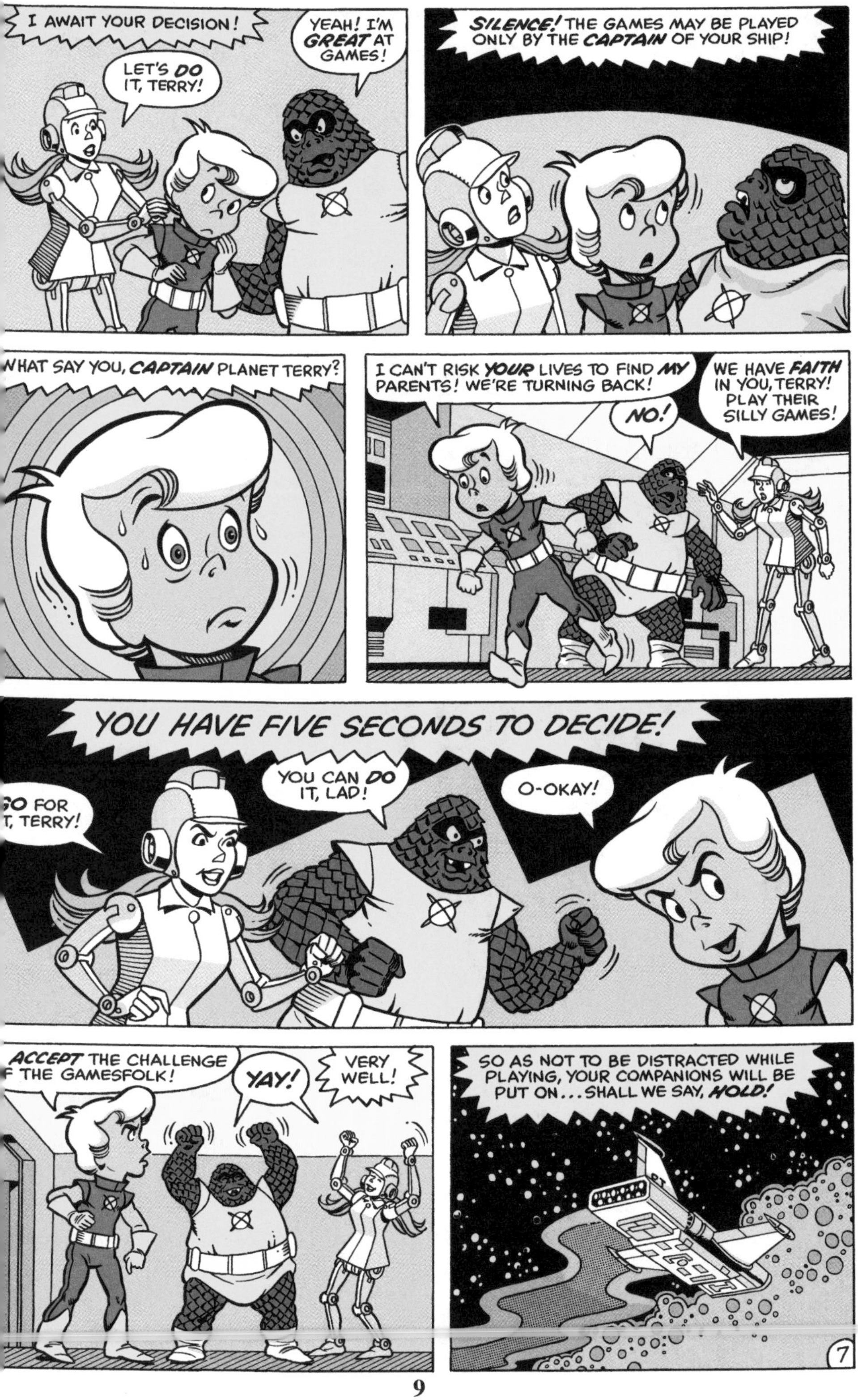
I AWAIT YOUR DECISION!
YEAH! I'M GREAT AT GAMES!
LET'S DO IT, TERRY!
SILENCE! THE GAMES MAY BE PLAYED ONLY BY THE CAPTAIN OF YOUR SHIP!
WHAT SAY YOU, CAPTAIN PLANET TERRY?
I CAN'T RISK YOUR LIVES TO FIND MY PARENTS! WE'RE TURNING BACK!
NO!
WE HAVE FAITH IN YOU, TERRY! PLAY THEIR SILLY GAMES!
YOU HAVE FIVE SECONDS TO DECIDE!
GO FOR IT, TERRY!
YOU CAN DO IT, LAD!
O-OKAY!
I ACCEPT THE CHALLENGE OF THE GAMESFOLK!
YAY!
VERY WELL!
SO AS NOT TO BE DISTRACTED WHILE PLAYING, YOUR COMPANIONS WILL BE PUT ON... SHALL WE SAY, HOLD!
7

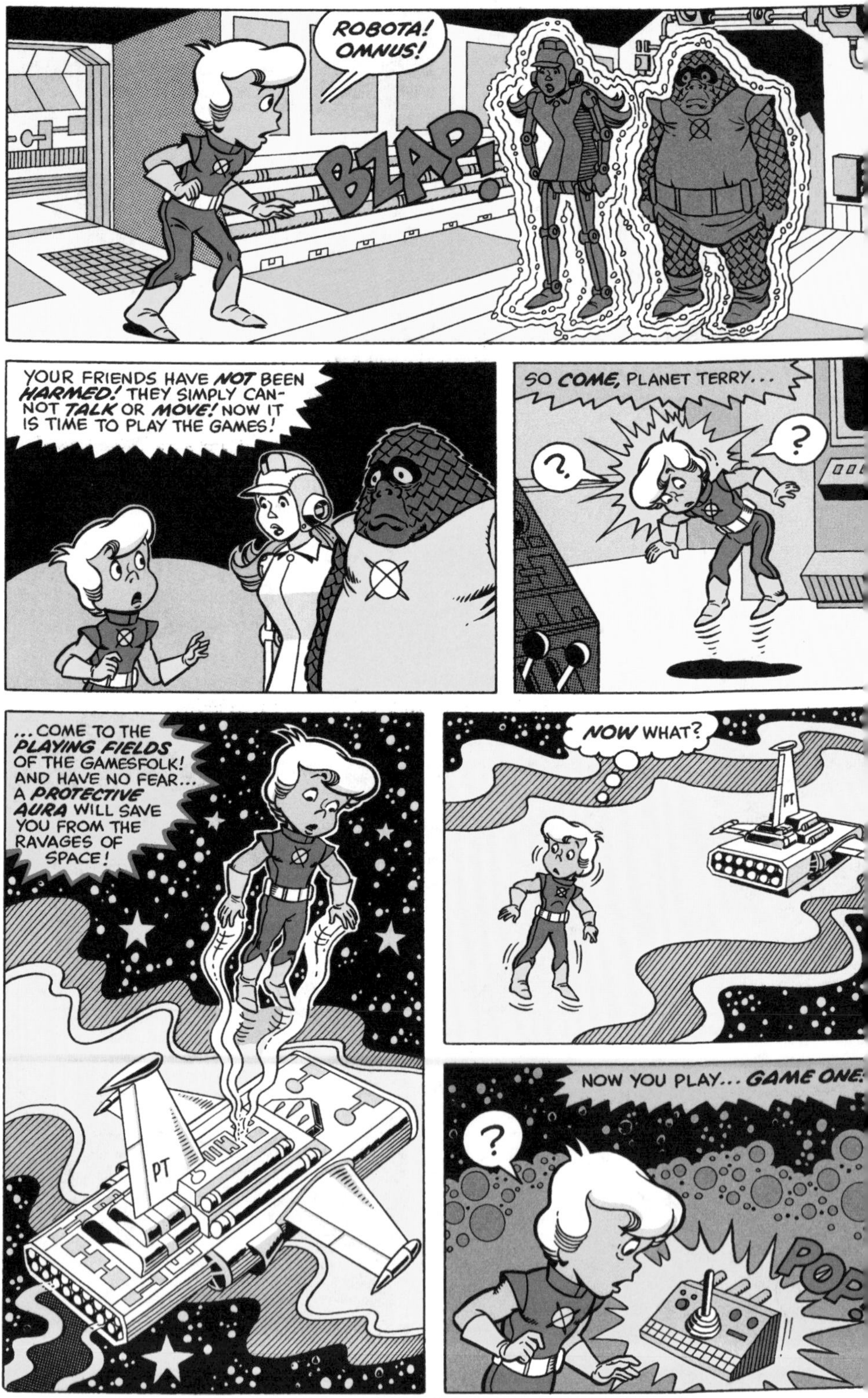
ROBOTA! OMNUS!
BZAP!
YOUR FRIENDS HAVE NOT BEEN HARMED! THEY SIMPLY CANNOT TALK OR MOVE! NOW IT IS TIME TO PLAY THE GAMES!
SO COME, PLANET TERRY...
?
?
...COME TO THE PLAYING FIELDS OF THE GAMESFOLK! AND HAVE NO FEAR... A PROTECTIVE AURA WILL SAVE YOU FROM THE RAVAGES OF SPACE!
NOW WHAT?
PT
PT
NOW YOU PLAY... GAME ONE!
?
POP!

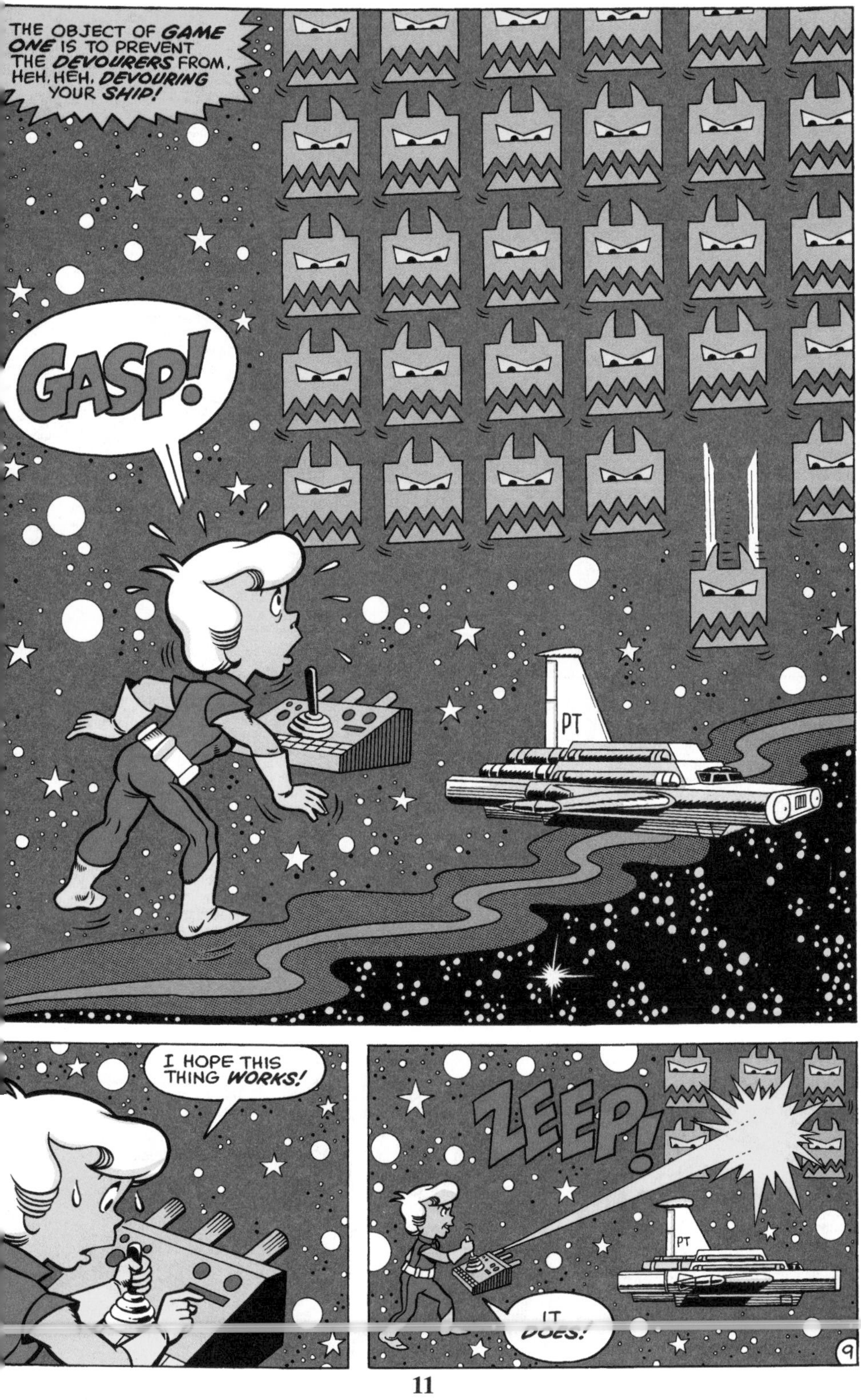
THE OBJECT OF GAME ONE IS TO PREVENT THE DEVOURERS FROM, HEH, HEH, DEVOURING YOUR SHIP!
GASP!
PT
I HOPE THIS THING WORKS!
ZEEP!
PT
IT DOES!
9

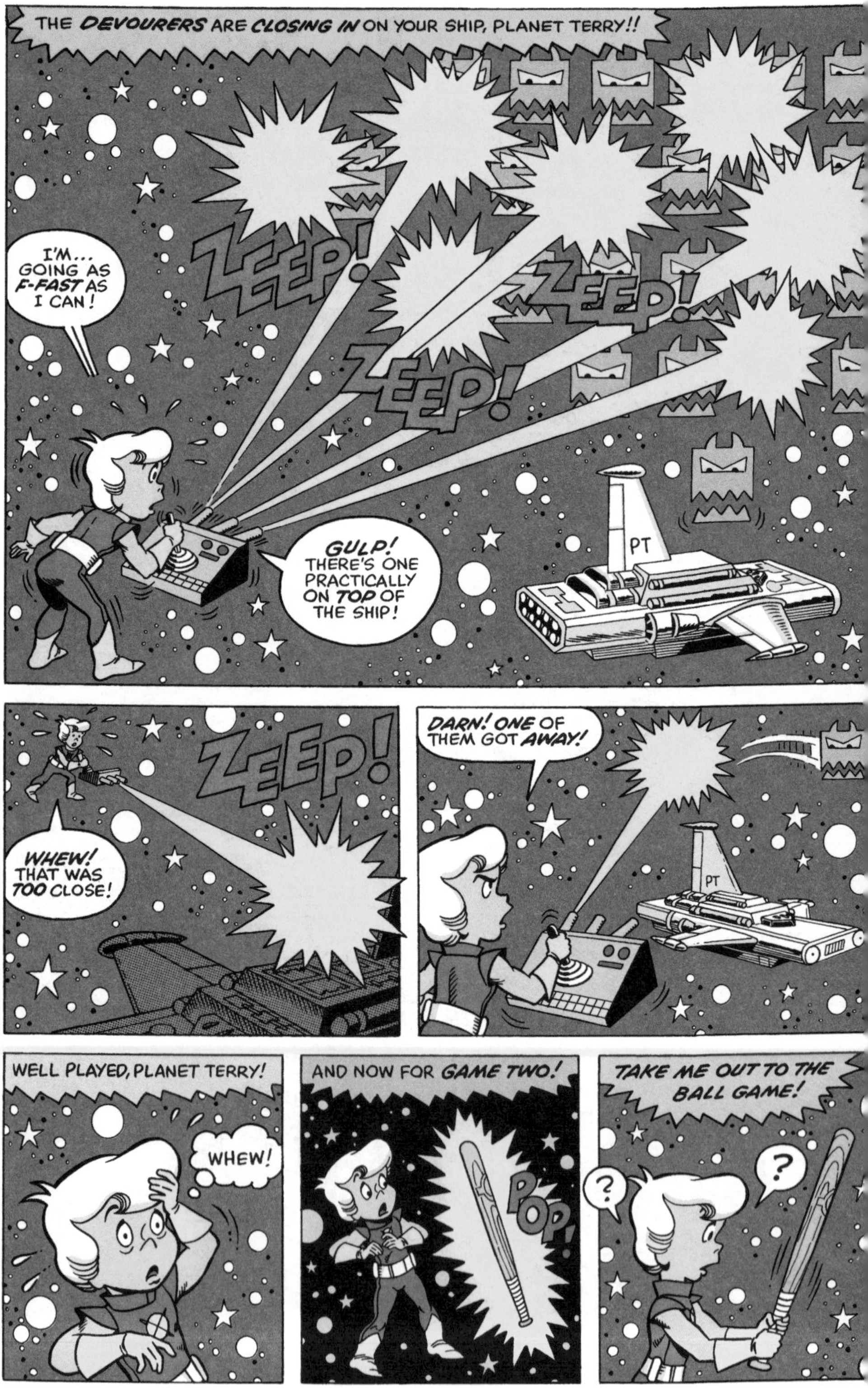
THE DEVOURERS ARE CLOSING IN ON YOUR SHIP, PLANET TERRY!!
I'M... GOING AS F-FAST AS I CAN!
ZEEP!
ZEEP!
ZEEP!
GULP! THERE'S ONE PRACTICALLY ON TOP OF THE SHIP!
PT
ZEEP!
WHEW! THAT WAS TOO CLOSE!
DARN! ONE OF THEM GOT AWAY!
PT
WELL PLAYED, PLANET TERRY!
WHEW!
AND NOW FOR GAME TWO!
POP!
TAKE ME OUT TO THE BALL GAME!
?
?

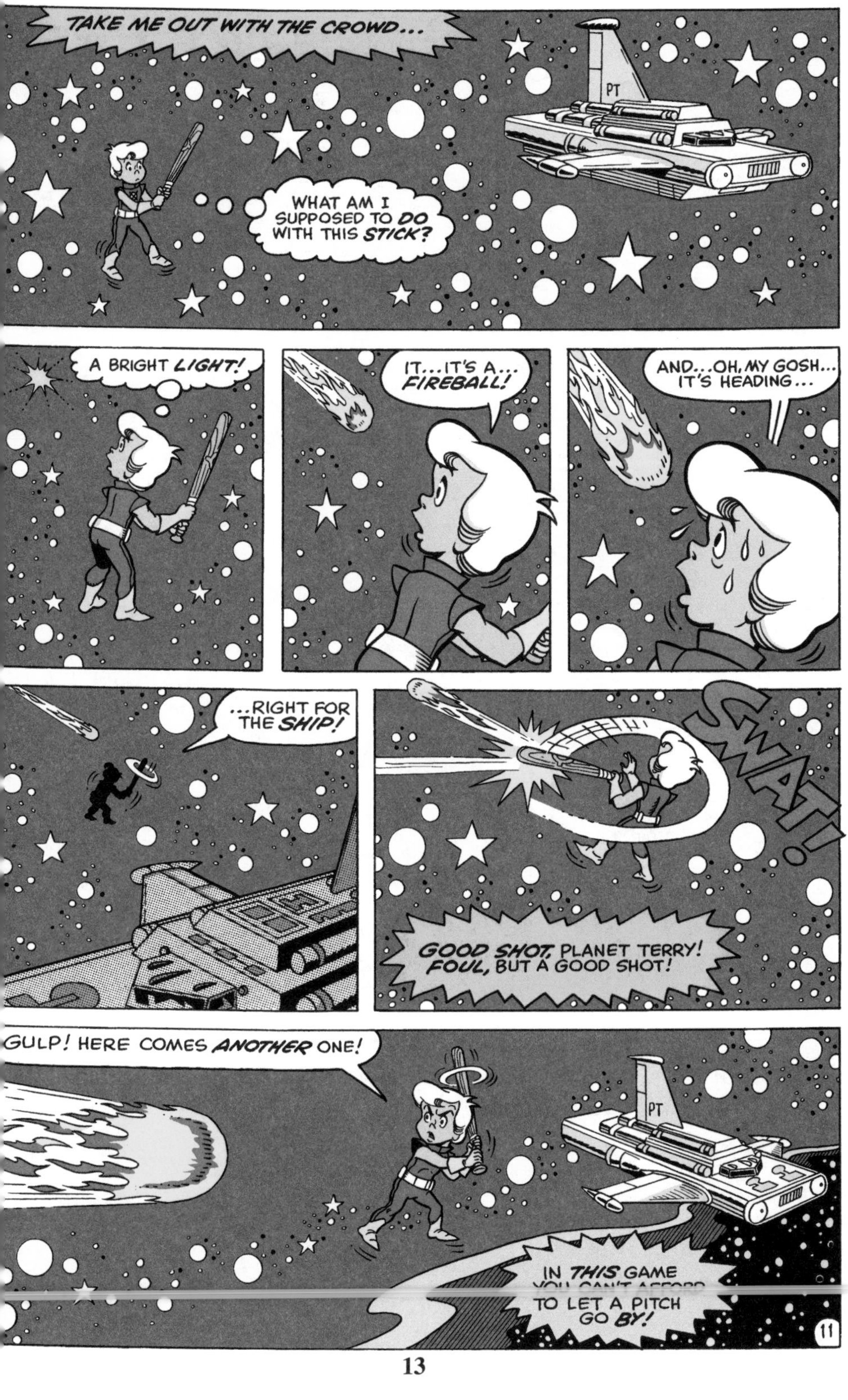

TAKE ME OUT WITH THE CROWD...
WHAT AM I SUPPOSED TO DO WITH THIS STICK?
PT
A BRIGHT LIGHT!
IT...IT'S A... FIREBALL!
AND...OH, MY GOSH... IT'S HEADING...
...RIGHT FOR THE SHIP!
SWAT!
GOOD SHOT, PLANET TERRY! FOUL, BUT A GOOD SHOT!
GULP! HERE COMES ANOTHER ONE!
PT
IN THIS GAME
TO LET A PITCH GO BY!
11

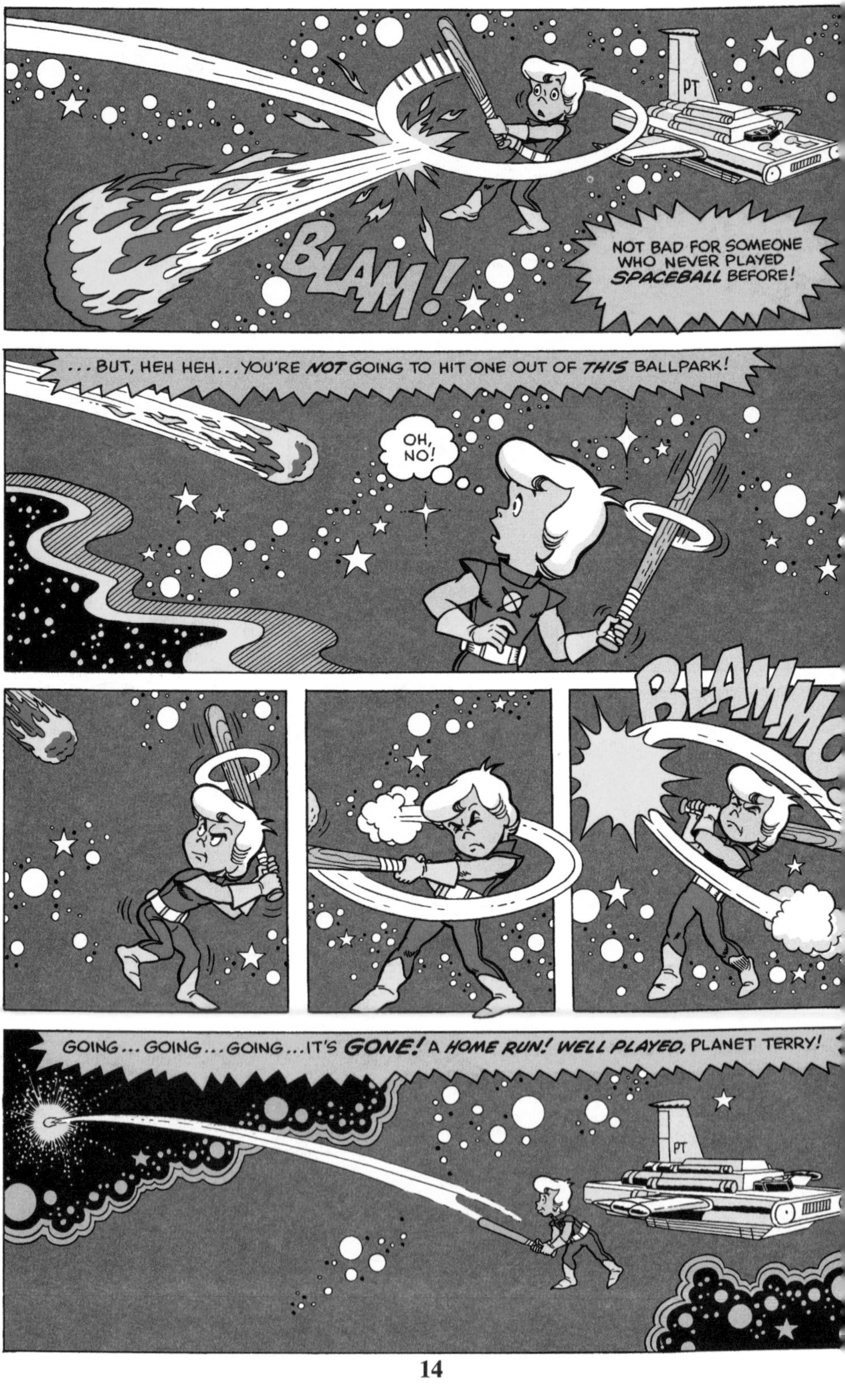

BLAM!
NOT BAD FOR SOMEONE WHO NEVER PLAYED SPACEBALL BEFORE!
...BUT, HEH HEH...YOU'RE NOT GOING TO HIT ONE OUT OF THIS BALLPARK!
OH, NO!
BLAMMO
GOING...GOING...GOING...IT'S GONE! A HOME RUN! WELL PLAYED, PLANET TERRY!
PT

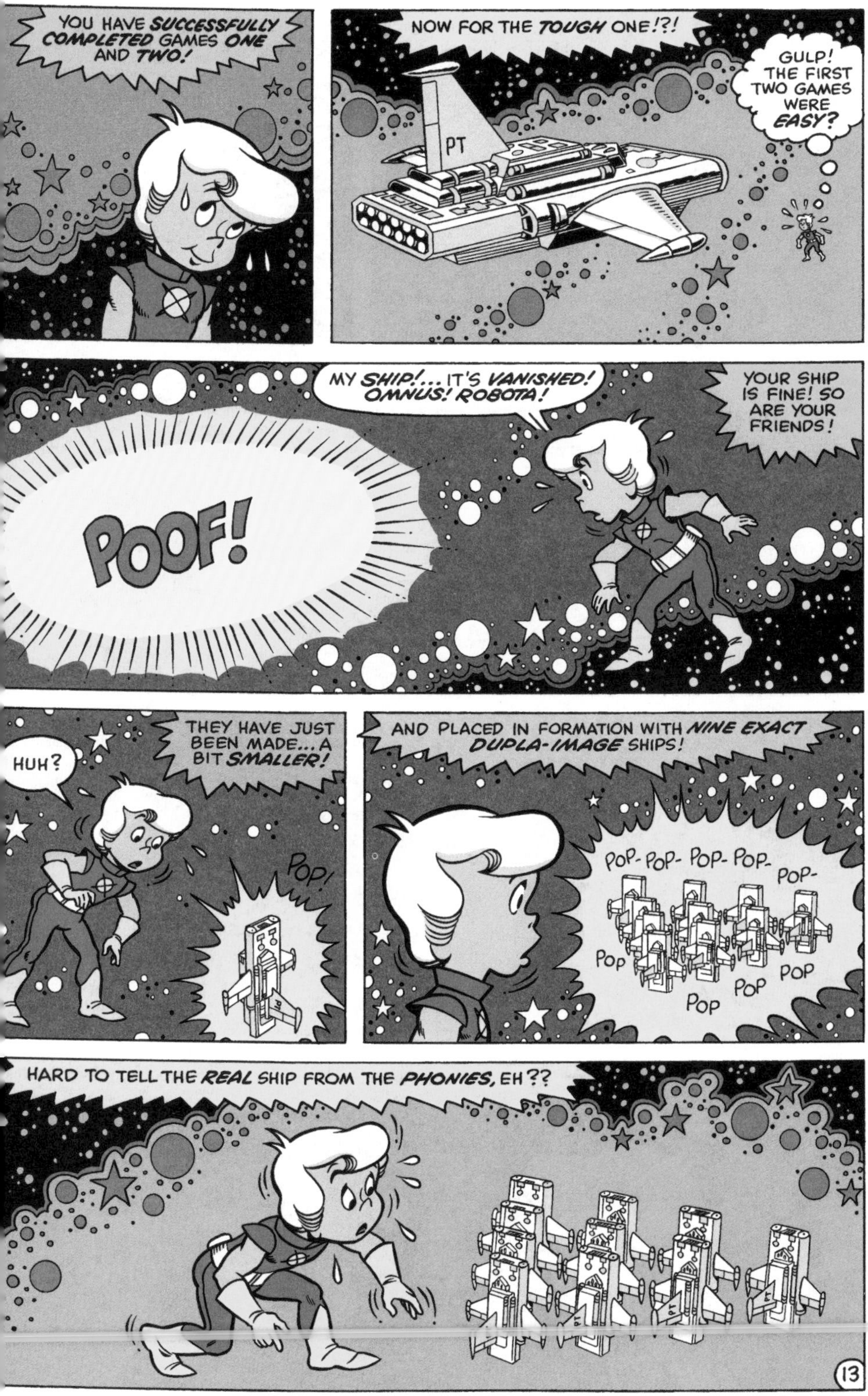
YOU HAVE SUCCESSFULLY COMPLETED GAMES ONE AND TWO!
NOW FOR THE TOUGH ONE!?!
GULP! THE FIRST TWO GAMES WERE EASY?
PT
POOF!
MY SHIP!... IT'S VANISHED! OMNUS! ROBOTA!
YOUR SHIP IS FINE! SO ARE YOUR FRIENDS!
THEY HAVE JUST BEEN MADE... A BIT SMALLER!
HUH?
POP!
AND PLACED IN FORMATION WITH NINE EXACT DUPLA-IMAGE SHIPS!
POP- POP- POP- POP- POP-
POP POP POP POP
HARD TO TELL THE REAL SHIP FROM THE PHONIES, EH??
13

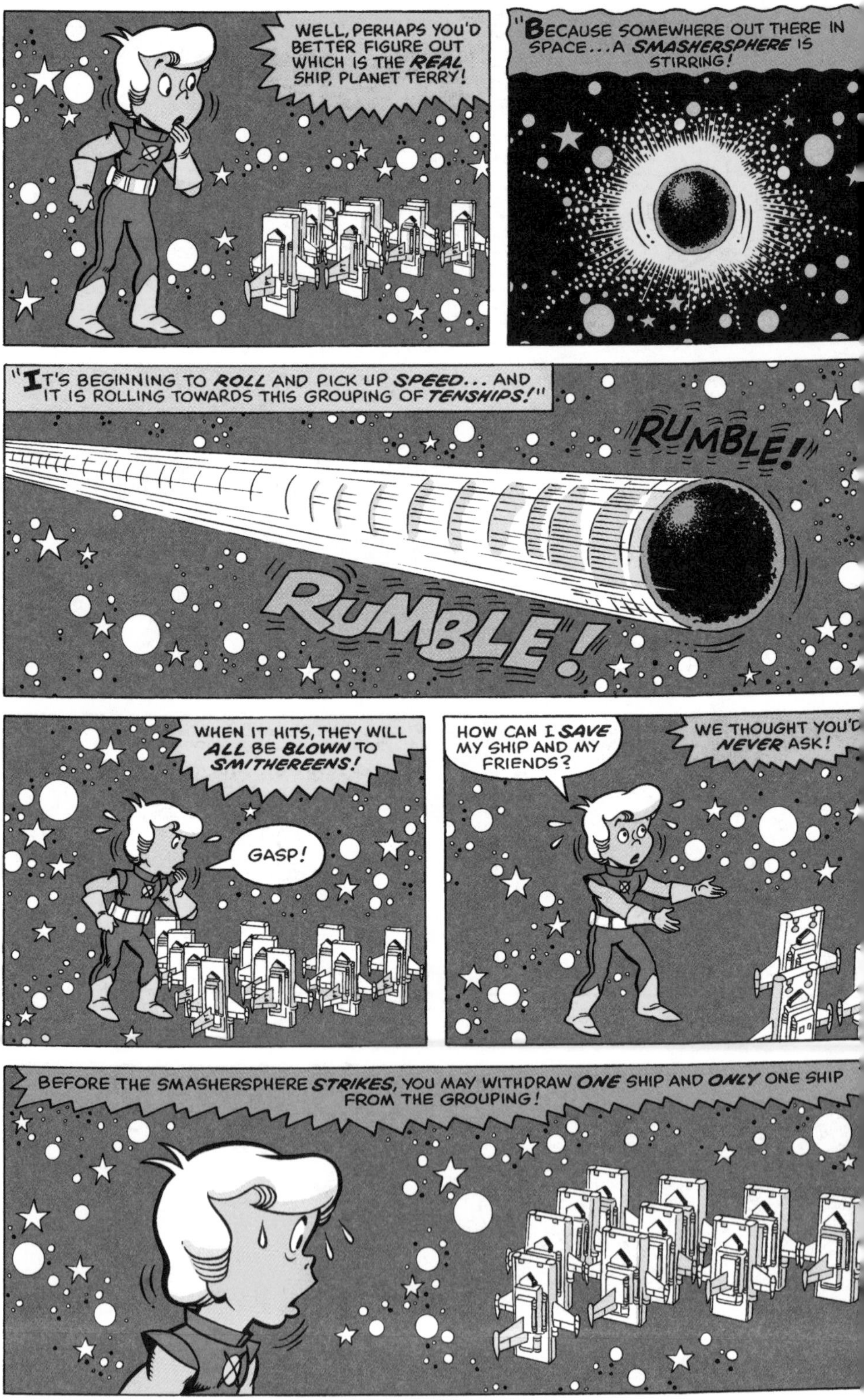
WELL, PERHAPS YOU'D BETTER FIGURE OUT WHICH IS THE REAL SHIP, PLANET TERRY!
"BECAUSE SOMEWHERE OUT THERE IN SPACE... A SMASHERSPHERE IS STIRRING!
"IT'S BEGINNING TO ROLL AND PICK UP SPEED... AND IT IS ROLLING TOWARDS THIS GROUPING OF TENSHIPS!"
RUMBLE!
RUMBLE!
WHEN IT HITS, THEY WILL ALL BE BLOWN TO SMITHEREENS!
GASP!
HOW CAN I SAVE MY SHIP AND MY FRIENDS?
WE THOUGHT YOU'D NEVER ASK!
BEFORE THE SMASHERSPHERE STRIKES, YOU MAY WITHDRAW ONE SHIP AND ONLY ONE SHIP FROM THE GROUPING!

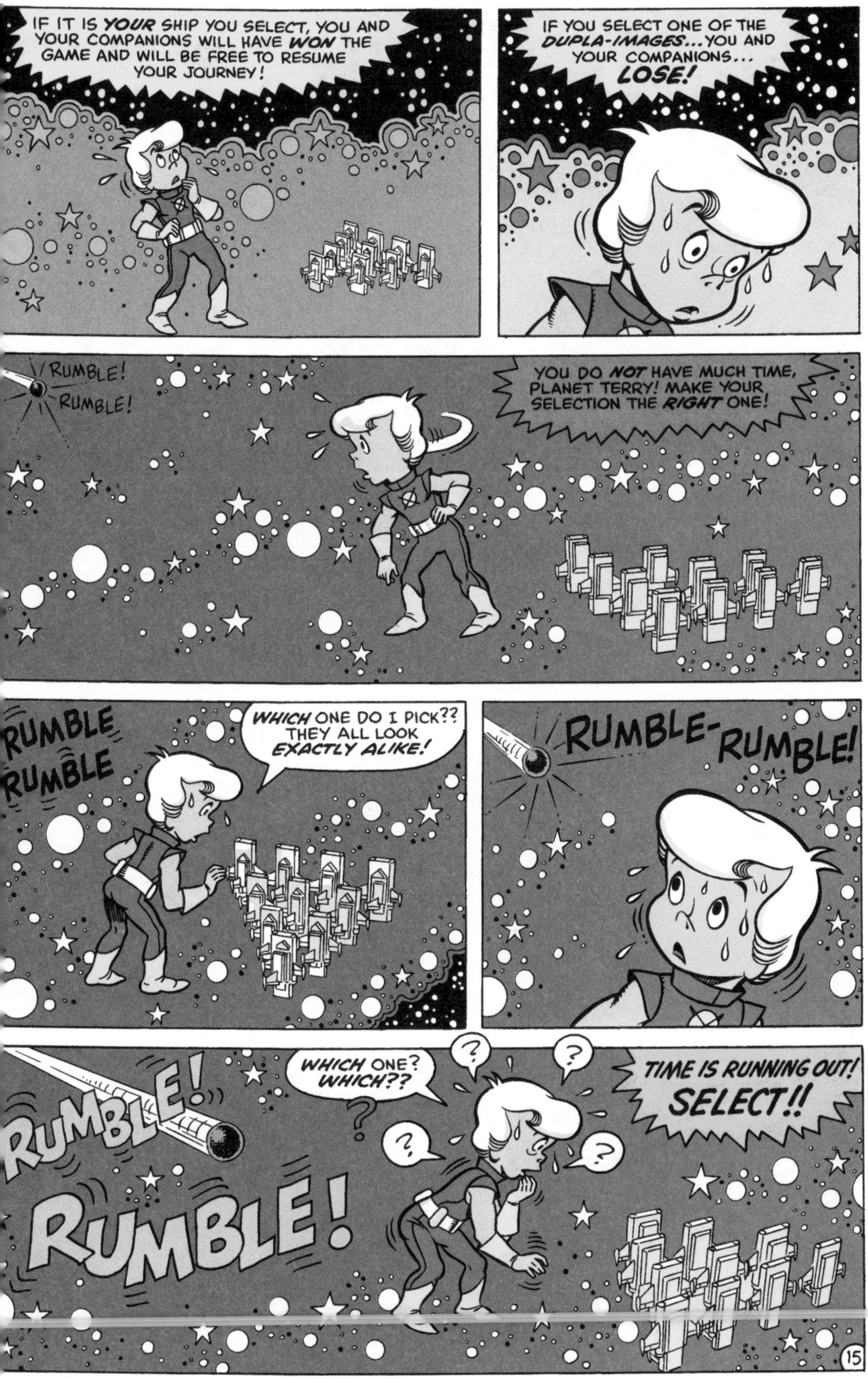
IF IT IS YOUR SHIP YOU SELECT, YOU AND YOUR COMPANIONS WILL HAVE WON THE GAME AND WILL BE FREE TO RESUME YOUR JOURNEY!
IF YOU SELECT ONE OF THE DUPLA-IMAGES... YOU AND YOUR COMPANIONS... LOSE!
RUMBLE! RUMBLE!
YOU DO NOT HAVE MUCH TIME, PLANET TERRY! MAKE YOUR SELECTION THE RIGHT ONE!
RUMBLE RUMBLE
WHICH ONE DO I PICK?? THEY ALL LOOK EXACTLY ALIKE!
RUMBLE-RUMBLE!
RUMBLE!
WHICH ONE? WHICH??
TIME IS RUNNING OUT! SELECT!!
RUMBLE!
15

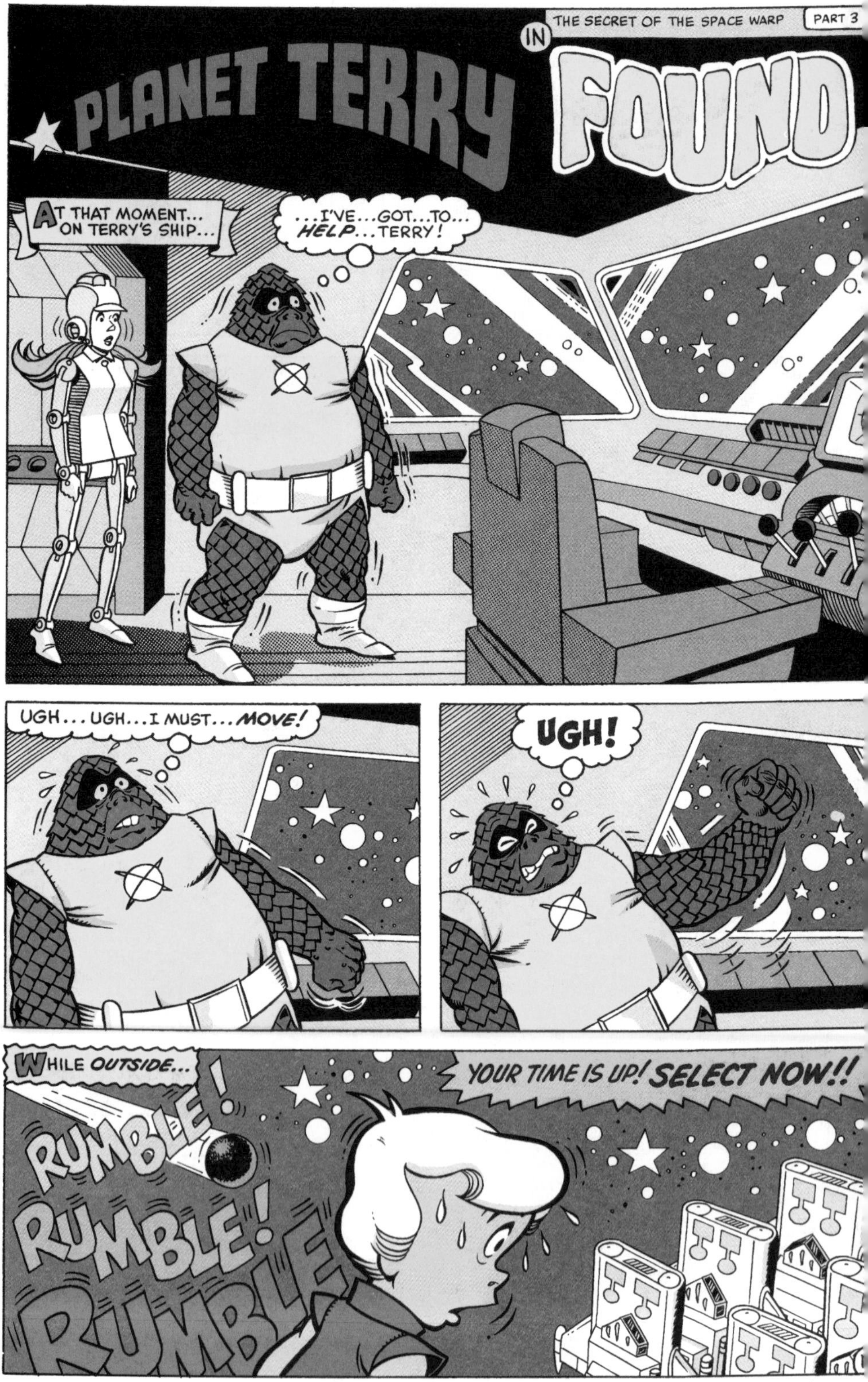
THE SECRET OF THE SPACE WARP
PART 3
PLANET TERRY
IN
FOUND
AT THAT MOMENT... ON TERRY'S SHIP...
...I'VE...GOT...TO... HELP...TERRY!
UGH...UGH...I MUST...MOVE!
UGH!
WHILE OUTSIDE...
YOUR TIME IS UP! SELECT NOW!!
RUMBLE!
RUMBLE!
RUMBLE

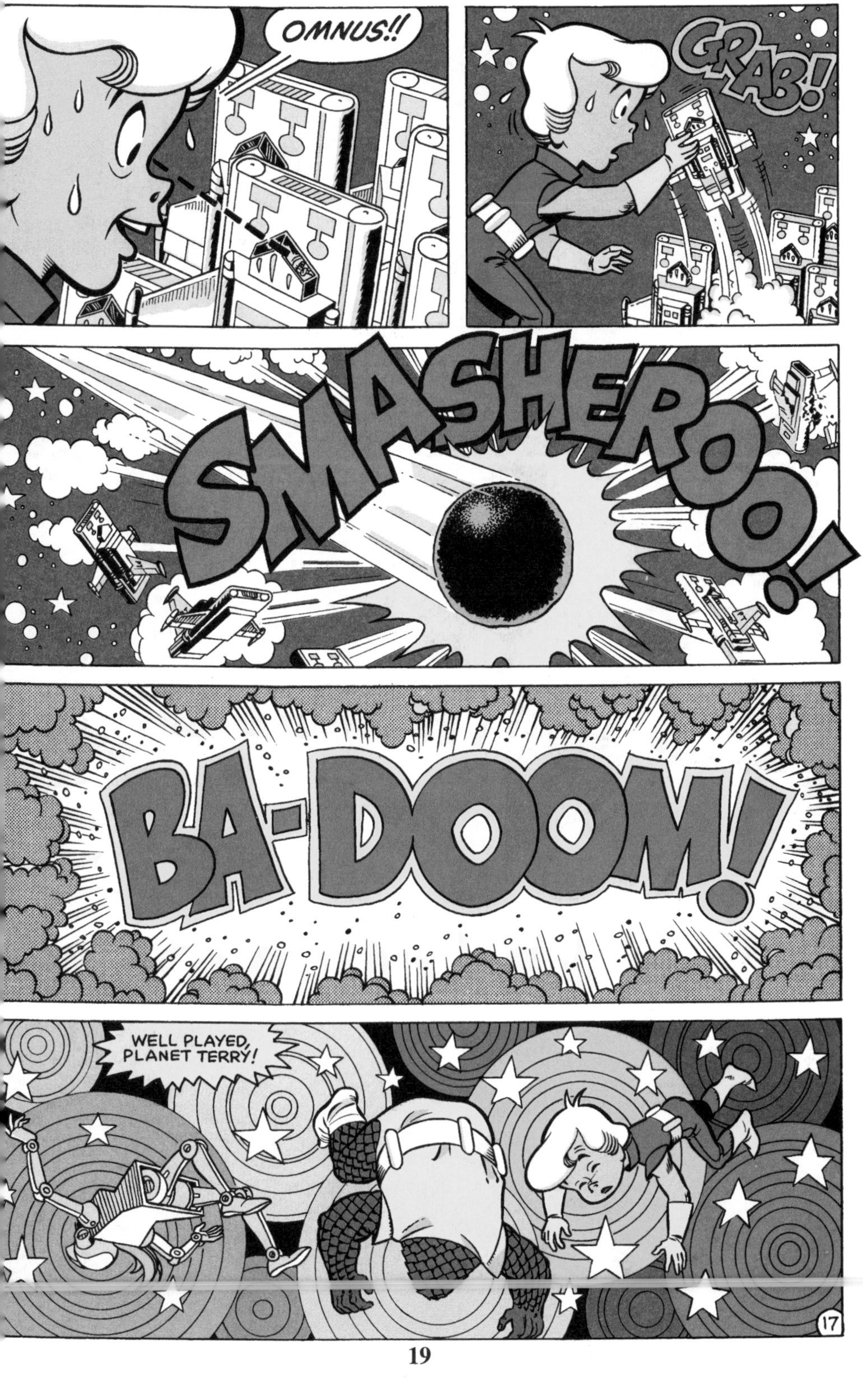

OMNUS!!
GRAB!
SMASHEROO!!
BA-DOOM!
WELL PLAYED, PLANET TERRY!
17

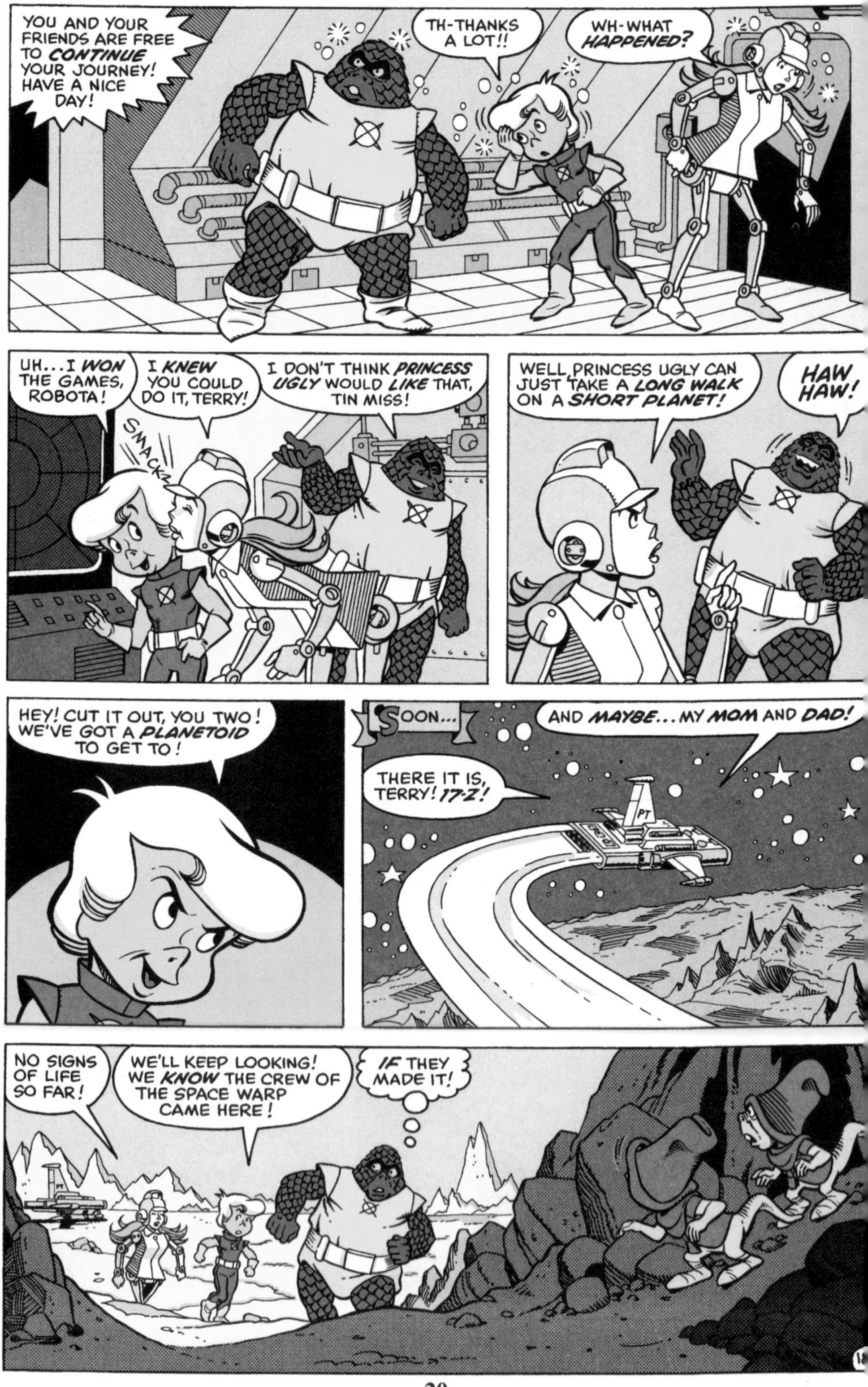
YOU AND YOUR FRIENDS ARE FREE TO CONTINUE YOUR JOURNEY! HAVE A NICE DAY!
TH-THANKS A LOT!!
WH-WHAT HAPPENED?
UH...I WON THE GAMES, ROBOTA!
I KNEW YOU COULD DO IT, TERRY!
SMACKZ
I DON'T THINK PRINCESS UGLY WOULD LIKE THAT, TIN MISS!
WELL, PRINCESS UGLY CAN JUST TAKE A LONG WALK ON A SHORT PLANET!
HAW HAW!
HEY! CUT IT OUT, YOU TWO! WE'VE GOT A PLANETOID TO GET TO!
SOON...
AND MAYBE... MY MOM AND DAD!
THERE IT IS, TERRY! 17-Z!
PT
NO SIGNS OF LIFE SO FAR!
WE'LL KEEP LOOKING! WE KNOW THE CREW OF THE SPACE WARP CAME HERE!
IF THEY MADE IT!

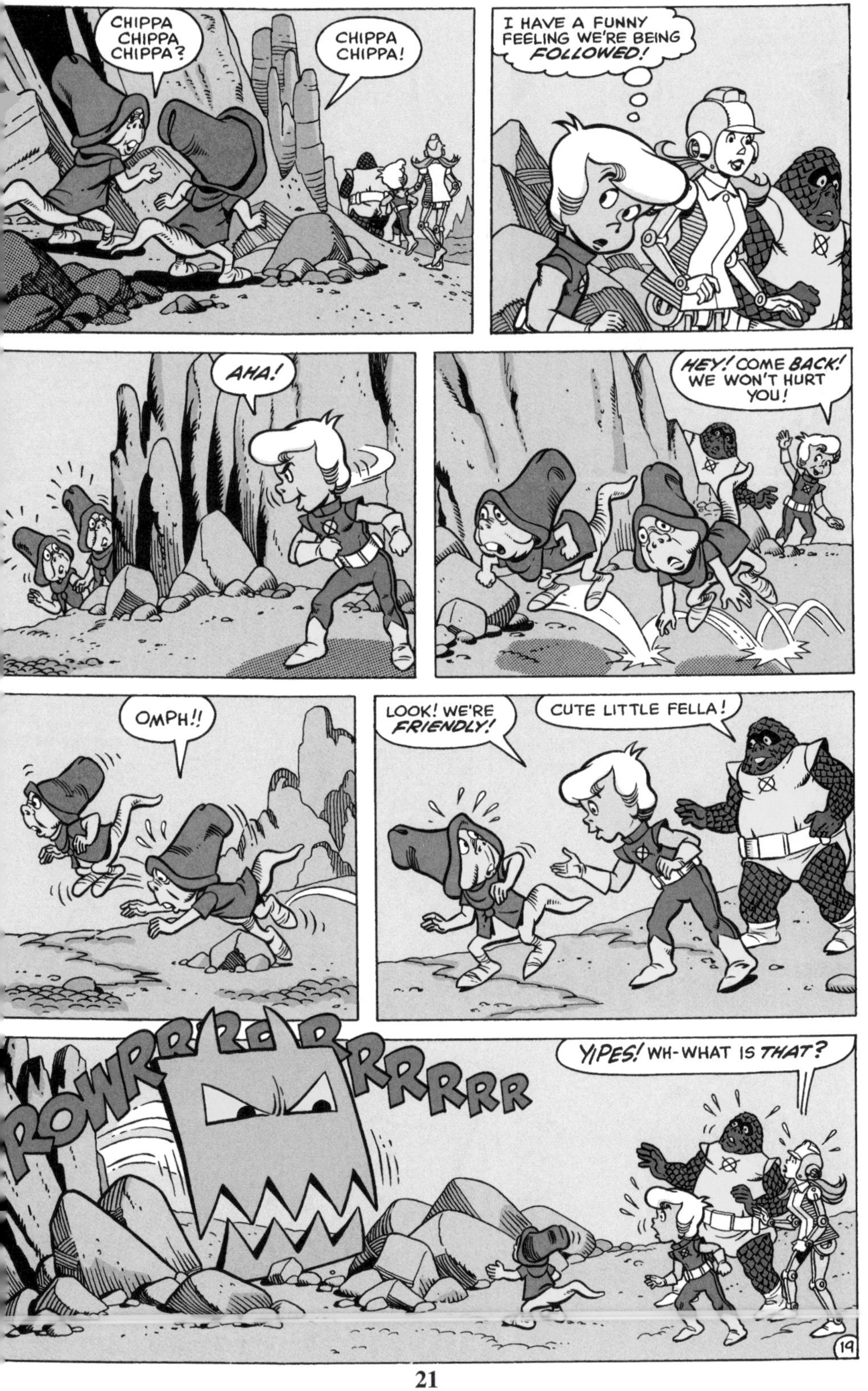
CHIPPA CHIPPA CHIPPA?
CHIPPA CHIPPA!
I HAVE A FUNNY FEELING WE'RE BEING FOLLOWED!
AHA!
HEY! COME BACK! WE WON'T HURT YOU!
OMPH!!
LOOK! WE'RE FRIENDLY!
CUTE LITTLE FELLA!
ROWRRRRRRRRRRR
YIPES! WH-WHAT IS THAT?
19

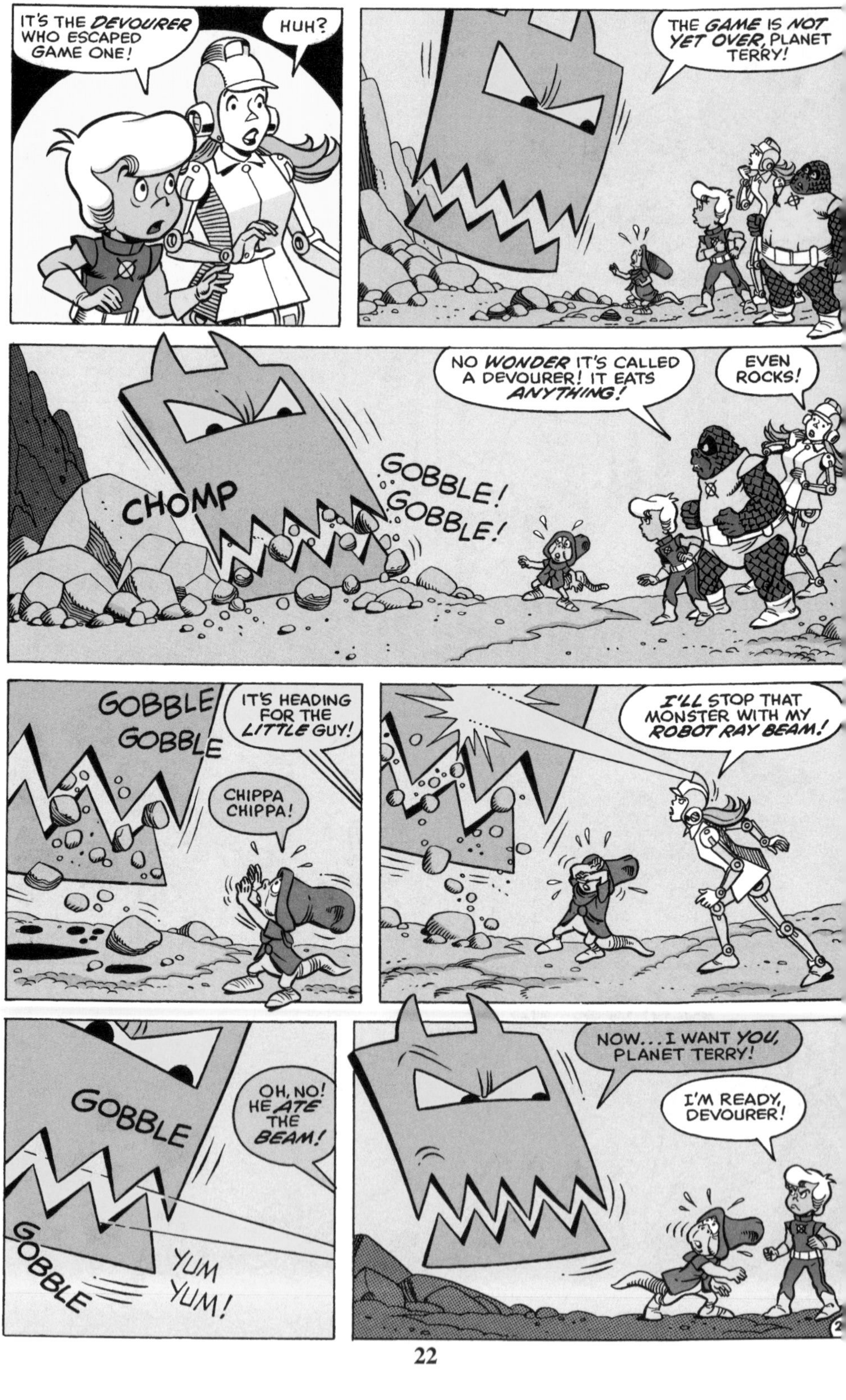
IT'S THE DEVOURER WHO ESCAPED GAME ONE!
HUH?
THE GAME IS NOT YET OVER, PLANET TERRY!
NO WONDER IT'S CALLED A DEVOURER! IT EATS ANYTHING!
EVEN ROCKS!
CHOMP
GOBBLE! GOBBLE!
GOBBLE GOBBLE
IT'S HEADING FOR THE LITTLE GUY!
CHIPPA CHIPPA!
I'LL STOP THAT MONSTER WITH MY ROBOT RAY BEAM!
GOBBLE
OH, NO! HE ATE THE BEAM!
GOBBLE
YUM YUM!
NOW... I WANT YOU, PLANET TERRY!
I'M READY, DEVOURER!

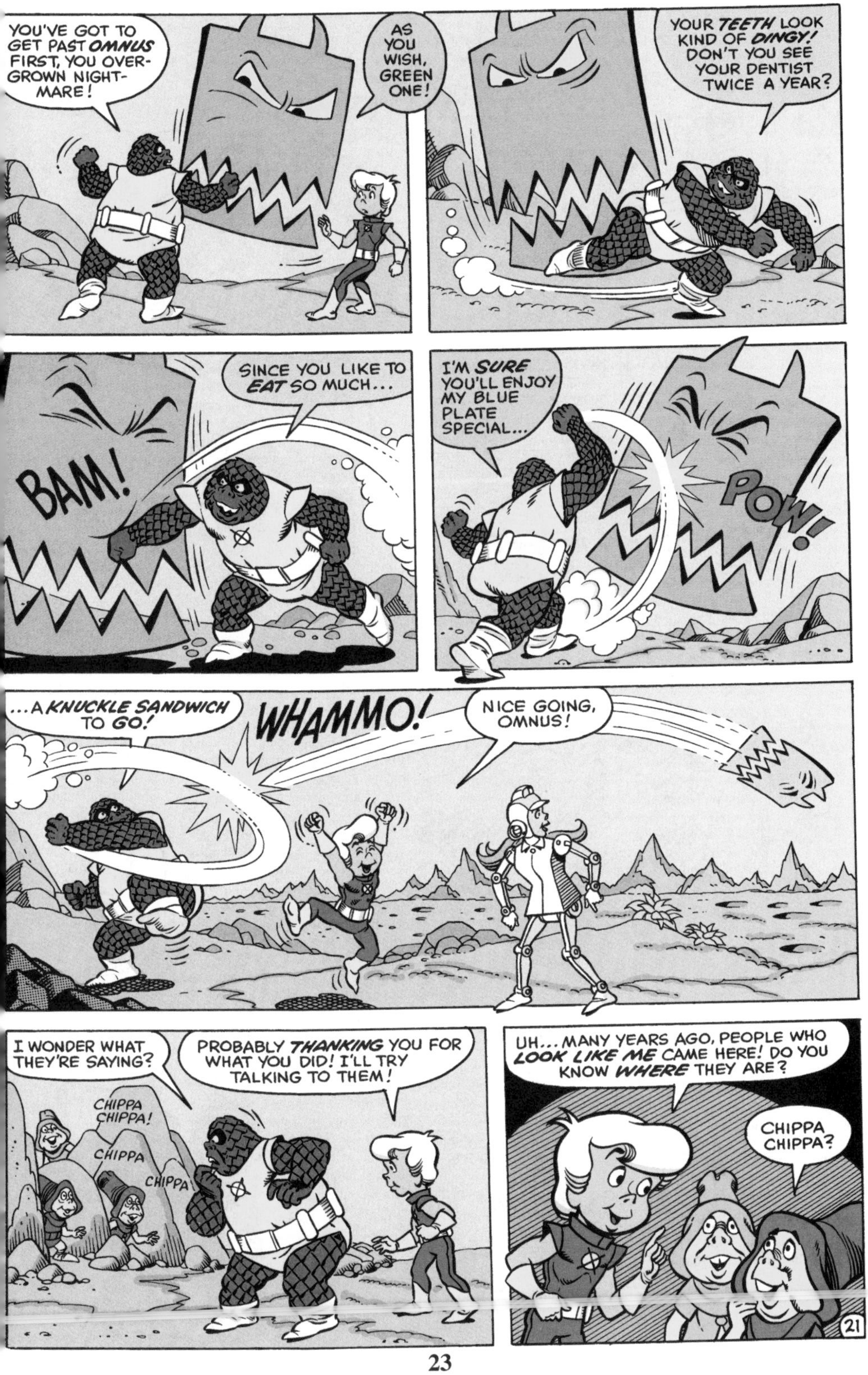
YOU'VE GOT TO GET PAST OMNUS FIRST, YOU OVER-GROWN NIGHT-MARE!
AS YOU WISH, GREEN ONE!
YOUR TEETH LOOK KIND OF DINGY! DON'T YOU SEE YOUR DENTIST TWICE A YEAR?
SINCE YOU LIKE TO EAT SO MUCH...
BAM!
I'M SURE YOU'LL ENJOY MY BLUE PLATE SPECIAL...
POW!
...A KNUCKLE SANDWICH TO GO!
WHAMMO!
NICE GOING, OMNUS!
I WONDER WHAT THEY'RE SAYING?
PROBABLY THANKING YOU FOR WHAT YOU DID! I'LL TRY TALKING TO THEM!
CHIPPA CHIPPA!
CHIPPA
CHIPPA
UH... MANY YEARS AGO, PEOPLE WHO LOOK LIKE ME CAME HERE! DO YOU KNOW WHERE THEY ARE?
CHIPPA CHIPPA?
21

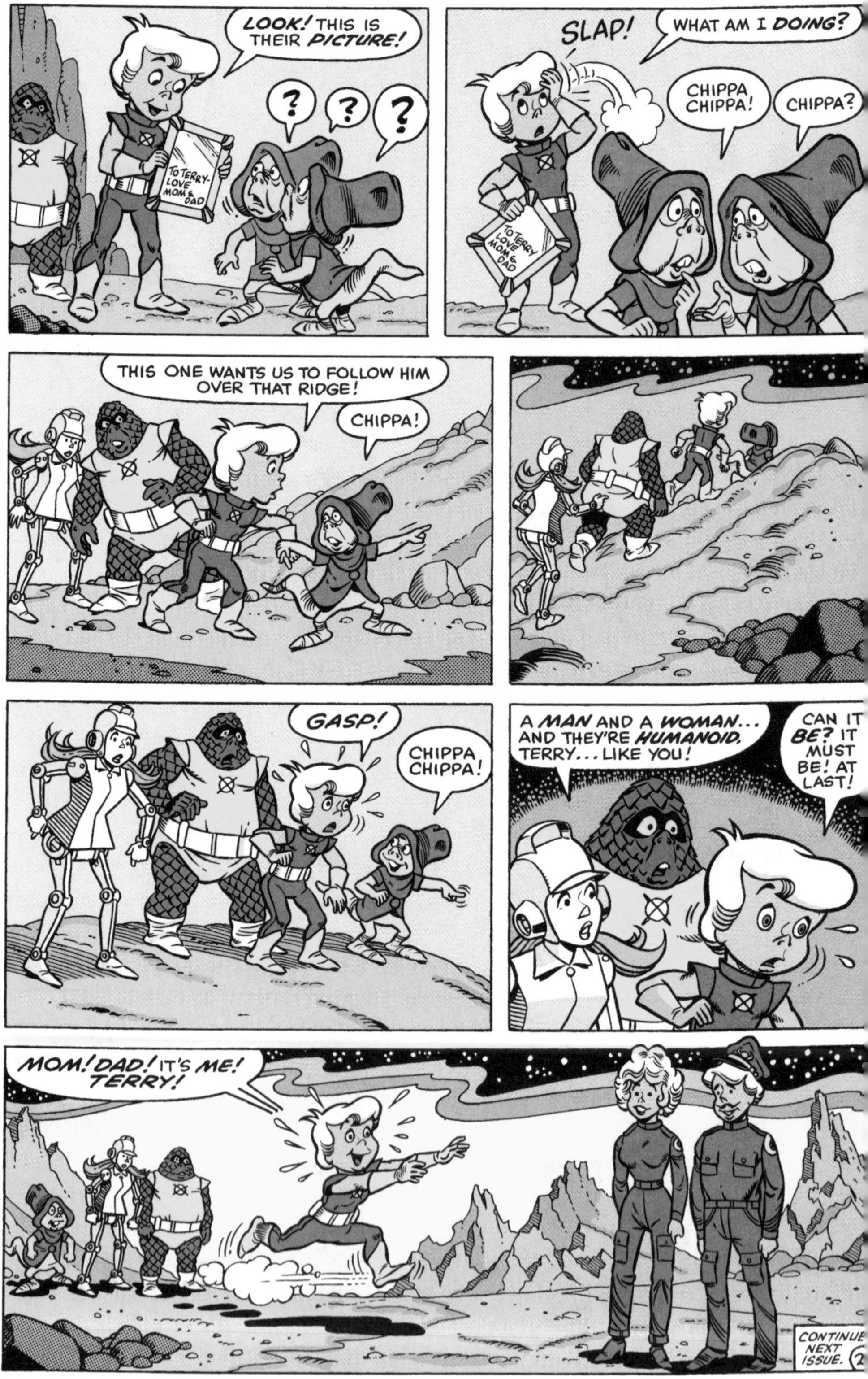
LOOK! THIS IS THEIR PICTURE!
?
?
?
TO TERRY- LOVE MOM & DAD
SLAP!
WHAT AM I DOING?
CHIPPA CHIPPA!
CHIPPA?
TO TERRY LOVE MOM & DAD
THIS ONE WANTS US TO FOLLOW HIM OVER THAT RIDGE!
CHIPPA!
GASP!
CHIPPA CHIPPA!
A MAN AND A WOMAN... AND THEY'RE HUMANOID, TERRY... LIKE YOU!
CAN IT BE? IT MUST BE! AT LAST!
MOM! DAD! IT'S ME! TERRY!
CONTINUE NEXT ISSUE.

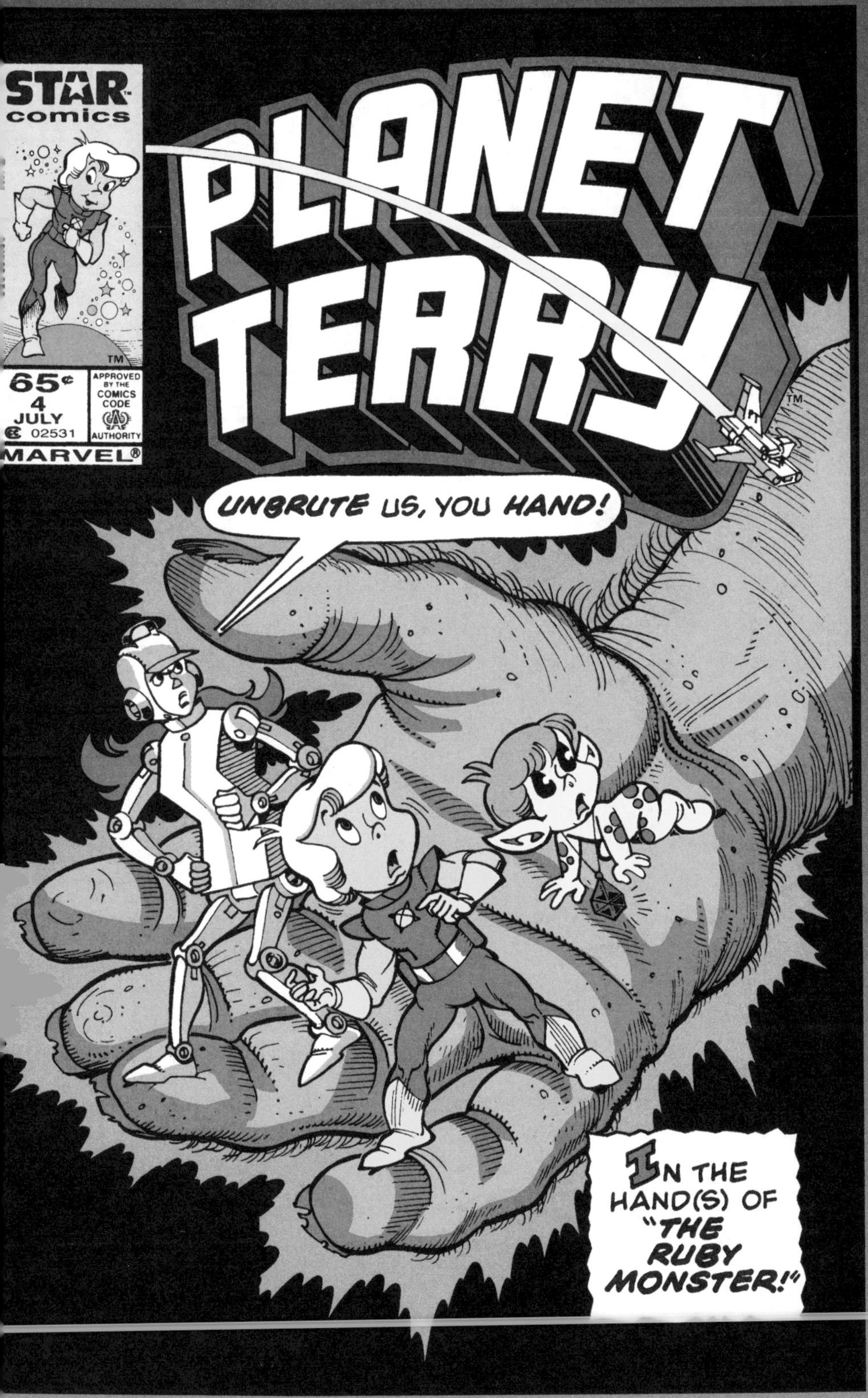
STAR comics
PLANET TERRY
65¢
4
JULY
02531
APPROVED BY THE COMICS CODE AUTHORITY
MARVEL®
UNBRUTE US, YOU HAND!
IN THE HAND(S) OF "THE RUBY MONSTER!"

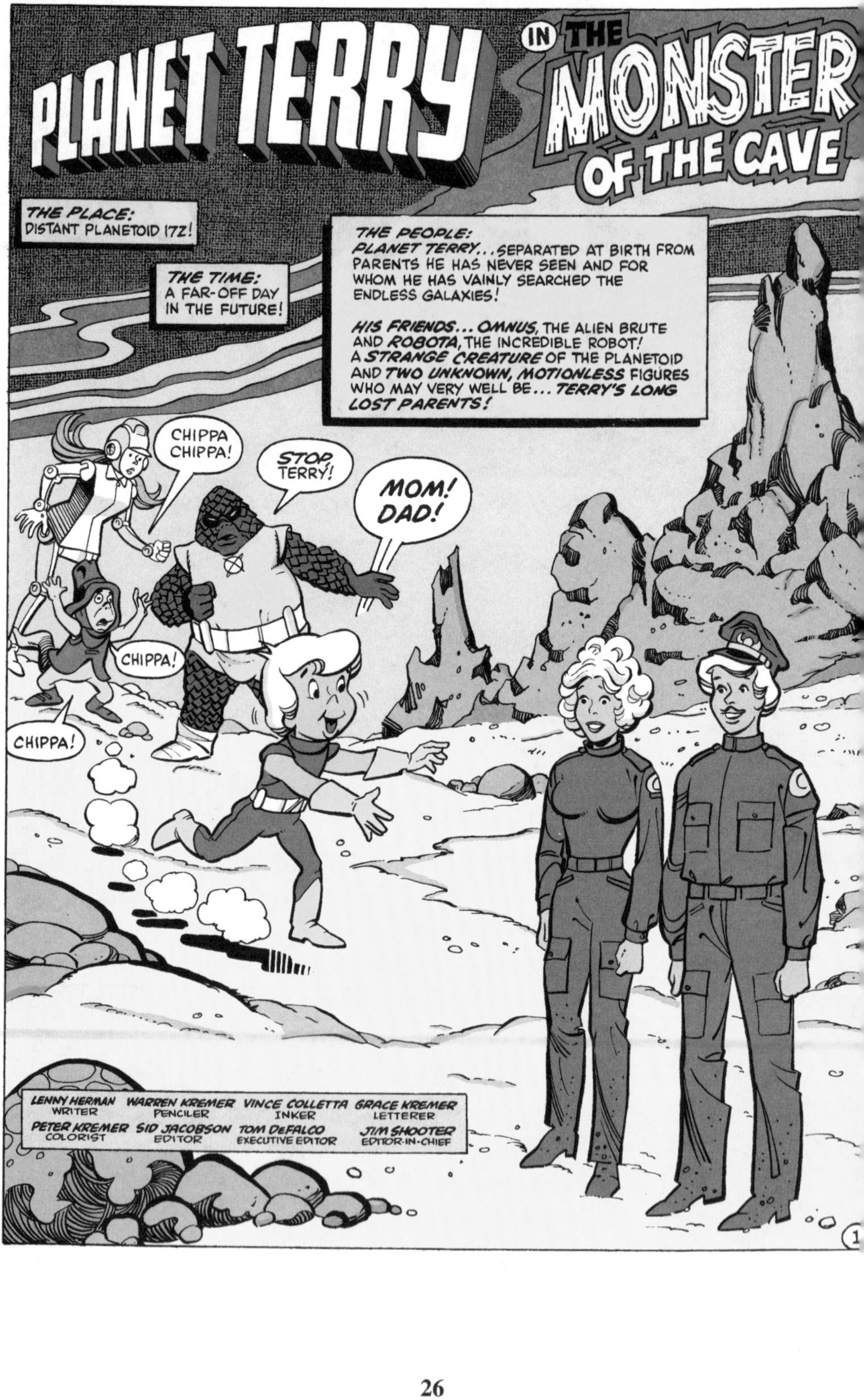
PLANET TERRY
IN THE MONSTER OF THE CAVE
THE PLACE: DISTANT PLANETOID 17Z!
THE TIME: A FAR-OFF DAY IN THE FUTURE!
THE PEOPLE: PLANET TERRY... SEPARATED AT BIRTH FROM PARENTS HE HAS NEVER SEEN AND FOR WHOM HE HAS VAINLY SEARCHED THE ENDLESS GALAXIES!
HIS FRIENDS... OMNUS, THE ALIEN BRUTE AND ROBOTA, THE INCREDIBLE ROBOT! A STRANGE CREATURE OF THE PLANETOID AND TWO UNKNOWN, MOTIONLESS FIGURES WHO MAY VERY WELL BE... TERRY'S LONG LOST PARENTS!
CHIPPA CHIPPA!
STOP, TERRY!
MOM! DAD!
CHIPPA!
CHIPPA!
LENNY HERMAN WRITER
WARREN KREMER PENCILER
VINCE COLLETTA INKER
GRACE KREMER LETTERER
PETER KREMER COLORIST
SID JACOBSON EDITOR
TOM DeFALCO EXECUTIVE EDITOR
JIM SHOOTER EDITOR-IN-CHIEF
1

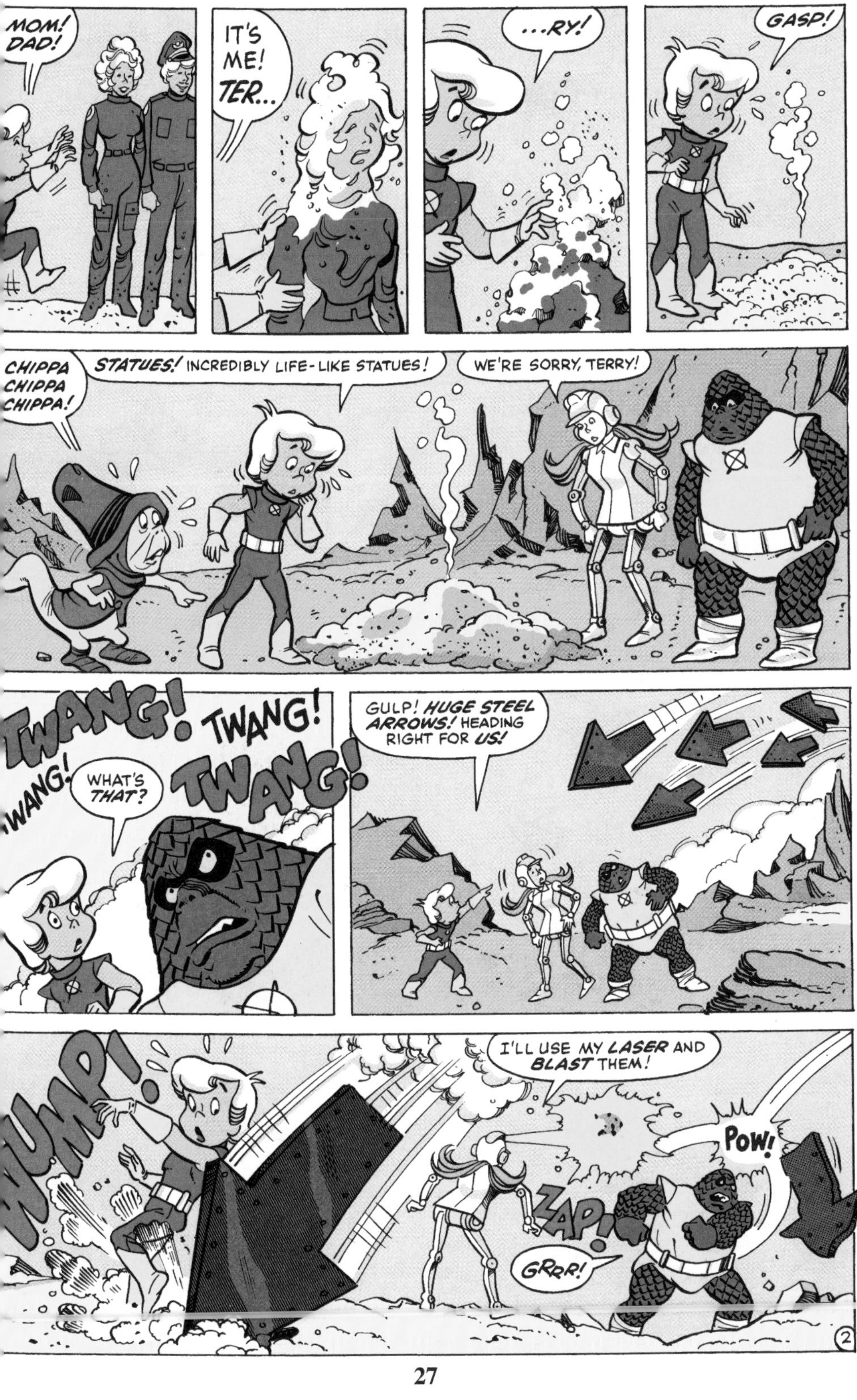
MOM! DAD!
IT'S ME! TER...
...RY!
GASP!
CHIPPA CHIPPA CHIPPA!
STATUES! INCREDIBLY LIFE-LIKE STATUES!
WE'RE SORRY, TERRY!
TWANG!
TWANG!
WANG!
WHAT'S THAT?
TWANG!
GULP! HUGE STEEL ARROWS! HEADING RIGHT FOR US!
WUMP!
I'LL USE MY LASER AND BLAST THEM!
POW!
ZAP!
GRRR!
2

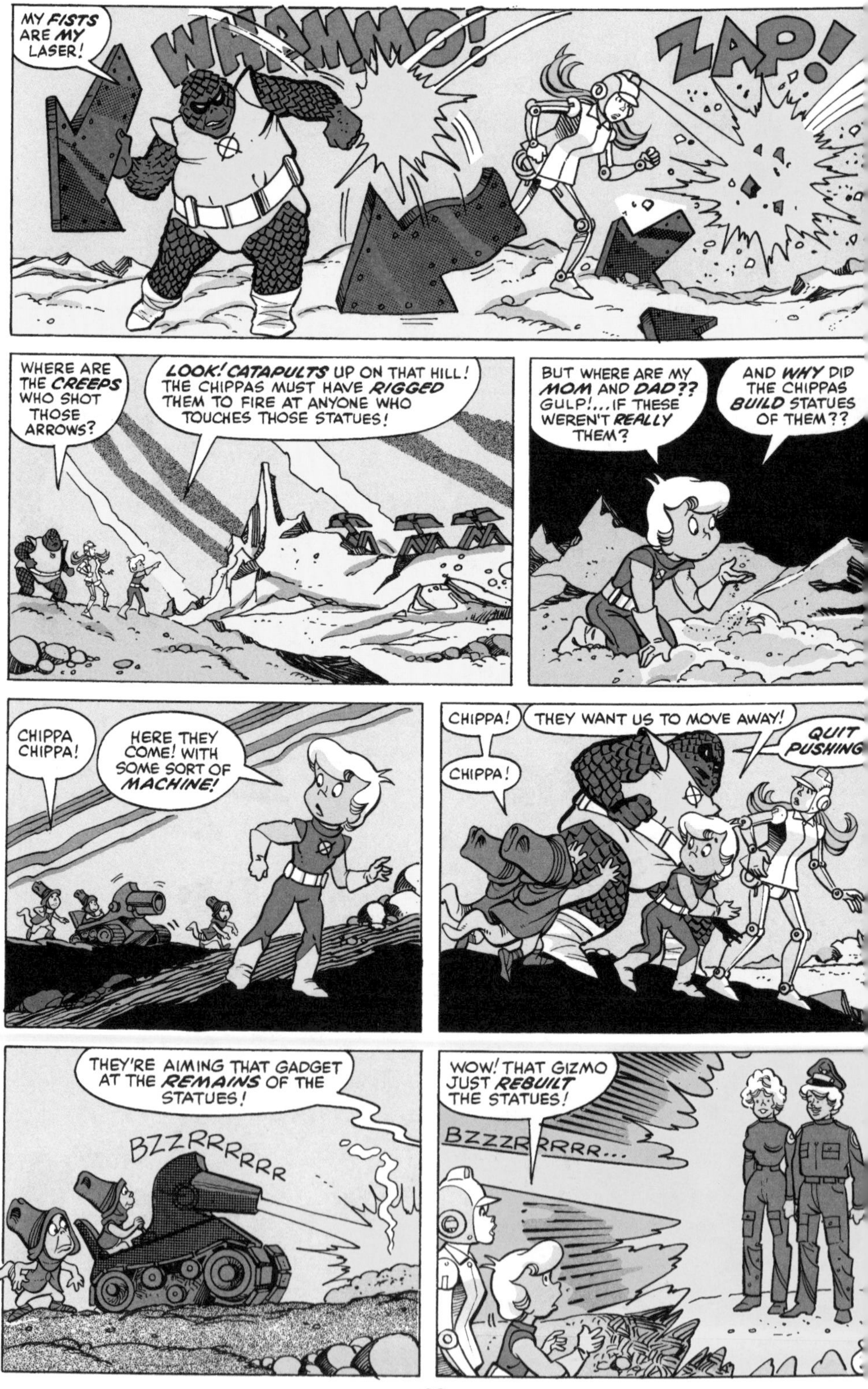
MY FISTS ARE MY LASER!
WHAMMO!
ZAP!
WHERE ARE THE CREEPS WHO SHOT THOSE ARROWS?
LOOK! CATAPULTS UP ON THAT HILL! THE CHIPPAS MUST HAVE RIGGED THEM TO FIRE AT ANYONE WHO TOUCHES THOSE STATUES!
BUT WHERE ARE MY MOM AND DAD?? GULP!... IF THESE WEREN'T REALLY THEM?
AND WHY DID THE CHIPPAS BUILD STATUES OF THEM??
CHIPPA CHIPPA!
HERE THEY COME! WITH SOME SORT OF MACHINE!
CHIPPA!
CHIPPA!
THEY WANT US TO MOVE AWAY!
QUIT PUSHING
THEY'RE AIMING THAT GADGET AT THE REMAINS OF THE STATUES!
BZZRRRRRR
WOW! THAT GIZMO JUST REBUILT THE STATUES!
BZZZRRRRR...

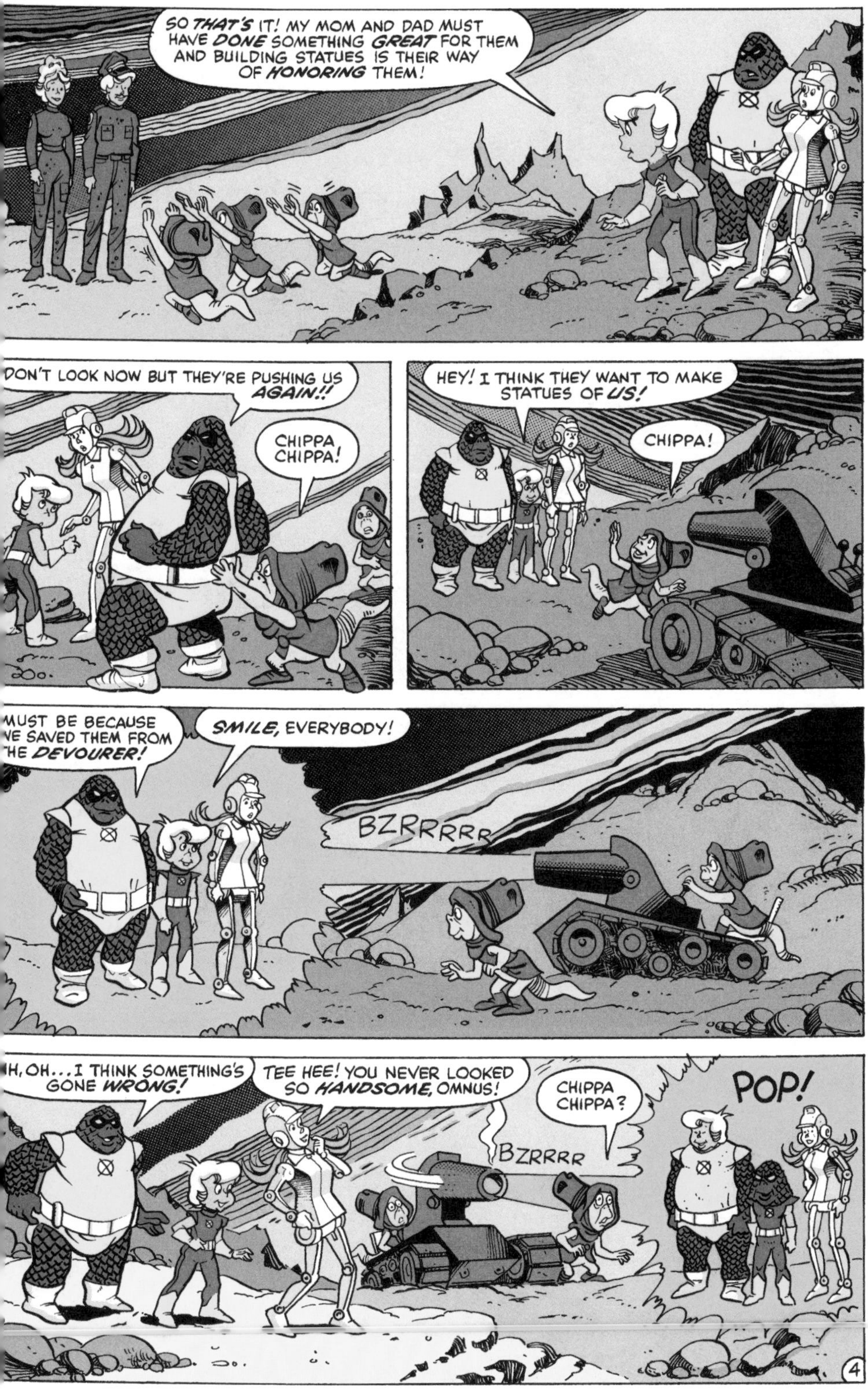
SO THAT'S IT! MY MOM AND DAD MUST HAVE DONE SOMETHING GREAT FOR THEM AND BUILDING STATUES IS THEIR WAY OF HONORING THEM!
DON'T LOOK NOW BUT THEY'RE PUSHING US AGAIN!!
CHIPPA CHIPPA!
HEY! I THINK THEY WANT TO MAKE STATUES OF US!
CHIPPA!
MUST BE BECAUSE WE SAVED THEM FROM THE DEVOURER!
SMILE, EVERYBODY!
BZRRRRRR
UH, OH... I THINK SOMETHING'S GONE WRONG!
TEE HEE! YOU NEVER LOOKED SO HANDSOME, OMNUS!
CHIPPA CHIPPA?
BZRRRR
POP!
4

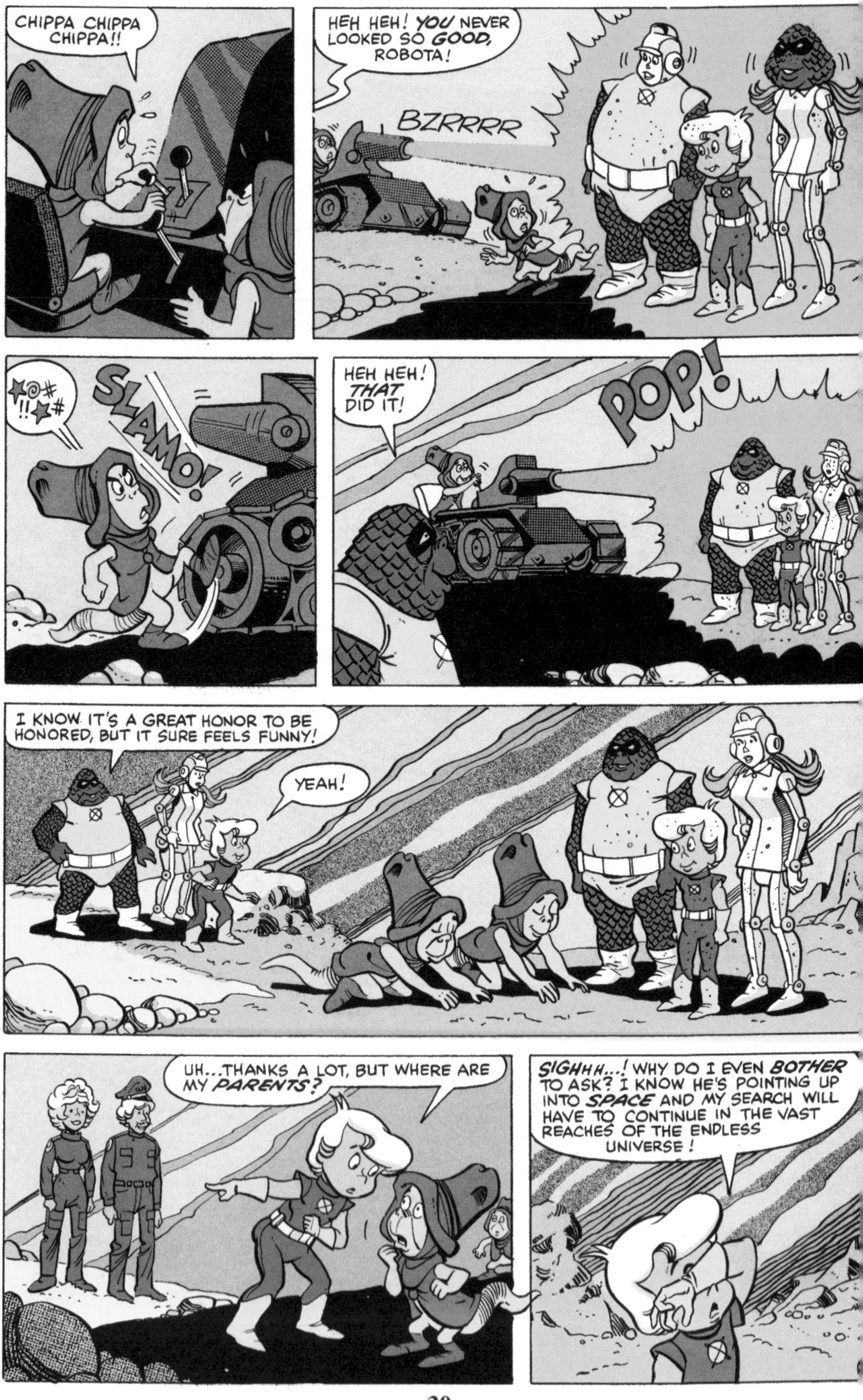
CHIPPA CHIPPA CHIPPA!!
HEH HEH! YOU NEVER LOOKED SO GOOD, ROBOTA!
BZRRRR
★@#
!!★#
SLAMO!
HEH HEH! THAT DID IT!
POP!
I KNOW IT'S A GREAT HONOR TO BE HONORED, BUT IT SURE FEELS FUNNY!
YEAH!
UH...THANKS A LOT, BUT WHERE ARE MY PARENTS?
SIGHHH...! WHY DO I EVEN BOTHER TO ASK? I KNOW HE'S POINTING UP INTO SPACE AND MY SEARCH WILL HAVE TO CONTINUE IN THE VAST REACHES OF THE ENDLESS UNIVERSE!

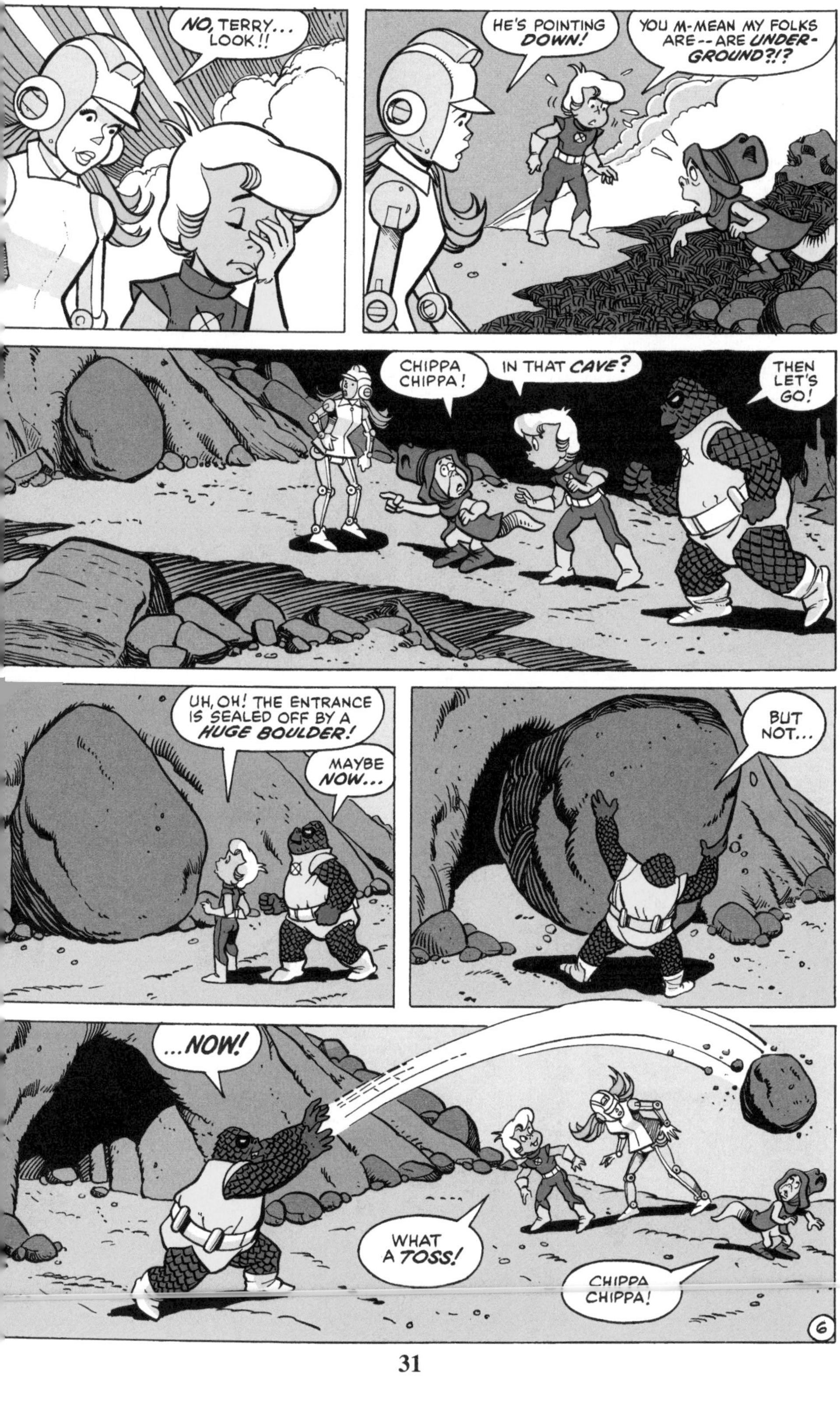
NO, TERRY... LOOK!!
HE'S POINTING DOWN!
YOU M-MEAN MY FOLKS ARE--ARE UNDER-GROUND?!?
CHIPPA CHIPPA!
IN THAT CAVE?
THEN LET'S GO!
UH, OH! THE ENTRANCE IS SEALED OFF BY A HUGE BOULDER!
MAYBE NOW...
BUT NOT...
...NOW!
WHAT A TOSS!
CHIPPA CHIPPA!
6

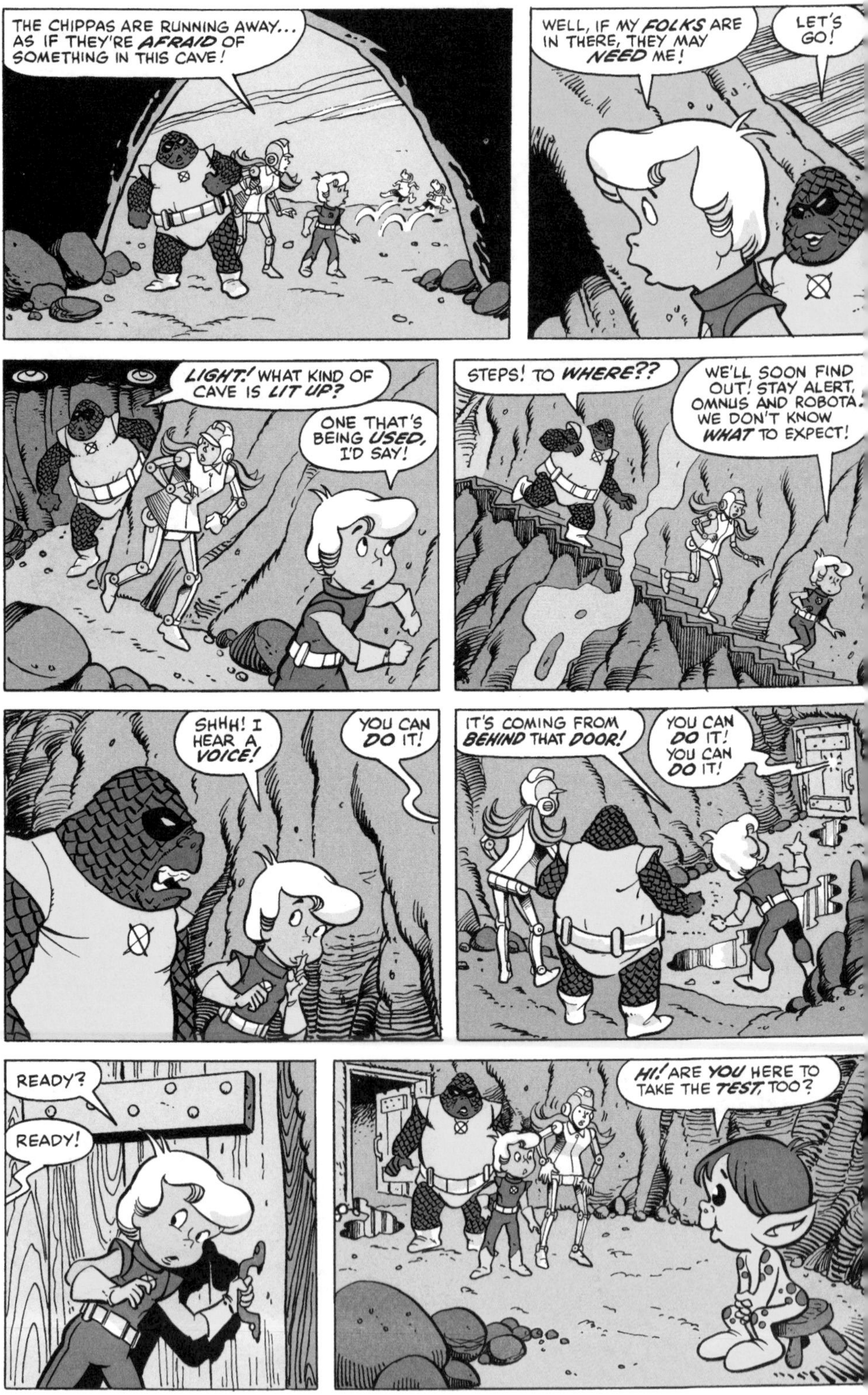
THE CHIPPAS ARE RUNNING AWAY... AS IF THEY'RE AFRAID OF SOMETHING IN THIS CAVE!
WELL, IF MY FOLKS ARE IN THERE, THEY MAY NEED ME!
LET'S GO!
LIGHT! WHAT KIND OF CAVE IS LIT UP?
ONE THAT'S BEING USED, I'D SAY!
STEPS! TO WHERE??
WE'LL SOON FIND OUT! STAY ALERT, OMNUS AND ROBOTA. WE DON'T KNOW WHAT TO EXPECT!
SHHH! I HEAR A VOICE!
YOU CAN DO IT!
IT'S COMING FROM BEHIND THAT DOOR!
YOU CAN DO IT! YOU CAN DO IT!
READY?
READY!
HI! ARE YOU HERE TO TAKE THE TEST, TOO?

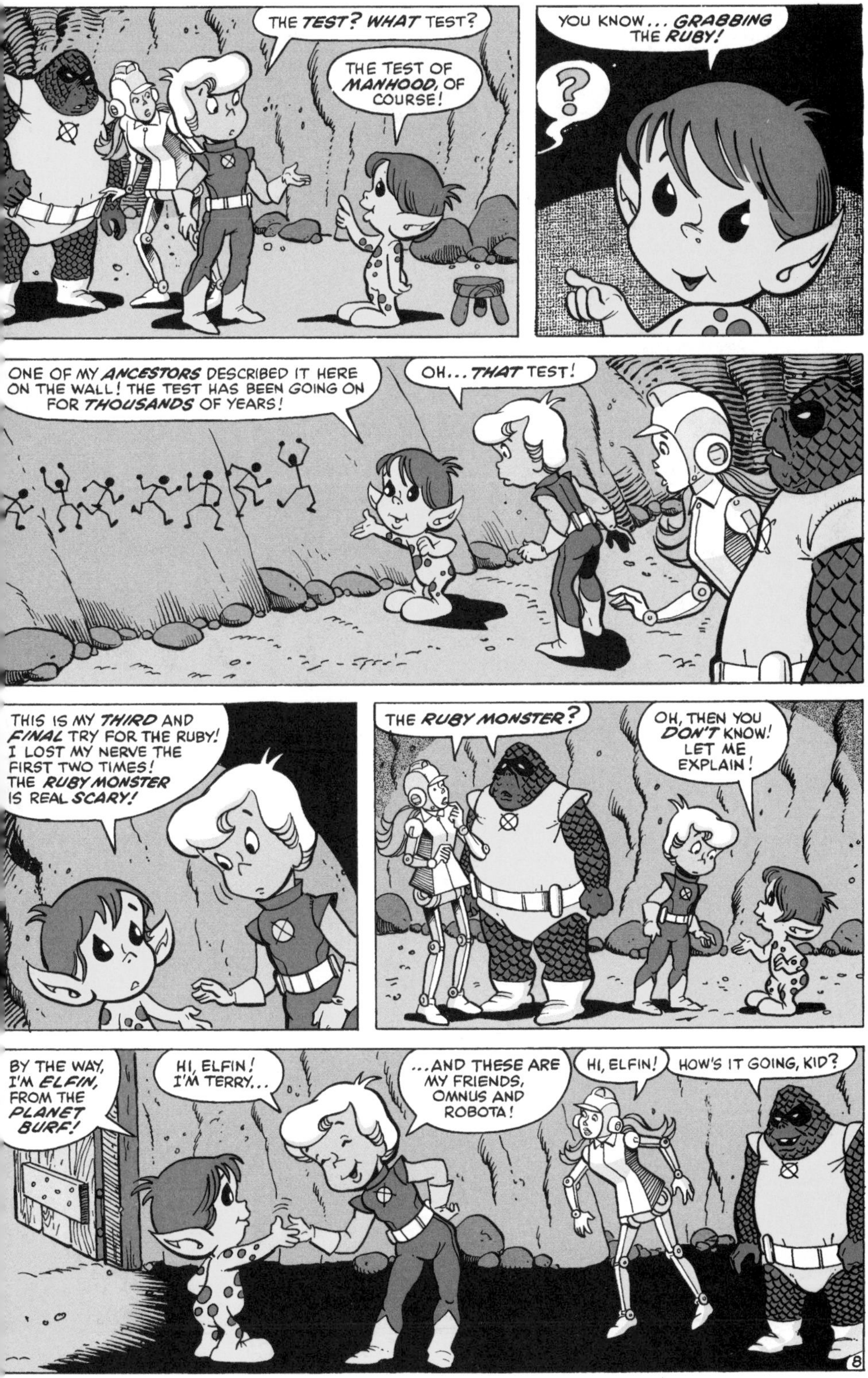
THE TEST? WHAT TEST?
THE TEST OF MANHOOD, OF COURSE!
YOU KNOW... GRABBING THE RUBY!
?
ONE OF MY ANCESTORS DESCRIBED IT HERE ON THE WALL! THE TEST HAS BEEN GOING ON FOR THOUSANDS OF YEARS!
OH... THAT TEST!
THIS IS MY THIRD AND FINAL TRY FOR THE RUBY! I LOST MY NERVE THE FIRST TWO TIMES! THE RUBY MONSTER IS REAL SCARY!
THE RUBY MONSTER?
OH, THEN YOU DON'T KNOW! LET ME EXPLAIN!
BY THE WAY, I'M ELFIN, FROM THE PLANET BURF!
HI, ELFIN! I'M TERRY...
...AND THESE ARE MY FRIENDS, OMNUS AND ROBOTA!
HI, ELFIN!
HOW'S IT GOING, KID?
8

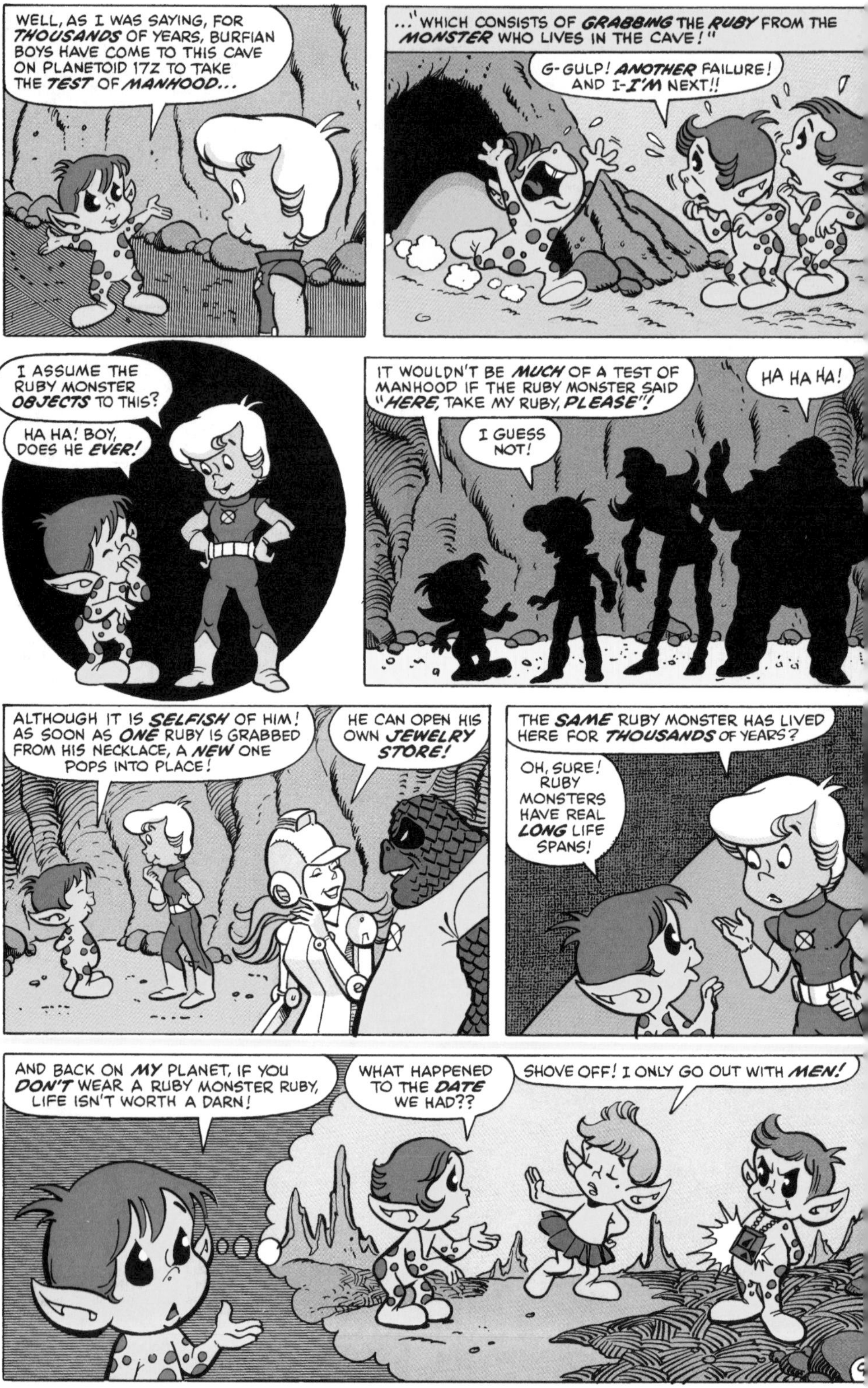

WELL, AS I WAS SAYING, FOR THOUSANDS OF YEARS, BURFIAN BOYS HAVE COME TO THIS CAVE ON PLANETOID 17Z TO TAKE THE TEST OF MANHOOD...
..."WHICH CONSISTS OF GRABBING THE RUBY FROM THE MONSTER WHO LIVES IN THE CAVE!"
G-GULP! ANOTHER FAILURE! AND I-I'M NEXT!!
I ASSUME THE RUBY MONSTER OBJECTS TO THIS?
HA HA! BOY, DOES HE EVER!
IT WOULDN'T BE MUCH OF A TEST OF MANHOOD IF THE RUBY MONSTER SAID "HERE, TAKE MY RUBY, PLEASE"!
HA HA HA!
I GUESS NOT!
ALTHOUGH IT IS SELFISH OF HIM! AS SOON AS ONE RUBY IS GRABBED FROM HIS NECKLACE, A NEW ONE POPS INTO PLACE!
HE CAN OPEN HIS OWN JEWELRY STORE!
THE SAME RUBY MONSTER HAS LIVED HERE FOR THOUSANDS OF YEARS?
OH, SURE! RUBY MONSTERS HAVE REAL LONG LIFE SPANS!
AND BACK ON MY PLANET, IF YOU DON'T WEAR A RUBY MONSTER RUBY, LIFE ISN'T WORTH A DARN!
WHAT HAPPENED TO THE DATE WE HAD??
SHOVE OFF! I ONLY GO OUT WITH MEN!

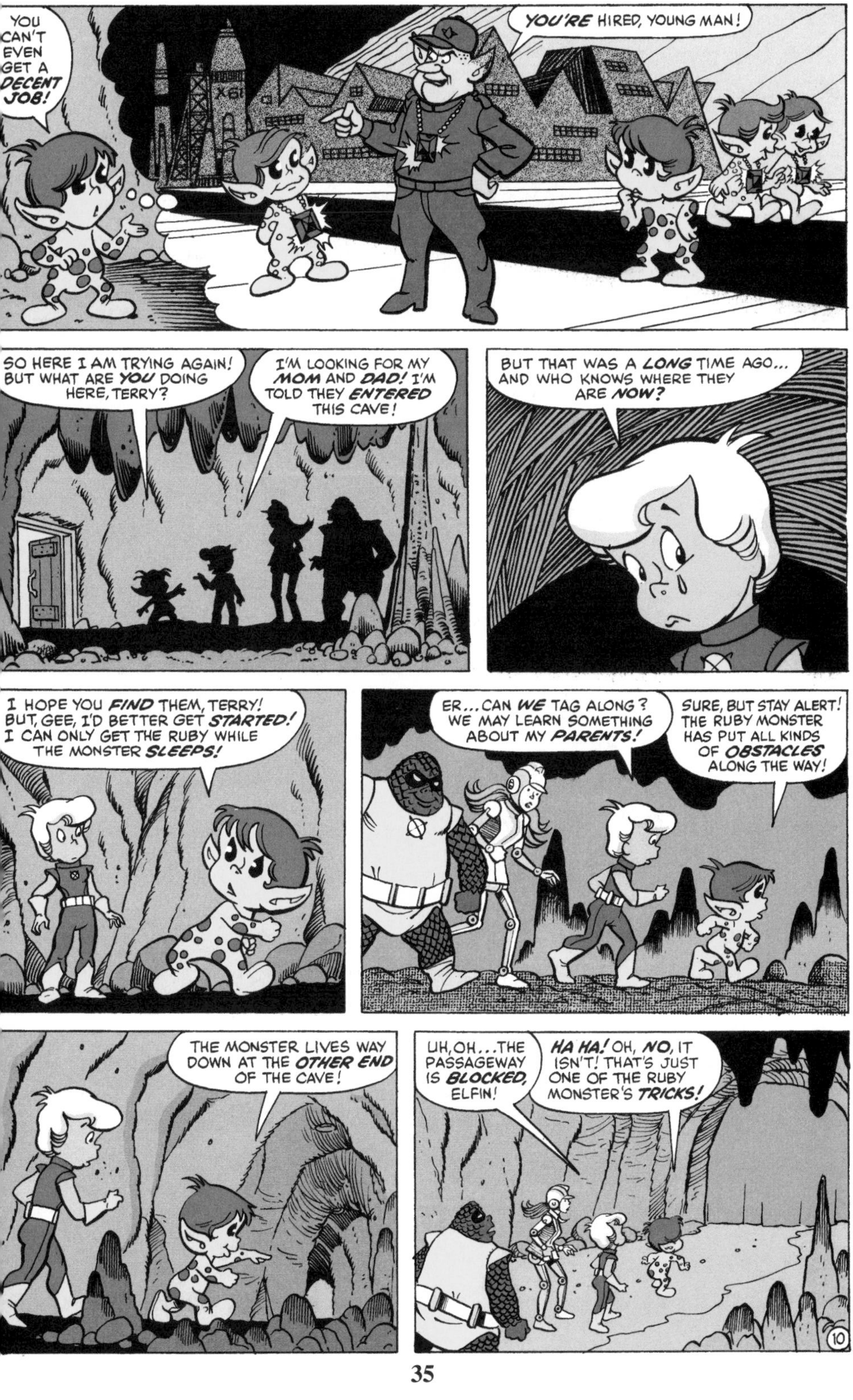
YOU CAN'T EVEN GET A DECENT JOB!
YOU'RE HIRED, YOUNG MAN!
X61
SO HERE I AM TRYING AGAIN! BUT WHAT ARE YOU DOING HERE, TERRY?
I'M LOOKING FOR MY MOM AND DAD! I'M TOLD THEY ENTERED THIS CAVE!
BUT THAT WAS A LONG TIME AGO... AND WHO KNOWS WHERE THEY ARE NOW?
I HOPE YOU FIND THEM, TERRY! BUT, GEE, I'D BETTER GET STARTED! I CAN ONLY GET THE RUBY WHILE THE MONSTER SLEEPS!
ER... CAN WE TAG ALONG? WE MAY LEARN SOMETHING ABOUT MY PARENTS!
SURE, BUT STAY ALERT! THE RUBY MONSTER HAS PUT ALL KINDS OF OBSTACLES ALONG THE WAY!
THE MONSTER LIVES WAY DOWN AT THE OTHER END OF THE CAVE!
UH, OH... THE PASSAGEWAY IS BLOCKED, ELFIN!
HA HA! OH, NO, IT ISN'T! THAT'S JUST ONE OF THE RUBY MONSTER'S TRICKS!
10

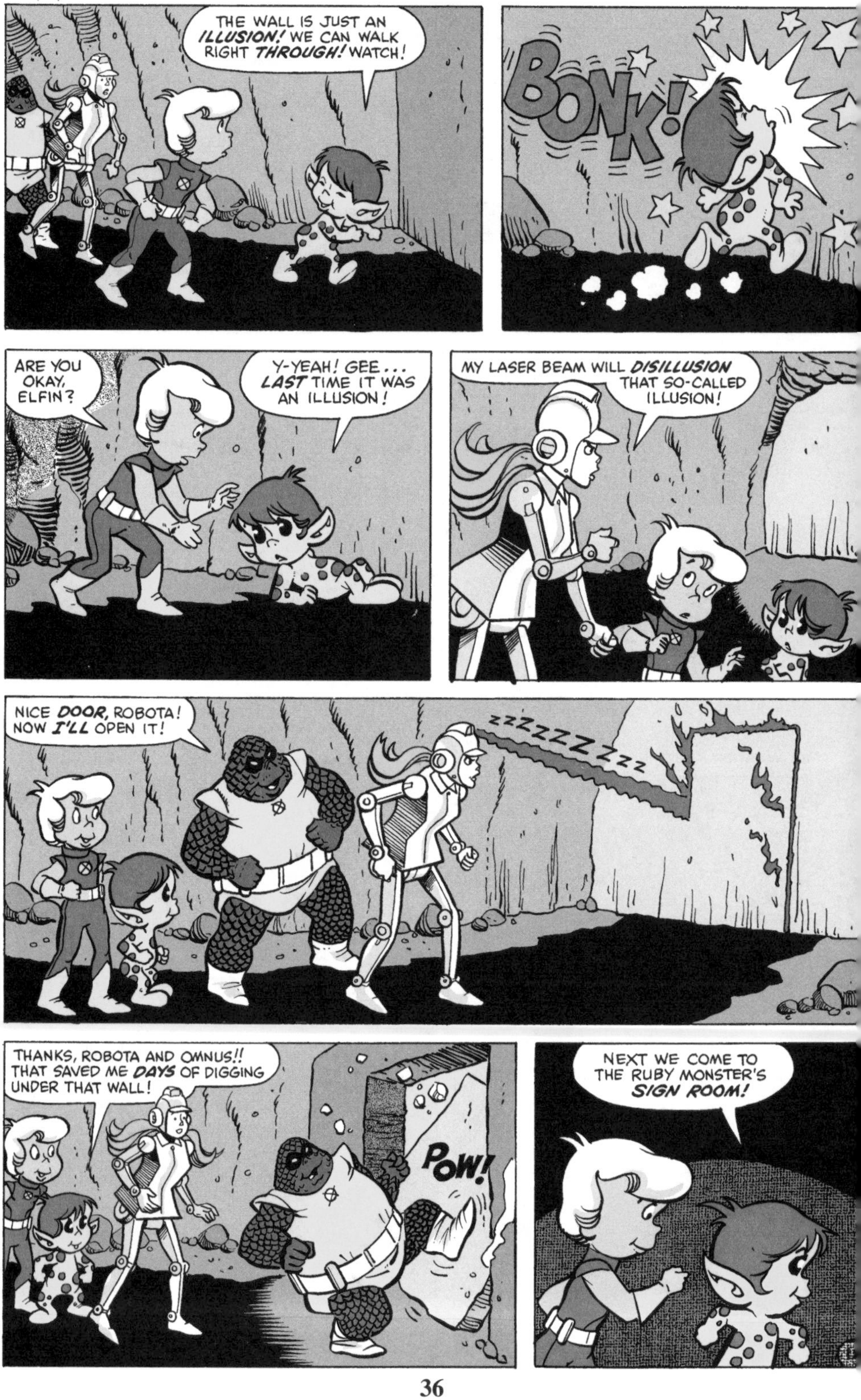
THE WALL IS JUST AN ILLUSION! WE CAN WALK RIGHT THROUGH! WATCH!
BONK!
ARE YOU OKAY, ELFIN?
Y-YEAH! GEE... LAST TIME IT WAS AN ILLUSION!
MY LASER BEAM WILL DISILLUSION THAT SO-CALLED ILLUSION!
NICE DOOR, ROBOTA! NOW I'LL OPEN IT!
zzZZZZZZzzz
THANKS, ROBOTA AND OMNUS!! THAT SAVED ME DAYS OF DIGGING UNDER THAT WALL!
POW!
NEXT WE COME TO THE RUBY MONSTER'S SIGN ROOM!

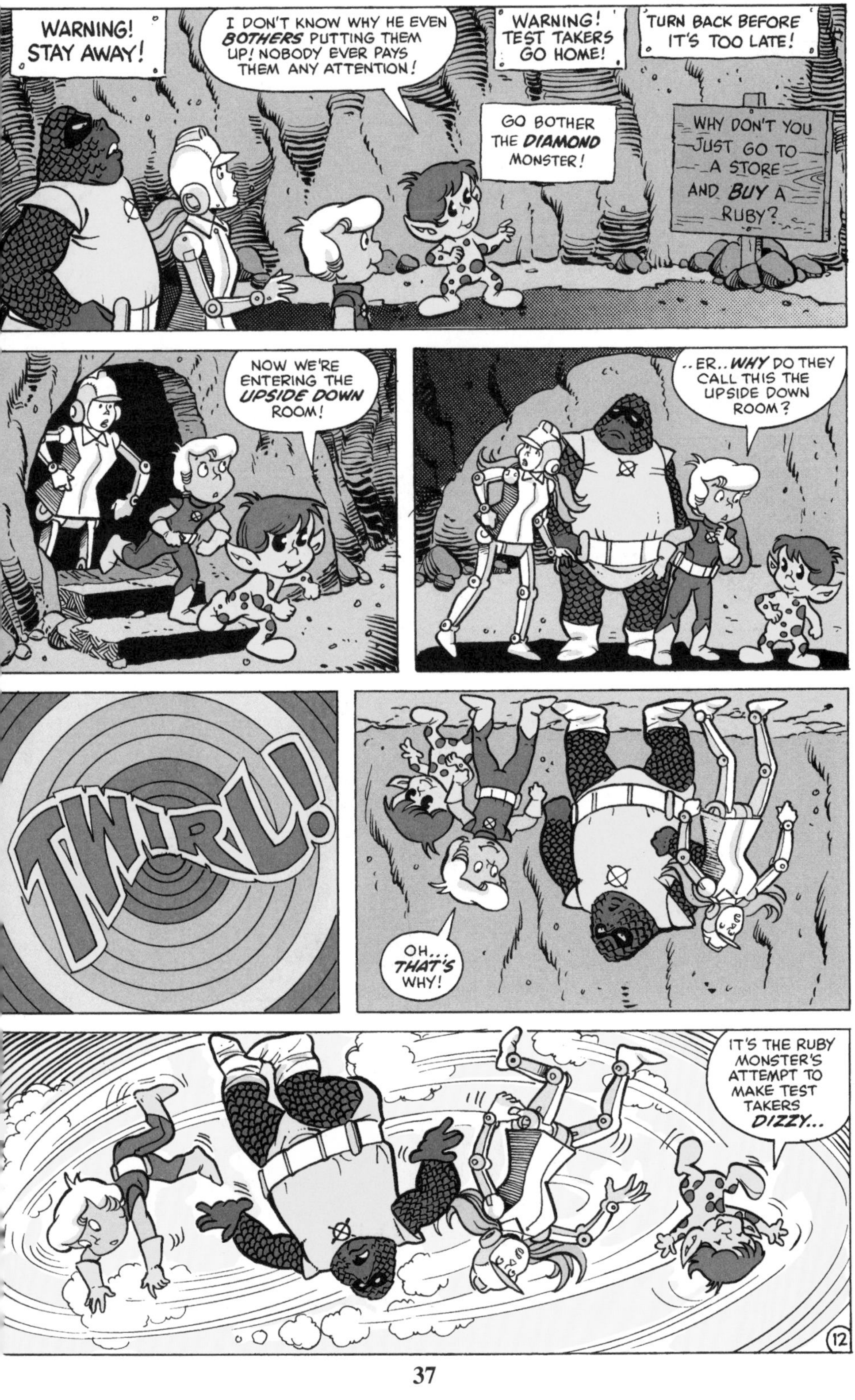
WARNING! STAY AWAY!
I DON'T KNOW WHY HE EVEN BOTHERS PUTTING THEM UP! NOBODY EVER PAYS THEM ANY ATTENTION!
WARNING! TEST TAKERS GO HOME!
TURN BACK BEFORE IT'S TOO LATE!
GO BOTHER THE DIAMOND MONSTER!
WHY DON'T YOU JUST GO TO A STORE AND BUY A RUBY?
NOW WE'RE ENTERING THE UPSIDE DOWN ROOM!
..ER.. WHY DO THEY CALL THIS THE UPSIDE DOWN ROOM?
TWIRL!
OH... THAT'S WHY!
IT'S THE RUBY MONSTER'S ATTEMPT TO MAKE TEST TAKERS DIZZY...
12

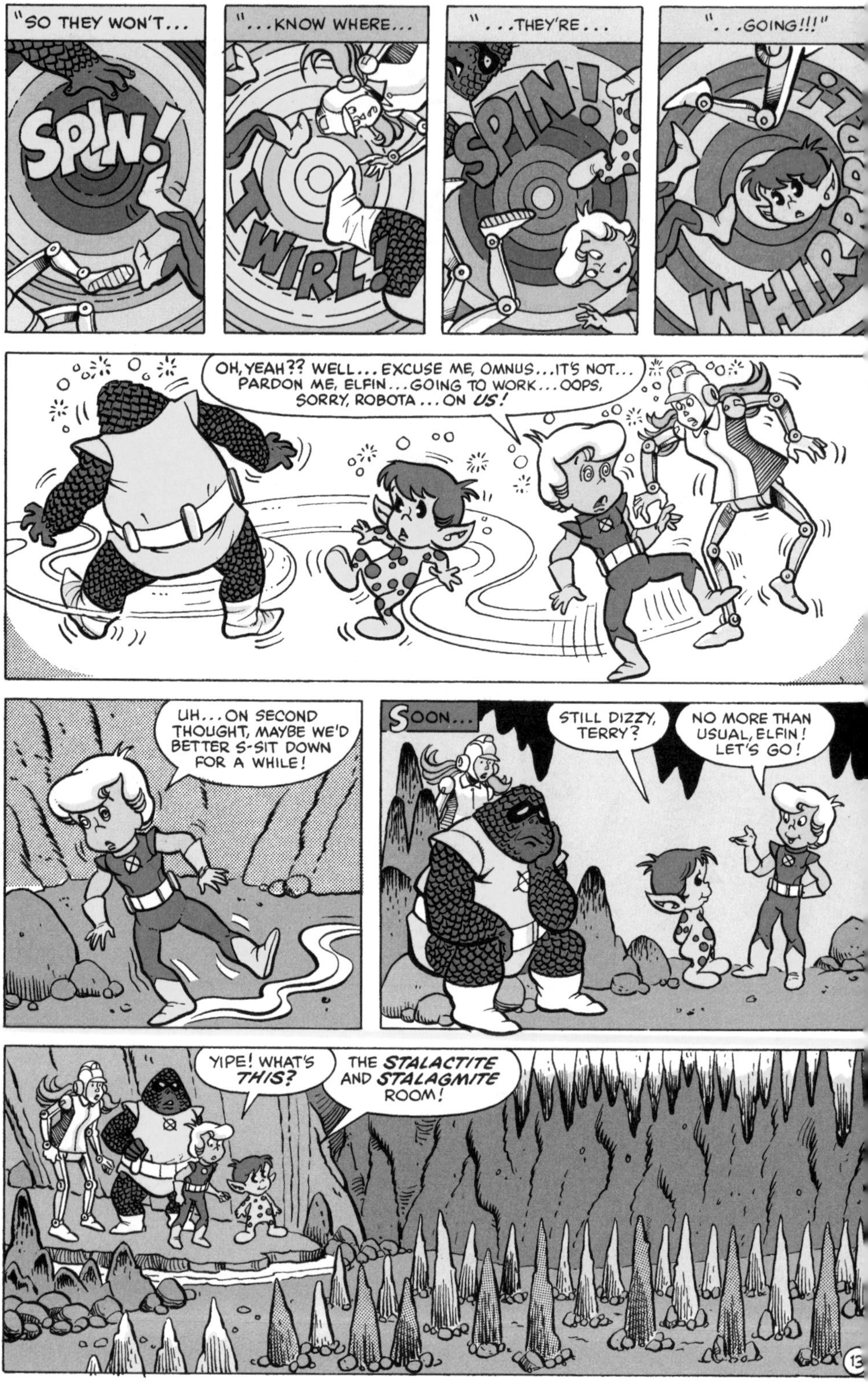
"SO THEY WON'T...
SPIN!
"...KNOW WHERE...
TWIRL!
"...THEY'RE...
SPIN!
"...GOING!!!"
WHIRRRL!
OH, YEAH?? WELL... EXCUSE ME, OMNUS...IT'S NOT... PARDON ME, ELFIN...GOING TO WORK...OOPS, SORRY, ROBOTA...ON US!
UH...ON SECOND THOUGHT, MAYBE WE'D BETTER S-SIT DOWN FOR A WHILE!
SOON...
STILL DIZZY, TERRY?
NO MORE THAN USUAL, ELFIN! LET'S GO!
YIPE! WHAT'S THIS?
THE STALACTITE AND STALAGMITE ROOM!
13

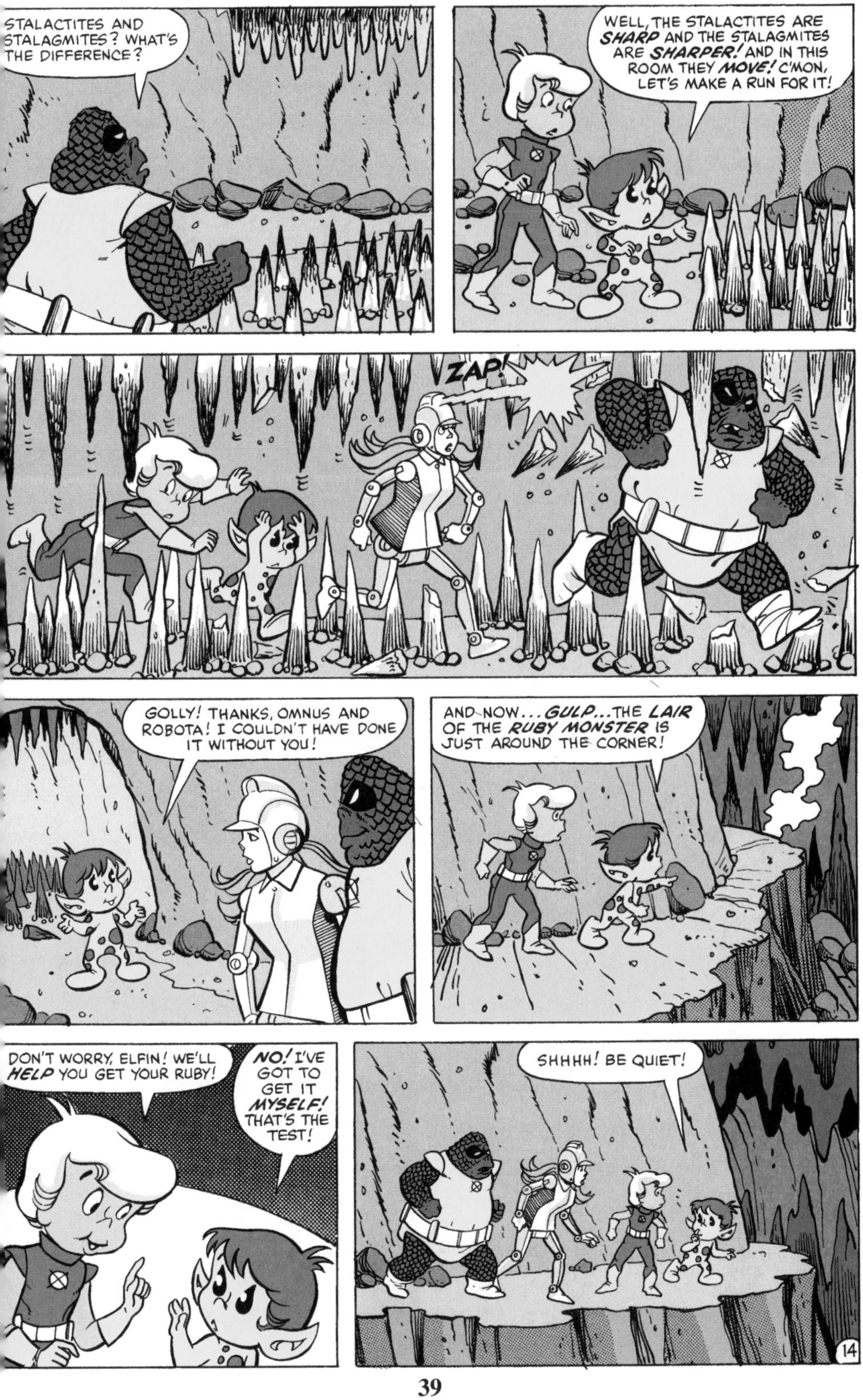
STALACTITES AND STALAGMITES? WHAT'S THE DIFFERENCE?
WELL, THE STALACTITES ARE SHARP AND THE STALAGMITES ARE SHARPER! AND IN THIS ROOM THEY MOVE! C'MON, LET'S MAKE A RUN FOR IT!
ZAP!
GOLLY! THANKS, OMNUS AND ROBOTA! I COULDN'T HAVE DONE IT WITHOUT YOU!
AND NOW... GULP... THE LAIR OF THE RUBY MONSTER IS JUST AROUND THE CORNER!
DON'T WORRY, ELFIN! WE'LL HELP YOU GET YOUR RUBY!
NO! I'VE GOT TO GET IT MYSELF! THAT'S THE TEST!
SHHHH! BE QUIET!
14

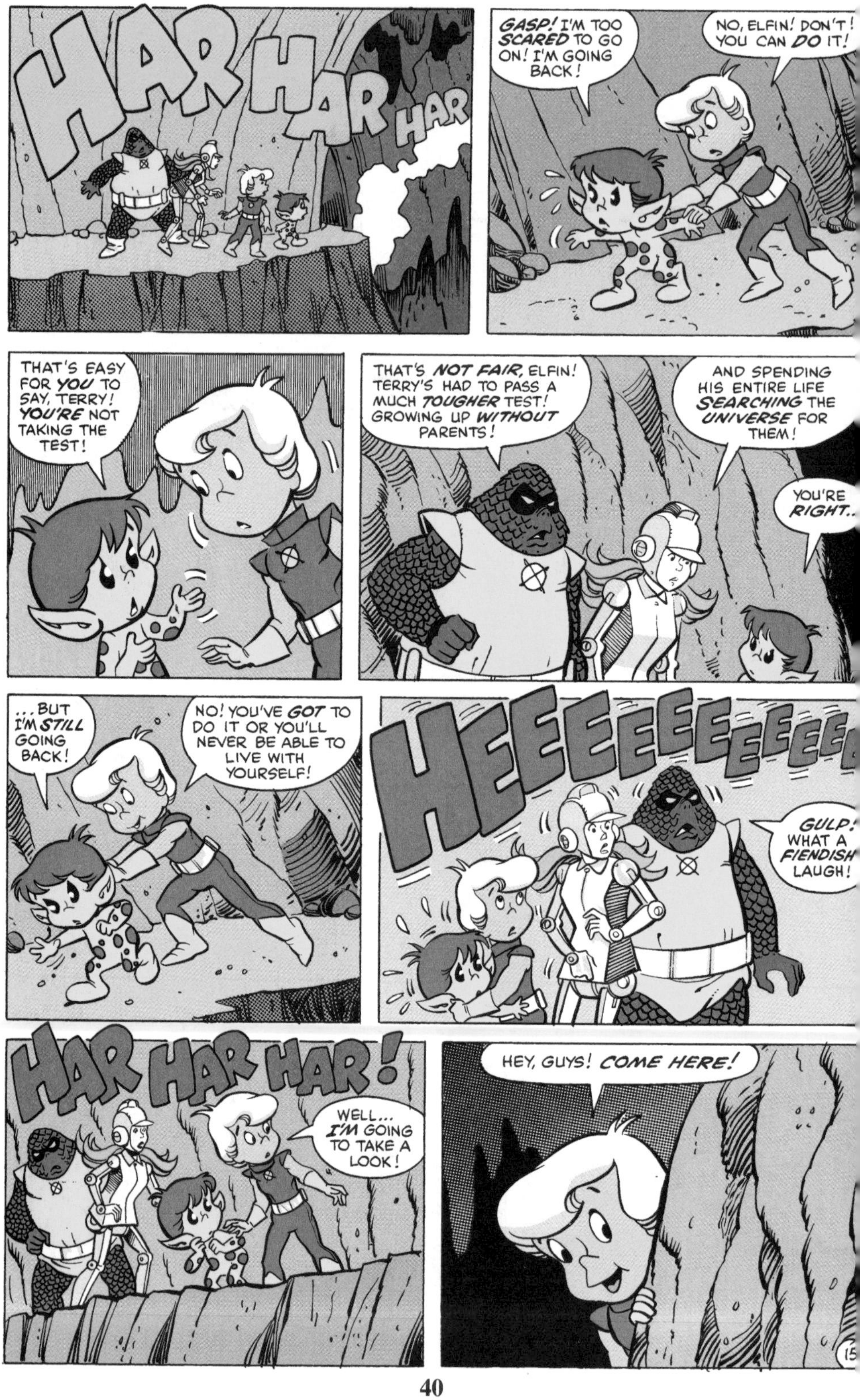
HAR HAR HAR
GASP! I'M TOO SCARED TO GO ON! I'M GOING BACK!
NO, ELFIN! DON'T! YOU CAN DO IT!
THAT'S EASY FOR YOU TO SAY, TERRY! YOU'RE NOT TAKING THE TEST!
THAT'S NOT FAIR, ELFIN! TERRY'S HAD TO PASS A MUCH TOUGHER TEST! GROWING UP WITHOUT PARENTS!
AND SPENDING HIS ENTIRE LIFE SEARCHING THE UNIVERSE FOR THEM!
YOU'RE RIGHT...
...BUT I'M STILL GOING BACK!
NO! YOU'VE GOT TO DO IT OR YOU'LL NEVER BE ABLE TO LIVE WITH YOURSELF!
HEEEEEEEEEE
GULP! WHAT A FIENDISH LAUGH!
HAR HAR HAR!
WELL... I'M GOING TO TAKE A LOOK!
HEY, GUYS! COME HERE!
15

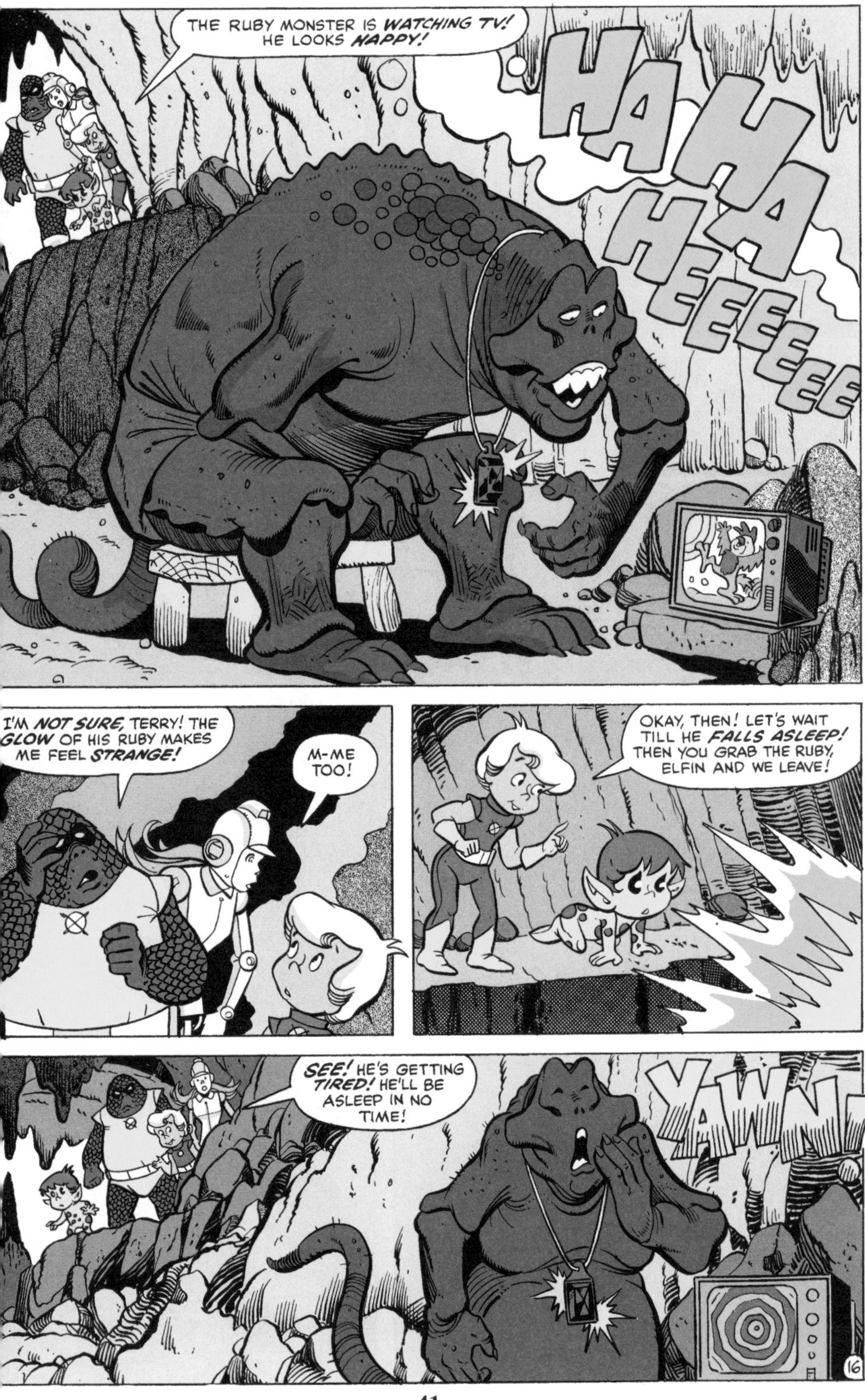
THE RUBY MONSTER IS WATCHING TV! HE LOOKS HAPPY!
HA HA HA HEEEEEEE
I'M NOT SURE, TERRY! THE GLOW OF HIS RUBY MAKES ME FEEL STRANGE!
M-ME TOO!
OKAY, THEN! LET'S WAIT TILL HE FALLS ASLEEP! THEN YOU GRAB THE RUBY, ELFIN AND WE LEAVE!
SEE! HE'S GETTING TIRED! HE'LL BE ASLEEP IN NO TIME!
YAWN!
16

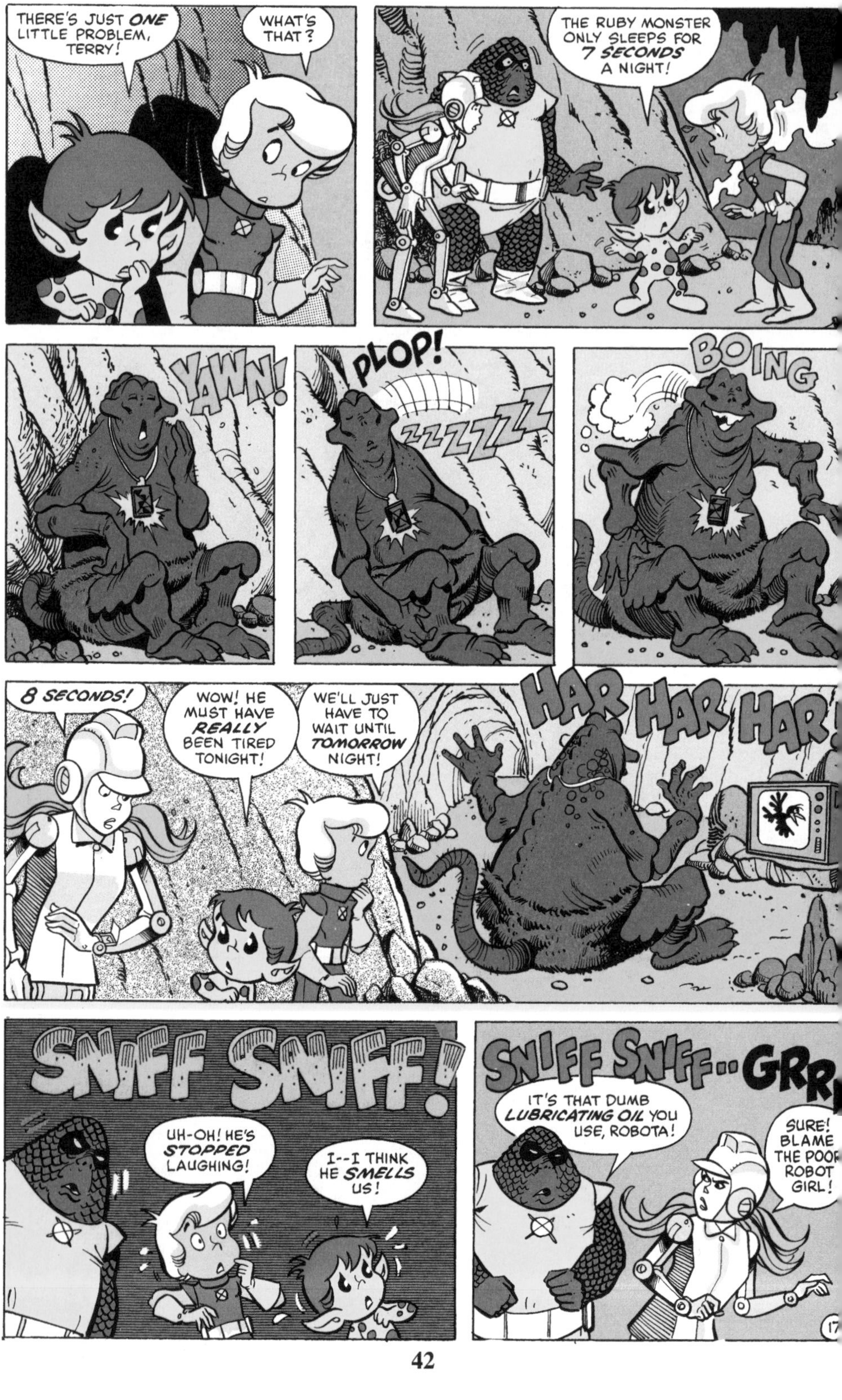
THERE'S JUST ONE LITTLE PROBLEM, TERRY!
WHAT'S THAT?
THE RUBY MONSTER ONLY SLEEPS FOR 7 SECONDS A NIGHT!
YAWN!
PLOP!
ZZZZZZZ
BOING
8 SECONDS!
WOW! HE MUST HAVE REALLY BEEN TIRED TONIGHT!
WE'LL JUST HAVE TO WAIT UNTIL TOMORROW NIGHT!
HAR HAR HAR!
SNIFF SNIFF!
UH-OH! HE'S STOPPED LAUGHING!
I--I THINK HE SMELLS US!
SNIFF SNIFF..GRR
IT'S THAT DUMB LUBRICATING OIL YOU USE, ROBOTA!
SURE! BLAME THE POOR ROBOT GIRL!
17

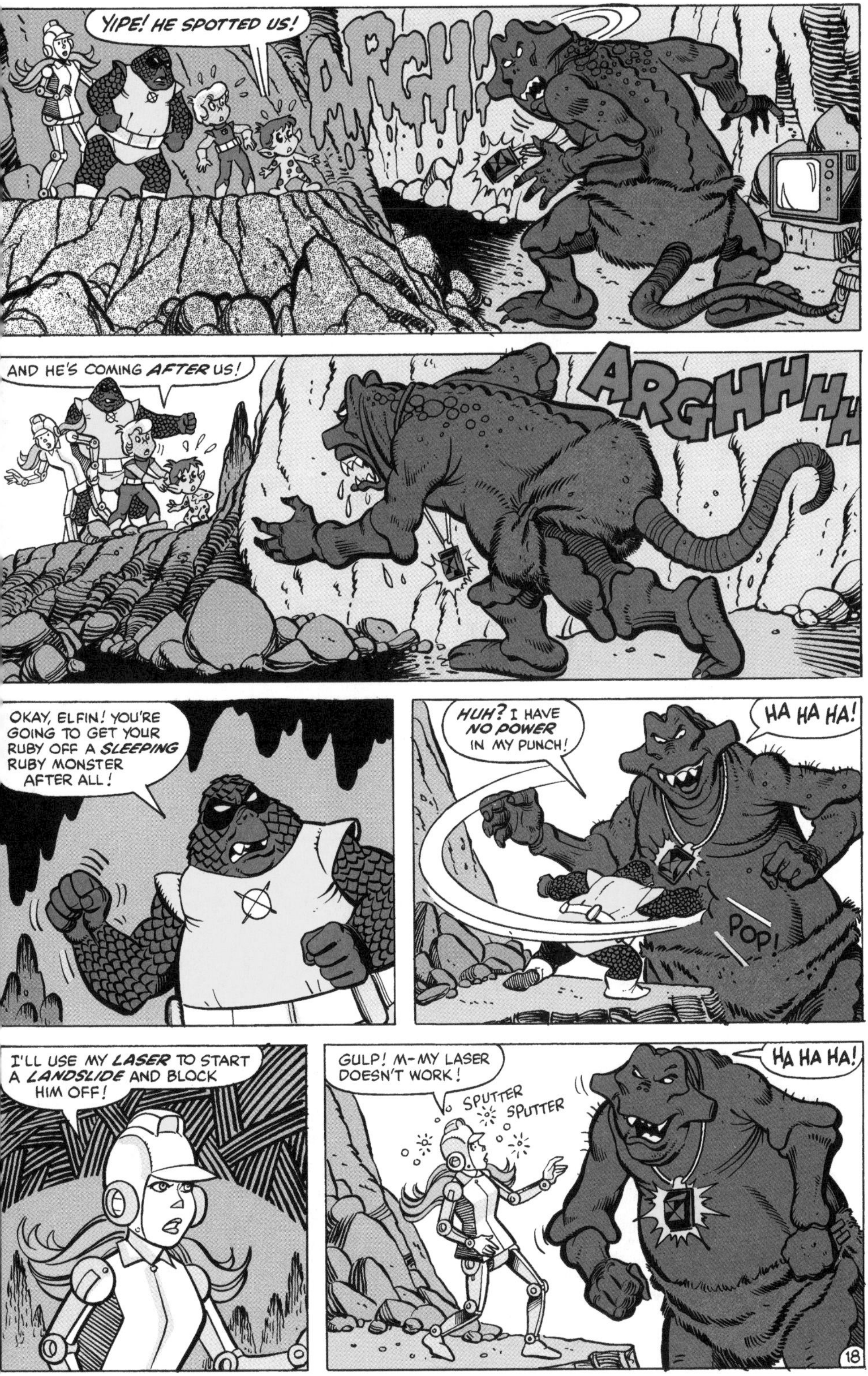
YIPE! HE SPOTTED US!
ARGH!
AND HE'S COMING AFTER US!
ARGHHHH
OKAY, ELFIN! YOU'RE GOING TO GET YOUR RUBY OFF A SLEEPING RUBY MONSTER AFTER ALL!
HUH? I HAVE NO POWER IN MY PUNCH!
HA HA HA!
POP!
I'LL USE MY LASER TO START A LANDSLIDE AND BLOCK HIM OFF!
GULP! M-MY LASER DOESN'T WORK!
SPUTTER
SPUTTER
HA HA HA!
18

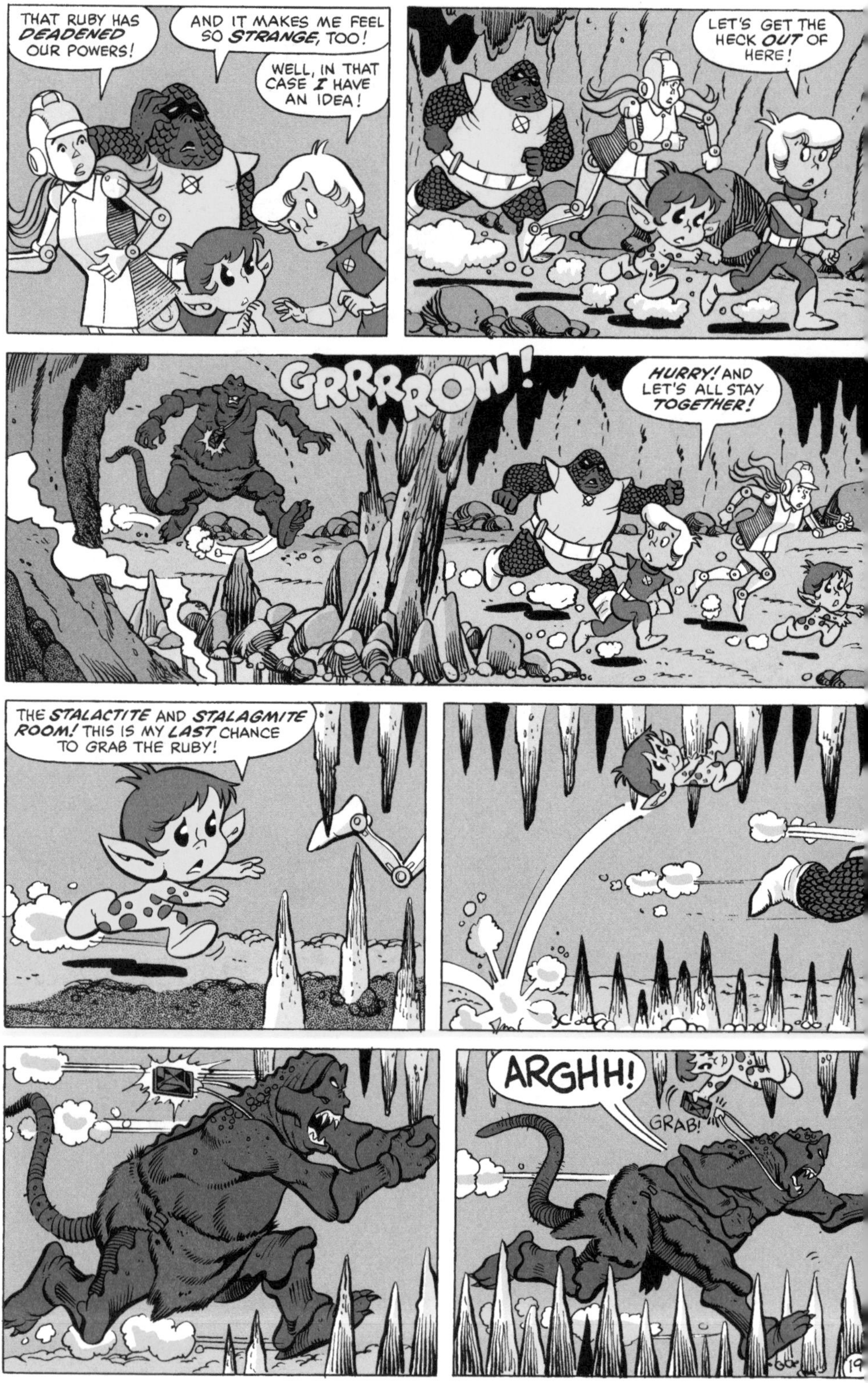
THAT RUBY HAS *DEADENED* OUR POWERS!
AND IT MAKES ME FEEL SO *STRANGE*, TOO!
WELL, IN THAT CASE *I* HAVE AN IDEA!
LET'S GET THE HECK *OUT* OF HERE!
GRRRROW!
HURRY! AND LET'S ALL STAY *TOGETHER!*
THE *STALACTITE* AND *STALAGMITE ROOM!* THIS IS MY *LAST* CHANCE TO GRAB THE RUBY!
ARGHH!
GRAB!
19

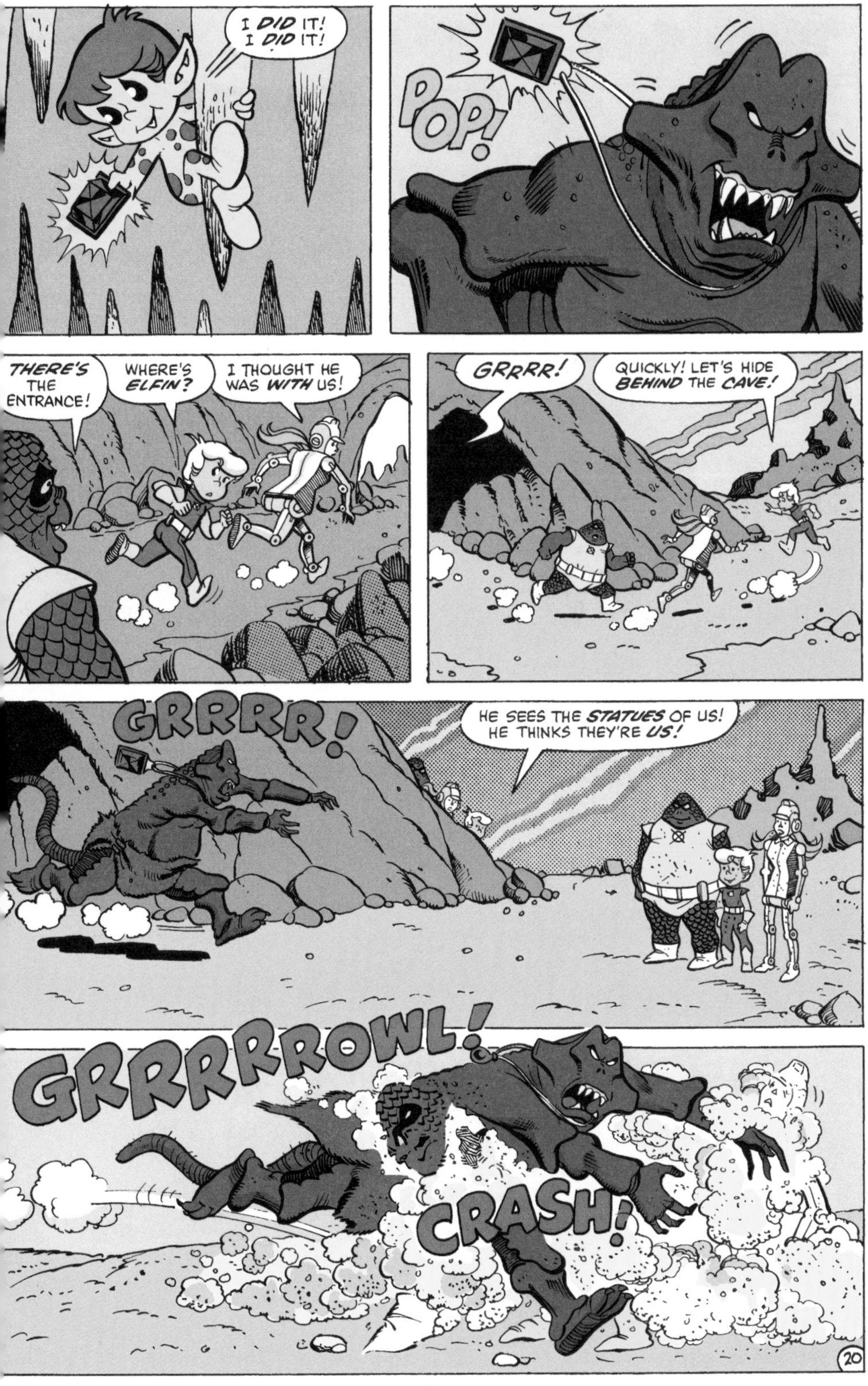

I DID IT! I DID IT!
POP!
THERE'S THE ENTRANCE!
WHERE'S ELFIN?
I THOUGHT HE WAS WITH US!
GRRRR!
QUICKLY! LET'S HIDE BEHIND THE CAVE!
GRRRRR!
HE SEES THE STATUES OF US! HE THINKS THEY'RE US!
GRRRRROWL!
CRASH!
20

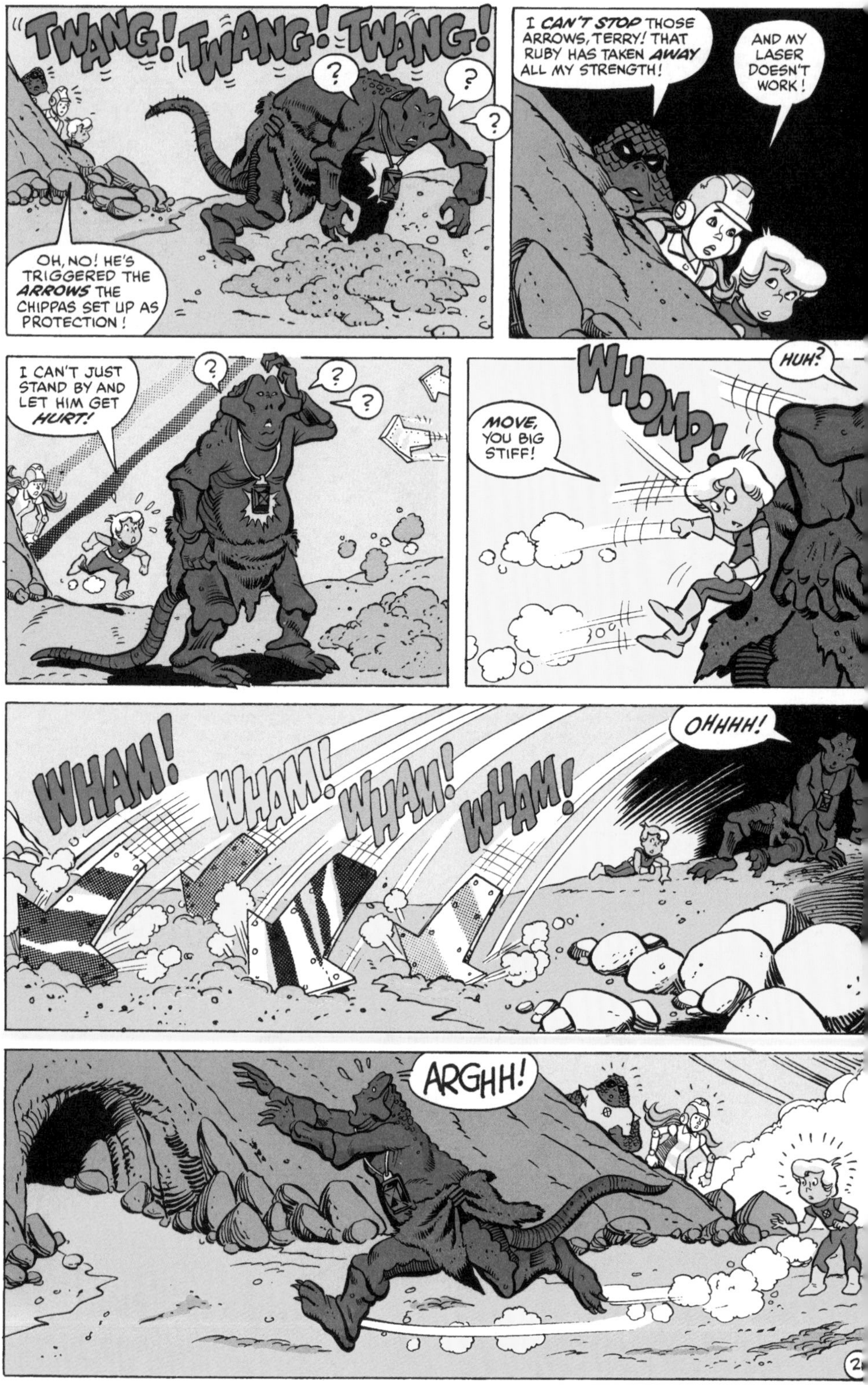
TWANG! TWANG! TWANG!
?
?
?
OH, NO! HE'S TRIGGERED THE ARROWS THE CHIPPAS SET UP AS PROTECTION!
I CAN'T STOP THOSE ARROWS, TERRY! THAT RUBY HAS TAKEN AWAY ALL MY STRENGTH!
AND MY LASER DOESN'T WORK!
I CAN'T JUST STAND BY AND LET HIM GET HURT!
?
?
?
WHOMP!
HUH?
MOVE, YOU BIG STIFF!
WHAM! WHAM! WHAM! WHAM!
OHHHH!
ARGHH!

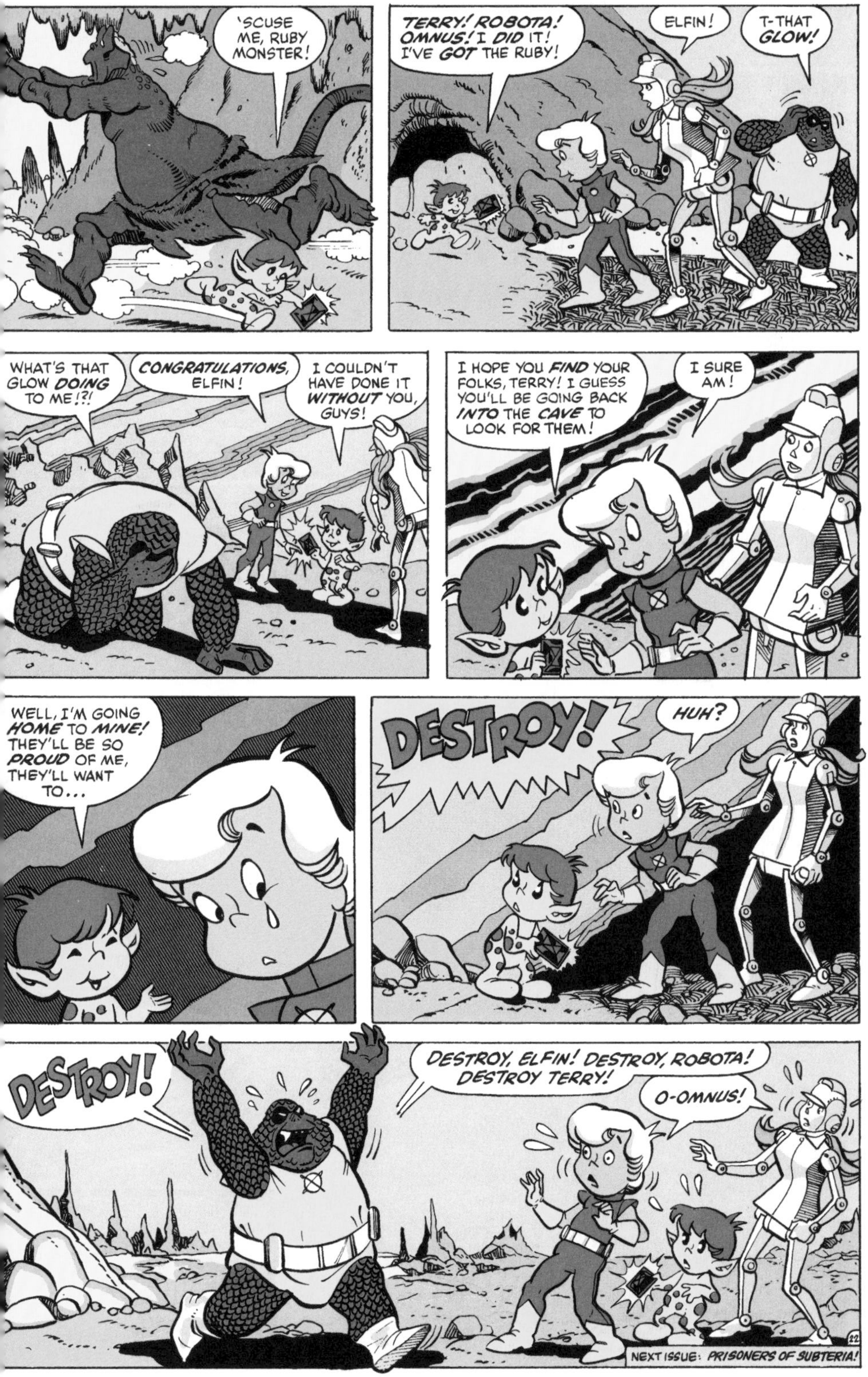
'SCUSE ME, RUBY MONSTER!
TERRY! ROBOTA! OMNUS! I DID IT! I'VE GOT THE RUBY!
ELFIN!
T-THAT GLOW!
WHAT'S THAT GLOW DOING TO ME!?!
CONGRATULATIONS, ELFIN!
I COULDN'T HAVE DONE IT WITHOUT YOU, GUYS!
I HOPE YOU FIND YOUR FOLKS, TERRY! I GUESS YOU'LL BE GOING BACK INTO THE CAVE TO LOOK FOR THEM!
I SURE AM!
WELL, I'M GOING HOME TO MINE! THEY'LL BE SO PROUD OF ME, THEY'LL WANT TO...
DESTROY!
HUH?
DESTROY!
DESTROY, ELFIN! DESTROY, ROBOTA! DESTROY TERRY!
O-OMNUS!
22
NEXT ISSUE: PRISONERS OF SUBTERIA!

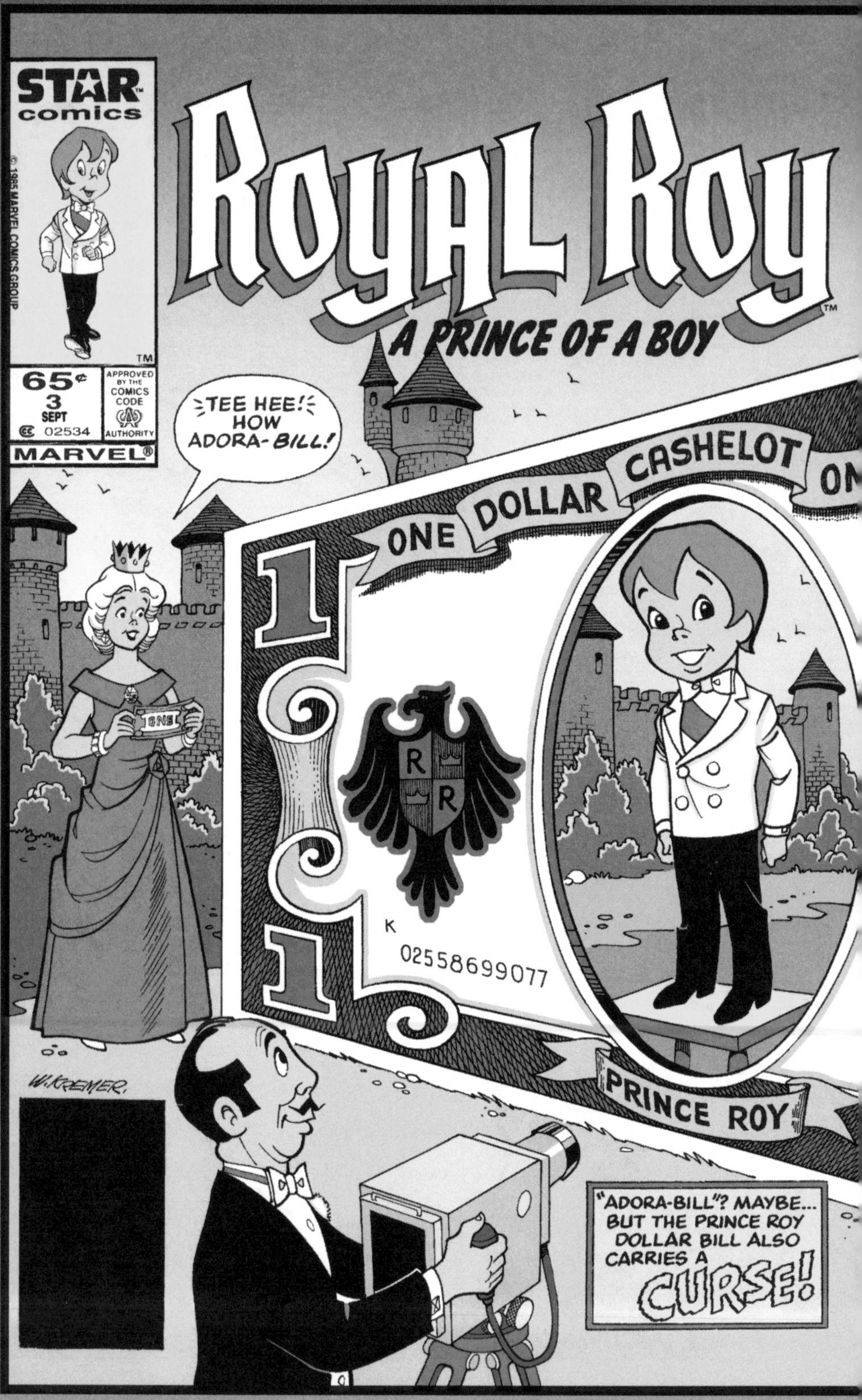

STAR comics
© 1985 MARVEL COMICS GROUP
TM
65¢
3
SEPT
02534
APPROVED BY THE COMICS CODE AUTHORITY
MARVEL®
Royal Roy™
A PRINCE OF A BOY
TEE HEE! HOW ADORA-BILL!
ONE
ONE DOLLAR CASHELOT
1
R R
K
02558699077
1
PRINCE ROY
W. KREMER.
"ADORA-BILL"? MAYBE... BUT THE PRINCE ROY DOLLAR BILL ALSO CARRIES A CURSE!

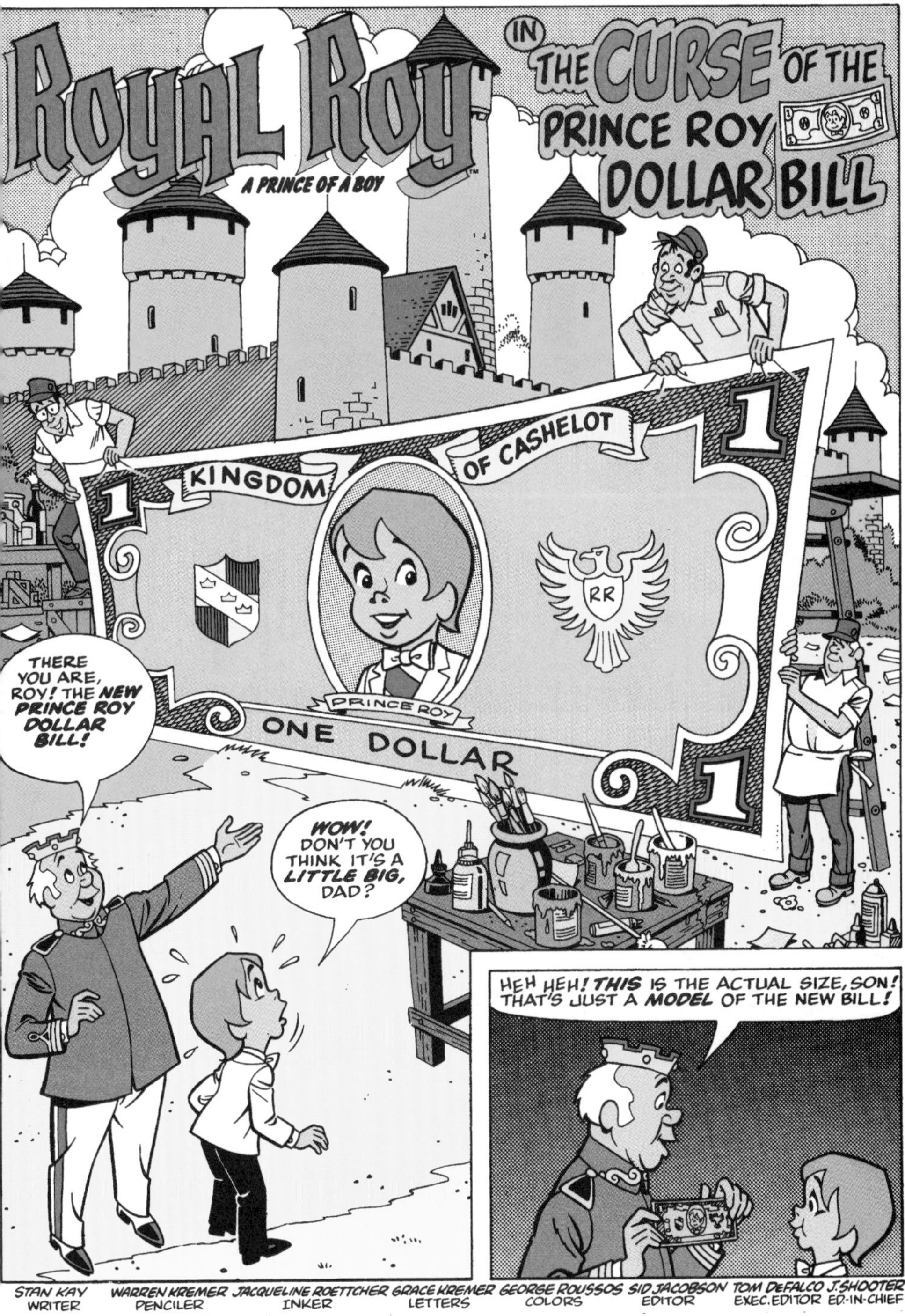

ROYAL ROY
A PRINCE OF A BOY
IN
THE CURSE OF THE PRINCE ROY DOLLAR BILL
KINGDOM
OF CASHELOT
PRINCE ROY
ONE DOLLAR
RR
THERE YOU ARE, ROY! THE NEW PRINCE ROY DOLLAR BILL!
WOW! DON'T YOU THINK IT'S A LITTLE BIG, DAD?
HEH HEH! THIS IS THE ACTUAL SIZE, SON! THAT'S JUST A MODEL OF THE NEW BILL!
STAN KAY WRITER
WARREN KREMER PENCILER
JACQUELINE ROETTCHER INKER
GRACE KREMER LETTERS
GEORGE ROUSSOS COLORS
SID JACOBSON EDITOR
TOM DEFALCO EXEC. EDITOR
J. SHOOTER ED.-IN-CHIEF

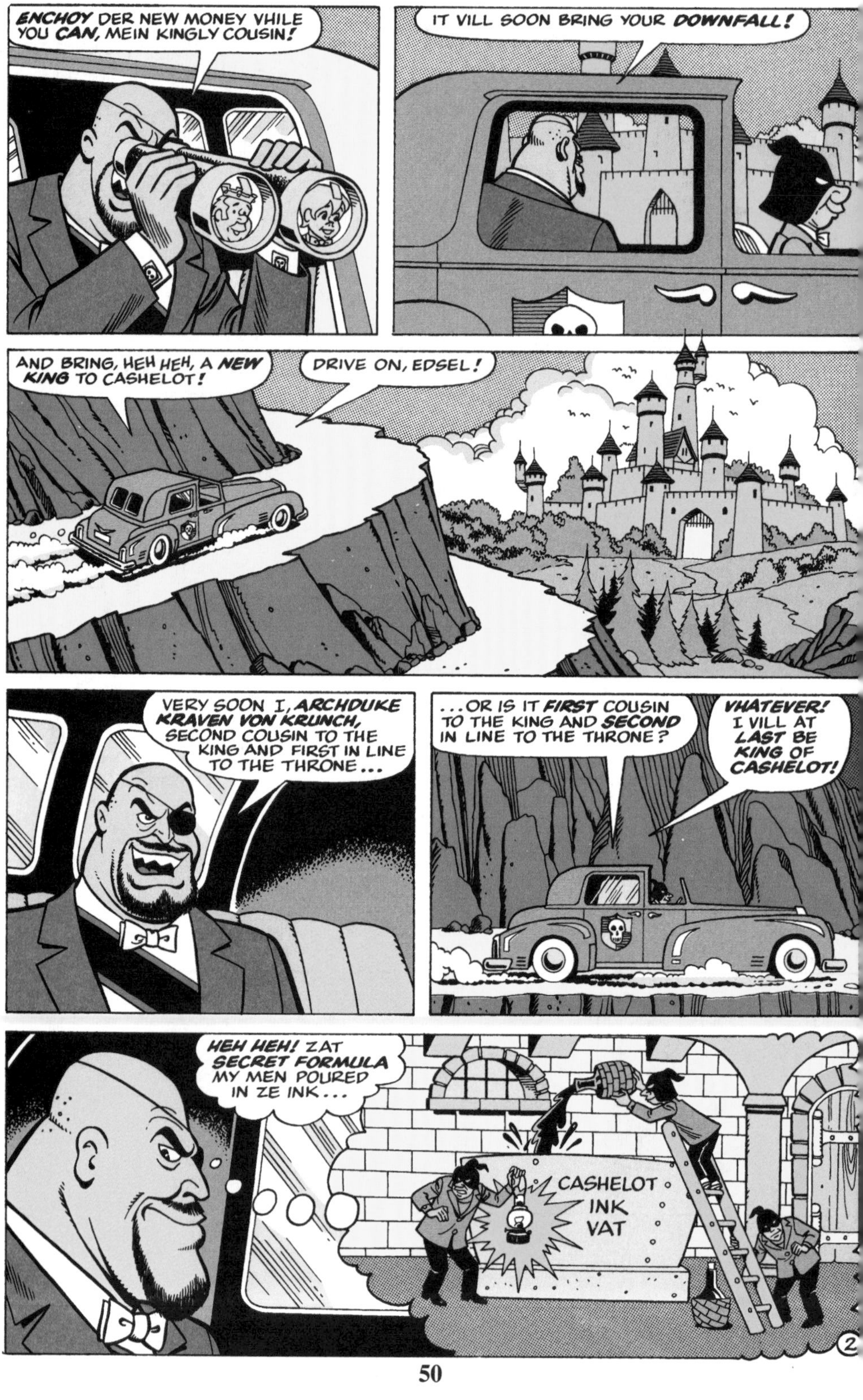

ENCHOY DER NEW MONEY VHILE YOU CAN, MEIN KINGLY COUSIN!
IT VILL SOON BRING YOUR DOWNFALL!
AND BRING, HEH HEH, A NEW KING TO CASHELOT!
DRIVE ON, EDSEL!
VERY SOON I, ARCHDUKE KRAVEN VON KRUNCH, SECOND COUSIN TO THE KING AND FIRST IN LINE TO THE THRONE...
...OR IS IT FIRST COUSIN TO THE KING AND SECOND IN LINE TO THE THRONE?
VHATEVER! I VILL AT LAST BE KING OF CASHELOT!
HEH HEH! ZAT SECRET FORMULA MY MEN POURED IN ZE INK...
CASHELOT INK VAT

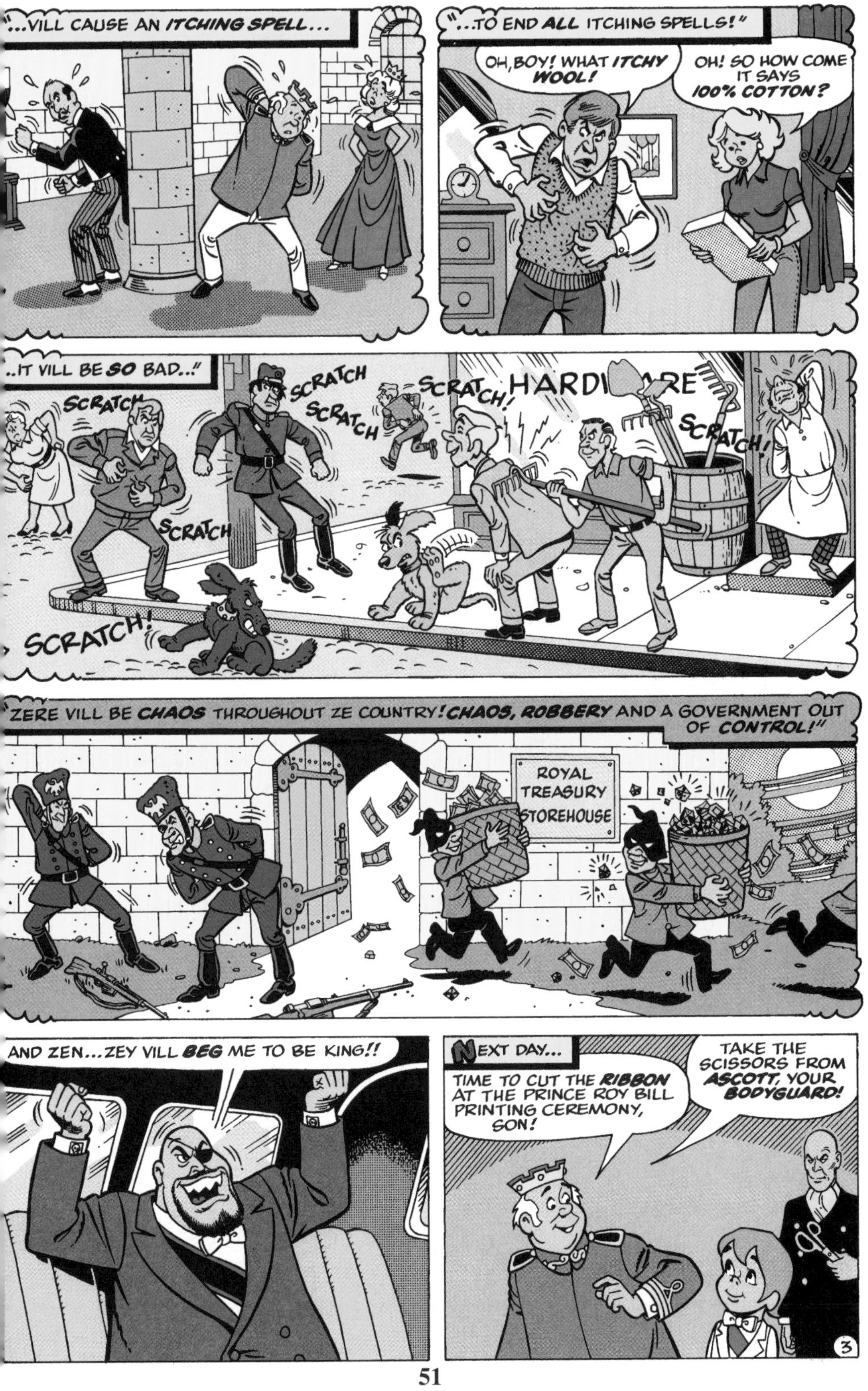
"...VILL CAUSE AN ITCHING SPELL...
"...TO END ALL ITCHING SPELLS!"
OH, BOY! WHAT ITCHY WOOL!
OH! SO HOW COME IT SAYS 100% COTTON?
..IT VILL BE SO BAD.."
SCRATCH
SCRATCH
SCRATCH
SCRATCH
SCRATCH!
SCRATCH!
SCRATCH!
SCRATCH!
HARDW ARE
"ZERE VILL BE CHAOS THROUGHOUT ZE COUNTRY! CHAOS, ROBBERY AND A GOVERNMENT OUT OF CONTROL!"
ROYAL TREASURY STOREHOUSE
AND ZEN...ZEY VILL BEG ME TO BE KING!!
NEXT DAY...
TIME TO CUT THE RIBBON AT THE PRINCE ROY BILL PRINTING CEREMONY, SON!
TAKE THE SCISSORS FROM ASCOTT, YOUR BODYGUARD!
3

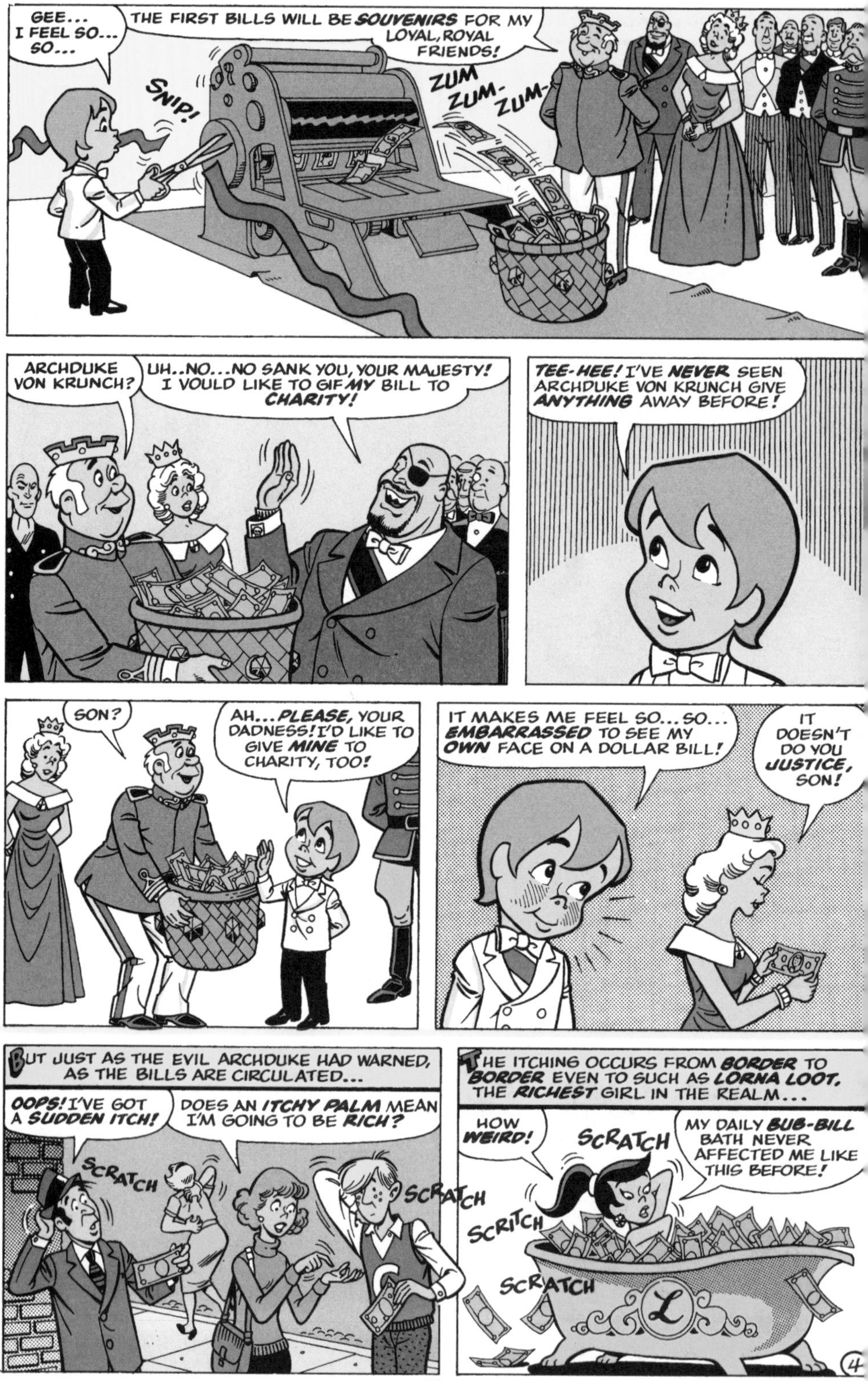
GEE... I FEEL SO... SO...
THE FIRST BILLS WILL BE SOUVENIRS FOR MY LOYAL, ROYAL FRIENDS!
SNIP!
ZUM ZUM- ZUM-
ARCHDUKE VON KRUNCH?
UH..NO...NO SANK YOU, YOUR MAJESTY! I VOULD LIKE TO GIF MY BILL TO CHARITY!
TEE-HEE! I'VE NEVER SEEN ARCHDUKE VON KRUNCH GIVE ANYTHING AWAY BEFORE!
SON?
AH...PLEASE, YOUR DADNESS! I'D LIKE TO GIVE MINE TO CHARITY, TOO!
IT MAKES ME FEEL SO...SO... EMBARRASSED TO SEE MY OWN FACE ON A DOLLAR BILL!
IT DOESN'T DO YOU JUSTICE, SON!
BUT JUST AS THE EVIL ARCHDUKE HAD WARNED, AS THE BILLS ARE CIRCULATED...
OOPS! I'VE GOT A SUDDEN ITCH!
DOES AN ITCHY PALM MEAN I'M GOING TO BE RICH?
SCRATCH
SCRATCH
THE ITCHING OCCURS FROM BORDER TO BORDER EVEN TO SUCH AS LORNA LOOT, THE RICHEST GIRL IN THE REALM...
HOW WEIRD!
SCRATCH
MY DAILY BUB-BILL BATH NEVER AFFECTED ME LIKE THIS BEFORE!
SCRITCH
SCRATCH
L
4

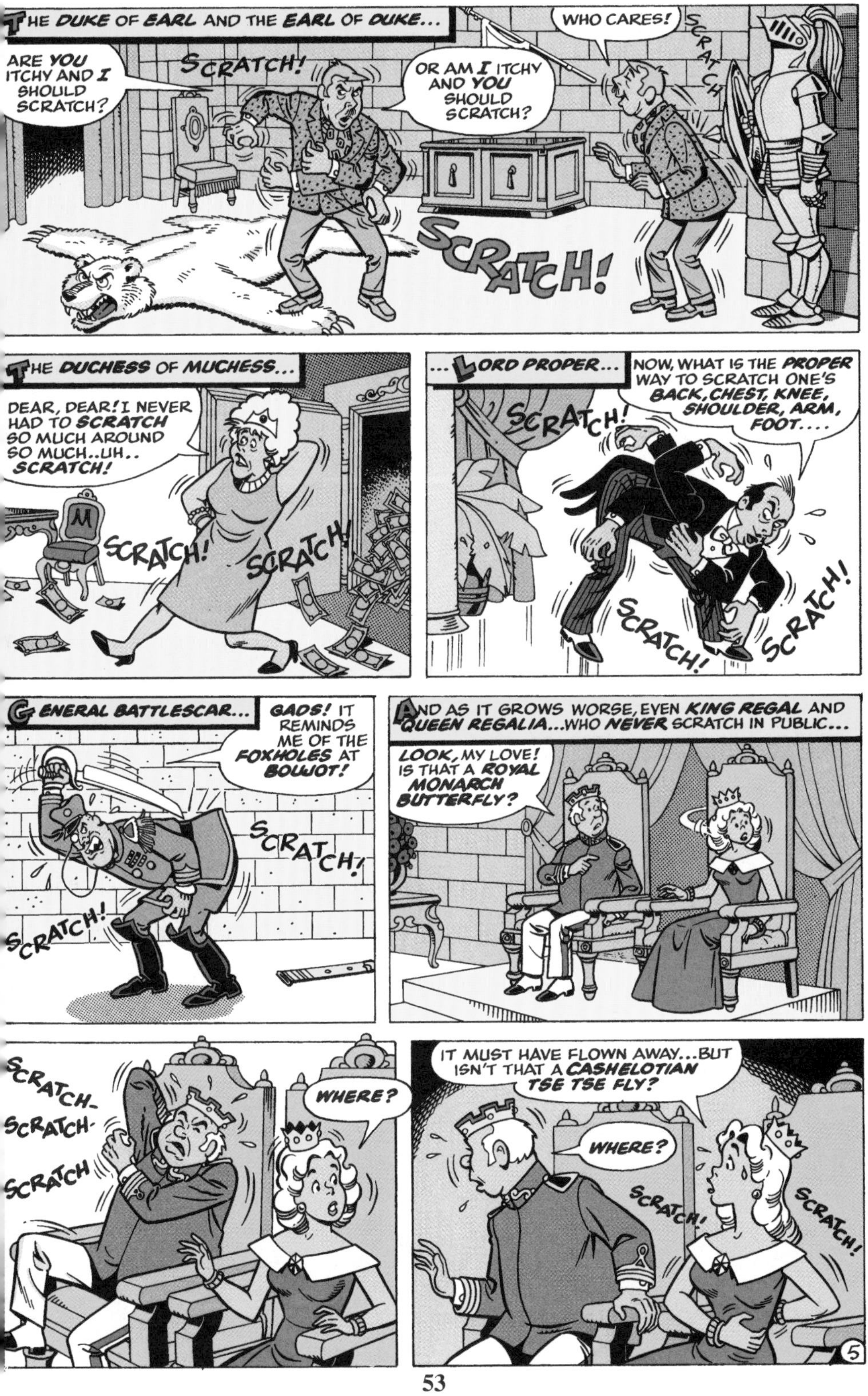
THE DUKE OF EARL AND THE EARL OF DUKE...
ARE YOU ITCHY AND I SHOULD SCRATCH?
SCRATCH!
OR AM I ITCHY AND YOU SHOULD SCRATCH?
WHO CARES!
SCRATCH
SCRATCH!
THE DUCHESS OF MUCHESS...
DEAR, DEAR! I NEVER HAD TO SCRATCH SO MUCH AROUND SO MUCH..UH.. SCRATCH!
SCRATCH!
SCRATCH!
...LORD PROPER...
NOW, WHAT IS THE PROPER WAY TO SCRATCH ONE'S BACK, CHEST, KNEE, SHOULDER, ARM, FOOT....
SCRATCH!
SCRATCH!
SCRATCH!
GENERAL BATTLESCAR...
GADS! IT REMINDS ME OF THE FOXHOLES AT BOWJOT!
SCRATCH!
SCRATCH!
AND AS IT GROWS WORSE, EVEN KING REGAL AND QUEEN REGALIA...WHO NEVER SCRATCH IN PUBLIC...
LOOK, MY LOVE! IS THAT A ROYAL MONARCH BUTTERFLY?
SCRATCH-
SCRATCH-
SCRATCH
WHERE?
IT MUST HAVE FLOWN AWAY...BUT ISN'T THAT A CASHELOTIAN TSE TSE FLY?
WHERE?
SCRATCH!
SCRATCH!
5

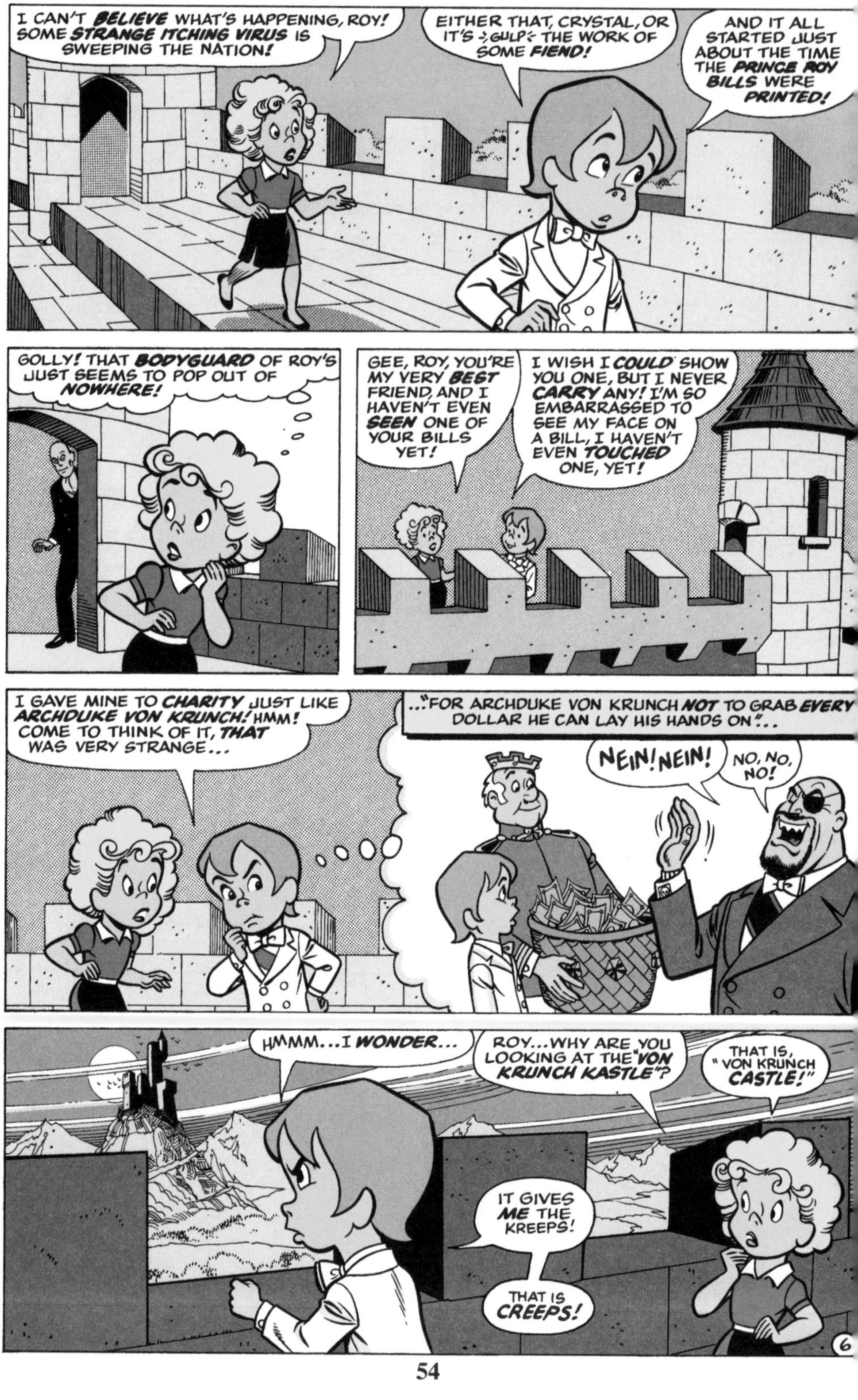
I CAN'T BELIEVE WHAT'S HAPPENING, ROY! SOME STRANGE ITCHING VIRUS IS SWEEPING THE NATION!
EITHER THAT, CRYSTAL, OR IT'S -GULP- THE WORK OF SOME FIEND!
AND IT ALL STARTED JUST ABOUT THE TIME THE PRINCE ROY BILLS WERE PRINTED!
GOLLY! THAT BODYGUARD OF ROY'S JUST SEEMS TO POP OUT OF NOWHERE!
GEE, ROY, YOU'RE MY VERY BEST FRIEND, AND I HAVEN'T EVEN SEEN ONE OF YOUR BILLS YET!
I WISH I COULD SHOW YOU ONE, BUT I NEVER CARRY ANY! I'M SO EMBARRASSED TO SEE MY FACE ON A BILL, I HAVEN'T EVEN TOUCHED ONE, YET!
I GAVE MINE TO CHARITY JUST LIKE ARCHDUKE VON KRUNCH! HMM! COME TO THINK OF IT, THAT WAS VERY STRANGE...
..."FOR ARCHDUKE VON KRUNCH NOT TO GRAB EVERY DOLLAR HE CAN LAY HIS HANDS ON"...
NEIN! NEIN!
NO, NO, NO!
HMMM...I WONDER...
ROY...WHY ARE YOU LOOKING AT THE "VON KRUNCH KASTLE"?
THAT IS, "VON KRUNCH CASTLE!"
IT GIVES ME THE KREEPS!
THAT IS CREEPS!
6

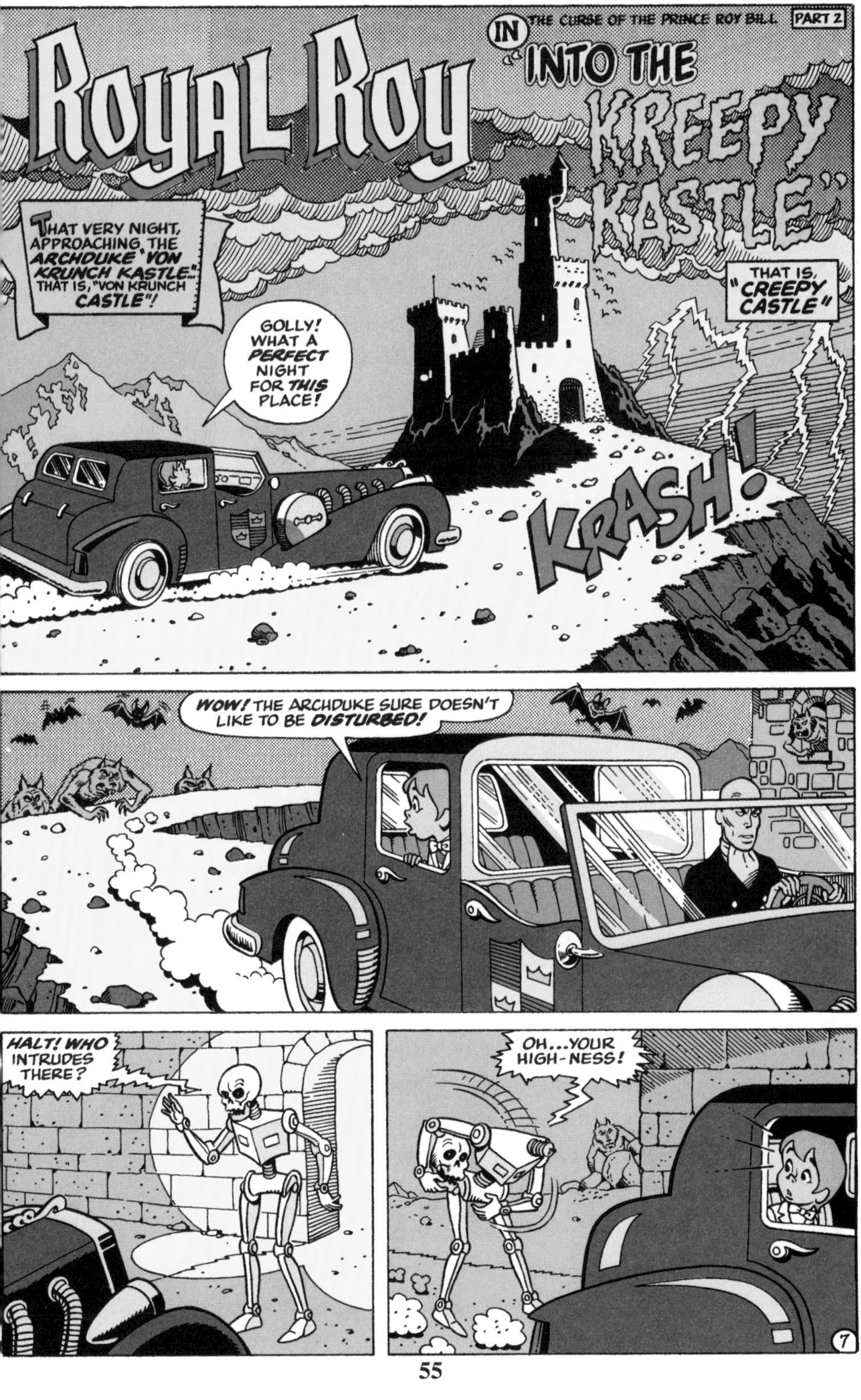
ROYAL ROY
IN THE CURSE OF THE PRINCE ROY BILL
PART 2
"INTO THE KREEPY KASTLE"
THAT VERY NIGHT, APPROACHING THE ARCHDUKE "VON KRUNCH KASTLE"... THAT IS, "VON KRUNCH CASTLE"!
THAT IS, "CREEPY CASTLE"
GOLLY! WHAT A PERFECT NIGHT FOR THIS PLACE!
KRASH!
WOW! THE ARCHDUKE SURE DOESN'T LIKE TO BE DISTURBED!
HALT! WHO INTRUDES THERE?
OH...YOUR HIGH-NESS!
7

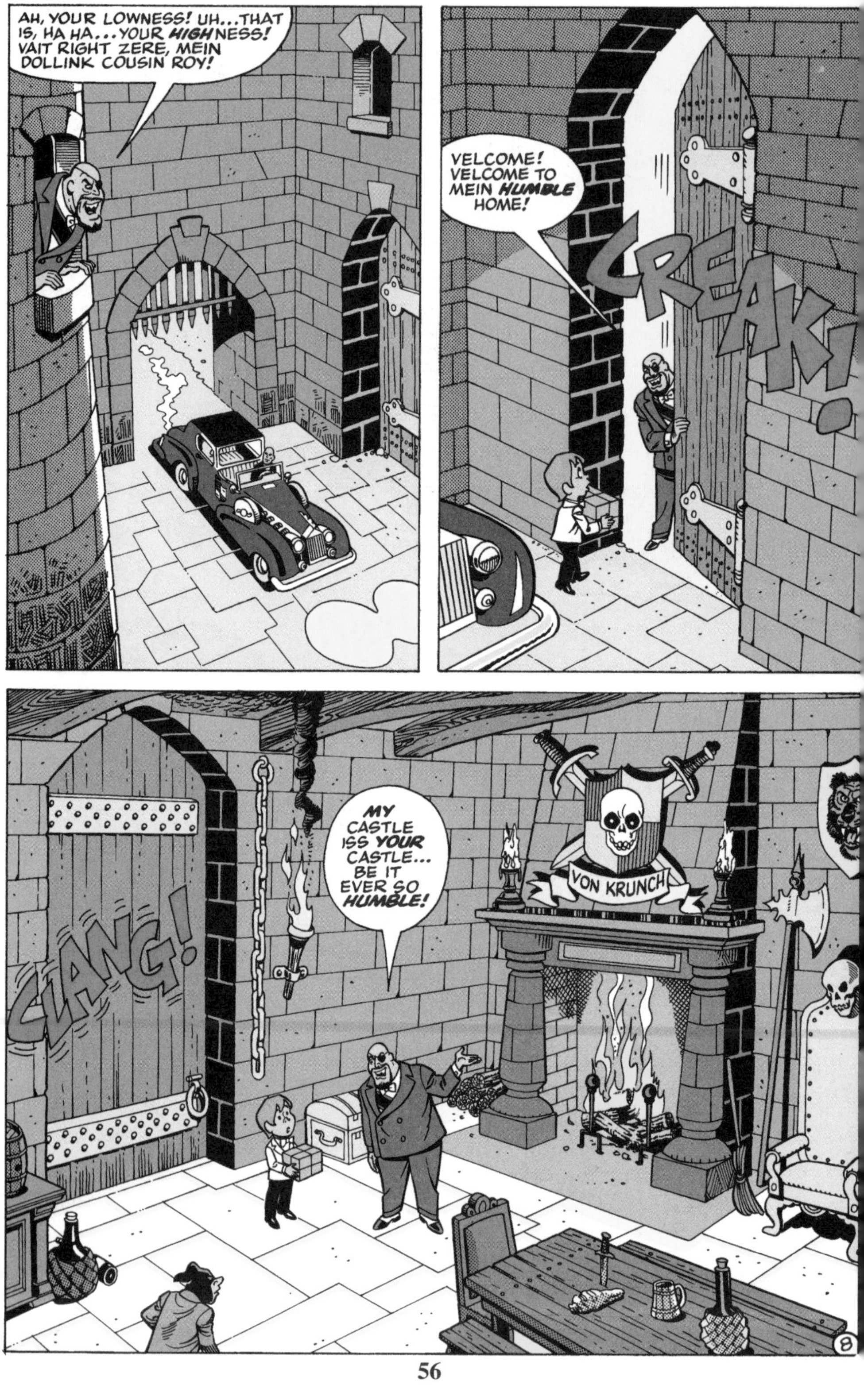

AH, YOUR LOWNESS! UH...THAT IS, HA HA...YOUR HIGHNESS! VAIT RIGHT ZERE, MEIN DOLLINK COUSIN ROY!
VELCOME! VELCOME TO MEIN HUMBLE HOME!
CREAK!
CLANG!
MY CASTLE ISS YOUR CASTLE... BE IT EVER SO HUMBLE!
VON KRUNCH
8

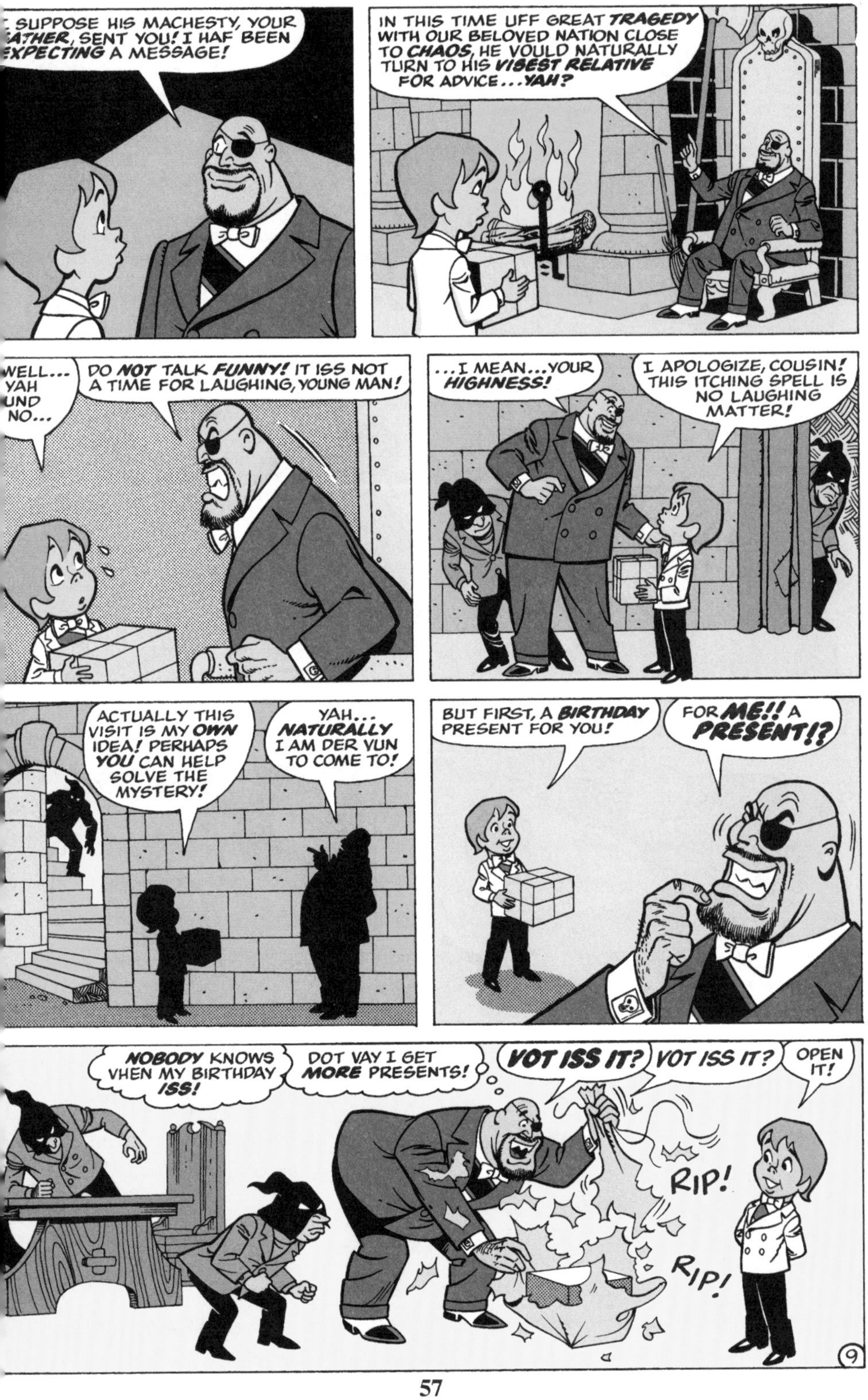

I SUPPOSE HIS MACHESTY, YOUR FATHER, SENT YOU! I HAF BEEN EXPECTING A MESSAGE!
IN THIS TIME UFF GREAT TRAGEDY WITH OUR BELOVED NATION CLOSE TO CHAOS, HE VOULD NATURALLY TURN TO HIS VISEST RELATIVE FOR ADVICE... YAH?
WELL... YAH UND NO...
DO NOT TALK FUNNY! IT ISS NOT A TIME FOR LAUGHING, YOUNG MAN!
...I MEAN... YOUR HIGHNESS!
I APOLOGIZE, COUSIN! THIS ITCHING SPELL IS NO LAUGHING MATTER!
ACTUALLY THIS VISIT IS MY OWN IDEA! PERHAPS YOU CAN HELP SOLVE THE MYSTERY!
YAH... NATURALLY I AM DER VUN TO COME TO!
BUT FIRST, A BIRTHDAY PRESENT FOR YOU!
FOR ME!! A PRESENT!?
NOBODY KNOWS VHEN MY BIRTHDAY ISS!
DOT VAY I GET MORE PRESENTS!
VOT ISS IT?
VOT ISS IT?
OPEN IT!
RIP!
RIP!
9

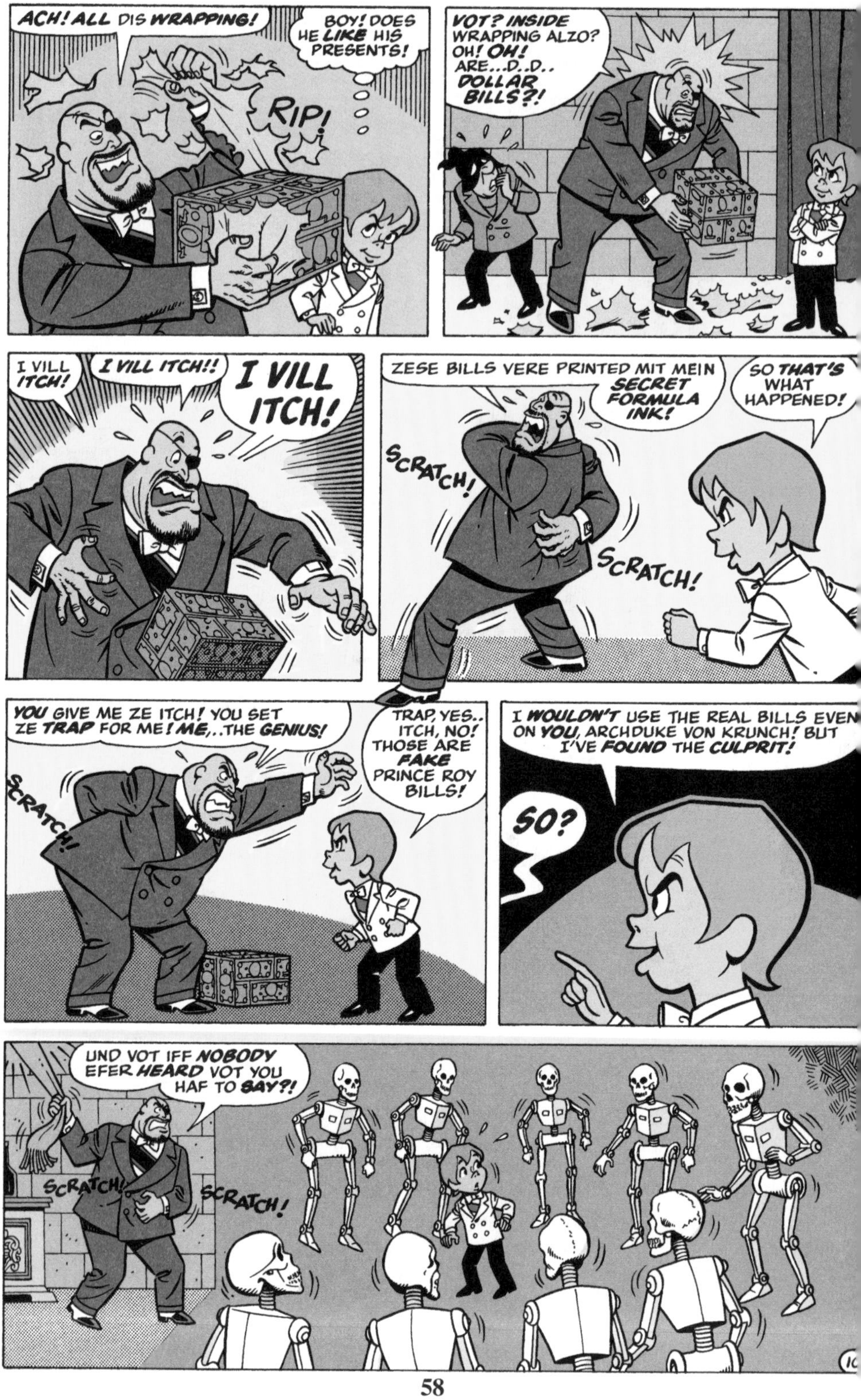
ACH! ALL DIS WRAPPING!
BOY! DOES HE LIKE HIS PRESENTS!
RIP!
VOT? INSIDE WRAPPING ALZO? OH! OH! ARE...D..D.. DOLLAR BILLS?!
I VILL ITCH!
I VILL ITCH!!
I VILL ITCH!
ZESE BILLS VERE PRINTED MIT MEIN SECRET FORMULA INK!
SCRATCH!
SCRATCH!
SO THAT'S WHAT HAPPENED!
YOU GIVE ME ZE ITCH! YOU SET ZE TRAP FOR ME! ME,..THE GENIUS!
SCRATCH!
TRAP, YES.. ITCH, NO! THOSE ARE FAKE PRINCE ROY BILLS!
I WOULDN'T USE THE REAL BILLS EVEN ON YOU, ARCHDUKE VON KRUNCH! BUT I'VE FOUND THE CULPRIT!
SO?
UND VOT IFF NOBODY EFER HEARD VOT YOU HAF TO SAY?!
SCRATCH!
SCRATCH!

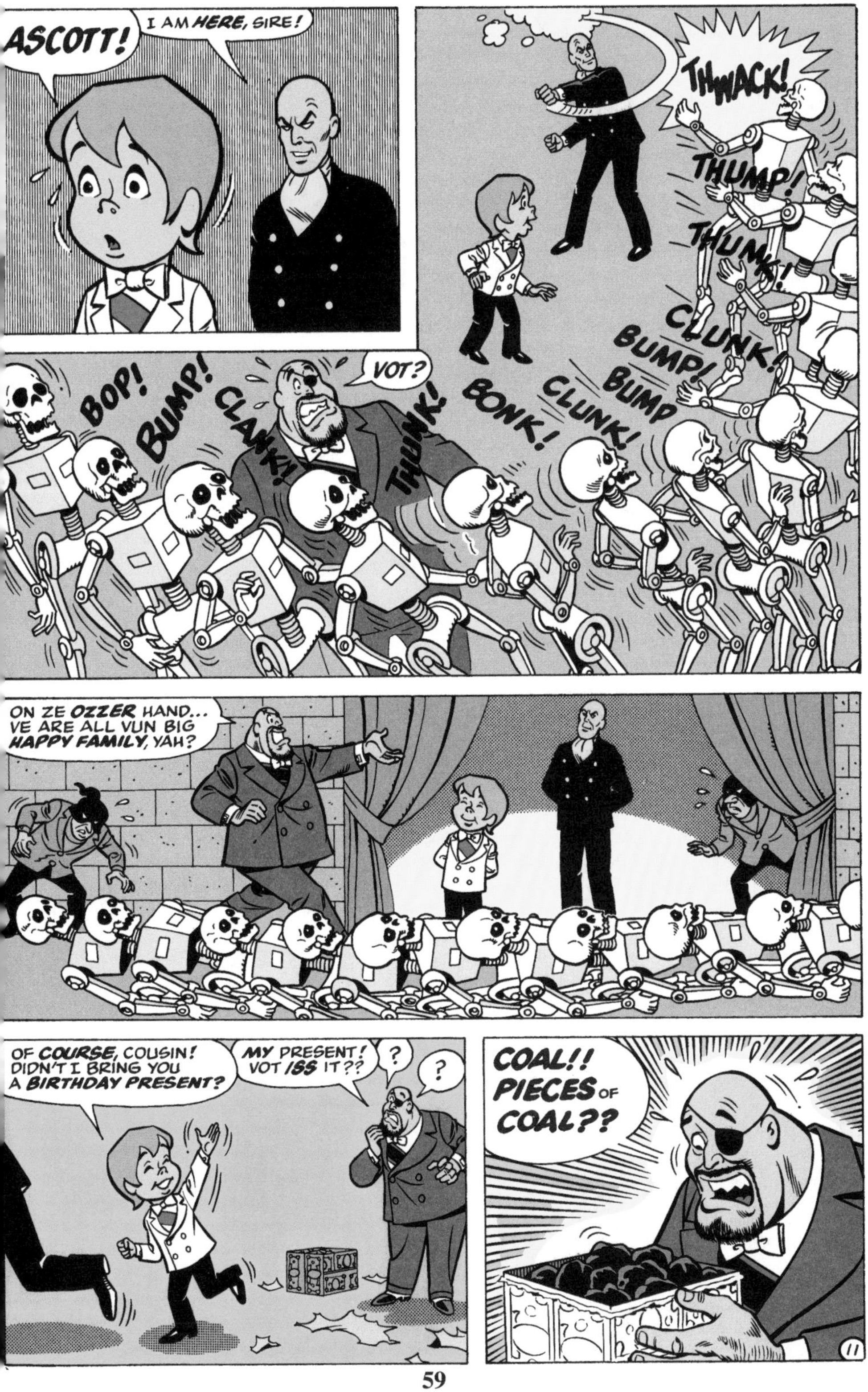

ASCOTT!
I AM HERE, SIRE!
THWACK!
THUMP!
THUNK!
CLUNK!
BUMP!
BUMP
VOT?
BOP!
BUMP!
CLANK!
THUNK!
BONK!
CLUNK!
ON ZE OZZER HAND... VE ARE ALL VUN BIG HAPPY FAMILY, YAH?
OF COURSE, COUSIN! DIDN'T I BRING YOU A BIRTHDAY PRESENT?
MY PRESENT! VOT ISS IT??
?
?
COAL!! PIECES OF COAL??
11

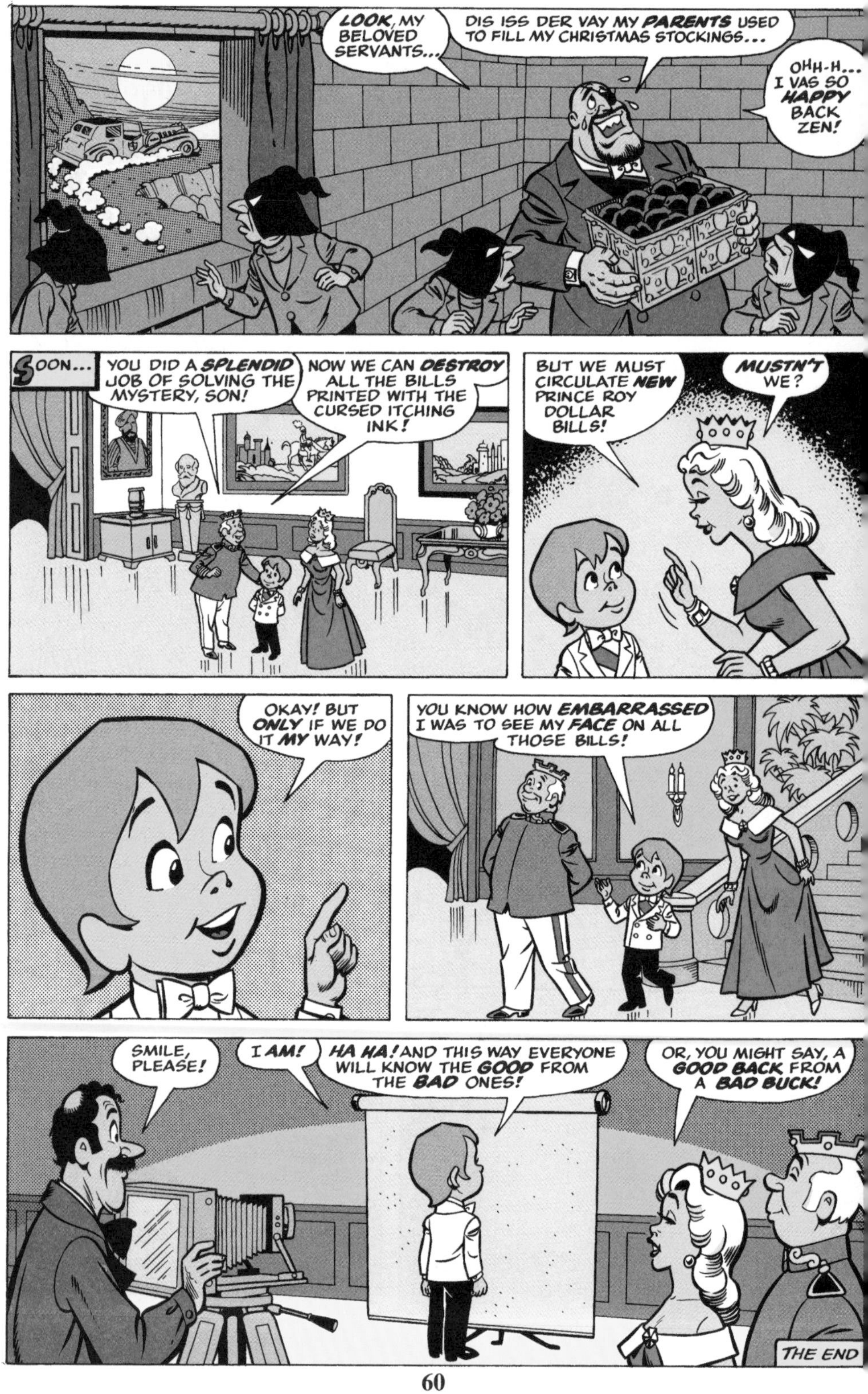
LOOK, MY BELOVED SERVANTS...
DIS ISS DER VAY MY PARENTS USED TO FILL MY CHRISTMAS STOCKINGS...
OHH-H... I VAS SO HAPPY BACK ZEN!
SOON...
YOU DID A SPLENDID JOB OF SOLVING THE MYSTERY, SON!
NOW WE CAN DESTROY ALL THE BILLS PRINTED WITH THE CURSED ITCHING INK!
BUT WE MUST CIRCULATE NEW PRINCE ROY DOLLAR BILLS!
MUSTN'T WE?
OKAY! BUT ONLY IF WE DO IT MY WAY!
YOU KNOW HOW EMBARRASSED I WAS TO SEE MY FACE ON ALL THOSE BILLS!
SMILE, PLEASE!
I AM!
HA HA! AND THIS WAY EVERYONE WILL KNOW THE GOOD FROM THE BAD ONES!
OR, YOU MIGHT SAY, A GOOD BACK FROM A BAD BUCK!
THE END

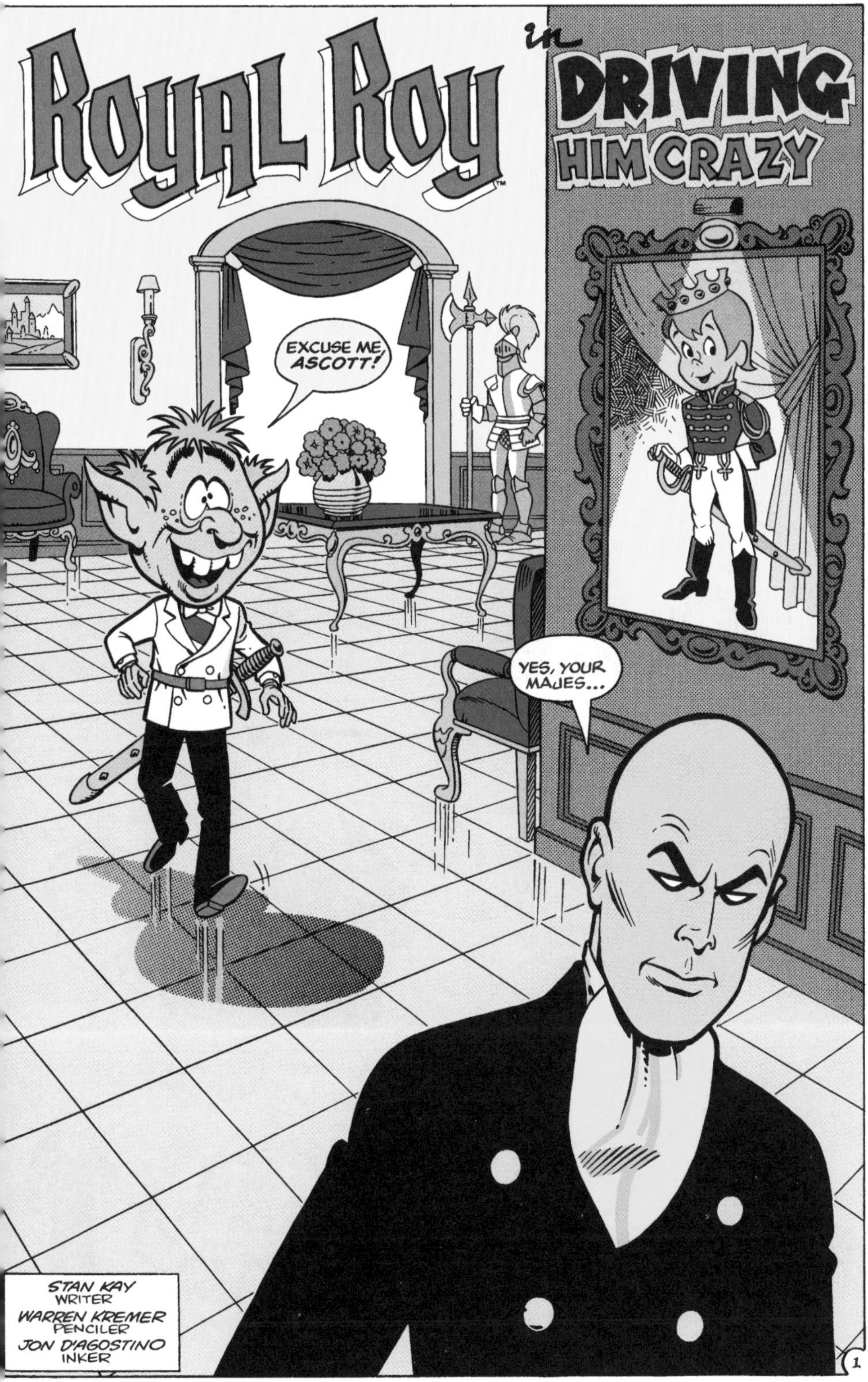
Royal Roy™
in
DRIVING HIM CRAZY
EXCUSE ME, ASCOTT!
YES, YOUR MAJES...
STAN KAY WRITER
WARREN KREMER PENCILER
JON D'AGOSTINO INKER
1

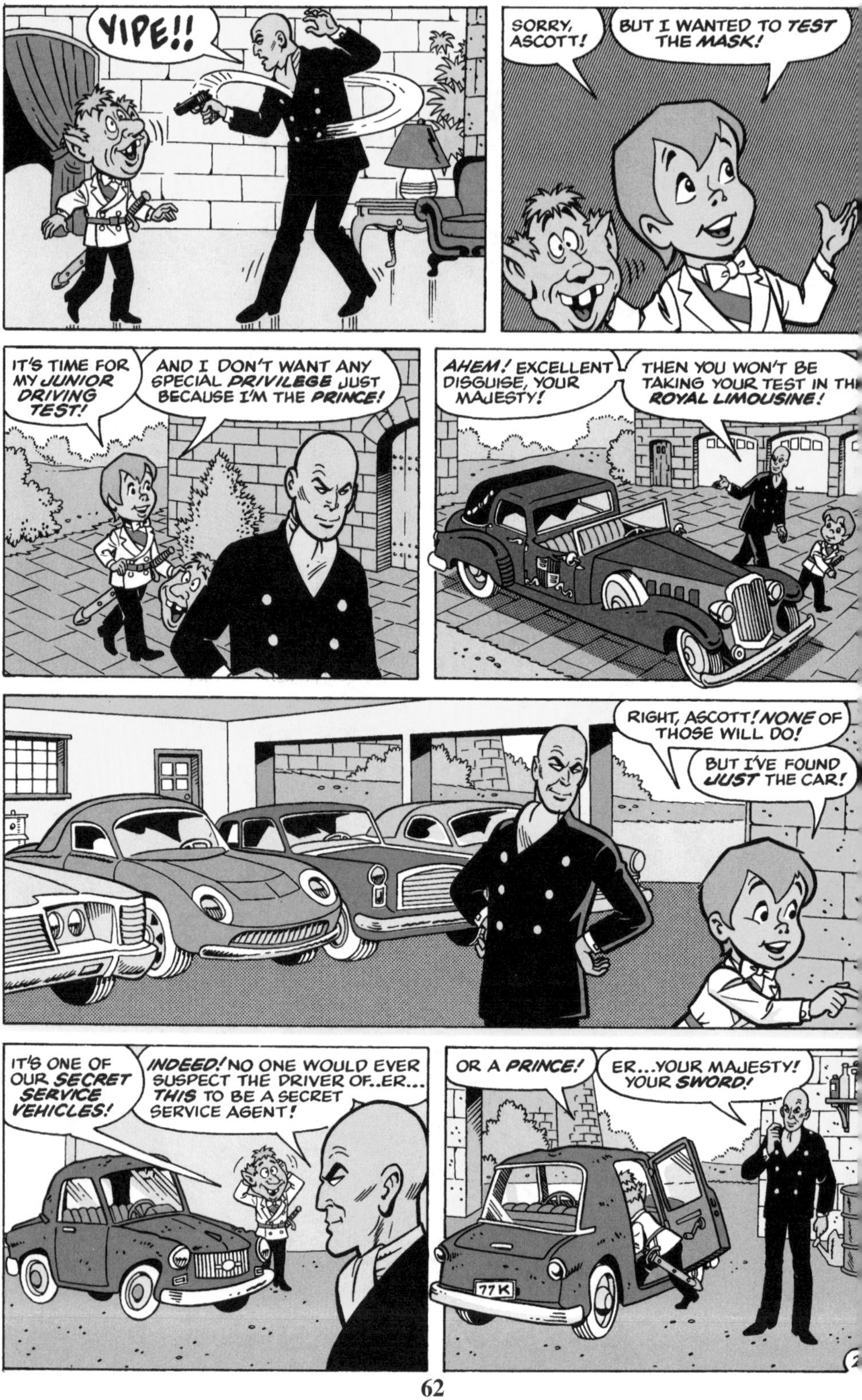
YIPE!!
SORRY, ASCOTT!
BUT I WANTED TO TEST THE MASK!
IT'S TIME FOR MY JUNIOR DRIVING TEST!
AND I DON'T WANT ANY SPECIAL PRIVILEGE JUST BECAUSE I'M THE PRINCE!
AHEM! EXCELLENT DISGUISE, YOUR MAJESTY!
THEN YOU WON'T BE TAKING YOUR TEST IN TH
ROYAL LIMOUSINE!
RIGHT, ASCOTT! NONE OF THOSE WILL DO!
BUT I'VE FOUND JUST THE CAR!
IT'S ONE OF OUR SECRET SERVICE VEHICLES!
INDEED! NO ONE WOULD EVER SUSPECT THE DRIVER OF..ER... THIS TO BE A SECRET SERVICE AGENT!
OR A PRINCE!
ER...YOUR MAJESTY! YOUR SWORD!
77K

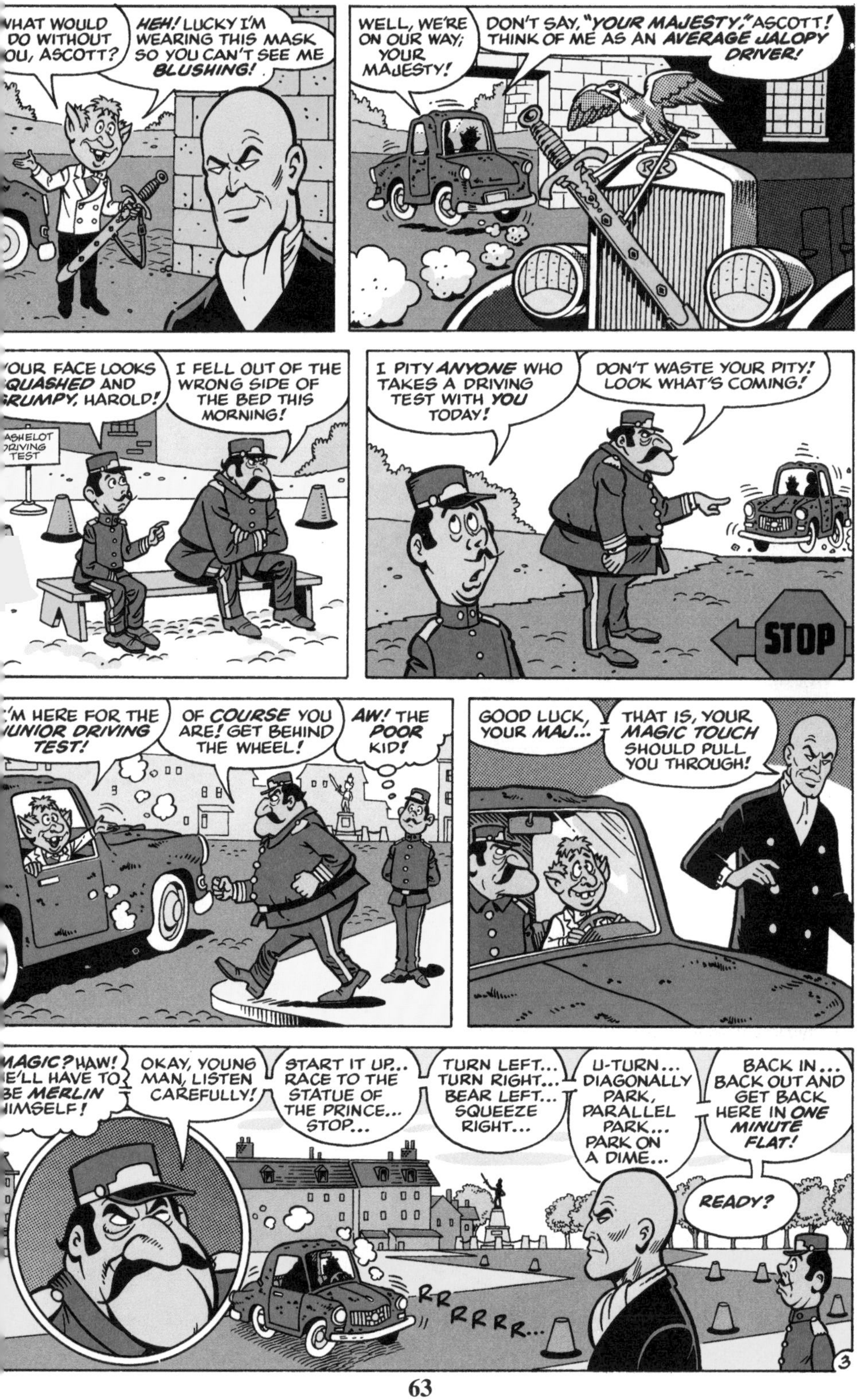

WHAT WOULD DO WITHOUT OU, ASCOTT?
HEH! LUCKY I'M WEARING THIS MASK SO YOU CAN'T SEE ME BLUSHING!
WELL, WE'RE ON OUR WAY; YOUR MAJESTY!
DON'T SAY, "YOUR MAJESTY," ASCOTT! THINK OF ME AS AN AVERAGE JALOPY DRIVER!
OUR FACE LOOKS QUASHED AND RUMPY, HAROLD!
I FELL OUT OF THE WRONG SIDE OF THE BED THIS MORNING!
ASHELOT DRIVING TEST
I PITY ANYONE WHO TAKES A DRIVING TEST WITH YOU TODAY!
DON'T WASTE YOUR PITY! LOOK WHAT'S COMING!
STOP
'M HERE FOR THE UNIOR DRIVING TEST!
OF COURSE YOU ARE! GET BEHIND THE WHEEL!
AW! THE POOR KID!
GOOD LUCK, YOUR MAJ...
THAT IS, YOUR MAGIC TOUCH SHOULD PULL YOU THROUGH!
MAGIC? HAW! E'LL HAVE TO BE MERLIN IMSELF!
OKAY, YOUNG MAN, LISTEN CAREFULLY!
START IT UP... RACE TO THE STATUE OF THE PRINCE... STOP...
TURN LEFT... TURN RIGHT... BEAR LEFT... SQUEEZE RIGHT...
U-TURN... DIAGONALLY PARK, PARALLEL PARK... PARK ON A DIME...
BACK IN... BACK OUT AND GET BACK HERE IN ONE MINUTE FLAT!
READY?
RRRRRR...
3

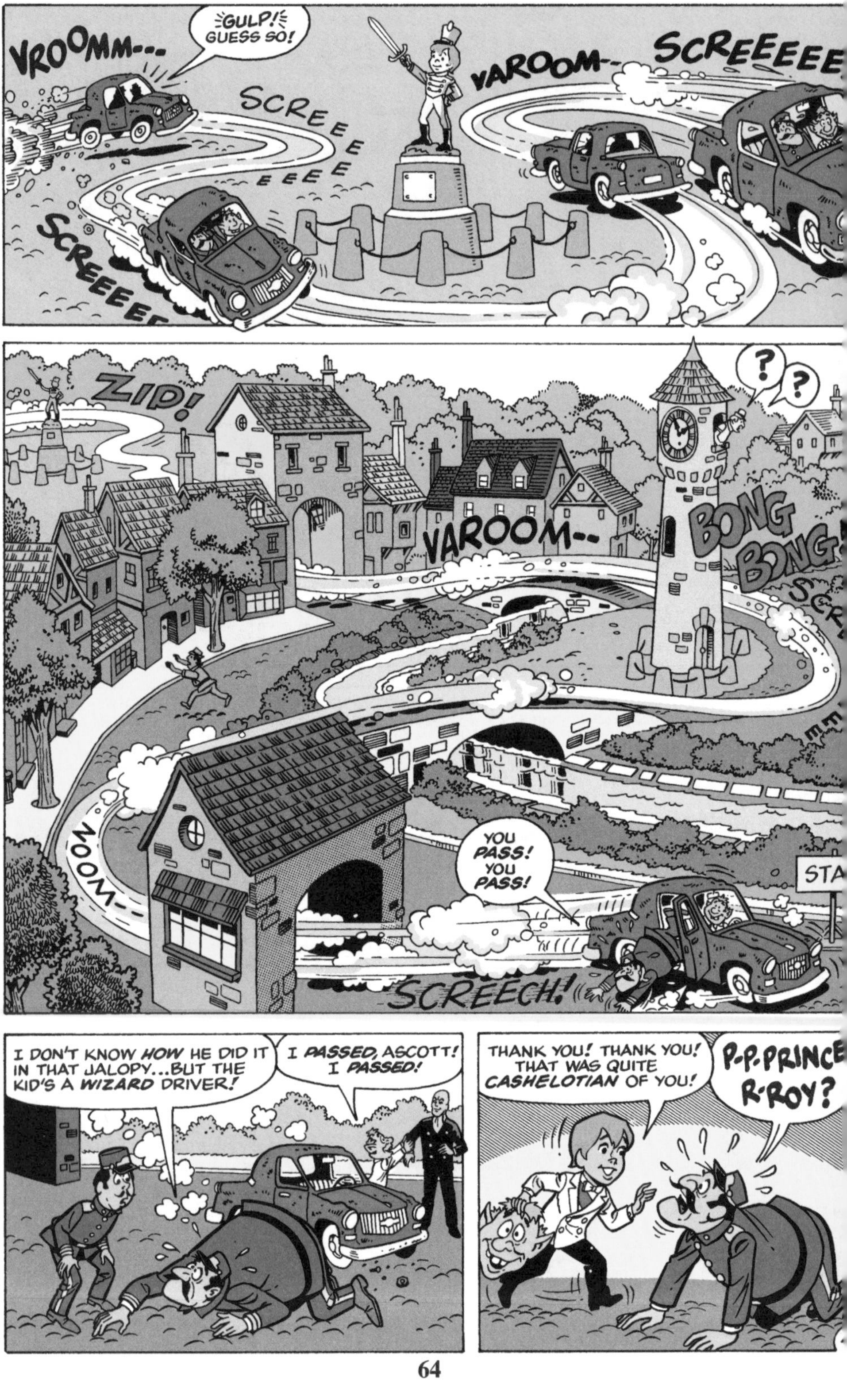
VROOMM...
GULP! GUESS SO!
SCREEEE EEEE
SCREEEEEE
VAROOM--
SCREEEEEE
ZIP!
??
VAROOM--
BONG BONG
SCR
WOOM--
YOU PASS! YOU PASS!
STA
SCREECH!
I DON'T KNOW HOW HE DID IT IN THAT JALOPY...BUT THE KID'S A WIZARD DRIVER!
I PASSED, ASCOTT! I PASSED!
THANK YOU! THANK YOU! THAT WAS QUITE CASHELOTIAN OF YOU!
P-P-PRINCE R-ROY?

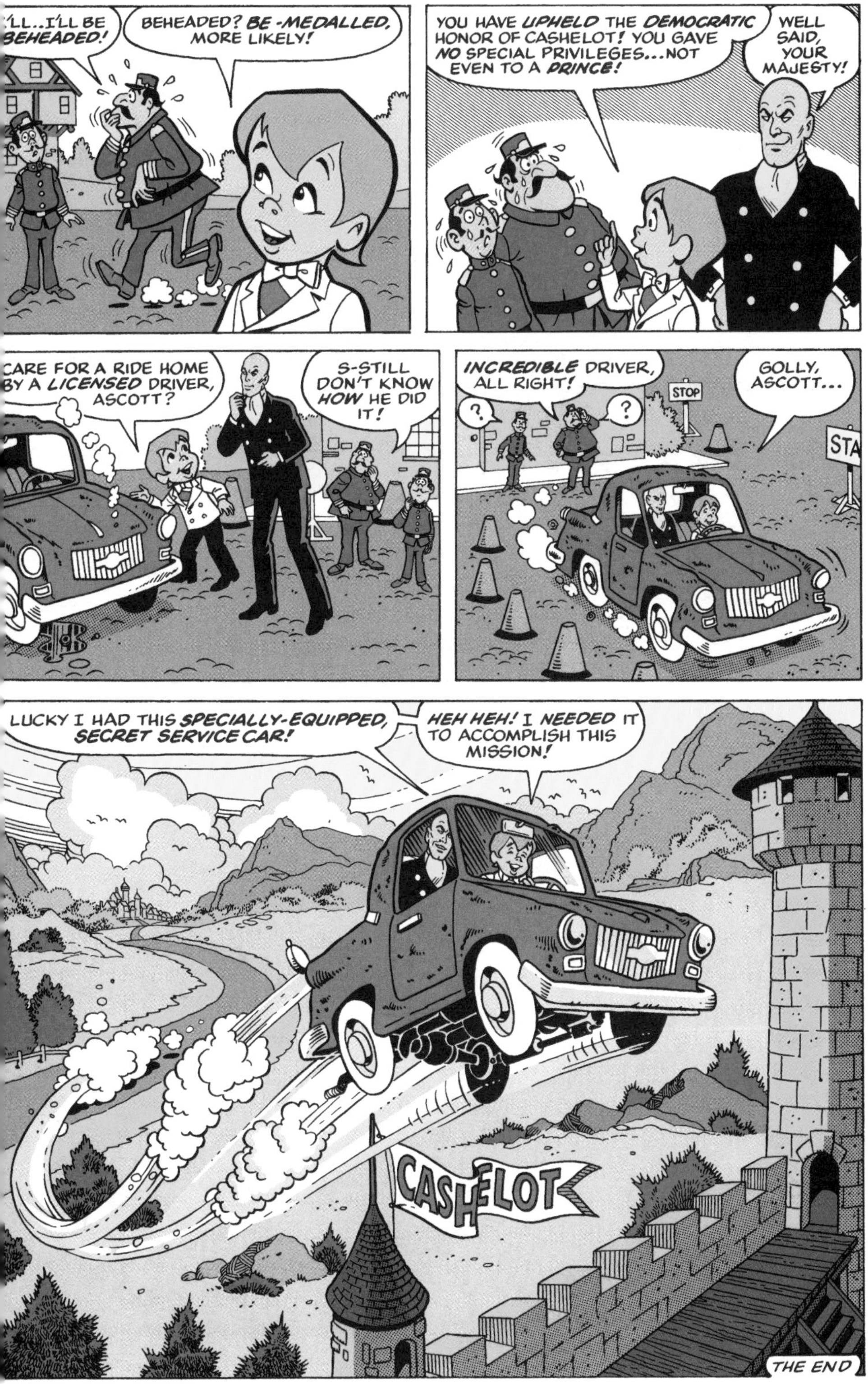
I'LL..I'LL BE BEHEADED!
BEHEADED? BE-MEDALLED, MORE LIKELY!
YOU HAVE UPHELD THE DEMOCRATIC HONOR OF CASHELOT! YOU GAVE NO SPECIAL PRIVILEGES...NOT EVEN TO A PRINCE!
WELL SAID, YOUR MAJESTY!
CARE FOR A RIDE HOME BY A LICENSED DRIVER, ASCOTT?
S-STILL DON'T KNOW HOW HE DID IT!
INCREDIBLE DRIVER, ALL RIGHT!
?
?
STOP
GOLLY, ASCOTT...
STA
LUCKY I HAD THIS SPECIALLY-EQUIPPED, SECRET SERVICE CAR!
HEH HEH! I NEEDED IT TO ACCOMPLISH THIS MISSION!
CASHELOT
THE END

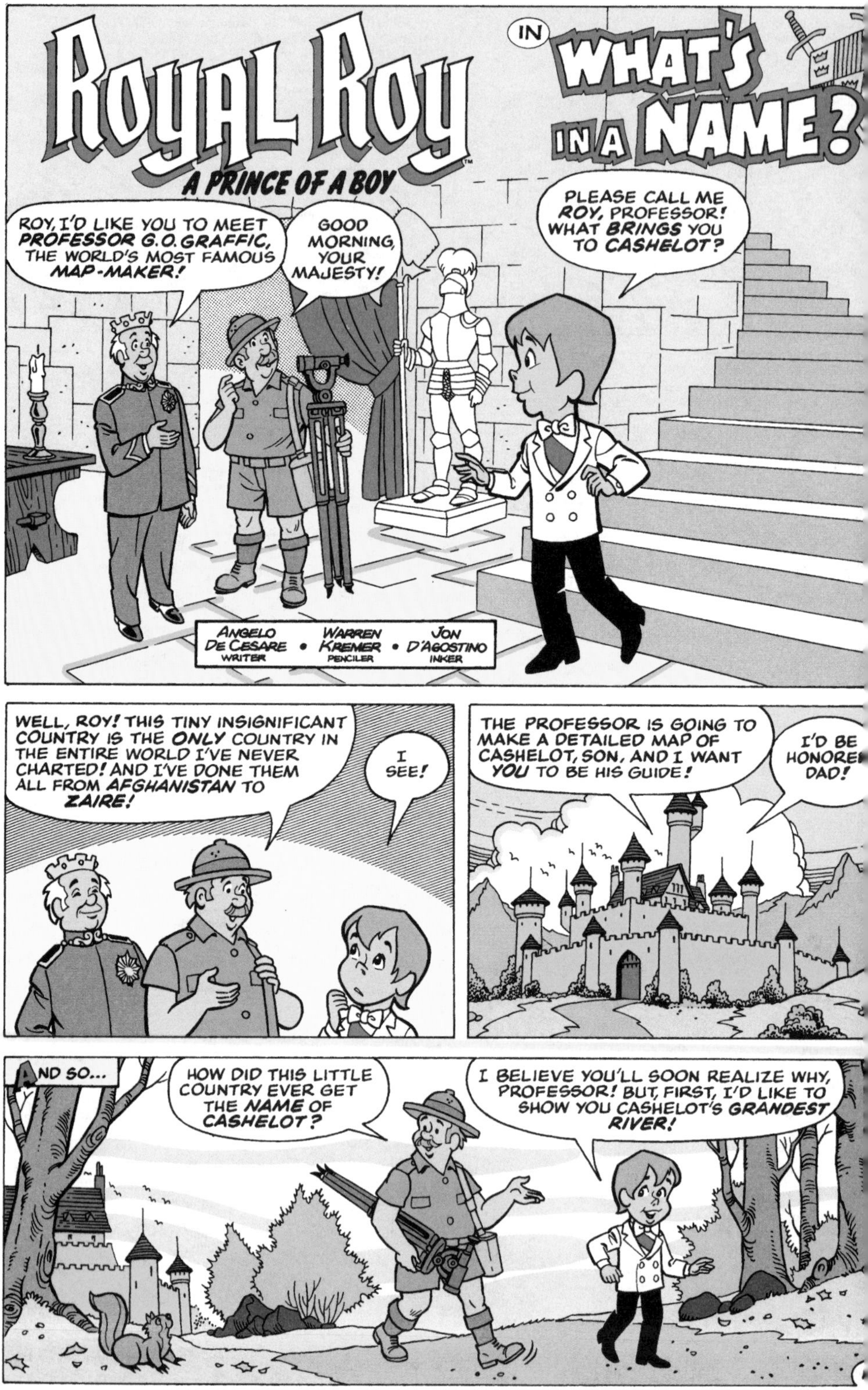

Royal Roy
A PRINCE OF A BOY
IN
WHAT'S IN A NAME?
ROY, I'D LIKE YOU TO MEET PROFESSOR G.O. GRAFFIC, THE WORLD'S MOST FAMOUS MAP-MAKER!
GOOD MORNING, YOUR MAJESTY!
PLEASE CALL ME ROY, PROFESSOR! WHAT BRINGS YOU TO CASHELOT?
ANGELO DE CESARE WRITER • WARREN KREMER PENCILER • JON D'AGOSTINO INKER
WELL, ROY! THIS TINY INSIGNIFICANT COUNTRY IS THE ONLY COUNTRY IN THE ENTIRE WORLD I'VE NEVER CHARTED! AND I'VE DONE THEM ALL FROM AFGHANISTAN TO ZAIRE!
I SEE!
THE PROFESSOR IS GOING TO MAKE A DETAILED MAP OF CASHELOT, SON, AND I WANT YOU TO BE HIS GUIDE!
I'D BE HONORED, DAD!
AND SO...
HOW DID THIS LITTLE COUNTRY EVER GET THE NAME OF CASHELOT?
I BELIEVE YOU'LL SOON REALIZE WHY, PROFESSOR! BUT, FIRST, I'D LIKE TO SHOW YOU CASHELOT'S GRANDEST RIVER!

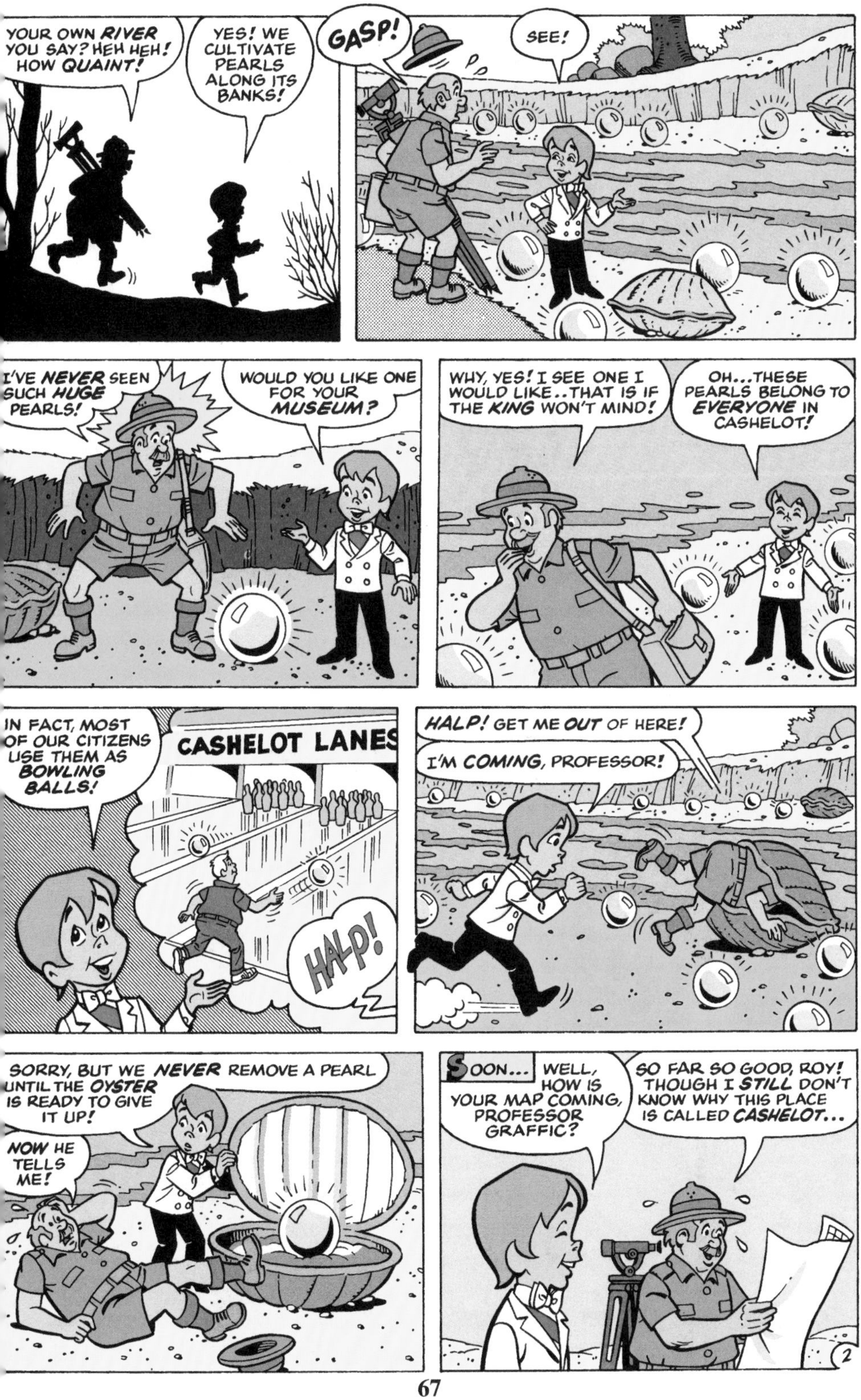

YOUR OWN RIVER YOU SAY? HEH HEH! HOW QUAINT!
YES! WE CULTIVATE PEARLS ALONG ITS BANKS!
GASP!
SEE!
I'VE NEVER SEEN SUCH HUGE PEARLS!
WOULD YOU LIKE ONE FOR YOUR MUSEUM?
WHY, YES! I SEE ONE I WOULD LIKE..THAT IS IF THE KING WON'T MIND!
OH...THESE PEARLS BELONG TO EVERYONE IN CASHELOT!
IN FACT, MOST OF OUR CITIZENS USE THEM AS BOWLING BALLS!
CASHELOT LANES
HALP!
HALP! GET ME OUT OF HERE!
I'M COMING, PROFESSOR!
SORRY, BUT WE NEVER REMOVE A PEARL UNTIL THE OYSTER IS READY TO GIVE IT UP!
NOW HE TELLS ME!
SOON...
WELL, HOW IS YOUR MAP COMING, PROFESSOR GRAFFIC?
SO FAR SO GOOD, ROY! THOUGH I STILL DON'T KNOW WHY THIS PLACE IS CALLED CASHELOT...
2

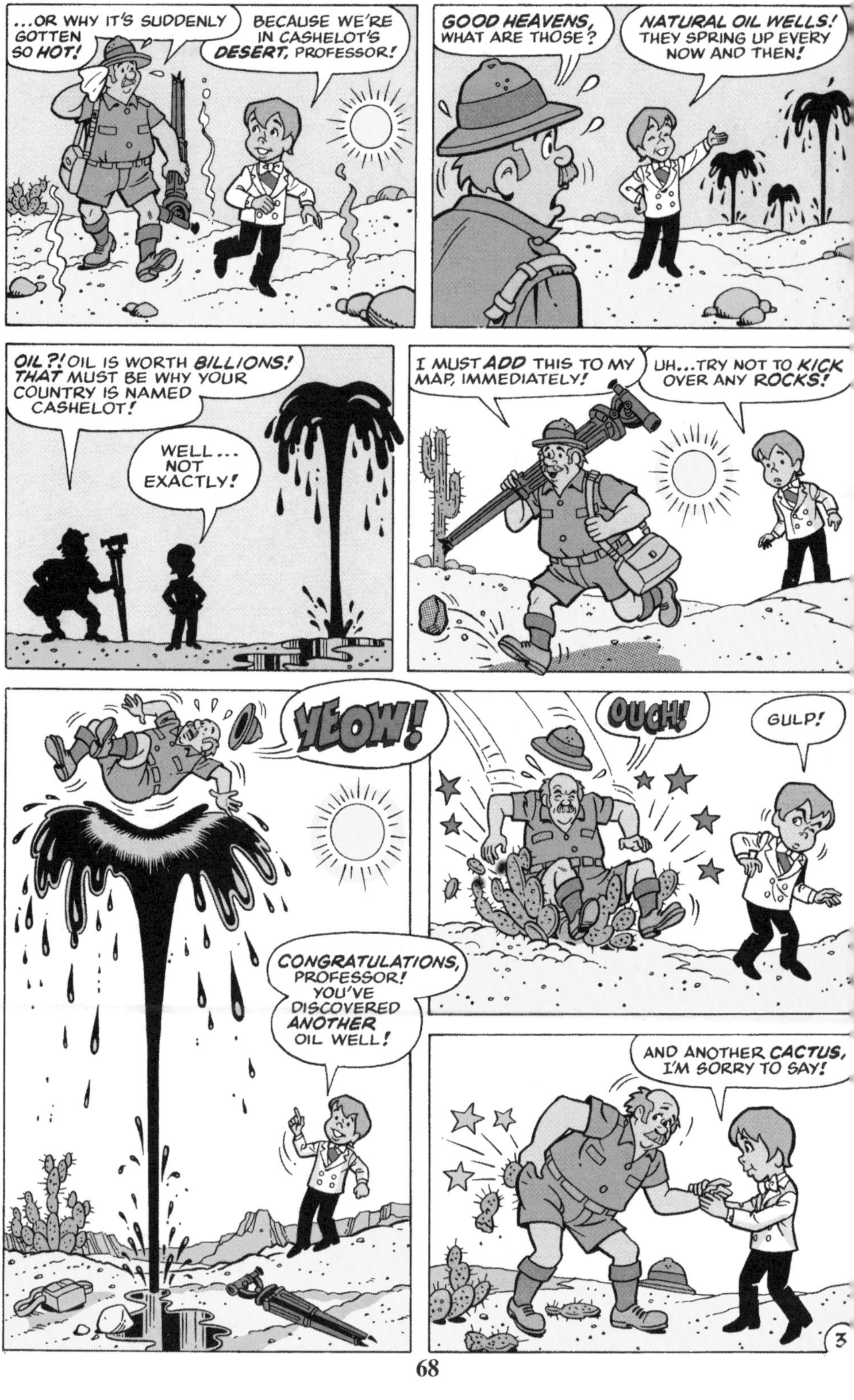
...OR WHY IT'S SUDDENLY GOTTEN SO HOT!
BECAUSE WE'RE IN CASHELOT'S DESERT, PROFESSOR!
GOOD HEAVENS, WHAT ARE THOSE?
NATURAL OIL WELLS! THEY SPRING UP EVERY NOW AND THEN!
OIL?! OIL IS WORTH BILLIONS! THAT MUST BE WHY YOUR COUNTRY IS NAMED CASHELOT!
WELL... NOT EXACTLY!
I MUST ADD THIS TO MY MAP, IMMEDIATELY!
UH...TRY NOT TO KICK OVER ANY ROCKS!
YEOW!
CONGRATULATIONS, PROFESSOR! YOU'VE DISCOVERED ANOTHER OIL WELL!
OUCH!
GULP!
AND ANOTHER CACTUS, I'M SORRY TO SAY!
3

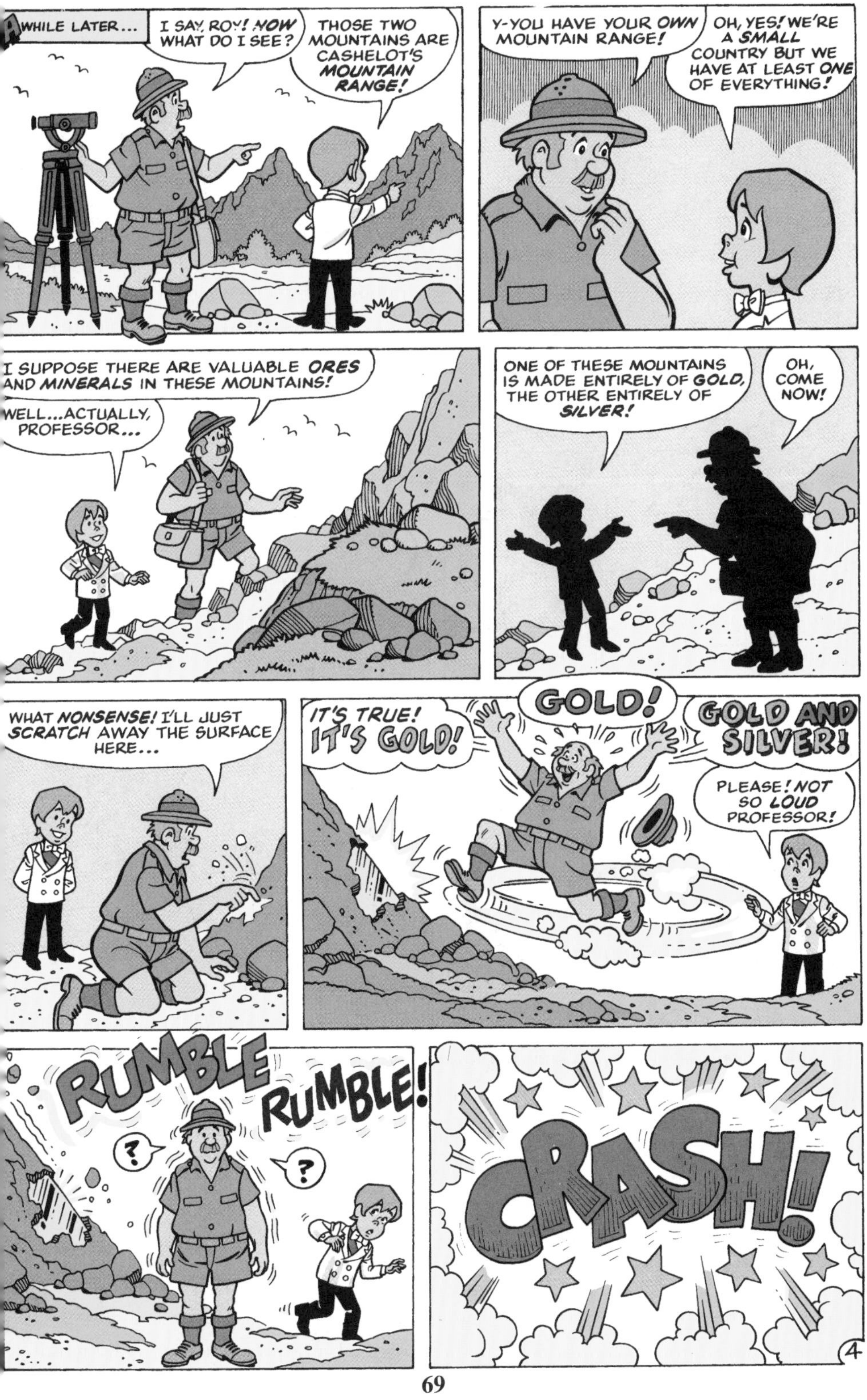

A WHILE LATER...
I SAY, ROY! NOW WHAT DO I SEE?
THOSE TWO MOUNTAINS ARE CASHELOT'S MOUNTAIN RANGE!
Y-YOU HAVE YOUR OWN MOUNTAIN RANGE!
OH, YES! WE'RE A SMALL COUNTRY BUT WE HAVE AT LEAST ONE OF EVERYTHING!
I SUPPOSE THERE ARE VALUABLE ORES AND MINERALS IN THESE MOUNTAINS!
WELL...ACTUALLY, PROFESSOR...
ONE OF THESE MOUNTAINS IS MADE ENTIRELY OF GOLD, THE OTHER ENTIRELY OF SILVER!
OH, COME NOW!
WHAT NONSENSE! I'LL JUST SCRATCH AWAY THE SURFACE HERE...
IT'S TRUE! IT'S GOLD!
GOLD!
GOLD AND SILVER!
PLEASE! NOT SO LOUD PROFESSOR!
RUMBLE RUMBLE!
?
?
CRASH!
4

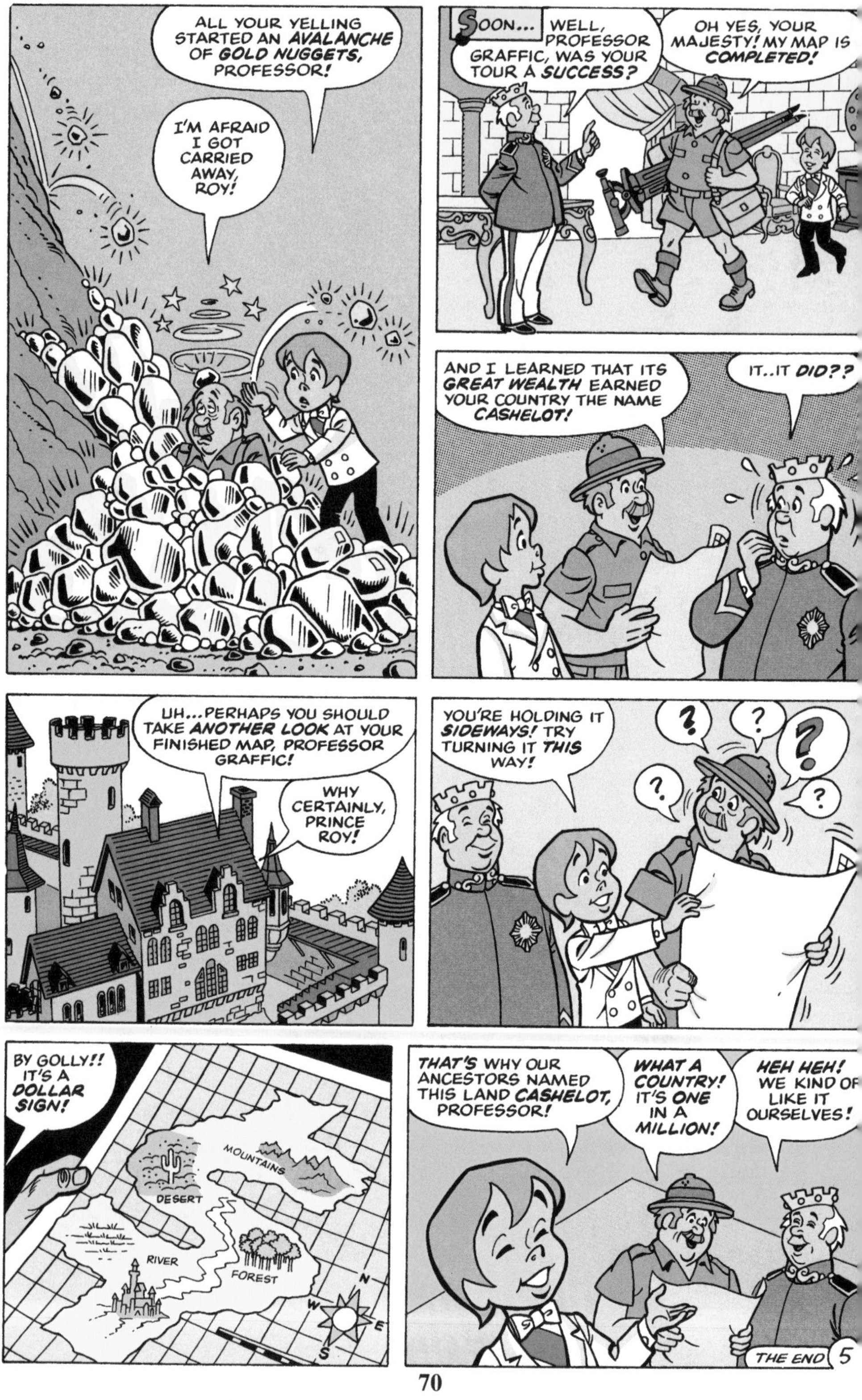
ALL YOUR YELLING STARTED AN AVALANCHE OF GOLD NUGGETS, PROFESSOR!
I'M AFRAID I GOT CARRIED AWAY, ROY!
SOON...
WELL, PROFESSOR GRAFFIC, WAS YOUR TOUR A SUCCESS?
OH YES, YOUR MAJESTY! MY MAP IS COMPLETED!
AND I LEARNED THAT ITS GREAT WEALTH EARNED YOUR COUNTRY THE NAME CASHELOT!
IT..IT DID??
UH...PERHAPS YOU SHOULD TAKE ANOTHER LOOK AT YOUR FINISHED MAP, PROFESSOR GRAFFIC!
WHY CERTAINLY, PRINCE ROY!
YOU'RE HOLDING IT SIDEWAYS! TRY TURNING IT THIS WAY!
BY GOLLY!! IT'S A DOLLAR SIGN!
MOUNTAINS
DESERT
RIVER
FOREST
N
W
E
S
THAT'S WHY OUR ANCESTORS NAMED THIS LAND CASHELOT, PROFESSOR!
WHAT A COUNTRY! IT'S ONE IN A MILLION!
HEH HEH! WE KIND OF LIKE IT OURSELVES!
THE END
5

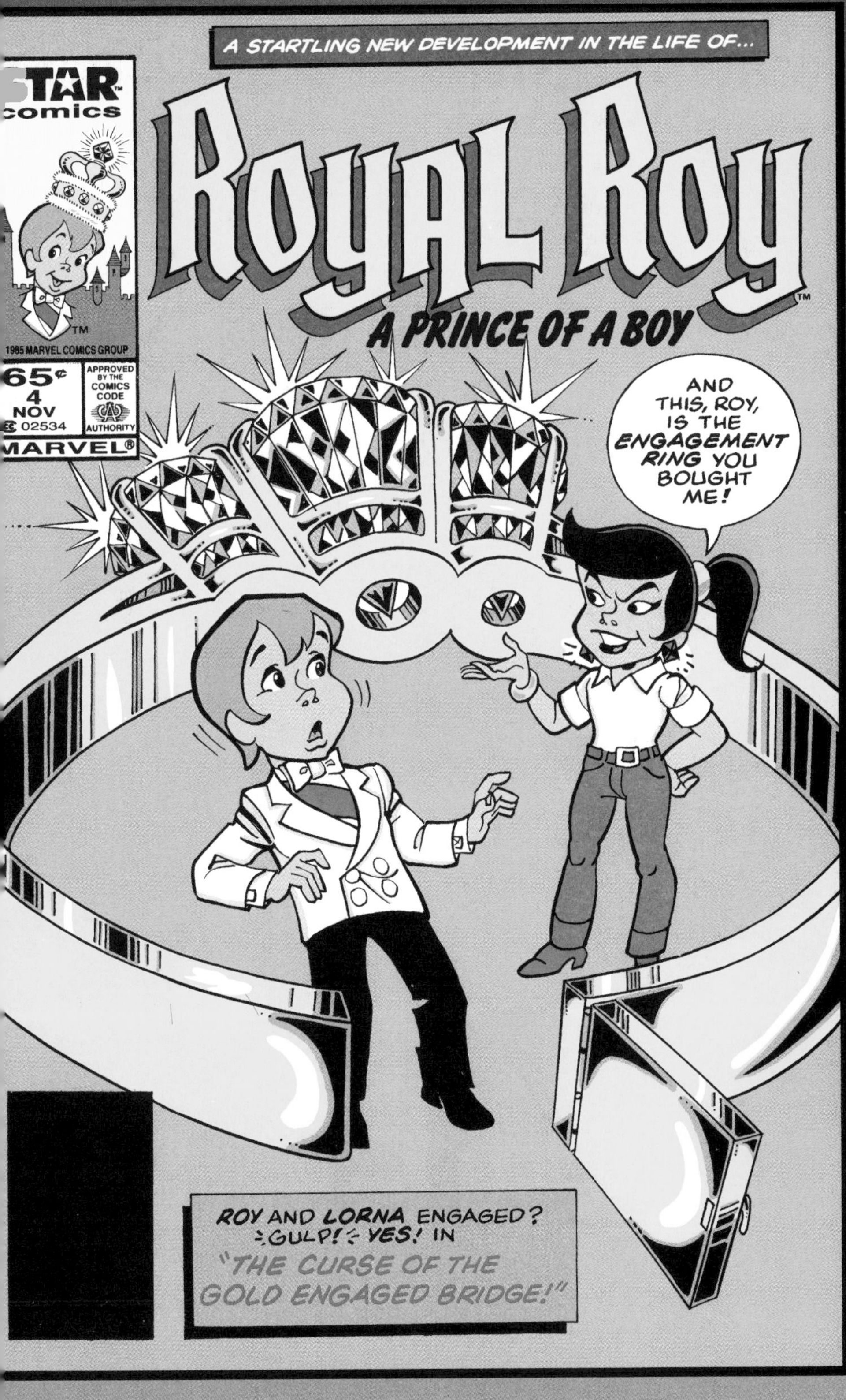
A STARTLING NEW DEVELOPMENT IN THE LIFE OF...
STAR comics
Royal Roy
A PRINCE OF A BOY
1985 MARVEL COMICS GROUP
65¢
4
NOV
02534
APPROVED BY THE COMICS CODE AUTHORITY
MARVEL
AND THIS, ROY, IS THE ENGAGEMENT RING YOU BOUGHT ME!
ROY AND LORNA ENGAGED? -GULP!- YES! IN
"THE CURSE OF THE GOLD ENGAGED BRIDGE!"

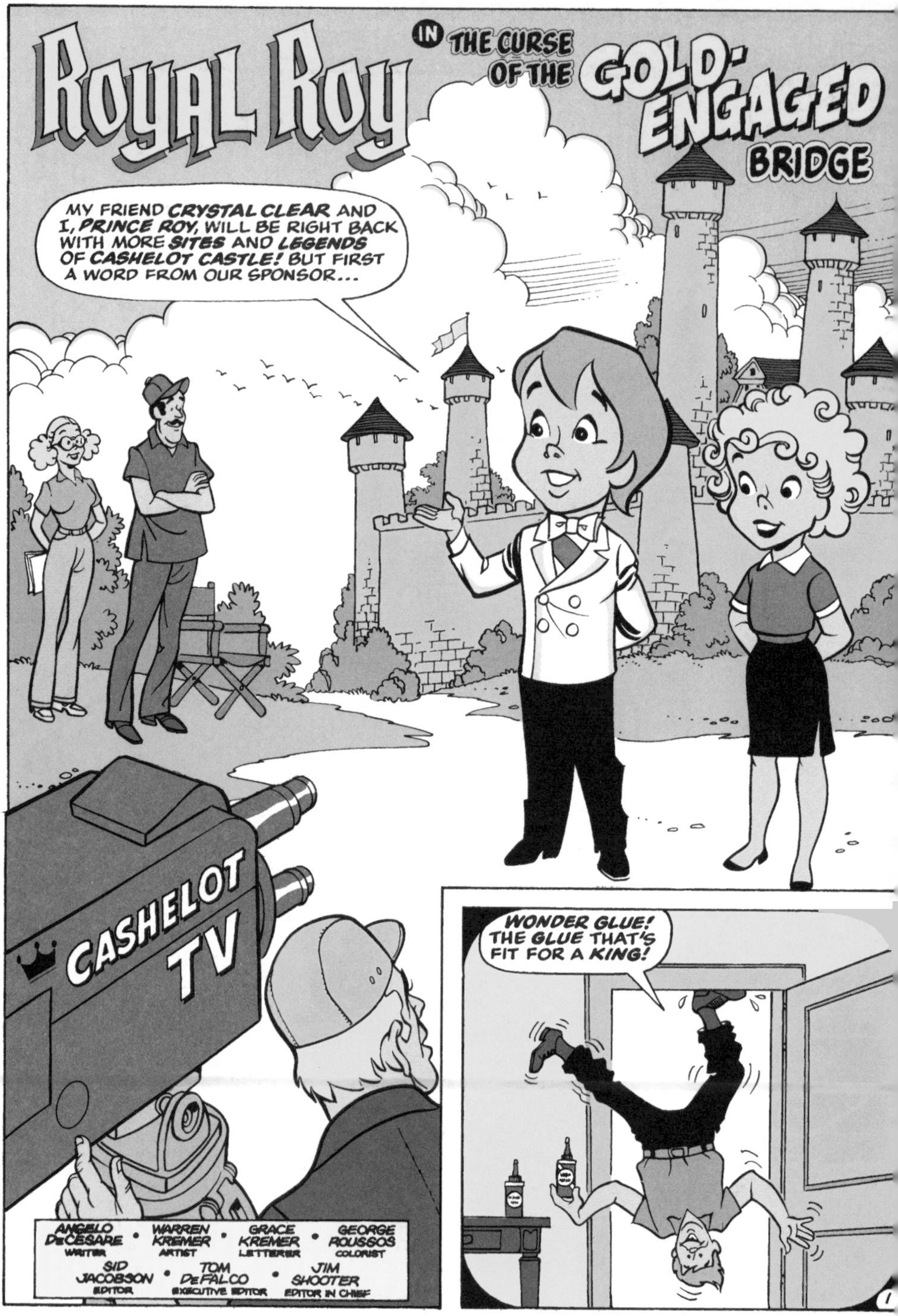
ROYAL ROY IN THE CURSE OF THE GOLD-ENGAGED BRIDGE
MY FRIEND CRYSTAL CLEAR AND I, PRINCE ROY, WILL BE RIGHT BACK WITH MORE SITES AND LEGENDS OF CASHELOT CASTLE! BUT FIRST A WORD FROM OUR SPONSOR...
CASHELOT TV
ANGELO DeCESARE WRITER • WARREN KREMER ARTIST • GRACE KREMER LETTERER • GEORGE ROUSSOS COLORIST
SID JACOBSON EDITOR • TOM DeFALCO EXECUTIVE EDITOR • JIM SHOOTER EDITOR IN CHIEF
WONDER GLUE! THE GLUE THAT'S FIT FOR A KING!

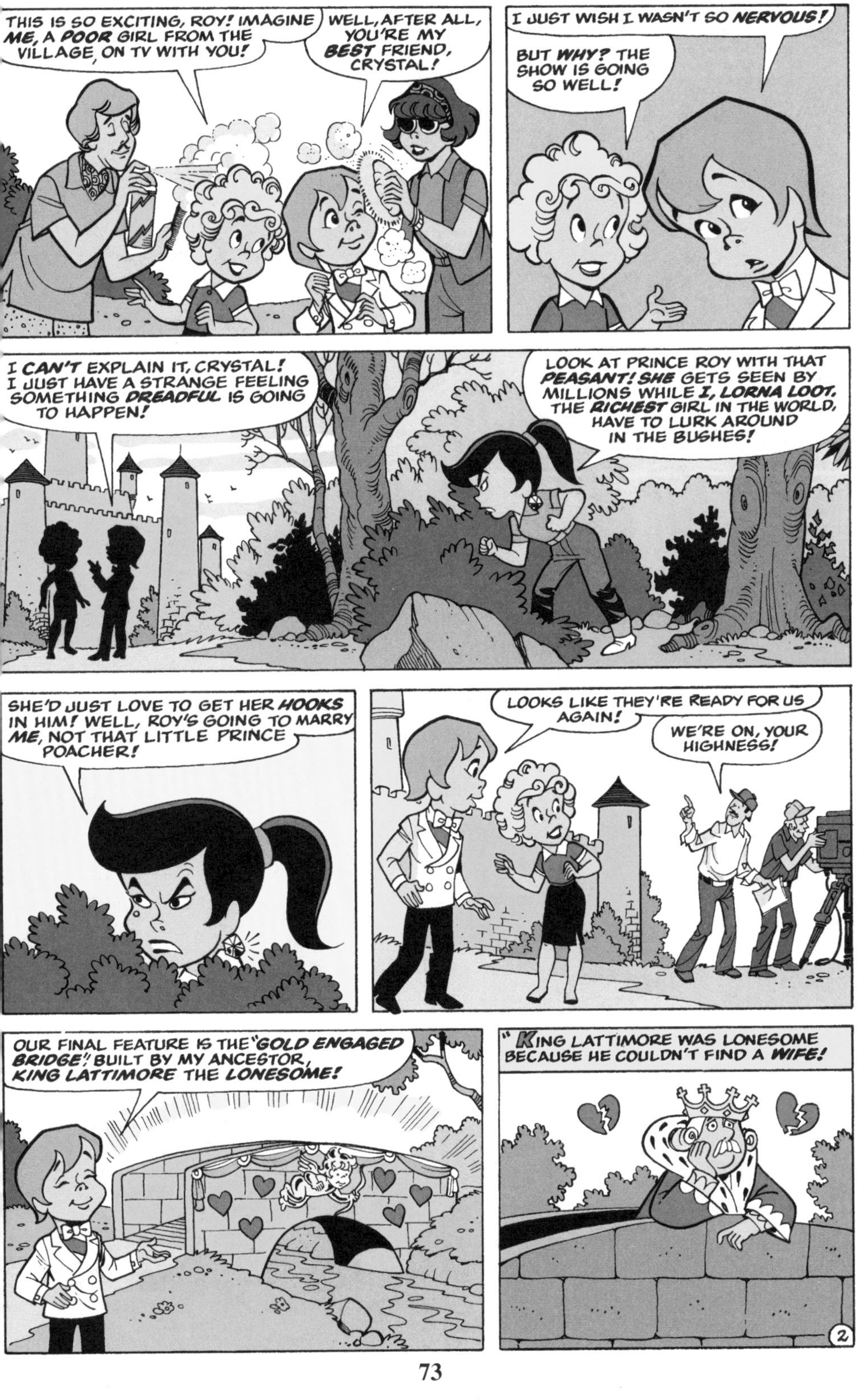
THIS IS SO EXCITING, ROY! IMAGINE ME, A POOR GIRL FROM THE VILLAGE, ON TV WITH YOU!
WELL, AFTER ALL, YOU'RE MY BEST FRIEND, CRYSTAL!
I JUST WISH I WASN'T SO NERVOUS!
BUT WHY? THE SHOW IS GOING SO WELL!
I CAN'T EXPLAIN IT, CRYSTAL! I JUST HAVE A STRANGE FEELING SOMETHING DREADFUL IS GOING TO HAPPEN!
LOOK AT PRINCE ROY WITH THAT PEASANT! SHE GETS SEEN BY MILLIONS WHILE I, LORNA LOOT, THE RICHEST GIRL IN THE WORLD, HAVE TO LURK AROUND IN THE BUSHES!
SHE'D JUST LOVE TO GET HER HOOKS IN HIM! WELL, ROY'S GOING TO MARRY ME, NOT THAT LITTLE PRINCE POACHER!
LOOKS LIKE THEY'RE READY FOR US AGAIN!
WE'RE ON, YOUR HIGHNESS!
OUR FINAL FEATURE IS THE "GOLD ENGAGED BRIDGE," BUILT BY MY ANCESTOR, KING LATTIMORE THE LONESOME!
"KING LATTIMORE WAS LONESOME BECAUSE HE COULDN'T FIND A WIFE!
2

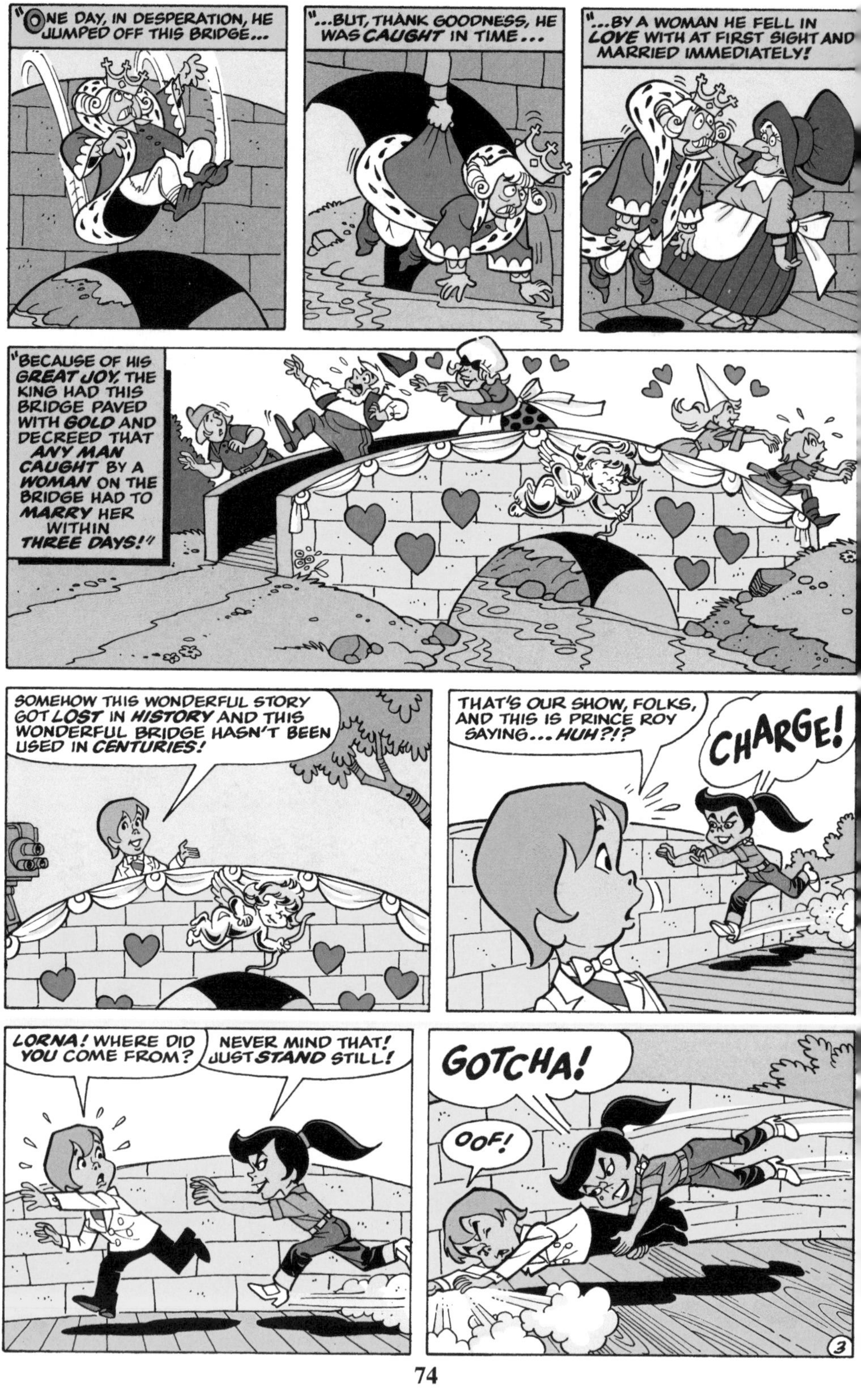
"ONE DAY, IN DESPERATION, HE JUMPED OFF THIS BRIDGE...
"...BUT, THANK GOODNESS, HE WAS CAUGHT IN TIME...
"...BY A WOMAN HE FELL IN LOVE WITH AT FIRST SIGHT AND MARRIED IMMEDIATELY!
"BECAUSE OF HIS GREAT JOY, THE KING HAD THIS BRIDGE PAVED WITH GOLD AND DECREED THAT ANY MAN CAUGHT BY A WOMAN ON THE BRIDGE HAD TO MARRY HER WITHIN THREE DAYS!"
SOMEHOW THIS WONDERFUL STORY GOT LOST IN HISTORY AND THIS WONDERFUL BRIDGE HASN'T BEEN USED IN CENTURIES!
THAT'S OUR SHOW, FOLKS, AND THIS IS PRINCE ROY SAYING... HUH?!?
CHARGE!
LORNA! WHERE DID YOU COME FROM?
NEVER MIND THAT! JUST STAND STILL!
GOTCHA!
OOF!
3

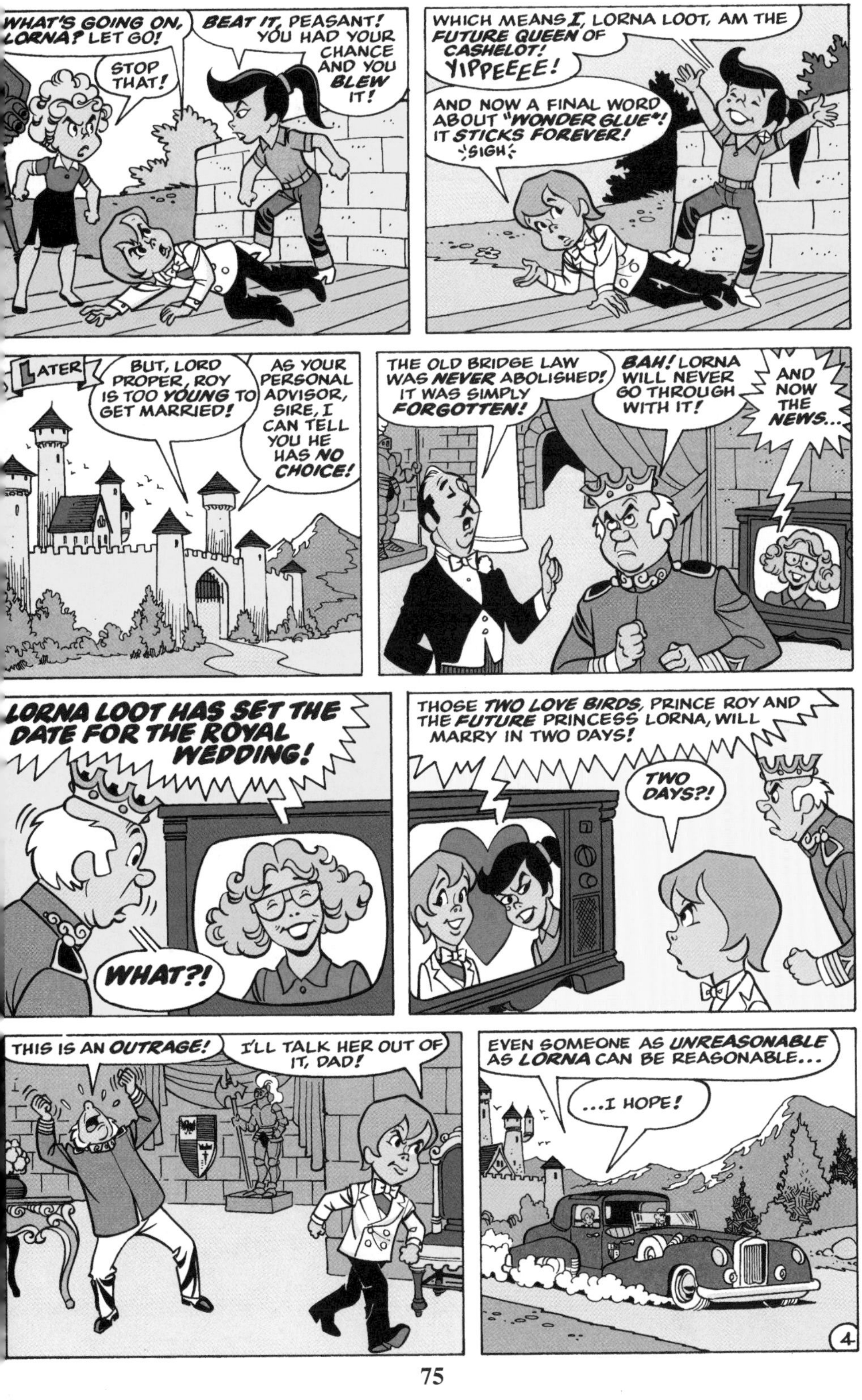
WHAT'S GOING ON, LORNA? LET GO!
STOP THAT!
BEAT IT, PEASANT! YOU HAD YOUR CHANCE AND YOU BLEW IT!
WHICH MEANS I, LORNA LOOT, AM THE FUTURE QUEEN OF CASHELOT! YIPPEEEEE!
AND NOW A FINAL WORD ABOUT "WONDER GLUE"! IT STICKS FOREVER!
SIGH
LATER
BUT, LORD PROPER, ROY IS TOO YOUNG TO GET MARRIED!
AS YOUR PERSONAL ADVISOR, SIRE, I CAN TELL YOU HE HAS NO CHOICE!
THE OLD BRIDGE LAW WAS NEVER ABOLISHED! IT WAS SIMPLY FORGOTTEN!
BAH! LORNA WILL NEVER GO THROUGH WITH IT!
AND NOW THE NEWS...
LORNA LOOT HAS SET THE DATE FOR THE ROYAL WEDDING!
WHAT?!
THOSE TWO LOVE BIRDS, PRINCE ROY AND THE FUTURE PRINCESS LORNA, WILL MARRY IN TWO DAYS!
TWO DAYS?!
THIS IS AN OUTRAGE!
I'LL TALK HER OUT OF IT, DAD!
EVEN SOMEONE AS UNREASONABLE AS LORNA CAN BE REASONABLE...
...I HOPE!
4

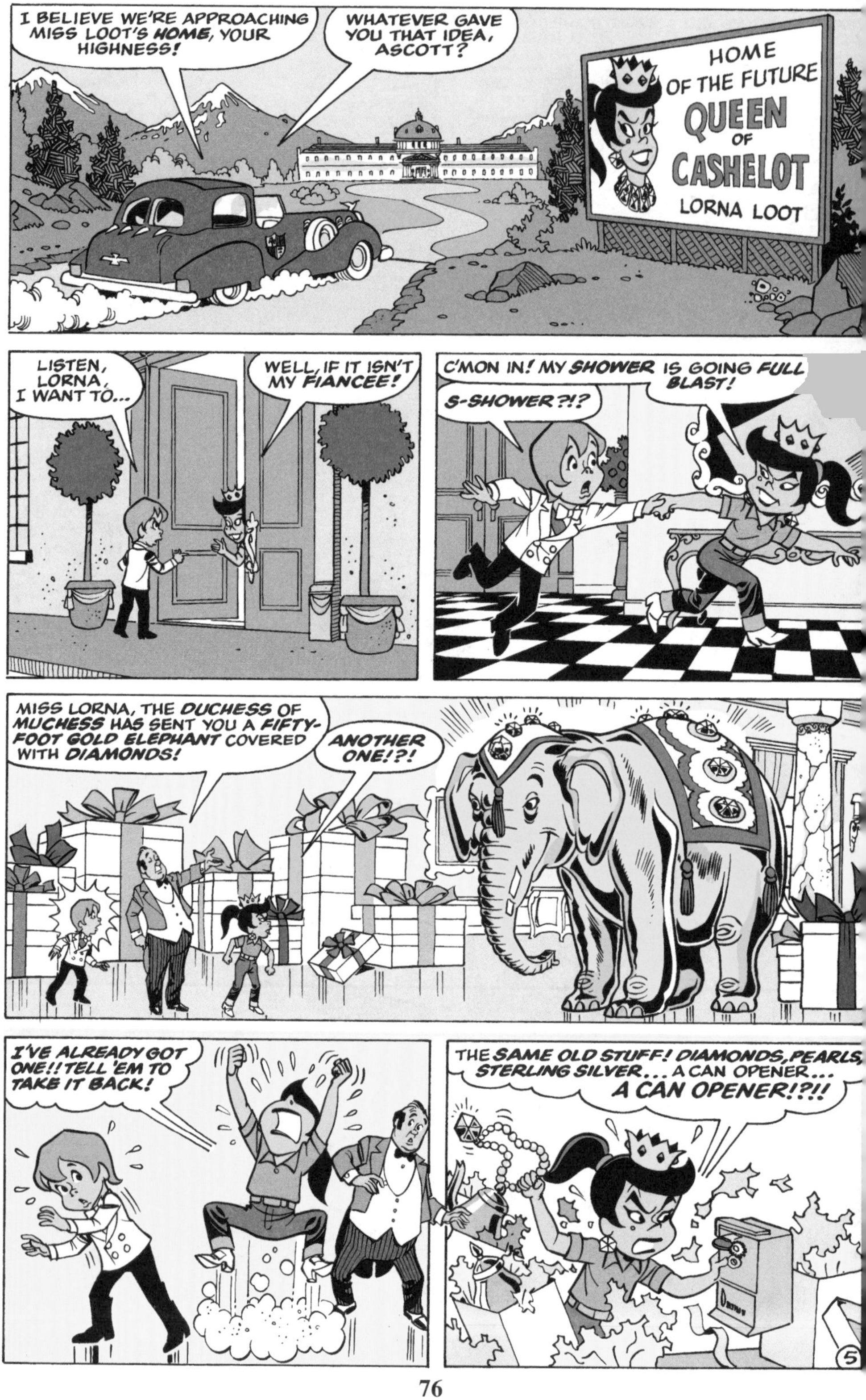

I BELIEVE WE'RE APPROACHING MISS LOOT'S HOME, YOUR HIGHNESS!
WHATEVER GAVE YOU THAT IDEA, ASCOTT?
HOME OF THE FUTURE QUEEN OF CASHELOT LORNA LOOT
LISTEN, LORNA, I WANT TO...
WELL, IF IT ISN'T MY FIANCEE!
C'MON IN! MY SHOWER IS GOING FULL BLAST!
S-SHOWER?!?
MISS LORNA, THE DUCHESS OF MUCHESS HAS SENT YOU A FIFTY-FOOT GOLD ELEPHANT COVERED WITH DIAMONDS!
ANOTHER ONE!?!
I'VE ALREADY GOT ONE!! TELL 'EM TO TAKE IT BACK!
THE SAME OLD STUFF! DIAMONDS, PEARLS, STERLING SILVER... A CAN OPENER... A CAN OPENER!?!!
5

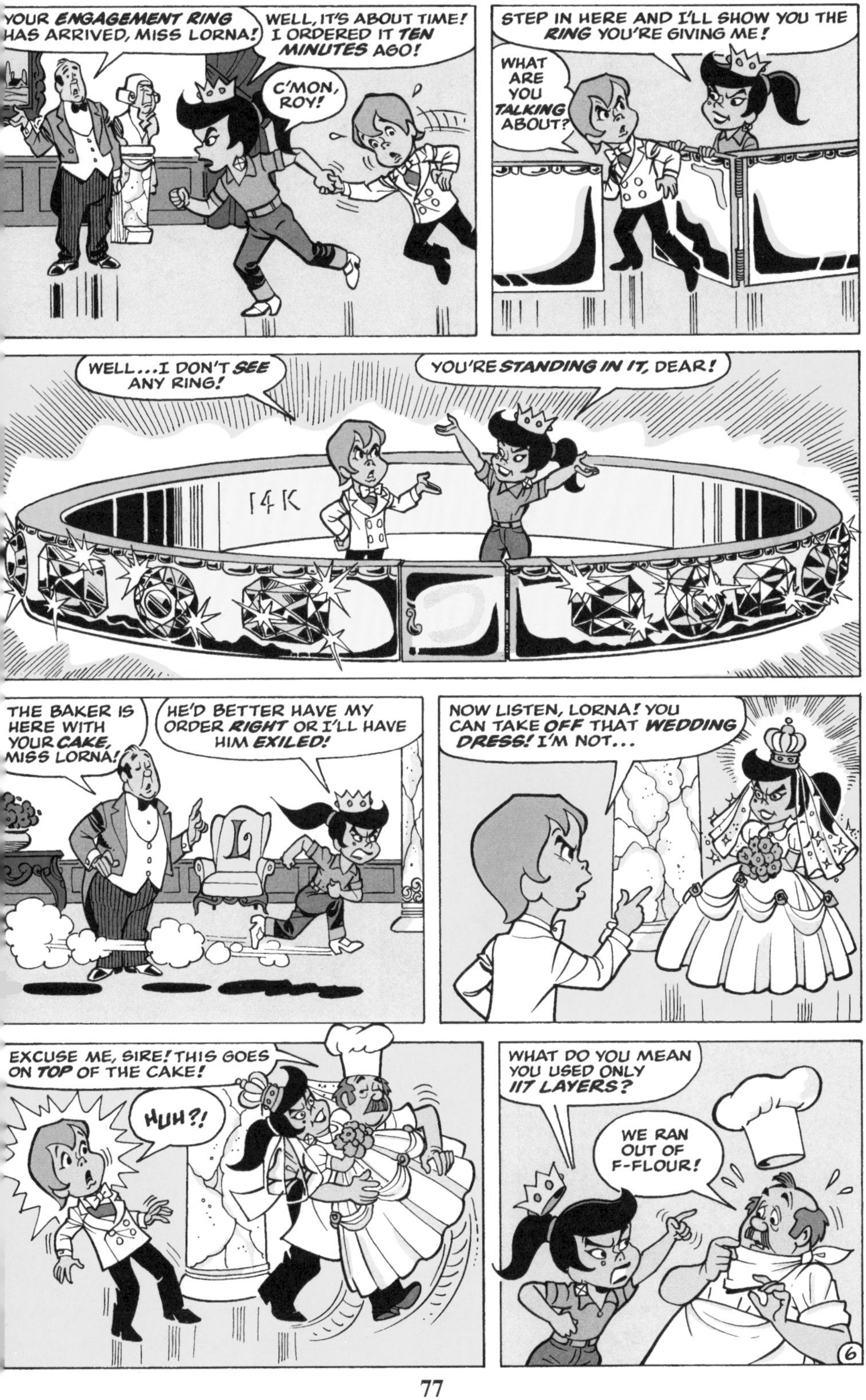
YOUR ENGAGEMENT RING HAS ARRIVED, MISS LORNA!
WELL, IT'S ABOUT TIME! I ORDERED IT TEN MINUTES AGO!
C'MON, ROY!
STEP IN HERE AND I'LL SHOW YOU THE RING YOU'RE GIVING ME!
WHAT ARE YOU TALKING ABOUT?
WELL...I DON'T SEE ANY RING!
YOU'RE STANDING IN IT, DEAR!
14K
THE BAKER IS HERE WITH YOUR CAKE, MISS LORNA!
HE'D BETTER HAVE MY ORDER RIGHT OR I'LL HAVE HIM EXILED!
NOW LISTEN, LORNA! YOU CAN TAKE OFF THAT WEDDING DRESS! I'M NOT...
EXCUSE ME, SIRE! THIS GOES ON TOP OF THE CAKE!
HUH?!
WHAT DO YOU MEAN YOU USED ONLY 117 LAYERS?
WE RAN OUT OF F-FLOUR!
6

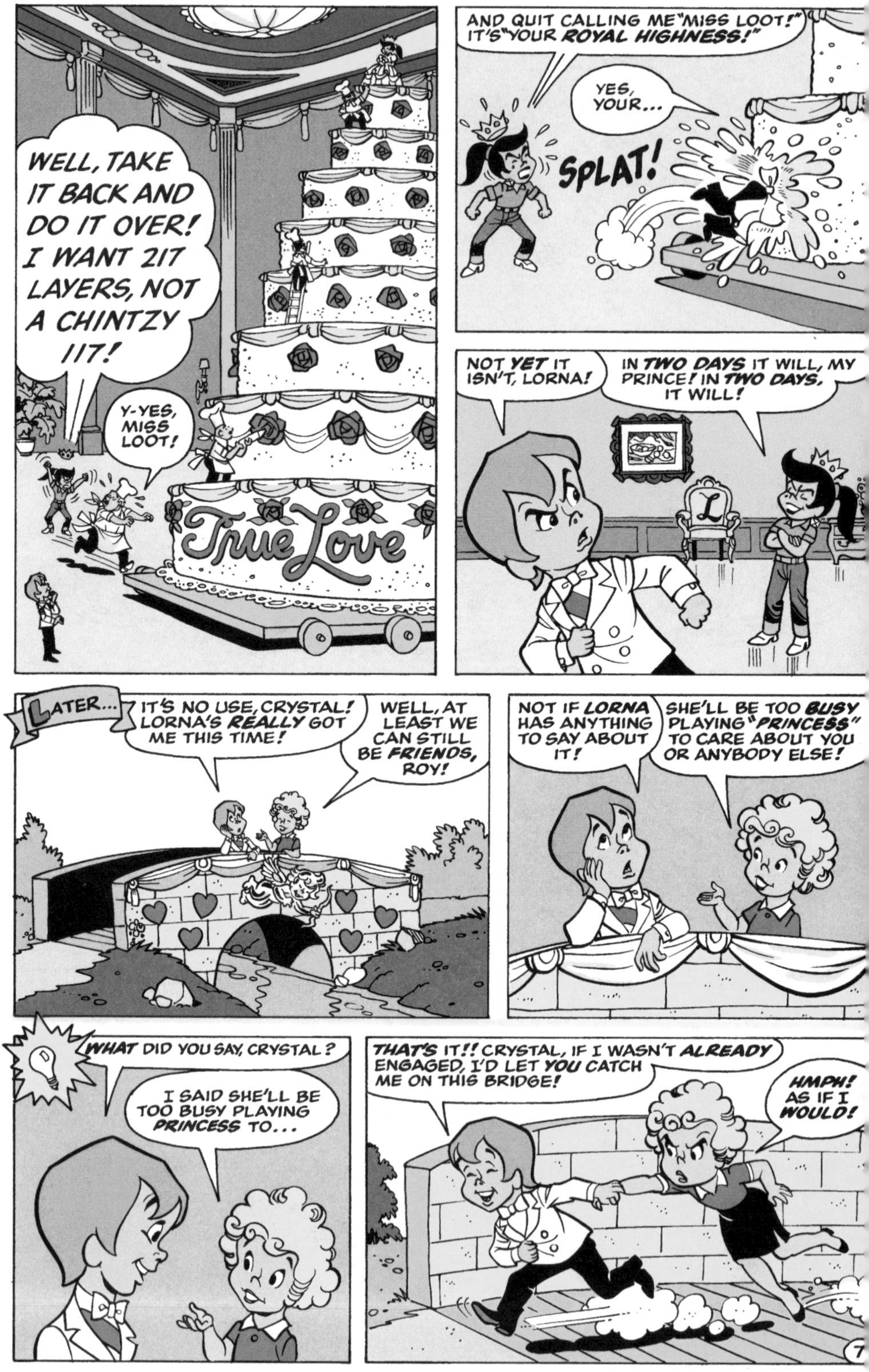

WELL, TAKE IT BACK AND DO IT OVER! I WANT 217 LAYERS, NOT A CHINTZY 117!
Y-YES, MISS LOOT!
True Love
AND QUIT CALLING ME "MISS LOOT!" IT'S "YOUR ROYAL HIGHNESS!"
YES, YOUR...
SPLAT!
NOT YET IT ISN'T, LORNA!
IN TWO DAYS IT WILL, MY PRINCE! IN TWO DAYS, IT WILL!
LATER...
IT'S NO USE, CRYSTAL! LORNA'S REALLY GOT ME THIS TIME!
WELL, AT LEAST WE CAN STILL BE FRIENDS, ROY!
NOT IF LORNA HAS ANYTHING TO SAY ABOUT IT!
SHE'LL BE TOO BUSY PLAYING "PRINCESS" TO CARE ABOUT YOU OR ANYBODY ELSE!
WHAT DID YOU SAY, CRYSTAL?
I SAID SHE'LL BE TOO BUSY PLAYING PRINCESS TO...
THAT'S IT!! CRYSTAL, IF I WASN'T ALREADY ENGAGED, I'D LET YOU CATCH ME ON THIS BRIDGE!
HMPH! AS IF I WOULD!

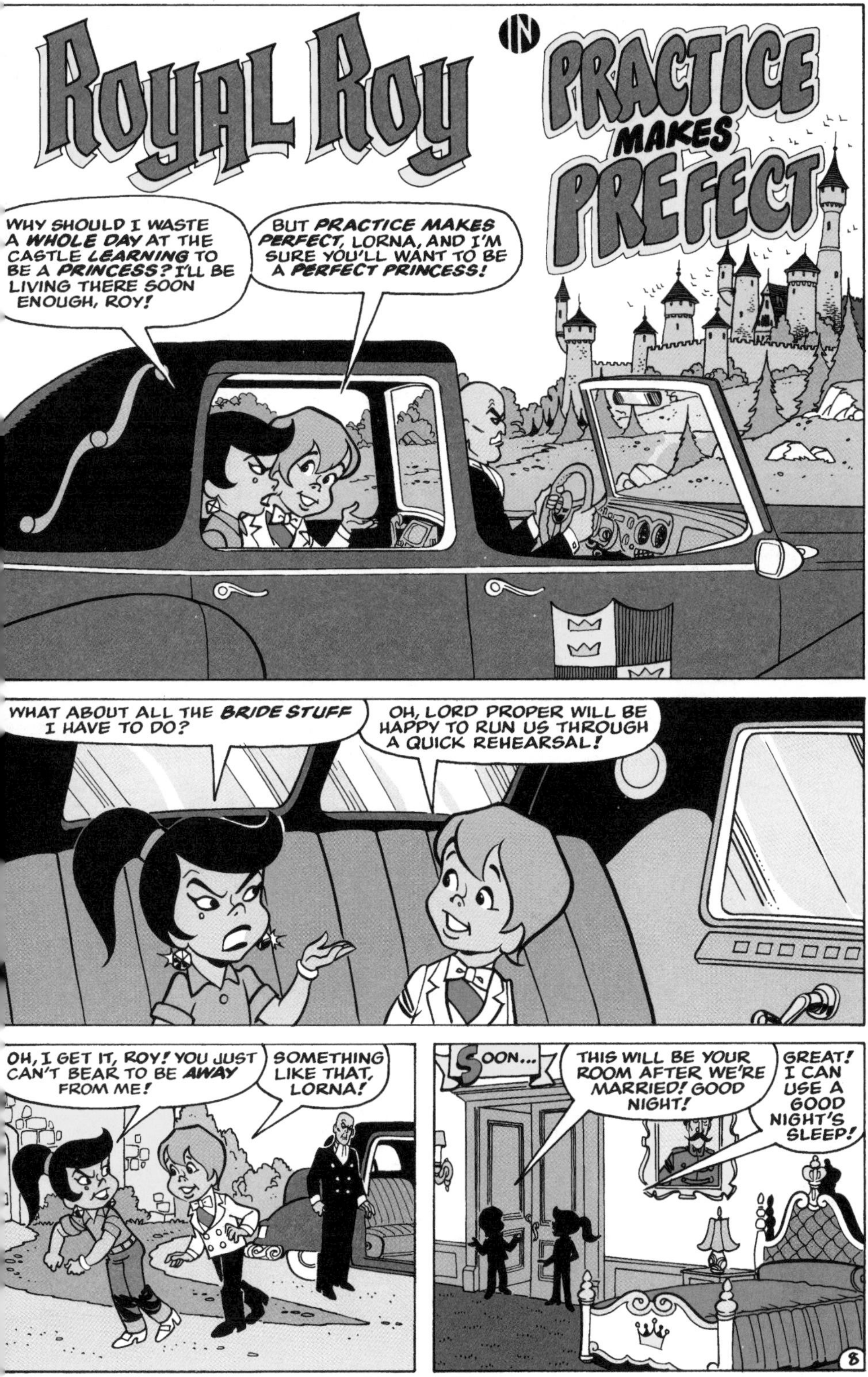
Royal Roy IN PRACTICE MAKES PREFECT
WHY SHOULD I WASTE A WHOLE DAY AT THE CASTLE LEARNING TO BE A PRINCESS? I'LL BE LIVING THERE SOON ENOUGH, ROY!
BUT PRACTICE MAKES PERFECT, LORNA, AND I'M SURE YOU'LL WANT TO BE A PERFECT PRINCESS!
WHAT ABOUT ALL THE BRIDE STUFF I HAVE TO DO?
OH, LORD PROPER WILL BE HAPPY TO RUN US THROUGH A QUICK REHEARSAL!
OH, I GET IT, ROY! YOU JUST CAN'T BEAR TO BE AWAY FROM ME!
SOMETHING LIKE THAT, LORNA!
SOON...
THIS WILL BE YOUR ROOM AFTER WE'RE MARRIED! GOOD NIGHT!
GREAT! I CAN USE A GOOD NIGHT'S SLEEP!
8

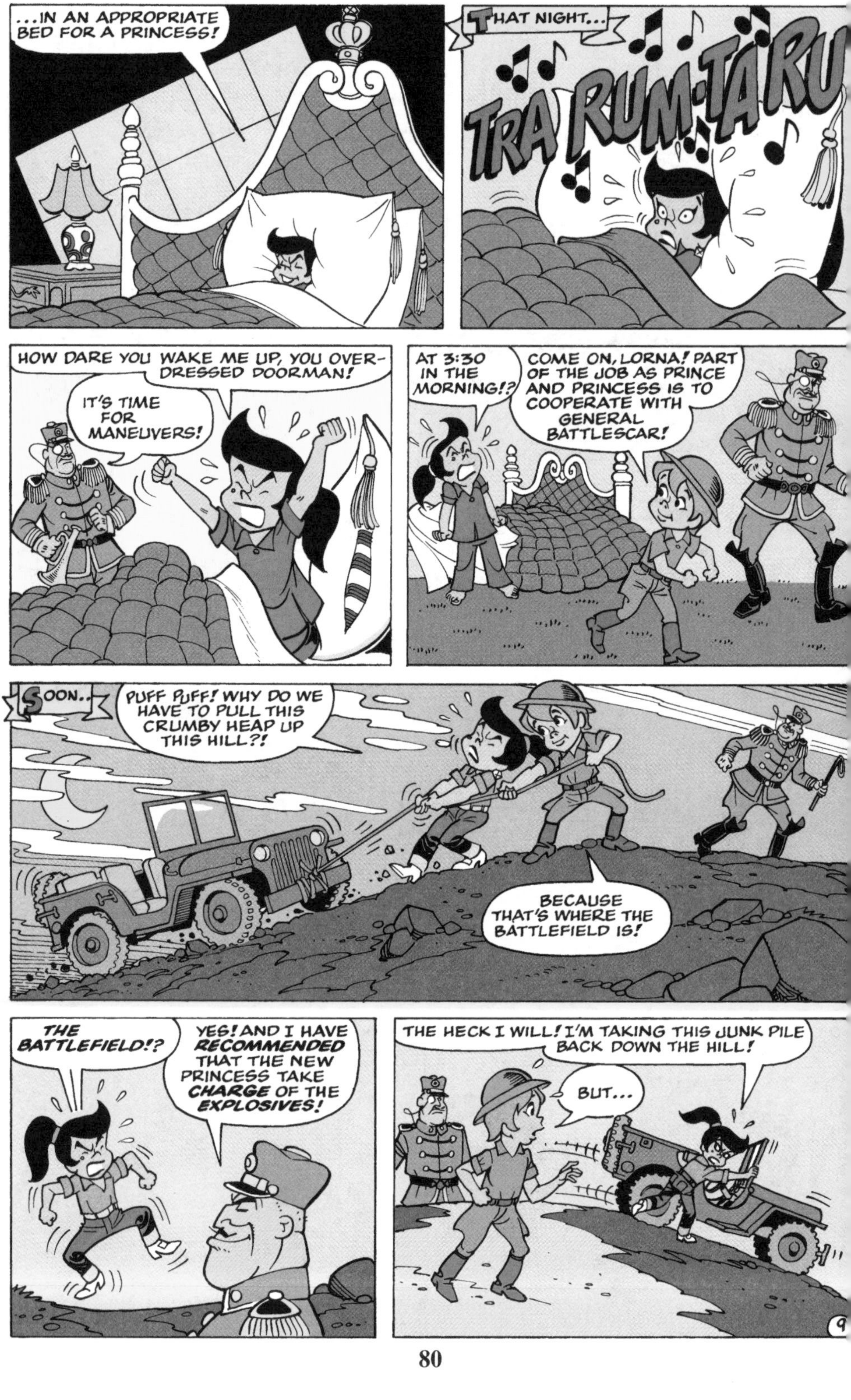
...IN AN APPROPRIATE BED FOR A PRINCESS!
THAT NIGHT...
TRA RUM-TA-RU
HOW DARE YOU WAKE ME UP, YOU OVER-DRESSED DOORMAN!
IT'S TIME FOR MANEUVERS!
AT 3:30 IN THE MORNING!?
COME ON, LORNA! PART OF THE JOB AS PRINCE AND PRINCESS IS TO COOPERATE WITH GENERAL BATTLESCAR!
SOON..
PUFF PUFF! WHY DO WE HAVE TO PULL THIS CRUMBY HEAP UP THIS HILL?!
BECAUSE THAT'S WHERE THE BATTLEFIELD IS!
THE BATTLEFIELD!?
YES! AND I HAVE RECOMMENDED THAT THE NEW PRINCESS TAKE CHARGE OF THE EXPLOSIVES!
THE HECK I WILL! I'M TAKING THIS JUNK PILE BACK DOWN THE HILL!
BUT...
9

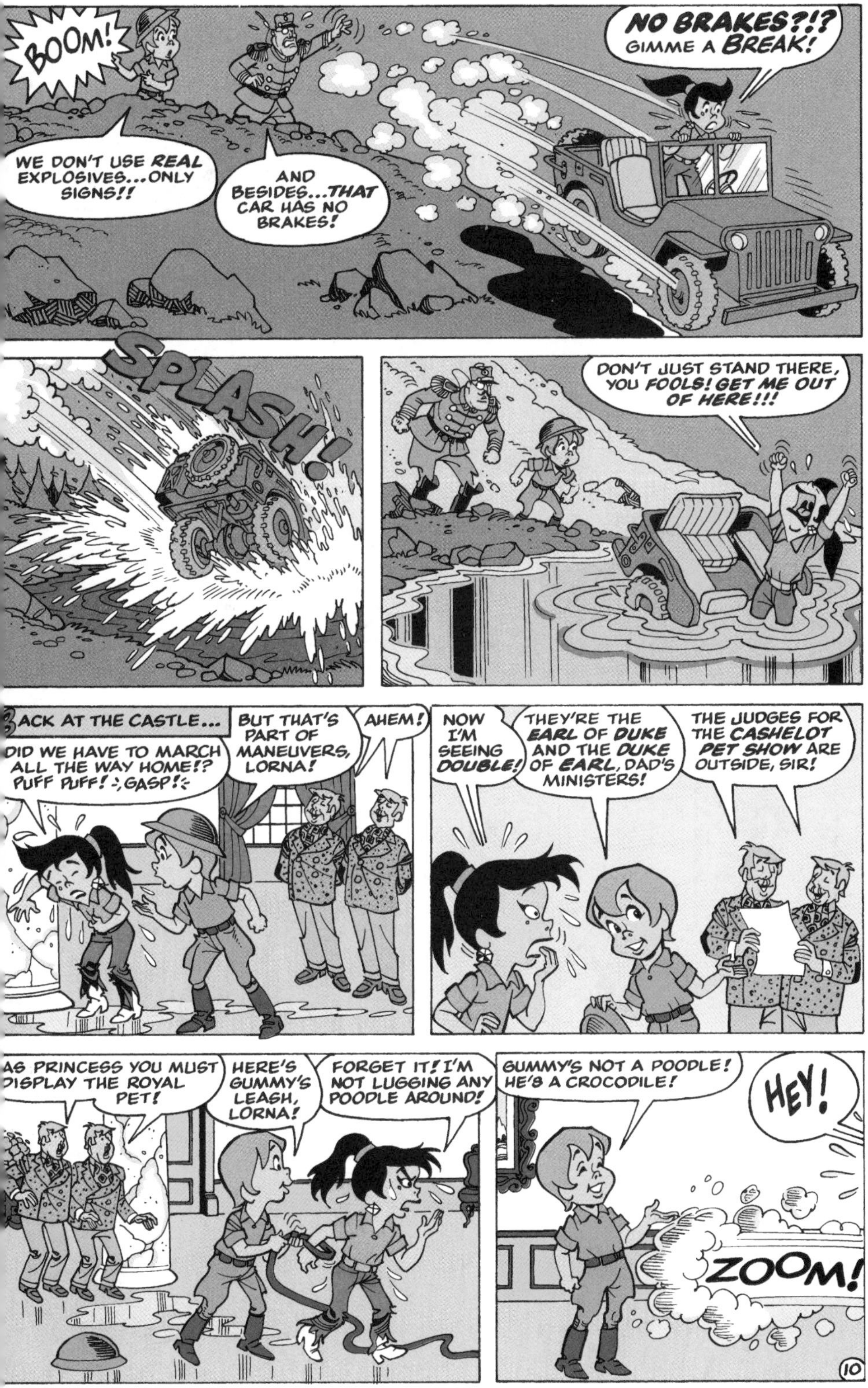

BOOM!
NO BRAKES?!? GIMME A BREAK!
WE DON'T USE REAL EXPLOSIVES...ONLY SIGNS!!
AND BESIDES...THAT CAR HAS NO BRAKES!
SPLASH!
DON'T JUST STAND THERE, YOU FOOLS! GET ME OUT OF HERE!!!
BACK AT THE CASTLE...
DID WE HAVE TO MARCH ALL THE WAY HOME!? PUFF PUFF! GASP!
BUT THAT'S PART OF MANEUVERS, LORNA!
AHEM!
NOW I'M SEEING DOUBLE!
THEY'RE THE EARL OF DUKE AND THE DUKE OF EARL, DAD'S MINISTERS!
THE JUDGES FOR THE CASHELOT PET SHOW ARE OUTSIDE, SIR!
AS PRINCESS YOU MUST DISPLAY THE ROYAL PET!
HERE'S GUMMY'S LEASH, LORNA!
FORGET IT! I'M NOT LUGGING ANY POODLE AROUND!
GUMMY'S NOT A POODLE! HE'S A CROCODILE!
HEY!
ZOOM!
10

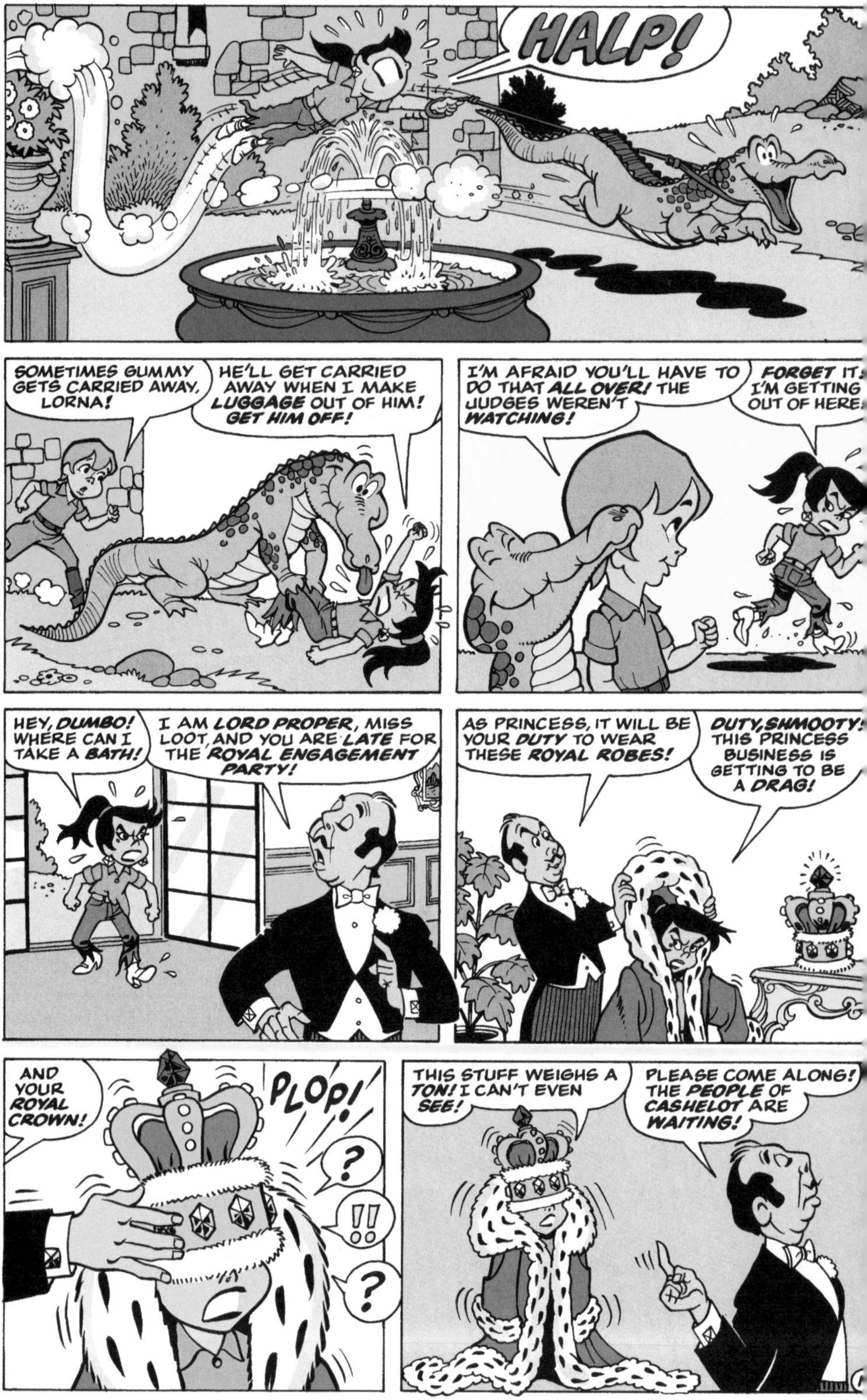

HALP!
SOMETIMES GUMMY GETS CARRIED AWAY, LORNA!
HE'LL GET CARRIED AWAY WHEN I MAKE LUGGAGE OUT OF HIM! GET HIM OFF!
I'M AFRAID YOU'LL HAVE TO DO THAT ALL OVER! THE JUDGES WEREN'T WATCHING!
FORGET IT! I'M GETTING OUT OF HERE!
HEY, DUMBO! WHERE CAN I TAKE A BATH!
I AM LORD PROPER, MISS LOOT, AND YOU ARE LATE FOR THE ROYAL ENGAGEMENT PARTY!
AS PRINCESS, IT WILL BE YOUR DUTY TO WEAR THESE ROYAL ROBES!
DUTY, SHMOOTY! THIS PRINCESS BUSINESS IS GETTING TO BE A DRAG!
AND YOUR ROYAL CROWN!
PLOP!
?
!!
?
THIS STUFF WEIGHS A TON! I CAN'T EVEN SEE!
PLEASE COME ALONG! THE PEOPLE OF CASHELOT ARE WAITING!

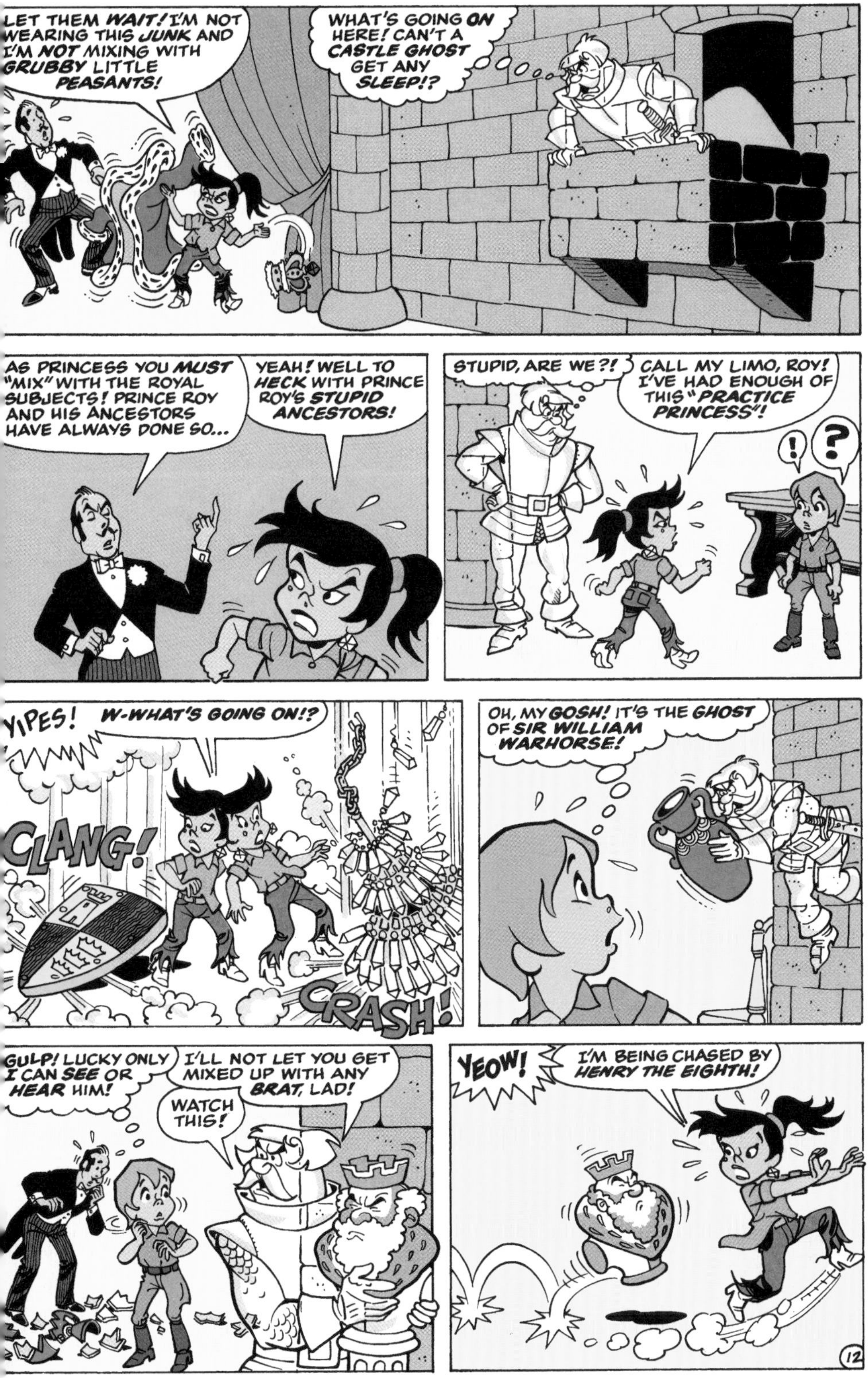
LET THEM WAIT! I'M NOT WEARING THIS JUNK AND I'M NOT MIXING WITH GRUBBY LITTLE PEASANTS!
WHAT'S GOING ON HERE! CAN'T A CASTLE GHOST GET ANY SLEEP!?
AS PRINCESS YOU MUST "MIX" WITH THE ROYAL SUBJECTS! PRINCE ROY AND HIS ANCESTORS HAVE ALWAYS DONE SO...
YEAH! WELL TO HECK WITH PRINCE ROY'S STUPID ANCESTORS!
STUPID, ARE WE?!
CALL MY LIMO, ROY! I'VE HAD ENOUGH OF THIS "PRACTICE PRINCESS"!
!
?
YIPES!
W-WHAT'S GOING ON!?
CLANG!
CRASH!
OH, MY GOSH! IT'S THE GHOST OF SIR WILLIAM WARHORSE!
GULP! LUCKY ONLY I CAN SEE OR HEAR HIM!
I'LL NOT LET YOU GET MIXED UP WITH ANY BRAT, LAD!
WATCH THIS!
YEOW!
I'M BEING CHASED BY HENRY THE EIGHTH!
12

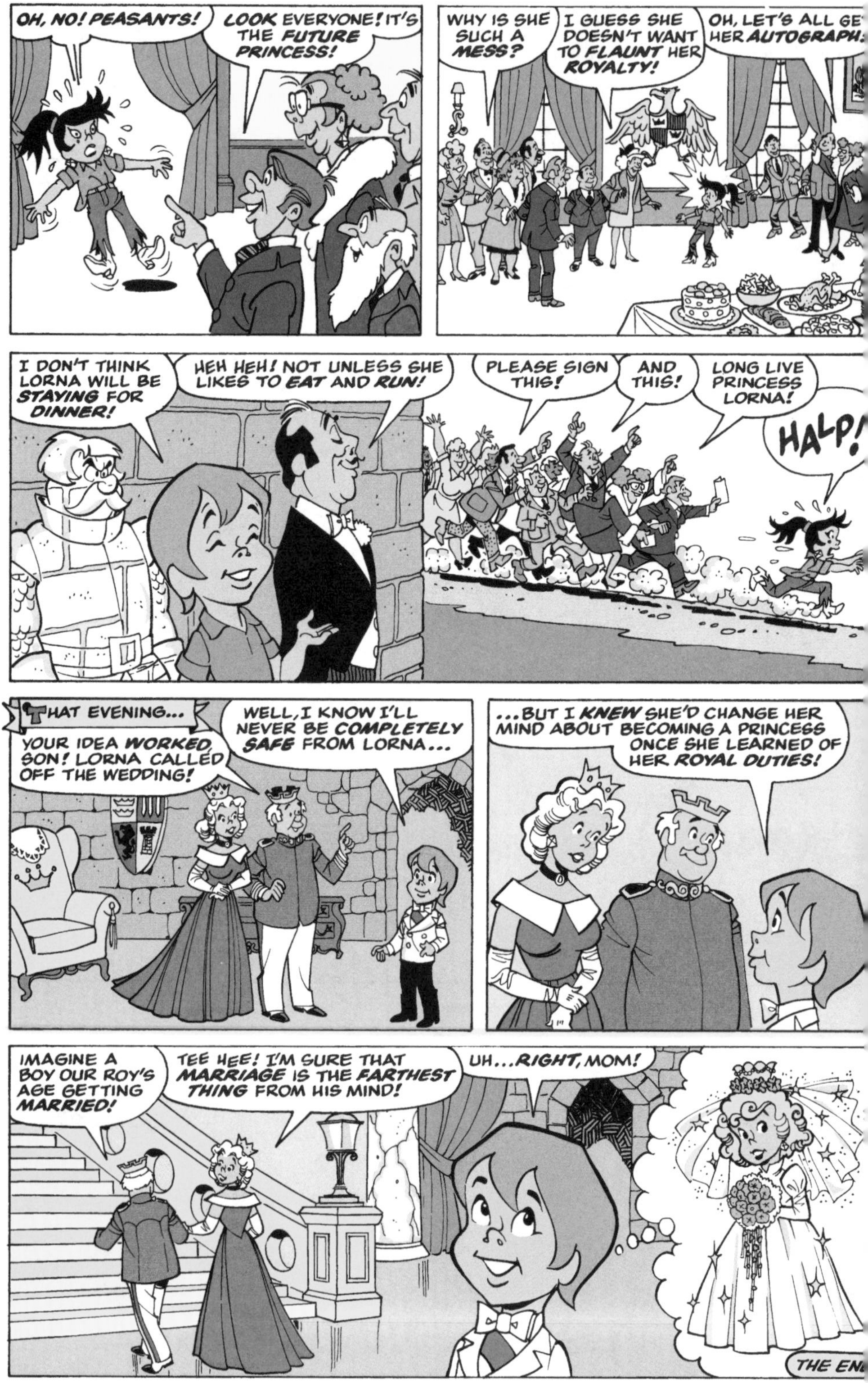
OH, NO! PEASANTS!
LOOK EVERYONE! IT'S THE FUTURE PRINCESS!
WHY IS SHE SUCH A MESS?
I GUESS SHE DOESN'T WANT TO FLAUNT HER ROYALTY!
OH, LET'S ALL GE HER AUTOGRAPH
I DON'T THINK LORNA WILL BE STAYING FOR DINNER!
HEH HEH! NOT UNLESS SHE LIKES TO EAT AND RUN!
PLEASE SIGN THIS!
AND THIS!
LONG LIVE PRINCESS LORNA!
HALP!
THAT EVENING...
YOUR IDEA WORKED, SON! LORNA CALLED OFF THE WEDDING!
WELL, I KNOW I'LL NEVER BE COMPLETELY SAFE FROM LORNA...
...BUT I KNEW SHE'D CHANGE HER MIND ABOUT BECOMING A PRINCESS ONCE SHE LEARNED OF HER ROYAL DUTIES!
IMAGINE A BOY OUR ROY'S AGE GETTING MARRIED!
TEE HEE! I'M SURE THAT MARRIAGE IS THE FARTHEST THING FROM HIS MIND!
UH...RIGHT, MOM!
THE EN

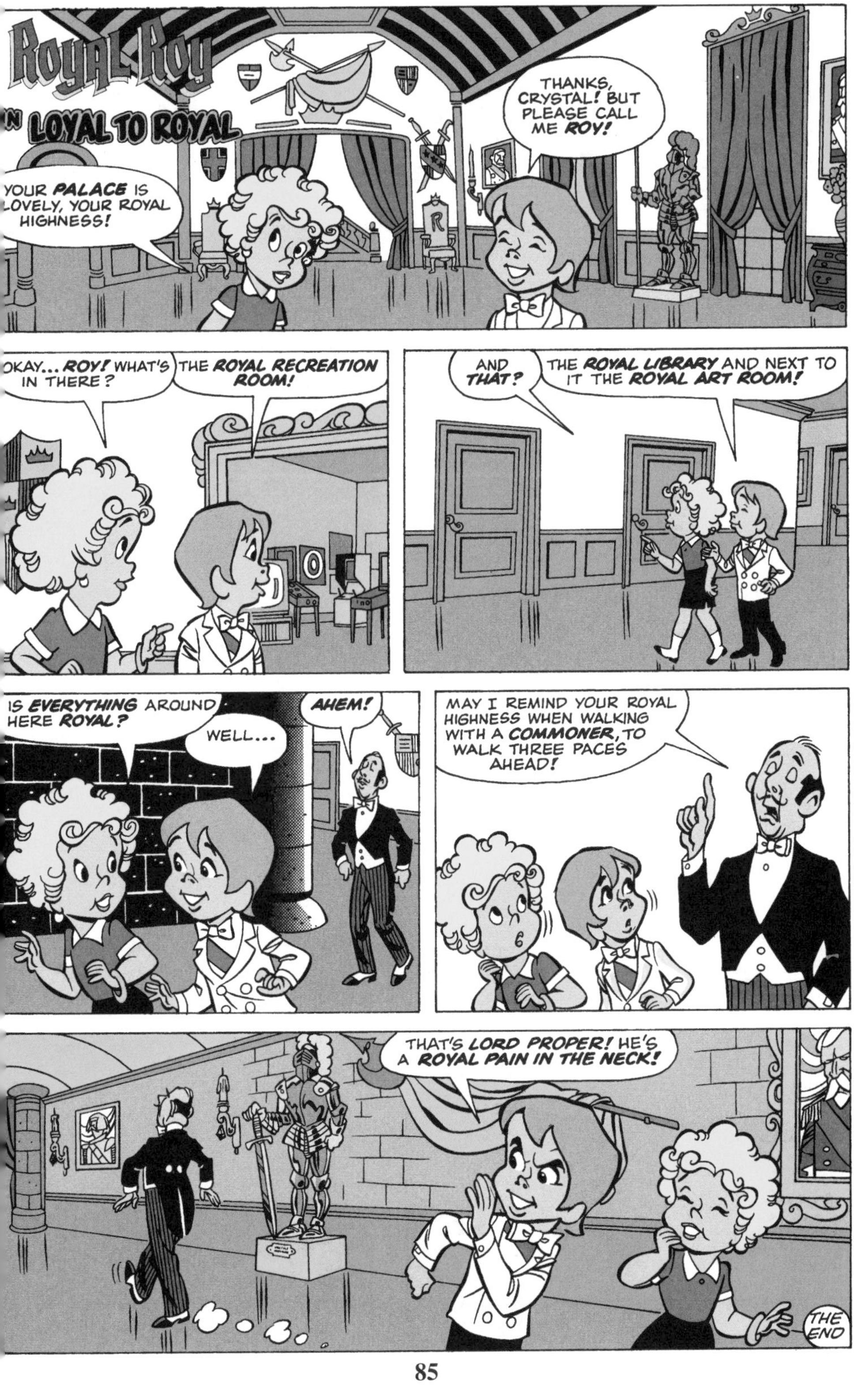
Royal Roy
IN LOYAL TO ROYAL
YOUR PALACE IS LOVELY, YOUR ROYAL HIGHNESS!
THANKS, CRYSTAL! BUT PLEASE CALL ME ROY!
OKAY... ROY! WHAT'S IN THERE?
THE ROYAL RECREATION ROOM!
AND THAT?
THE ROYAL LIBRARY AND NEXT TO IT THE ROYAL ART ROOM!
IS EVERYTHING AROUND HERE ROYAL?
WELL...
AHEM!
MAY I REMIND YOUR ROYAL HIGHNESS WHEN WALKING WITH A COMMONER, TO WALK THREE PACES AHEAD!
THAT'S LORD PROPER! HE'S A ROYAL PAIN IN THE NECK!
THE END

Royal Roy in Space Race Ace

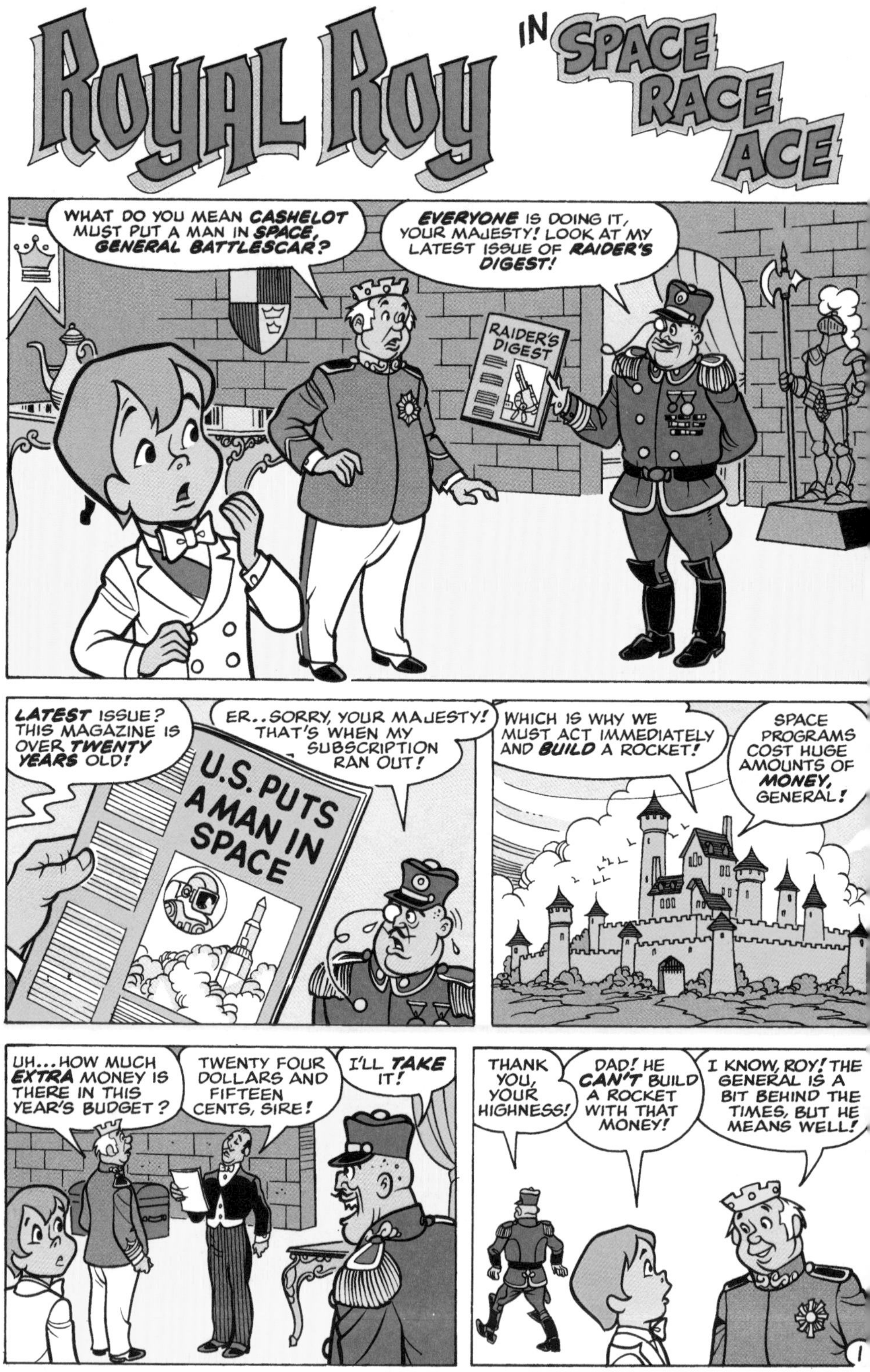

WHAT DO YOU MEAN CASHELOT MUST PUT A MAN IN SPACE, GENERAL BATTLESCAR?
EVERYONE IS DOING IT, YOUR MAJESTY! LOOK AT MY LATEST ISSUE OF RAIDER'S DIGEST!
RAIDER'S DIGEST
LATEST ISSUE? THIS MAGAZINE IS OVER TWENTY YEARS OLD!
ER.. SORRY, YOUR MAJESTY! THAT'S WHEN MY SUBSCRIPTION RAN OUT!
U.S. PUTS A MAN IN SPACE
WHICH IS WHY WE MUST ACT IMMEDIATELY AND BUILD A ROCKET!
SPACE PROGRAMS COST HUGE AMOUNTS OF MONEY, GENERAL!
UH... HOW MUCH EXTRA MONEY IS THERE IN THIS YEAR'S BUDGET?
TWENTY FOUR DOLLARS AND FIFTEEN CENTS, SIRE!
I'LL TAKE IT!
THANK YOU, YOUR HIGHNESS!
DAD! HE CAN'T BUILD A ROCKET WITH THAT MONEY!
I KNOW, ROY! THE GENERAL IS A BIT BEHIND THE TIMES, BUT HE MEANS WELL!
1

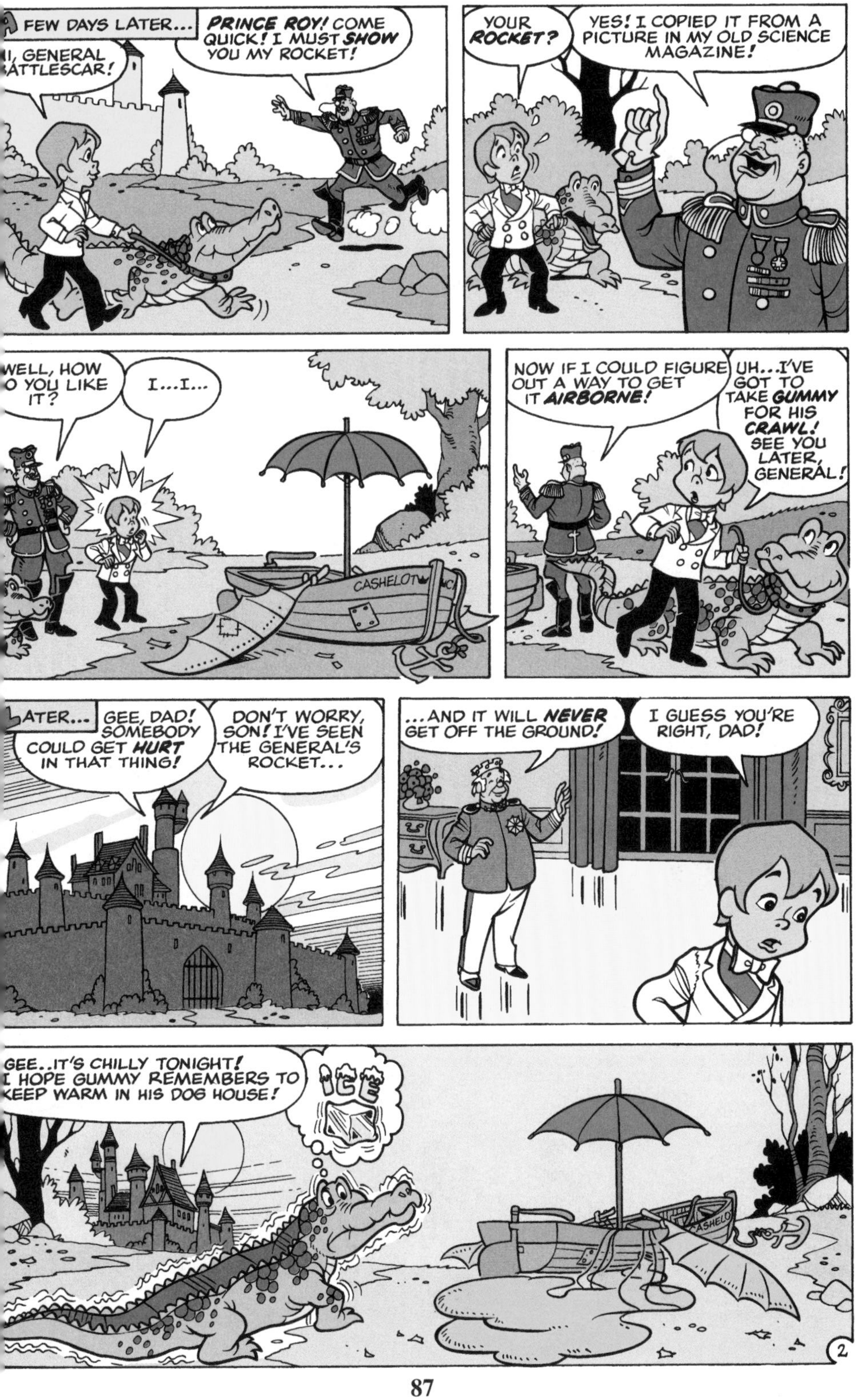

FEW DAYS LATER...
I, GENERAL ATTLESCAR!
PRINCE ROY! COME QUICK! I MUST SHOW YOU MY ROCKET!
YOUR ROCKET?
YES! I COPIED IT FROM A PICTURE IN MY OLD SCIENCE MAGAZINE!
WELL, HOW O YOU LIKE IT?
I...I...
CASHELOT
NOW IF I COULD FIGURE OUT A WAY TO GET IT AIRBORNE!
UH...I'VE GOT TO TAKE GUMMY FOR HIS CRAWL! SEE YOU LATER, GENERAL!
ATER...
GEE, DAD! SOMEBODY COULD GET HURT IN THAT THING!
DON'T WORRY, SON! I'VE SEEN THE GENERAL'S ROCKET...
...AND IT WILL NEVER GET OFF THE GROUND!
I GUESS YOU'RE RIGHT, DAD!
GEE..IT'S CHILLY TONIGHT! I HOPE GUMMY REMEMBERS TO KEEP WARM IN HIS DOG HOUSE!
ICE
2

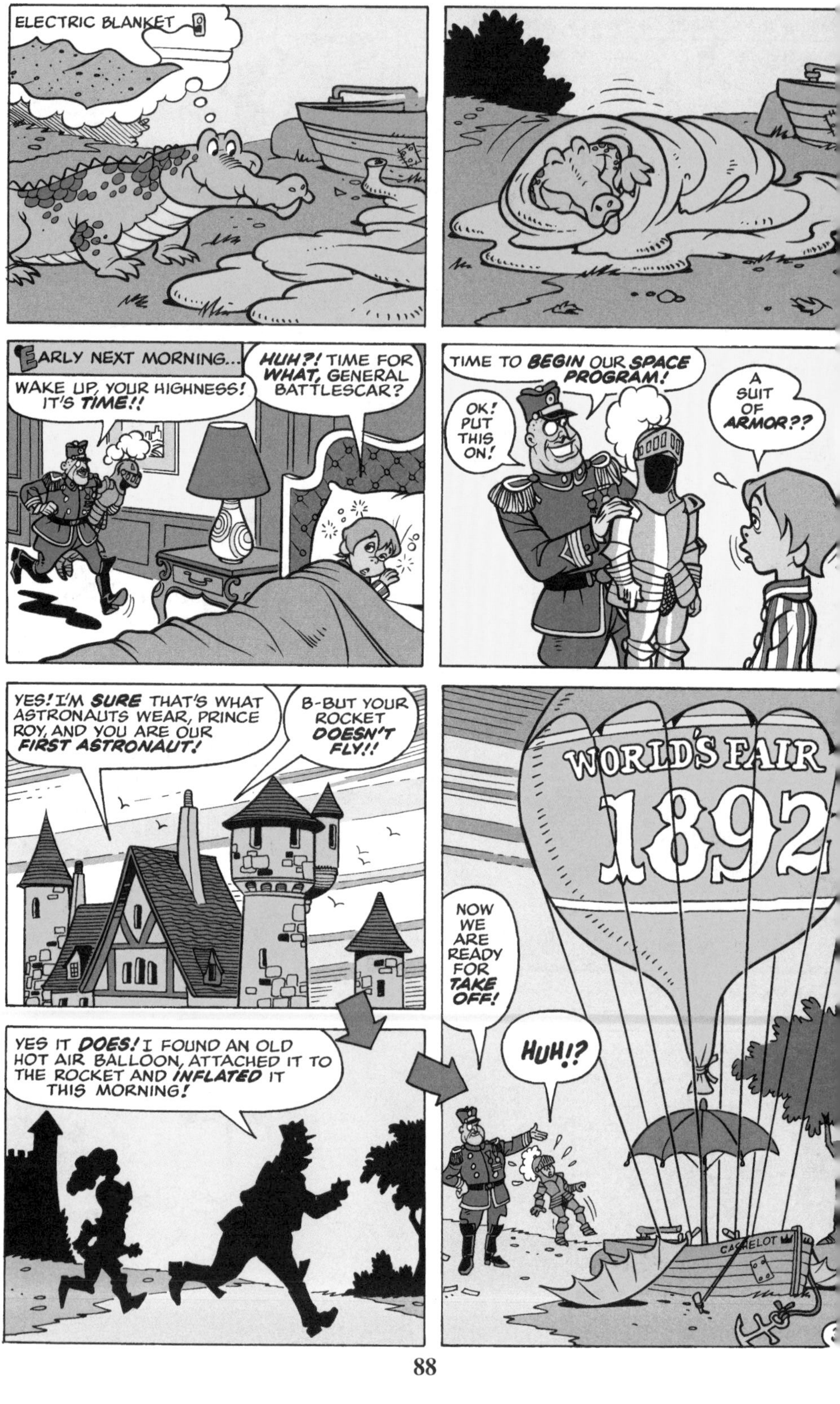
ELECTRIC BLANKET
EARLY NEXT MORNING...
WAKE UP, YOUR HIGHNESS! IT'S TIME!!
HUH?! TIME FOR WHAT, GENERAL BATTLESCAR?
TIME TO BEGIN OUR SPACE PROGRAM!
OK! PUT THIS ON!
A SUIT OF ARMOR??
YES! I'M SURE THAT'S WHAT ASTRONAUTS WEAR, PRINCE ROY, AND YOU ARE OUR FIRST ASTRONAUT!
B-BUT YOUR ROCKET DOESN'T FLY!!
WORLD'S FAIR
1892
YES IT DOES! I FOUND AN OLD HOT AIR BALLOON, ATTACHED IT TO THE ROCKET AND INFLATED IT THIS MORNING!
NOW WE ARE READY FOR TAKE OFF!
HUH!?
CAMELOT

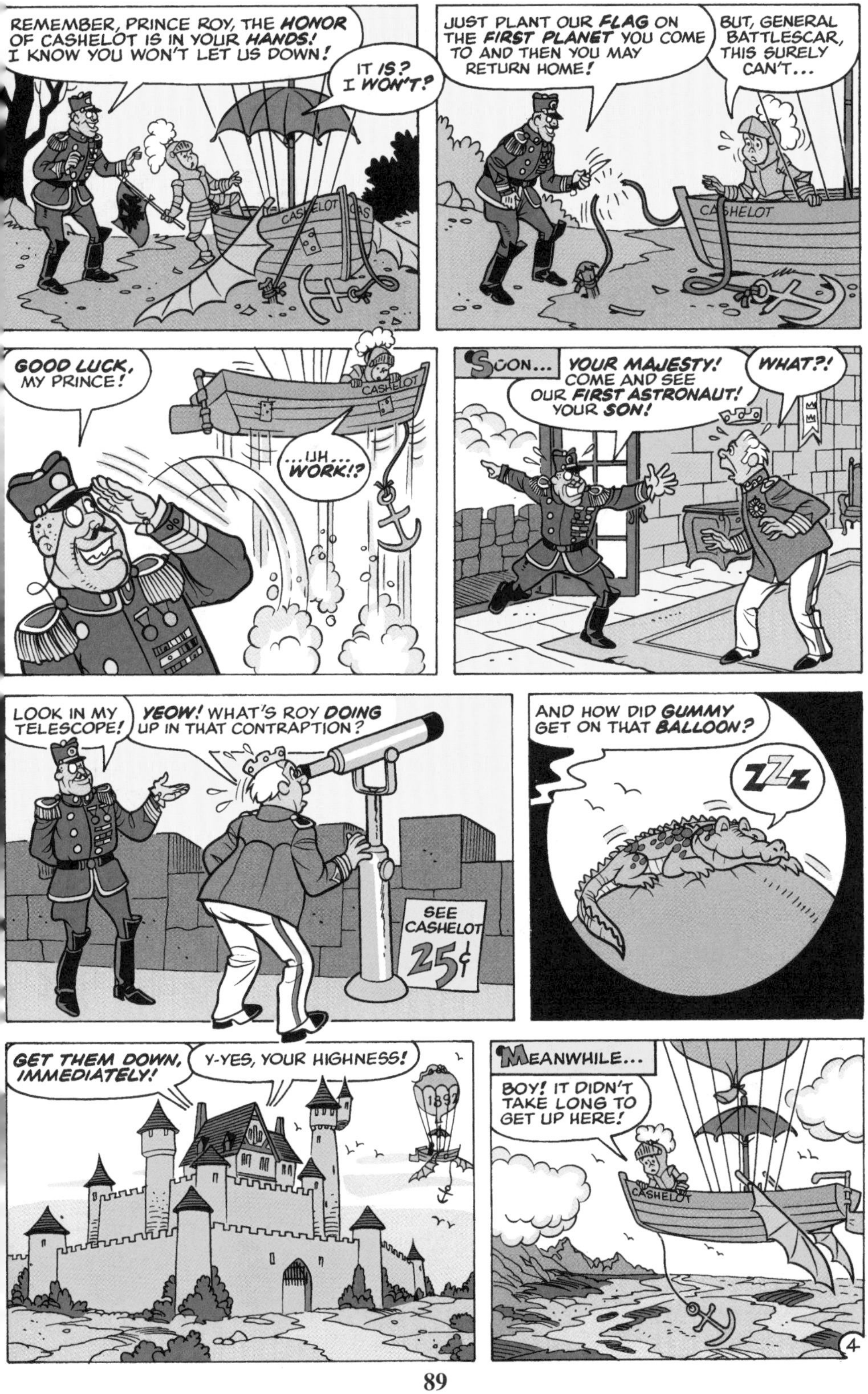
REMEMBER, PRINCE ROY, THE HONOR OF CASHELOT IS IN YOUR HANDS! I KNOW YOU WON'T LET US DOWN!
IT IS? I WON'T?
CASHELOT
JUST PLANT OUR FLAG ON THE FIRST PLANET YOU COME TO AND THEN YOU MAY RETURN HOME!
BUT, GENERAL BATTLESCAR, THIS SURELY CAN'T...
CASHELOT
GOOD LUCK, MY PRINCE!
CASHELOT
...UH... WORK!?
SOON...
YOUR MAJESTY! COME AND SEE OUR FIRST ASTRONAUT! YOUR SON!
WHAT?!
LOOK IN MY TELESCOPE!
YEOW! WHAT'S ROY DOING UP IN THAT CONTRAPTION?
SEE CASHELOT 25¢
AND HOW DID GUMMY GET ON THAT BALLOON?
ZZZ
GET THEM DOWN, IMMEDIATELY!
Y-YES, YOUR HIGHNESS!
1892
MEANWHILE...
BOY! IT DIDN'T TAKE LONG TO GET UP HERE!
CASHELOT
4

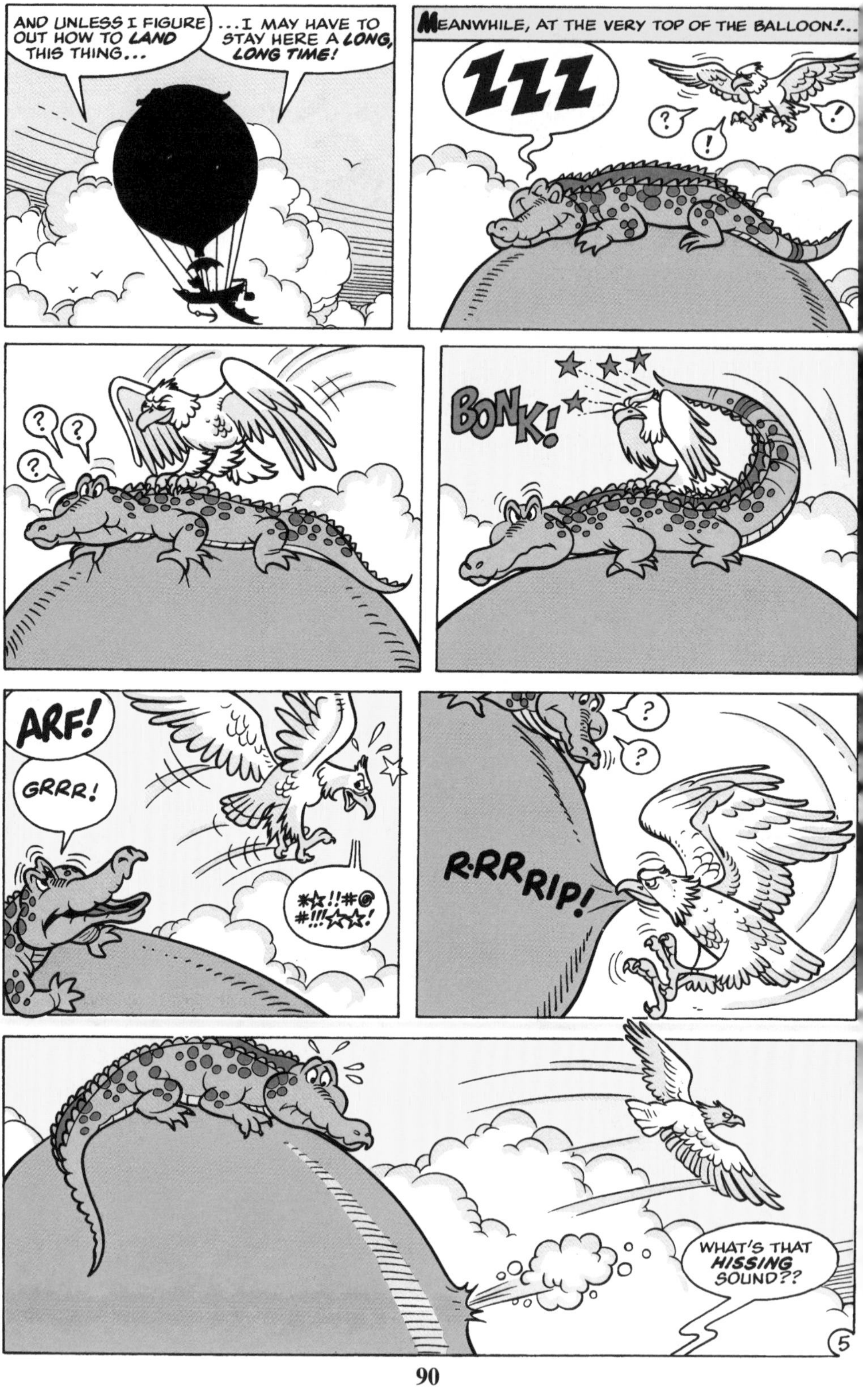
AND UNLESS I FIGURE OUT HOW TO LAND THIS THING...
...I MAY HAVE TO STAY HERE A LONG, LONG TIME!
MEANWHILE, AT THE VERY TOP OF THE BALLOON!...
ZZZ
?
!
!
?
?
?
BONK!
ARF!
GRRR!
*☆!!#@ #!!!☆☆!
?
?
R-RRRIP!
WHAT'S THAT HISSING SOUND??
5

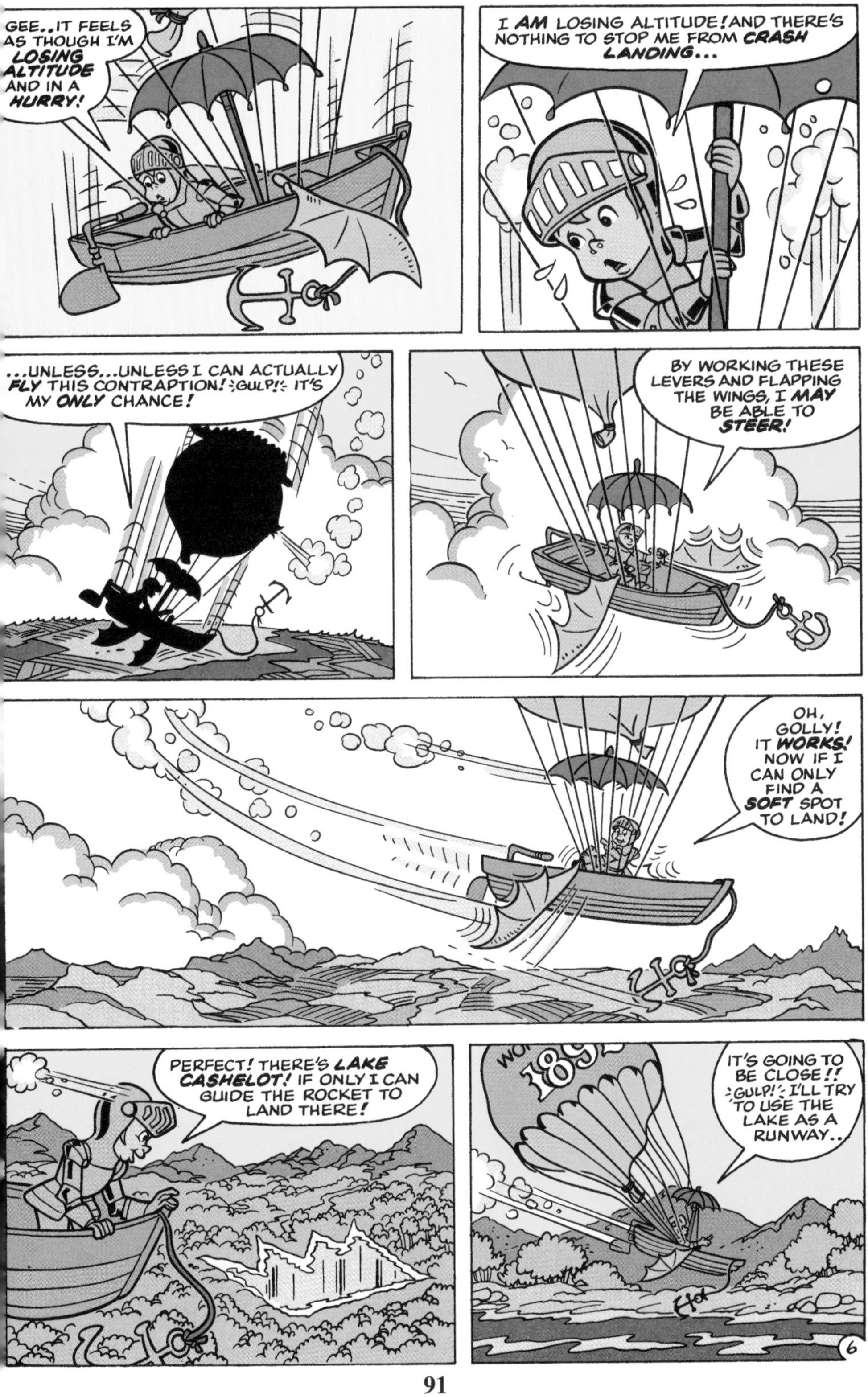
GEE..IT FEELS AS THOUGH I'M LOSING ALTITUDE AND IN A HURRY!
I AM LOSING ALTITUDE! AND THERE'S NOTHING TO STOP ME FROM CRASH LANDING...
...UNLESS...UNLESS I CAN ACTUALLY FLY THIS CONTRAPTION! GULP! IT'S MY ONLY CHANCE!
BY WORKING THESE LEVERS AND FLAPPING THE WINGS, I MAY BE ABLE TO STEER!
OH, GOLLY! IT WORKS! NOW IF I CAN ONLY FIND A SOFT SPOT TO LAND!
PERFECT! THERE'S LAKE CASHELOT! IF ONLY I CAN GUIDE THE ROCKET TO LAND THERE!
IT'S GOING TO BE CLOSE!! GULP! I'LL TRY TO USE THE LAKE AS A RUNWAY..
6

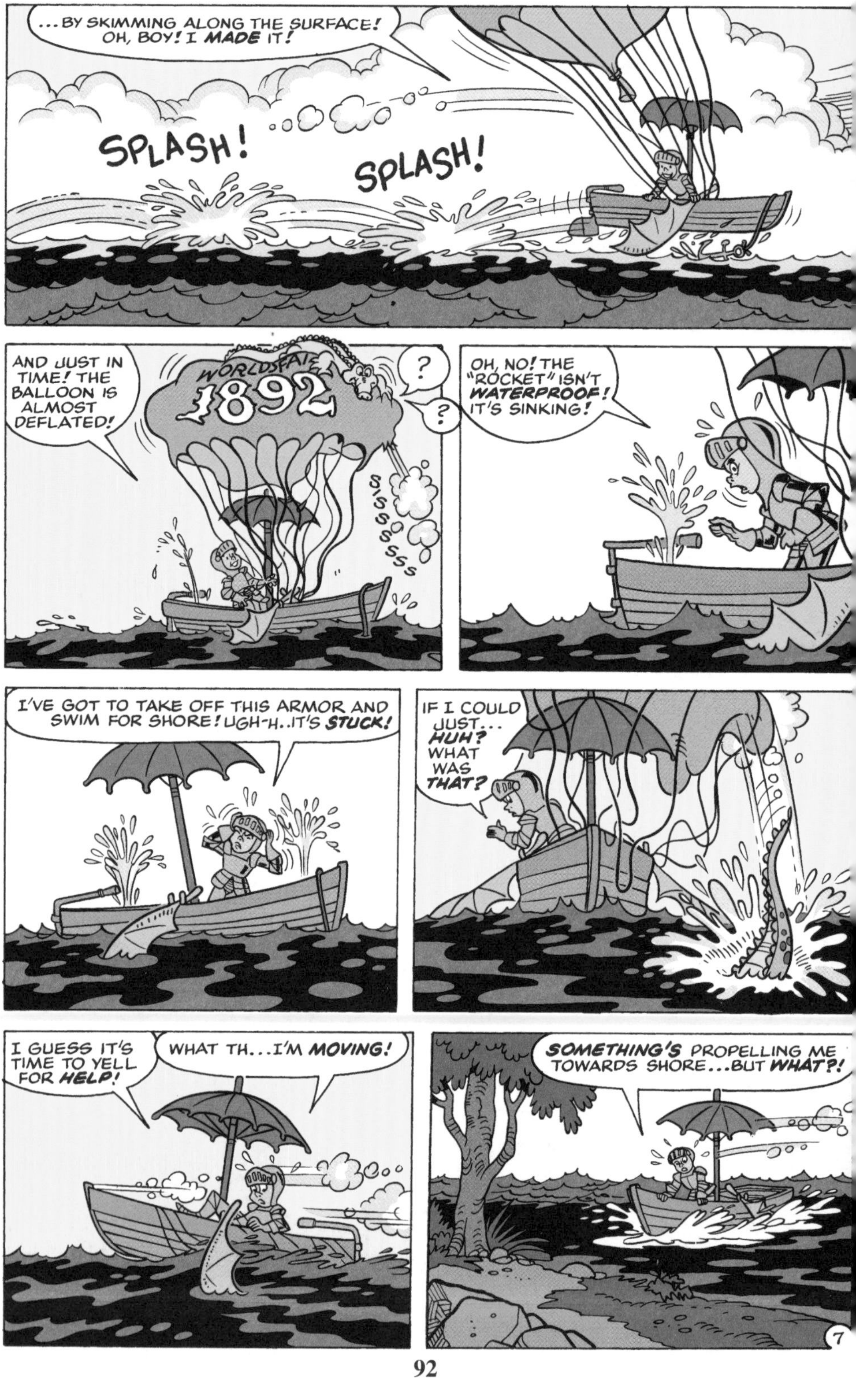

...BY SKIMMING ALONG THE SURFACE! OH, BOY! I MADE IT!
SPLASH!
SPLASH!
AND JUST IN TIME! THE BALLOON IS ALMOST DEFLATED!
WORLDSFAIR 1892
?
?
SSSSSSSSS
OH, NO! THE "ROCKET" ISN'T WATERPROOF! IT'S SINKING!
I'VE GOT TO TAKE OFF THIS ARMOR AND SWIM FOR SHORE! UGH-H..IT'S STUCK!
IF I COULD JUST... HUH? WHAT WAS THAT?
I GUESS IT'S TIME TO YELL FOR HELP!
WHAT TH...I'M MOVING!
SOMETHING'S PROPELLING ME TOWARDS SHORE...BUT WHAT?!
7

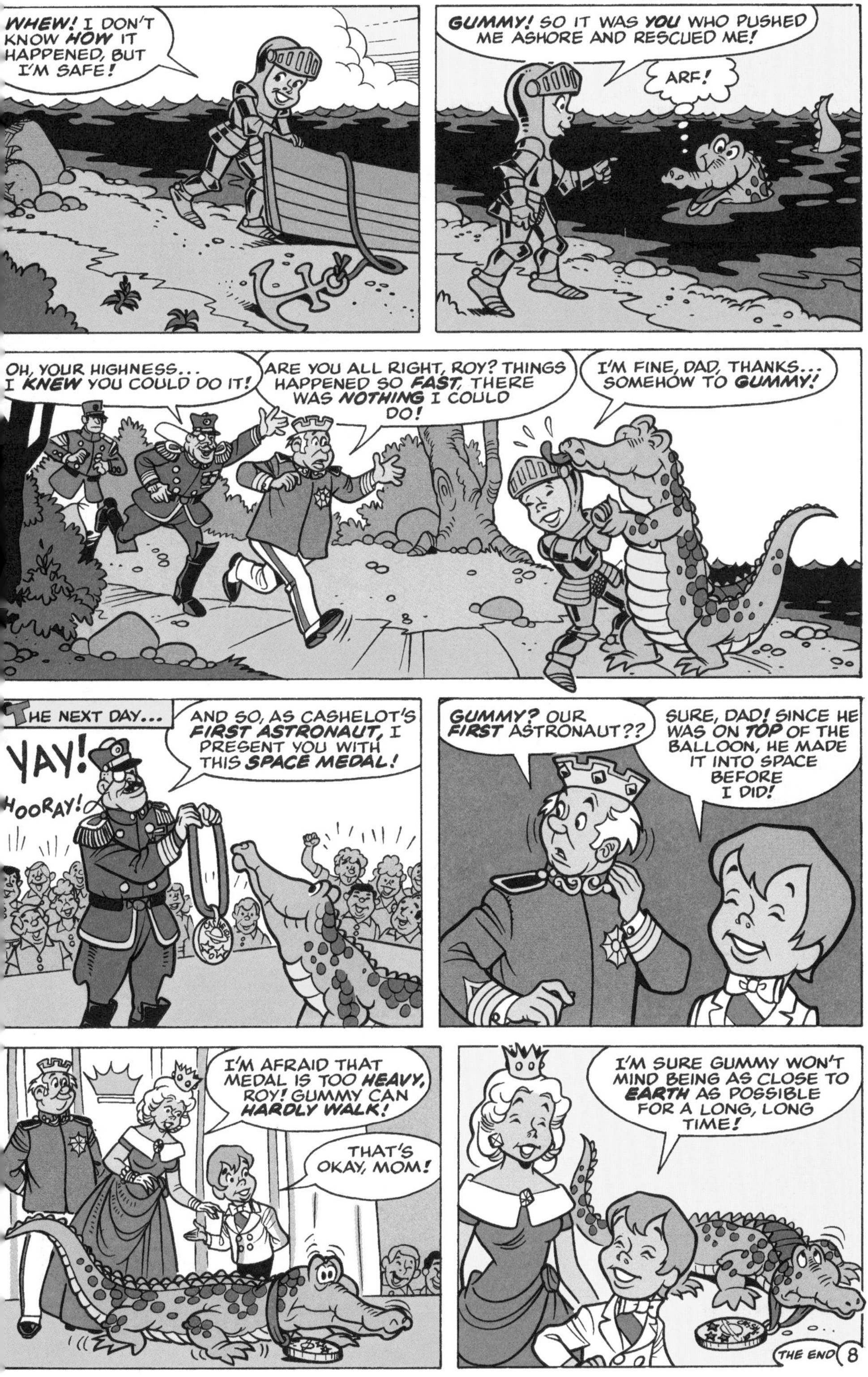
WHEW! I DON'T KNOW HOW IT HAPPENED, BUT I'M SAFE!
GUMMY! SO IT WAS YOU WHO PUSHED ME ASHORE AND RESCUED ME!
ARF!
OH, YOUR HIGHNESS... I KNEW YOU COULD DO IT!
ARE YOU ALL RIGHT, ROY? THINGS HAPPENED SO FAST, THERE WAS NOTHING I COULD DO!
I'M FINE, DAD, THANKS... SOMEHOW TO GUMMY!
THE NEXT DAY...
YAY!
HOORAY!
AND SO, AS CASHELOT'S FIRST ASTRONAUT, I PRESENT YOU WITH THIS SPACE MEDAL!
GUMMY? OUR FIRST ASTRONAUT??
SURE, DAD! SINCE HE WAS ON TOP OF THE BALLOON, HE MADE IT INTO SPACE BEFORE I DID!
I'M AFRAID THAT MEDAL IS TOO HEAVY, ROY! GUMMY CAN HARDLY WALK!
THAT'S OKAY, MOM!
I'M SURE GUMMY WON'T MIND BEING AS CLOSE TO EARTH AS POSSIBLE FOR A LONG, LONG TIME!
THE END 8

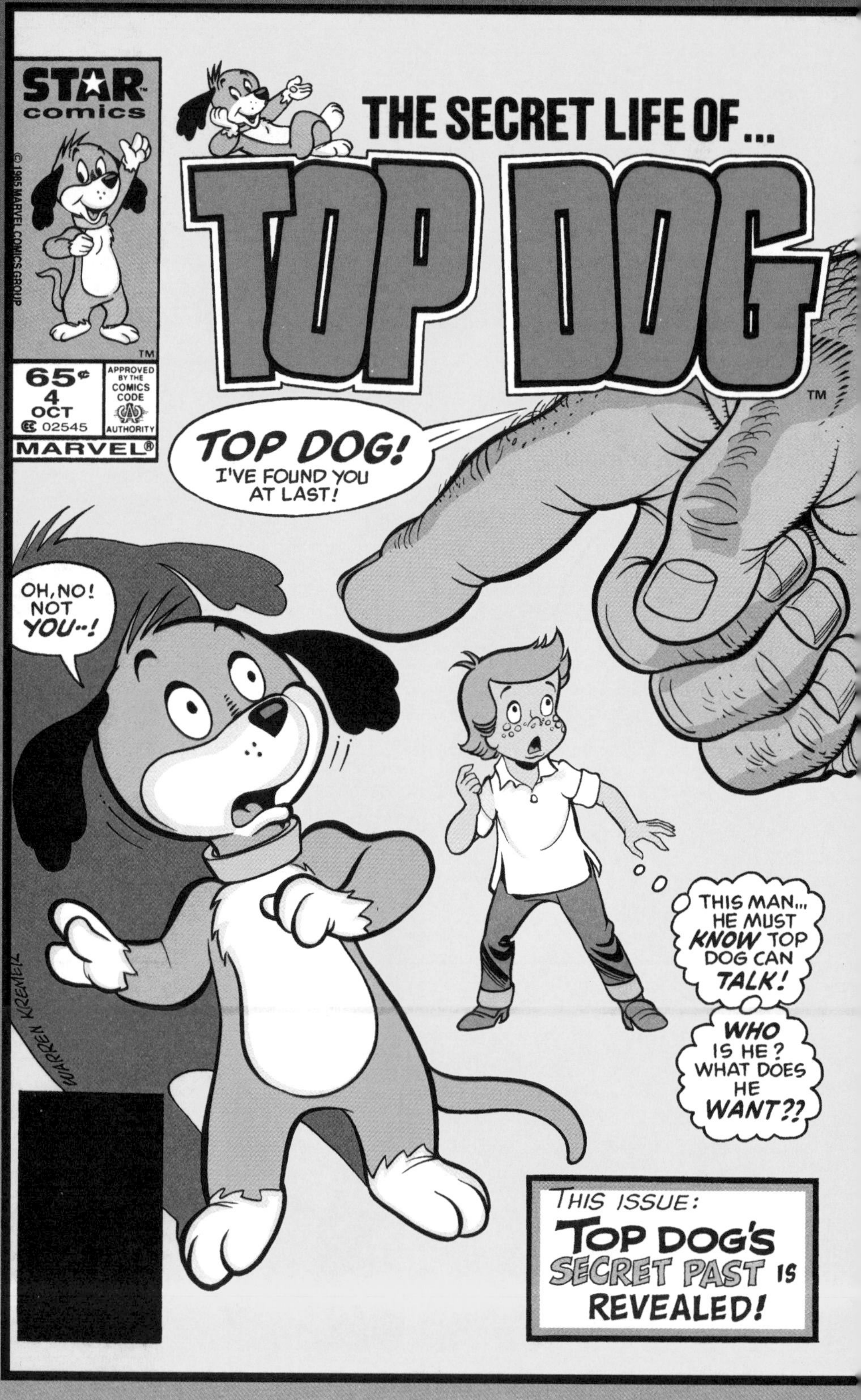
STAR comics
© 1985 MARVEL COMICS GROUP
TM
65¢
4
OCT
02545
APPROVED BY THE COMICS CODE AUTHORITY
MARVEL®
THE SECRET LIFE OF...
TOP DOG
TM
TOP DOG! I'VE FOUND YOU AT LAST!
OH, NO! NOT YOU--!
THIS MAN... HE MUST KNOW TOP DOG CAN TALK!
WHO IS HE? WHAT DOES HE WANT??
WARREN KREMER
THIS ISSUE:
TOP DOG'S SECRET PAST IS REVEALED!

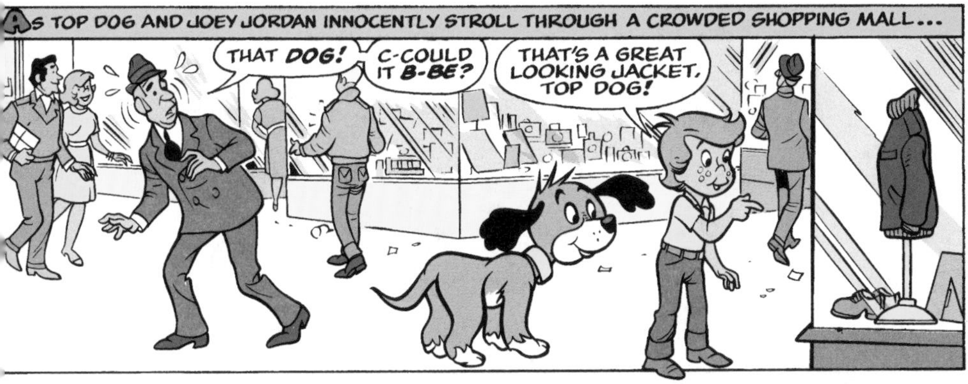
AS TOP DOG AND JOEY JORDAN INNOCENTLY STROLL THROUGH A CROWDED SHOPPING MALL...
THAT DOG!
C-COULD IT B-BE?
THAT'S A GREAT LOOKING JACKET, TOP DOG!

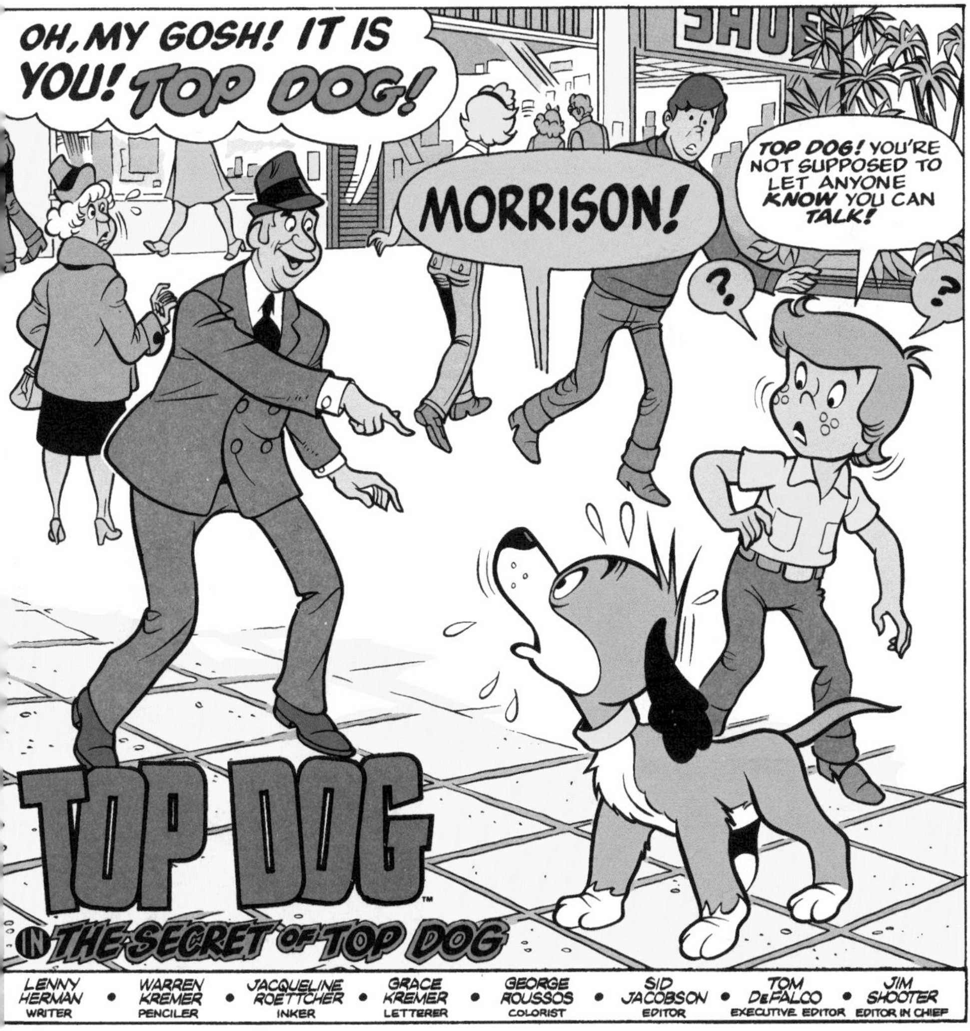
OH, MY GOSH! IT IS YOU! TOP DOG!
SHOE
MORRISON!
TOP DOG! YOU'RE NOT SUPPOSED TO LET ANYONE KNOW YOU CAN TALK!
?
?
TOP DOG™
IN THE SECRET OF TOP DOG

LENNY HERMAN WRITER • WARREN KREMER PENCILER • JACQUELINE ROETTCHER INKER • GRACE KREMER LETTERER • GEORGE ROUSSOS COLORIST • SID JACOBSON EDITOR • TOM DeFALCO EXECUTIVE EDITOR • JIM SHOOTER EDITOR IN CHIEF

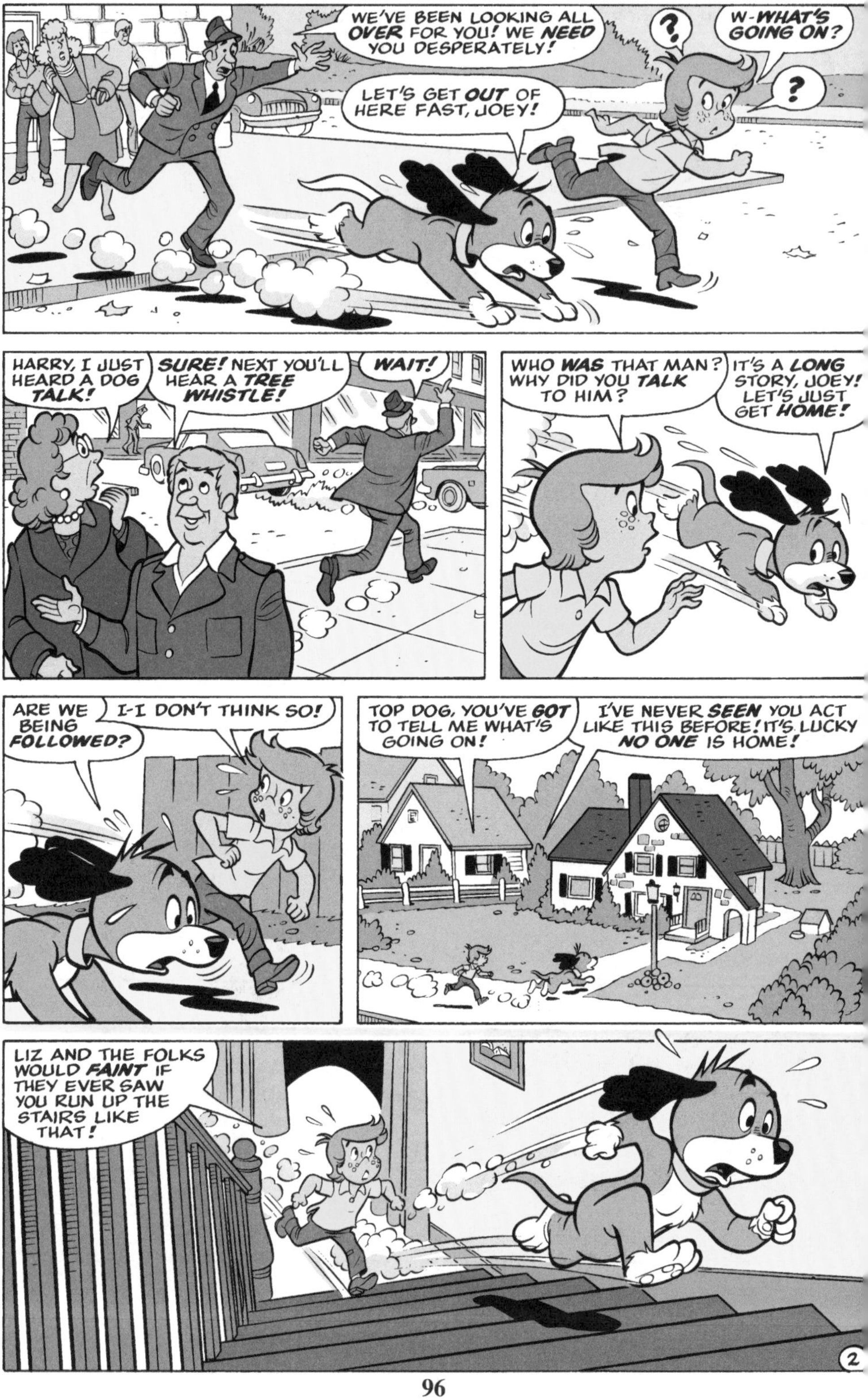
WE'VE BEEN LOOKING ALL OVER FOR YOU! WE NEED YOU DESPERATELY!
?
W-WHAT'S GOING ON?
?
LET'S GET OUT OF HERE FAST, JOEY!
HARRY, I JUST HEARD A DOG TALK!
SURE! NEXT YOU'LL HEAR A TREE WHISTLE!
WAIT!
WHO WAS THAT MAN? WHY DID YOU TALK TO HIM?
IT'S A LONG STORY, JOEY! LET'S JUST GET HOME!
ARE WE BEING FOLLOWED?
I-I DON'T THINK SO!
TOP DOG, YOU'VE GOT TO TELL ME WHAT'S GOING ON!
I'VE NEVER SEEN YOU ACT LIKE THIS BEFORE! IT'S LUCKY NO ONE IS HOME!
LIZ AND THE FOLKS WOULD FAINT IF THEY EVER SAW YOU RUN UP THE STAIRS LIKE THAT!
2

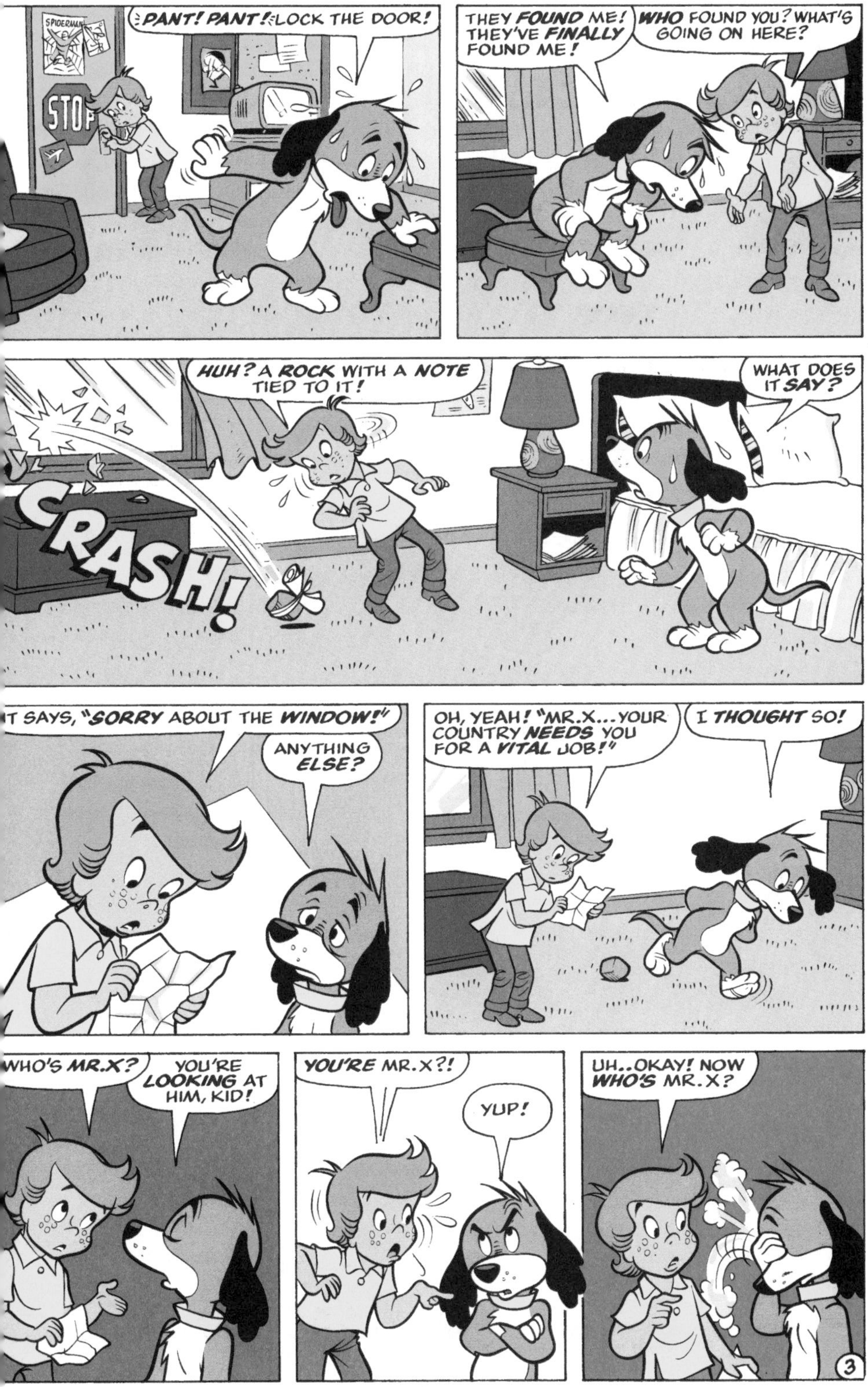

PANT! PANT! LOCK THE DOOR!
SPIDERMAN
STOP
THEY FOUND ME! THEY'VE FINALLY FOUND ME!
WHO FOUND YOU? WHAT'S GOING ON HERE?
CRASH!
HUH? A ROCK WITH A NOTE TIED TO IT!
WHAT DOES IT SAY?
IT SAYS, "SORRY ABOUT THE WINDOW!"
ANYTHING ELSE?
OH, YEAH! "MR.X... YOUR COUNTRY NEEDS YOU FOR A VITAL JOB!"
I THOUGHT SO!
WHO'S MR.X?
YOU'RE LOOKING AT HIM, KID!
YOU'RE MR.X?!
YUP!
UH..OKAY! NOW WHO'S MR.X?
3

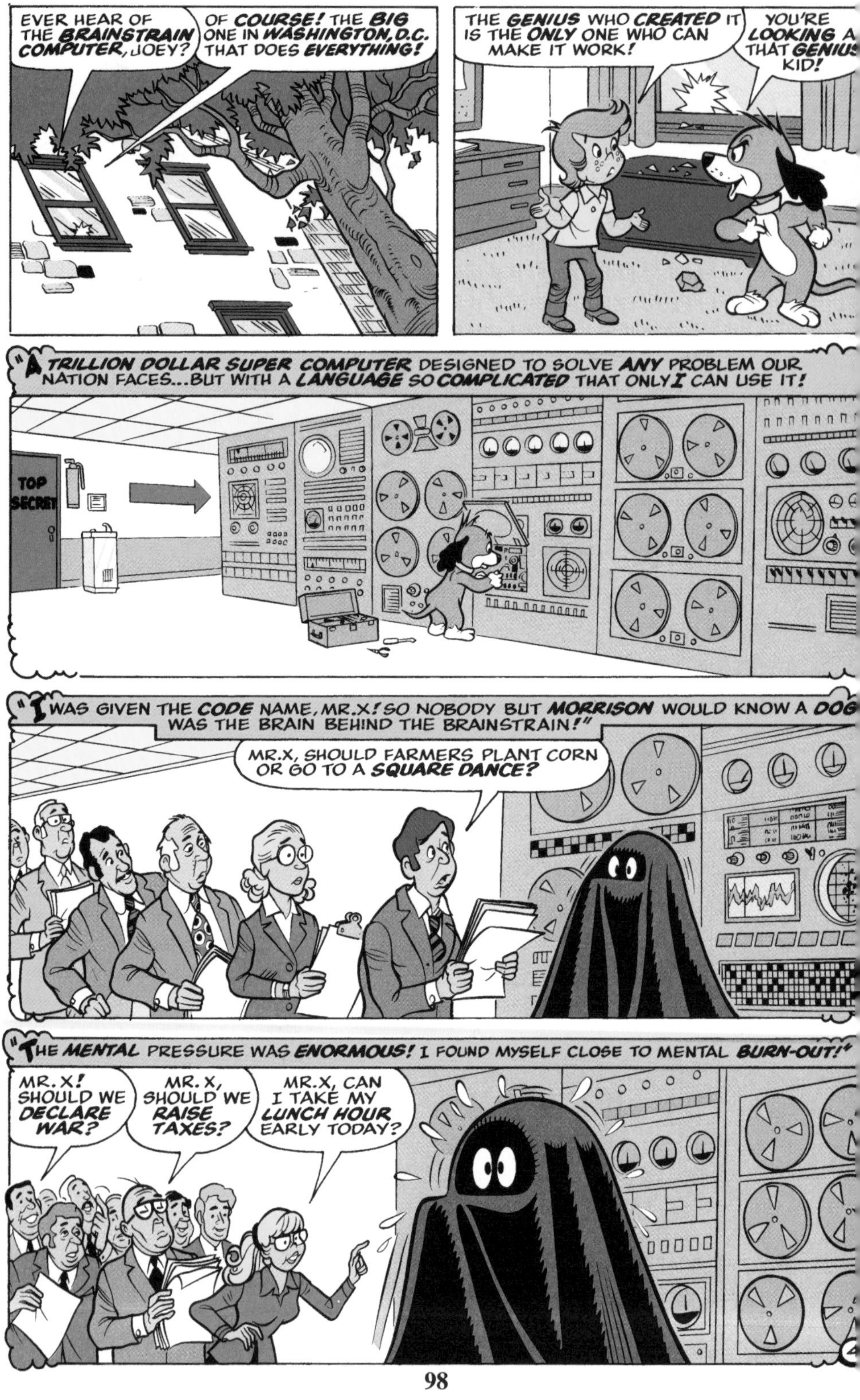
EVER HEAR OF THE BRAINSTRAIN COMPUTER, JOEY?
OF COURSE! THE BIG ONE IN WASHINGTON, D.C. THAT DOES EVERYTHING!
THE GENIUS WHO CREATED IT IS THE ONLY ONE WHO CAN MAKE IT WORK!
YOU'RE LOOKING A THAT GENIUS KID!
"A TRILLION DOLLAR SUPER COMPUTER DESIGNED TO SOLVE ANY PROBLEM OUR NATION FACES...BUT WITH A LANGUAGE SO COMPLICATED THAT ONLY I CAN USE IT!
TOP SECRET
"I WAS GIVEN THE CODE NAME, MR.X! SO NOBODY BUT MORRISON WOULD KNOW A DOG WAS THE BRAIN BEHIND THE BRAINSTRAIN!"
MR.X, SHOULD FARMERS PLANT CORN OR GO TO A SQUARE DANCE?
"THE MENTAL PRESSURE WAS ENORMOUS! I FOUND MYSELF CLOSE TO MENTAL BURN-OUT!"
MR.X! SHOULD WE DECLARE WAR?
MR.X, SHOULD WE RAISE TAXES?
MR.X, CAN I TAKE MY LUNCH HOUR EARLY TODAY?

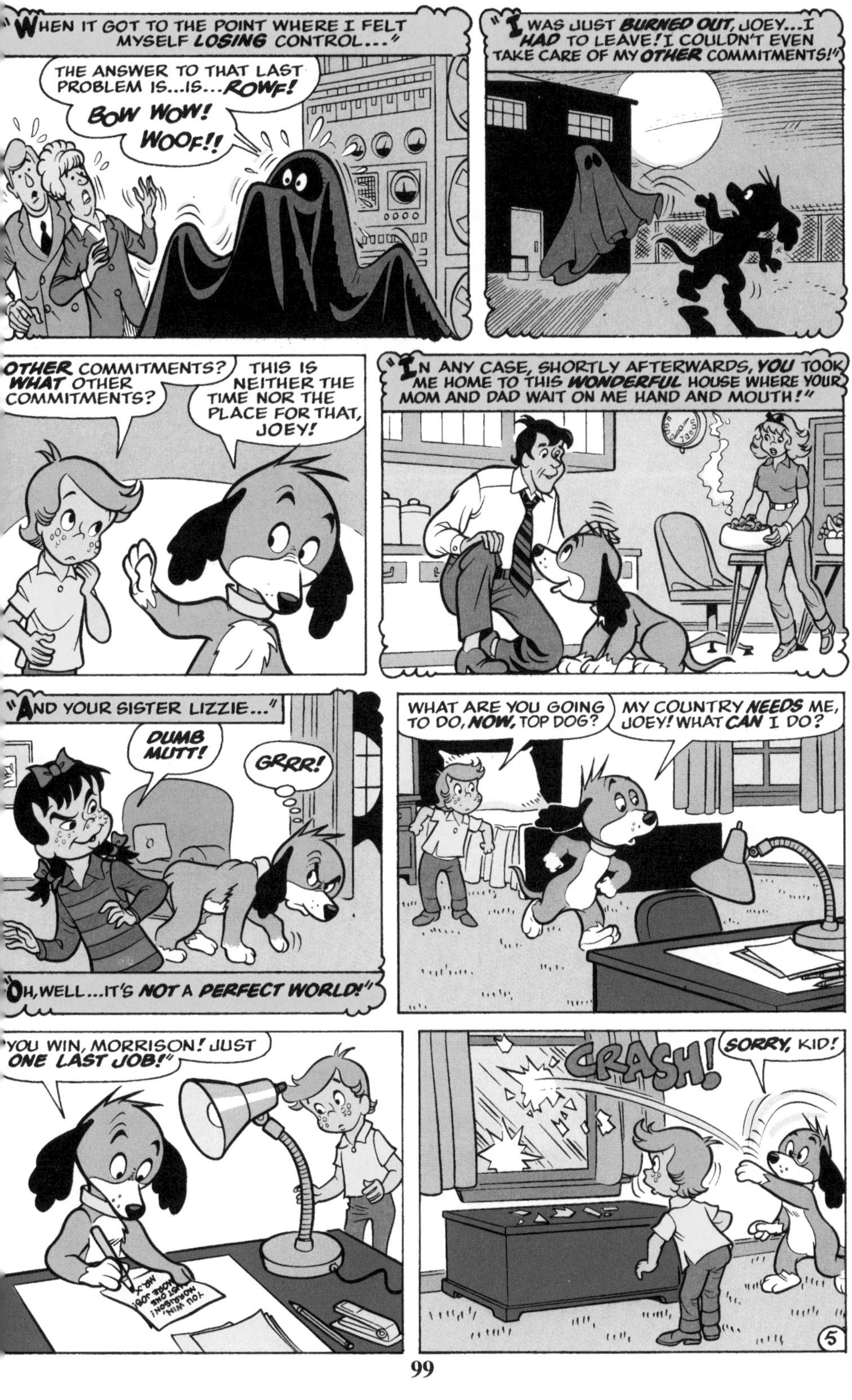
"WHEN IT GOT TO THE POINT WHERE I FELT MYSELF LOSING CONTROL..."
THE ANSWER TO THAT LAST PROBLEM IS...IS...ROWF!
BOW WOW! WOOF!!
"I WAS JUST BURNED OUT, JOEY...I HAD TO LEAVE! I COULDN'T EVEN TAKE CARE OF MY OTHER COMMITMENTS!"
OTHER COMMITMENTS? WHAT OTHER COMMITMENTS?
THIS IS NEITHER THE TIME NOR THE PLACE FOR THAT, JOEY!
"IN ANY CASE, SHORTLY AFTERWARDS, YOU TOOK ME HOME TO THIS WONDERFUL HOUSE WHERE YOUR MOM AND DAD WAIT ON ME HAND AND MOUTH!"
"AND YOUR SISTER LIZZIE..."
DUMB MUTT!
GRRR!
"OH, WELL...IT'S NOT A PERFECT WORLD!"
WHAT ARE YOU GOING TO DO, NOW, TOP DOG?
MY COUNTRY NEEDS ME, JOEY! WHAT CAN I DO?
"YOU WIN, MORRISON! JUST ONE LAST JOB!"
CRASH!
SORRY, KID!
5

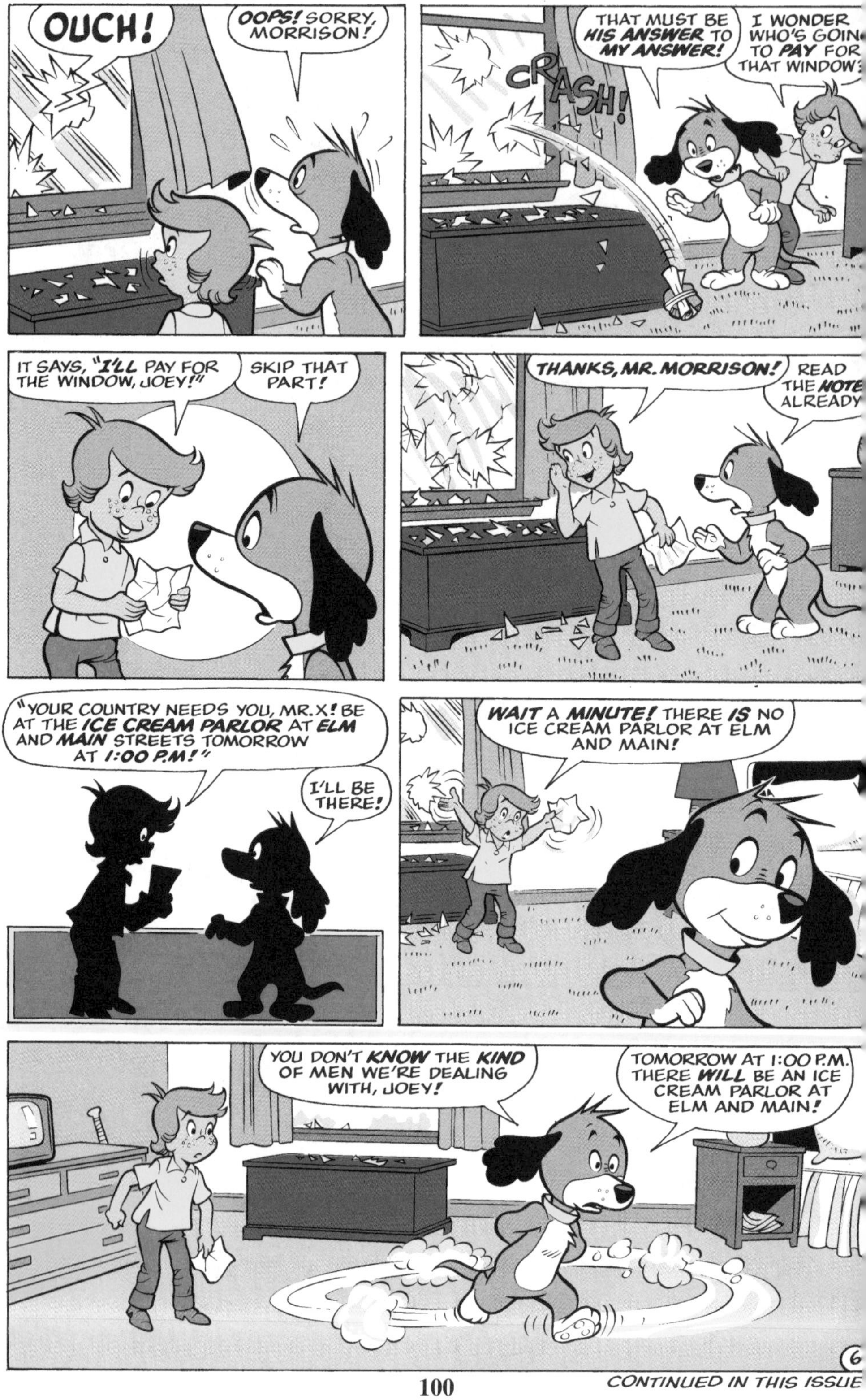
OUCH!
OOPS! SORRY, MORRISON!
CRASH!
THAT MUST BE HIS ANSWER TO MY ANSWER!
I WONDER WHO'S GOIN TO PAY FOR THAT WINDOW?
IT SAYS, "I'LL PAY FOR THE WINDOW, JOEY!"
SKIP THAT PART!
THANKS, MR. MORRISON!
READ THE NOTE ALREADY
"YOUR COUNTRY NEEDS YOU, MR. X! BE AT THE ICE CREAM PARLOR AT ELM AND MAIN STREETS TOMORROW AT 1:00 P.M!"
I'LL BE THERE!
WAIT A MINUTE! THERE IS NO ICE CREAM PARLOR AT ELM AND MAIN!
YOU DON'T KNOW THE KIND OF MEN WE'RE DEALING WITH, JOEY!
TOMORROW AT 1:00 P.M. THERE WILL BE AN ICE CREAM PARLOR AT ELM AND MAIN!
6

CONTINUED IN THIS ISSUE

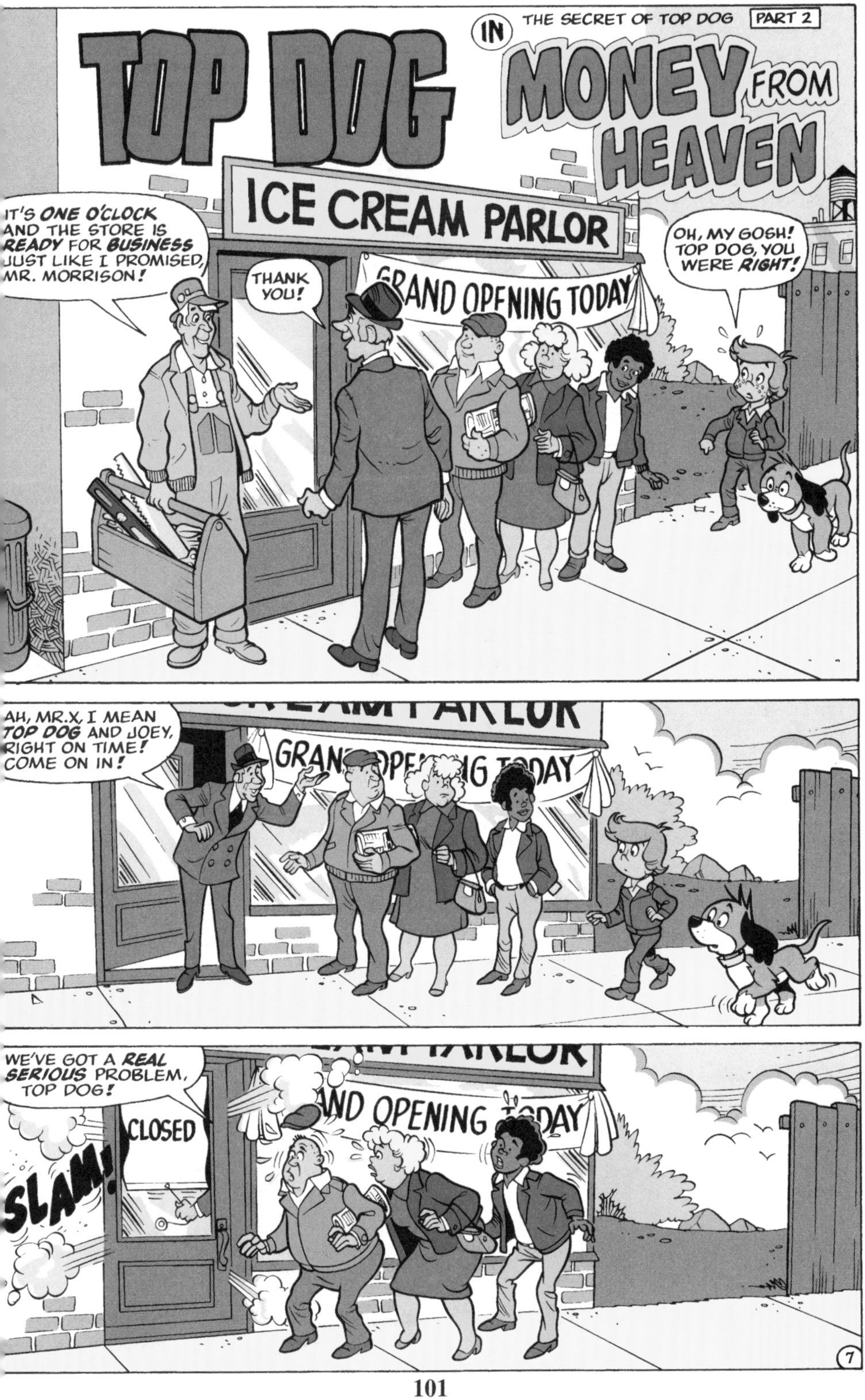
TOP DOG
IN
THE SECRET OF TOP DOG
PART 2
MONEY FROM HEAVEN
ICE CREAM PARLOR
IT'S ONE O'CLOCK AND THE STORE IS READY FOR BUSINESS JUST LIKE I PROMISED, MR. MORRISON!
THANK YOU!
GRAND OPENING TODAY
OH, MY GOSH! TOP DOG, YOU WERE RIGHT!
AH, MR. X, I MEAN TOP DOG AND JOEY, RIGHT ON TIME! COME ON IN!
WE'VE GOT A REAL SERIOUS PROBLEM, TOP DOG!
CLOSED
SLAM!
7

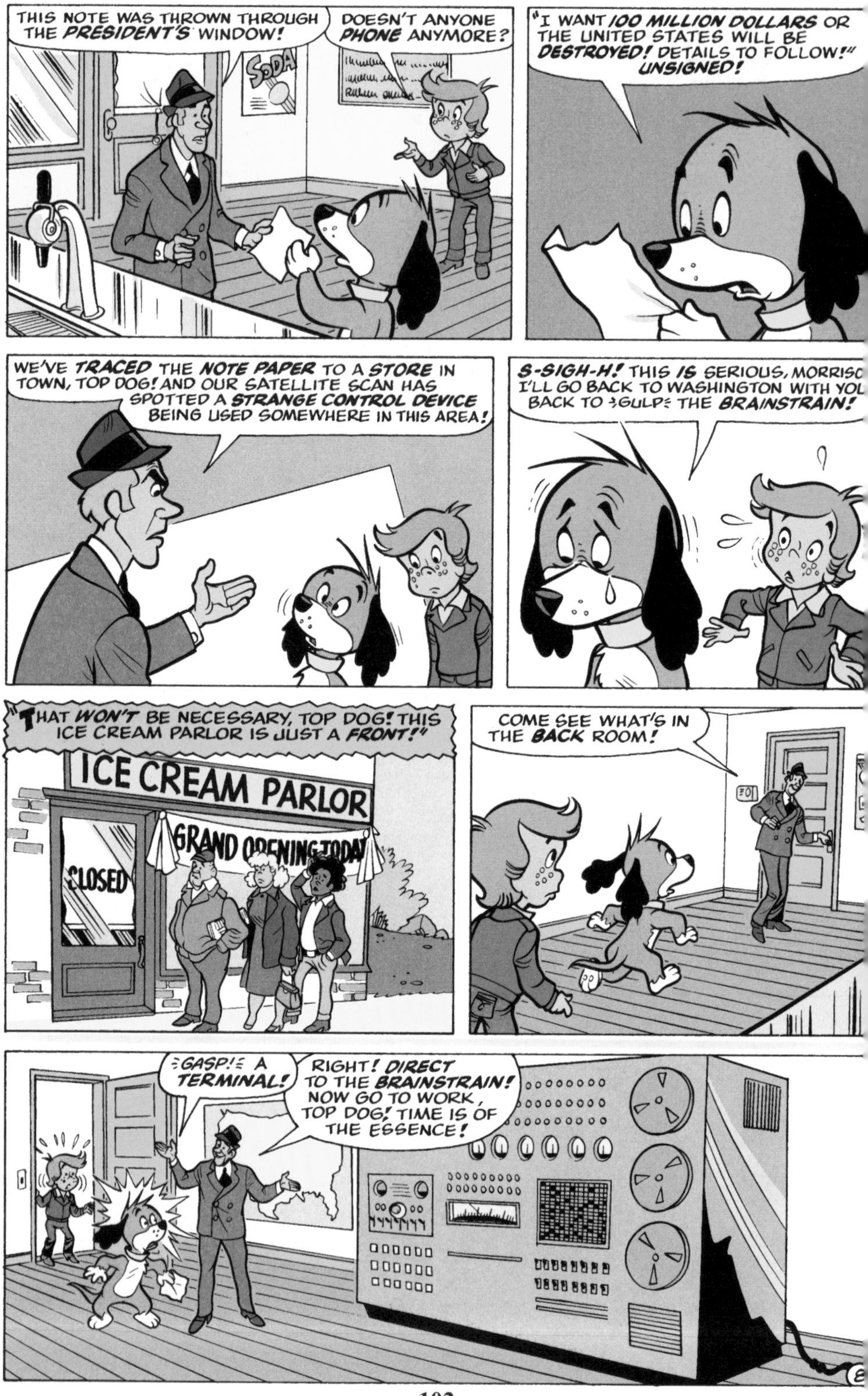
THIS NOTE WAS THROWN THROUGH THE *PRESIDENT'S* WINDOW!
DOESN'T ANYONE *PHONE* ANYMORE?
SODA
"I WANT *100 MILLION DOLLARS* OR THE UNITED STATES WILL BE *DESTROYED!* DETAILS TO FOLLOW!" *UNSIGNED!*
WE'VE *TRACED* THE *NOTE PAPER* TO A *STORE* IN TOWN, TOP DOG! AND OUR SATELLITE SCAN HAS SPOTTED A *STRANGE CONTROL DEVICE* BEING USED SOMEWHERE IN THIS AREA!
S-SIGH-H! THIS *IS* SERIOUS, MORRISO I'LL GO BACK TO WASHINGTON WITH YOU BACK TO *GULP* THE *BRAINSTRAIN!*
"THAT *WON'T* BE NECESSARY, TOP DOG! THIS ICE CREAM PARLOR IS JUST A *FRONT!*"
ICE CREAM PARLOR
GRAND OPENING TODAY
CLOSED
COME SEE WHAT'S IN THE *BACK* ROOM!
GASP! A *TERMINAL!*
RIGHT! *DIRECT* TO THE *BRAINSTRAIN!* NOW GO TO WORK, TOP DOG! TIME IS OF THE ESSENCE!

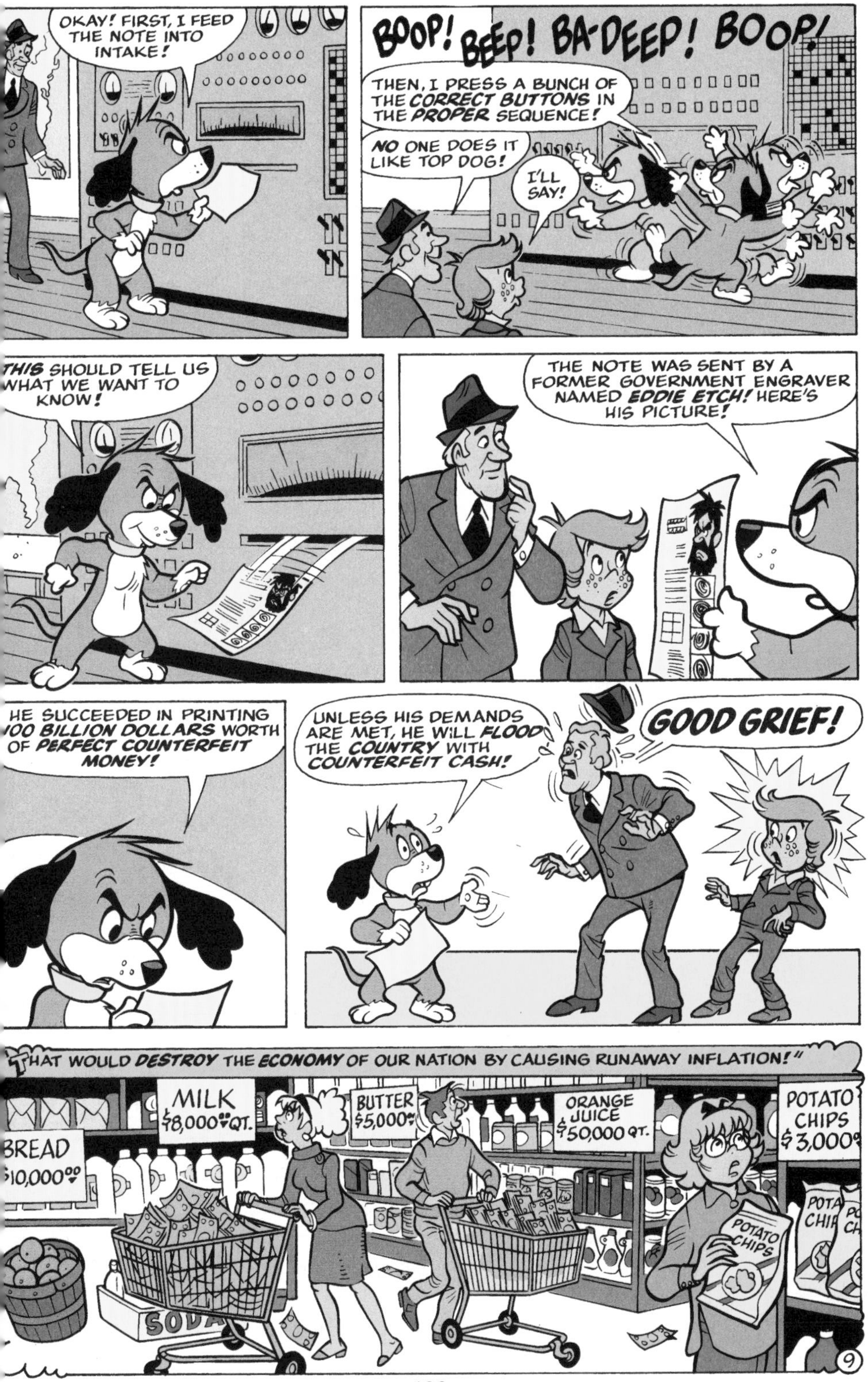
OKAY! FIRST, I FEED THE NOTE INTO INTAKE!
BOOP! BEEP! BA-DEEP! BOOP!
THEN, I PRESS A BUNCH OF THE CORRECT BUTTONS IN THE PROPER SEQUENCE!
NO ONE DOES IT LIKE TOP DOG!
I'LL SAY!
THIS SHOULD TELL US WHAT WE WANT TO KNOW!
THE NOTE WAS SENT BY A FORMER GOVERNMENT ENGRAVER NAMED EDDIE ETCH! HERE'S HIS PICTURE!
HE SUCCEEDED IN PRINTING 100 BILLION DOLLARS WORTH OF PERFECT COUNTERFEIT MONEY!
UNLESS HIS DEMANDS ARE MET, HE WILL FLOOD THE COUNTRY WITH COUNTERFEIT CASH!
GOOD GRIEF!
THAT WOULD DESTROY THE ECONOMY OF OUR NATION BY CAUSING RUNAWAY INFLATION!"
BREAD $10,000.00
MILK $8,000.00 QT.
BUTTER $5,000.00
ORANGE JUICE $50,000 QT.
POTATO CHIPS $3,000.00
POTATO CHIPS
SODA
9

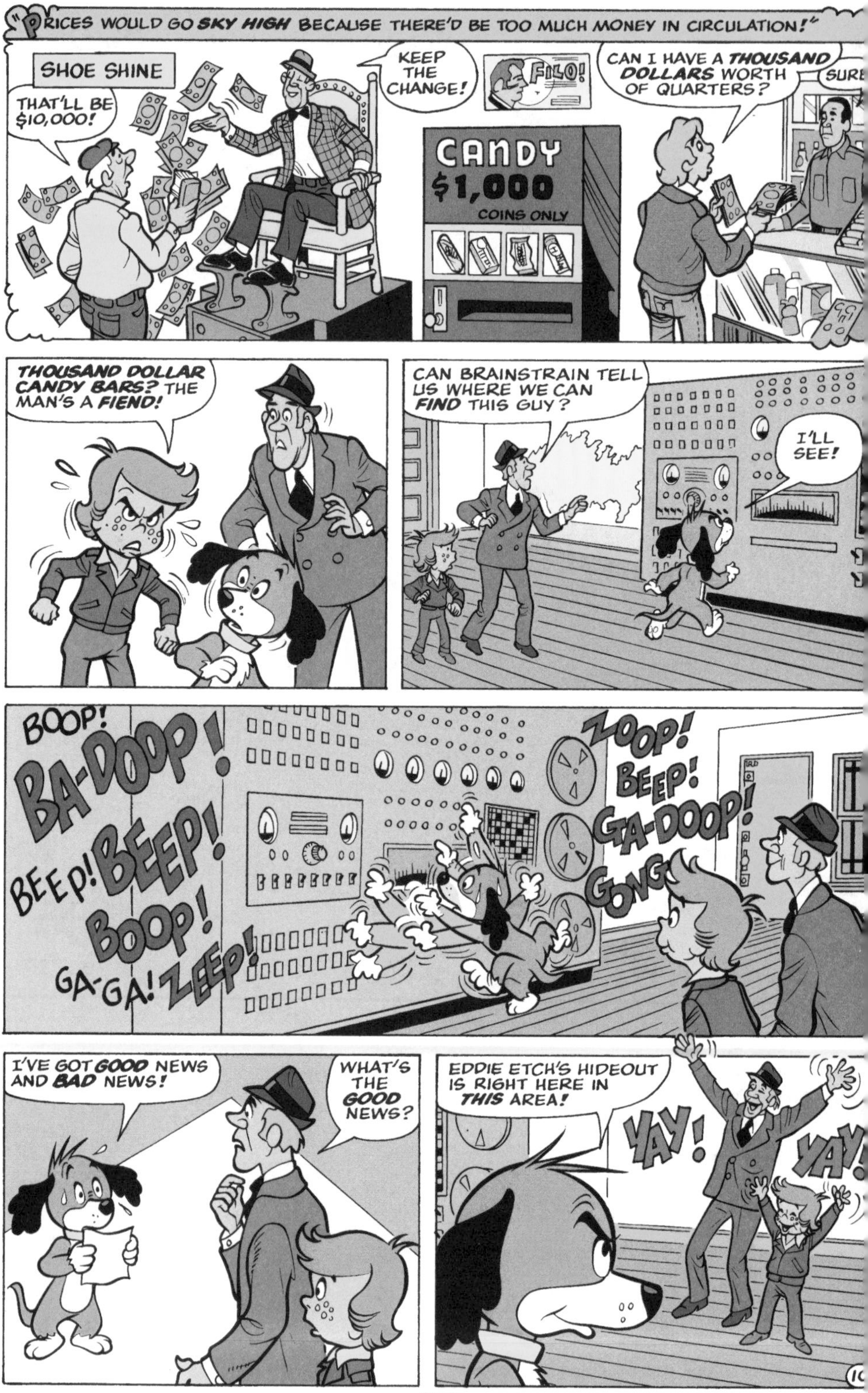
"PRICES WOULD GO SKY HIGH BECAUSE THERE'D BE TOO MUCH MONEY IN CIRCULATION!"
SHOE SHINE
THAT'LL BE $10,000!
KEEP THE CHANGE!
FILO!
CANDY $1,000 COINS ONLY
CAN I HAVE A THOUSAND DOLLARS WORTH OF QUARTERS?
SURE
THOUSAND DOLLAR CANDY BARS? THE MAN'S A FIEND!
CAN BRAINSTRAIN TELL US WHERE WE CAN FIND THIS GUY?
I'LL SEE!
BOOP! BA-DOOP!
BEEP! BEEP!
BOOP!
GA-GA! ZEEP!
ZOOP! BEEP! GA-DOOP!
GONG
I'VE GOT GOOD NEWS AND BAD NEWS!
WHAT'S THE GOOD NEWS?
EDDIE ETCH'S HIDEOUT IS RIGHT HERE IN THIS AREA!
YAY!
YAY!

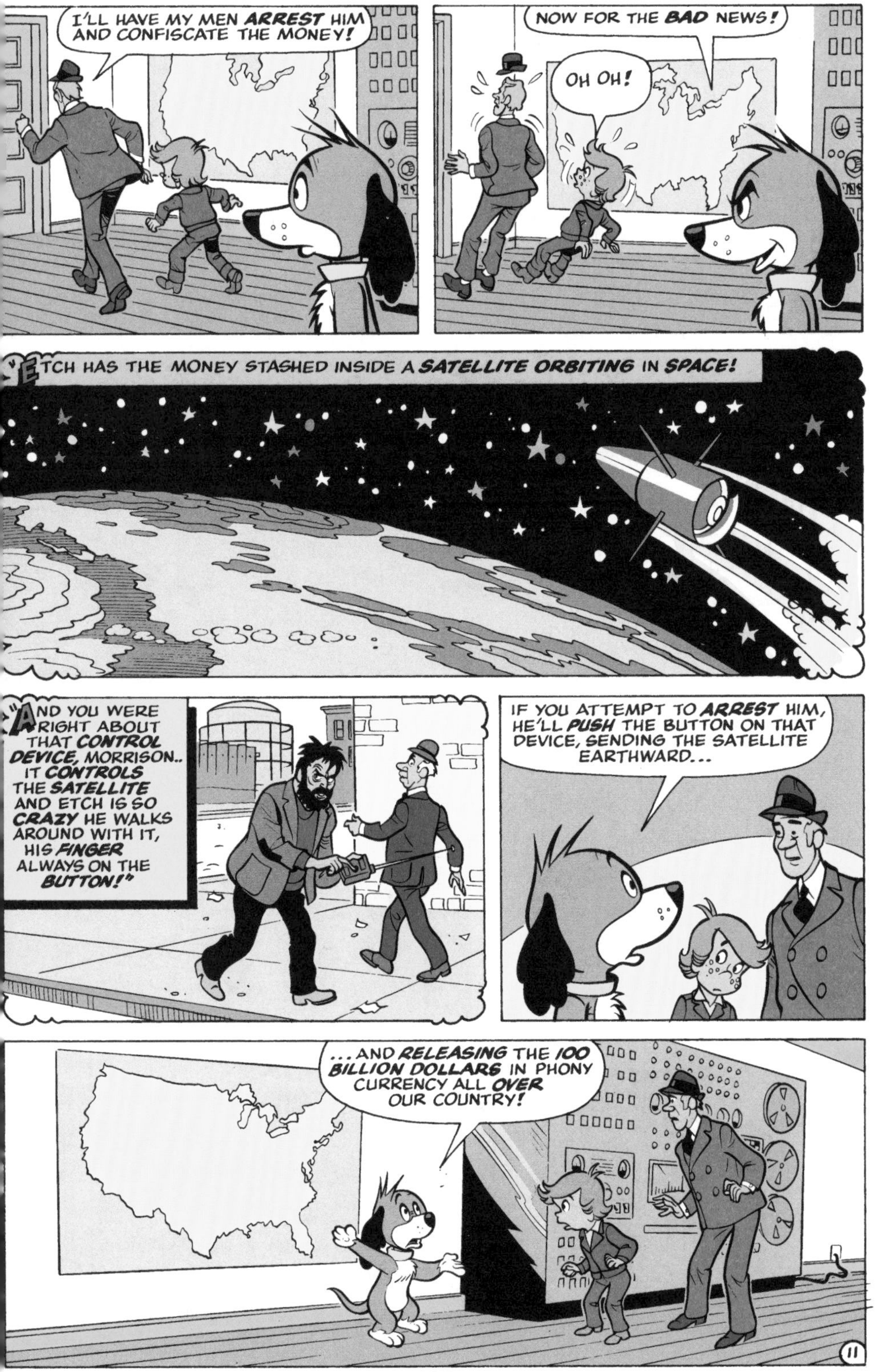
I'LL HAVE MY MEN ARREST HIM AND CONFISCATE THE MONEY!
NOW FOR THE BAD NEWS!
OH OH!
ETCH HAS THE MONEY STASHED INSIDE A SATELLITE ORBITING IN SPACE!
"AND YOU WERE RIGHT ABOUT THAT CONTROL DEVICE, MORRISON.. IT CONTROLS THE SATELLITE AND ETCH IS SO CRAZY HE WALKS AROUND WITH IT, HIS FINGER ALWAYS ON THE BUTTON!"
IF YOU ATTEMPT TO ARREST HIM, HE'LL PUSH THE BUTTON ON THAT DEVICE, SENDING THE SATELLITE EARTHWARD...
...AND RELEASING THE 100 BILLION DOLLARS IN PHONY CURRENCY ALL OVER OUR COUNTRY!
11

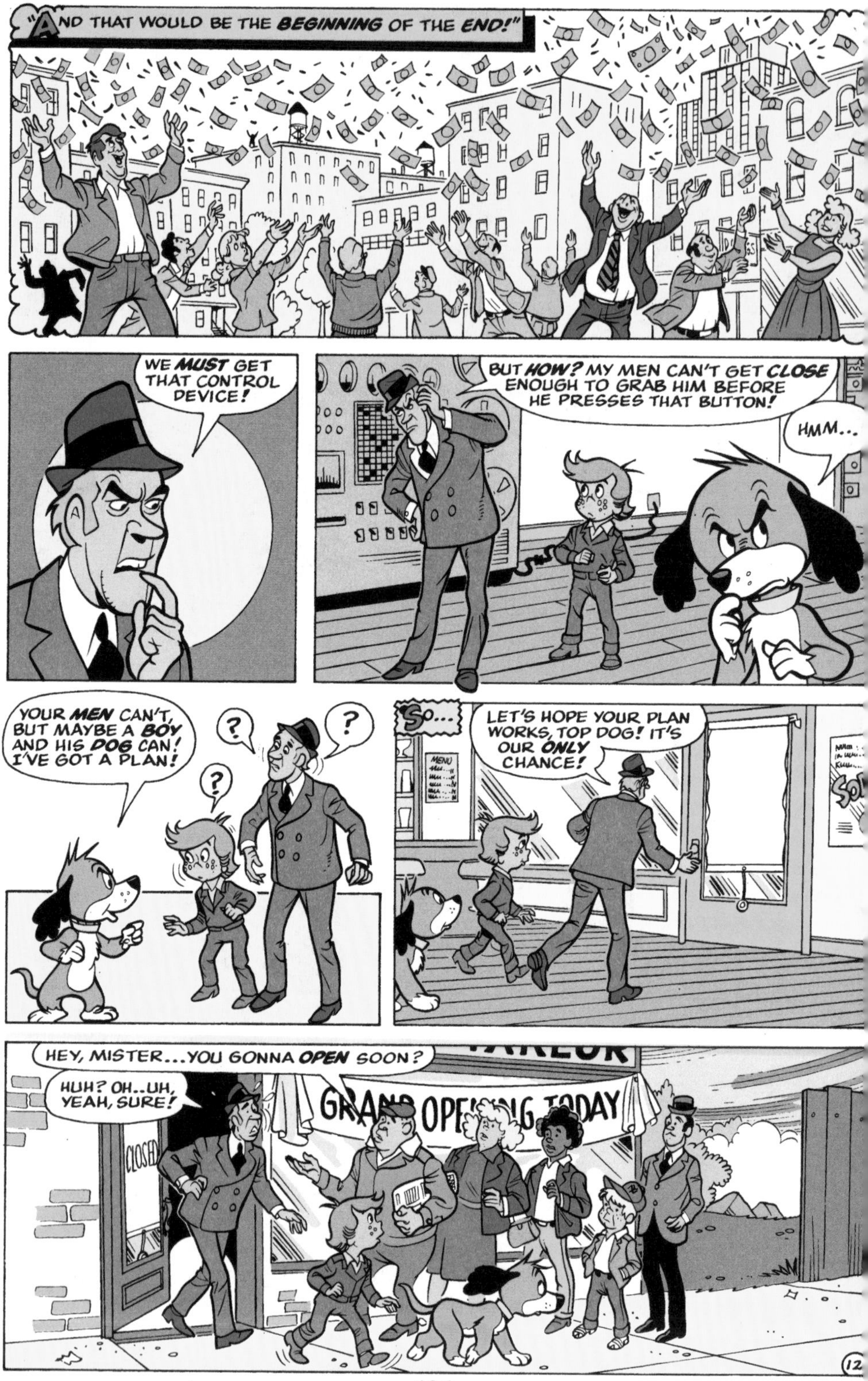
"AND THAT WOULD BE THE BEGINNING OF THE END!"
WE MUST GET THAT CONTROL DEVICE!
BUT HOW? MY MEN CAN'T GET CLOSE ENOUGH TO GRAB HIM BEFORE HE PRESSES THAT BUTTON!
HMM...
YOUR MEN CAN'T, BUT MAYBE A BOY AND HIS DOG CAN! I'VE GOT A PLAN!
?
?
?
SO...
LET'S HOPE YOUR PLAN WORKS, TOP DOG! IT'S OUR ONLY CHANCE!
MENU
HEY, MISTER...YOU GONNA OPEN SOON?
HUH? OH..UH, YEAH, SURE!
CLOSED
12

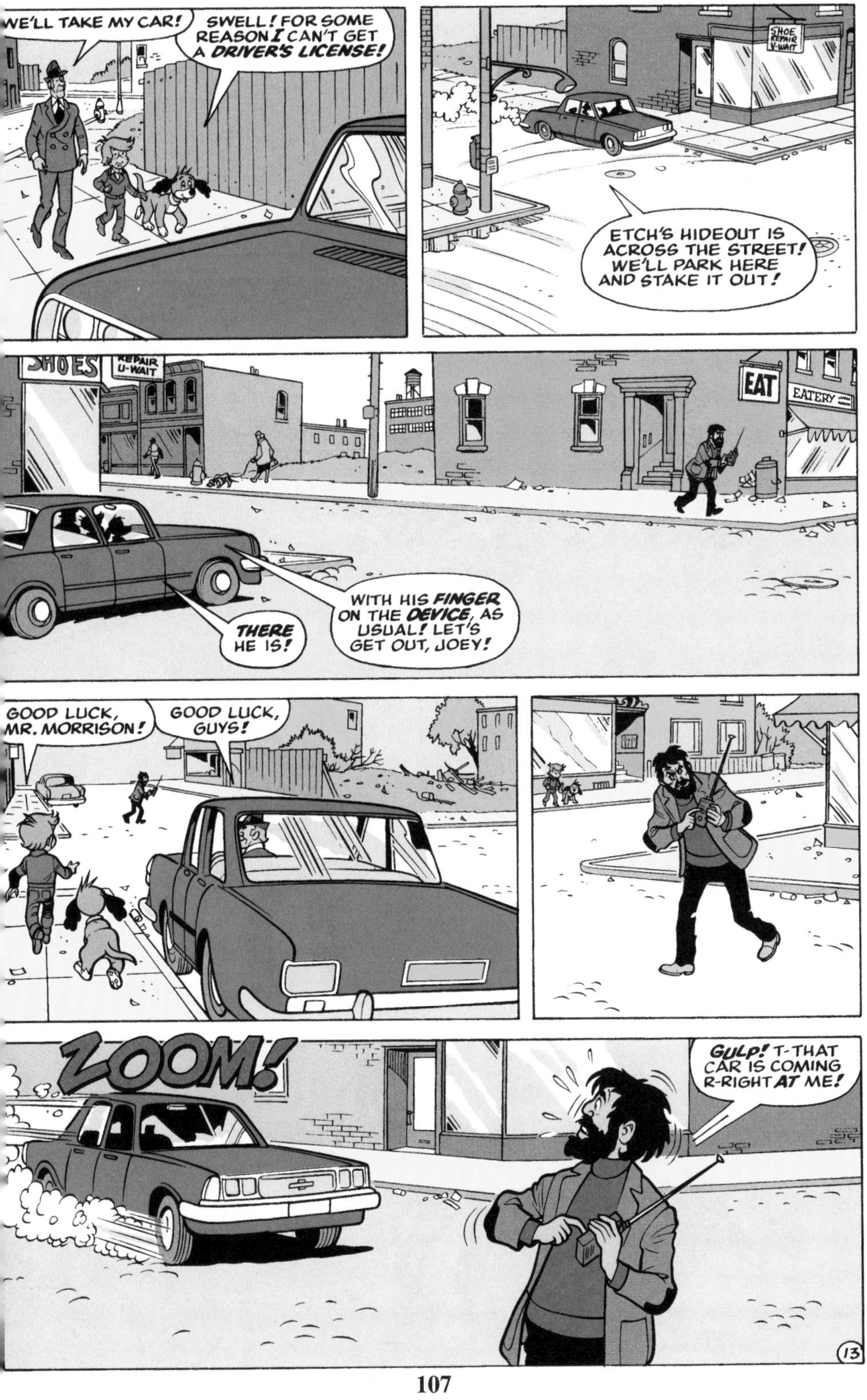
WE'LL TAKE MY CAR!
SWELL! FOR SOME REASON I CAN'T GET A DRIVER'S LICENSE!
SHOE REPAIR U-WAIT
ETCH'S HIDEOUT IS ACROSS THE STREET! WE'LL PARK HERE AND STAKE IT OUT!
SHOES
REPAIR U-WAIT
EAT
EATERY
THERE HE IS!
WITH HIS FINGER ON THE DEVICE, AS USUAL! LET'S GET OUT, JOEY!
GOOD LUCK, MR. MORRISON!
GOOD LUCK, GUYS!
ZOOM!
GULP! T-THAT CAR IS COMING R-RIGHT AT ME!
13

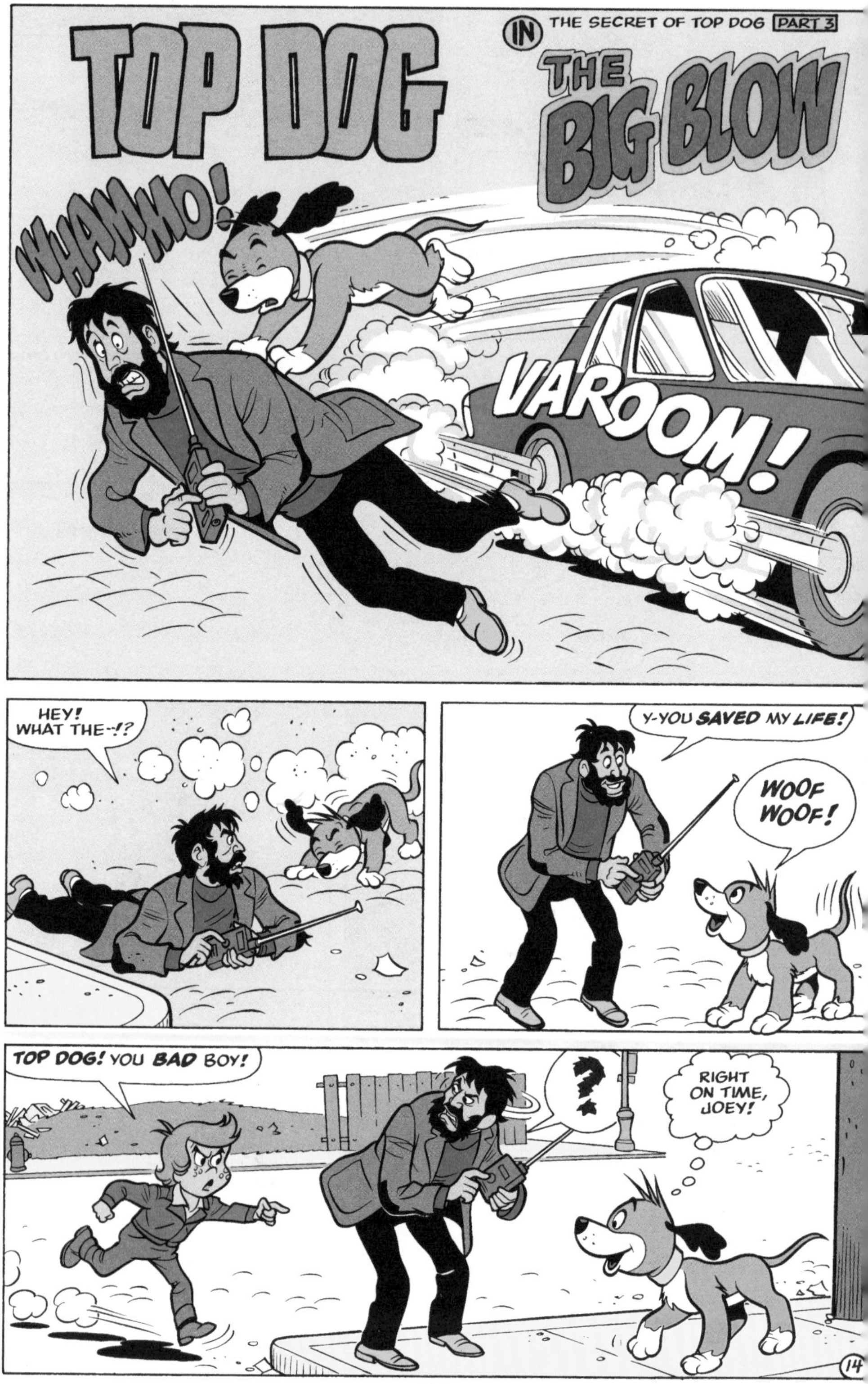
TOP DOG
IN THE SECRET OF TOP DOG PART 3
THE BIG BLOW
WHAMMO!
VAROOM!
HEY! WHAT THE--!?
Y-YOU SAVED MY LIFE!
WOOF WOOF!
TOP DOG! YOU BAD BOY!
?!
RIGHT ON TIME, JOEY!
14

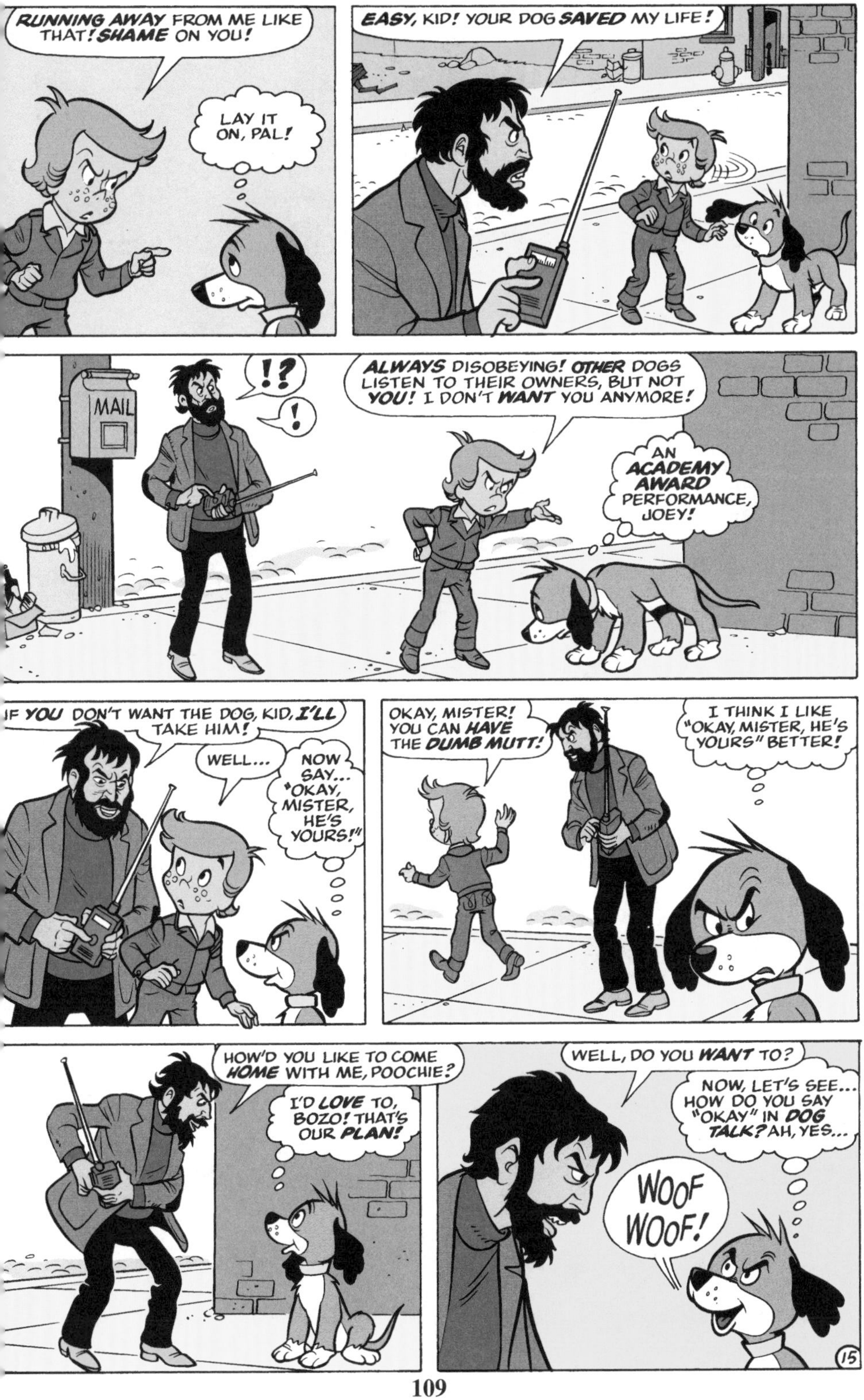
RUNNING AWAY FROM ME LIKE THAT! SHAME ON YOU!
LAY IT ON, PAL!
EASY, KID! YOUR DOG SAVED MY LIFE!
!?
!
ALWAYS DISOBEYING! OTHER DOGS LISTEN TO THEIR OWNERS, BUT NOT YOU! I DON'T WANT YOU ANYMORE!
AN ACADEMY AWARD PERFORMANCE, JOEY!
MAIL
IF YOU DON'T WANT THE DOG, KID, I'LL TAKE HIM!
WELL...
NOW SAY... "OKAY, MISTER, HE'S YOURS!"
OKAY, MISTER! YOU CAN HAVE THE DUMB MUTT!
I THINK I LIKE "OKAY, MISTER, HE'S YOURS" BETTER!
HOW'D YOU LIKE TO COME HOME WITH ME, POOCHIE?
I'D LOVE TO, BOZO! THAT'S OUR PLAN!
WELL, DO YOU WANT TO?
NOW, LET'S SEE... HOW DO YOU SAY "OKAY" IN DOG TALK? AH, YES...
WOOF WOOF!
15

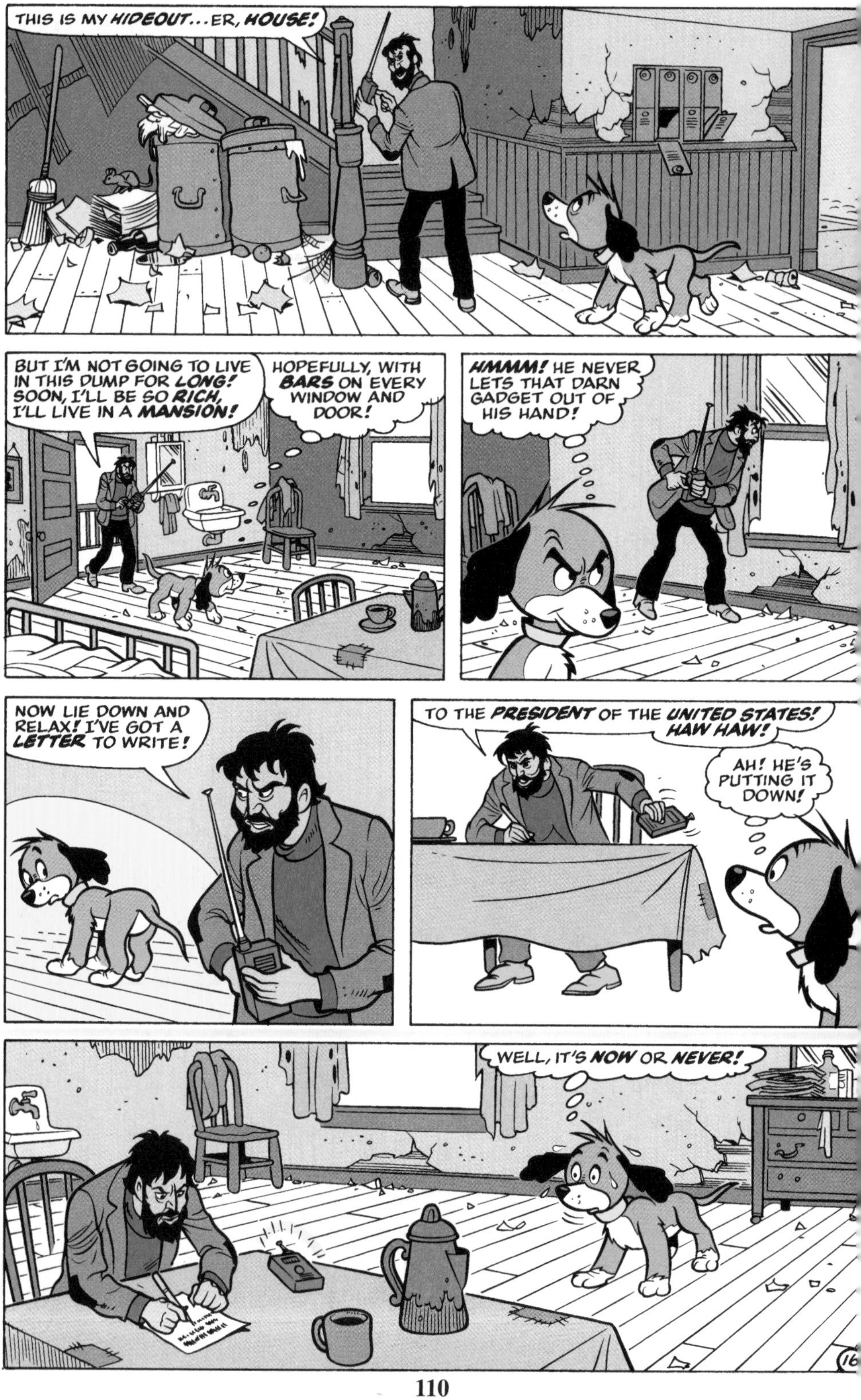
THIS IS MY HIDEOUT... ER, HOUSE!
BUT I'M NOT GOING TO LIVE IN THIS DUMP FOR LONG! SOON, I'LL BE SO RICH, I'LL LIVE IN A MANSION!
HOPEFULLY, WITH BARS ON EVERY WINDOW AND DOOR!
HMMM! HE NEVER LETS THAT DARN GADGET OUT OF HIS HAND!
NOW LIE DOWN AND RELAX! I'VE GOT A LETTER TO WRITE!
TO THE PRESIDENT OF THE UNITED STATES! HAW HAW!
AH! HE'S PUTTING IT DOWN!
WELL, IT'S NOW OR NEVER!
16

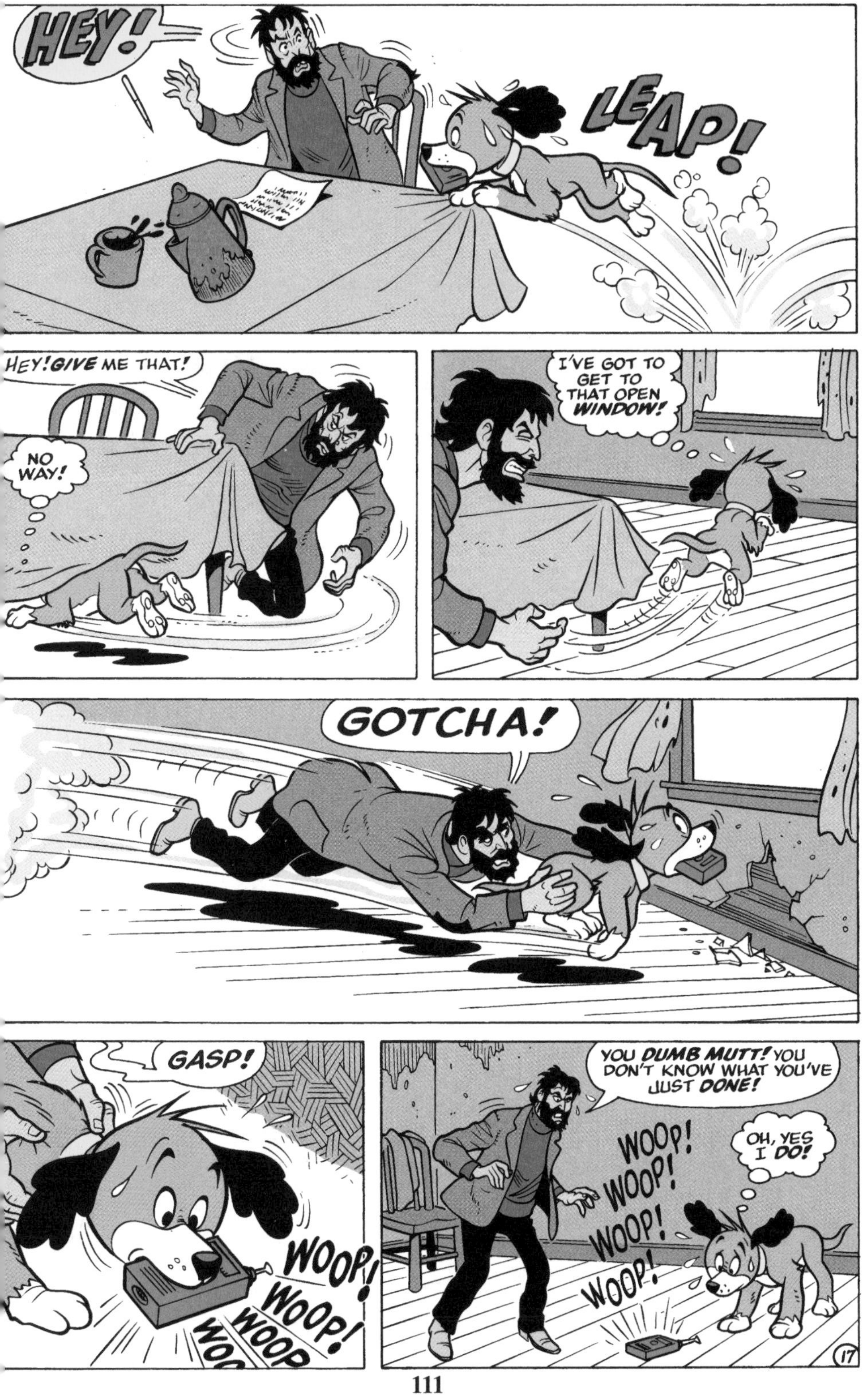

HEY!
LEAP!
HEY! GIVE ME THAT!
NO WAY!
I'VE GOT TO GET TO THAT OPEN WINDOW!
GOTCHA!
GASP!
WOOP!
WOOP!
WOOP
YOU DUMB MUTT! YOU DON'T KNOW WHAT YOU'VE JUST DONE!
WOOP! WOOP! WOOP! WOOP!
OH, YES I DO!
17

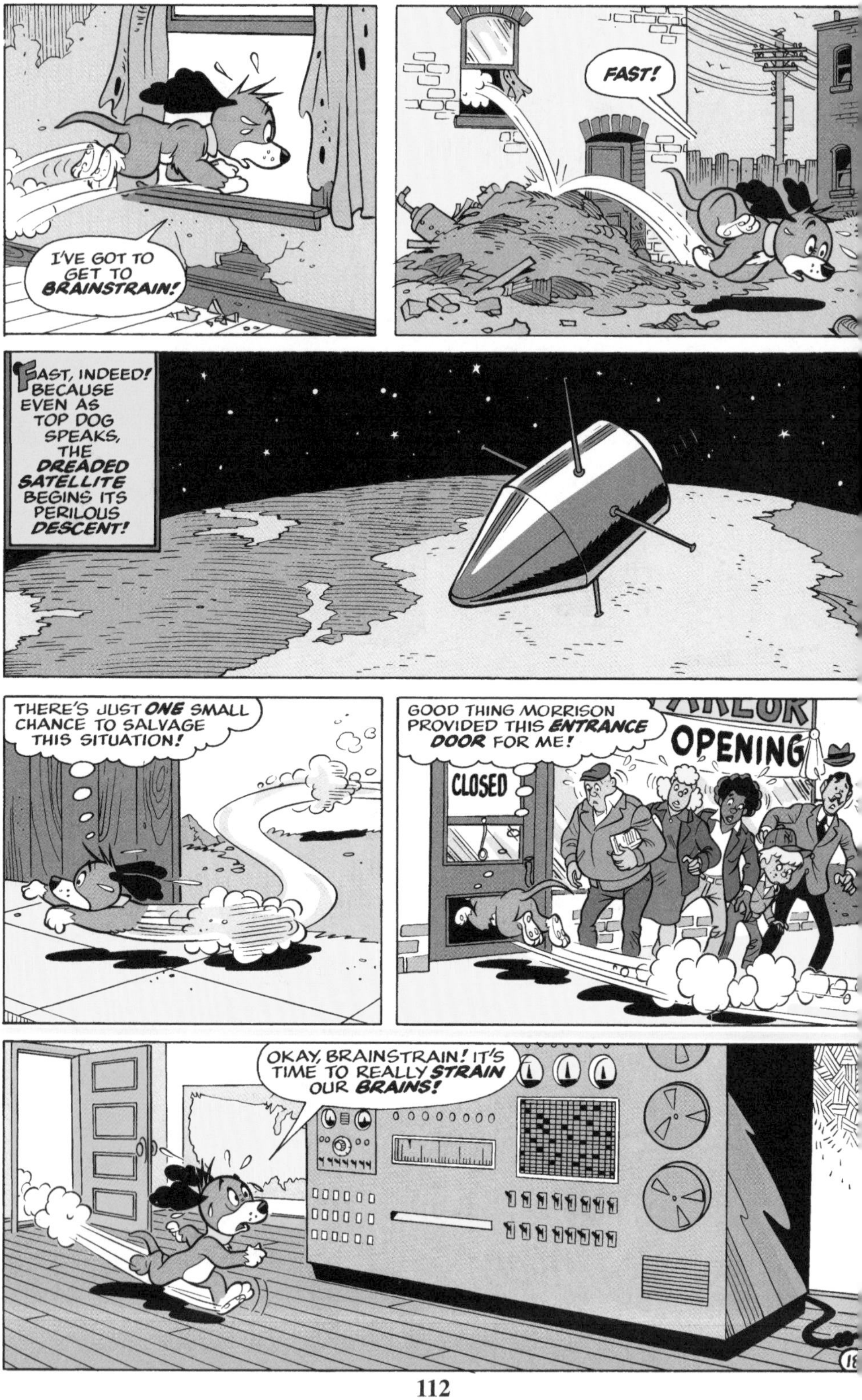

I'VE GOT TO GET TO BRAINSTRAIN!
FAST!
FAST, INDEED! BECAUSE EVEN AS TOP DOG SPEAKS, THE DREADED SATELLITE BEGINS ITS PERILOUS DESCENT!
THERE'S JUST ONE SMALL CHANCE TO SALVAGE THIS SITUATION!
GOOD THING MORRISON PROVIDED THIS ENTRANCE DOOR FOR ME!
CLOSED
OPENING
OKAY, BRAINSTRAIN! IT'S TIME TO REALLY STRAIN OUR BRAINS!

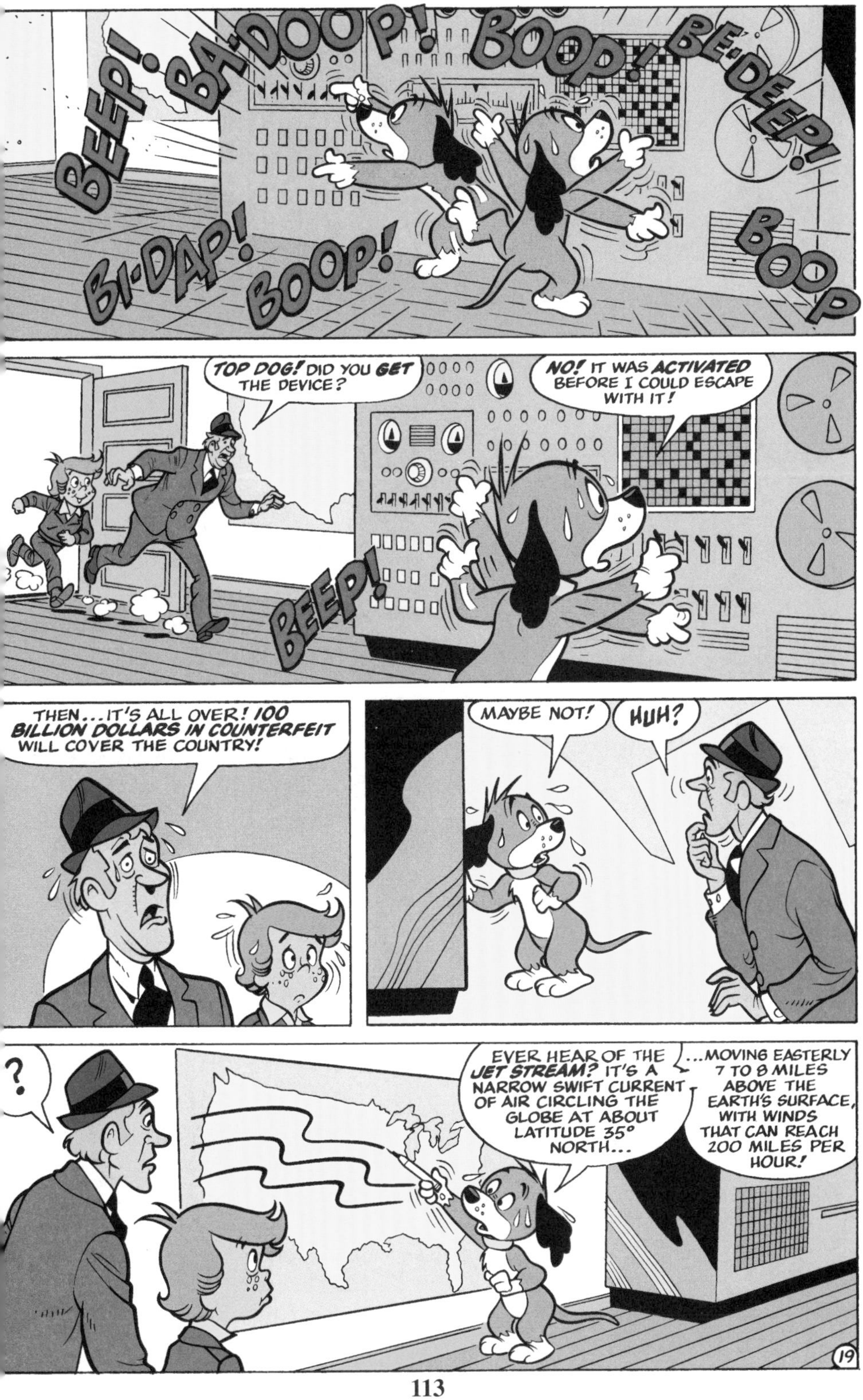
BEEP!
BA-DOOP!
BOOP!
BE-DEEP!
BI-DAP!
BOOP!
BOOP
TOP DOG! DID YOU GET THE DEVICE?
NO! IT WAS ACTIVATED BEFORE I COULD ESCAPE WITH IT!
BEEP!
THEN... IT'S ALL OVER! 100 BILLION DOLLARS IN COUNTERFEIT WILL COVER THE COUNTRY!
MAYBE NOT!
HUH?
?
EVER HEAR OF THE JET STREAM? IT'S A NARROW SWIFT CURRENT OF AIR CIRCLING THE GLOBE AT ABOUT LATITUDE 35° NORTH...
...MOVING EASTERLY 7 TO 8 MILES ABOVE THE EARTH'S SURFACE, WITH WINDS THAT CAN REACH 200 MILES PER HOUR!
19

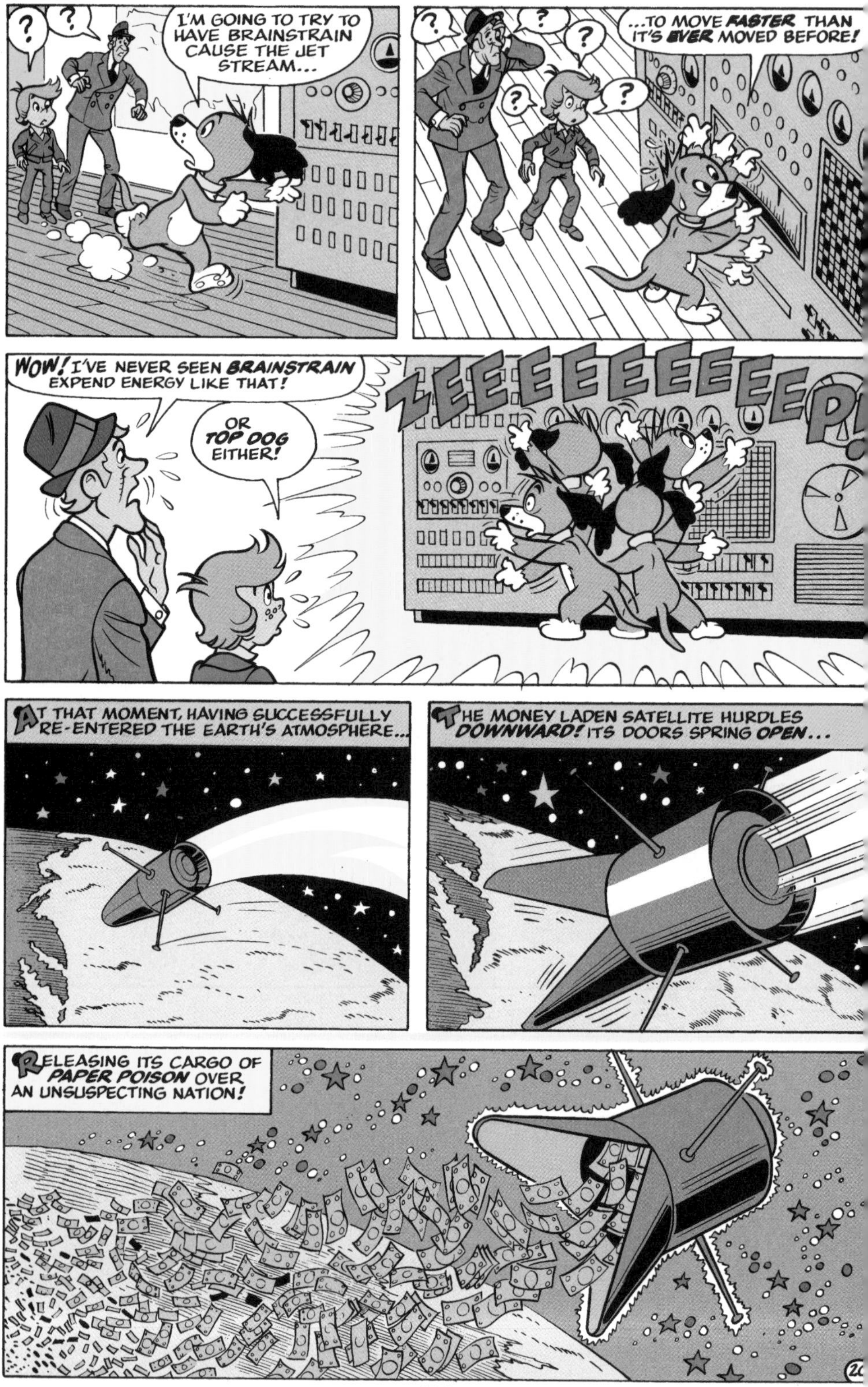
I'M GOING TO TRY TO HAVE BRAINSTRAIN CAUSE THE JET STREAM...
...TO MOVE FASTER THAN IT'S EVER MOVED BEFORE!
WOW! I'VE NEVER SEEN BRAINSTRAIN EXPEND ENERGY LIKE THAT!
OR TOP DOG EITHER!
ZEEEEEEEEEP!
AT THAT MOMENT, HAVING SUCCESSFULLY RE-ENTERED THE EARTH'S ATMOSPHERE...
THE MONEY LADEN SATELLITE HURDLES DOWNWARD! ITS DOORS SPRING OPEN...
RELEASING ITS CARGO OF PAPER POISON OVER AN UNSUSPECTING NATION!

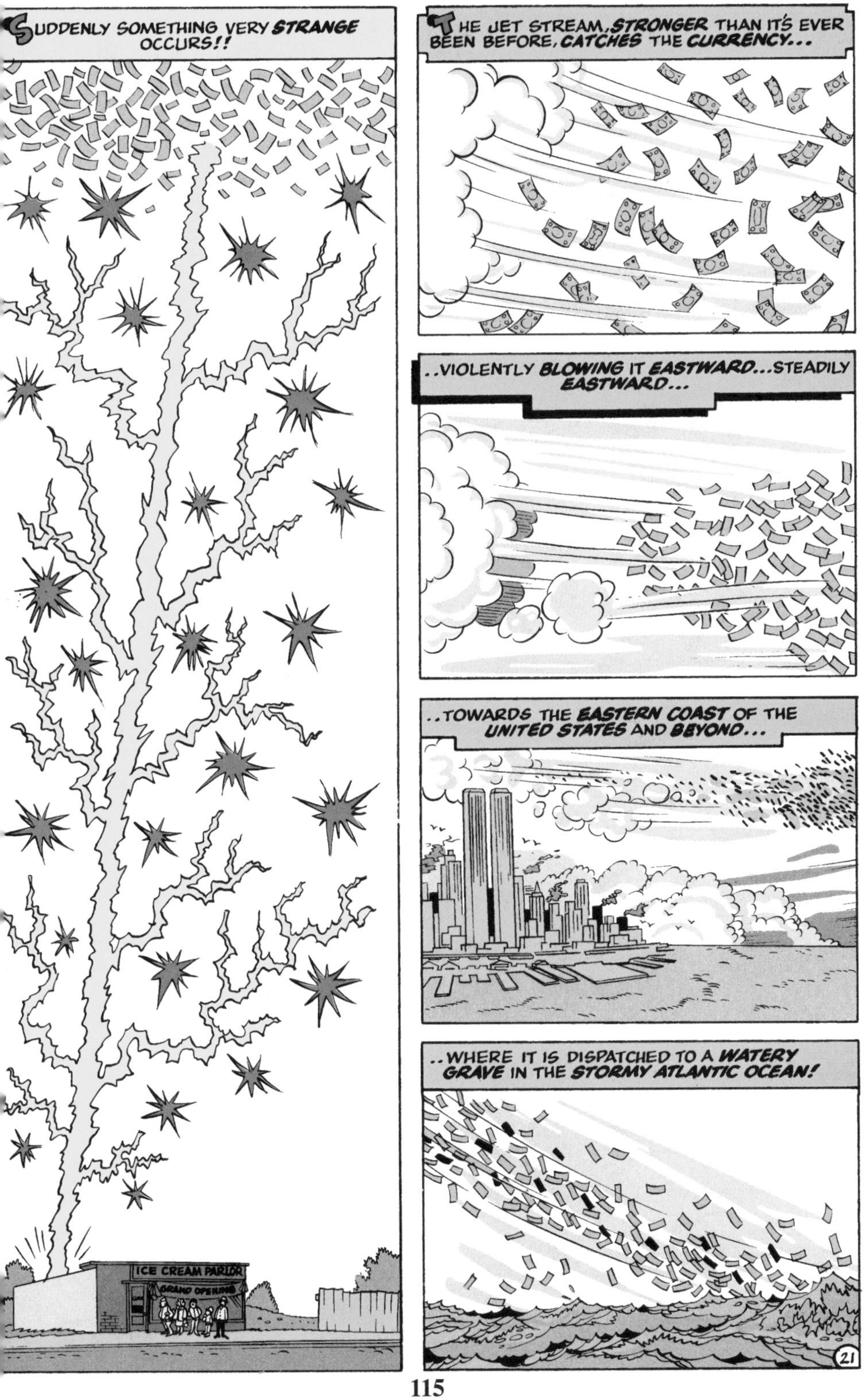
SUDDENLY SOMETHING VERY STRANGE OCCURS!!
ICE CREAM PARLOR
GRAND OPENING
THE JET STREAM, STRONGER THAN IT'S EVER BEEN BEFORE, CATCHES THE CURRENCY...
..VIOLENTLY BLOWING IT EASTWARD...STEADILY EASTWARD...
..TOWARDS THE EASTERN COAST OF THE UNITED STATES AND BEYOND...
..WHERE IT IS DISPATCHED TO A WATERY GRAVE IN THE STORMY ATLANTIC OCEAN!
21

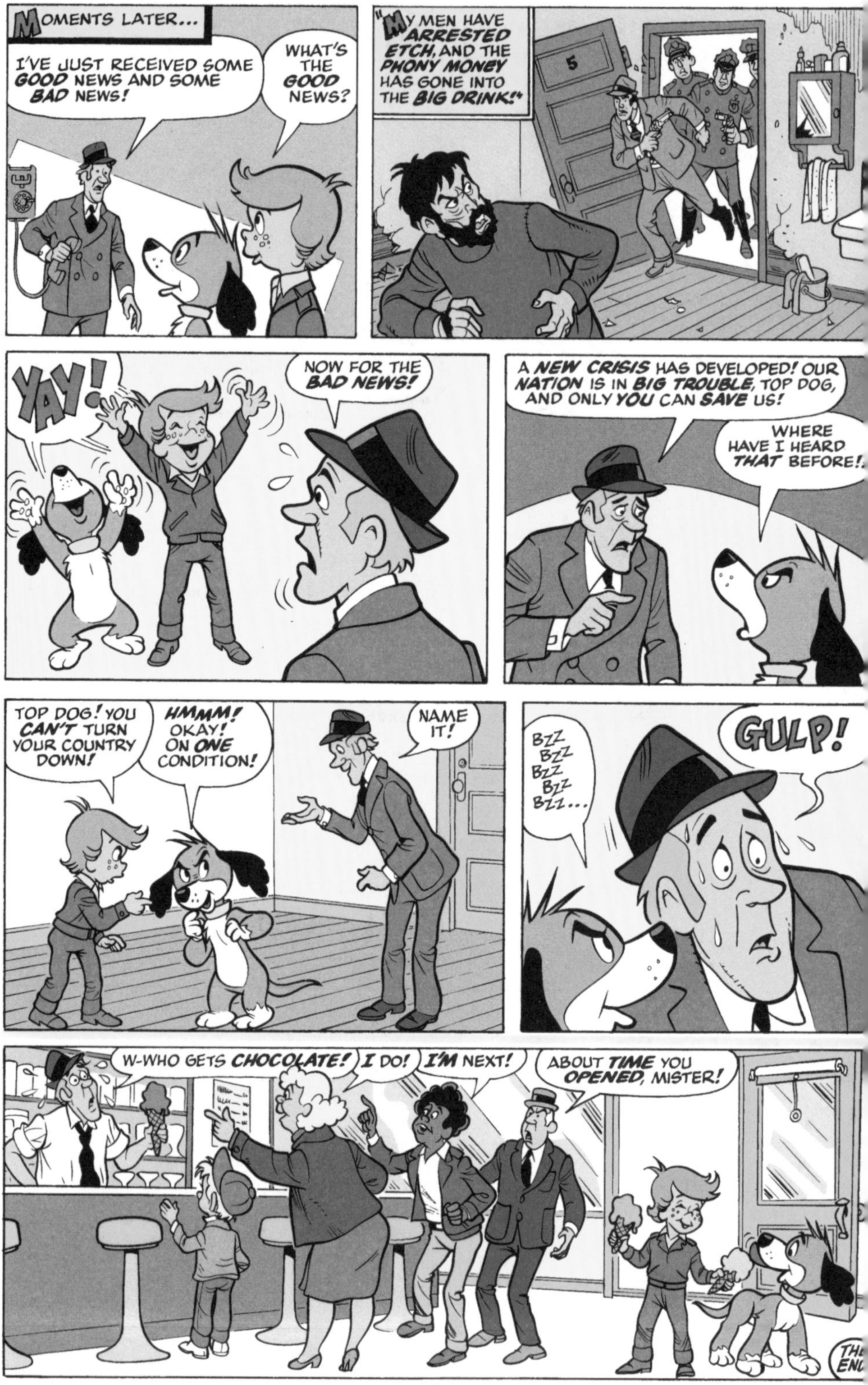

MOMENTS LATER...
I'VE JUST RECEIVED SOME GOOD NEWS AND SOME BAD NEWS!
WHAT'S THE GOOD NEWS?
"MY MEN HAVE ARRESTED ETCH, AND THE PHONY MONEY HAS GONE INTO THE BIG DRINK!"
5
YAY!
NOW FOR THE BAD NEWS!
A NEW CRISIS HAS DEVELOPED! OUR NATION IS IN BIG TROUBLE, TOP DOG, AND ONLY YOU CAN SAVE US!
WHERE HAVE I HEARD THAT BEFORE!
TOP DOG! YOU CAN'T TURN YOUR COUNTRY DOWN!
HMMM! OKAY! ON ONE CONDITION!
NAME IT!
BZZ BZZ BZZ BZZ BZZ...
GULP!
W-WHO GETS CHOCOLATE!
I DO!
I'M NEXT!
ABOUT TIME YOU OPENED, MISTER!

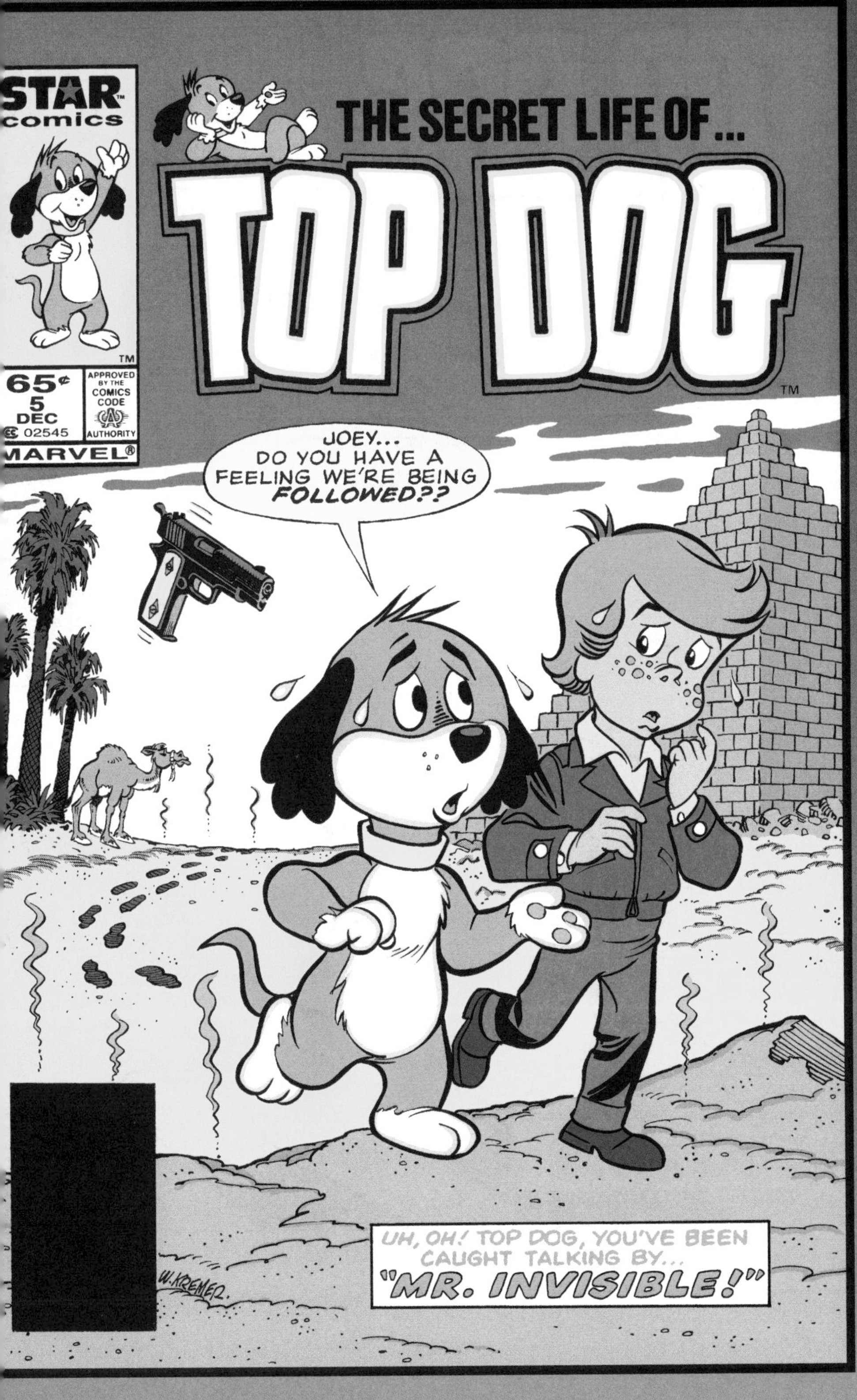
STAR comics
THE SECRET LIFE OF...
TOP DOG
65¢
5
DEC
02545
APPROVED BY THE COMICS CODE AUTHORITY
MARVEL®
JOEY... DO YOU HAVE A FEELING WE'RE BEING FOLLOWED??
UH, OH! TOP DOG, YOU'VE BEEN CAUGHT TALKING BY... "MR. INVISIBLE!"
W. KREMER

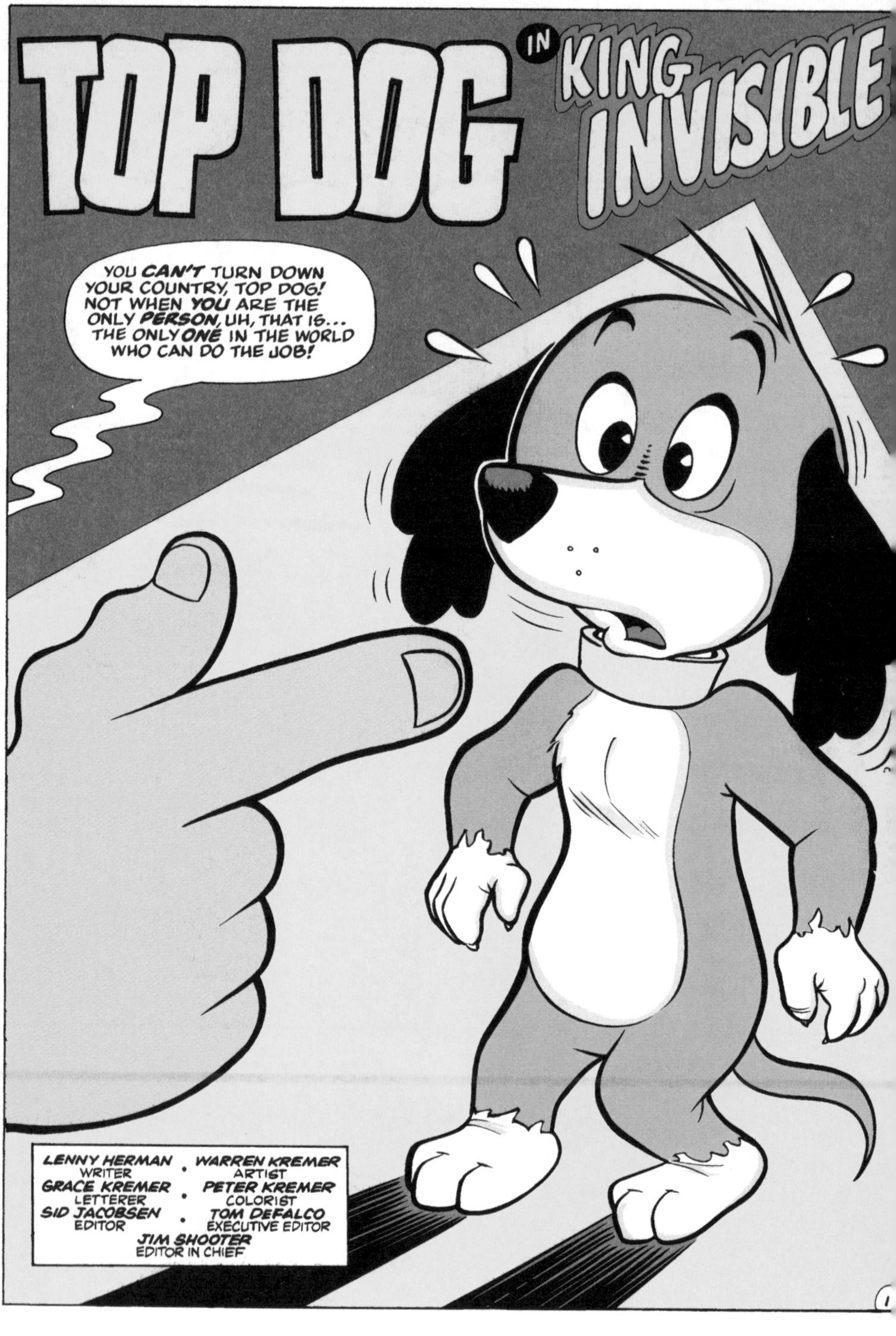
TOP DOG IN KING INVISIBLE
YOU CAN'T TURN DOWN YOUR COUNTRY, TOP DOG! NOT WHEN YOU ARE THE ONLY PERSON, UH, THAT IS... THE ONLY ONE IN THE WORLD WHO CAN DO THE JOB!
LENNY HERMAN WRITER • WARREN KREMER ARTIST
GRACE KREMER LETTERER • PETER KREMER COLORIST
SID JACOBSEN EDITOR • TOM DEFALCO EXECUTIVE EDITOR
JIM SHOOTER EDITOR IN CHIEF

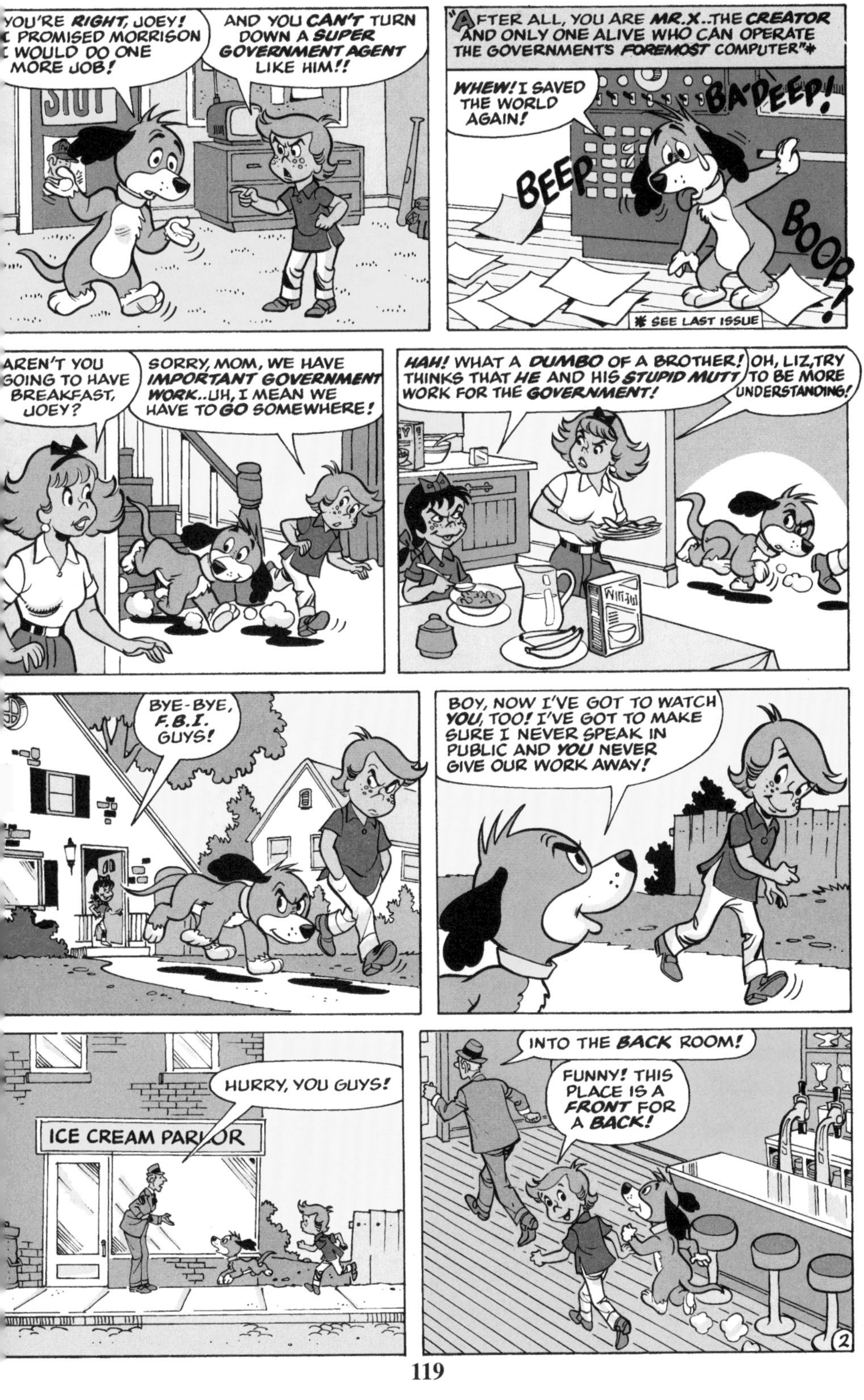
YOU'RE RIGHT, JOEY! I PROMISED MORRISON I WOULD DO ONE MORE JOB!
AND YOU CAN'T TURN DOWN A SUPER GOVERNMENT AGENT LIKE HIM!!
"AFTER ALL, YOU ARE MR.X..THE CREATOR AND ONLY ONE ALIVE WHO CAN OPERATE THE GOVERNMENT'S FOREMOST COMPUTER"*
WHEW! I SAVED THE WORLD AGAIN!
BA'DEEP!
BEEP
BOOP!
* SEE LAST ISSUE
AREN'T YOU GOING TO HAVE BREAKFAST, JOEY?
SORRY, MOM, WE HAVE IMPORTANT GOVERNMENT WORK..UH, I MEAN WE HAVE TO GO SOMEWHERE!
HAH! WHAT A DUMBO OF A BROTHER! THINKS THAT HE AND HIS STUPID MUTT WORK FOR THE GOVERNMENT!
OH, LIZ, TRY TO BE MORE UNDERSTANDING!
BYE-BYE, F.B.I. GUYS!
BOY, NOW I'VE GOT TO WATCH YOU, TOO! I'VE GOT TO MAKE SURE I NEVER SPEAK IN PUBLIC AND YOU NEVER GIVE OUR WORK AWAY!
ICE CREAM PARLOR
HURRY, YOU GUYS!
INTO THE BACK ROOM!
FUNNY! THIS PLACE IS A FRONT FOR A BACK!
2

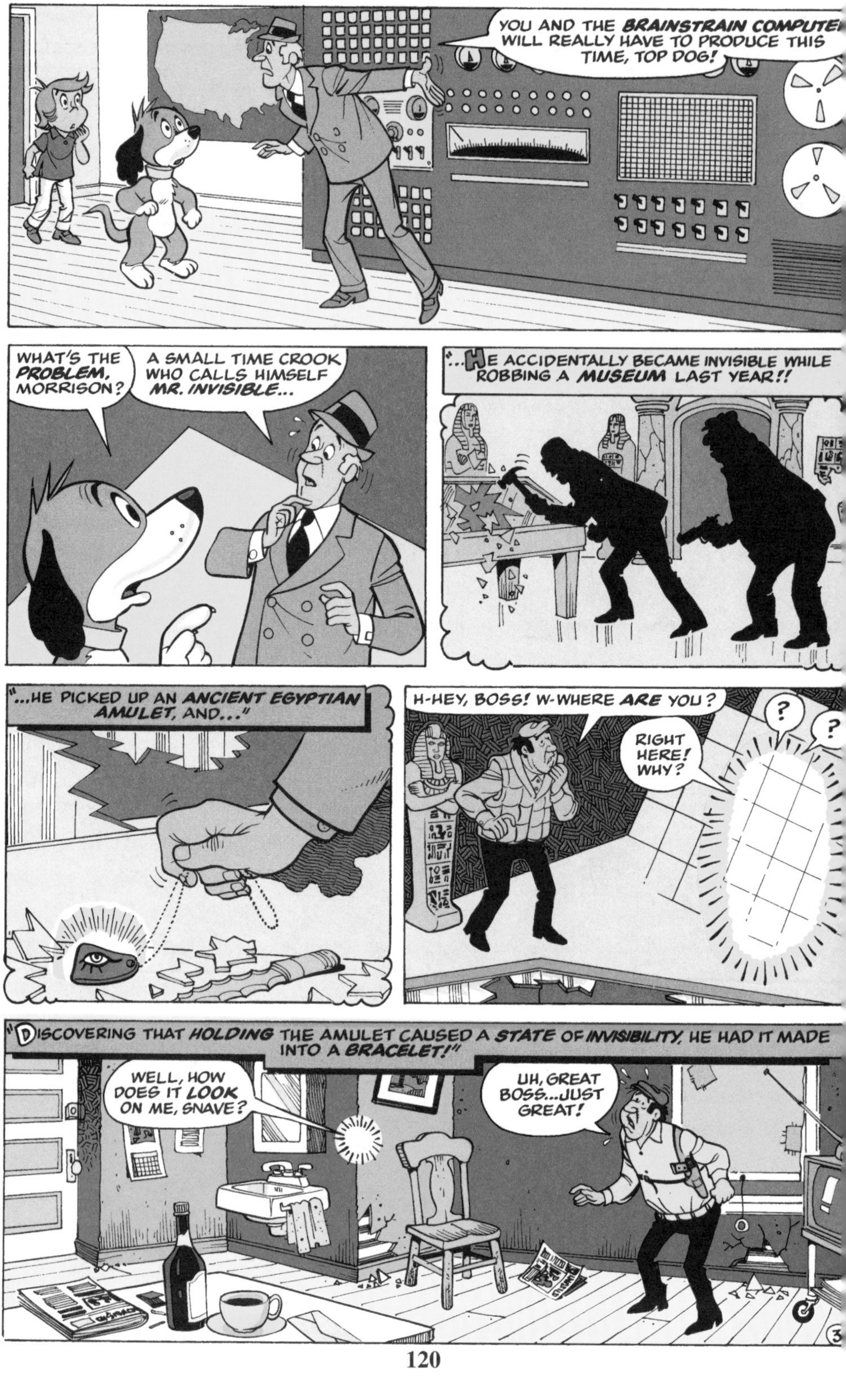
YOU AND THE BRAINSTRAIN COMPUTER WILL REALLY HAVE TO PRODUCE THIS TIME, TOP DOG!
WHAT'S THE PROBLEM, MORRISON?
A SMALL TIME CROOK WHO CALLS HIMSELF MR. INVISIBLE...
"...HE ACCIDENTALLY BECAME INVISIBLE WHILE ROBBING A MUSEUM LAST YEAR!!
"...HE PICKED UP AN ANCIENT EGYPTIAN AMULET, AND..."
H-HEY, BOSS! W-WHERE ARE YOU?
RIGHT HERE! WHY?
?
?
"DISCOVERING THAT HOLDING THE AMULET CAUSED A STATE OF INVISIBILITY, HE HAD IT MADE INTO A BRACELET!"
WELL, HOW DOES IT LOOK ON ME, SNAVE?
UH, GREAT BOSS...JUST GREAT!

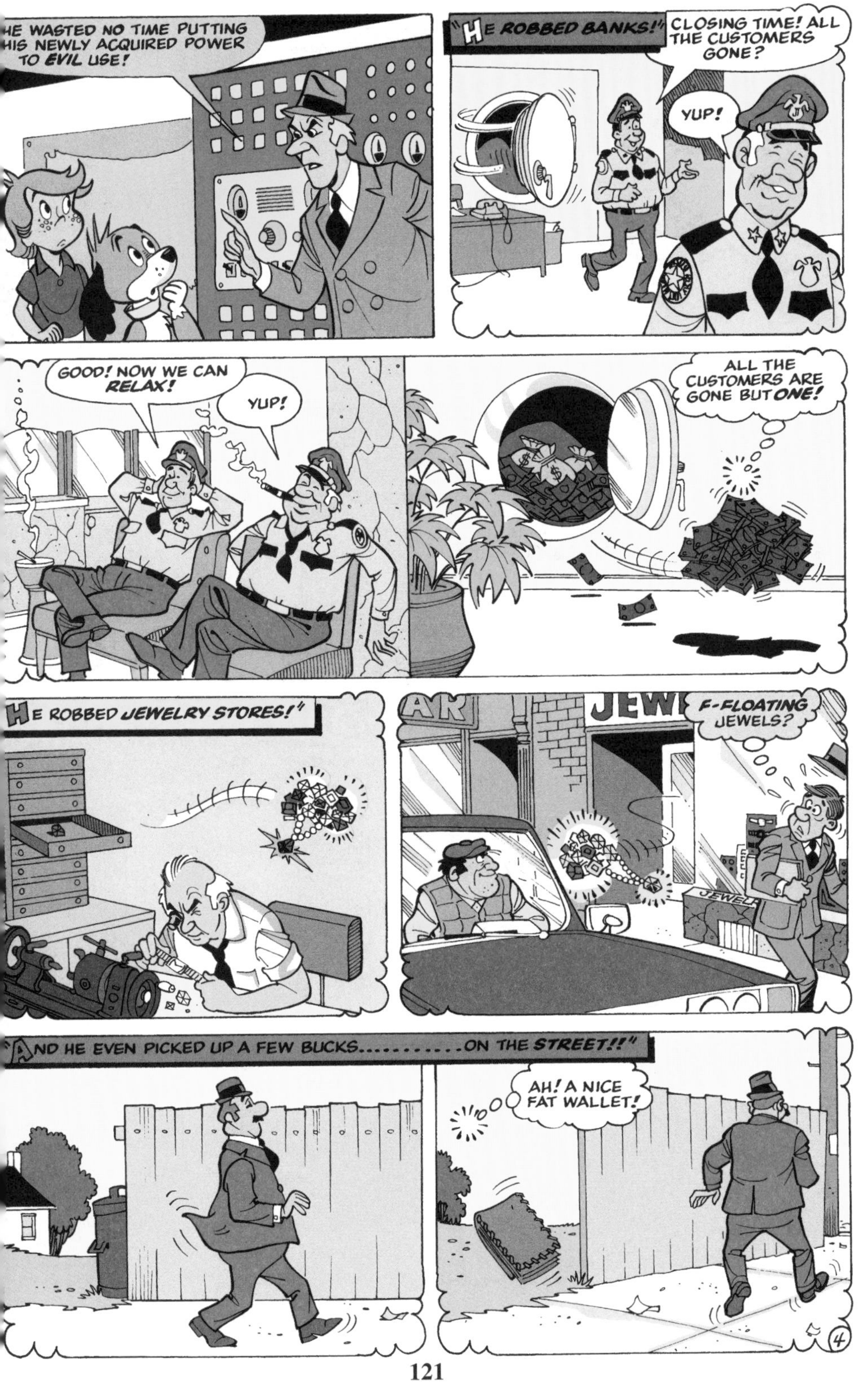
HE WASTED NO TIME PUTTING HIS NEWLY ACQUIRED POWER TO EVIL USE!
"HE ROBBED BANKS!"
CLOSING TIME! ALL THE CUSTOMERS GONE?
YUP!
GOOD! NOW WE CAN RELAX!
YUP!
ALL THE CUSTOMERS ARE GONE BUT ONE!
HE ROBBED JEWELRY STORES!"
F-FLOATING JEWELS?
"AND HE EVEN PICKED UP A FEW BUCKS..........ON THE STREET!!"
AH! A NICE FAT WALLET!
4

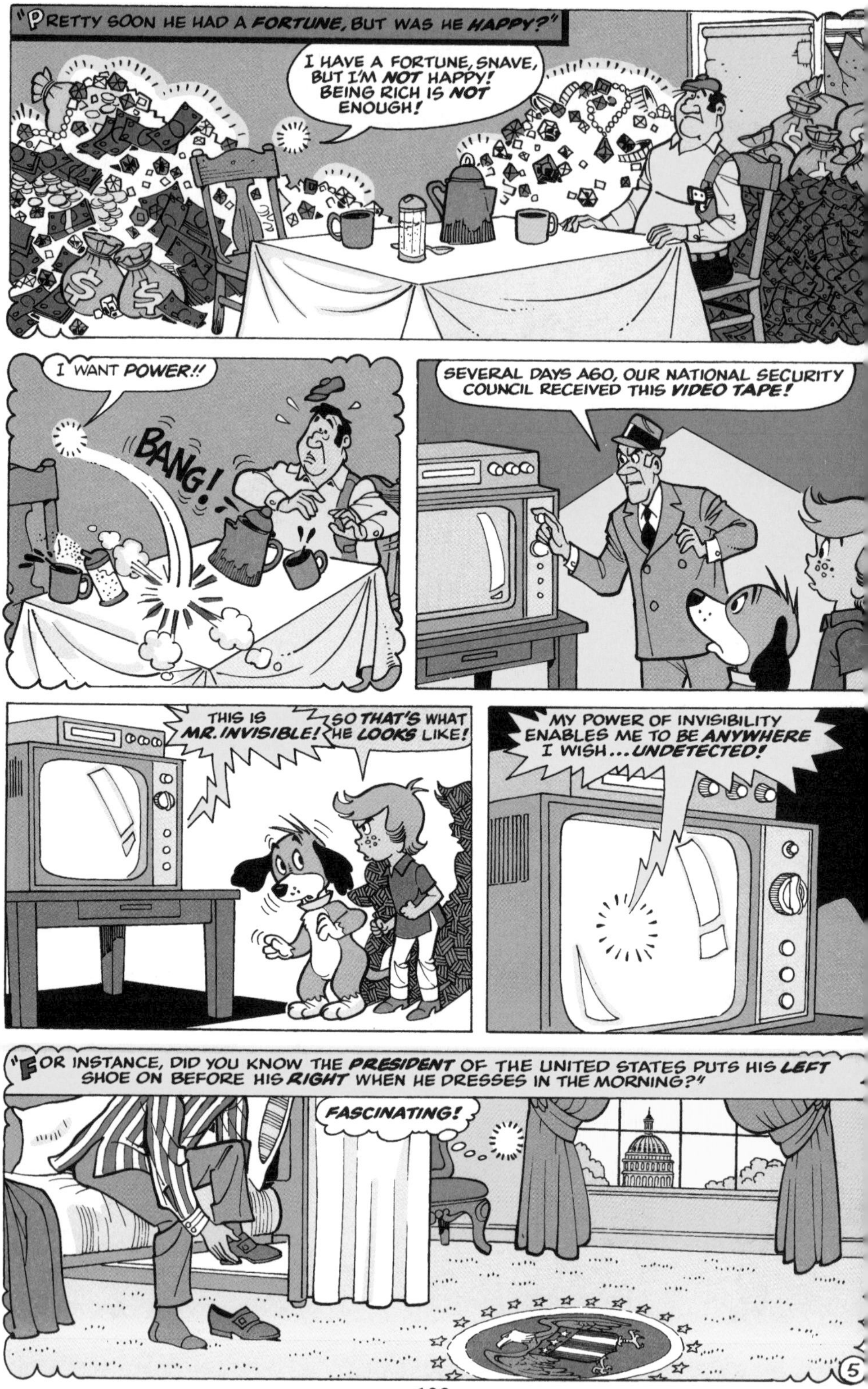
"PRETTY SOON HE HAD A FORTUNE, BUT WAS HE HAPPY?"
I HAVE A FORTUNE, SNAVE, BUT I'M NOT HAPPY! BEING RICH IS NOT ENOUGH!
I WANT POWER!!
BANG!
SEVERAL DAYS AGO, OUR NATIONAL SECURITY COUNCIL RECEIVED THIS VIDEO TAPE!
THIS IS MR. INVISIBLE!
SO THAT'S WHAT HE LOOKS LIKE!
MY POWER OF INVISIBILITY ENABLES ME TO BE ANYWHERE I WISH... UNDETECTED!
"FOR INSTANCE, DID YOU KNOW THE PRESIDENT OF THE UNITED STATES PUTS HIS LEFT SHOE ON BEFORE HIS RIGHT WHEN HE DRESSES IN THE MORNING?"
FASCINATING!
5

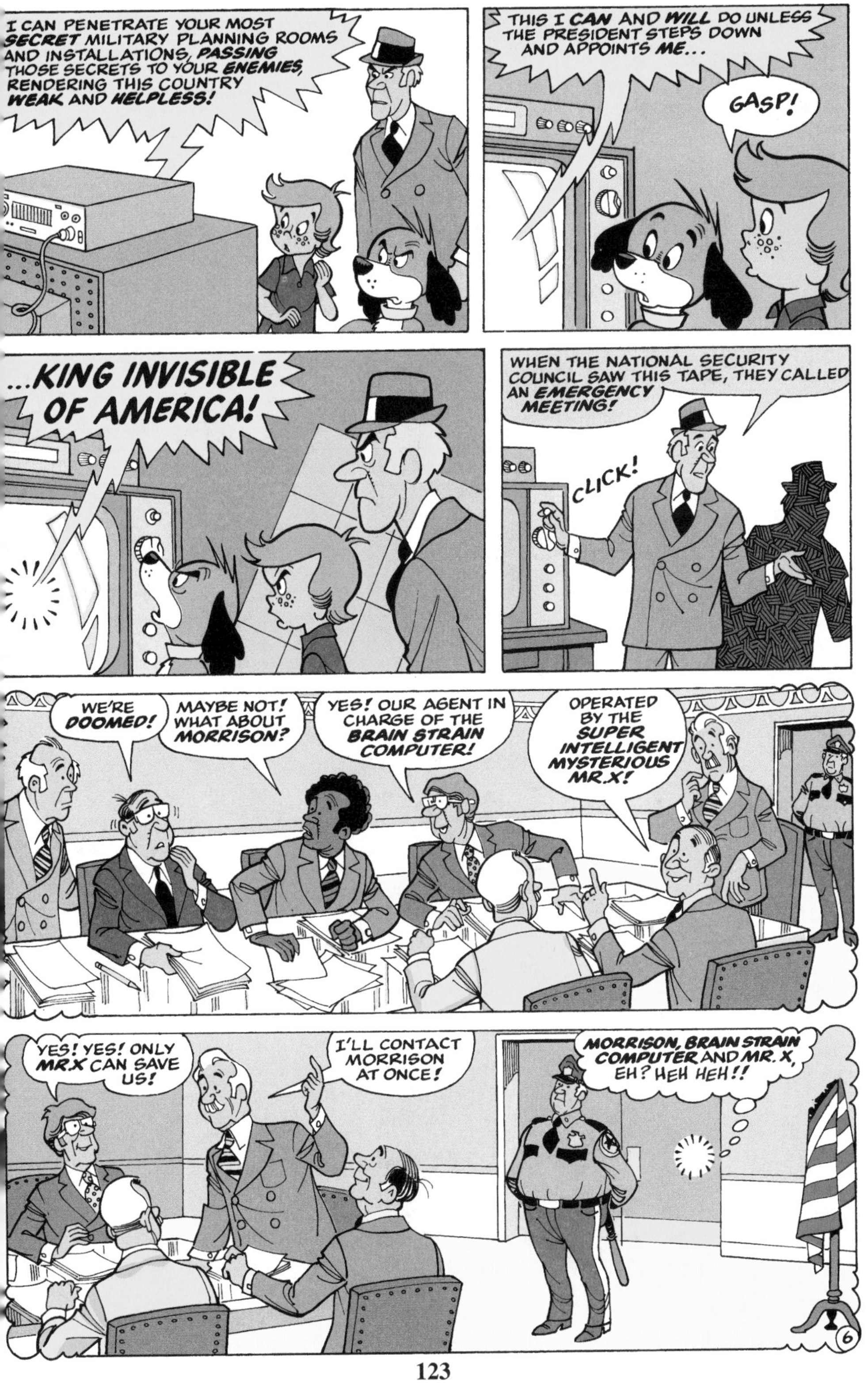
I CAN PENETRATE YOUR MOST SECRET MILITARY PLANNING ROOMS AND INSTALLATIONS, PASSING THOSE SECRETS TO YOUR ENEMIES, RENDERING THIS COUNTRY WEAK AND HELPLESS!
THIS I CAN AND WILL DO UNLESS THE PRESIDENT STEPS DOWN AND APPOINTS ME...
GASP!
...KING INVISIBLE OF AMERICA!
WHEN THE NATIONAL SECURITY COUNCIL SAW THIS TAPE, THEY CALLED AN EMERGENCY MEETING!
CLICK!
WE'RE DOOMED!
MAYBE NOT! WHAT ABOUT MORRISON?
YES! OUR AGENT IN CHARGE OF THE BRAIN STRAIN COMPUTER!
OPERATED BY THE SUPER INTELLIGENT MYSTERIOUS MR. X!
YES! YES! ONLY MR. X CAN SAVE US!
I'LL CONTACT MORRISON AT ONCE!
MORRISON, BRAIN STRAIN COMPUTER AND MR. X, EH? HEH HEH!!
6

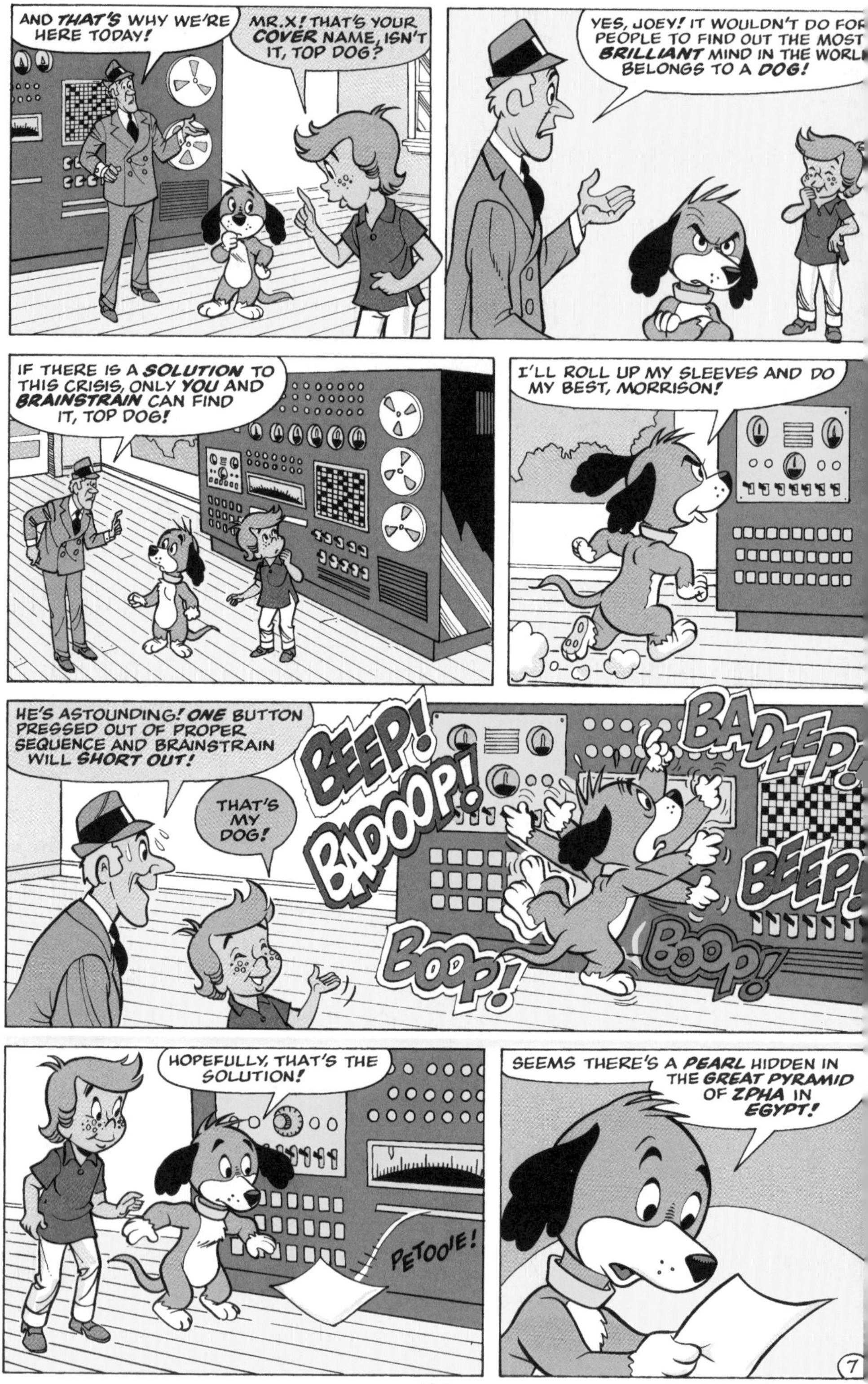
AND THAT'S WHY WE'RE HERE TODAY!
MR.X! THAT'S YOUR COVER NAME, ISN'T IT, TOP DOG?
YES, JOEY! IT WOULDN'T DO FOR PEOPLE TO FIND OUT THE MOST BRILLIANT MIND IN THE WORLD BELONGS TO A DOG!
IF THERE IS A SOLUTION TO THIS CRISIS, ONLY YOU AND BRAINSTRAIN CAN FIND IT, TOP DOG!
I'LL ROLL UP MY SLEEVES AND DO MY BEST, MORRISON!
HE'S ASTOUNDING! ONE BUTTON PRESSED OUT OF PROPER SEQUENCE AND BRAINSTRAIN WILL SHORT OUT!
THAT'S MY DOG!
BEEP!
BADOOP!
BADEEP!
BEEP!
BOOP!
BOOP!
HOPEFULLY, THAT'S THE SOLUTION!
PETOOIE!
SEEMS THERE'S A PEARL HIDDEN IN THE GREAT PYRAMID OF ZPHA IN EGYPT!
7

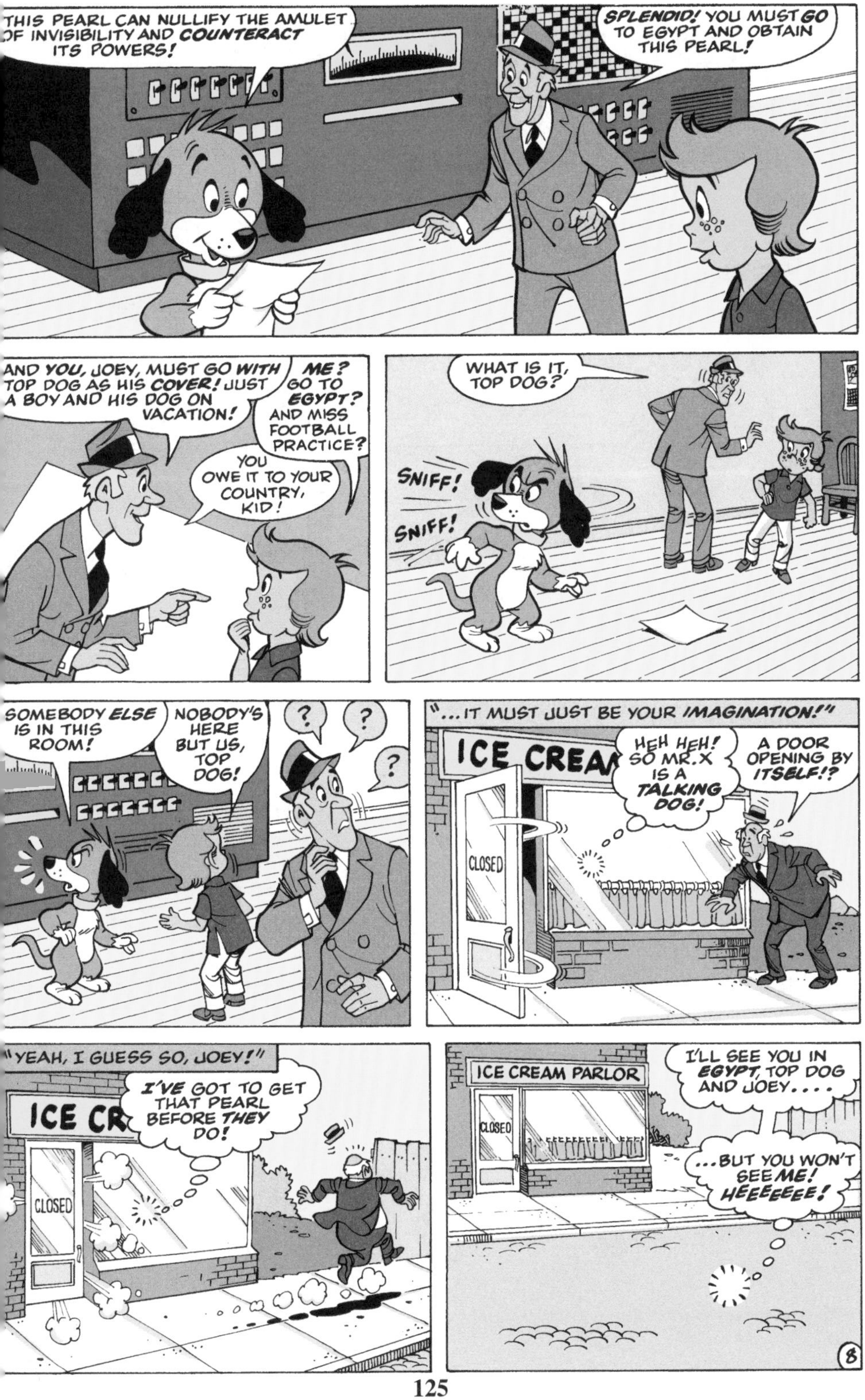

THIS PEARL CAN NULLIFY THE AMULET OF INVISIBILITY AND COUNTERACT ITS POWERS!
SPLENDID! YOU MUST GO TO EGYPT AND OBTAIN THIS PEARL!
AND YOU, JOEY, MUST GO WITH TOP DOG AS HIS COVER! JUST A BOY AND HIS DOG ON VACATION!
ME? GO TO EGYPT? AND MISS FOOTBALL PRACTICE?
YOU OWE IT TO YOUR COUNTRY, KID!
WHAT IS IT, TOP DOG?
SNIFF!
SNIFF!
SOMEBODY ELSE IS IN THIS ROOM!
NOBODY'S HERE BUT US, TOP DOG!
?
?
?
"...IT MUST JUST BE YOUR IMAGINATION!"
ICE CREA
CLOSED
HEH HEH! SO MR. X IS A TALKING DOG!
A DOOR OPENING BY ITSELF!?
"YEAH, I GUESS SO, JOEY!"
ICE CR
CLOSED
I'VE GOT TO GET THAT PEARL BEFORE THEY DO!
ICE CREAM PARLOR
CLOSED
I'LL SEE YOU IN EGYPT, TOP DOG AND JOEY....
...BUT YOU WON'T SEE ME! HEEEEEEE!
8

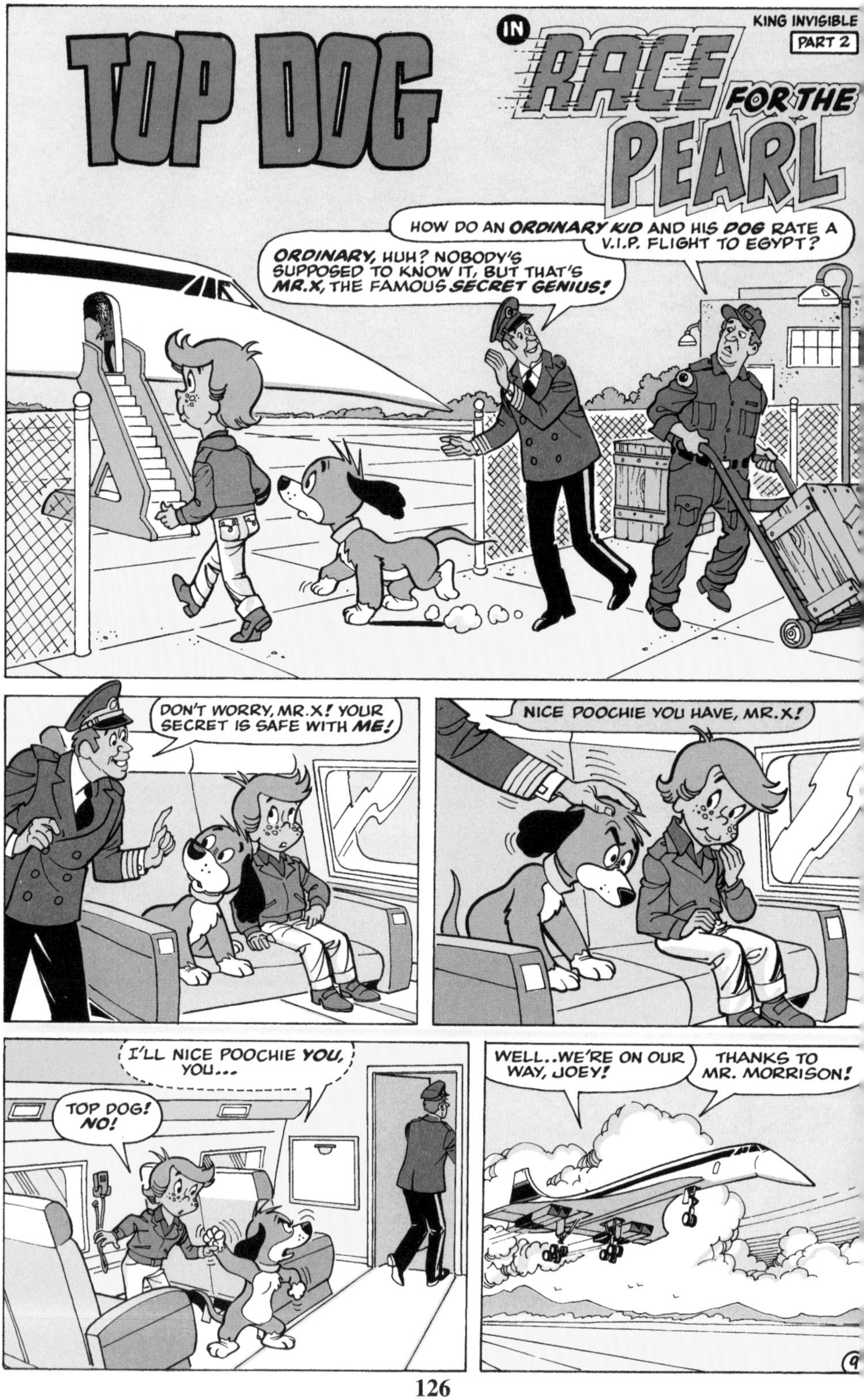

TOP DOG
IN
RACE FOR THE PEARL
KING INVISIBLE
PART 2
HOW DO AN ORDINARY KID AND HIS DOG RATE A V.I.P. FLIGHT TO EGYPT?
ORDINARY, HUH? NOBODY'S SUPPOSED TO KNOW IT, BUT THAT'S MR.X, THE FAMOUS SECRET GENIUS!
DON'T WORRY, MR.X! YOUR SECRET IS SAFE WITH ME!
NICE POOCHIE YOU HAVE, MR.X!
I'LL NICE POOCHIE YOU, YOU...
TOP DOG! NO!
WELL..WE'RE ON OUR WAY, JOEY!
THANKS TO MR. MORRISON!
9

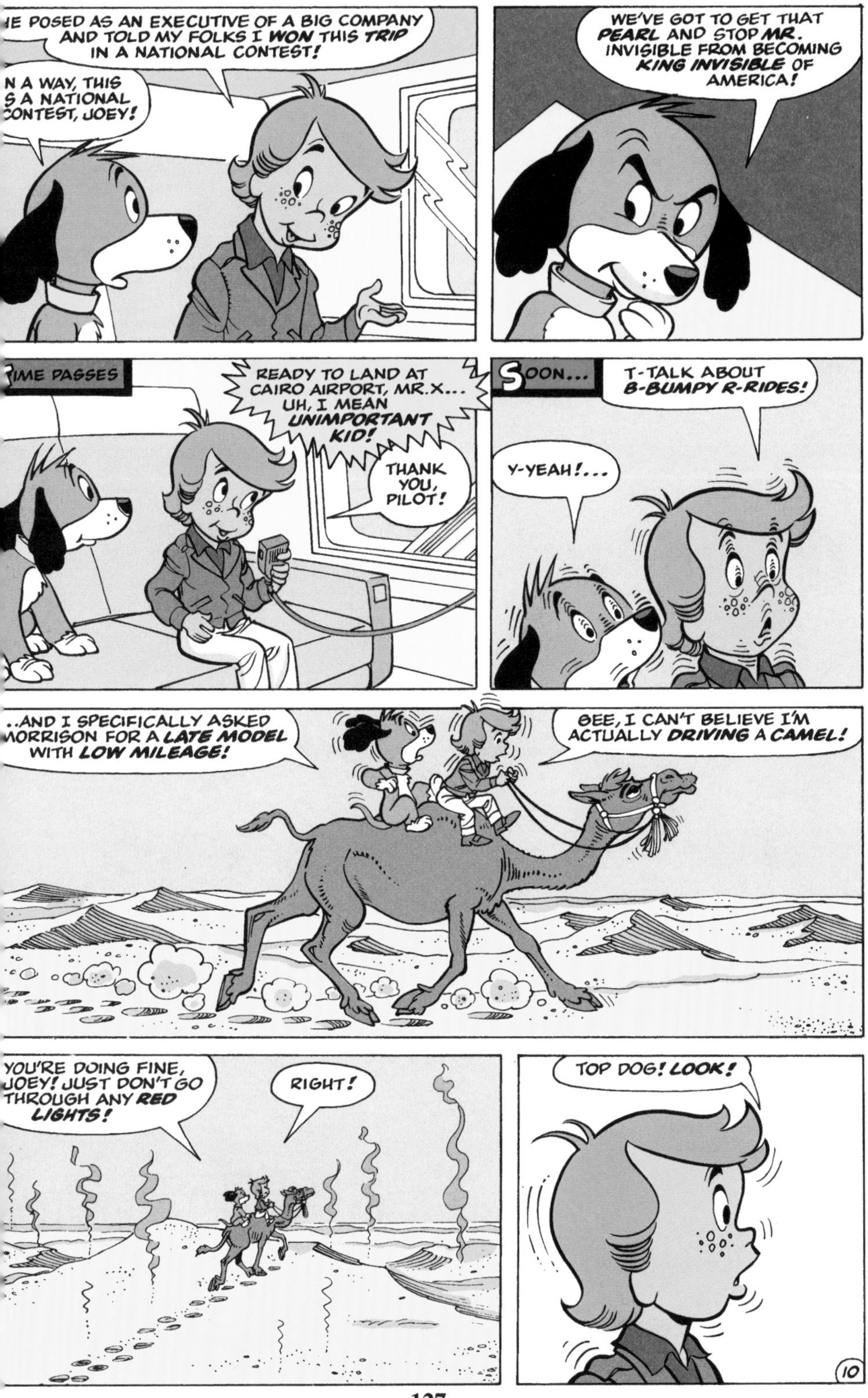

IE POSED AS AN EXECUTIVE OF A BIG COMPANY AND TOLD MY FOLKS I WON THIS TRIP IN A NATIONAL CONTEST!
N A WAY, THIS S A NATIONAL CONTEST, JOEY!
WE'VE GOT TO GET THAT PEARL AND STOP MR. INVISIBLE FROM BECOMING KING INVISIBLE OF AMERICA!
TIME PASSES
READY TO LAND AT CAIRO AIRPORT, MR. X... UH, I MEAN UNIMPORTANT KID!
THANK YOU, PILOT!
SOON...
T-TALK ABOUT B-BUMPY R-RIDES!
Y-YEAH!...
..AND I SPECIFICALLY ASKED MORRISON FOR A LATE MODEL WITH LOW MILEAGE!
GEE, I CAN'T BELIEVE I'M ACTUALLY DRIVING A CAMEL!
YOU'RE DOING FINE, JOEY! JUST DON'T GO THROUGH ANY RED LIGHTS!
RIGHT!
TOP DOG! LOOK!
10

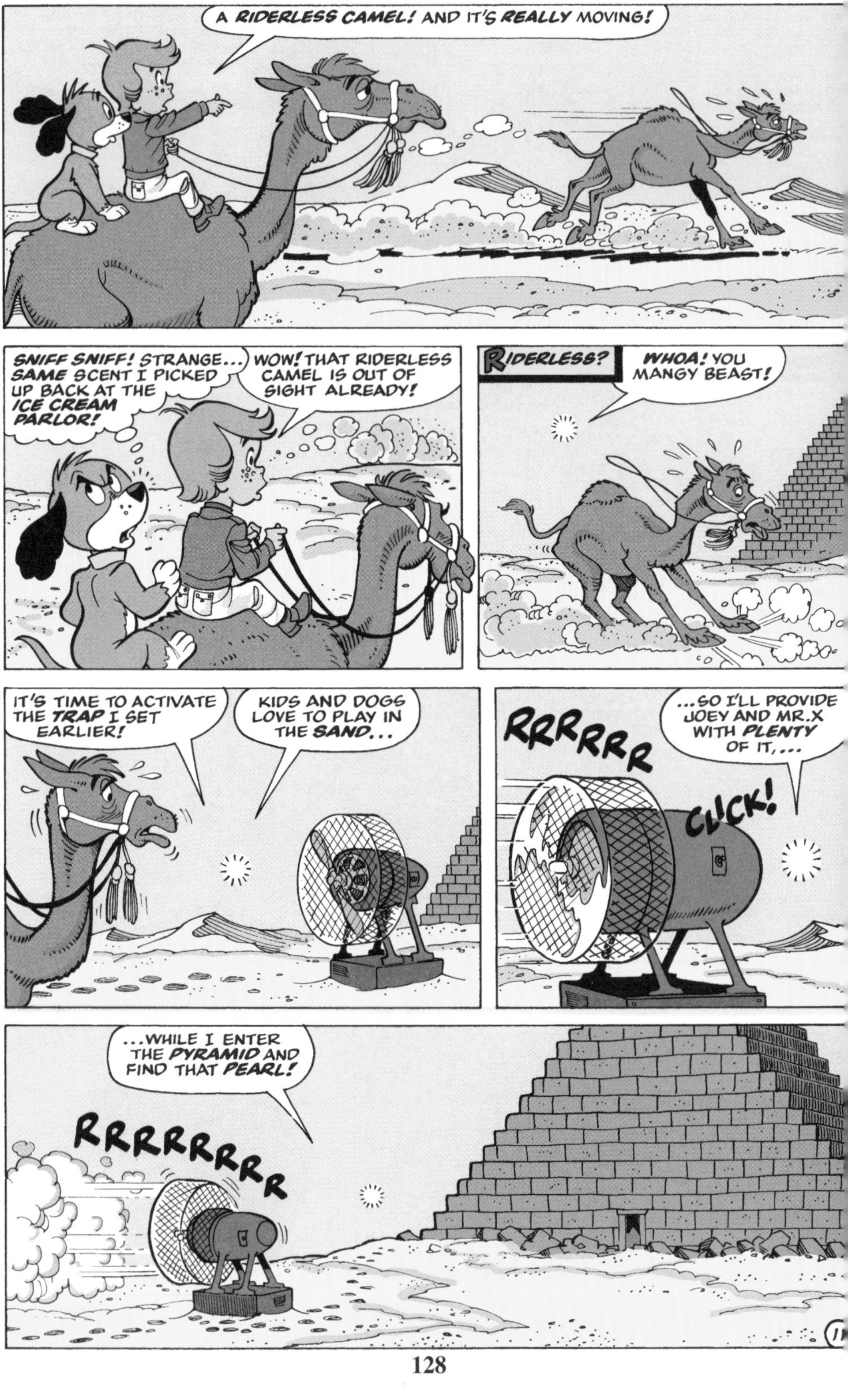
A RIDERLESS CAMEL! AND IT'S REALLY MOVING!
SNIFF SNIFF! STRANGE... SAME SCENT I PICKED UP BACK AT THE ICE CREAM PARLOR!
WOW! THAT RIDERLESS CAMEL IS OUT OF SIGHT ALREADY!
RIDERLESS?
WHOA! YOU MANGY BEAST!
IT'S TIME TO ACTIVATE THE TRAP I SET EARLIER!
KIDS AND DOGS LOVE TO PLAY IN THE SAND...
RRRRRRR
CLICK!
...SO I'LL PROVIDE JOEY AND MR.X WITH PLENTY OF IT,...
...WHILE I ENTER THE PYRAMID AND FIND THAT PEARL!
RRRRRRRRR

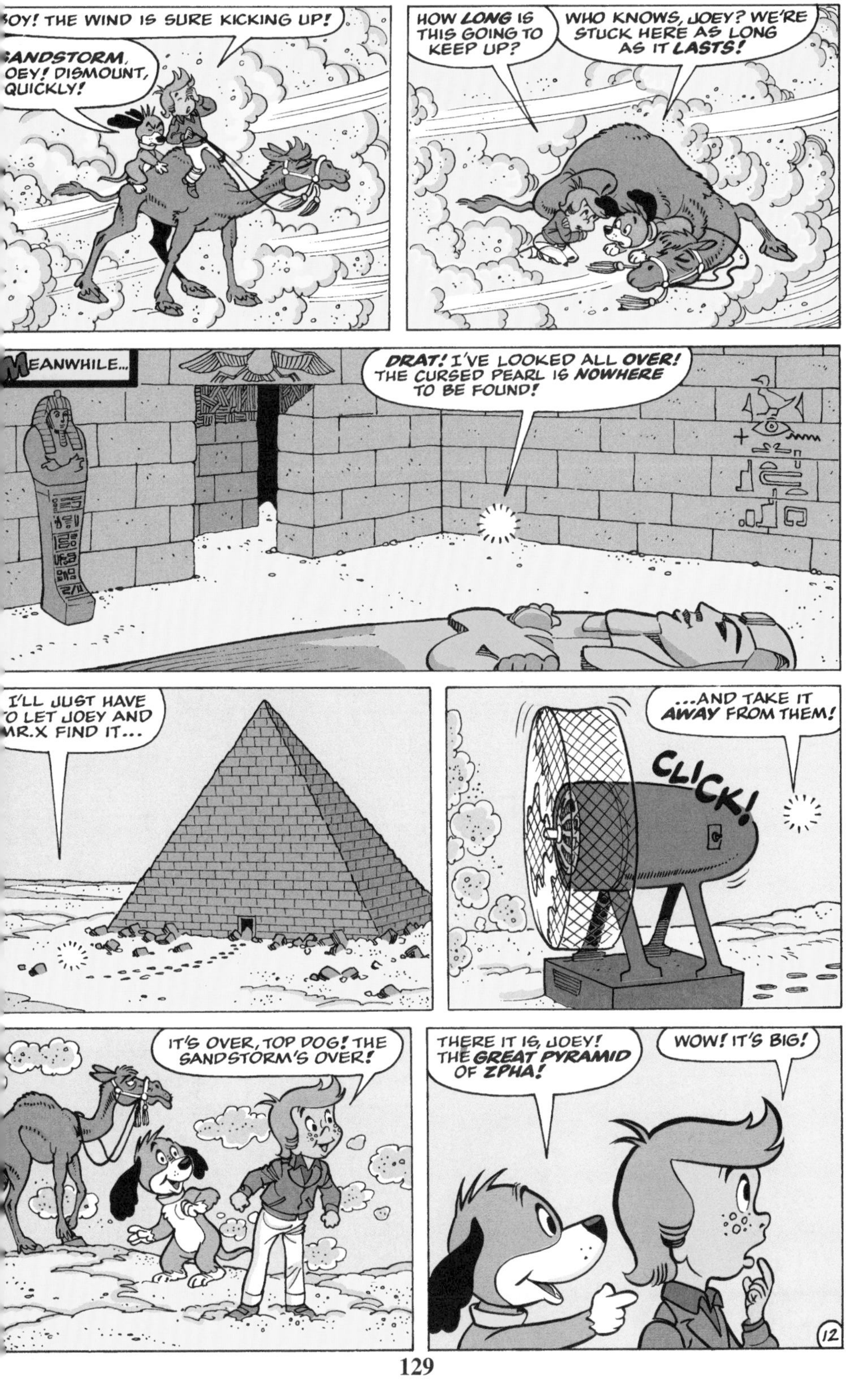
BOY! THE WIND IS SURE KICKING UP!
SANDSTORM, JOEY! DISMOUNT, QUICKLY!
HOW LONG IS THIS GOING TO KEEP UP?
WHO KNOWS, JOEY? WE'RE STUCK HERE AS LONG AS IT LASTS!
MEANWHILE...
DRAT! I'VE LOOKED ALL OVER! THE CURSED PEARL IS NOWHERE TO BE FOUND!
I'LL JUST HAVE TO LET JOEY AND MR.X FIND IT...
...AND TAKE IT AWAY FROM THEM!
CLICK!
IT'S OVER, TOP DOG! THE SANDSTORM'S OVER!
THERE IT IS, JOEY! THE GREAT PYRAMID OF ZPHA!
WOW! IT'S BIG!
12

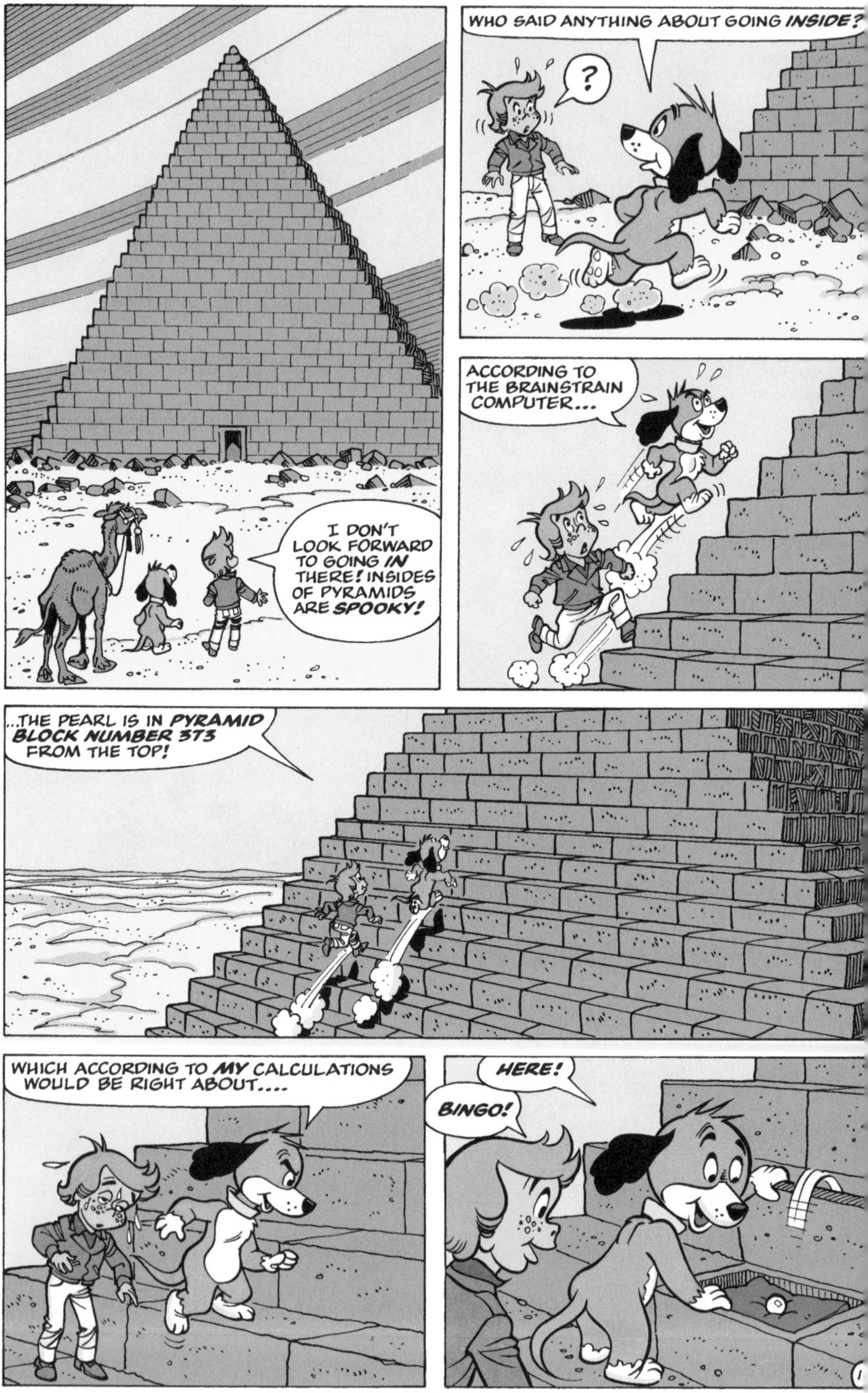
I DON'T LOOK FORWARD TO GOING IN THERE! INSIDES OF PYRAMIDS ARE SPOOKY!
WHO SAID ANYTHING ABOUT GOING INSIDE?
?
ACCORDING TO THE BRAINSTRAIN COMPUTER...
...THE PEARL IS IN PYRAMID BLOCK NUMBER 373 FROM THE TOP!
WHICH ACCORDING TO MY CALCULATIONS WOULD BE RIGHT ABOUT....
HERE!
BINGO!

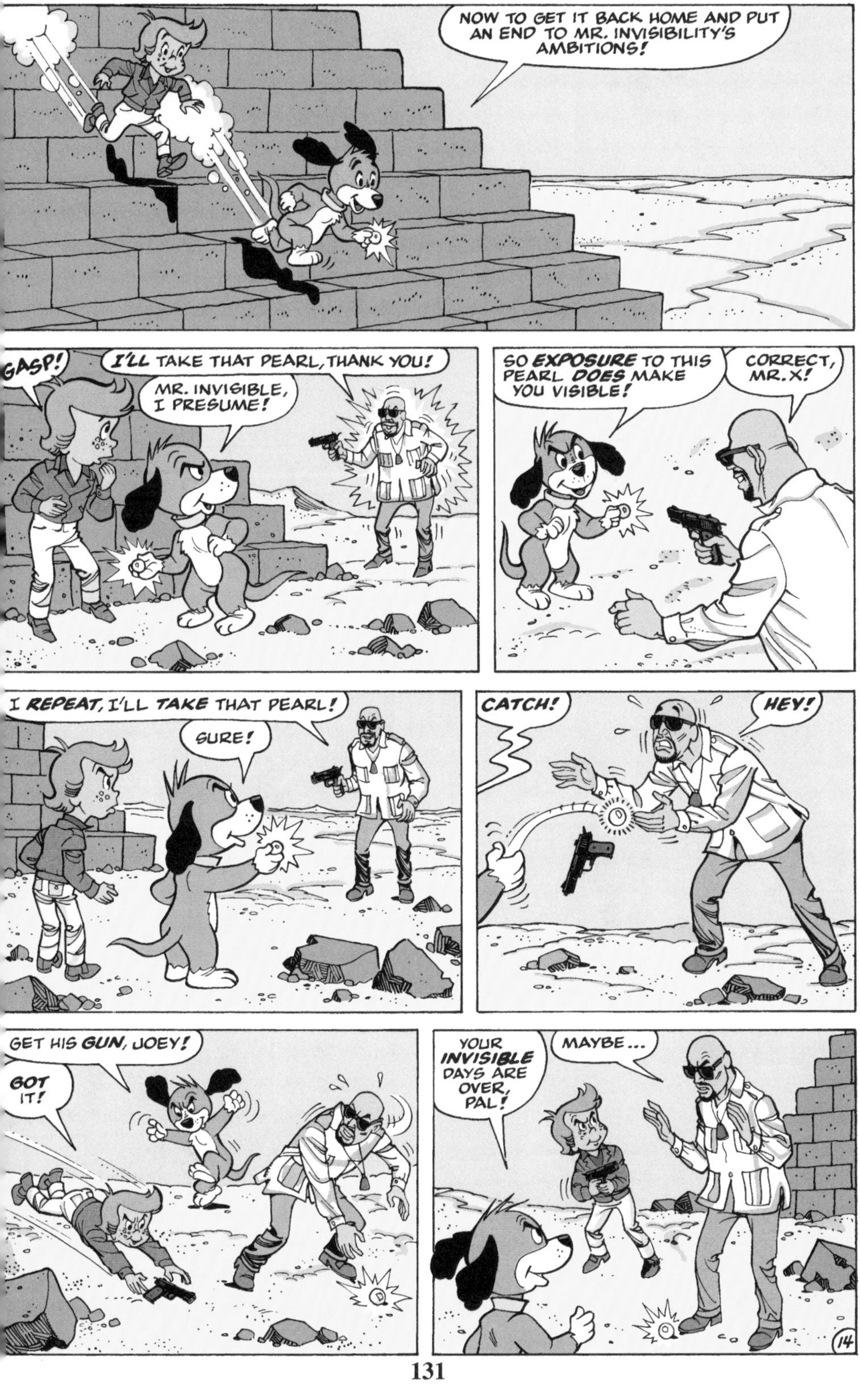
NOW TO GET IT BACK HOME AND PUT AN END TO MR. INVISIBILITY'S AMBITIONS!
GASP!
I'LL TAKE THAT PEARL, THANK YOU!
MR. INVISIBLE, I PRESUME!
SO EXPOSURE TO THIS PEARL DOES MAKE YOU VISIBLE!
CORRECT, MR. X!
I REPEAT, I'LL TAKE THAT PEARL!
SURE!
CATCH!
HEY!
GET HIS GUN, JOEY!
GOT IT!
YOUR INVISIBLE DAYS ARE OVER, PAL!
MAYBE...
14

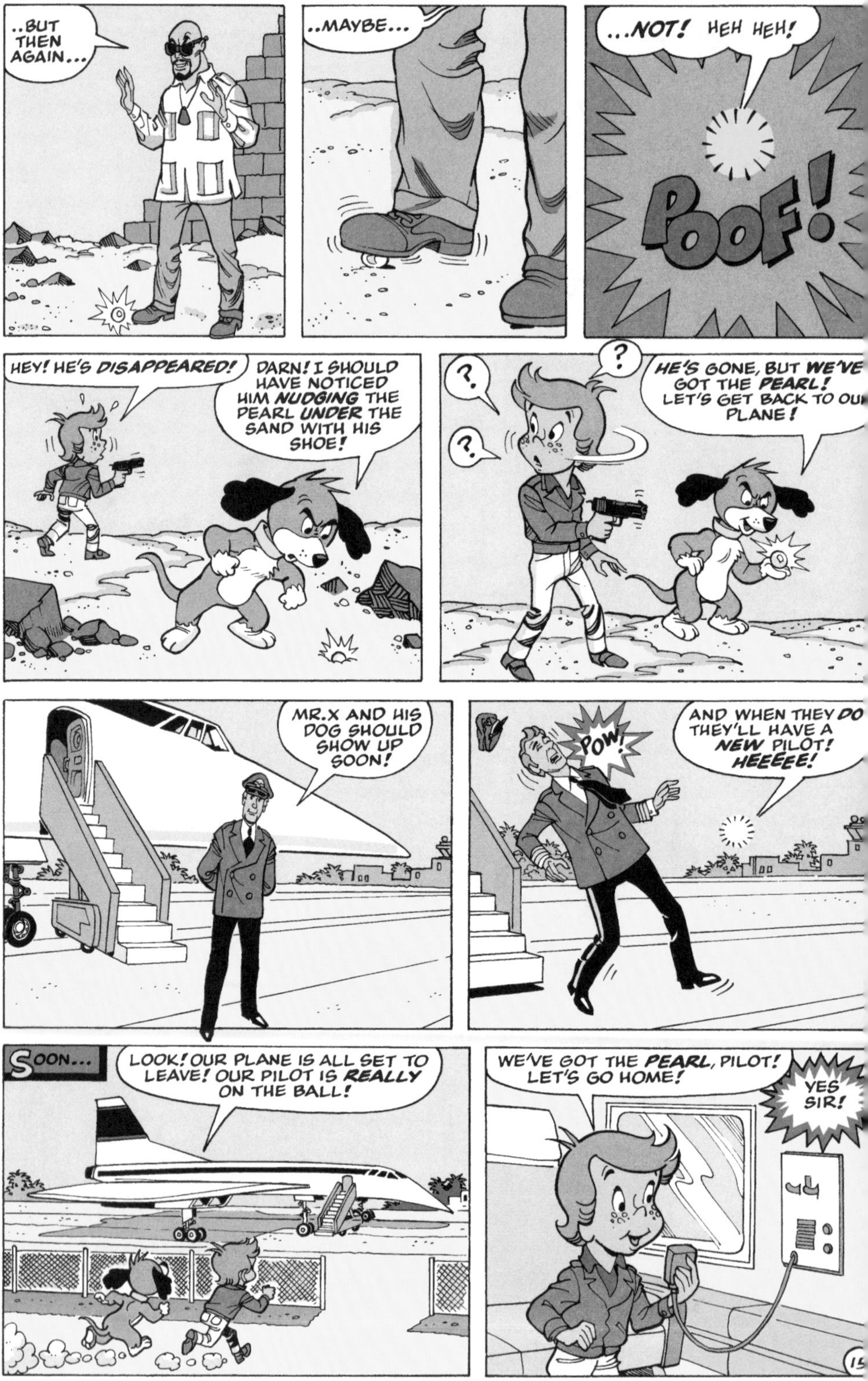
..BUT THEN AGAIN...
..MAYBE...
...NOT! HEH HEH!
POOF!
HEY! HE'S DISAPPEARED!
DARN! I SHOULD HAVE NOTICED HIM NUDGING THE PEARL UNDER THE SAND WITH HIS SHOE!
?
?
?
HE'S GONE, BUT WE'VE GOT THE PEARL! LET'S GET BACK TO OU PLANE!
MR.X AND HIS DOG SHOULD SHOW UP SOON!
POW!
AND WHEN THEY DO THEY'LL HAVE A NEW PILOT! HEEEEE!
SOON...
LOOK! OUR PLANE IS ALL SET TO LEAVE! OUR PILOT IS REALLY ON THE BALL!
WE'VE GOT THE PEARL, PILOT! LET'S GO HOME!
YES SIR!

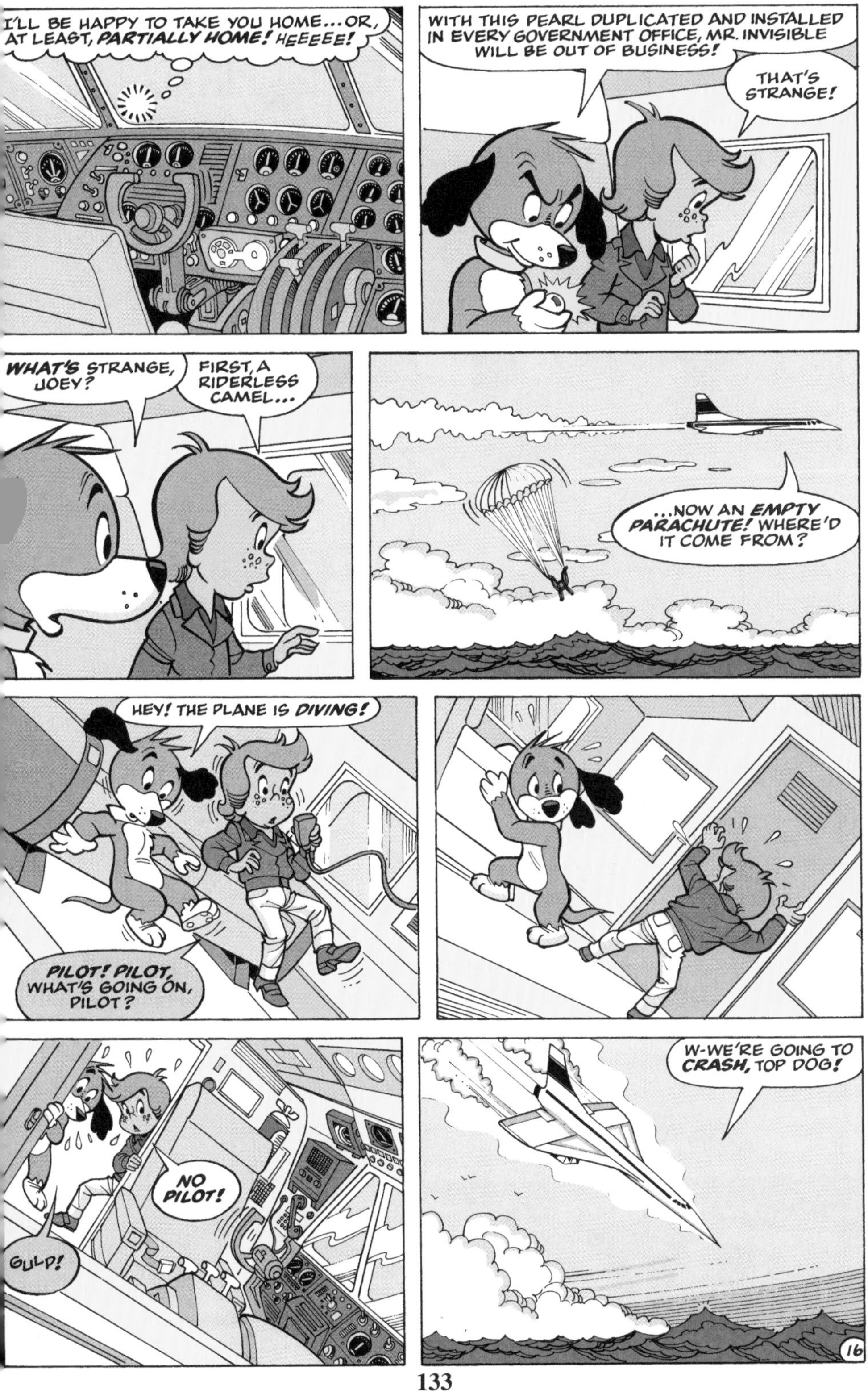
I'LL BE HAPPY TO TAKE YOU HOME...OR, AT LEAST, PARTIALLY HOME! HEEEEE!
WITH THIS PEARL DUPLICATED AND INSTALLED IN EVERY GOVERNMENT OFFICE, MR. INVISIBLE WILL BE OUT OF BUSINESS!
THAT'S STRANGE!
WHAT'S STRANGE, JOEY?
FIRST, A RIDERLESS CAMEL...
...NOW AN EMPTY PARACHUTE! WHERE'D IT COME FROM?
HEY! THE PLANE IS DIVING!
PILOT! PILOT, WHAT'S GOING ON, PILOT?
NO PILOT!
GULP!
W-WE'RE GOING TO CRASH, TOP DOG!
16

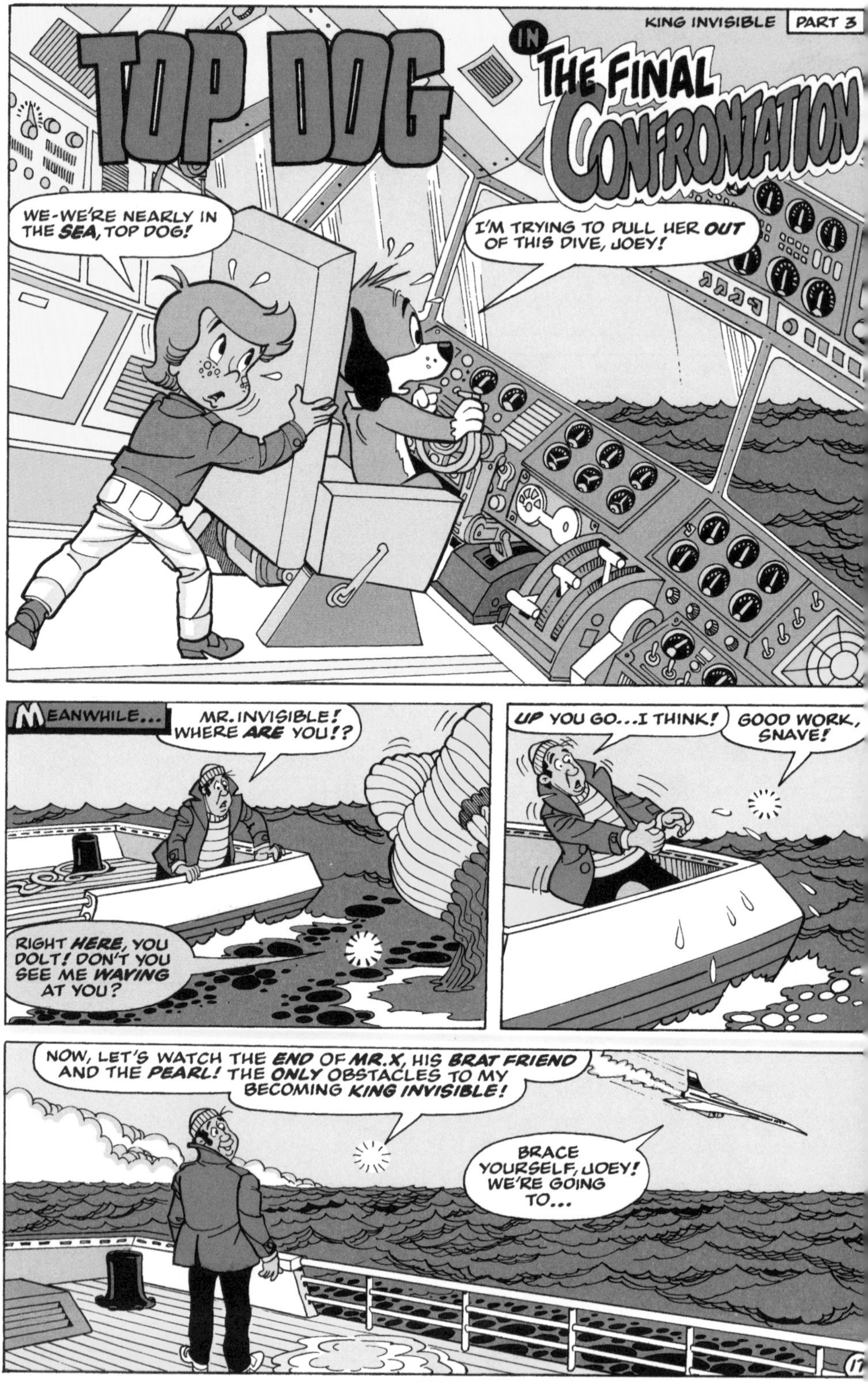
KING INVISIBLE | PART 3
TOP DOG IN THE FINAL CONFRONTATION
WE-WE'RE NEARLY IN THE SEA, TOP DOG!
I'M TRYING TO PULL HER OUT OF THIS DIVE, JOEY!
MEANWHILE...
MR. INVISIBLE! WHERE ARE YOU!?
RIGHT HERE, YOU DOLT! DON'T YOU SEE ME WAVING AT YOU?
UP YOU GO...I THINK!
GOOD WORK, SNAVE!
NOW, LET'S WATCH THE END OF MR. X, HIS BRAT FRIEND AND THE PEARL! THE ONLY OBSTACLES TO MY BECOMING KING INVISIBLE!
BRACE YOURSELF, JOEY! WE'RE GOING TO...
17

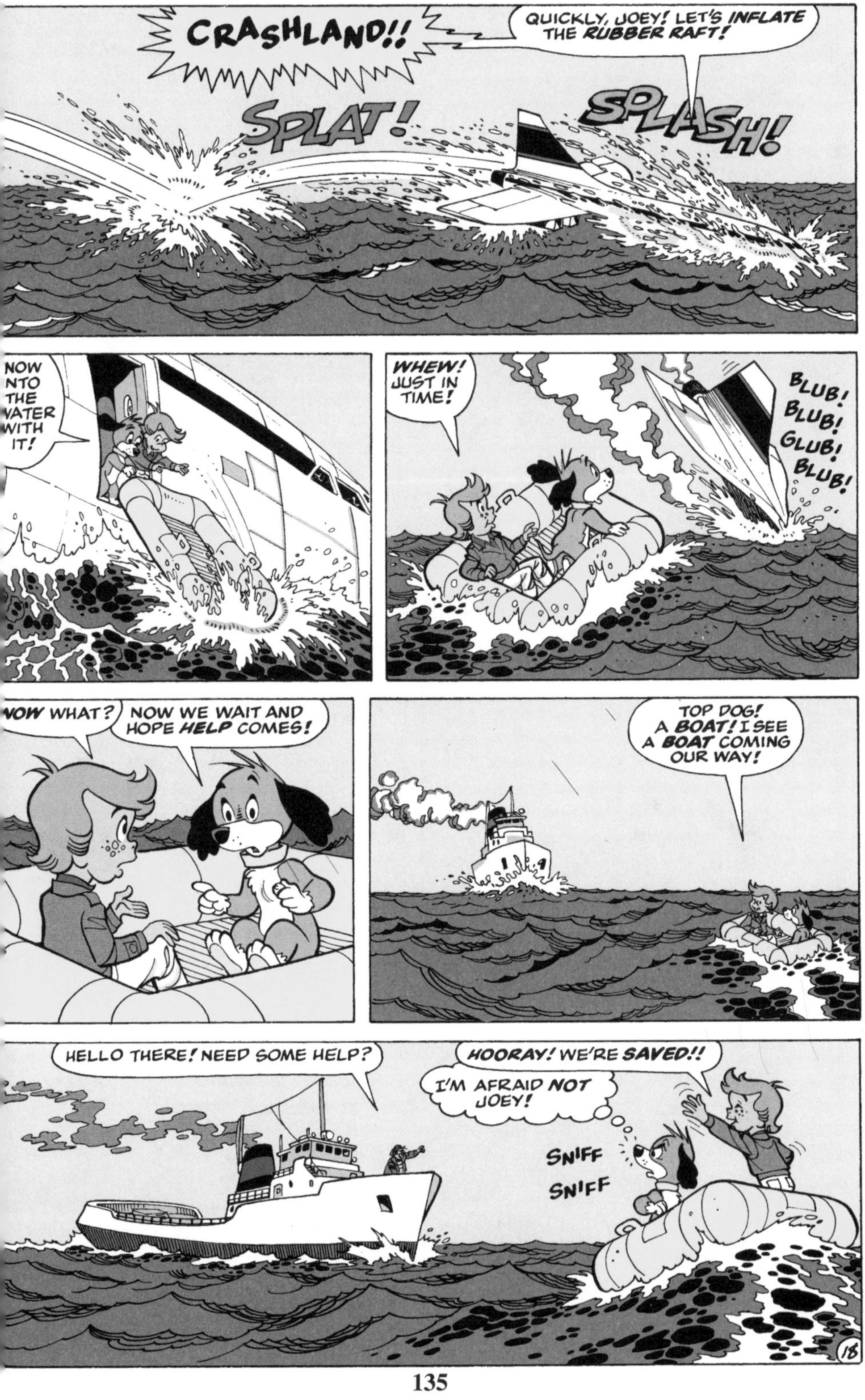
CRASHLAND!!
QUICKLY, JOEY! LET'S INFLATE THE RUBBER RAFT!
SPLAT!
SPLASH!
NOW NTO THE VATER WITH IT!
WHEW! JUST IN TIME!
BLUB! BLUB! GLUB! BLUB!
NOW WHAT?
NOW WE WAIT AND HOPE HELP COMES!
TOP DOG! A BOAT! I SEE A BOAT COMING OUR WAY!
HELLO THERE! NEED SOME HELP?
HOORAY! WE'RE SAVED!!
I'M AFRAID NOT JOEY!
SNIFF
SNIFF
18

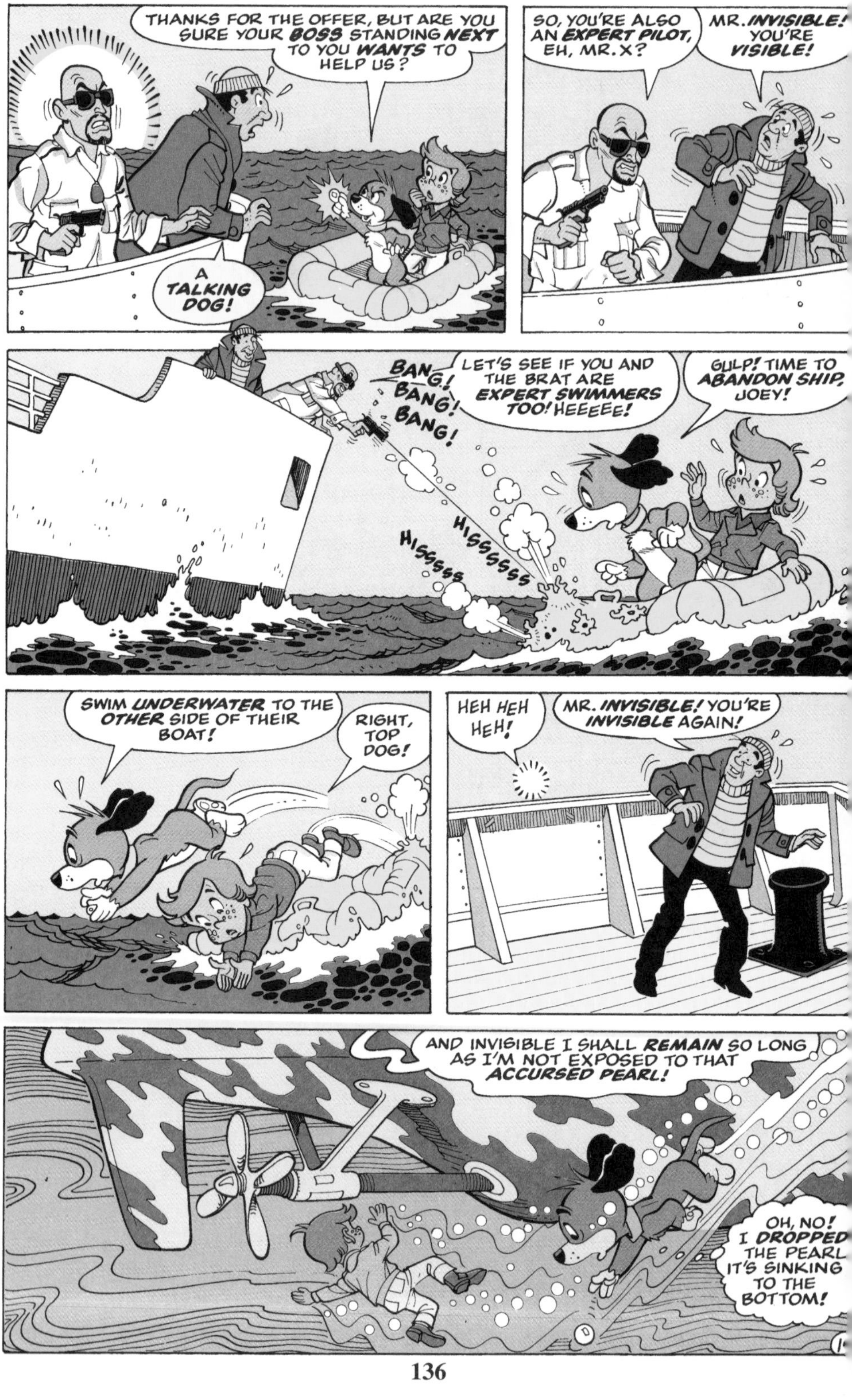
THANKS FOR THE OFFER, BUT ARE YOU SURE YOUR BOSS STANDING NEXT TO YOU WANTS TO HELP US?
A TALKING DOG!
SO, YOU'RE ALSO AN EXPERT PILOT, EH, MR. X?
MR. INVISIBLE! YOU'RE VISIBLE!
BANG! BANG! BANG!
LET'S SEE IF YOU AND THE BRAT ARE EXPERT SWIMMERS TOO! HEEEEEE!
GULP! TIME TO ABANDON SHIP, JOEY!
HISSSSSSS
HISSSSSS
SWIM UNDERWATER TO THE OTHER SIDE OF THEIR BOAT!
RIGHT, TOP DOG!
HEH HEH HEH!
MR. INVISIBLE! YOU'RE INVISIBLE AGAIN!
AND INVISIBLE I SHALL REMAIN SO LONG AS I'M NOT EXPOSED TO THAT ACCURSED PEARL!
OH, NO! I DROPPED THE PEARL IT'S SINKING TO THE BOTTOM!

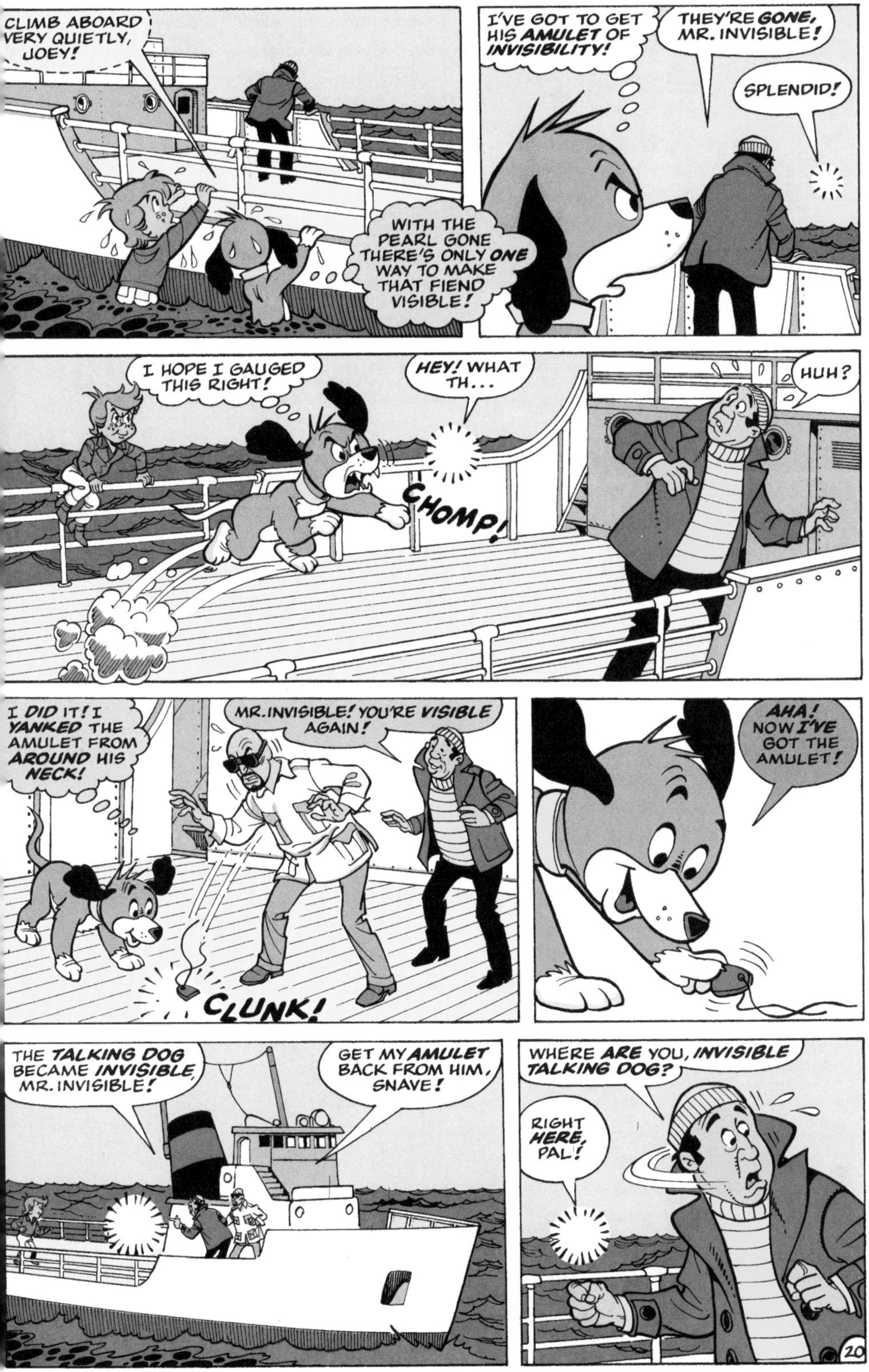

CLIMB ABOARD VERY QUIETLY, JOEY!
I'VE GOT TO GET HIS AMULET OF INVISIBILITY!
THEY'RE GONE, MR. INVISIBLE!
SPLENDID!
WITH THE PEARL GONE THERE'S ONLY ONE WAY TO MAKE THAT FIEND VISIBLE!
I HOPE I GAUGED THIS RIGHT!
HEY! WHAT TH...
HUH?
CHOMP!
I DID IT! I YANKED THE AMULET FROM AROUND HIS NECK!
MR. INVISIBLE! YOU'RE VISIBLE AGAIN!
CLUNK!
AHA! NOW I'VE GOT THE AMULET!
THE TALKING DOG BECAME INVISIBLE, MR. INVISIBLE!
GET MY AMULET BACK FROM HIM, SNAVE!
WHERE ARE YOU, INVISIBLE TALKING DOG?
RIGHT HERE, PAL!
20

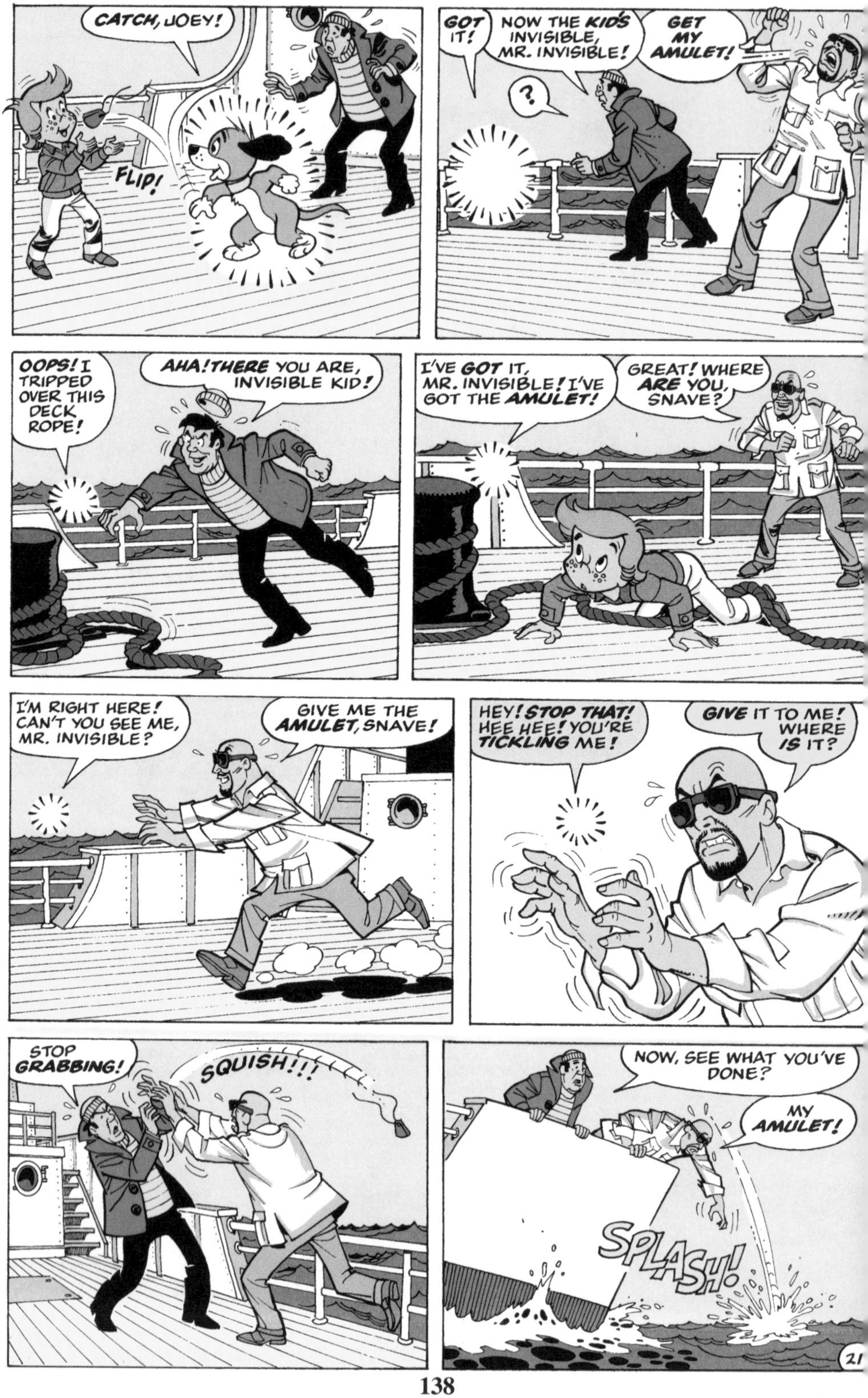
CATCH, JOEY!
FLIP!
GOT IT!
NOW THE KID'S INVISIBLE, MR. INVISIBLE!
GET MY AMULET!
?
OOPS! I TRIPPED OVER THIS DECK ROPE!
AHA! THERE YOU ARE, INVISIBLE KID!
I'VE GOT IT, MR. INVISIBLE! I'VE GOT THE AMULET!
GREAT! WHERE ARE YOU, SNAVE?
I'M RIGHT HERE! CAN'T YOU SEE ME, MR. INVISIBLE?
GIVE ME THE AMULET, SNAVE!
HEY! STOP THAT! HEE HEE! YOU'RE TICKLING ME!
GIVE IT TO ME! WHERE IS IT?
STOP GRABBING!
SQUISH!!!
NOW, SEE WHAT YOU'VE DONE?
MY AMULET!
SPLASH!
21

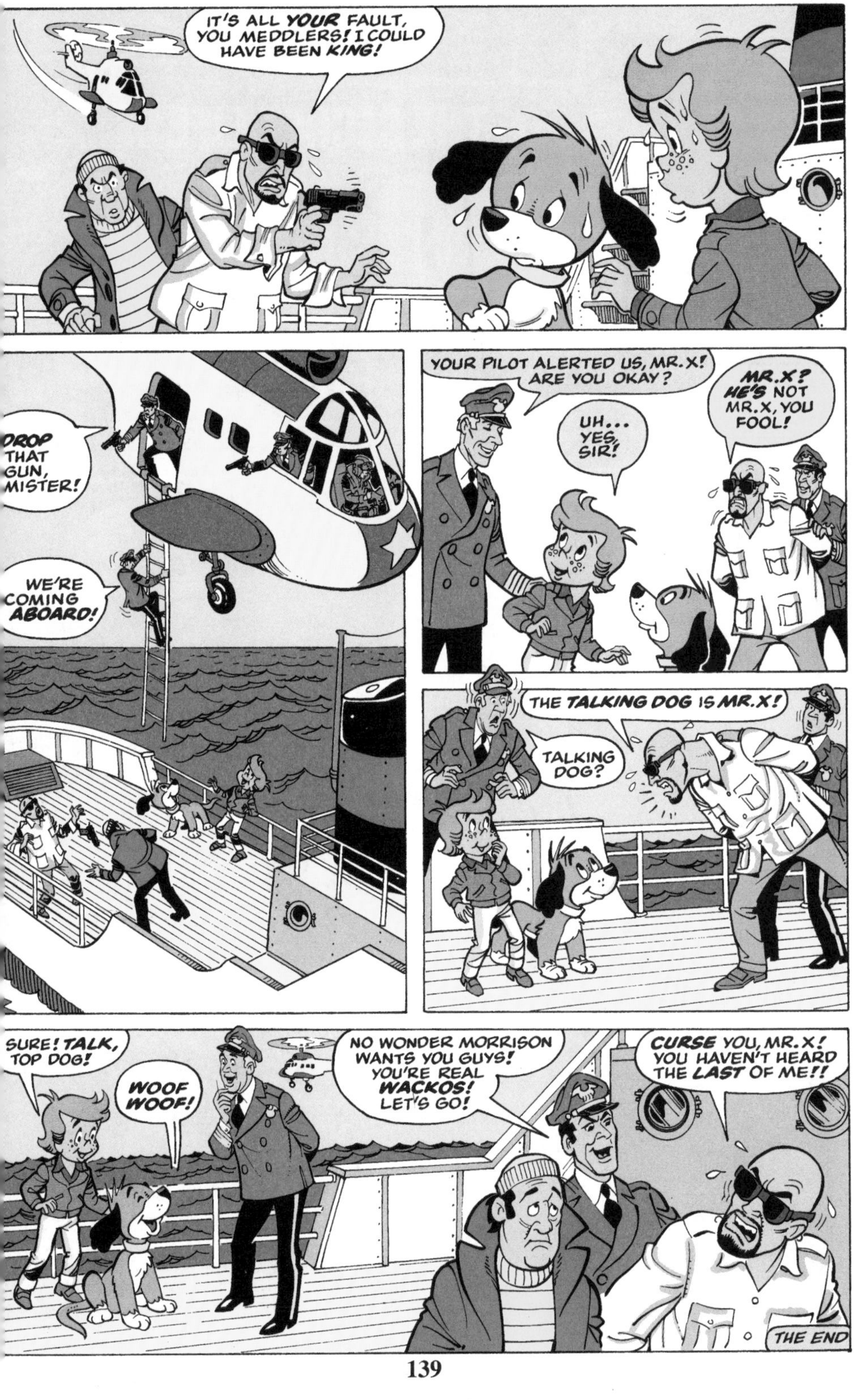

IT'S ALL YOUR FAULT, YOU MEDDLERS! I COULD HAVE BEEN KING!
DROP THAT GUN, MISTER!
WE'RE COMING ABOARD!
YOUR PILOT ALERTED US, MR. X! ARE YOU OKAY?
UH... YES, SIR!
MR. X? HE'S NOT MR. X, YOU FOOL!
THE TALKING DOG IS MR. X!
TALKING DOG?
SURE! TALK, TOP DOG!
WOOF WOOF!
NO WONDER MORRISON WANTS YOU GUYS! YOU'RE REAL WACKOS! LET'S GO!
CURSE YOU, MR. X! YOU HAVEN'T HEARD THE LAST OF ME!!
THE END

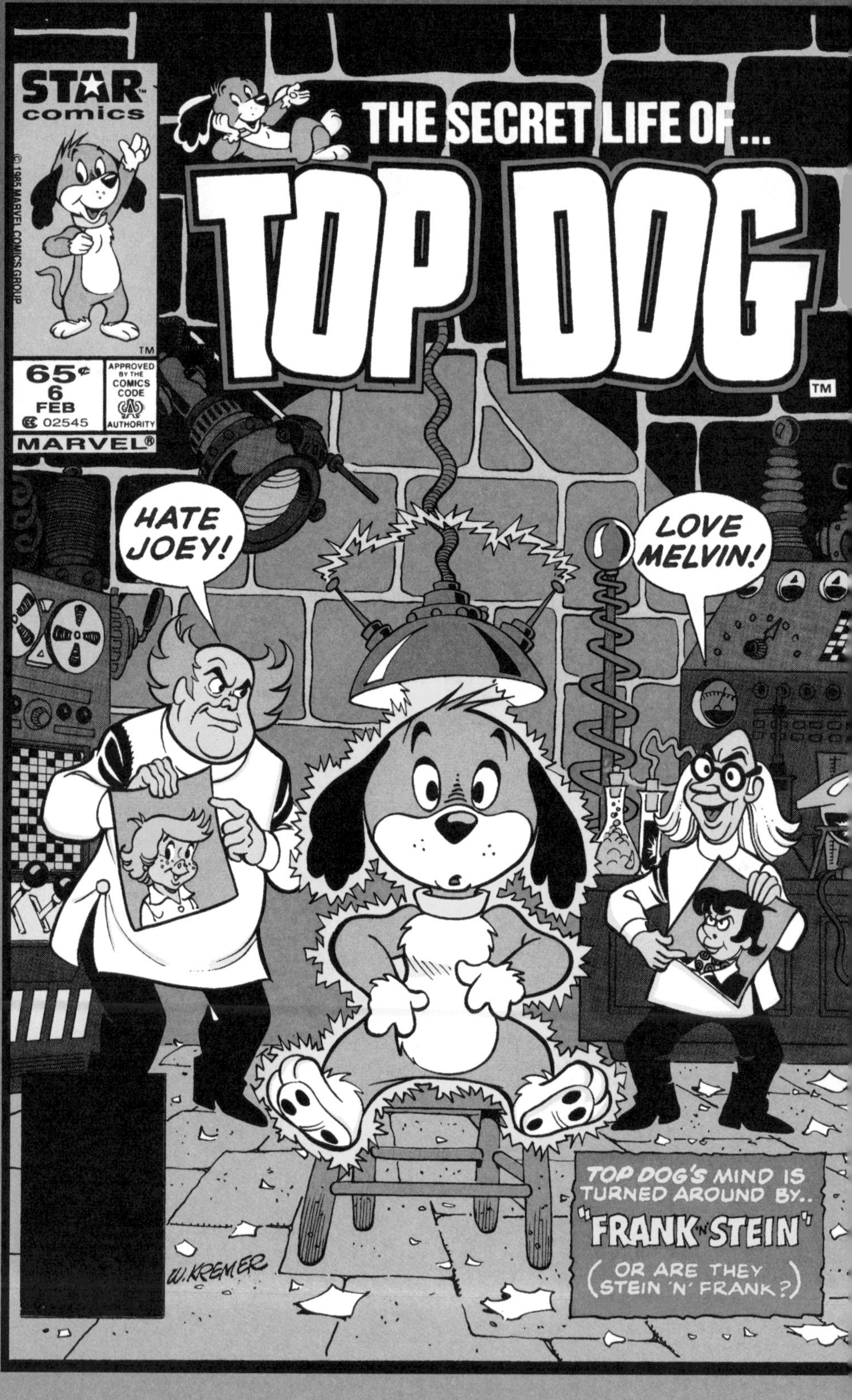
STAR comics
© 1985 MARVEL COMICS GROUP
THE SECRET LIFE OF...
TOP DOG
65¢
6
FEB
02545
APPROVED BY THE COMICS CODE AUTHORITY
MARVEL®
HATE JOEY!
LOVE MELVIN!
W. KREMER
TOP DOG'S MIND IS TURNED AROUND BY..
"FRANK 'N' STEIN"
(OR ARE THEY STEIN 'N' FRANK?)

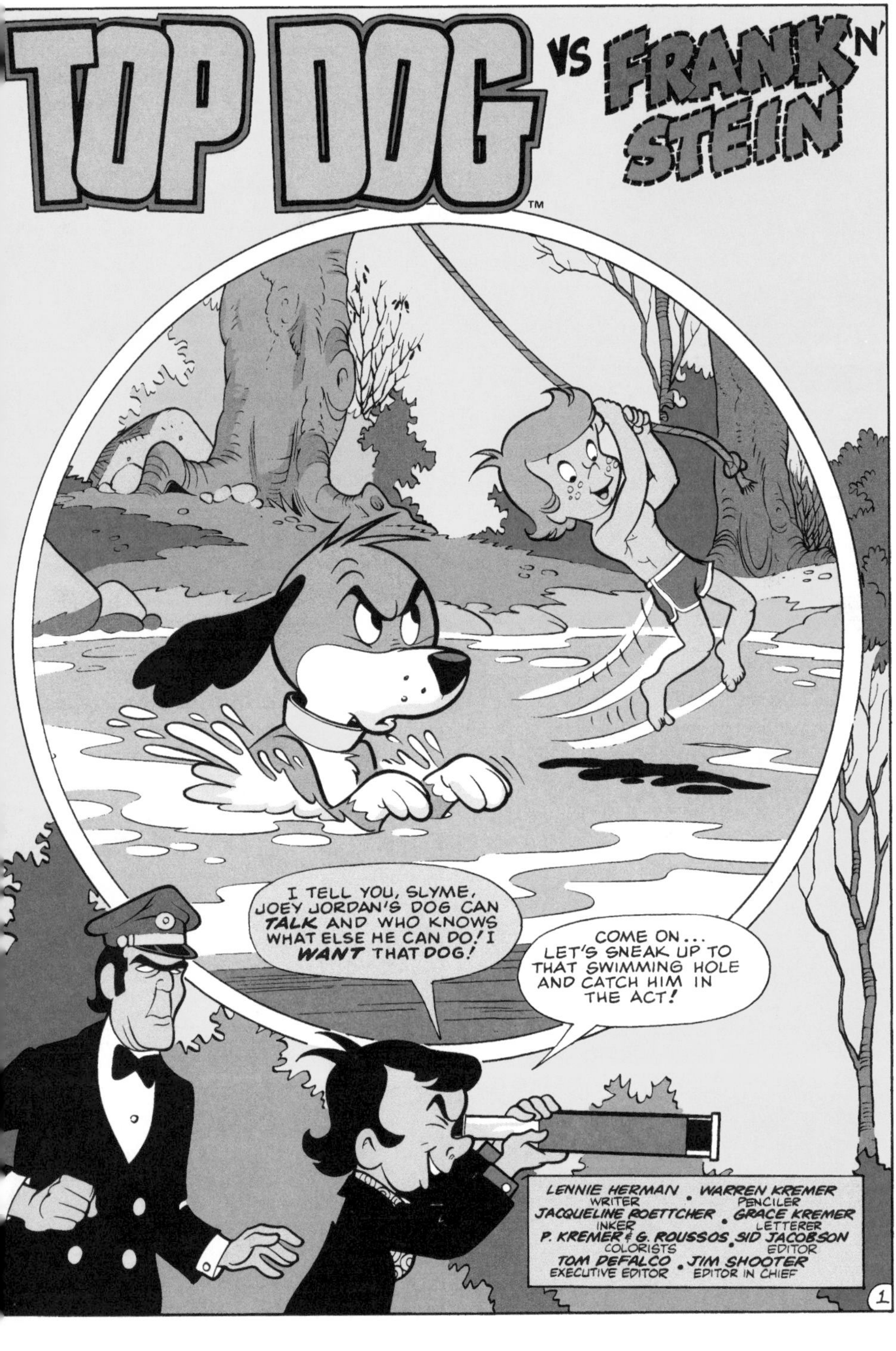
TOP DOG VS FRANK 'N' STEIN
I TELL YOU, SLYME, JOEY JORDAN'S DOG CAN TALK AND WHO KNOWS WHAT ELSE HE CAN DO! I WANT THAT DOG!
COME ON... LET'S SNEAK UP TO THAT SWIMMING HOLE AND CATCH HIM IN THE ACT!
LENNIE HERMAN WRITER • WARREN KREMER PENCILER
JACQUELINE ROETTCHER INKER • GRACE KREMER LETTERER
P. KREMER & G. ROUSSOS COLORISTS • SID JACOBSON EDITOR
TOM DEFALCO EXECUTIVE EDITOR • JIM SHOOTER EDITOR IN CHIEF
1

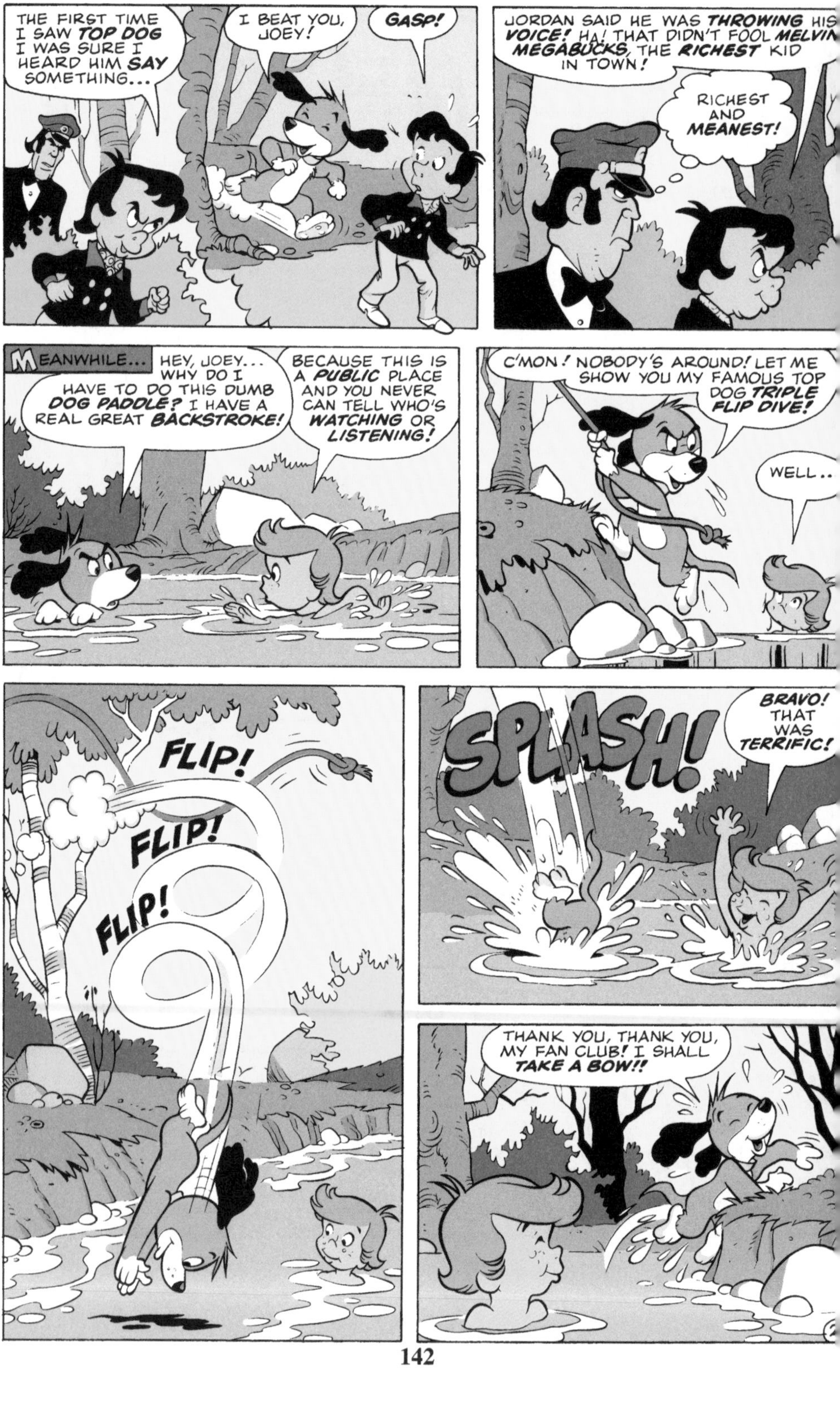
THE FIRST TIME I SAW TOP DOG I WAS SURE I HEARD HIM SAY SOMETHING...
I BEAT YOU, JOEY!
GASP!
JORDAN SAID HE WAS THROWING HIS VOICE! HA! THAT DIDN'T FOOL MELVIN MEGABUCKS, THE RICHEST KID IN TOWN!
RICHEST AND MEANEST!
MEANWHILE...
HEY, JOEY... WHY DO I HAVE TO DO THIS DUMB DOG PADDLE? I HAVE A REAL GREAT BACKSTROKE!
BECAUSE THIS IS A PUBLIC PLACE AND YOU NEVER CAN TELL WHO'S WATCHING OR LISTENING!
C'MON! NOBODY'S AROUND! LET ME SHOW YOU MY FAMOUS TOP DOG TRIPLE FLIP DIVE!
WELL...
FLIP!
FLIP!
FLIP!
SPLASH!
BRAVO! THAT WAS TERRIFIC!
THANK YOU, THANK YOU, MY FAN CLUB! I SHALL TAKE A BOW!!

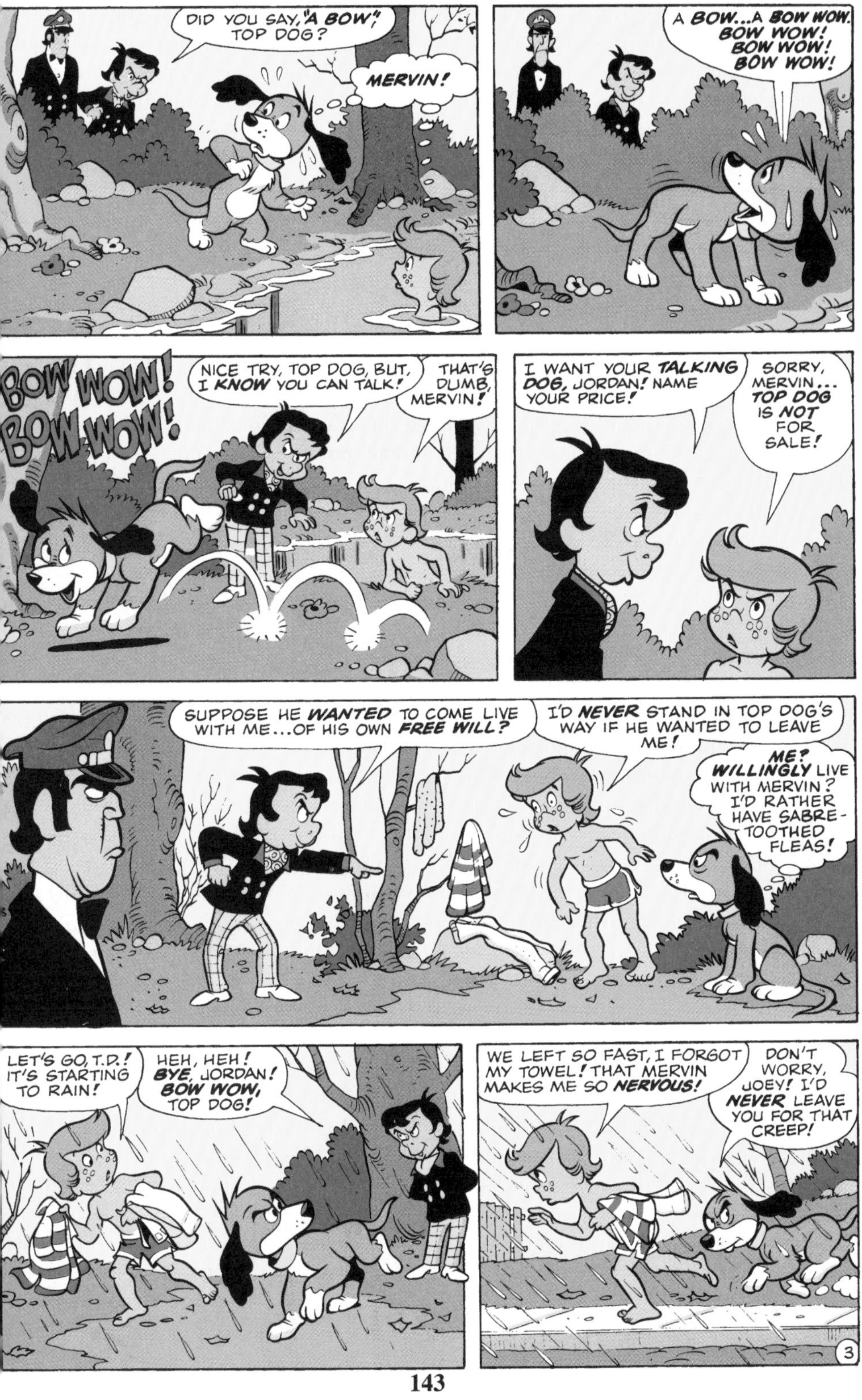
DID YOU SAY, "A BOW", TOP DOG?
MERVIN!
A BOW...A BOW WOW. BOW WOW! BOW WOW! BOW WOW!
BOW WOW! BOW WOW!
NICE TRY, TOP DOG, BUT, I KNOW YOU CAN TALK!
THAT'S DUMB, MERVIN!
I WANT YOUR TALKING DOG, JORDAN! NAME YOUR PRICE!
SORRY, MERVIN... TOP DOG IS NOT FOR SALE!
SUPPOSE HE WANTED TO COME LIVE WITH ME...OF HIS OWN FREE WILL?
I'D NEVER STAND IN TOP DOG'S WAY IF HE WANTED TO LEAVE ME!
ME? WILLINGLY LIVE WITH MERVIN? I'D RATHER HAVE SABRE-TOOTHED FLEAS!
LET'S GO, T.D.! IT'S STARTING TO RAIN!
HEH, HEH! BYE, JORDAN! BOW WOW, TOP DOG!
WE LEFT SO FAST, I FORGOT MY TOWEL! THAT MERVIN MAKES ME SO NERVOUS!
DON'T WORRY, JOEY! I'D NEVER LEAVE YOU FOR THAT CREEP!
3

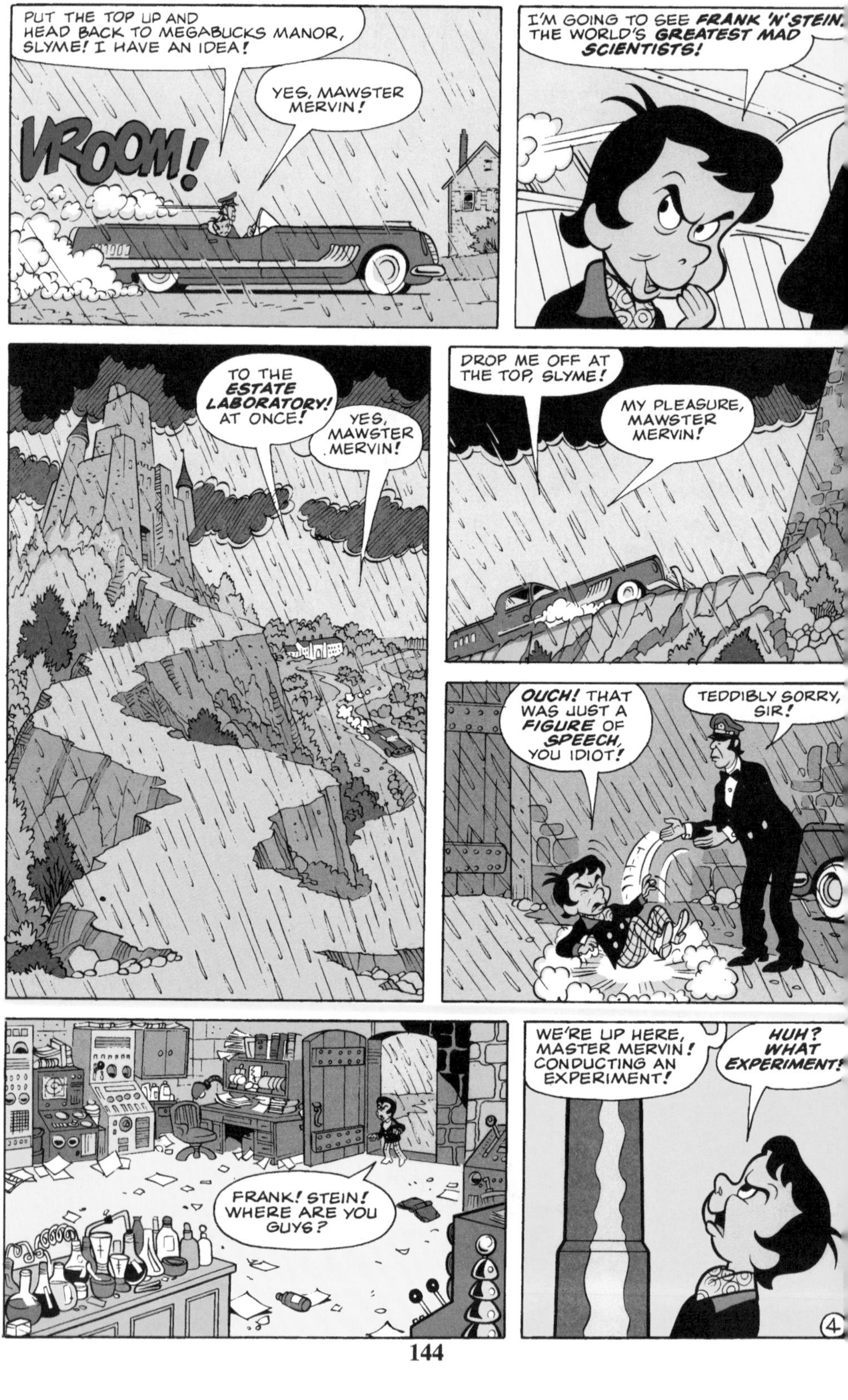
PUT THE TOP UP AND HEAD BACK TO MEGABUCKS MANOR, SLYME! I HAVE AN IDEA!
YES, MAWSTER MERVIN!
VROOM!
I'M GOING TO SEE FRANK 'N' STEIN, THE WORLD'S GREATEST MAD SCIENTISTS!
TO THE ESTATE LABORATORY! AT ONCE!
YES, MAWSTER MERVIN!
DROP ME OFF AT THE TOP, SLYME!
MY PLEASURE, MAWSTER MERVIN!
OUCH! THAT WAS JUST A FIGURE OF SPEECH, YOU IDIOT!
TEDDIBLY SORRY, SIR!
FRANK! STEIN! WHERE ARE YOU GUYS?
WE'RE UP HERE, MASTER MERVIN! CONDUCTING AN EXPERIMENT!
HUH? WHAT EXPERIMENT!
4

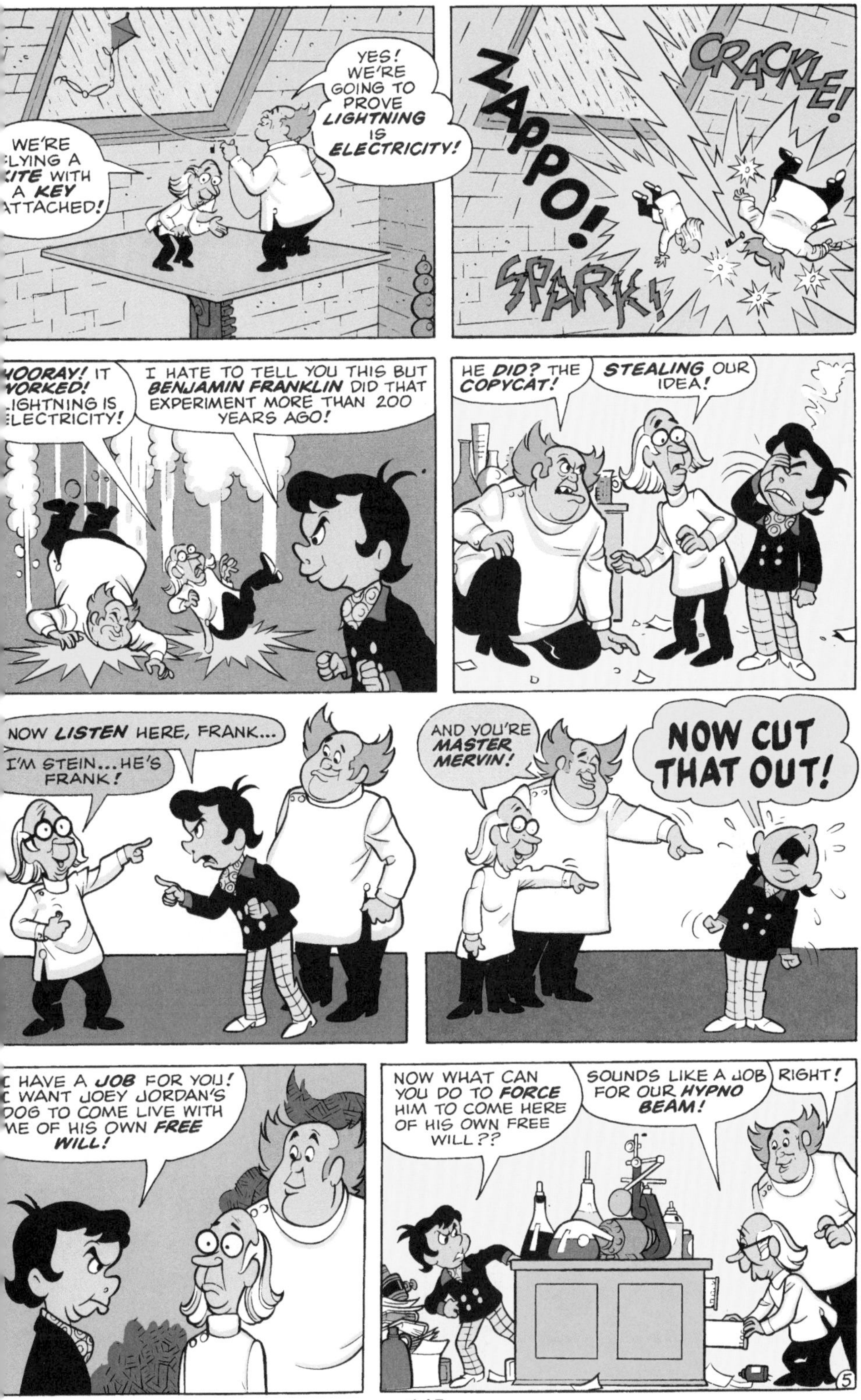

WE'RE
FLYING A
KITE WITH
A KEY
ATTACHED!
YES! WE'RE GOING TO PROVE LIGHTNING IS ELECTRICITY!
ZAPPO!
CRACKLE!
SPARK!
HOORAY! IT WORKED! LIGHTNING IS ELECTRICITY!
I HATE TO TELL YOU THIS BUT BENJAMIN FRANKLIN DID THAT EXPERIMENT MORE THAN 200 YEARS AGO!
HE DID? THE COPYCAT!
STEALING OUR IDEA!
NOW LISTEN HERE, FRANK...
I'M STEIN...HE'S FRANK!
AND YOU'RE MASTER MERVIN!
NOW CUT THAT OUT!
I HAVE A JOB FOR YOU! I WANT JOEY JORDAN'S DOG TO COME LIVE WITH ME OF HIS OWN FREE WILL!
NOW WHAT CAN YOU DO TO FORCE HIM TO COME HERE OF HIS OWN FREE WILL??
SOUNDS LIKE A JOB FOR OUR HYPNO BEAM!
RIGHT!
5

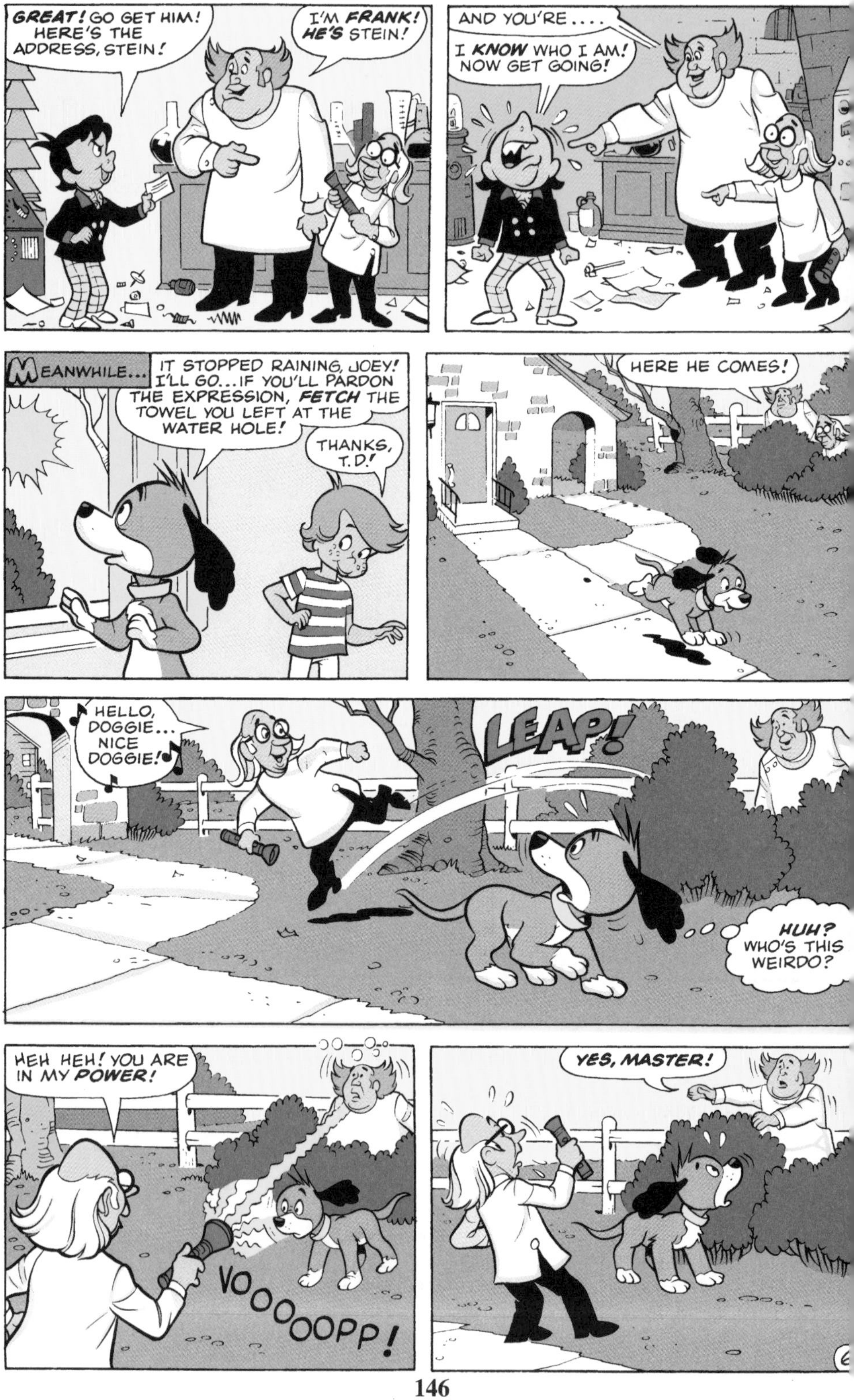

GREAT! GO GET HIM! HERE'S THE ADDRESS, STEIN!
I'M FRANK! HE'S STEIN!
AND YOU'RE....
I KNOW WHO I AM! NOW GET GOING!
MEANWHILE...
IT STOPPED RAINING, JOEY! I'LL GO...IF YOU'LL PARDON THE EXPRESSION, FETCH THE TOWEL YOU LEFT AT THE WATER HOLE!
THANKS, T.D.!
HERE HE COMES!
HELLO, DOGGIE... NICE DOGGIE!
LEAP!
HUH? WHO'S THIS WEIRDO?
HEH HEH! YOU ARE IN MY POWER!
VOOOOOPP!
YES, MASTER!

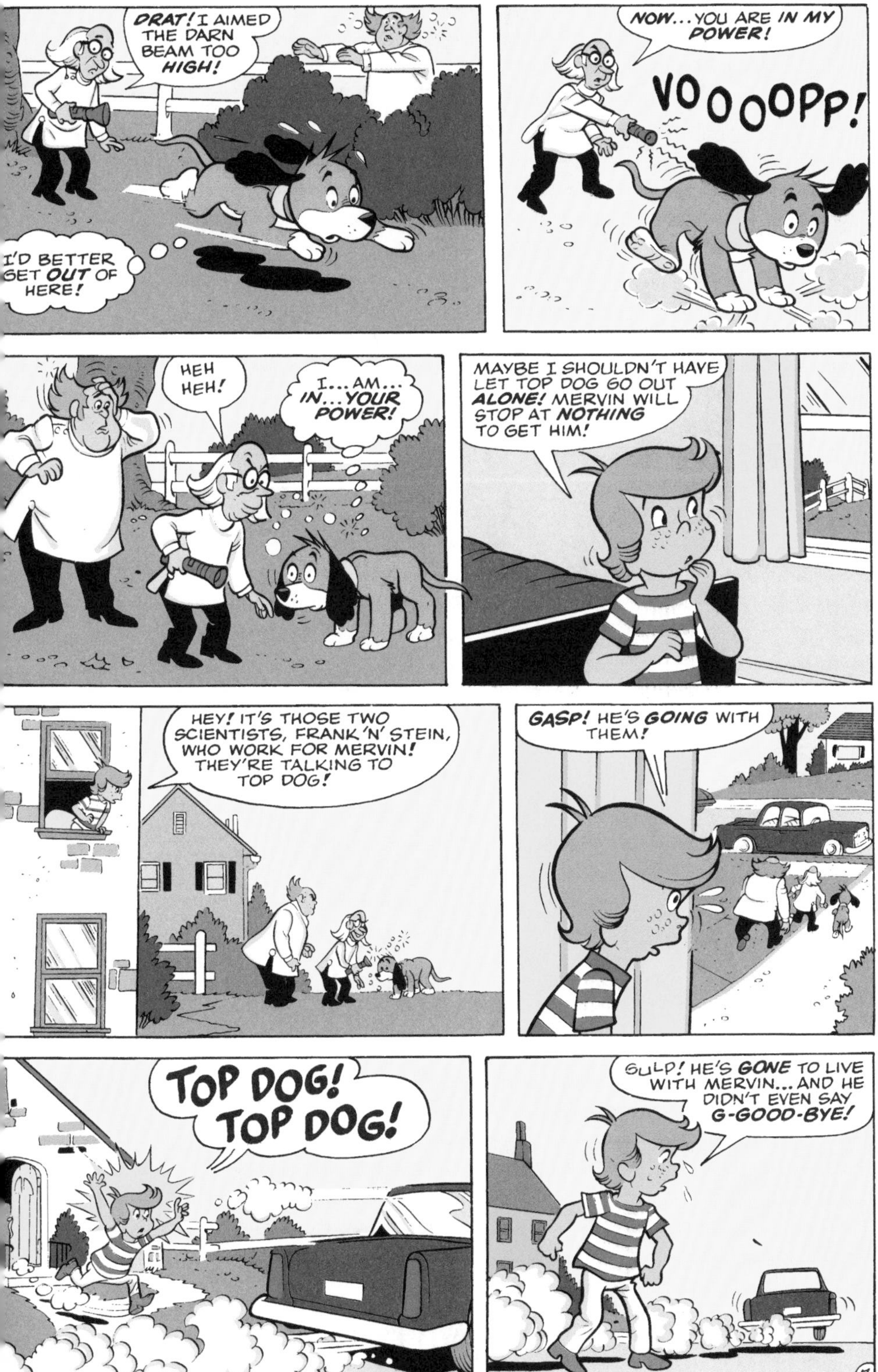

DRAT! I AIMED THE DARN BEAM TOO HIGH!
I'D BETTER GET OUT OF HERE!
NOW... YOU ARE IN MY POWER!
VOOOOPP!
HEH HEH!
I... AM... IN... YOUR POWER!
MAYBE I SHOULDN'T HAVE LET TOP DOG GO OUT ALONE! MERVIN WILL STOP AT NOTHING TO GET HIM!
HEY! IT'S THOSE TWO SCIENTISTS, FRANK 'N' STEIN, WHO WORK FOR MERVIN! THEY'RE TALKING TO TOP DOG!
GASP! HE'S GOING WITH THEM!
TOP DOG! TOP DOG!
GULP! HE'S GONE TO LIVE WITH MERVIN... AND HE DIDN'T EVEN SAY G-GOOD-BYE!
7

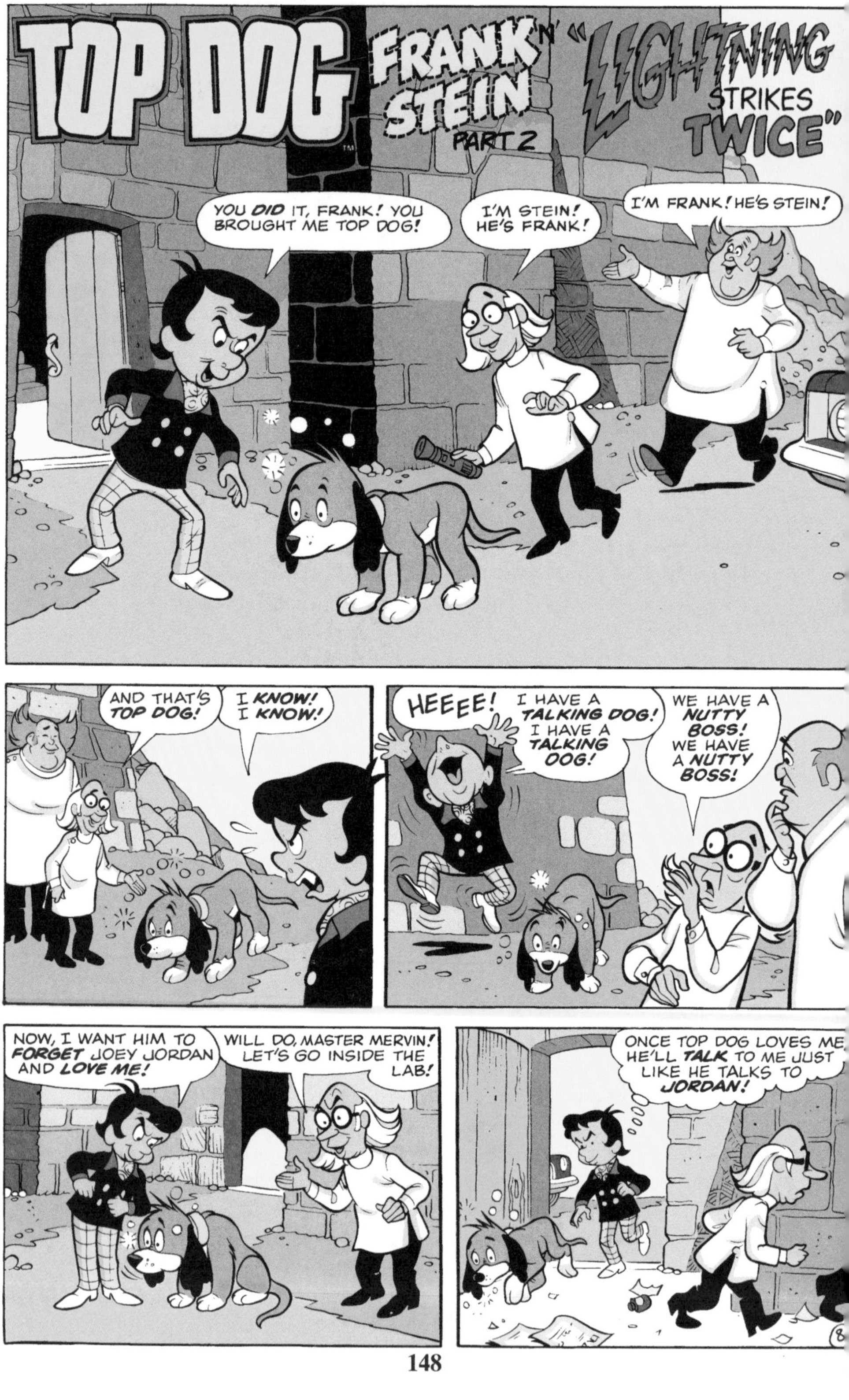
TOP DOG
FRANK N' STEIN
PART 2
"LIGHTNING STRIKES TWICE"
YOU DID IT, FRANK! YOU BROUGHT ME TOP DOG!
I'M STEIN! HE'S FRANK!
I'M FRANK! HE'S STEIN!
AND THAT'S TOP DOG!
I KNOW! I KNOW!
HEEEEE!
I HAVE A TALKING DOG! I HAVE A TALKING DOG!
WE HAVE A NUTTY BOSS! WE HAVE A NUTTY BOSS!
NOW, I WANT HIM TO FORGET JOEY JORDAN AND LOVE ME!
WILL DO, MASTER MERVIN! LET'S GO INSIDE THE LAB!
ONCE TOP DOG LOVES ME, HE'LL TALK TO ME JUST LIKE HE TALKS TO JORDAN!
8

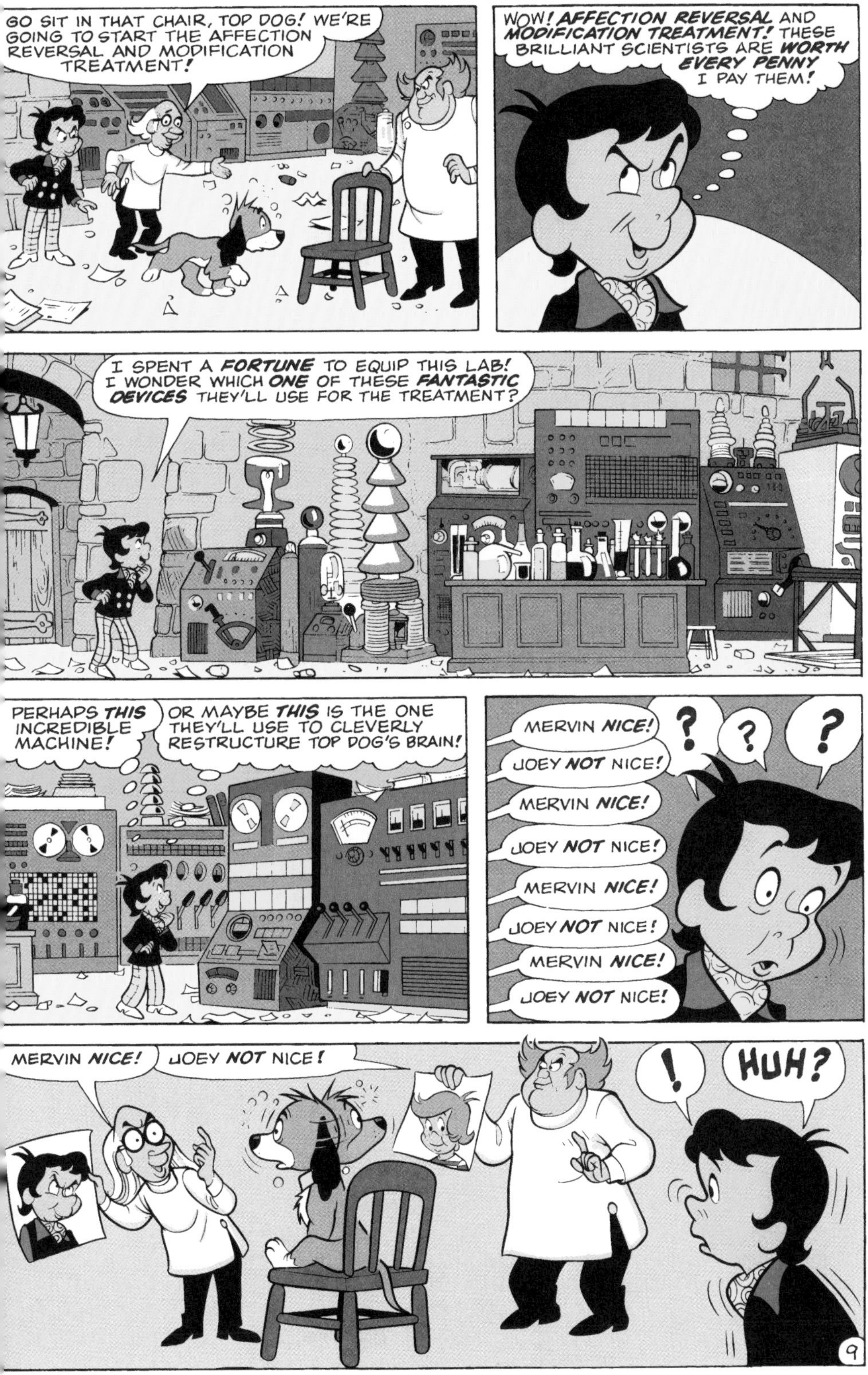
GO SIT IN THAT CHAIR, TOP DOG! WE'RE GOING TO START THE AFFECTION REVERSAL AND MODIFICATION TREATMENT!
WOW! AFFECTION REVERSAL AND MODIFICATION TREATMENT! THESE BRILLIANT SCIENTISTS ARE WORTH EVERY PENNY I PAY THEM!
I SPENT A FORTUNE TO EQUIP THIS LAB! I WONDER WHICH ONE OF THESE FANTASTIC DEVICES THEY'LL USE FOR THE TREATMENT?
PERHAPS THIS INCREDIBLE MACHINE!
OR MAYBE THIS IS THE ONE THEY'LL USE TO CLEVERLY RESTRUCTURE TOP DOG'S BRAIN!
MERVIN NICE!
JOEY NOT NICE!
MERVIN NICE!
JOEY NOT NICE!
MERVIN NICE!
JOEY NOT NICE!
MERVIN NICE!
JOEY NOT NICE!
?
?
?
MERVIN NICE!
JOEY NOT NICE!
!
HUH?
9

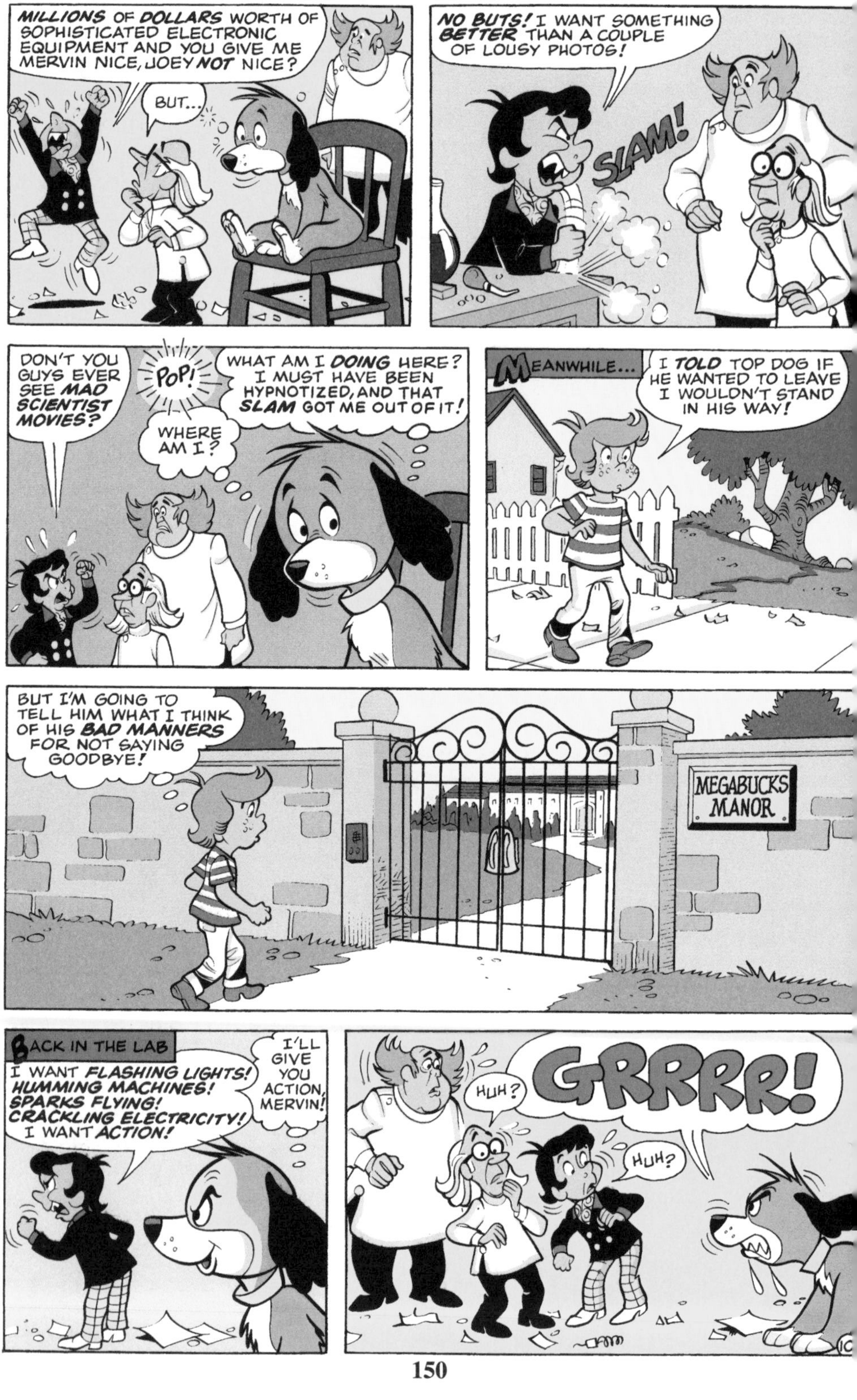

MILLIONS OF DOLLARS WORTH OF SOPHISTICATED ELECTRONIC EQUIPMENT AND YOU GIVE ME MERVIN NICE, JOEY NOT NICE?
BUT...
NO BUTS! I WANT SOMETHING BETTER THAN A COUPLE OF LOUSY PHOTOS!
SLAM!
DON'T YOU GUYS EVER SEE MAD SCIENTIST MOVIES?
POP!
WHAT AM I DOING HERE? I MUST HAVE BEEN HYPNOTIZED, AND THAT SLAM GOT ME OUT OF IT!
WHERE AM I?
MEANWHILE...
I TOLD TOP DOG IF HE WANTED TO LEAVE I WOULDN'T STAND IN HIS WAY!
BUT I'M GOING TO TELL HIM WHAT I THINK OF HIS BAD MANNERS FOR NOT SAYING GOODBYE!
MEGABUCKS MANOR
BACK IN THE LAB
I WANT FLASHING LIGHTS! HUMMING MACHINES! SPARKS FLYING! CRACKLING ELECTRICITY! I WANT ACTION!
I'LL GIVE YOU ACTION, MERVIN!
HUH?
GRRRR!
HUH?

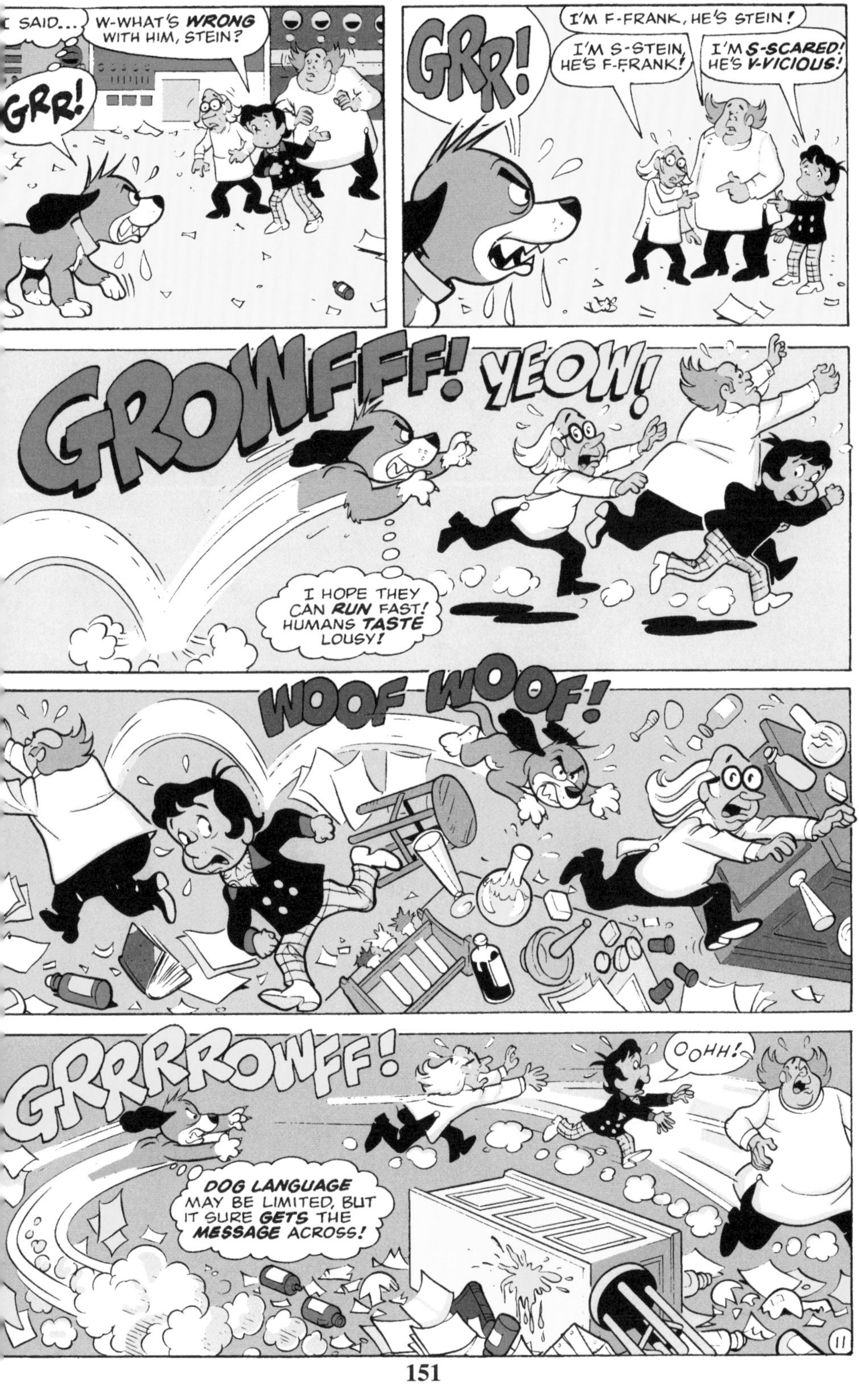
I SAID...
W-WHAT'S WRONG WITH HIM, STEIN?
GRR!
GRR!
I'M F-FRANK, HE'S STEIN!
I'M S-STEIN, HE'S F-FRANK!
I'M S-SCARED! HE'S V-VICIOUS!
GROWFFF!
YEOW!
I HOPE THEY CAN RUN FAST! HUMANS TASTE LOUSY!
WOOF WOOF!
GRRRROWFF!
OOHH!
DOG LANGUAGE MAY BE LIMITED, BUT IT SURE GETS THE MESSAGE ACROSS!
11

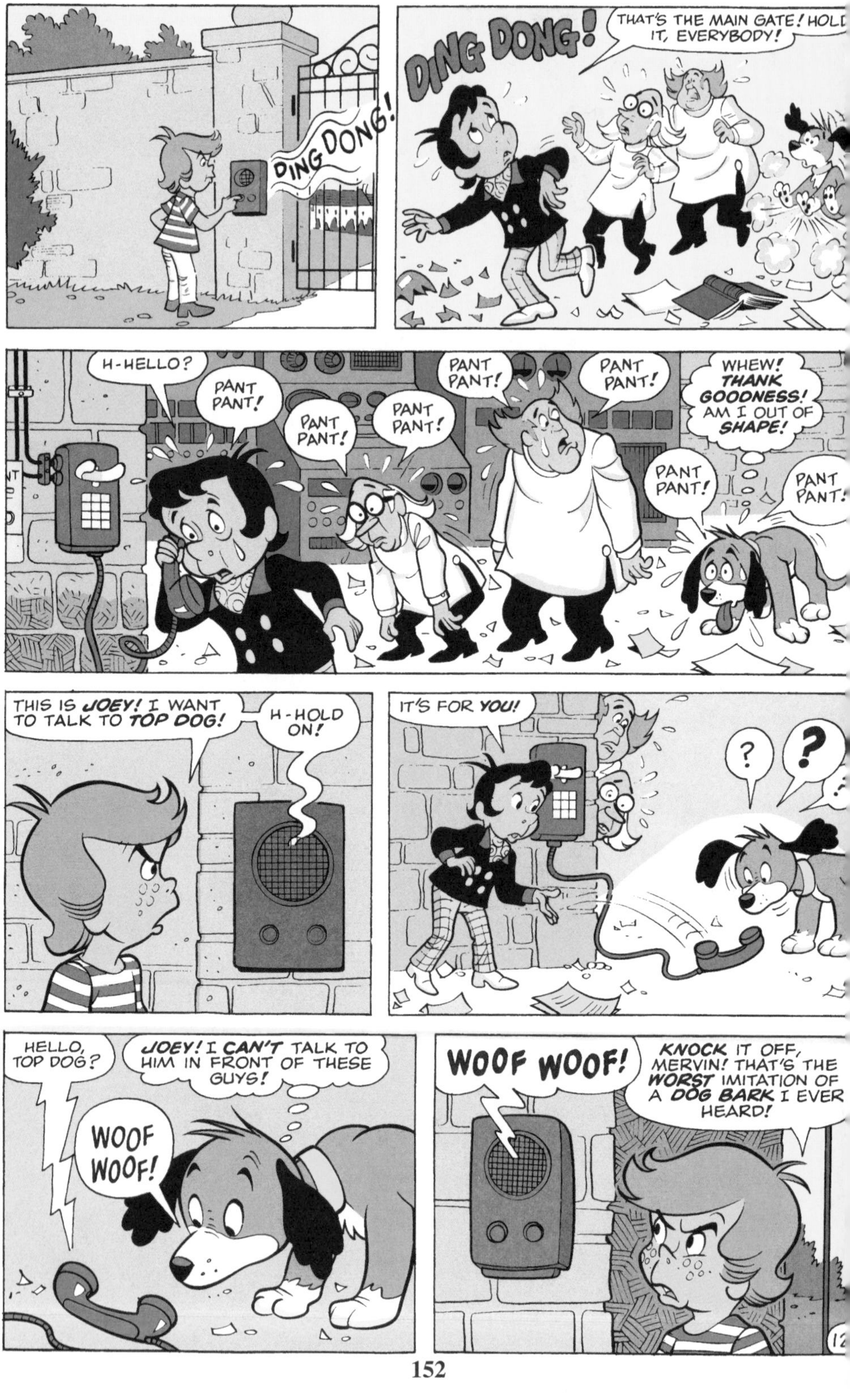
DING DONG!
DING DONG!
THAT'S THE MAIN GATE! HOLD IT, EVERYBODY!
H-HELLO?
PANT PANT!
PANT PANT!
PANT PANT!
PANT PANT!
PANT PANT!
WHEW! THANK GOODNESS! AM I OUT OF SHAPE!
PANT PANT!
PANT PANT!
THIS IS JOEY! I WANT TO TALK TO TOP DOG!
H-HOLD ON!
IT'S FOR YOU!
?
?
HELLO, TOP DOG?
JOEY! I CAN'T TALK TO HIM IN FRONT OF THESE GUYS!
WOOF WOOF!
WOOF WOOF!
KNOCK IT OFF, MERVIN! THAT'S THE WORST IMITATION OF A DOG BARK I EVER HEARD!

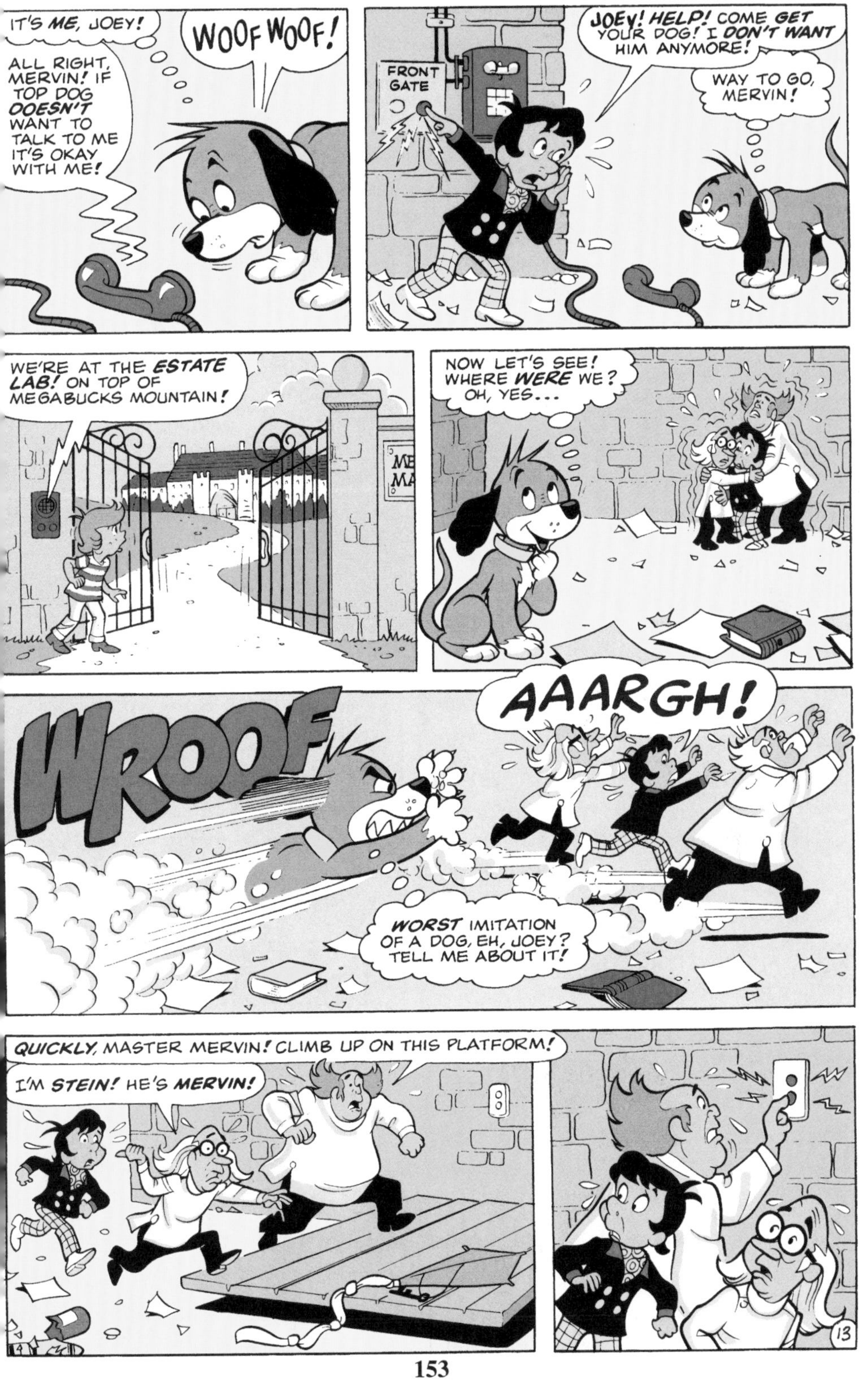
IT'S ME, JOEY!
WOOF WOOF!
ALL RIGHT, MERVIN! IF TOP DOG DOESN'T WANT TO TALK TO ME IT'S OKAY WITH ME!
FRONT GATE
JOEY! HELP! COME GET YOUR DOG! I DON'T WANT HIM ANYMORE!
WAY TO GO, MERVIN!
WE'RE AT THE ESTATE LAB! ON TOP OF MEGABUCKS MOUNTAIN!
NOW LET'S SEE! WHERE WERE WE? OH, YES...
WROOF
AAARGH!
WORST IMITATION OF A DOG, EH, JOEY? TELL ME ABOUT IT!
QUICKLY, MASTER MERVIN! CLIMB UP ON THIS PLATFORM!
I'M STEIN! HE'S MERVIN!
13

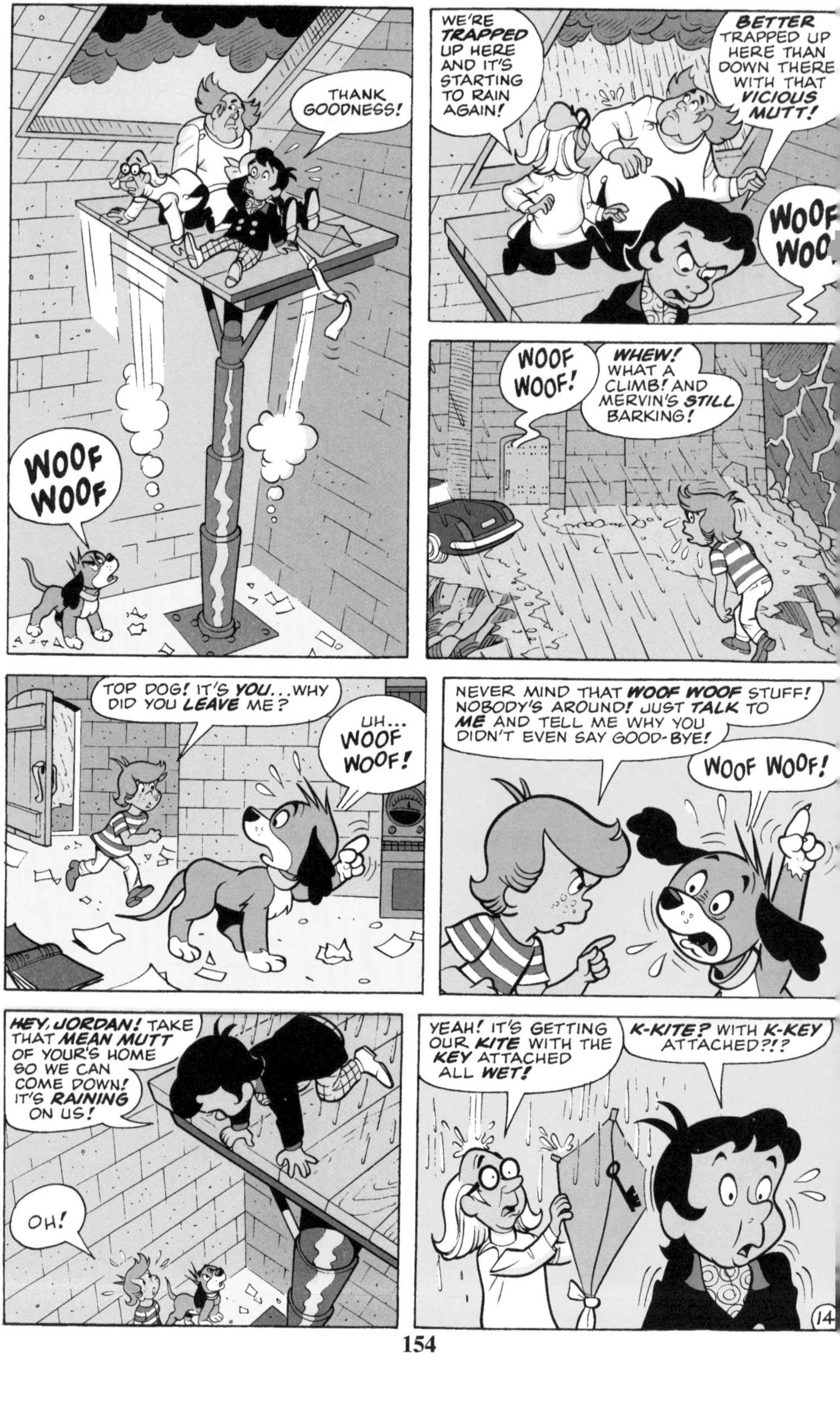
THANK GOODNESS!
WOOF WOOF
WE'RE TRAPPED UP HERE AND IT'S STARTING TO RAIN AGAIN!
BETTER TRAPPED UP HERE THAN DOWN THERE WITH THAT VICIOUS MUTT!
WOOF WOO
WOOF WOOF!
WHEW! WHAT A CLIMB! AND MERVIN'S STILL BARKING!
TOP DOG! IT'S YOU...WHY DID YOU LEAVE ME?
UH... WOOF WOOF!
NEVER MIND THAT WOOF WOOF STUFF! NOBODY'S AROUND! JUST TALK TO ME AND TELL ME WHY YOU DIDN'T EVEN SAY GOOD-BYE!
WOOF WOOF!
HEY, JORDAN! TAKE THAT MEAN MUTT OF YOUR'S HOME SO WE CAN COME DOWN! IT'S RAINING ON US!
OH!
YEAH! IT'S GETTING OUR KITE WITH THE KEY ATTACHED ALL WET!
K-KITE? WITH K-KEY ATTACHED?!?
14

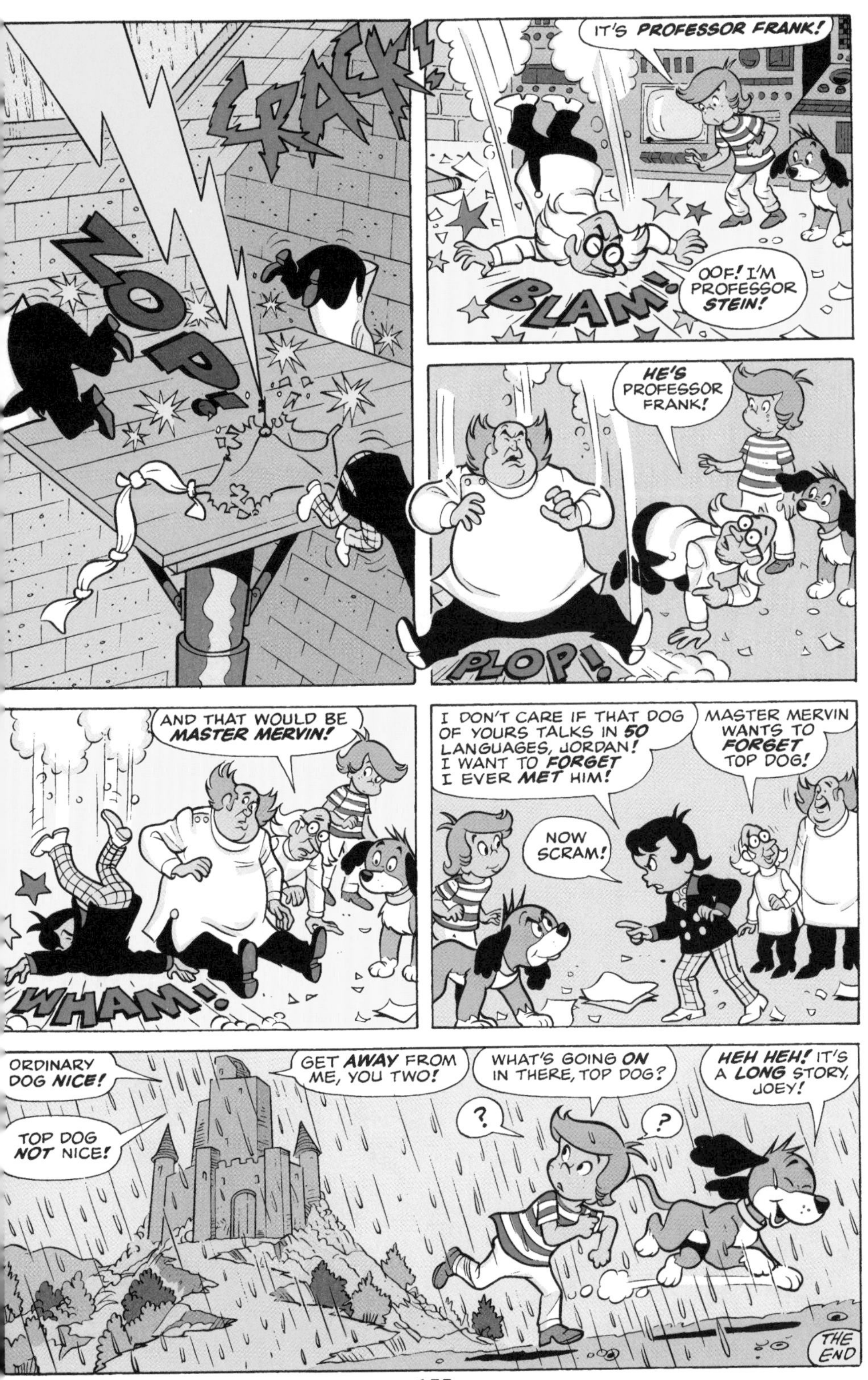
CRACK!
ZOOP!
IT'S PROFESSOR FRANK!
OOF! I'M PROFESSOR STEIN!
BLAM!
HE'S PROFESSOR FRANK!
PLOP!
AND THAT WOULD BE MASTER MERVIN!
WHAM!
I DON'T CARE IF THAT DOG OF YOURS TALKS IN 50 LANGUAGES, JORDAN! I WANT TO FORGET I EVER MET HIM!
MASTER MERVIN WANTS TO FORGET TOP DOG!
NOW SCRAM!
ORDINARY DOG NICE!
TOP DOG NOT NICE!
GET AWAY FROM ME, YOU TWO!
WHAT'S GOING ON IN THERE, TOP DOG?
?
?
HEH HEH! IT'S A LONG STORY, JOEY!
THE END

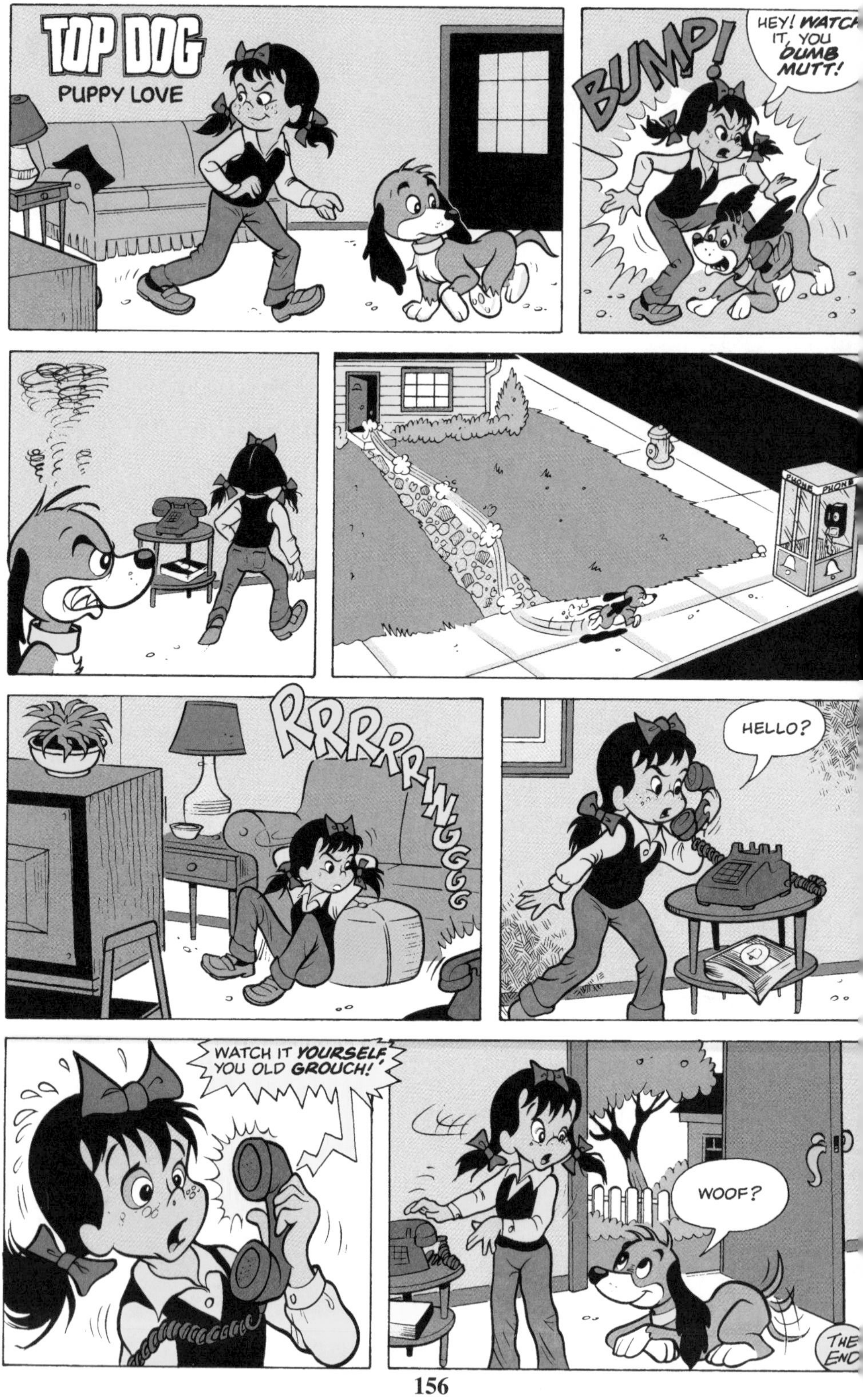
TOP DOG
PUPPY LOVE
BUMP!
HEY! WATCH IT, YOU DUMB MUTT!
PHONE PHONE
RRRRRINGGGG
HELLO?
WATCH IT YOURSELF, YOU OLD GROUCH!
WOOF?
THE END

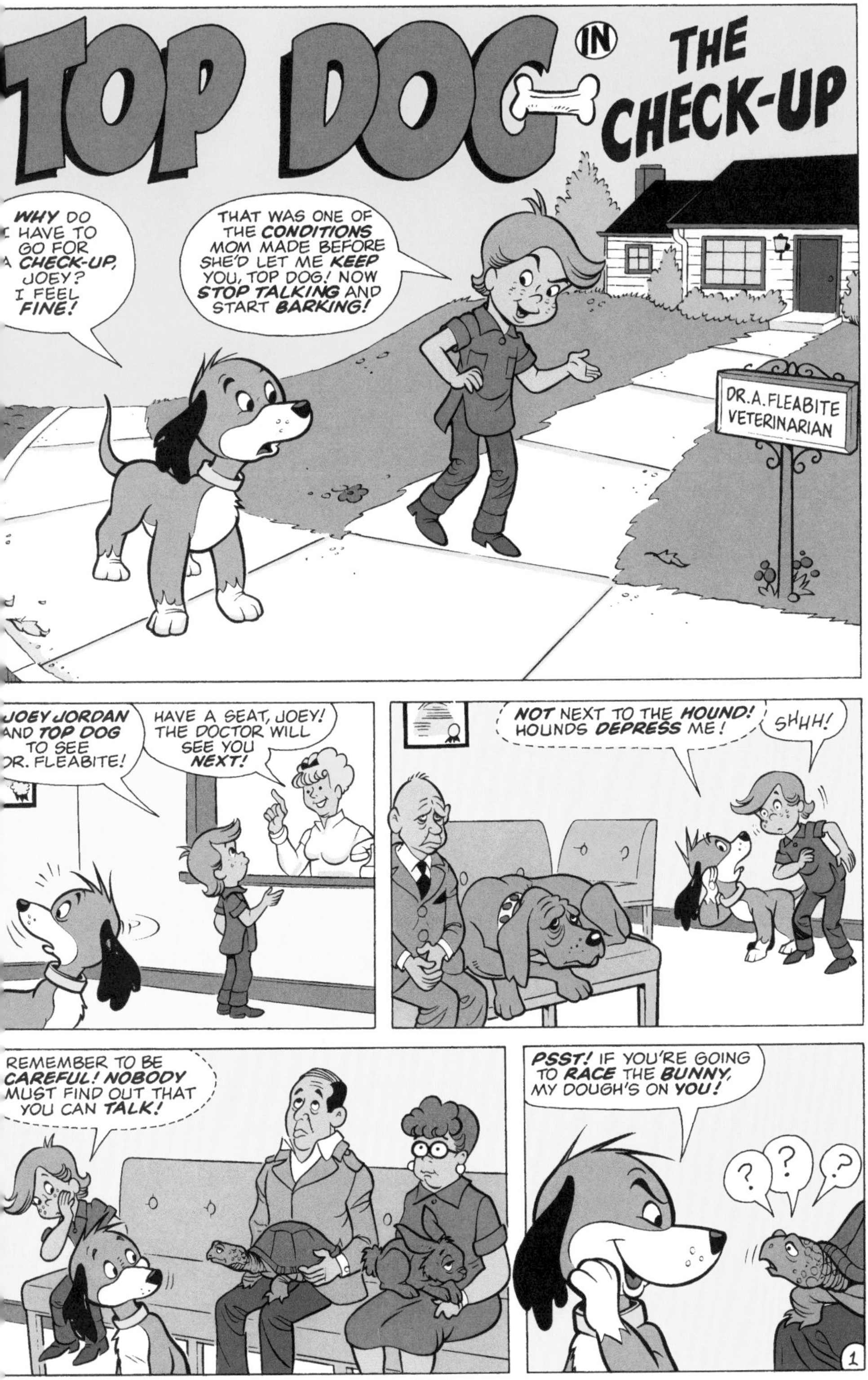
TOP DOG IN THE CHECK-UP
WHY DO I HAVE TO GO FOR A CHECK-UP, JOEY? I FEEL FINE!
THAT WAS ONE OF THE CONDITIONS MOM MADE BEFORE SHE'D LET ME KEEP YOU, TOP DOG! NOW STOP TALKING AND START BARKING!
DR. A. FLEABITE VETERINARIAN
JOEY JORDAN AND TOP DOG TO SEE DR. FLEABITE!
HAVE A SEAT, JOEY! THE DOCTOR WILL SEE YOU NEXT!
NOT NEXT TO THE HOUND! HOUNDS DEPRESS ME!
SHHH!
REMEMBER TO BE CAREFUL! NOBODY MUST FIND OUT THAT YOU CAN TALK!
PSST! IF YOU'RE GOING TO RACE THE BUNNY, MY DOUGH'S ON YOU!
? ? ?
1

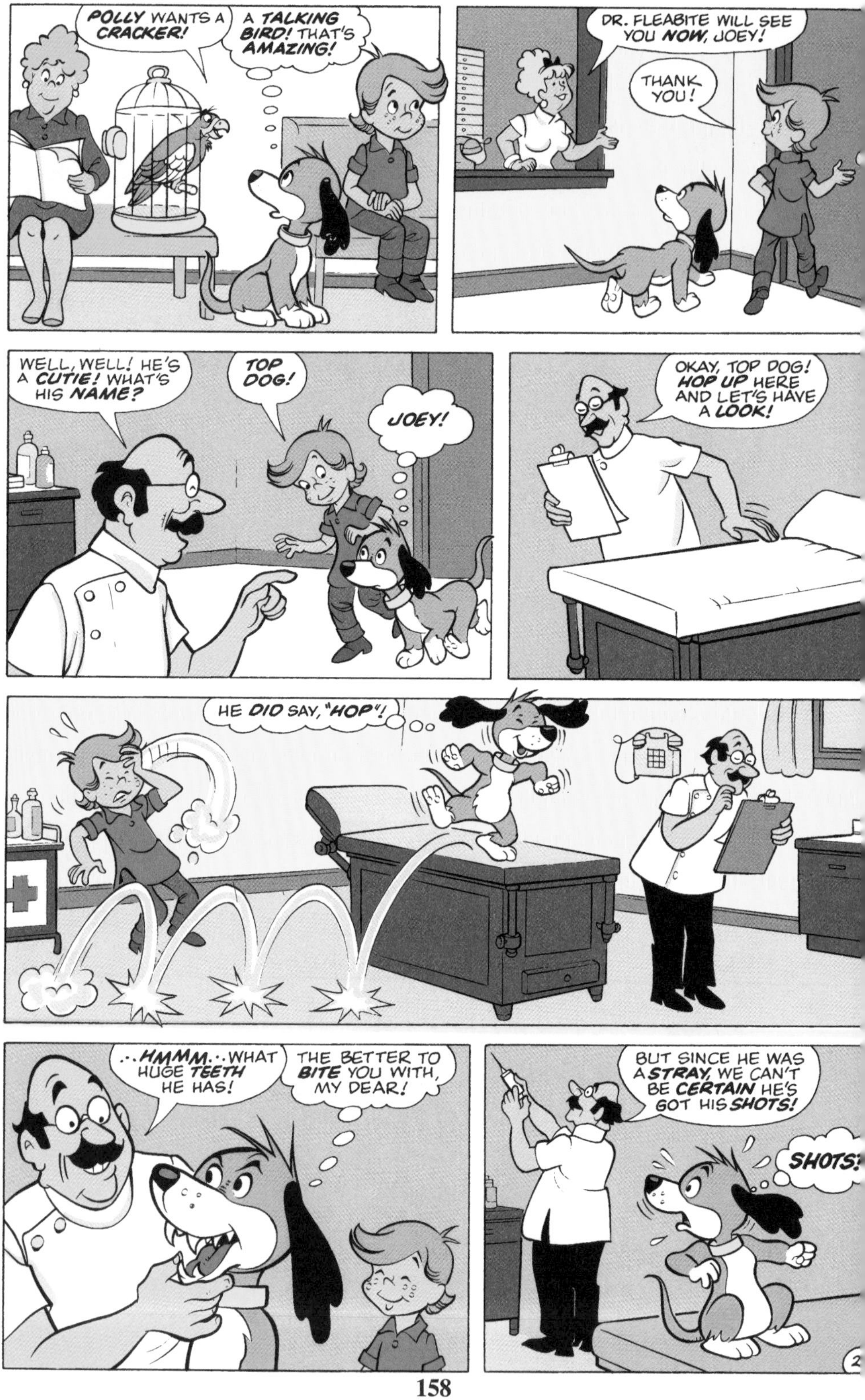
POLLY WANTS A CRACKER!
A TALKING BIRD! THAT'S AMAZING!
DR. FLEABITE WILL SEE YOU NOW, JOEY!
THANK YOU!
WELL, WELL! HE'S A CUTIE! WHAT'S HIS NAME?
TOP DOG!
JOEY!
OKAY, TOP DOG! HOP UP HERE AND LET'S HAVE A LOOK!
HE DID SAY, "HOP"!
..HMMM..WHAT HUGE TEETH HE HAS!
THE BETTER TO BITE YOU WITH, MY DEAR!
BUT SINCE HE WAS A STRAY, WE CAN'T BE CERTAIN HE'S GOT HIS SHOTS!
SHOTS!

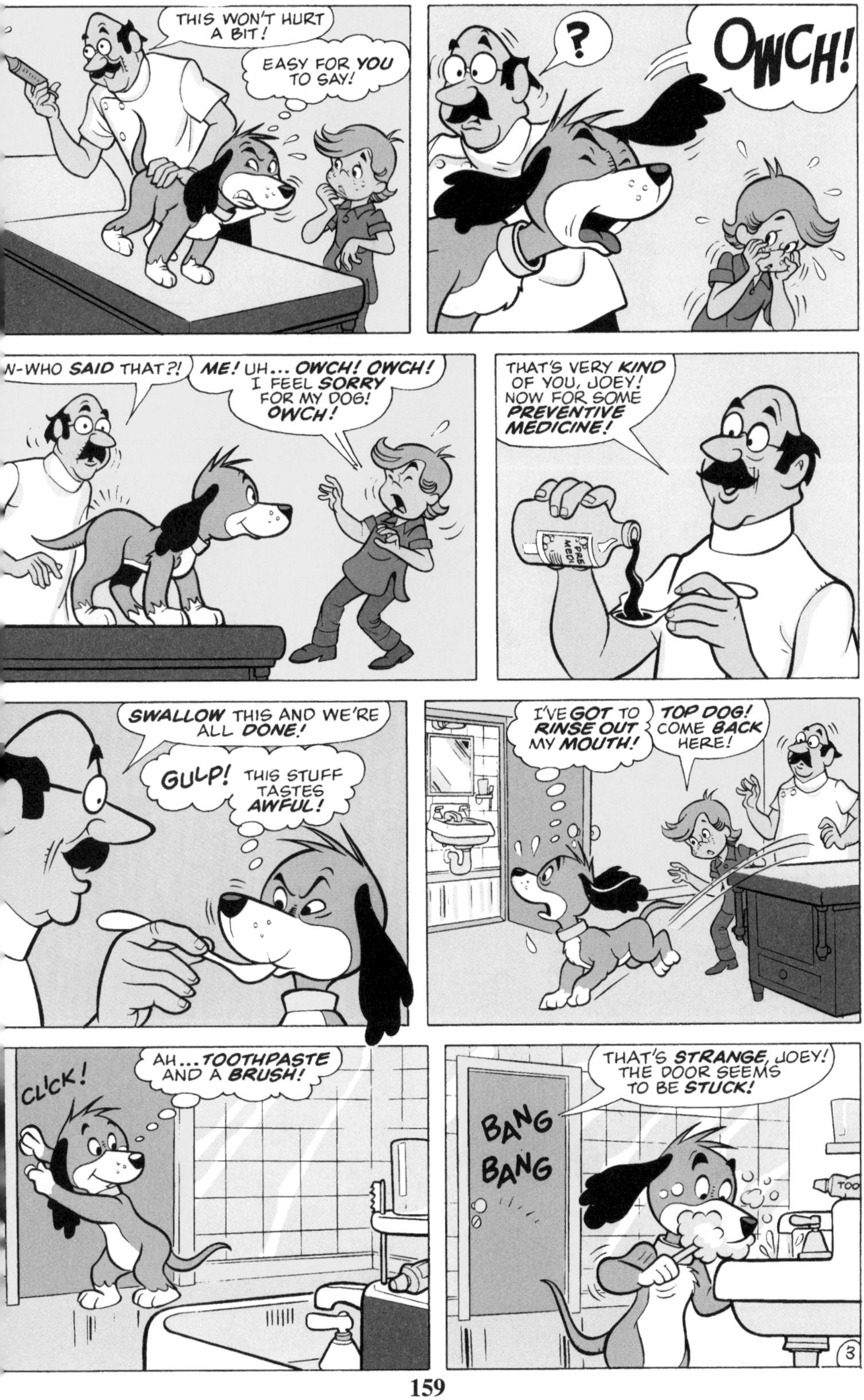
THIS WON'T HURT A BIT!
EASY FOR YOU TO SAY!
?
OWCH!
W-WHO SAID THAT?!
ME! UH... OWCH! OWCH! I FEEL SORRY FOR MY DOG! OWCH!
THAT'S VERY KIND OF YOU, JOEY! NOW FOR SOME PREVENTIVE MEDICINE!
SWALLOW THIS AND WE'RE ALL DONE!
GULP! THIS STUFF TASTES AWFUL!
I'VE GOT TO RINSE OUT MY MOUTH!
TOP DOG! COME BACK HERE!
CLICK!
AH... TOOTHPASTE AND A BRUSH!
THAT'S STRANGE, JOEY! THE DOOR SEEMS TO BE STUCK!
BANG
BANG
3

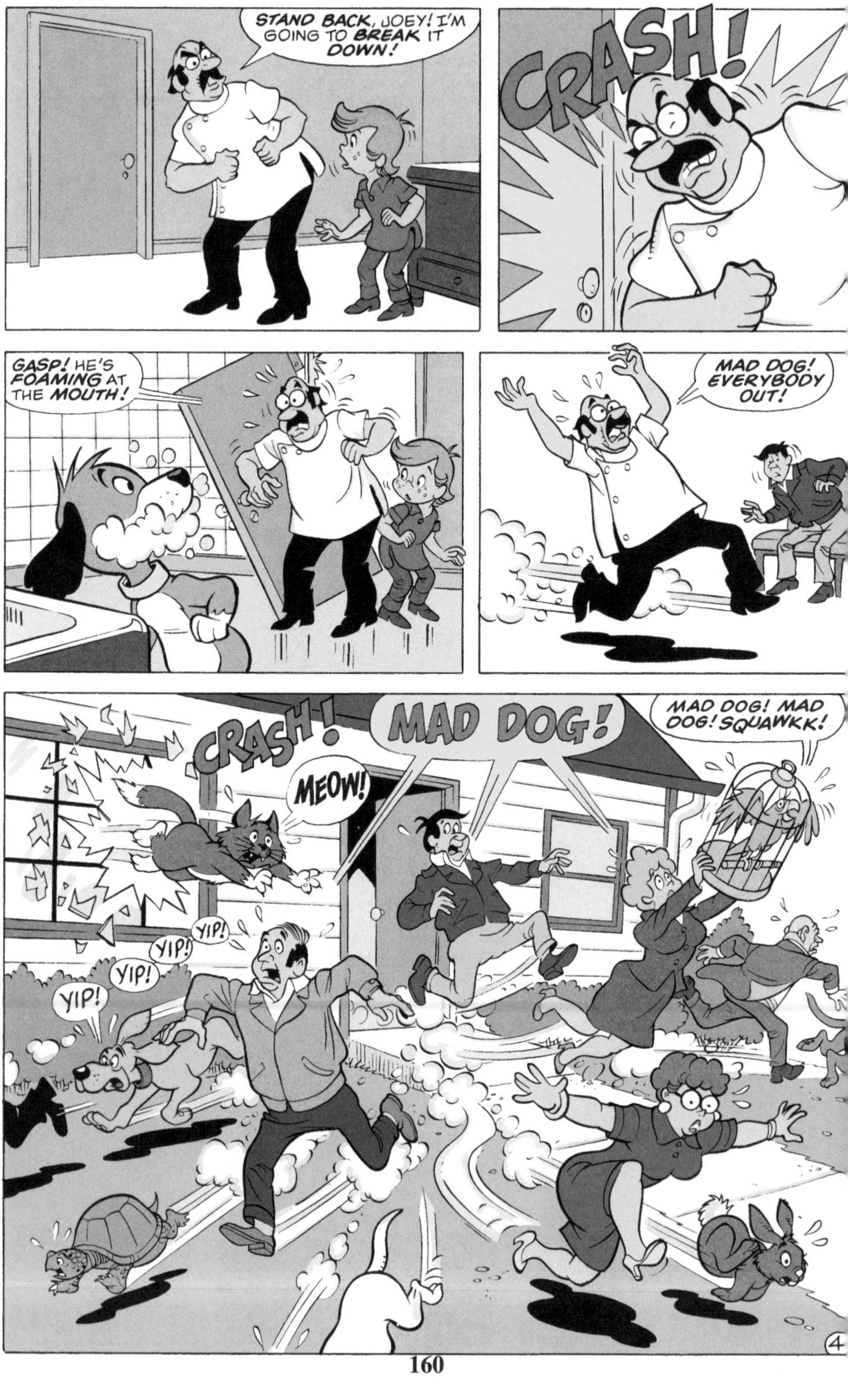
STAND BACK, JOEY! I'M GOING TO BREAK IT DOWN!
CRASH!
GASP! HE'S FOAMING AT THE MOUTH!
MAD DOG! EVERYBODY OUT!
CRASH!
MAD DOG!
MAD DOG! MAD DOG! SQUAWKK!
MEOW!
YIP!
YIP!
YIP!
YIP!
4

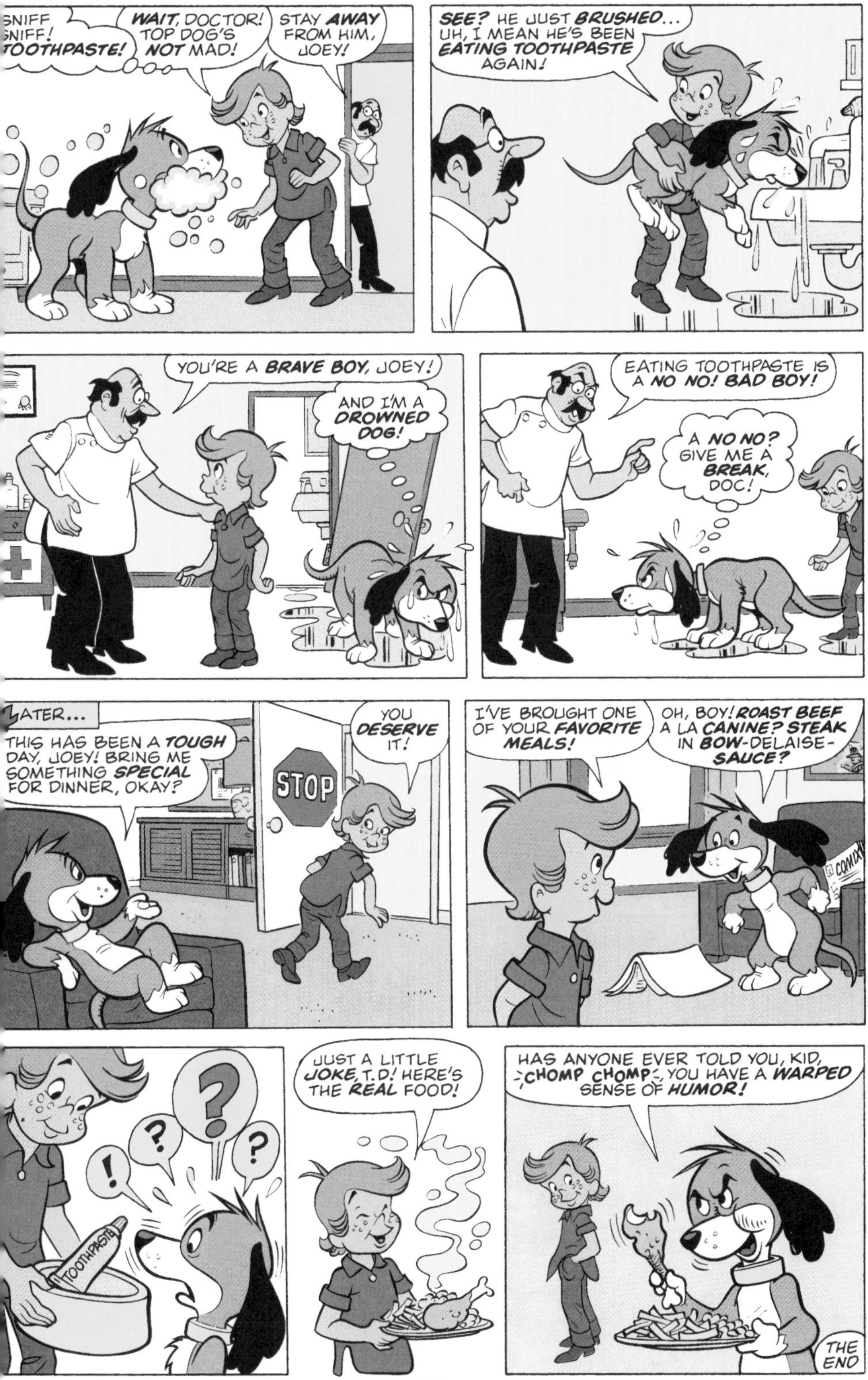
SNIFF SNIFF! TOOTHPASTE!
WAIT, DOCTOR! TOP DOG'S NOT MAD!
STAY AWAY FROM HIM, JOEY!
SEE? HE JUST BRUSHED... UH, I MEAN HE'S BEEN EATING TOOTHPASTE AGAIN!
YOU'RE A BRAVE BOY, JOEY!
AND I'M A DROWNED DOG!
EATING TOOTHPASTE IS A NO NO! BAD BOY!
A NO NO? GIVE ME A BREAK, DOC!
LATER...
THIS HAS BEEN A TOUGH DAY, JOEY! BRING ME SOMETHING SPECIAL FOR DINNER, OKAY?
STOP
YOU DESERVE IT!
I'VE BROUGHT ONE OF YOUR FAVORITE MEALS!
OH, BOY! ROAST BEEF A LA CANINE? STEAK IN BOW-DELAISE-SAUCE?
COMIX
TOOTHPASTE
!
?
?
?
JUST A LITTLE JOKE, T.D! HERE'S THE REAL FOOD!
HAS ANYONE EVER TOLD YOU, KID, CHOMP CHOMP, YOU HAVE A WARPED SENSE OF HUMOR!
THE END

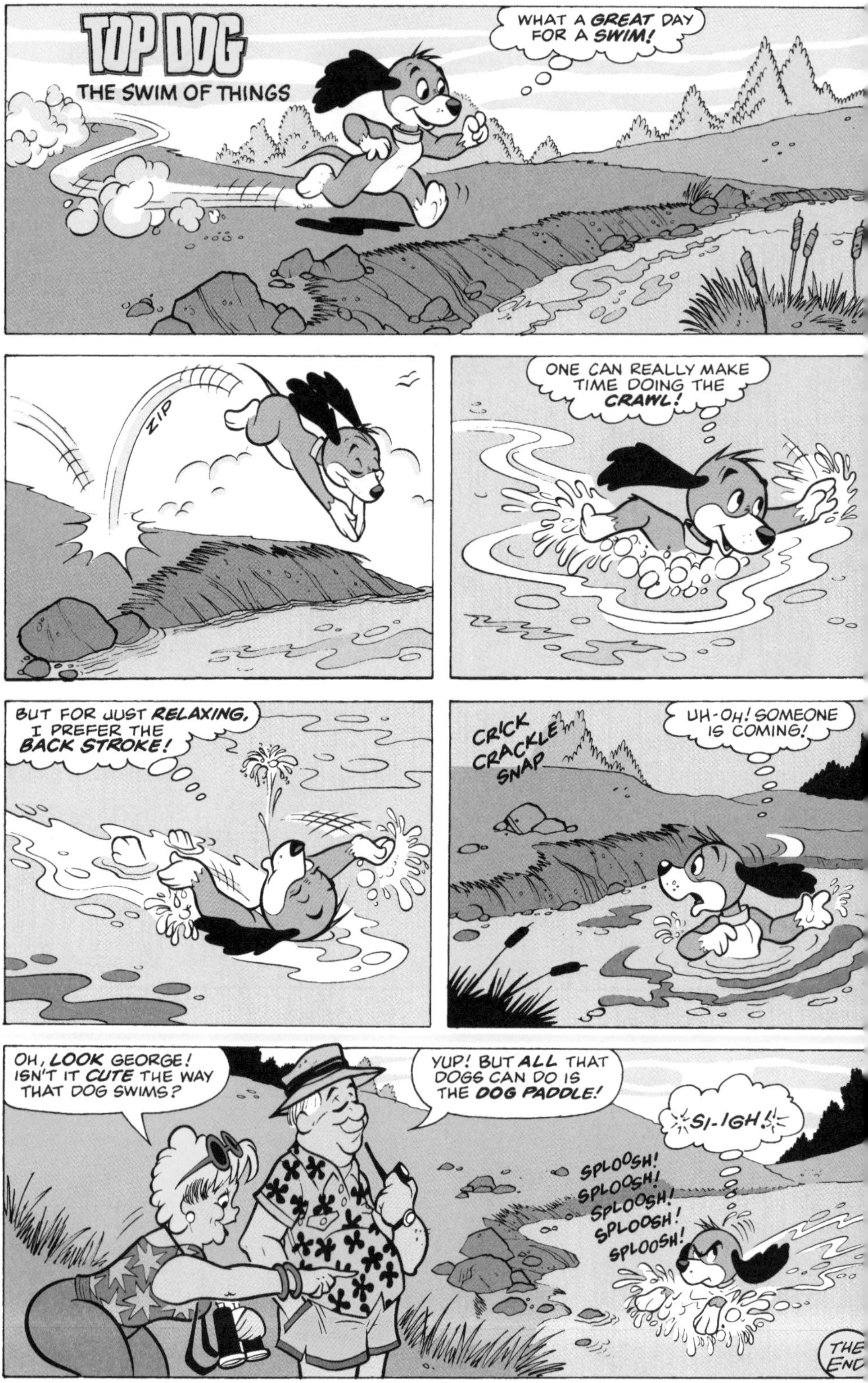
TOP DOG
THE SWIM OF THINGS
WHAT A GREAT DAY FOR A SWIM!
ZIP
ONE CAN REALLY MAKE TIME DOING THE CRAWL!
BUT FOR JUST RELAXING, I PREFER THE BACK STROKE!
CRICK CRACKLE SNAP
UH-OH! SOMEONE IS COMING!
OH, LOOK GEORGE! ISN'T IT CUTE THE WAY THAT DOG SWIMS?
YUP! BUT ALL THAT DOGS CAN DO IS THE DOG PADDLE!
SI-IGH!
SPLOOSH! SPLOOSH! SPLOOSH! SPLOOSH! SPLOOSH!
THE END

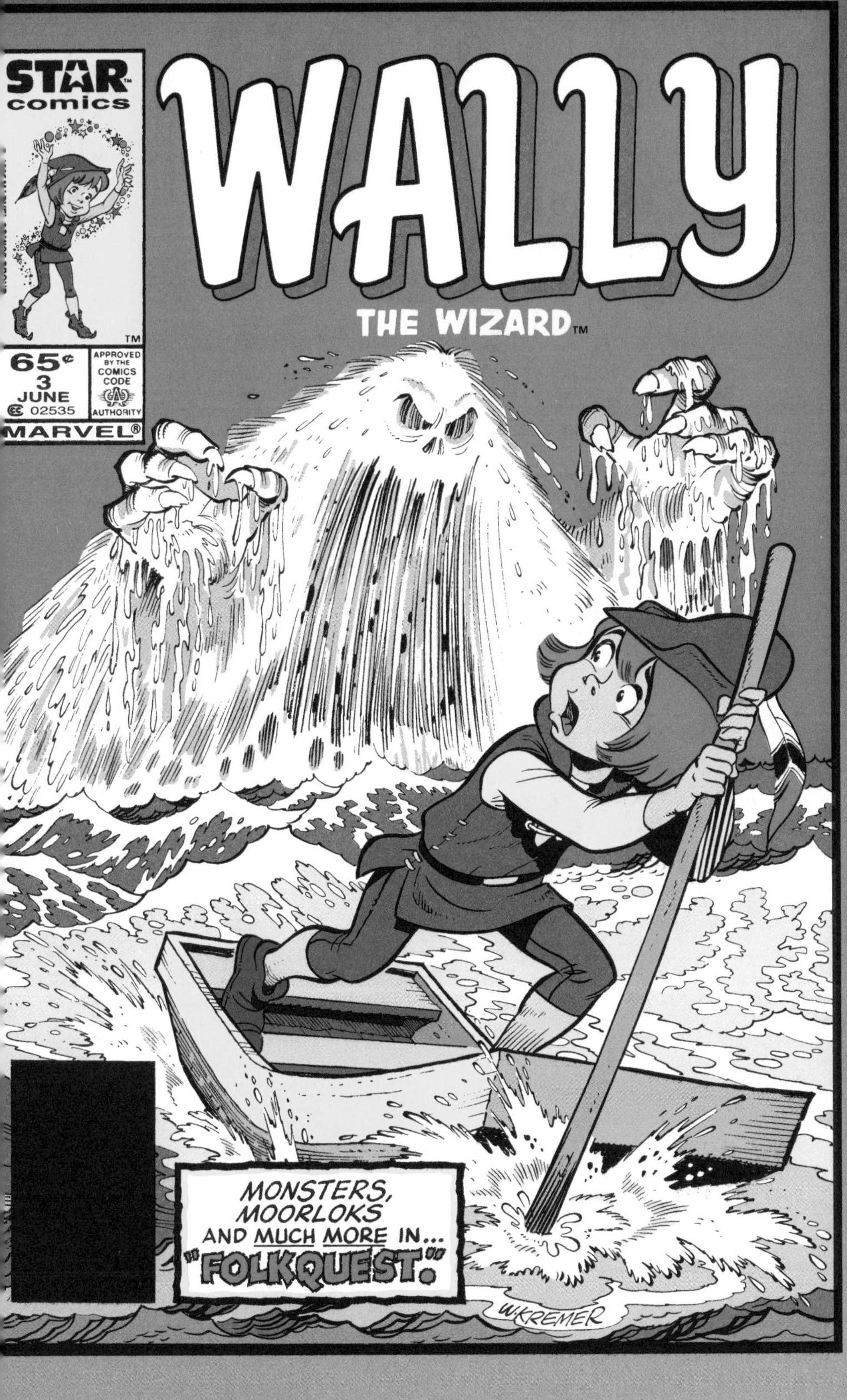
STAR comics
65¢
3
JUNE
02535
APPROVED BY THE COMICS CODE AUTHORITY
MARVEL®
WALLY
THE WIZARD™
MONSTERS, MOORLOKS AND MUCH MORE IN... "FOLKQUEST."
W.KREMER

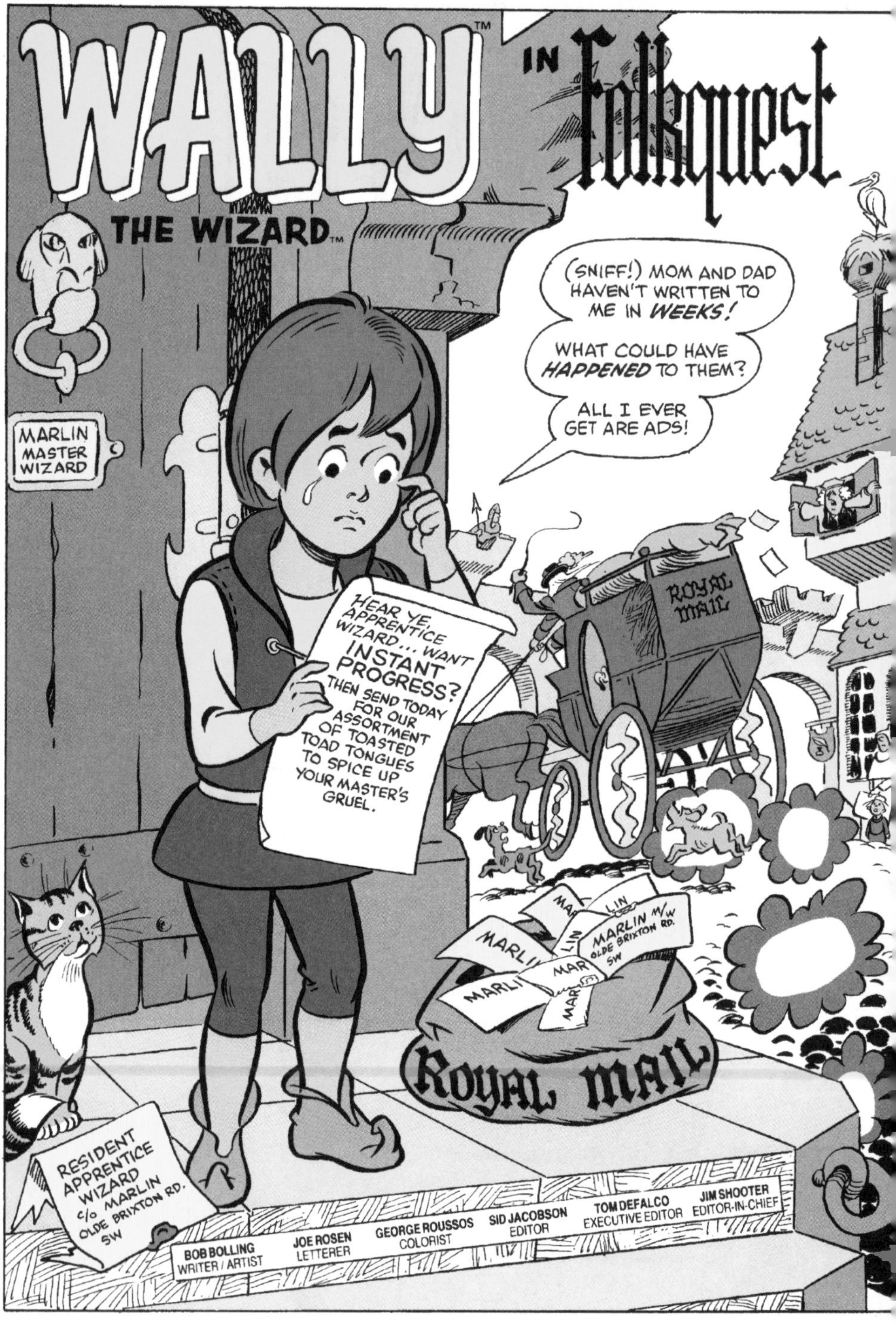

WALLY™ THE WIZARD™ IN Folkquest
(SNIFF!) MOM AND DAD HAVEN'T WRITTEN TO ME IN WEEKS!
WHAT COULD HAVE HAPPENED TO THEM?
ALL I EVER GET ARE ADS!
MARLIN MASTER WIZARD
HEAR YE, APPRENTICE WIZARD... WANT INSTANT PROGRESS? THEN SEND TODAY FOR OUR ASSORTMENT OF TOASTED TOAD TONGUES TO SPICE UP YOUR MASTER'S GRUEL.
ROYAL MAIL
MARLIN M/W OLDE BRIXTON RD. SW
ROYAL MAIL
RESIDENT APPRENTICE WIZARD c/o MARLIN OLDE BRIXTON RD. SW
BOB BOLLING WRITER / ARTIST
JOE ROSEN LETTERER
GEORGE ROUSSOS COLORIST
SID JACOBSON EDITOR
TOM DEFALCO EXECUTIVE EDITOR
JIM SHOOTER EDITOR-IN-CHIEF

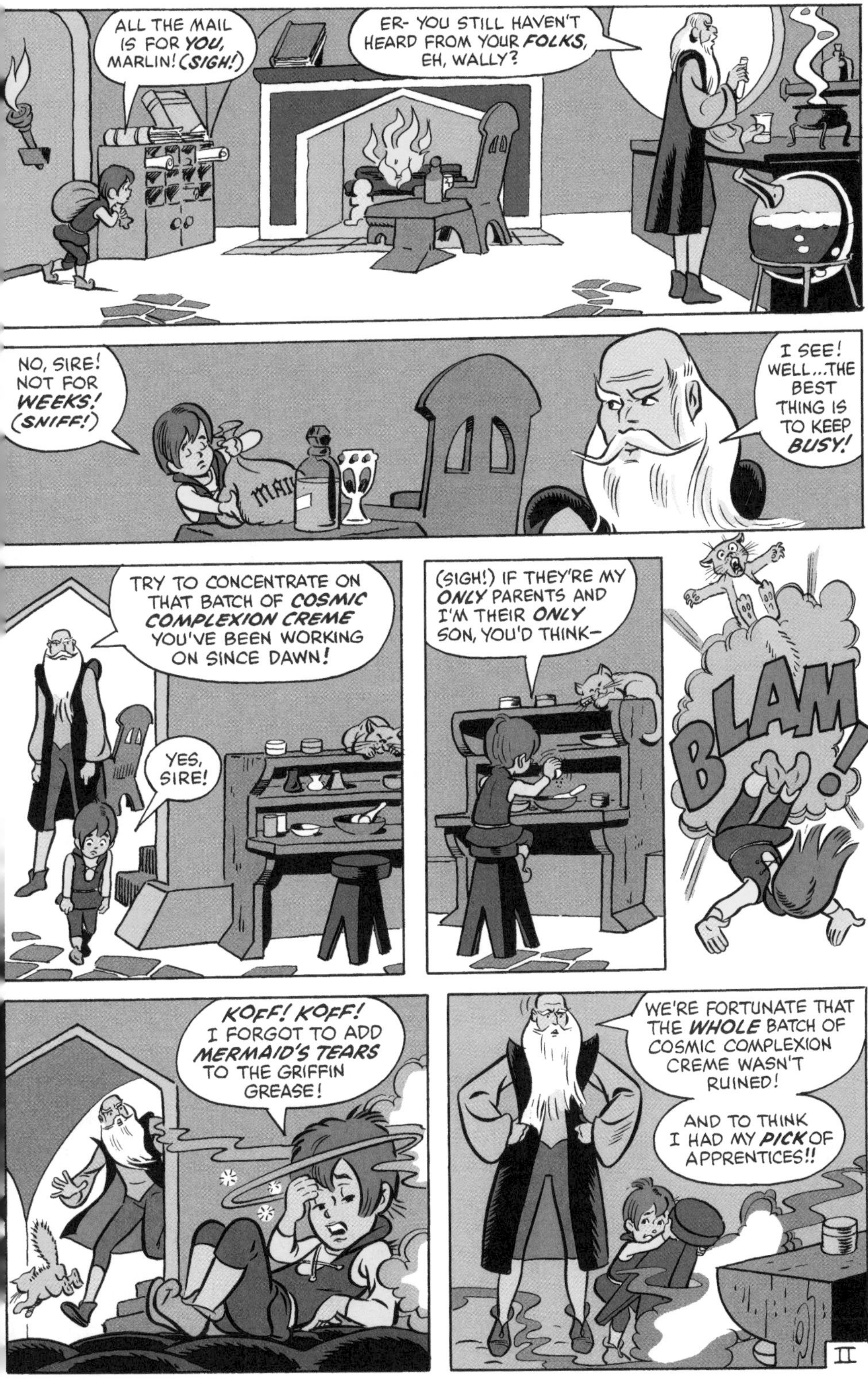
ALL THE MAIL IS FOR YOU, MARLIN! (SIGH!)
ER- YOU STILL HAVEN'T HEARD FROM YOUR FOLKS, EH, WALLY?
NO, SIRE! NOT FOR WEEKS! (SNIFF!)
MAIL
I SEE! WELL...THE BEST THING IS TO KEEP BUSY!
TRY TO CONCENTRATE ON THAT BATCH OF COSMIC COMPLEXION CREME YOU'VE BEEN WORKING ON SINCE DAWN!
YES, SIRE!
(SIGH!) IF THEY'RE MY ONLY PARENTS AND I'M THEIR ONLY SON, YOU'D THINK—
BLAM!
KOFF! KOFF! I FORGOT TO ADD MERMAID'S TEARS TO THE GRIFFIN GREASE!
WE'RE FORTUNATE THAT THE WHOLE BATCH OF COSMIC COMPLEXION CREME WASN'T RUINED!
AND TO THINK I HAD MY PICK OF APPRENTICES!!
II

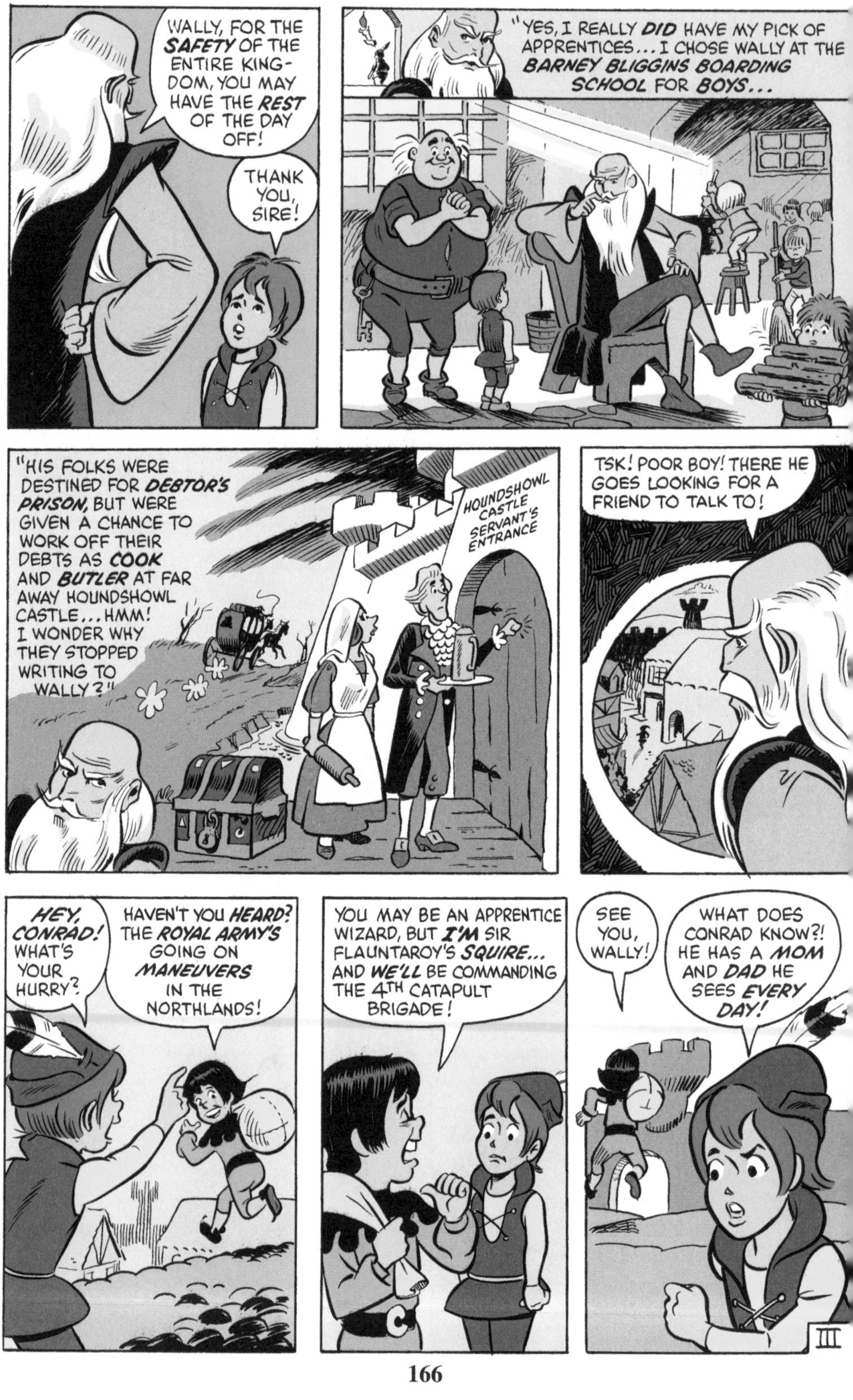

WALLY, FOR THE SAFETY OF THE ENTIRE KINGDOM, YOU MAY HAVE THE REST OF THE DAY OFF!
THANK YOU, SIRE!
"YES, I REALLY DID HAVE MY PICK OF APPRENTICES... I CHOSE WALLY AT THE BARNEY BLIGGINS BOARDING SCHOOL FOR BOYS...
"HIS FOLKS WERE DESTINED FOR DEBTOR'S PRISON, BUT WERE GIVEN A CHANCE TO WORK OFF THEIR DEBTS AS COOK AND BUTLER AT FAR AWAY HOUNDSHOWL CASTLE,.. HMM! I WONDER WHY THEY STOPPED WRITING TO WALLY?"
HOUNDSHOWL CASTLE SERVANT'S ENTRANCE
TSK! POOR BOY! THERE HE GOES LOOKING FOR A FRIEND TO TALK TO!
HEY, CONRAD! WHAT'S YOUR HURRY?
HAVEN'T YOU HEARD? THE ROYAL ARMY'S GOING ON MANEUVERS IN THE NORTHLANDS!
YOU MAY BE AN APPRENTICE WIZARD, BUT I'M SIR FLAUNTAROY'S SQUIRE... AND WE'LL BE COMMANDING THE 4TH CATAPULT BRIGADE!
SEE YOU, WALLY!
WHAT DOES CONRAD KNOW?! HE HAS A MOM AND DAD HE SEES EVERY DAY!
III

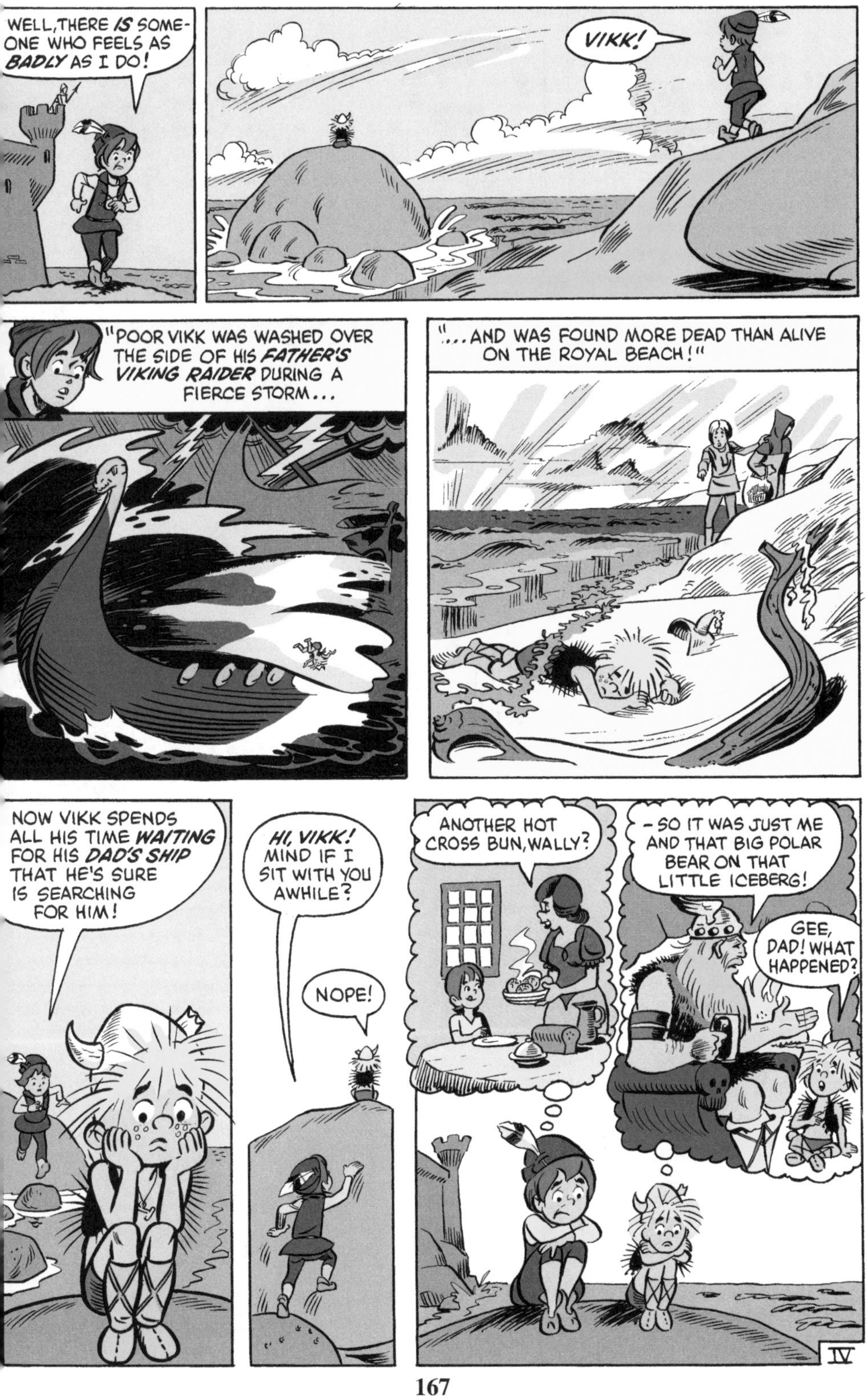
WELL, THERE *IS* SOMEONE WHO FEELS AS *BADLY* AS I DO!
VIKK!
"POOR VIKK WAS WASHED OVER THE SIDE OF HIS *FATHER'S VIKING RAIDER* DURING A FIERCE STORM...
"...AND WAS FOUND MORE DEAD THAN ALIVE ON THE ROYAL BEACH!"
NOW VIKK SPENDS ALL HIS TIME *WAITING* FOR HIS *DAD'S SHIP* THAT HE'S SURE IS SEARCHING FOR HIM!
HI, VIKK! MIND IF I SIT WITH YOU AWHILE?
NOPE!
ANOTHER HOT CROSS BUN, WALLY?
–SO IT WAS JUST ME AND THAT BIG POLAR BEAR ON THAT LITTLE ICEBERG!
GEE, DAD! WHAT HAPPENED?
IV

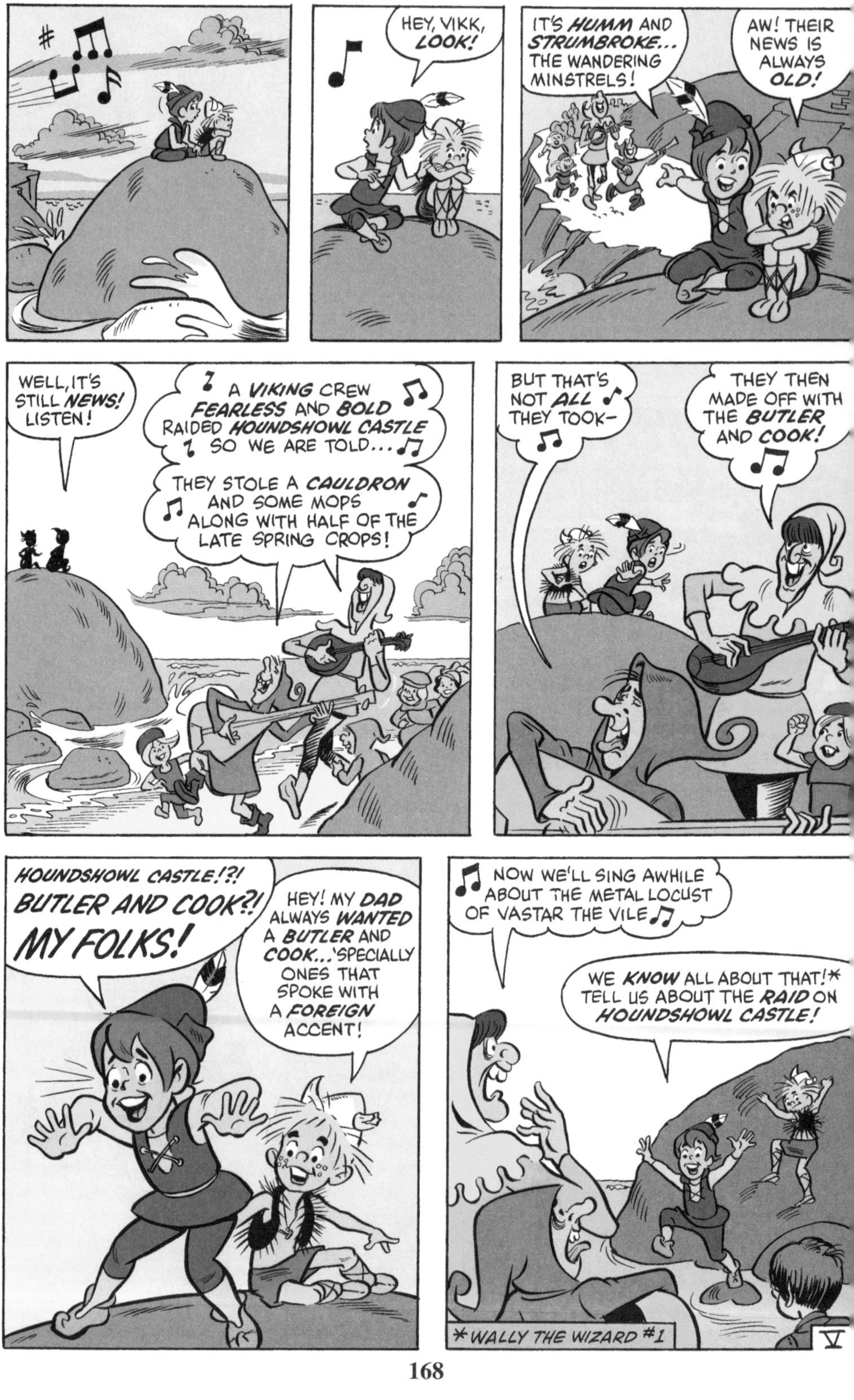

HEY, VIKK, LOOK!
IT'S HUMM AND STRUMBROKE... THE WANDERING MINSTRELS!
AW! THEIR NEWS IS ALWAYS OLD!
WELL, IT'S STILL NEWS! LISTEN!
A VIKING CREW FEARLESS AND BOLD RAIDED HOUNDSHOWL CASTLE SO WE ARE TOLD...
THEY STOLE A CAULDRON AND SOME MOPS ALONG WITH HALF OF THE LATE SPRING CROPS!
BUT THAT'S NOT ALL THEY TOOK-
THEY THEN MADE OFF WITH THE BUTLER AND COOK!
HOUNDSHOWL CASTLE!?! BUTLER AND COOK?! MY FOLKS!
HEY! MY DAD ALWAYS WANTED A BUTLER AND COOK...'SPECIALLY ONES THAT SPOKE WITH A FOREIGN ACCENT!
NOW WE'LL SING AWHILE ABOUT THE METAL LOCUST OF VASTAR THE VILE
WE KNOW ALL ABOUT THAT!* TELL US ABOUT THE RAID ON HOUNDSHOWL CASTLE!
*WALLY THE WIZARD #1

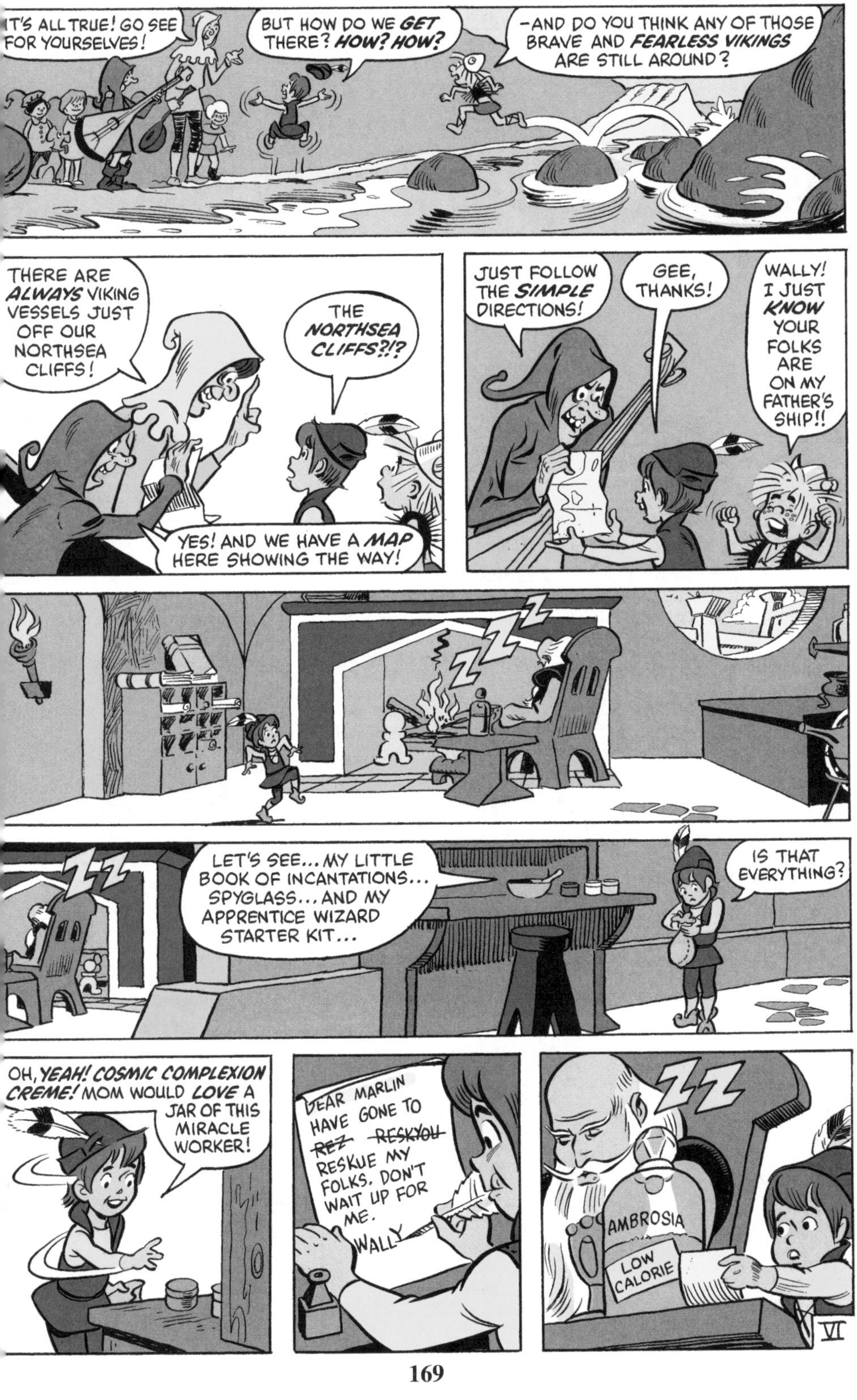
IT'S ALL TRUE! GO SEE FOR YOURSELVES!
BUT HOW DO WE GET THERE? HOW? HOW?
–AND DO YOU THINK ANY OF THOSE BRAVE AND FEARLESS VIKINGS ARE STILL AROUND?
THERE ARE ALWAYS VIKING VESSELS JUST OFF OUR NORTHSEA CLIFFS!
THE NORTHSEA CLIFFS?!?
YES! AND WE HAVE A MAP HERE SHOWING THE WAY!
JUST FOLLOW THE SIMPLE DIRECTIONS!
GEE, THANKS!
WALLY! I JUST KNOW YOUR FOLKS ARE ON MY FATHER'S SHIP!!
LET'S SEE... MY LITTLE BOOK OF INCANTATIONS... SPYGLASS... AND MY APPRENTICE WIZARD STARTER KIT...
IS THAT EVERYTHING?
OH, YEAH! COSMIC COMPLEXION CREME! MOM WOULD LOVE A JAR OF THIS MIRACLE WORKER!
DEAR MARLIN HAVE GONE TO REZ RESKYOU RESKUE MY FOLKS. DON'T WAIT UP FOR ME. WALLY
AMBROSIA
LOW CALORIE
VI

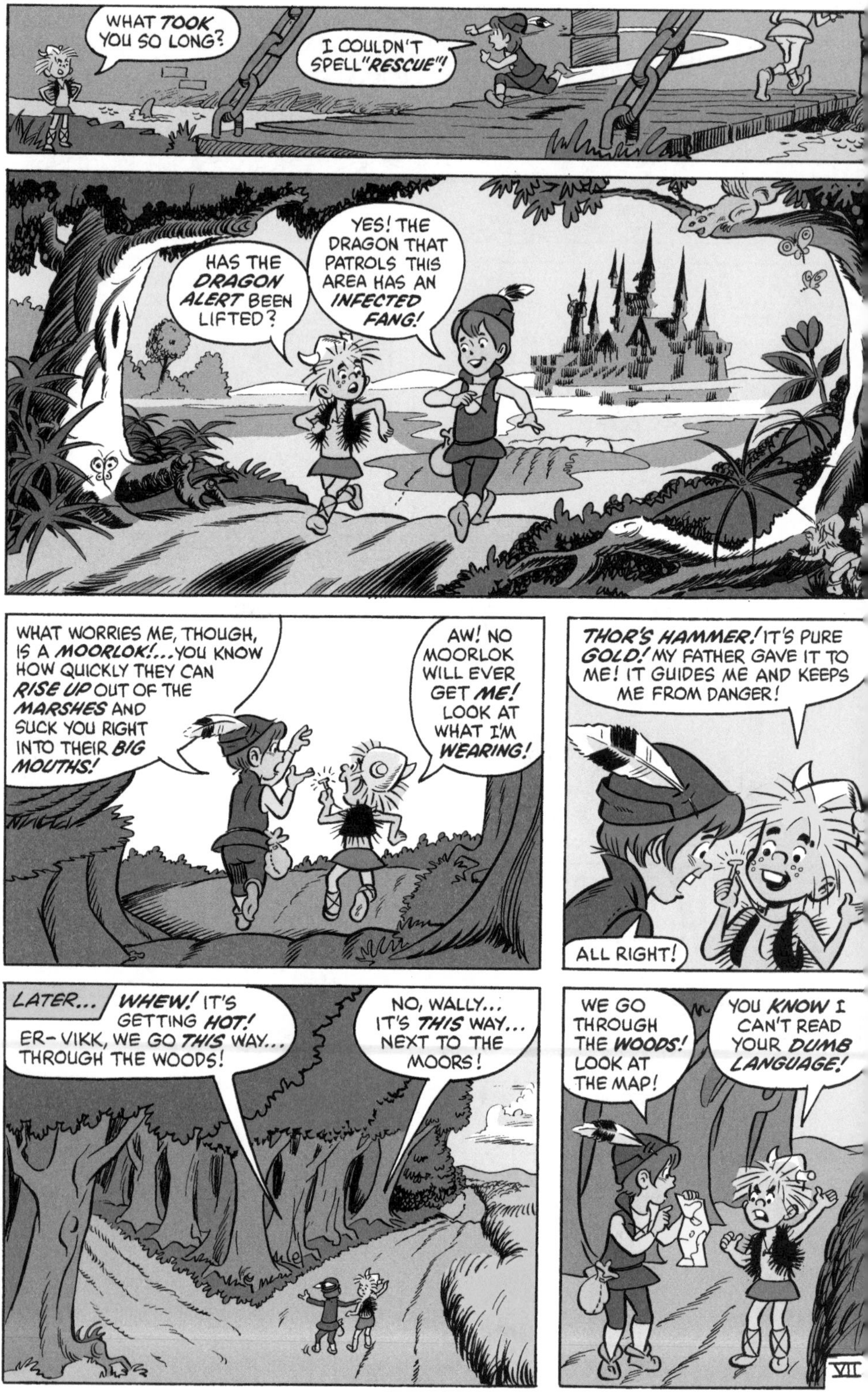
WHAT TOOK YOU SO LONG?
I COULDN'T SPELL "RESCUE"!
HAS THE DRAGON ALERT BEEN LIFTED?
YES! THE DRAGON THAT PATROLS THIS AREA HAS AN INFECTED FANG!
WHAT WORRIES ME, THOUGH, IS A MOORLOK!... YOU KNOW HOW QUICKLY THEY CAN RISE UP OUT OF THE MARSHES AND SUCK YOU RIGHT INTO THEIR BIG MOUTHS!
AW! NO MOORLOK WILL EVER GET ME! LOOK AT WHAT I'M WEARING!
THOR'S HAMMER! IT'S PURE GOLD! MY FATHER GAVE IT TO ME! IT GUIDES ME AND KEEPS ME FROM DANGER!
ALL RIGHT!
LATER...
WHEW! IT'S GETTING HOT! ER-VIKK, WE GO THIS WAY... THROUGH THE WOODS!
NO, WALLY... IT'S THIS WAY... NEXT TO THE MOORS!
WE GO THROUGH THE WOODS! LOOK AT THE MAP!
YOU KNOW I CAN'T READ YOUR DUMB LANGUAGE!
VII

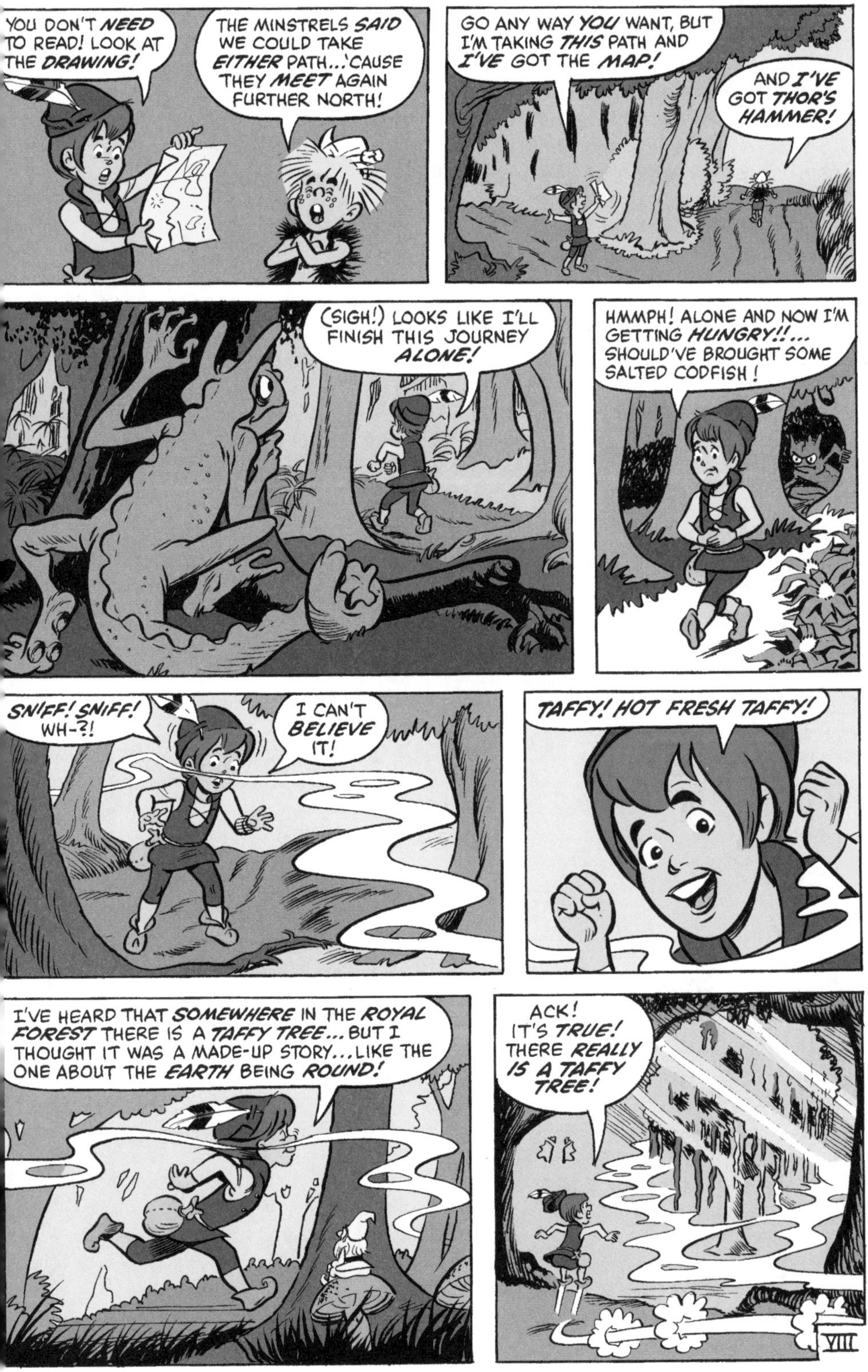
YOU DON'T NEED TO READ! LOOK AT THE DRAWING!
THE MINSTRELS SAID WE COULD TAKE EITHER PATH...'CAUSE THEY MEET AGAIN FURTHER NORTH!
GO ANY WAY YOU WANT, BUT I'M TAKING THIS PATH AND I'VE GOT THE MAP!
AND I'VE GOT THOR'S HAMMER!
(SIGH!) LOOKS LIKE I'LL FINISH THIS JOURNEY ALONE!
HMMPH! ALONE AND NOW I'M GETTING HUNGRY!!... SHOULD'VE BROUGHT SOME SALTED CODFISH!
SNIFF! SNIFF! WH-?!
I CAN'T BELIEVE IT!
TAFFY! HOT FRESH TAFFY!
I'VE HEARD THAT SOMEWHERE IN THE ROYAL FOREST THERE IS A TAFFY TREE... BUT I THOUGHT IT WAS A MADE-UP STORY... LIKE THE ONE ABOUT THE EARTH BEING ROUND!
ACK! IT'S TRUE! THERE REALLY IS A TAFFY TREE!
VIII

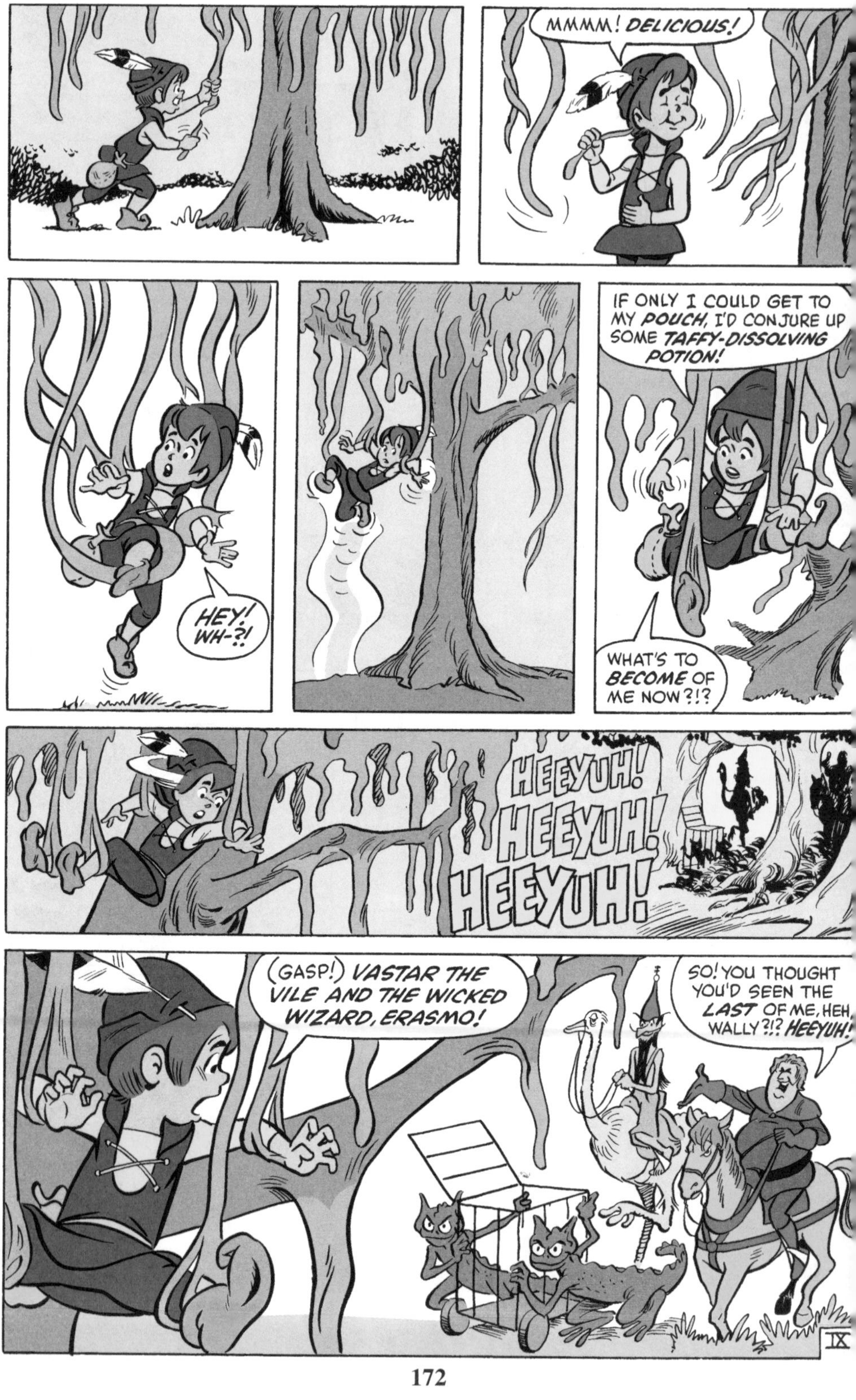
MMMM! DELICIOUS!
HEY! WH-?!
IF ONLY I COULD GET TO MY POUCH, I'D CONJURE UP SOME TAFFY-DISSOLVING POTION!
WHAT'S TO BECOME OF ME NOW?!?
HEEYUH! HEEYUH! HEEYUH!
(GASP!) VASTAR THE VILE AND THE WICKED WIZARD, ERASMO!
SO! YOU THOUGHT YOU'D SEEN THE LAST OF ME, HEH, WALLY?!? HEEYUH!
IX

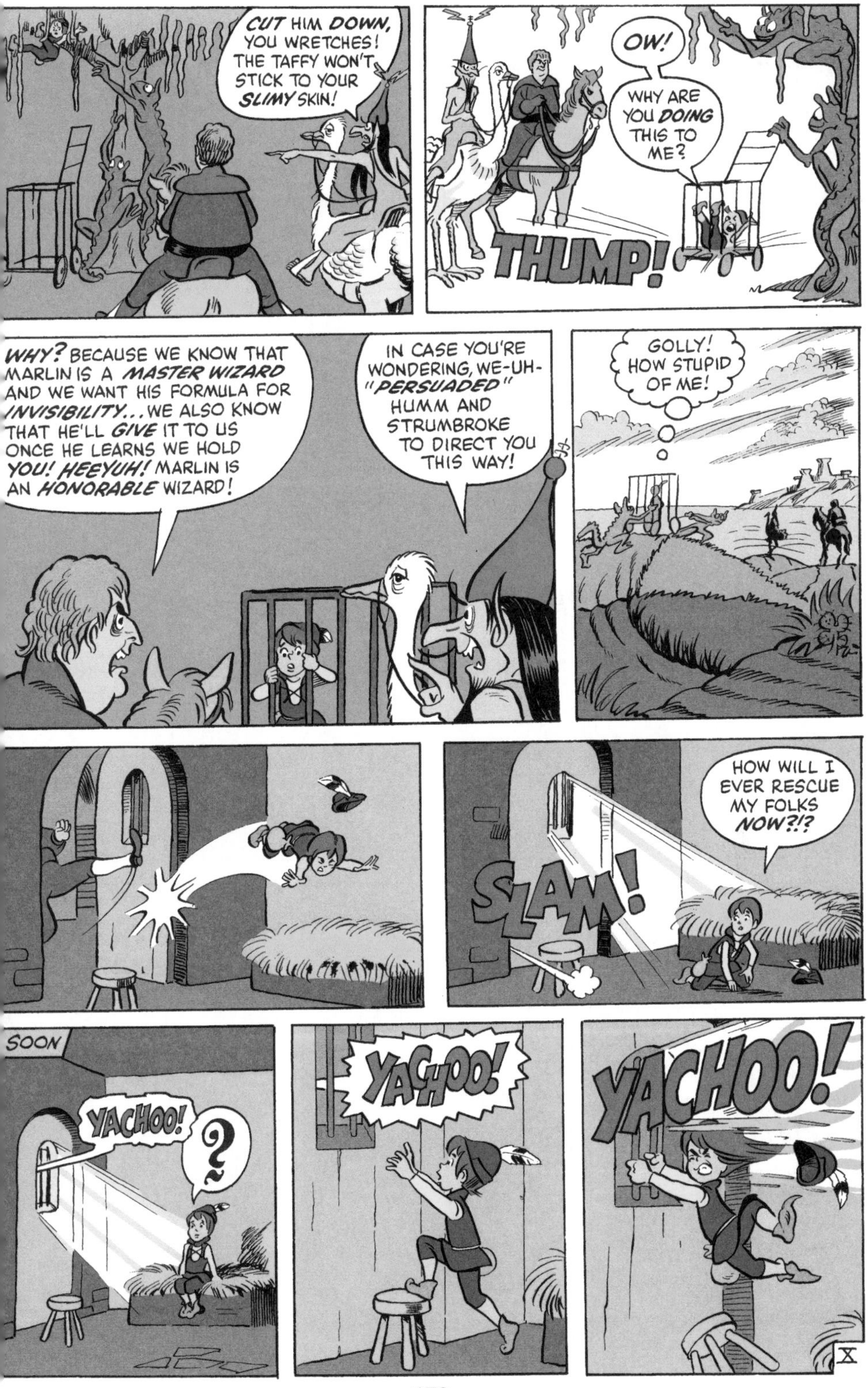
CUT HIM DOWN, YOU WRETCHES! THE TAFFY WON'T STICK TO YOUR SLIMY SKIN!
OW!
WHY ARE YOU DOING THIS TO ME?
THUMP!
WHY? BECAUSE WE KNOW THAT MARLIN IS A MASTER WIZARD AND WE WANT HIS FORMULA FOR INVISIBILITY... WE ALSO KNOW THAT HE'LL GIVE IT TO US ONCE HE LEARNS WE HOLD YOU! HEEYUH! MARLIN IS AN HONORABLE WIZARD!
IN CASE YOU'RE WONDERING, WE-UH- "PERSUADED" HUMM AND STRUMBROKE TO DIRECT YOU THIS WAY!
GOLLY! HOW STUPID OF ME!
SLAM!
HOW WILL I EVER RESCUE MY FOLKS NOW?!?
SOON
YACHOO!
?
YACHOO!
YACHOO!

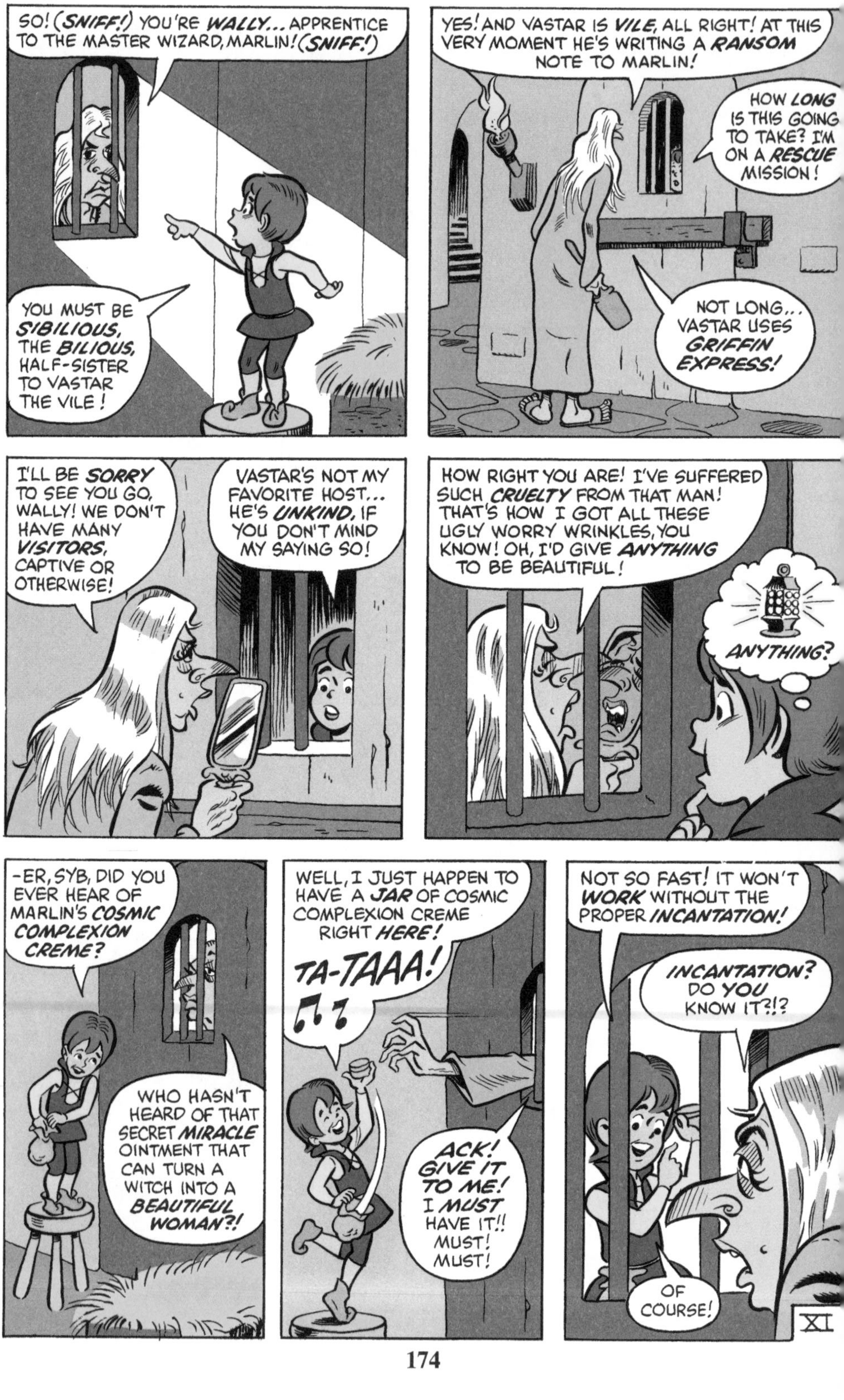
SO! (SNIFF!) YOU'RE WALLY... APPRENTICE TO THE MASTER WIZARD, MARLIN! (SNIFF!)
YOU MUST BE SIBILIOUS, THE BILIOUS, HALF-SISTER TO VASTAR THE VILE!
YES! AND VASTAR IS VILE, ALL RIGHT! AT THIS VERY MOMENT HE'S WRITING A RANSOM NOTE TO MARLIN!
HOW LONG IS THIS GOING TO TAKE? I'M ON A RESCUE MISSION!
NOT LONG... VASTAR USES GRIFFIN EXPRESS!
I'LL BE SORRY TO SEE YOU GO, WALLY! WE DON'T HAVE MANY VISITORS, CAPTIVE OR OTHERWISE!
VASTAR'S NOT MY FAVORITE HOST... HE'S UNKIND, IF YOU DON'T MIND MY SAYING SO!
HOW RIGHT YOU ARE! I'VE SUFFERED SUCH CRUELTY FROM THAT MAN! THAT'S HOW I GOT ALL THESE UGLY WORRY WRINKLES, YOU KNOW! OH, I'D GIVE ANYTHING TO BE BEAUTIFUL!
ANYTHING?
-ER, SYB, DID YOU EVER HEAR OF MARLIN'S COSMIC COMPLEXION CREME?
WHO HASN'T HEARD OF THAT SECRET MIRACLE OINTMENT THAT CAN TURN A WITCH INTO A BEAUTIFUL WOMAN?!
WELL, I JUST HAPPEN TO HAVE A JAR OF COSMIC COMPLEXION CREME RIGHT HERE!
TA-TAAA!
ACK! GIVE IT TO ME! I MUST HAVE IT!! MUST! MUST!
NOT SO FAST! IT WON'T WORK WITHOUT THE PROPER INCANTATION!
INCANTATION? DO YOU KNOW IT?!?
OF COURSE!
XI

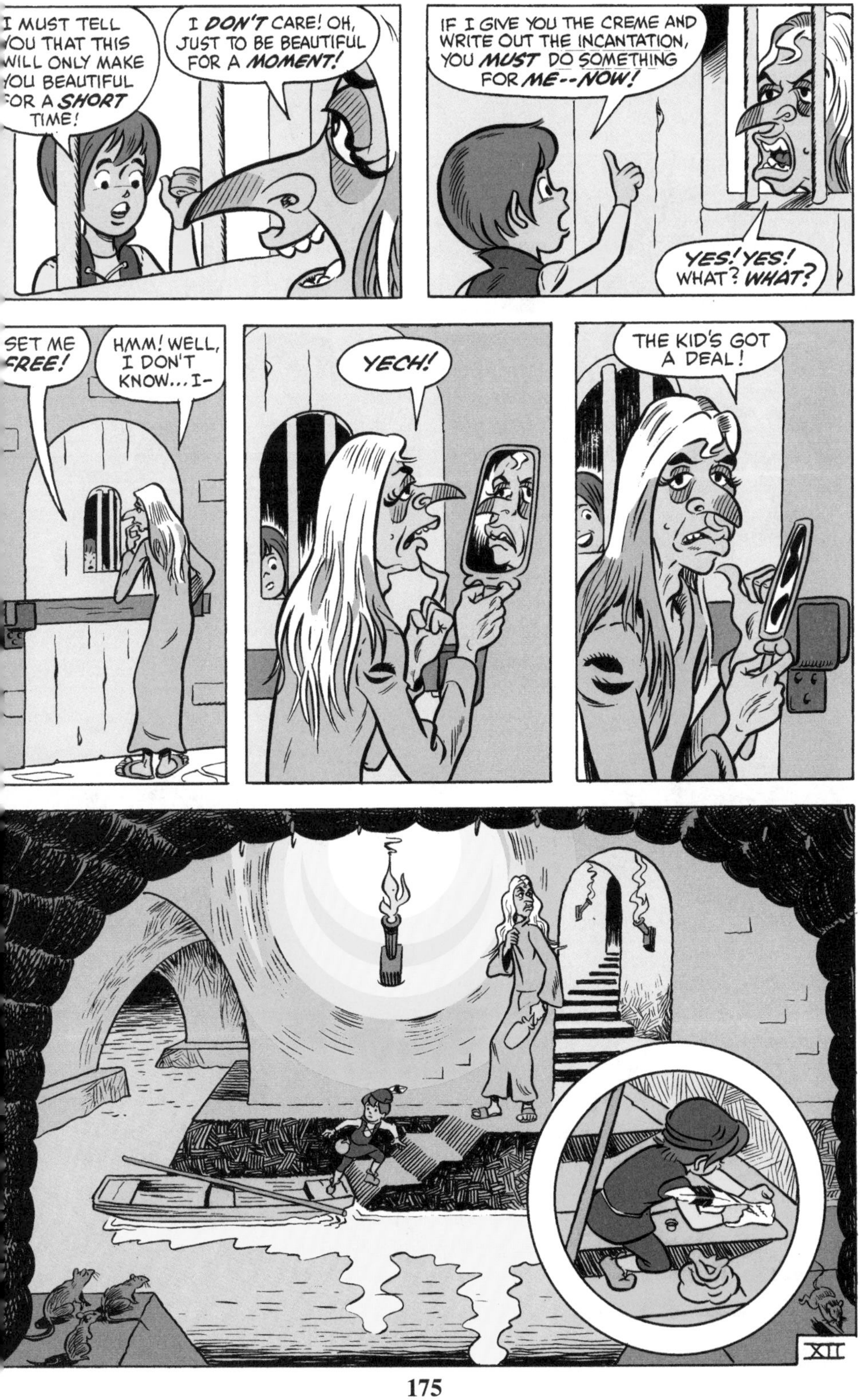
I MUST TELL YOU THAT THIS WILL ONLY MAKE YOU BEAUTIFUL FOR A SHORT TIME!
I DON'T CARE! OH, JUST TO BE BEAUTIFUL FOR A MOMENT!
IF I GIVE YOU THE CREME AND WRITE OUT THE INCANTATION, YOU MUST DO SOMETHING FOR ME--NOW!
YES! YES! WHAT? WHAT?
SET ME FREE!
HMM! WELL, I DON'T KNOW... I-
YECH!
THE KID'S GOT A DEAL!
XII

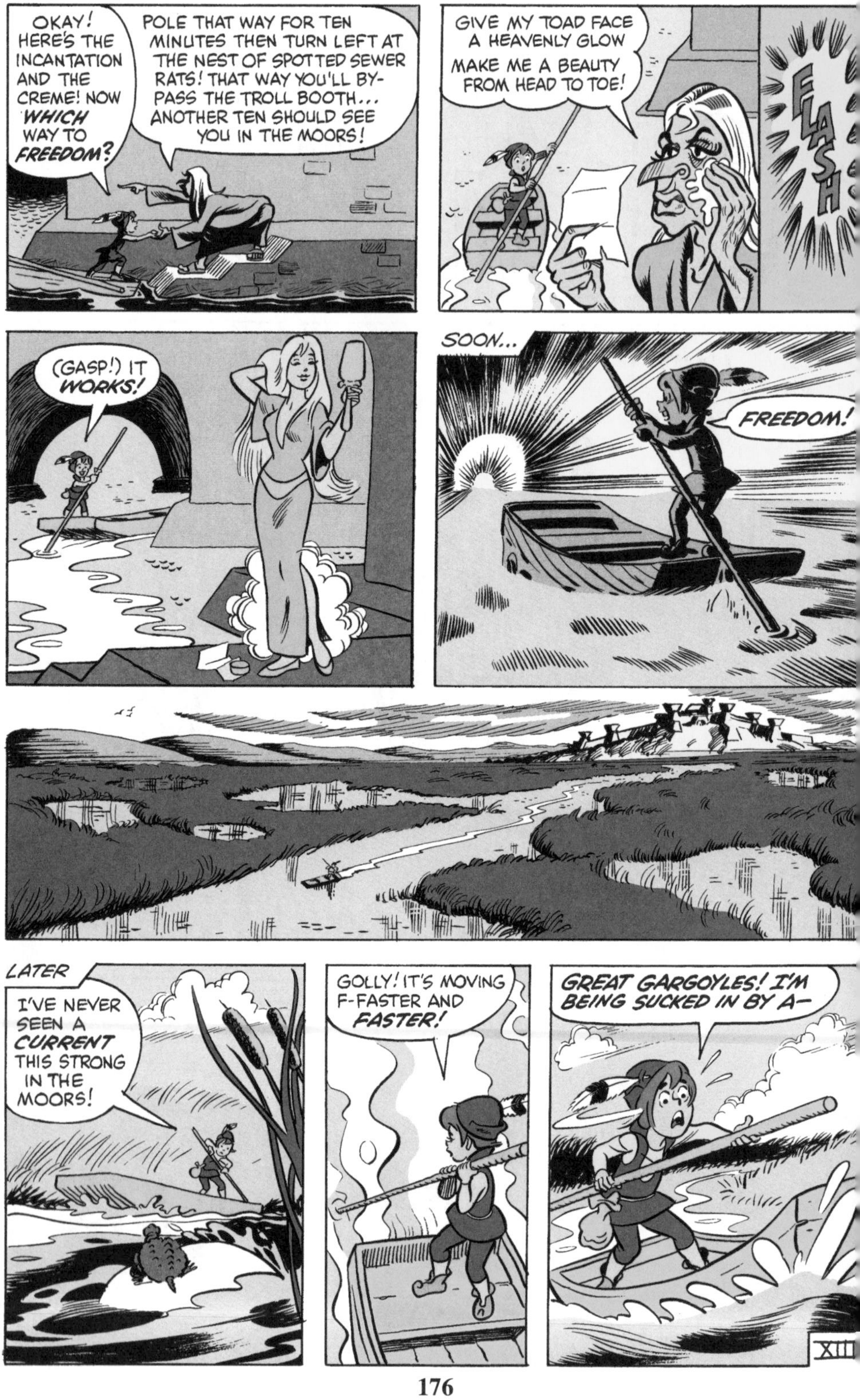

OKAY! HERE'S THE INCANTATION AND THE CREME! NOW WHICH WAY TO FREEDOM?
POLE THAT WAY FOR TEN MINUTES THEN TURN LEFT AT THE NEST OF SPOTTED SEWER RATS! THAT WAY YOU'LL BY-PASS THE TROLL BOOTH... ANOTHER TEN SHOULD SEE YOU IN THE MOORS!
GIVE MY TOAD FACE A HEAVENLY GLOW
MAKE ME A BEAUTY FROM HEAD TO TOE!
FLASH
(GASP!) IT WORKS!
SOON...
FREEDOM!
LATER
I'VE NEVER SEEN A CURRENT THIS STRONG IN THE MOORS!
GOLLY! IT'S MOVING F-FASTER AND FASTER!
GREAT GARGOYLES! I'M BEING SUCKED IN BY A—
XIII

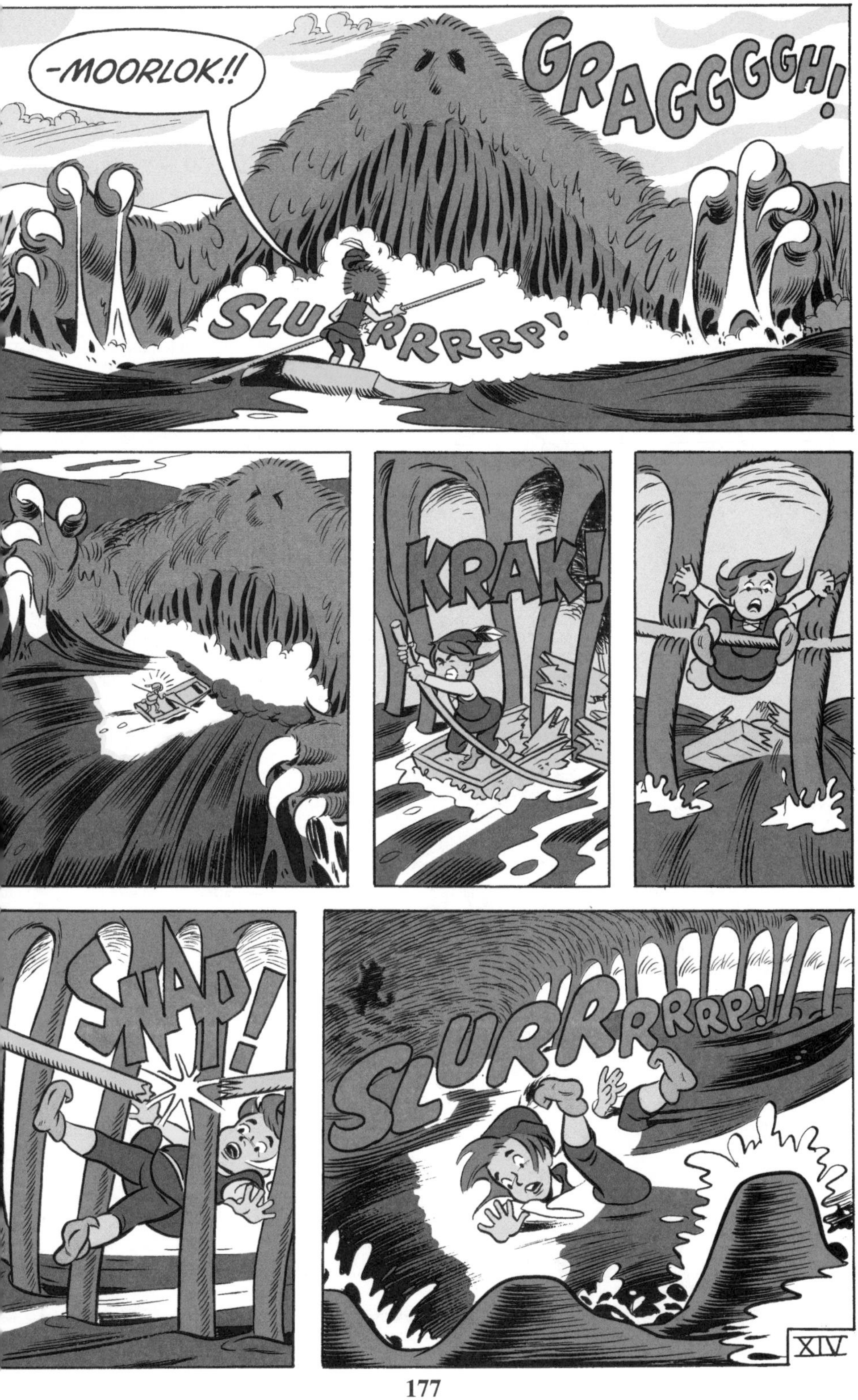

-MOORLOK!!
GRAGGGGH!
SLURRRRRP!
KRAK!
SNAP!
SLURRRRRP!!!
XIV

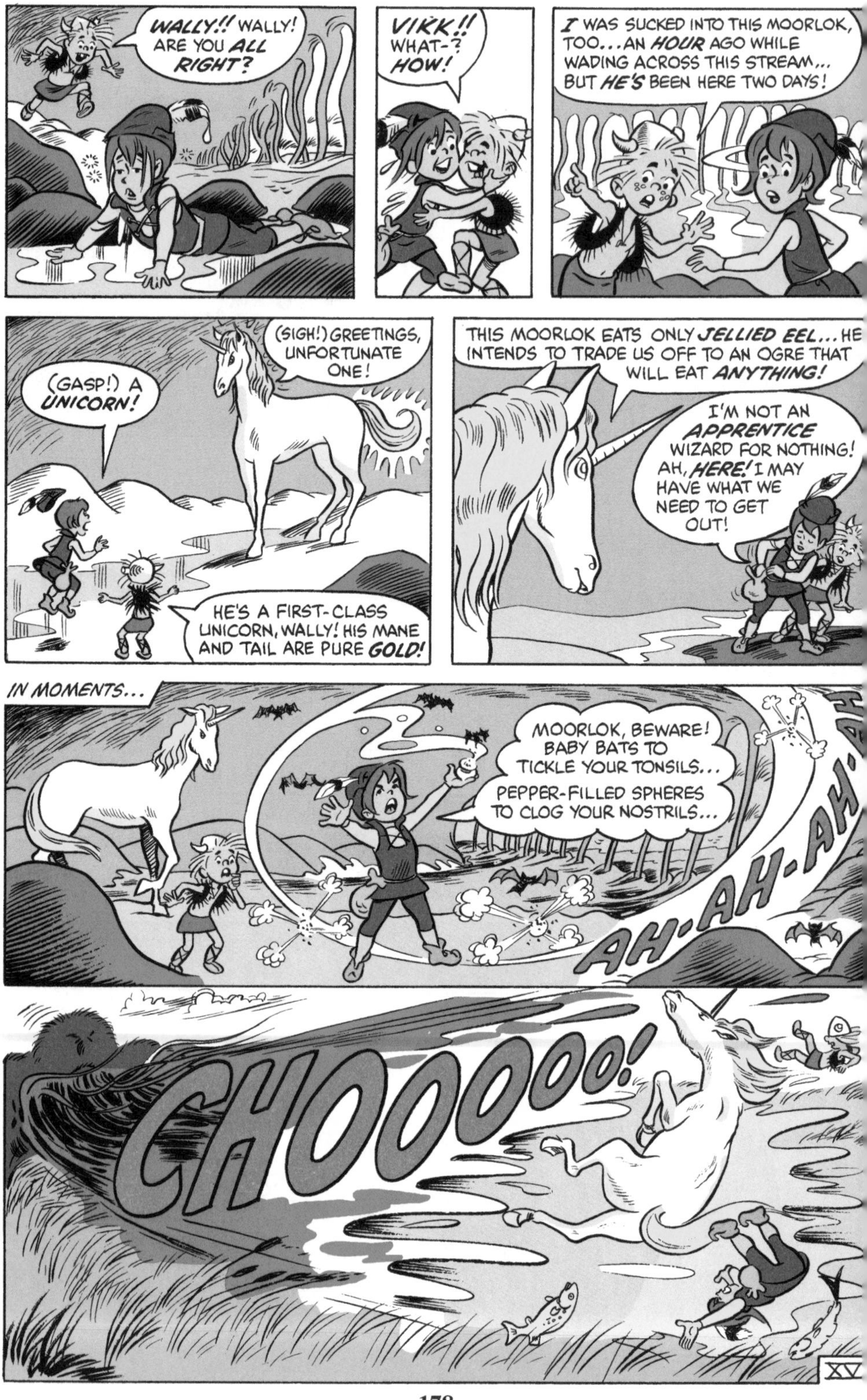
WALLY!! WALLY! ARE YOU ALL RIGHT?
VIKK!! WHAT-? HOW!
I WAS SUCKED INTO THIS MOORLOK, TOO...AN HOUR AGO WHILE WADING ACROSS THIS STREAM... BUT HE'S BEEN HERE TWO DAYS!
(GASP!) A UNICORN!
(SIGH!) GREETINGS, UNFORTUNATE ONE!
HE'S A FIRST-CLASS UNICORN, WALLY! HIS MANE AND TAIL ARE PURE GOLD!
THIS MOORLOK EATS ONLY JELLIED EEL...HE INTENDS TO TRADE US OFF TO AN OGRE THAT WILL EAT ANYTHING!
I'M NOT AN APPRENTICE WIZARD FOR NOTHING! AH, HERE! I MAY HAVE WHAT WE NEED TO GET OUT!
IN MOMENTS...
MOORLOK, BEWARE! BABY BATS TO TICKLE YOUR TONSILS... PEPPER-FILLED SPHERES TO CLOG YOUR NOSTRILS...
AH-AH-AH-AH
CHOOOOOO!
XV

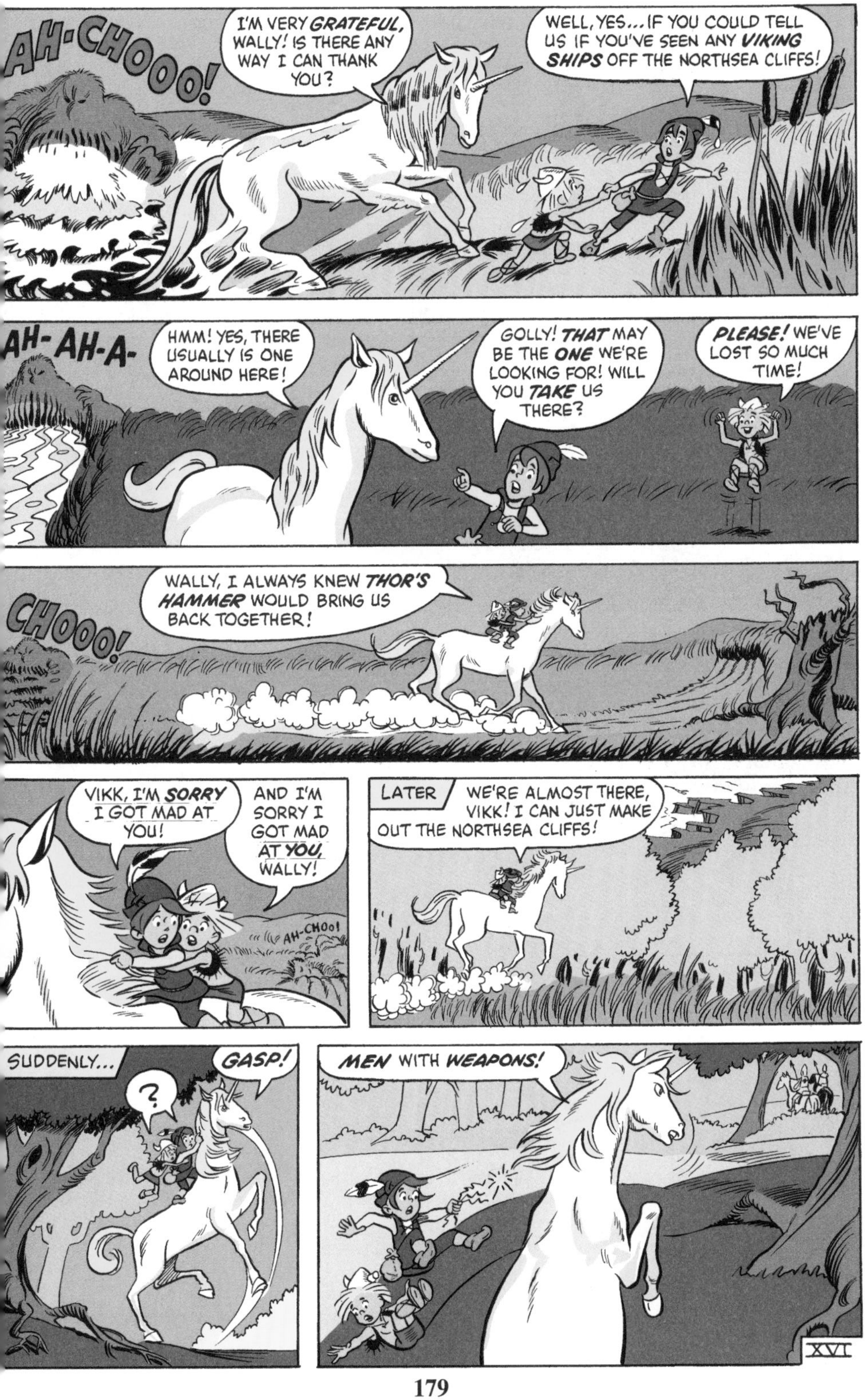

AH-CHOOO!
I'M VERY GRATEFUL, WALLY! IS THERE ANY WAY I CAN THANK YOU?
WELL, YES... IF YOU COULD TELL US IF YOU'VE SEEN ANY VIKING SHIPS OFF THE NORTHSEA CLIFFS!
AH-AH-A-
HMM! YES, THERE USUALLY IS ONE AROUND HERE!
GOLLY! THAT MAY BE THE ONE WE'RE LOOKING FOR! WILL YOU TAKE US THERE?
PLEASE! WE'VE LOST SO MUCH TIME!
CHOOO!
WALLY, I ALWAYS KNEW THOR'S HAMMER WOULD BRING US BACK TOGETHER!
VIKK, I'M SORRY I GOT MAD AT YOU!
AND I'M SORRY I GOT MAD AT YOU, WALLY!
AH-CHOO!
LATER
WE'RE ALMOST THERE, VIKK! I CAN JUST MAKE OUT THE NORTHSEA CLIFFS!
SUDDENLY...
?
GASP!
MEN WITH WEAPONS!
XVI

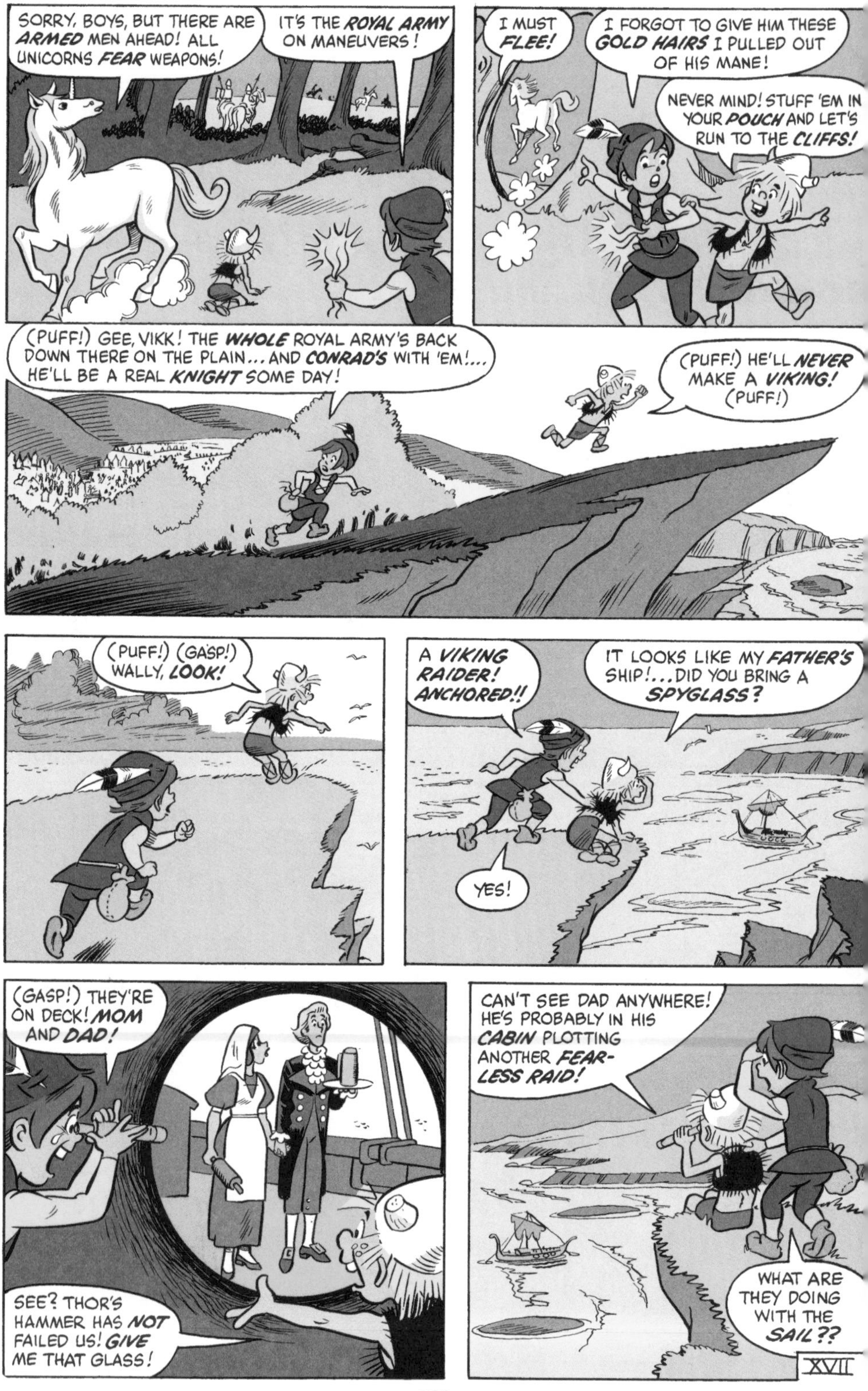
SORRY, BOYS, BUT THERE ARE ARMED MEN AHEAD! ALL UNICORNS FEAR WEAPONS!
IT'S THE ROYAL ARMY ON MANEUVERS!
I MUST FLEE!
I FORGOT TO GIVE HIM THESE GOLD HAIRS I PULLED OUT OF HIS MANE!
NEVER MIND! STUFF 'EM IN YOUR POUCH AND LET'S RUN TO THE CLIFFS!
(PUFF!) GEE, VIKK! THE WHOLE ROYAL ARMY'S BACK DOWN THERE ON THE PLAIN... AND CONRAD'S WITH 'EM!... HE'LL BE A REAL KNIGHT SOME DAY!
(PUFF!) HE'LL NEVER MAKE A VIKING! (PUFF!)
(PUFF!) (GASP!) WALLY, LOOK!
A VIKING RAIDER! ANCHORED!!
IT LOOKS LIKE MY FATHER'S SHIP!... DID YOU BRING A SPYGLASS?
YES!
(GASP!) THEY'RE ON DECK! MOM AND DAD!
SEE? THOR'S HAMMER HAS NOT FAILED US! GIVE ME THAT GLASS!
CAN'T SEE DAD ANYWHERE! HE'S PROBABLY IN HIS CABIN PLOTTING ANOTHER FEAR-LESS RAID!
WHAT ARE THEY DOING WITH THE SAIL??
XVII

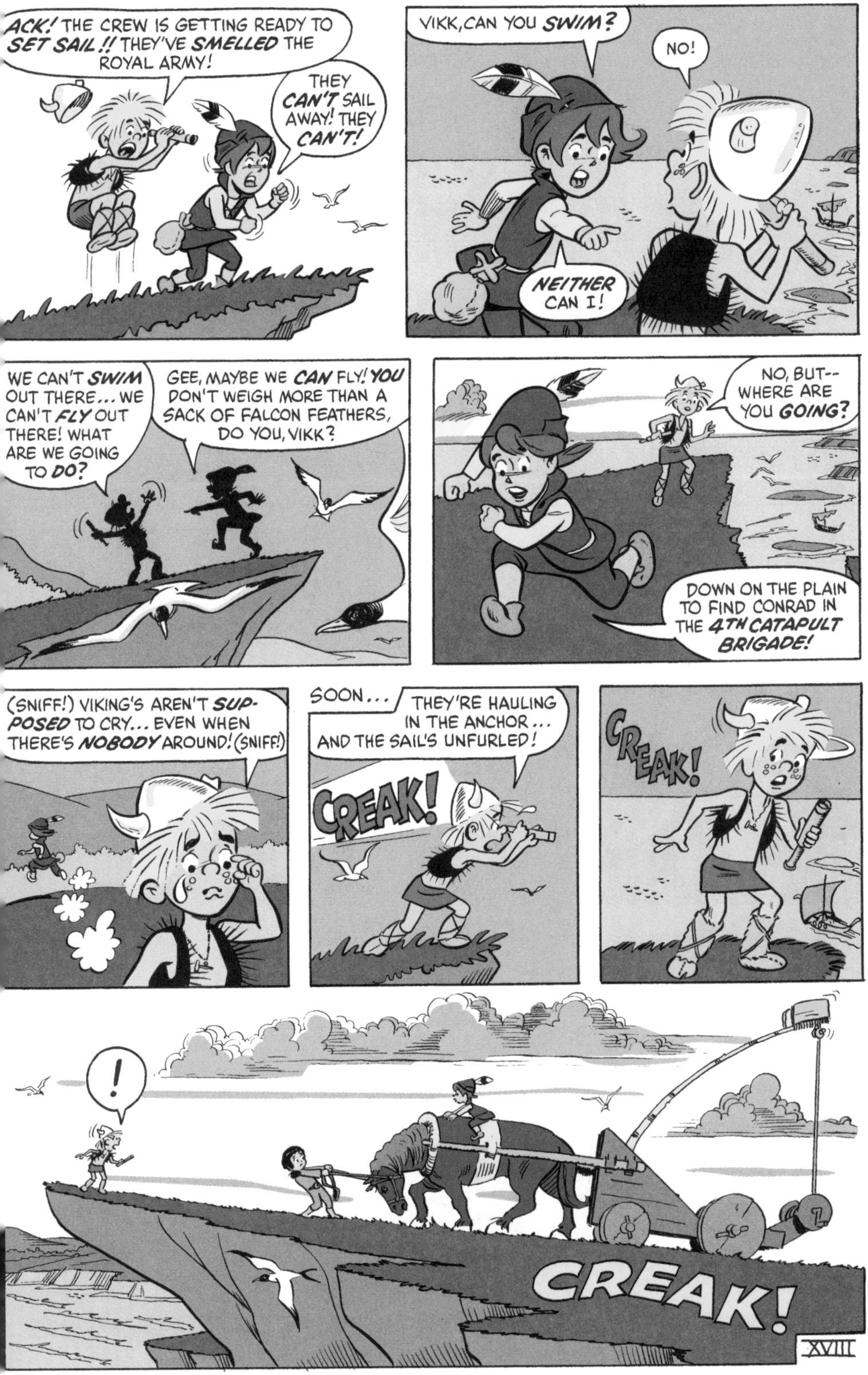
ACK! THE CREW IS GETTING READY TO SET SAIL!! THEY'VE SMELLED THE ROYAL ARMY!
THEY CAN'T SAIL AWAY! THEY CAN'T!
VIKK, CAN YOU SWIM?
NO!
NEITHER CAN I!
WE CAN'T SWIM OUT THERE... WE CAN'T FLY OUT THERE! WHAT ARE WE GOING TO DO?
GEE, MAYBE WE CAN FLY! YOU DON'T WEIGH MORE THAN A SACK OF FALCON FEATHERS, DO YOU, VIKK?
NO, BUT-- WHERE ARE YOU GOING?
DOWN ON THE PLAIN TO FIND CONRAD IN THE 4TH CATAPULT BRIGADE!
(SNIFF!) VIKING'S AREN'T SUPPOSED TO CRY... EVEN WHEN THERE'S NOBODY AROUND! (SNIFF!)
SOON...
THEY'RE HAULING IN THE ANCHOR... AND THE SAIL'S UNFURLED!
CREAK!
CREAK!
!
CREAK!
XVIII

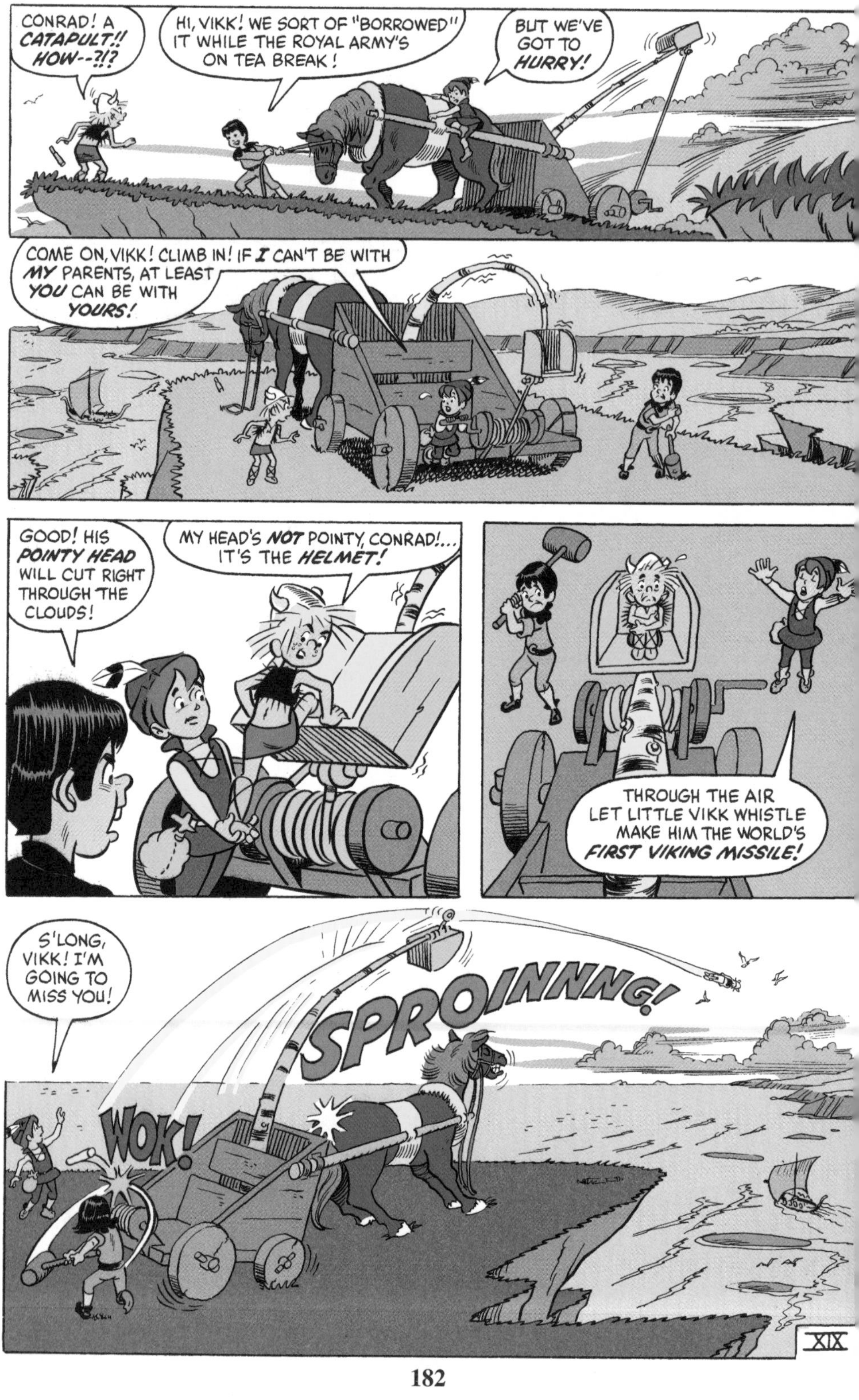

CONRAD! A CATAPULT!! HOW--?!?
HI, VIKK! WE SORT OF "BORROWED" IT WHILE THE ROYAL ARMY'S ON TEA BREAK!
BUT WE'VE GOT TO HURRY!
COME ON, VIKK! CLIMB IN! IF I CAN'T BE WITH MY PARENTS, AT LEAST YOU CAN BE WITH YOURS!
GOOD! HIS POINTY HEAD WILL CUT RIGHT THROUGH THE CLOUDS!
MY HEAD'S NOT POINTY, CONRAD!... IT'S THE HELMET!
THROUGH THE AIR LET LITTLE VIKK WHISTLE MAKE HIM THE WORLD'S FIRST VIKING MISSILE!
S'LONG, VIKK! I'M GOING TO MISS YOU!
SPROINNNG!
WOK!
XIX

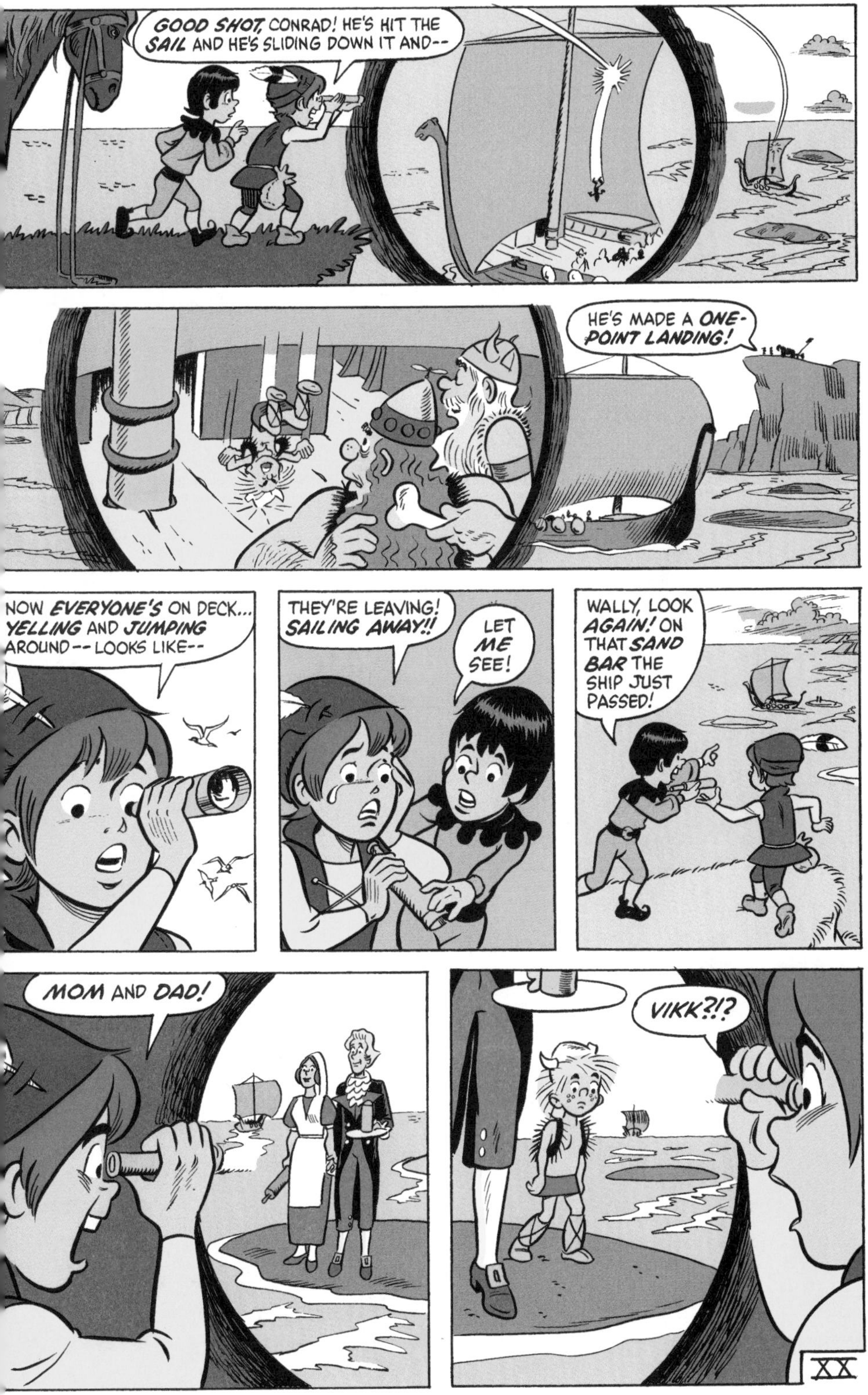
GOOD SHOT, CONRAD! HE'S HIT THE SAIL AND HE'S SLIDING DOWN IT AND--
HE'S MADE A ONE-POINT LANDING!
NOW EVERYONE'S ON DECK... YELLING AND JUMPING AROUND--LOOKS LIKE--
THEY'RE LEAVING! SAILING AWAY!!
LET ME SEE!
WALLY, LOOK AGAIN! ON THAT SAND BAR THE SHIP JUST PASSED!
MOM AND DAD!
VIKK?!?
XX

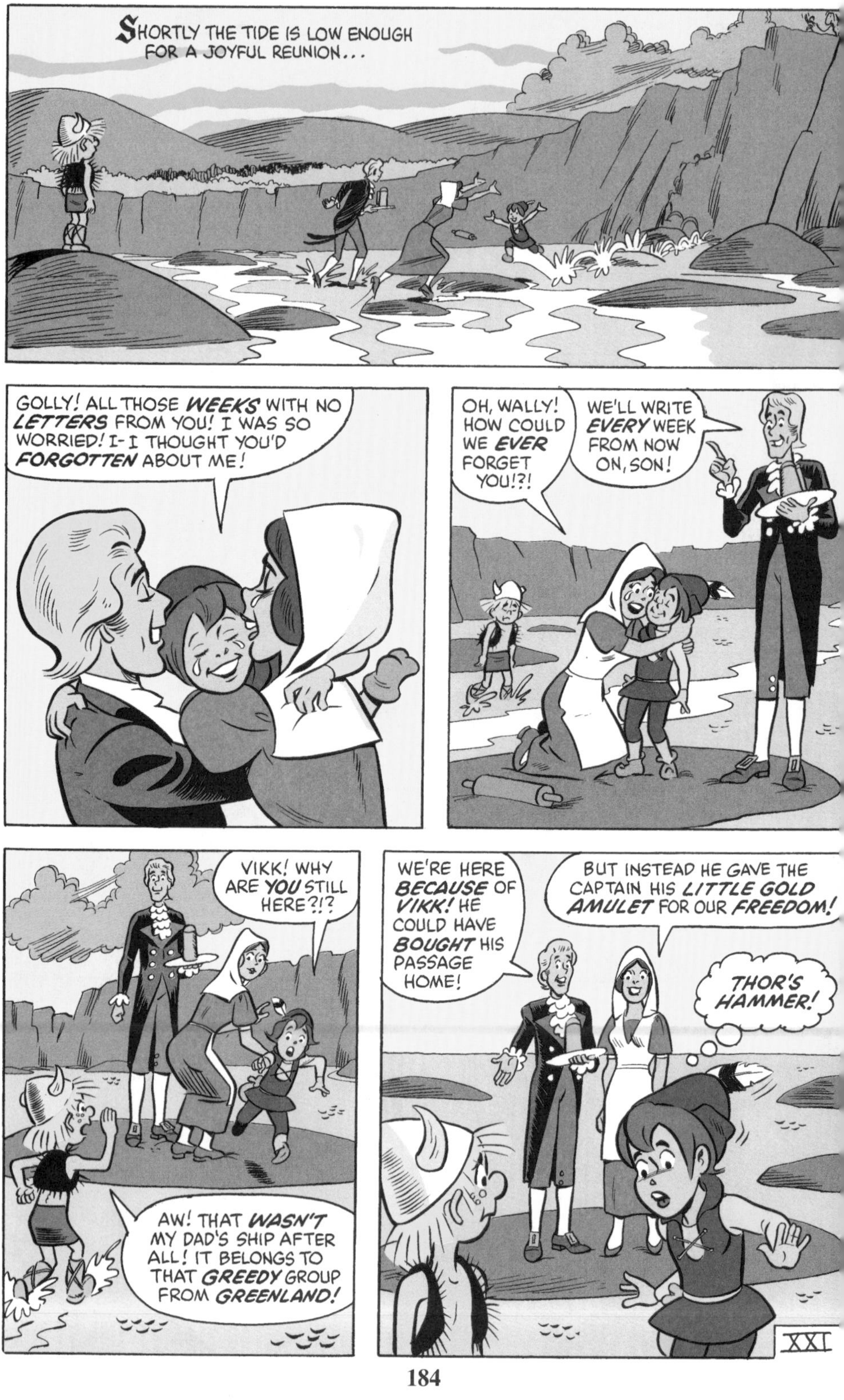
SHORTLY THE TIDE IS LOW ENOUGH FOR A JOYFUL REUNION...
GOLLY! ALL THOSE WEEKS WITH NO LETTERS FROM YOU! I WAS SO WORRIED! I-I THOUGHT YOU'D FORGOTTEN ABOUT ME!
OH, WALLY! HOW COULD WE EVER FORGET YOU!?!
WE'LL WRITE EVERY WEEK FROM NOW ON, SON!
VIKK! WHY ARE YOU STILL HERE?!?
AW! THAT WASN'T MY DAD'S SHIP AFTER ALL! IT BELONGS TO THAT GREEDY GROUP FROM GREENLAND!
WE'RE HERE BECAUSE OF VIKK! HE COULD HAVE BOUGHT HIS PASSAGE HOME!
BUT INSTEAD HE GAVE THE CAPTAIN HIS LITTLE GOLD AMULET FOR OUR FREEDOM!
THOR'S HAMMER!
XXI

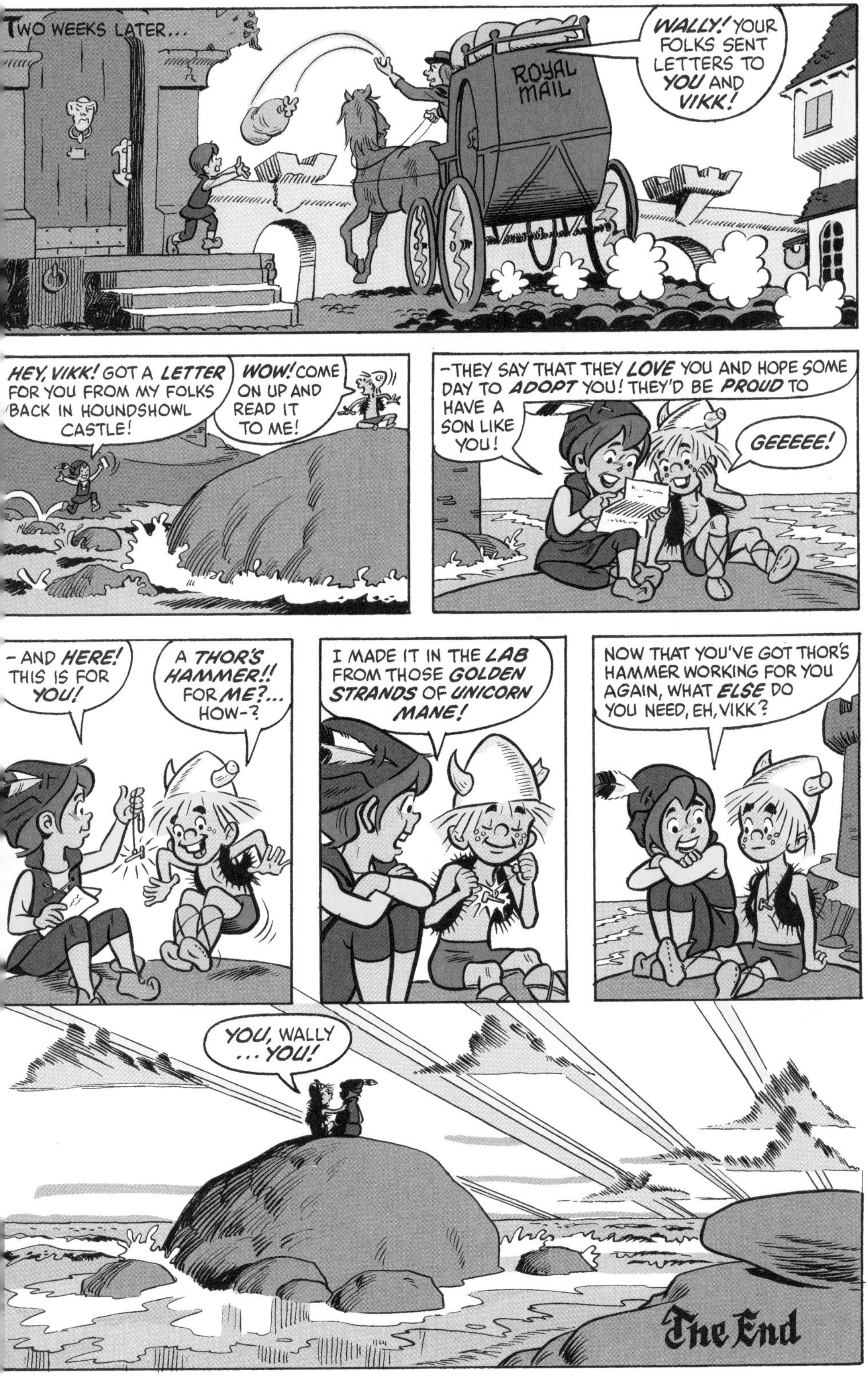
TWO WEEKS LATER...
ROYAL MAIL
WALLY! YOUR FOLKS SENT LETTERS TO YOU AND VIKK!
HEY, VIKK! GOT A LETTER FOR YOU FROM MY FOLKS BACK IN HOUNDSHOWL CASTLE!
WOW! COME ON UP AND READ IT TO ME!
-THEY SAY THAT THEY LOVE YOU AND HOPE SOME DAY TO ADOPT YOU! THEY'D BE PROUD TO HAVE A SON LIKE YOU!
GEEEEE!
-AND HERE! THIS IS FOR YOU!
A THOR'S HAMMER!! FOR ME?... HOW-?
I MADE IT IN THE LAB FROM THOSE GOLDEN STRANDS OF UNICORN MANE!
NOW THAT YOU'VE GOT THOR'S HAMMER WORKING FOR YOU AGAIN, WHAT ELSE DO YOU NEED, EH, VIKK?
YOU, WALLY ... YOU!
The End

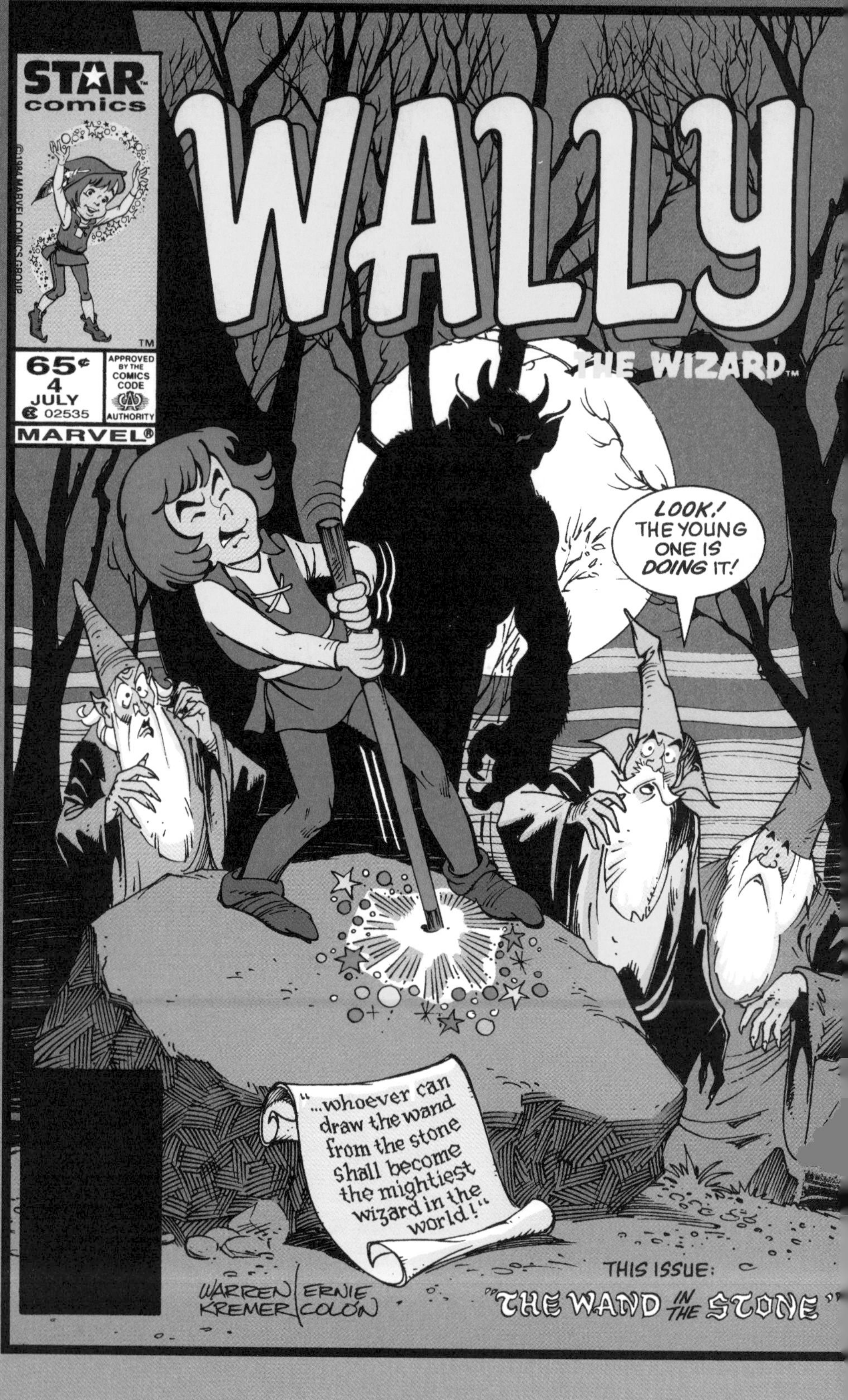
STAR comics
©1984 MARVEL COMICS GROUP
WALLY
THE WIZARD
65¢
4
JULY
02535
APPROVED BY THE COMICS CODE AUTHORITY
MARVEL
LOOK! THE YOUNG ONE IS DOING IT!
"...whoever can draw the wand from the stone shall become the mightiest wizard in the world!"
WARREN KREMER
ERNIE COLÓN
THIS ISSUE:
"THE WAND IN THE STONE"

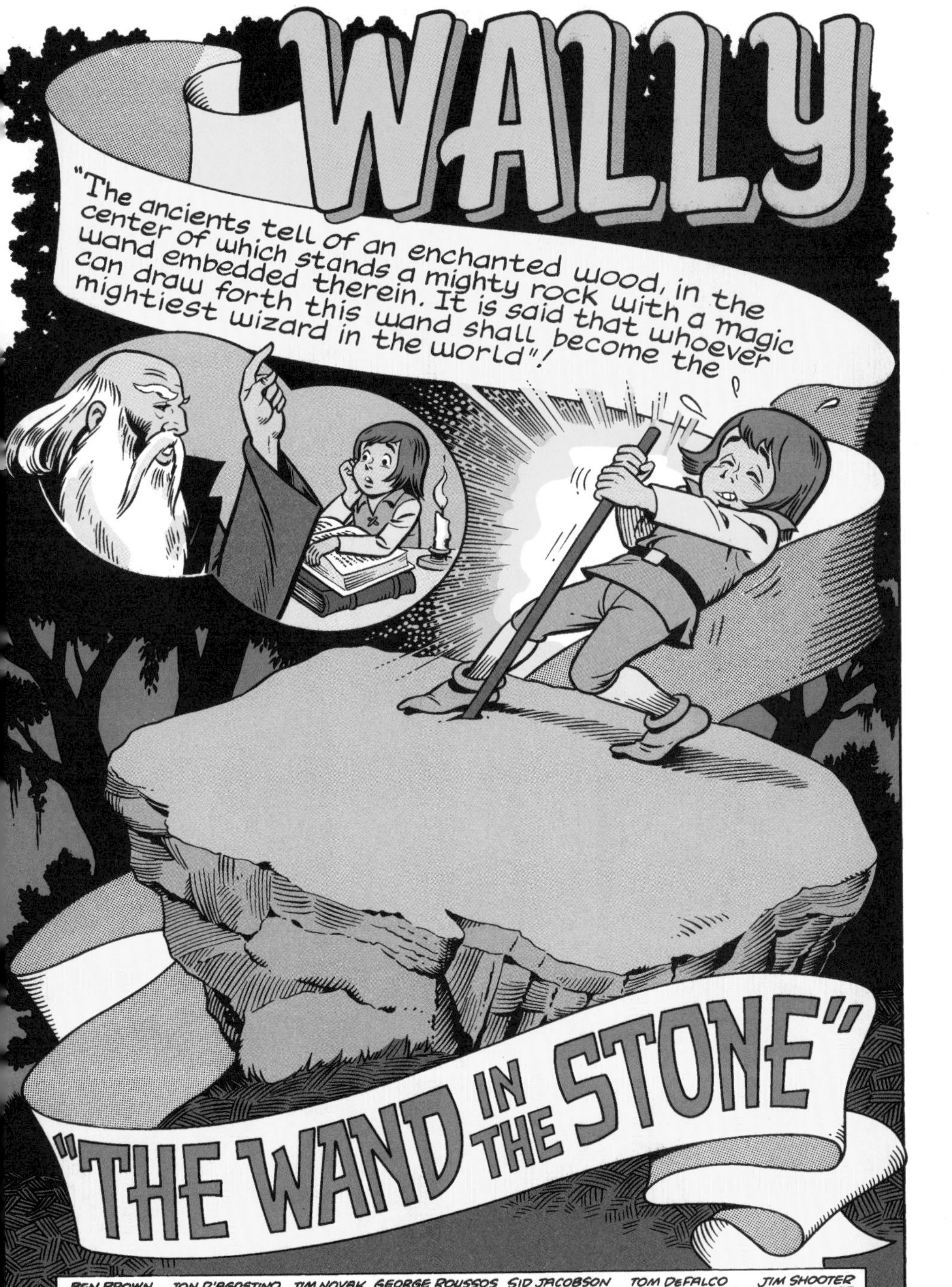
WALLY
"The ancients tell of an enchanted wood, in the center of which stands a mighty rock with a magic wand embedded therein. It is said that whoever can draw forth this wand shall become the mightiest wizard in the world"!
"THE WAND IN THE STONE"
BEN BROWN WRITER/ARTIST
JON D'AGOSTINO INKER
JIM NOVAK LETTERER
GEORGE ROUSSOS COLORIST
SID JACOBSON EDITOR
TOM DEFALCO EXECUTIVE EDITOR
JIM SHOOTER EDITOR-IN-CHIEF
1

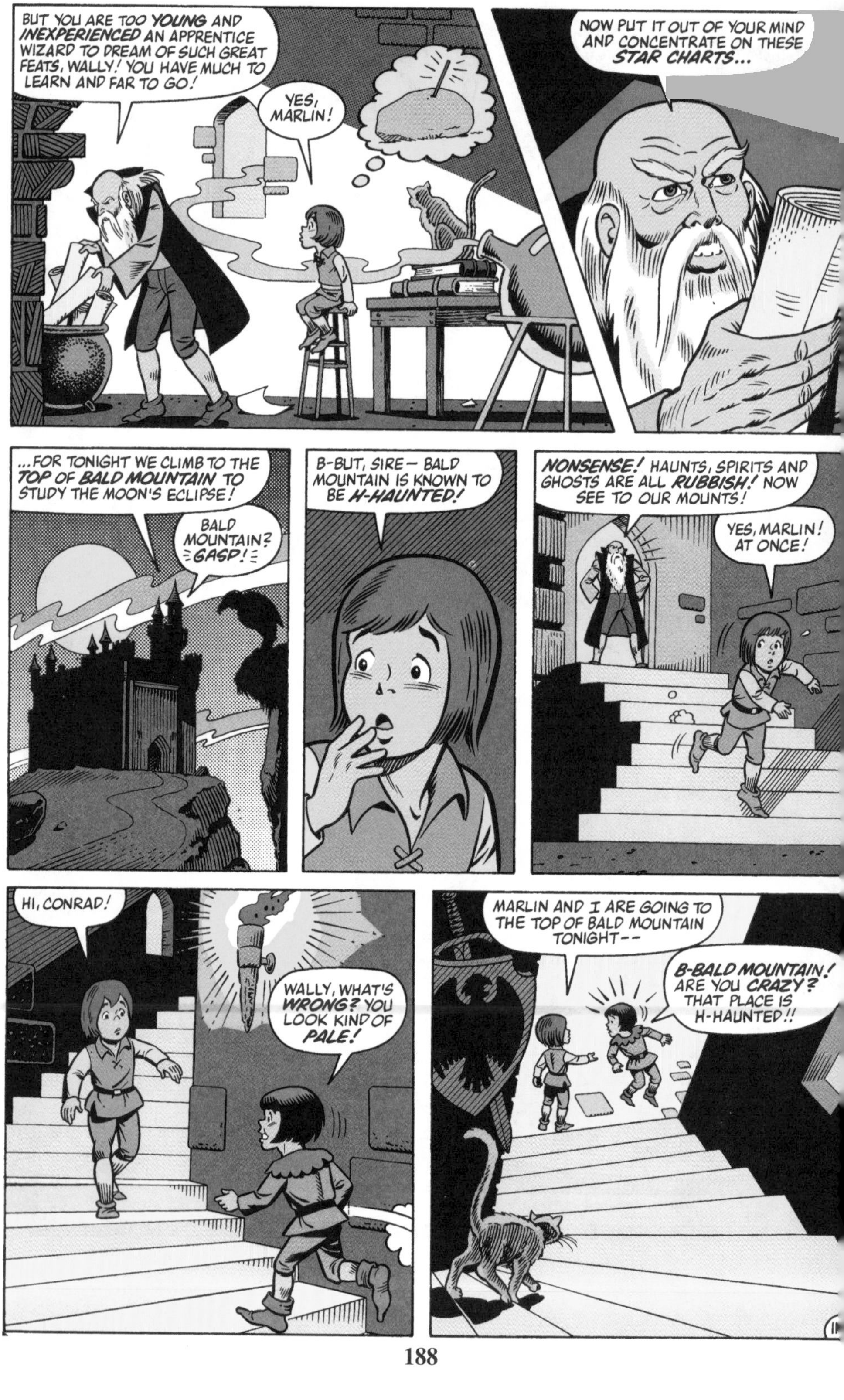
BUT YOU ARE TOO YOUNG AND INEXPERIENCED AN APPRENTICE WIZARD TO DREAM OF SUCH GREAT FEATS, WALLY! YOU HAVE MUCH TO LEARN AND FAR TO GO!
YES, MARLIN!
NOW PUT IT OUT OF YOUR MIND AND CONCENTRATE ON THESE STAR CHARTS...
...FOR TONIGHT WE CLIMB TO THE TOP OF BALD MOUNTAIN TO STUDY THE MOON'S ECLIPSE!
BALD MOUNTAIN? GASP!
B-BUT, SIRE— BALD MOUNTAIN IS KNOWN TO BE H-HAUNTED!
NONSENSE! HAUNTS, SPIRITS AND GHOSTS ARE ALL RUBBISH! NOW SEE TO OUR MOUNTS!
YES, MARLIN! AT ONCE!
HI, CONRAD!
WALLY, WHAT'S WRONG? YOU LOOK KIND OF PALE!
MARLIN AND I ARE GOING TO THE TOP OF BALD MOUNTAIN TONIGHT--
B-BALD MOUNTAIN! ARE YOU CRAZY? THAT PLACE IS H-HAUNTED!!

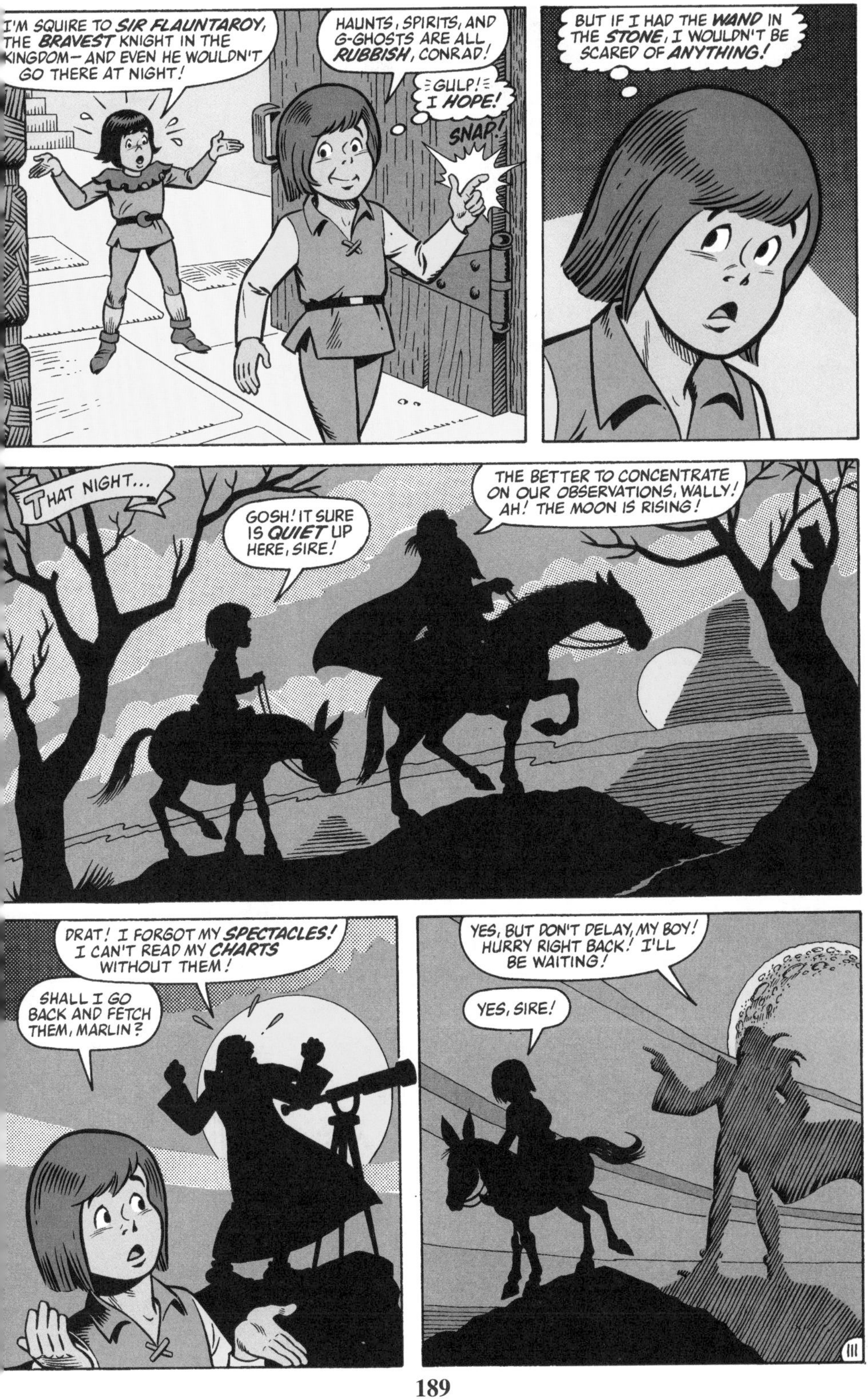
I'M SQUIRE TO SIR FLAUNTAROY, THE BRAVEST KNIGHT IN THE KINGDOM—AND EVEN HE WOULDN'T GO THERE AT NIGHT!
HAUNTS, SPIRITS, AND G-GHOSTS ARE ALL RUBBISH, CONRAD!
GULP! I HOPE!
SNAP!
BUT IF I HAD THE WAND IN THE STONE, I WOULDN'T BE SCARED OF ANYTHING!
THAT NIGHT...
GOSH! IT SURE IS QUIET UP HERE, SIRE!
THE BETTER TO CONCENTRATE ON OUR OBSERVATIONS, WALLY! AH! THE MOON IS RISING!
DRAT! I FORGOT MY SPECTACLES! I CAN'T READ MY CHARTS WITHOUT THEM!
SHALL I GO BACK AND FETCH THEM, MARLIN?
YES, BUT DON'T DELAY, MY BOY! HURRY RIGHT BACK! I'LL BE WAITING!
YES, SIRE!
111

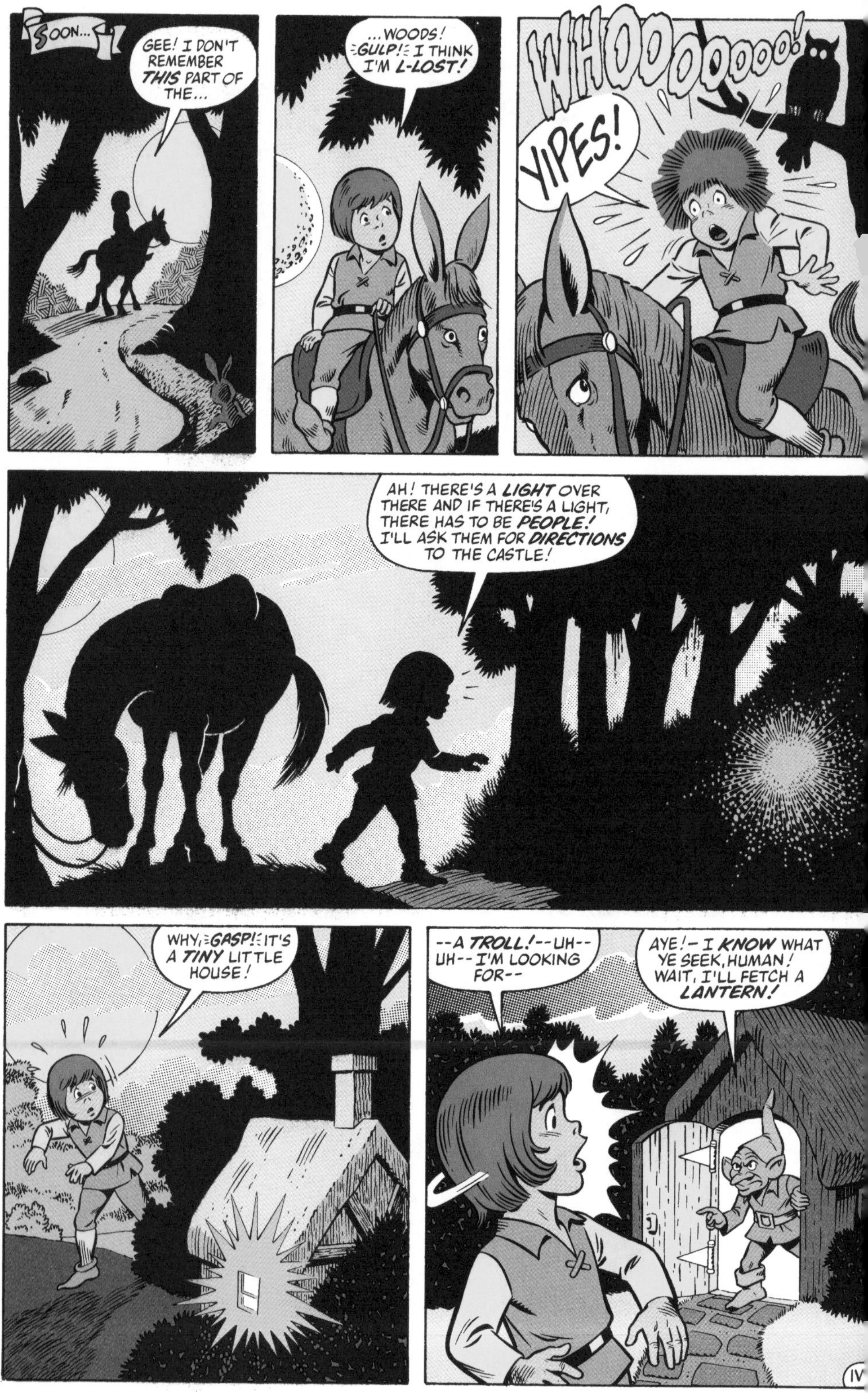
SOON...
GEE! I DON'T REMEMBER THIS PART OF THE...
...WOODS! GULP! I THINK I'M L-LOST!
WHOOOOOOOO!
YIPES!
AH! THERE'S A LIGHT OVER THERE AND IF THERE'S A LIGHT, THERE HAS TO BE PEOPLE! I'LL ASK THEM FOR DIRECTIONS TO THE CASTLE!
WHY, GASP! IT'S A TINY LITTLE HOUSE!
--A TROLL!--UH-- UH--I'M LOOKING FOR--
AYE!-- I KNOW WHAT YE SEEK, HUMAN! WAIT, I'LL FETCH A LANTERN!
IV

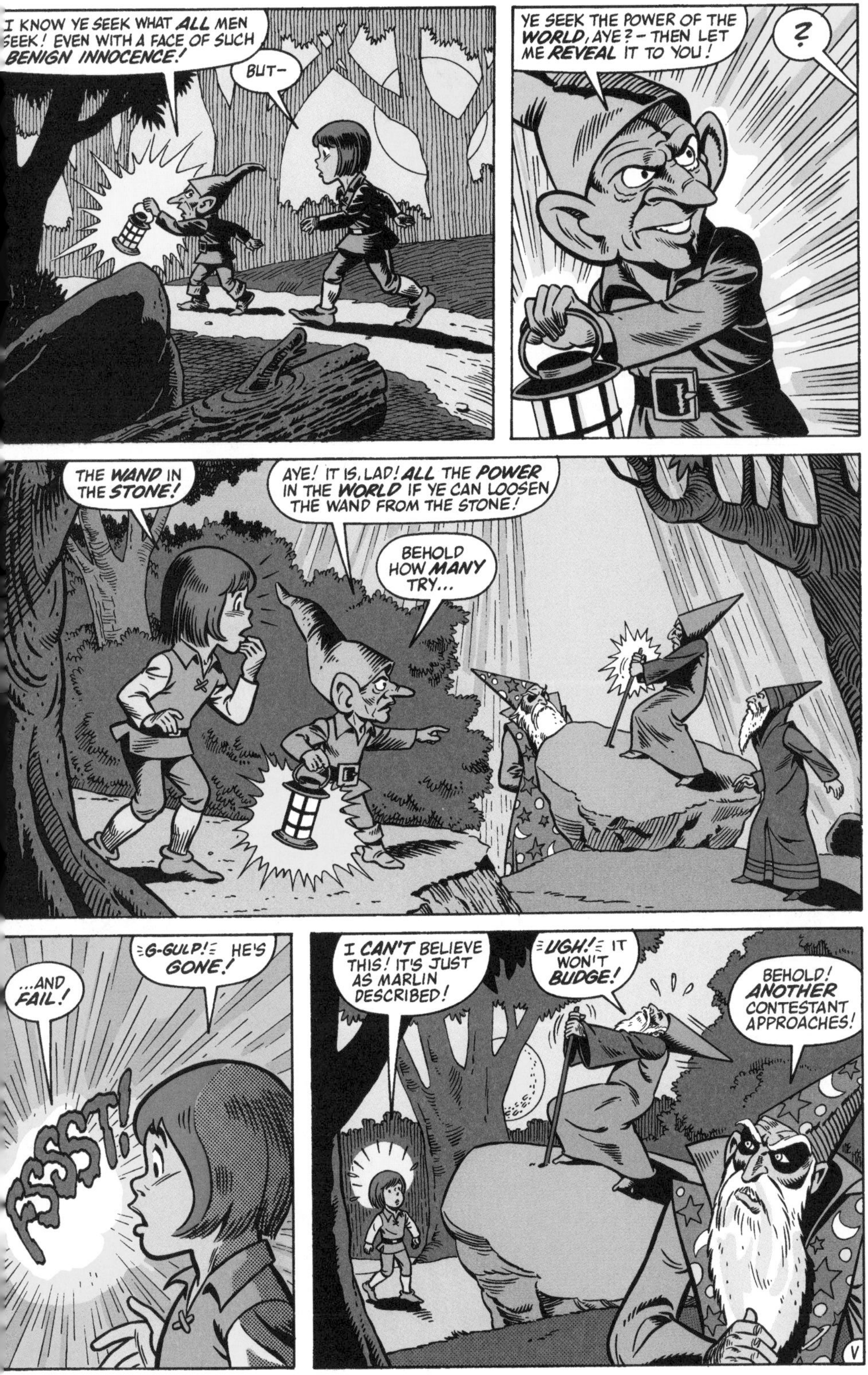

I KNOW YE SEEK WHAT ALL MEN SEEK! EVEN WITH A FACE OF SUCH BENIGN INNOCENCE!
BUT-
YE SEEK THE POWER OF THE WORLD, AYE? - THEN LET ME REVEAL IT TO YOU!
?
THE WAND IN THE STONE!
AYE! IT IS, LAD! ALL THE POWER IN THE WORLD IF YE CAN LOOSEN THE WAND FROM THE STONE!
BEHOLD HOW MANY TRY...
...AND FAIL!
G-GULP! HE'S GONE!
SSST!
I CAN'T BELIEVE THIS! IT'S JUST AS MARLIN DESCRIBED!
UGH! IT WON'T BUDGE!
BEHOLD! ANOTHER CONTESTANT APPROACHES!
V

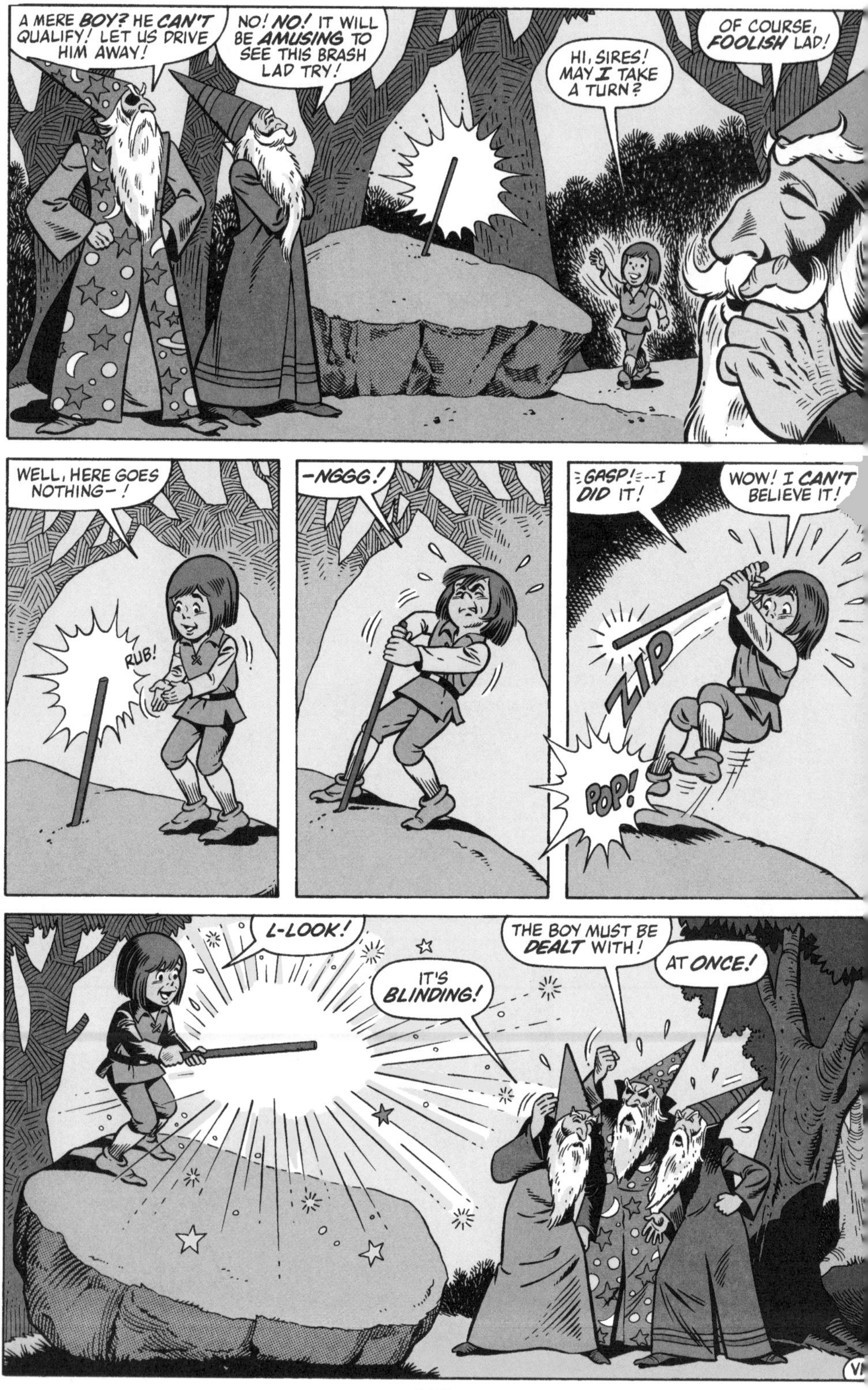

A MERE BOY? HE CAN'T QUALIFY! LET US DRIVE HIM AWAY!
NO! NO! IT WILL BE AMUSING TO SEE THIS BRASH LAD TRY!
HI, SIRES! MAY I TAKE A TURN?
OF COURSE, FOOLISH LAD!
WELL, HERE GOES NOTHING-!
RUB!
-NGGG!
GASP!--I DID IT!
WOW! I CAN'T BELIEVE IT!
ZIP
POP!
L-LOOK!
IT'S BLINDING!
THE BOY MUST BE DEALT WITH!
AT ONCE!

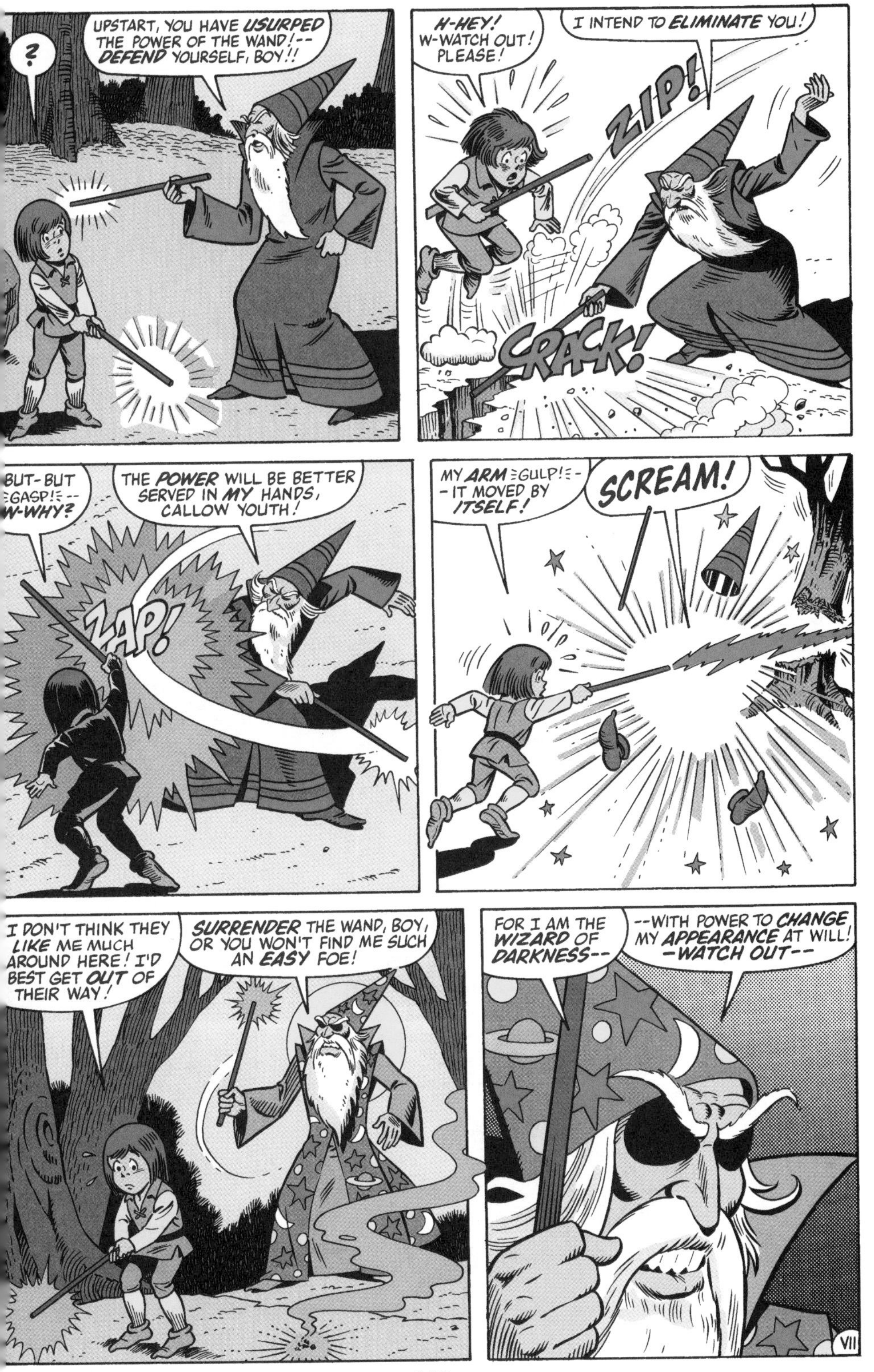
?
UPSTART, YOU HAVE USURPED THE POWER OF THE WAND!-- DEFEND YOURSELF, BOY!!
H-HEY! W-WATCH OUT! PLEASE!
I INTEND TO ELIMINATE YOU!
ZIP!
CRACK!
BUT-BUT GASP!-- W-WHY?
THE POWER WILL BE BETTER SERVED IN MY HANDS, CALLOW YOUTH!
ZAP!
MY ARM GULP!-- IT MOVED BY ITSELF!
SCREAM!
I DON'T THINK THEY LIKE ME MUCH AROUND HERE! I'D BEST GET OUT OF THEIR WAY!
SURRENDER THE WAND, BOY, OR YOU WON'T FIND ME SUCH AN EASY FOE!
FOR I AM THE WIZARD OF DARKNESS--
--WITH POWER TO CHANGE MY APPEARANCE AT WILL! --WATCH OUT--
VII

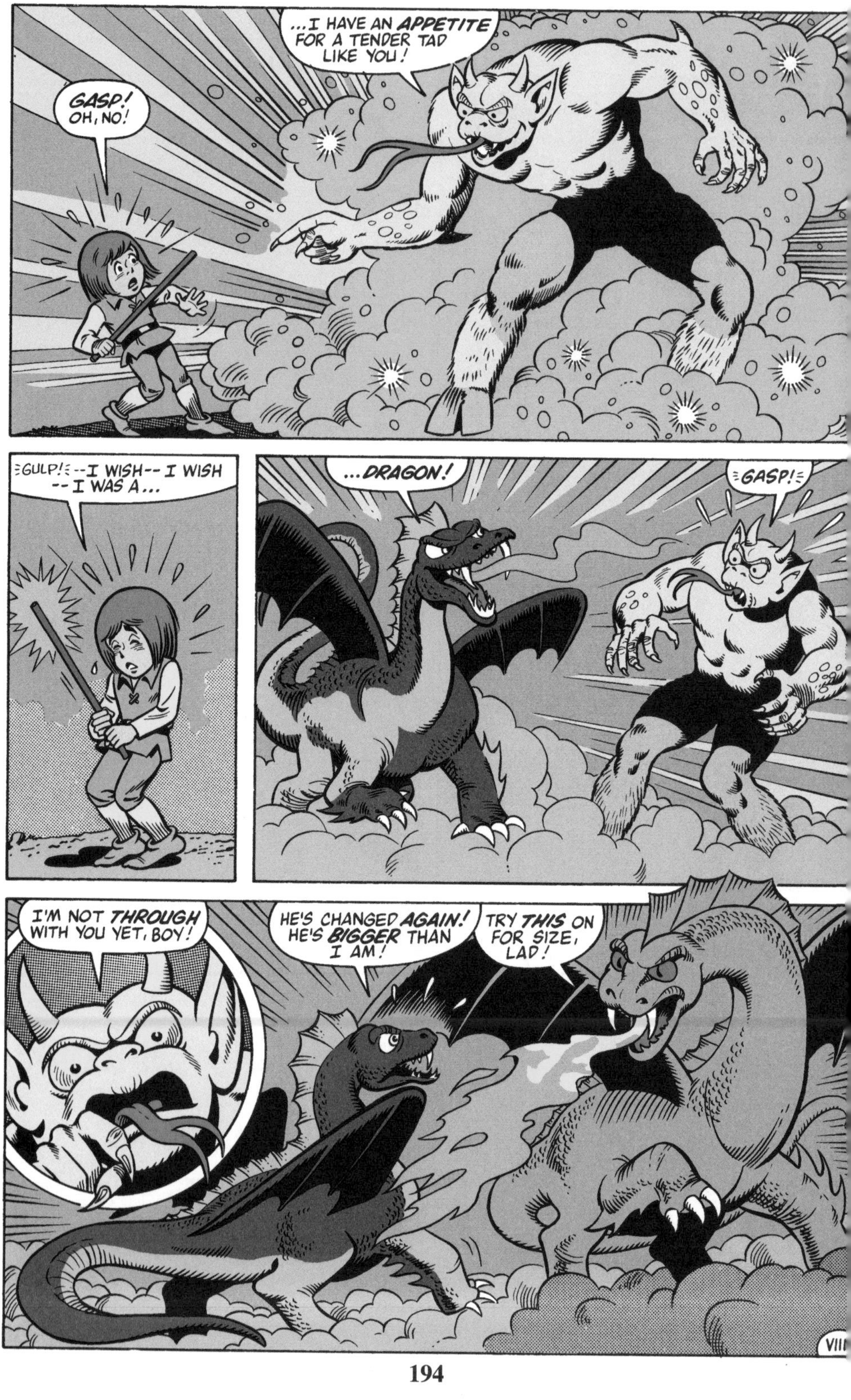
...I HAVE AN APPETITE FOR A TENDER TAD LIKE YOU!
GASP! OH, NO!
GULP! --I WISH-- I WISH --I WAS A...
...DRAGON!
GASP!
I'M NOT THROUGH WITH YOU YET, BOY!
HE'S CHANGED AGAIN! HE'S BIGGER THAN I AM!
TRY THIS ON FOR SIZE, LAD!
VIII

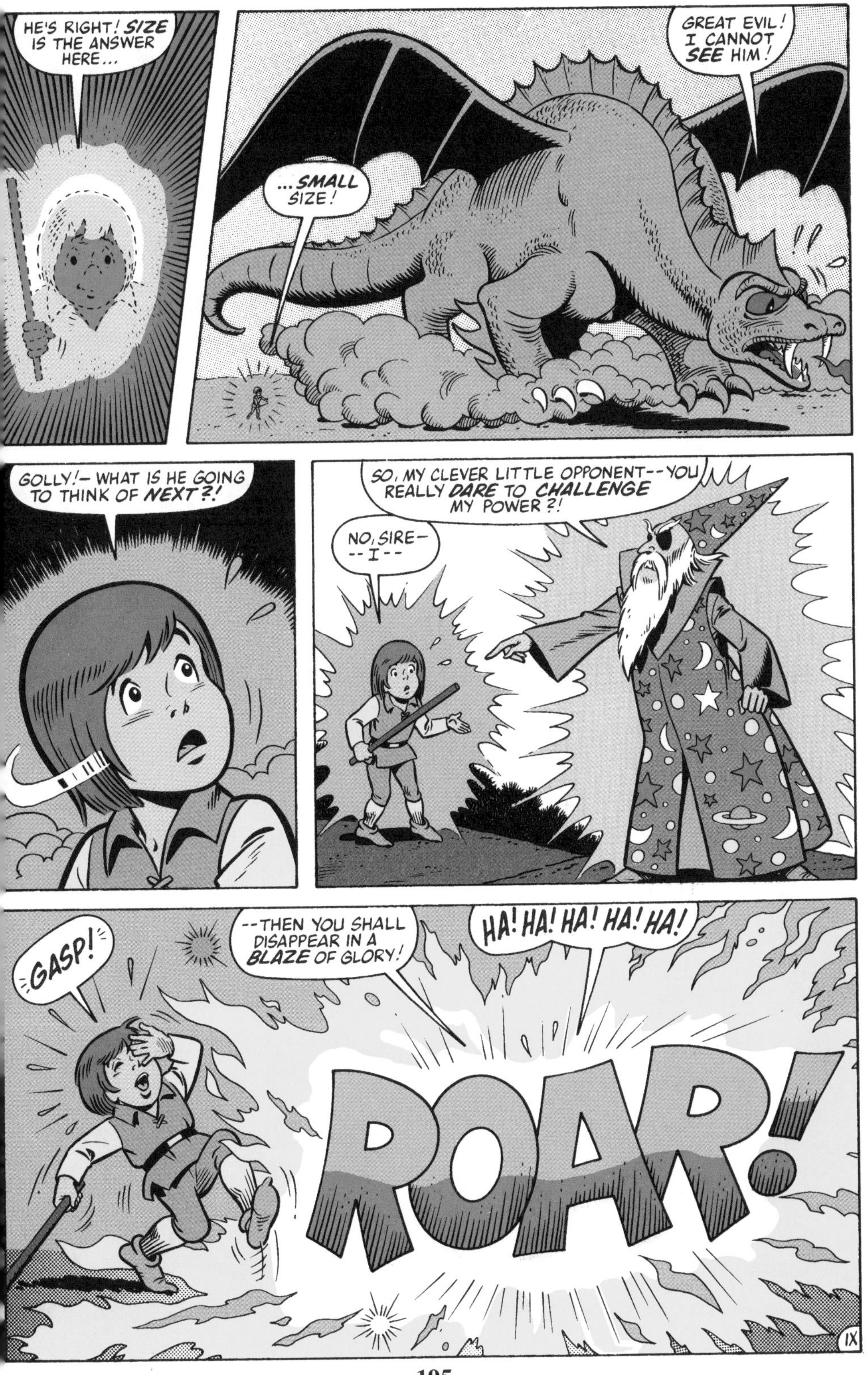

HE'S RIGHT! SIZE IS THE ANSWER HERE...
GREAT EVIL! I CANNOT SEE HIM!
...SMALL SIZE!
GOLLY!– WHAT IS HE GOING TO THINK OF NEXT?!
SO, MY CLEVER LITTLE OPPONENT--YOU REALLY DARE TO CHALLENGE MY POWER?!
NO, SIRE– --I--
GASP!
--THEN YOU SHALL DISAPPEAR IN A BLAZE OF GLORY!
HA! HA! HA! HA! HA!
ROAR!
IX

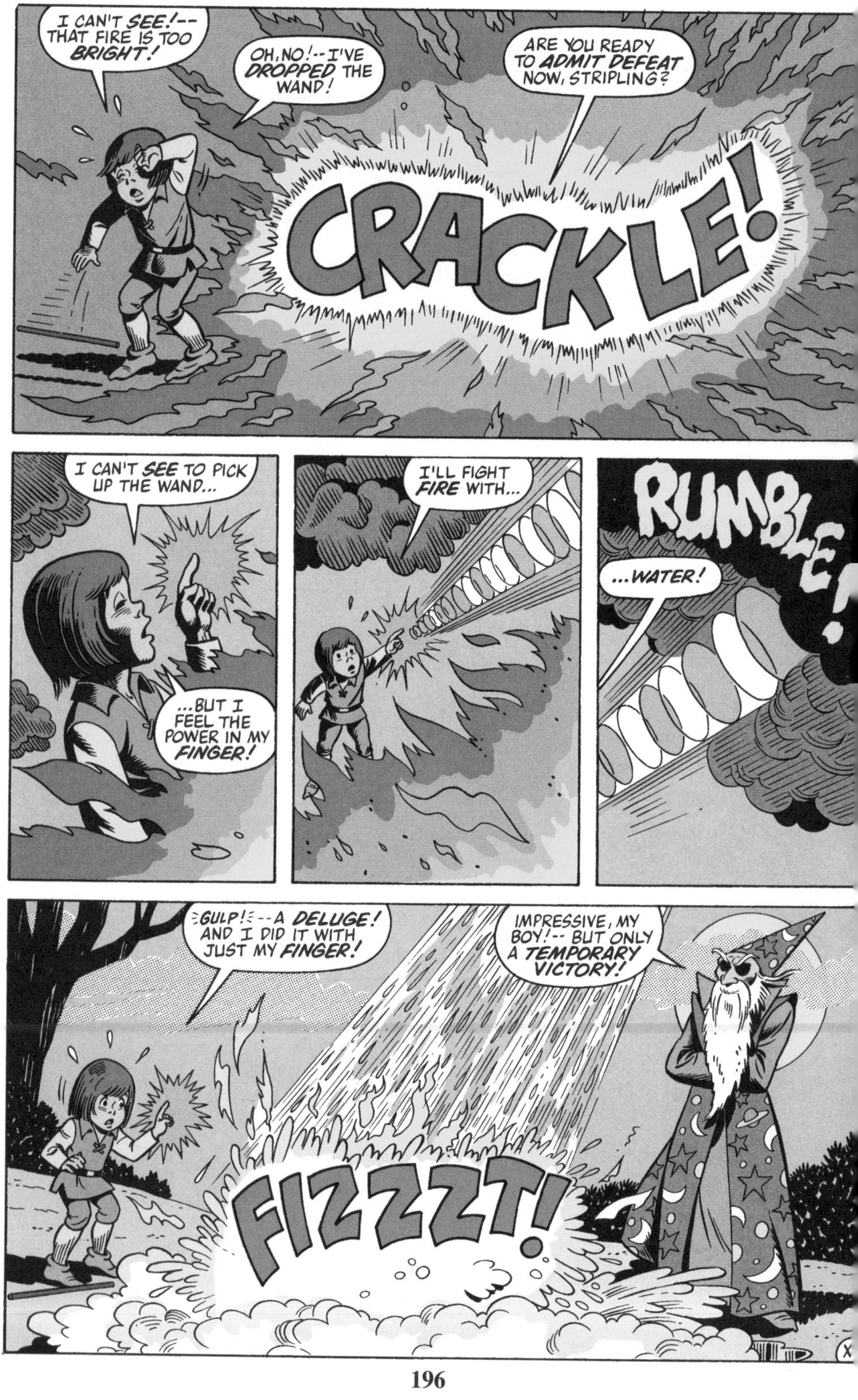

I CAN'T SEE!-- THAT FIRE IS TOO BRIGHT!
OH, NO!--I'VE DROPPED THE WAND!
ARE YOU READY TO ADMIT DEFEAT NOW, STRIPLING?
CRACKLE!
I CAN'T SEE TO PICK UP THE WAND...
...BUT I FEEL THE POWER IN MY FINGER!
I'LL FIGHT FIRE WITH...
RUMBLE!
...WATER!
GULP!--A DELUGE! AND I DID IT WITH JUST MY FINGER!
IMPRESSIVE, MY BOY!-- BUT ONLY A TEMPORARY VICTORY!
FIZZZT!

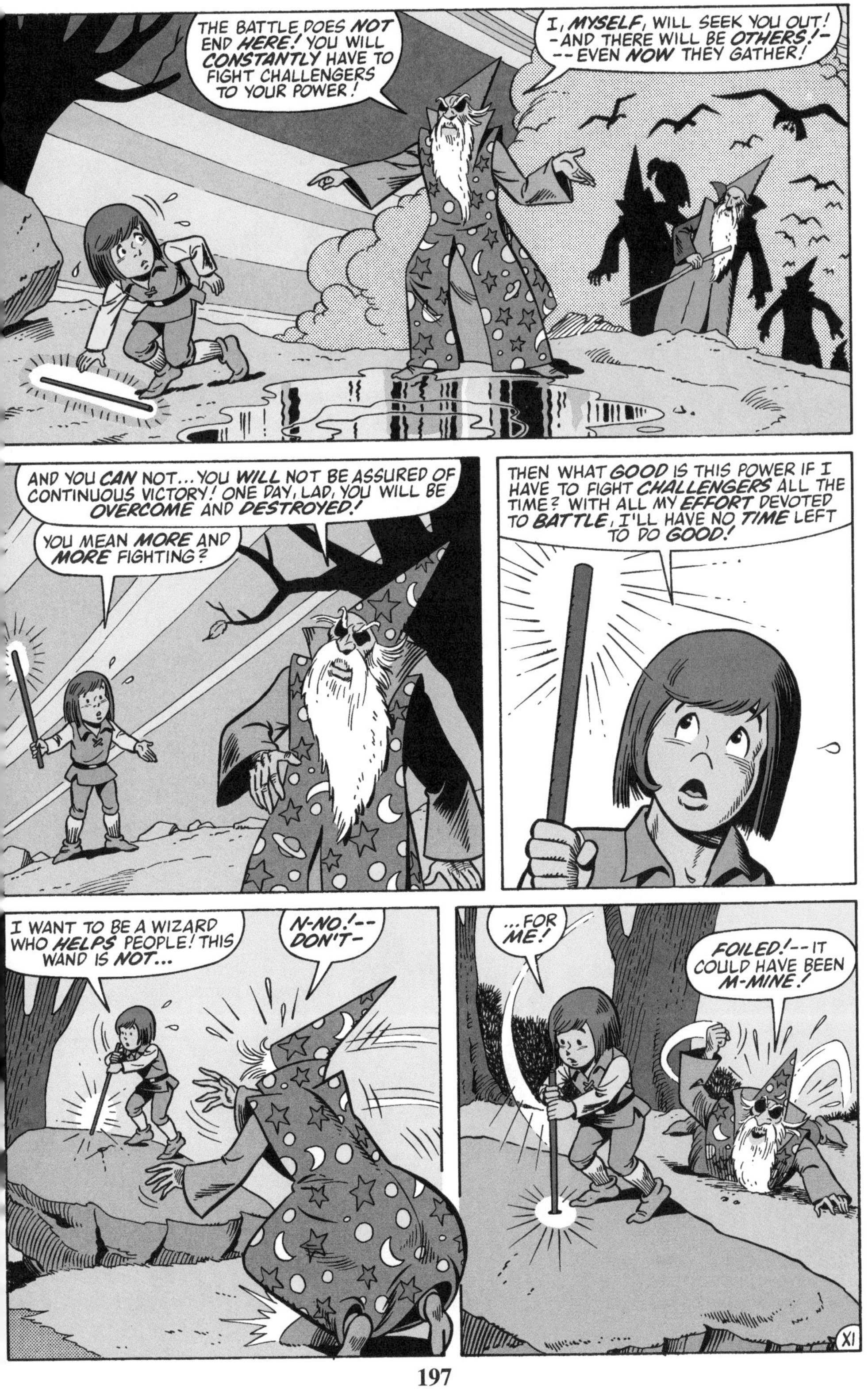
THE BATTLE DOES NOT END HERE! YOU WILL CONSTANTLY HAVE TO FIGHT CHALLENGERS TO YOUR POWER!
I, MYSELF, WILL SEEK YOU OUT! -AND THERE WILL BE OTHERS!- --EVEN NOW THEY GATHER!
AND YOU CAN NOT... YOU WILL NOT BE ASSURED OF CONTINUOUS VICTORY! ONE DAY, LAD, YOU WILL BE OVERCOME AND DESTROYED!
YOU MEAN MORE AND MORE FIGHTING?
THEN WHAT GOOD IS THIS POWER IF I HAVE TO FIGHT CHALLENGERS ALL THE TIME? WITH ALL MY EFFORT DEVOTED TO BATTLE, I'LL HAVE NO TIME LEFT TO DO GOOD!
I WANT TO BE A WIZARD WHO HELPS PEOPLE! THIS WAND IS NOT...
N-NO!-- DON'T-
...FOR ME!
FOILED!--IT COULD HAVE BEEN M-MINE!
XI

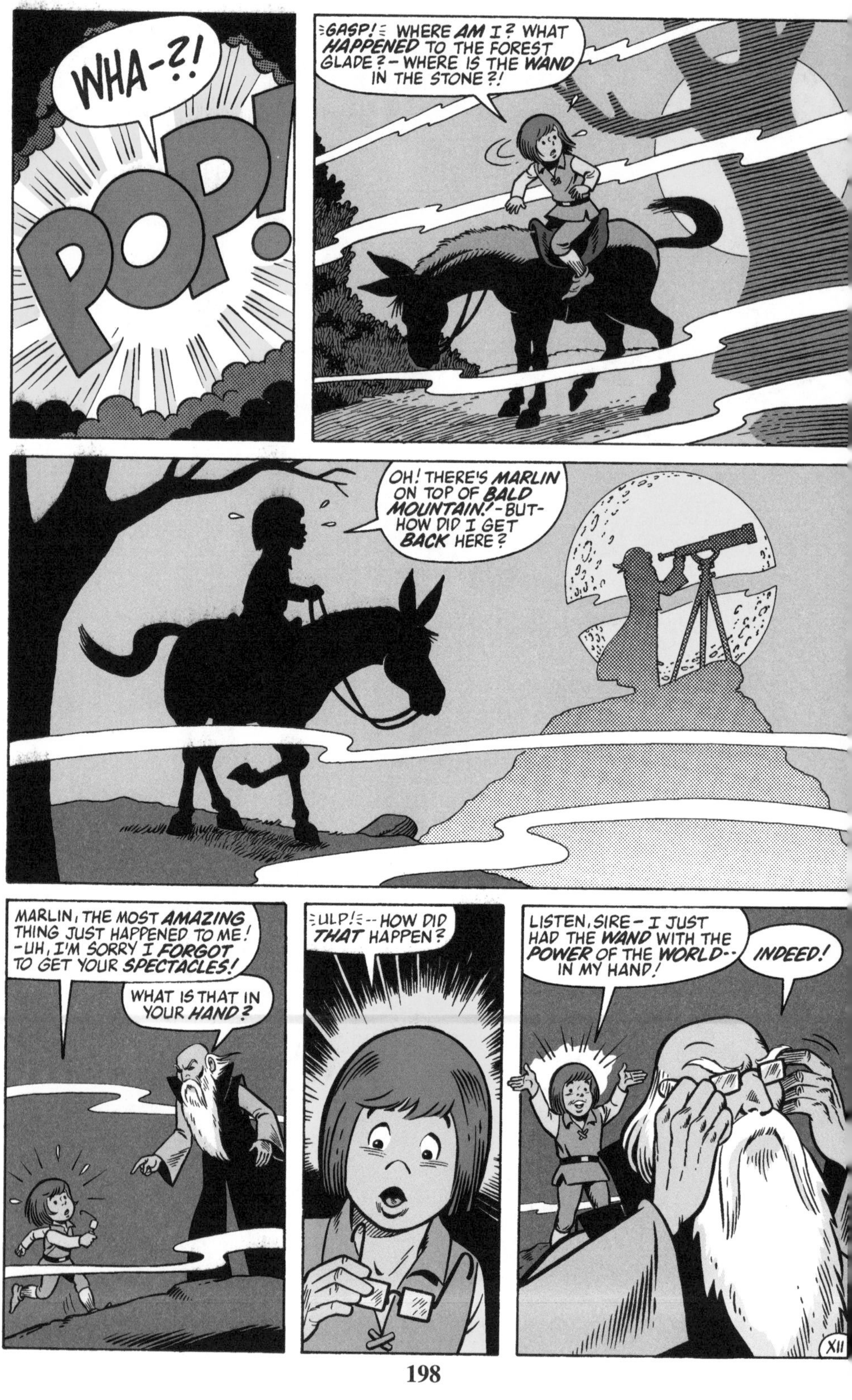
WHA-?!
POP!
=GASP!= WHERE AM I? WHAT HAPPENED TO THE FOREST GLADE?-WHERE IS THE WAND IN THE STONE?!
OH! THERE'S MARLIN ON TOP OF BALD MOUNTAIN!-BUT-HOW DID I GET BACK HERE?
MARLIN, THE MOST AMAZING THING JUST HAPPENED TO ME! -UH, I'M SORRY I FORGOT TO GET YOUR SPECTACLES!
WHAT IS THAT IN YOUR HAND?
=ULP!=--HOW DID THAT HAPPEN?
LISTEN, SIRE-I JUST HAD THE WAND WITH THE POWER OF THE WORLD--IN MY HAND!
INDEED!
XII

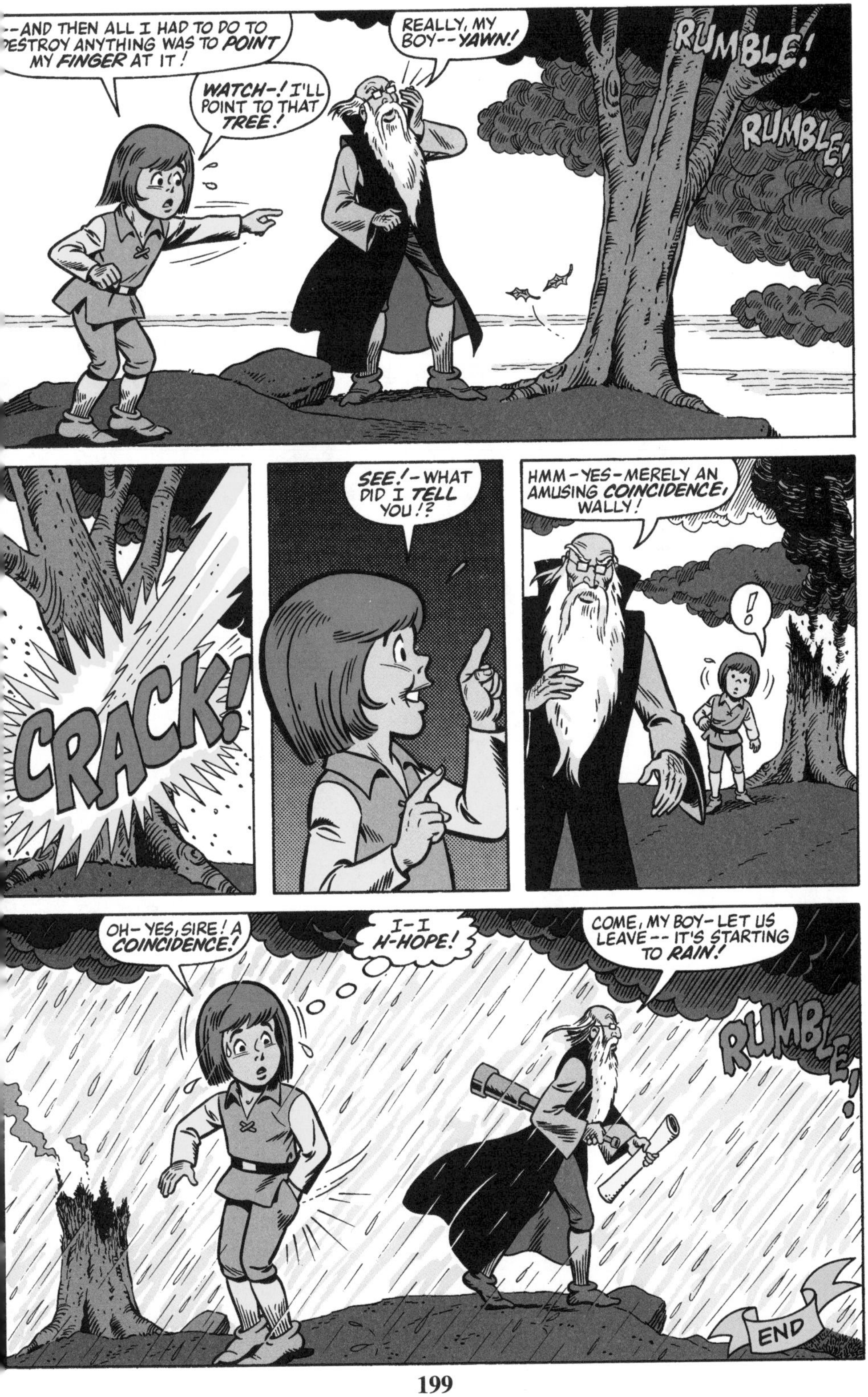
--AND THEN ALL I HAD TO DO TO DESTROY ANYTHING WAS TO POINT MY FINGER AT IT!
WATCH-! I'LL POINT TO THAT TREE!
REALLY, MY BOY--YAWN!
RUMBLE!
RUMBLE!
CRACK!
SEE!-WHAT DID I TELL YOU!?
HMM-YES-MERELY AN AMUSING COINCIDENCE, WALLY!
!
OH-YES, SIRE! A COINCIDENCE!
I-I H-HOPE!
COME, MY BOY-LET US LEAVE--IT'S STARTING TO RAIN!
RUMBLE!
END

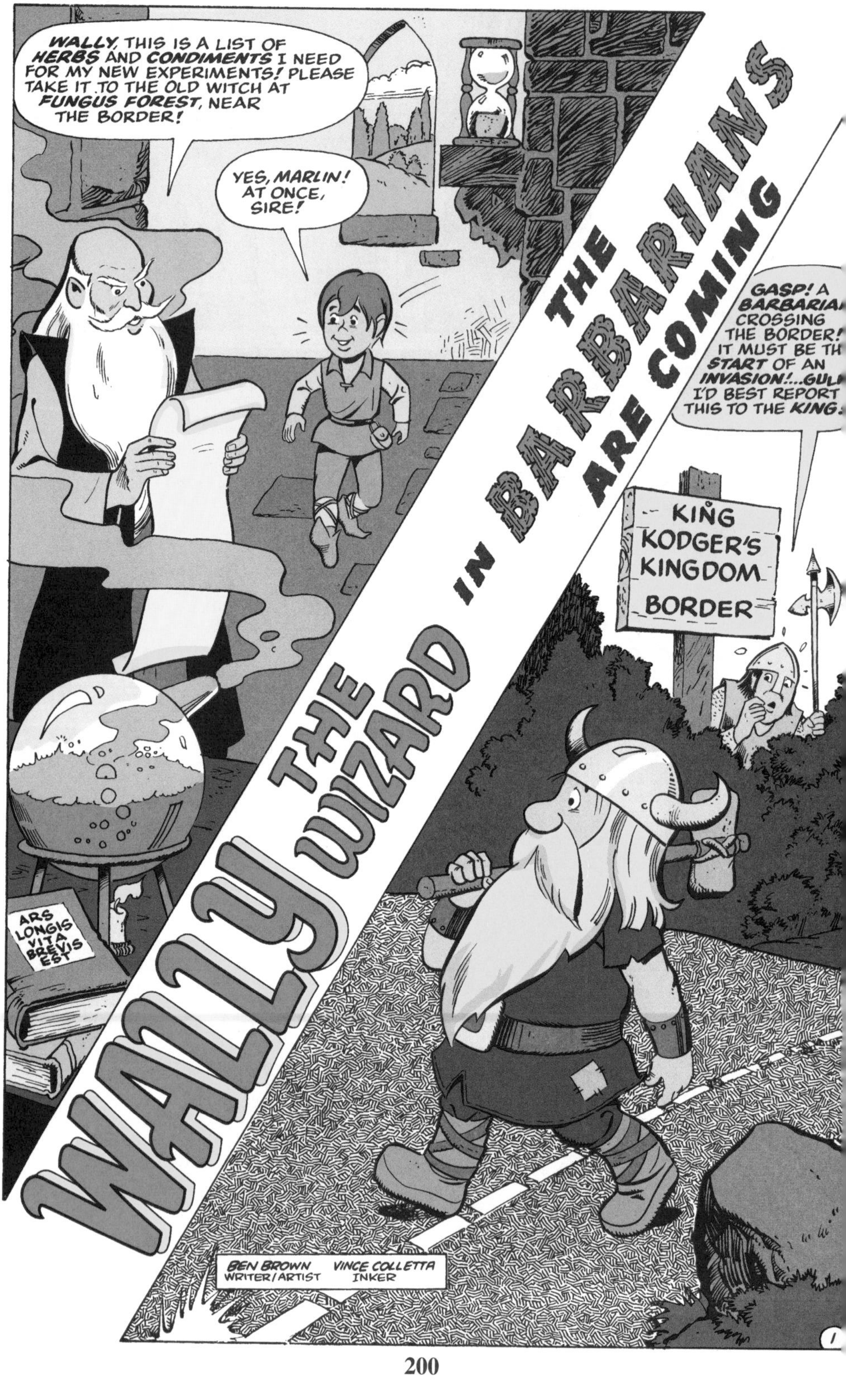
WALLY, THIS IS A LIST OF HERBS AND CONDIMENTS I NEED FOR MY NEW EXPERIMENTS! PLEASE TAKE IT TO THE OLD WITCH AT FUNGUS FOREST, NEAR THE BORDER!
YES, MARLIN! AT ONCE, SIRE!
WALLY THE WIZARD
IN THE BARBARIANS ARE COMING
ARS LONGIS VITA BREVIS EST
GASP! A BARBARIA CROSSING THE BORDER! IT MUST BE TH START OF AN INVASION!...GUL I'D BEST REPORT THIS TO THE KING.
KING KODGER'S KINGDOM BORDER
BEN BROWN WRITER/ARTIST
VINCE COLLETTA INKER
1

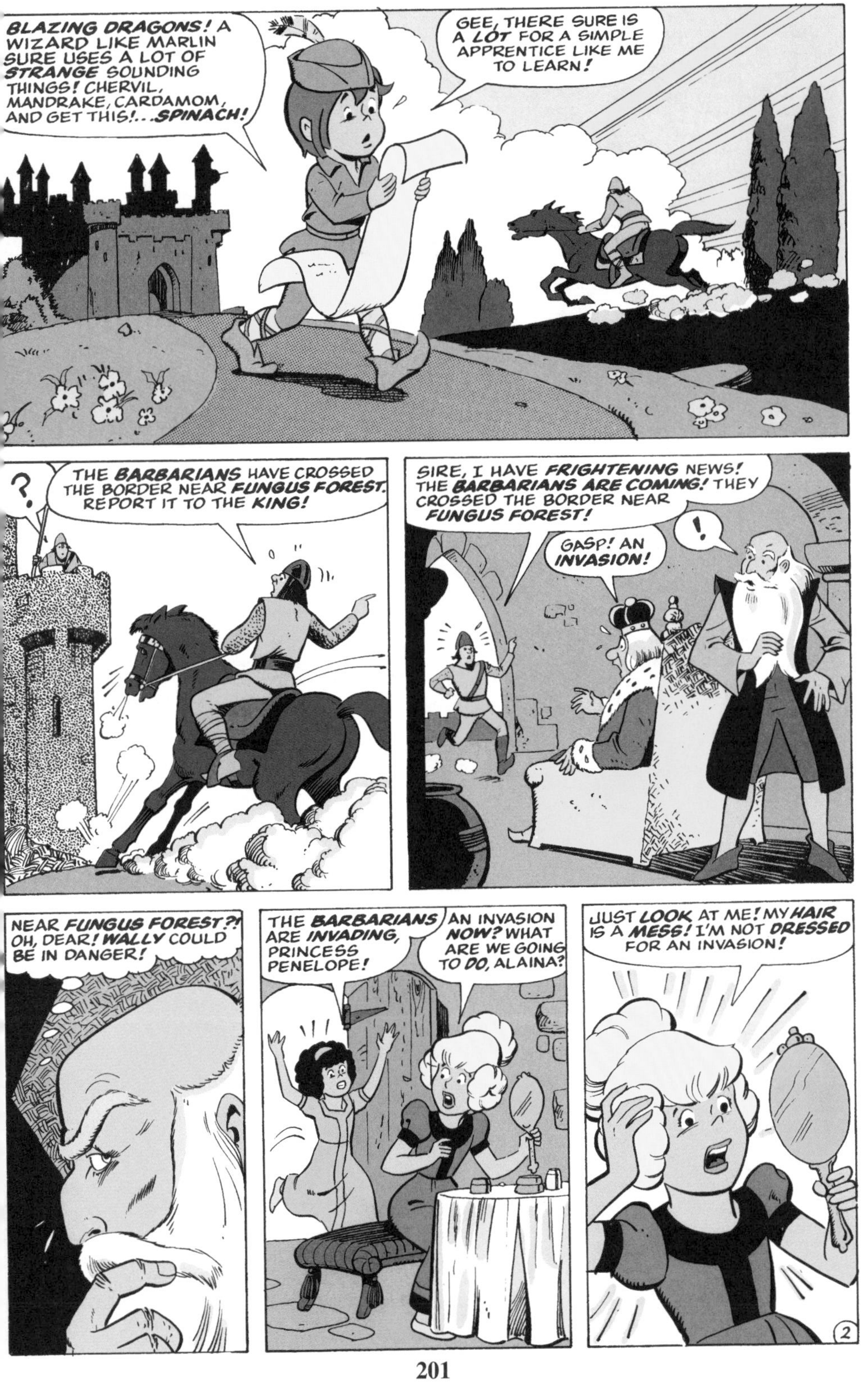
BLAZING DRAGONS! A WIZARD LIKE MARLIN SURE USES A LOT OF STRANGE SOUNDING THINGS! CHERVIL, MANDRAKE, CARDAMOM, AND GET THIS!...SPINACH!
GEE, THERE SURE IS A LOT FOR A SIMPLE APPRENTICE LIKE ME TO LEARN!
?
THE BARBARIANS HAVE CROSSED THE BORDER NEAR FUNGUS FOREST. REPORT IT TO THE KING!
SIRE, I HAVE FRIGHTENING NEWS! THE BARBARIANS ARE COMING! THEY CROSSED THE BORDER NEAR FUNGUS FOREST!
GASP! AN INVASION!
!
NEAR FUNGUS FOREST?! OH, DEAR! WALLY COULD BE IN DANGER!
THE BARBARIANS ARE INVADING, PRINCESS PENELOPE!
AN INVASION NOW? WHAT ARE WE GOING TO DO, ALAINA?
JUST LOOK AT ME! MY HAIR IS A MESS! I'M NOT DRESSED FOR AN INVASION!
2

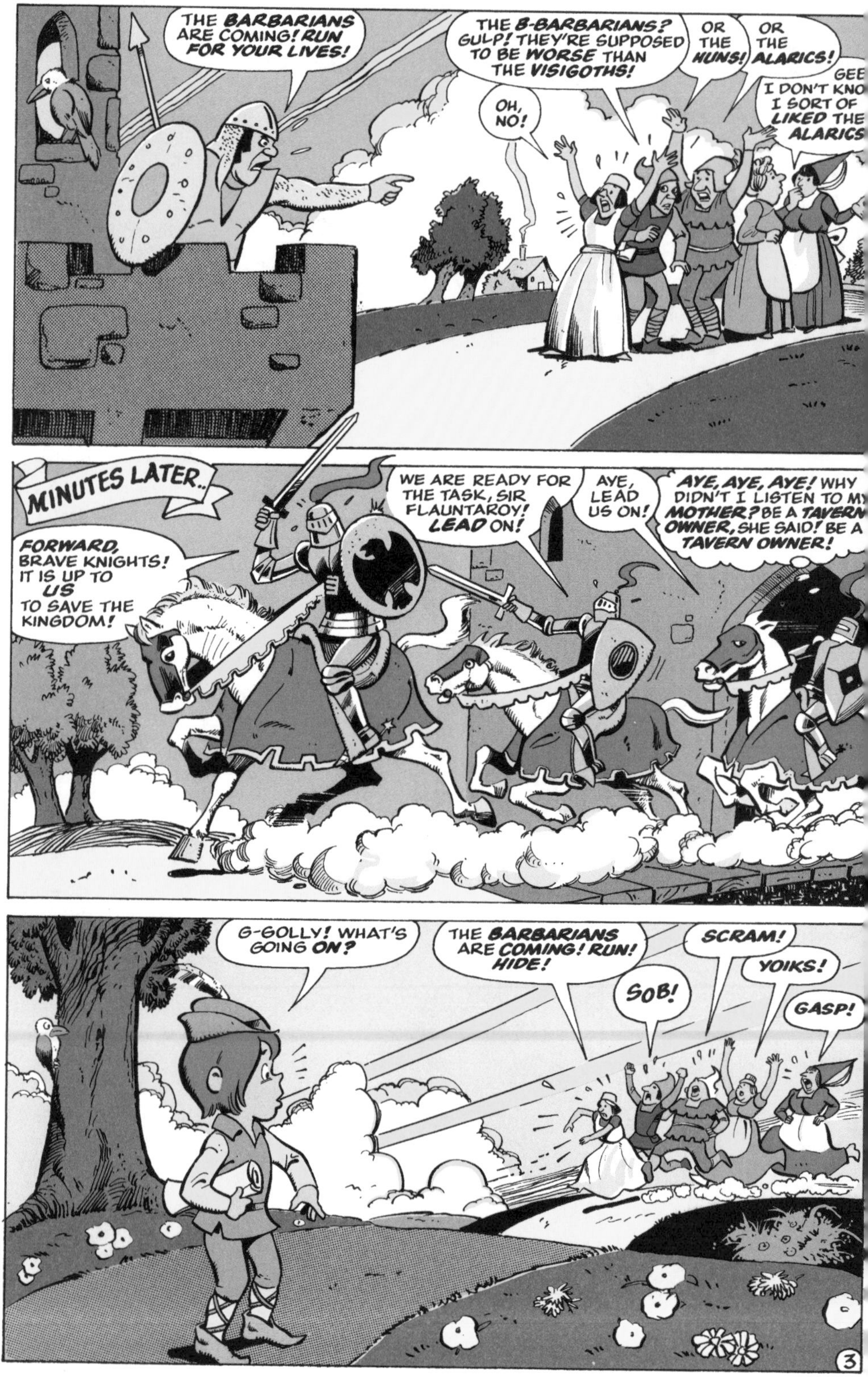

THE BARBARIANS ARE COMING! RUN FOR YOUR LIVES!
THE B-BARBARIANS? GULP! THEY'RE SUPPOSED TO BE WORSE THAN THE VISIGOTHS!
OH, NO!
OR THE HUNS!
OR THE ALARICS!
GEE I DON'T KNO I SORT OF LIKED THE ALARICS
MINUTES LATER..
FORWARD, BRAVE KNIGHTS! IT IS UP TO US TO SAVE THE KINGDOM!
WE ARE READY FOR THE TASK, SIR FLAUNTAROY! LEAD ON!
AYE, LEAD US ON!
AYE, AYE, AYE! WHY DIDN'T I LISTEN TO MY MOTHER? BE A TAVERN OWNER, SHE SAID! BE A TAVERN OWNER!
G-GOLLY! WHAT'S GOING ON?
THE BARBARIANS ARE COMING! RUN! HIDE!
SOB!
SCRAM!
YOIKS!
GASP!
3

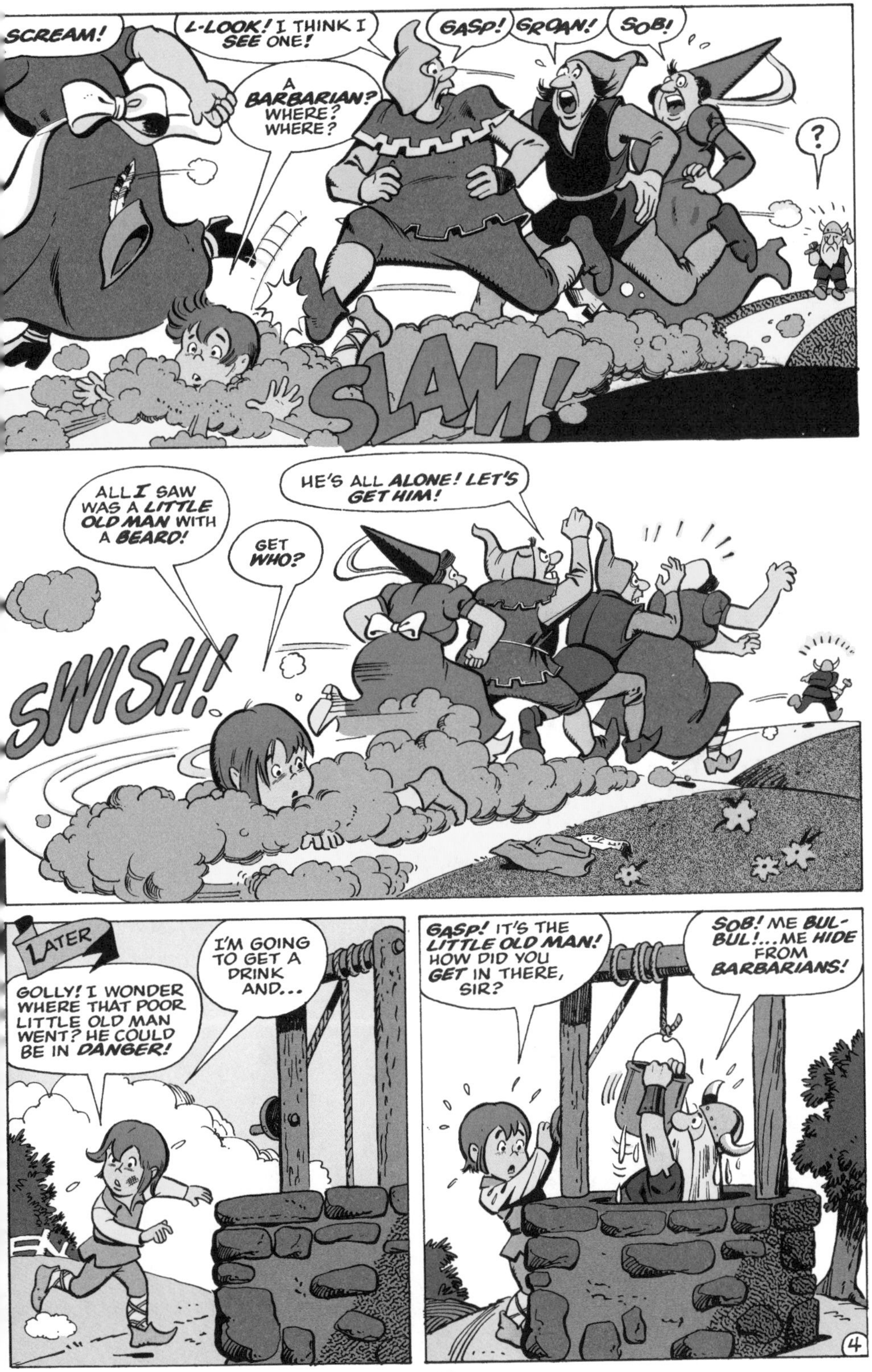

SCREAM!
L-LOOK! I THINK I SEE ONE!
A BARBARIAN? WHERE? WHERE?
GASP!
GROAN!
SOB!
?
SLAM!
ALL I SAW WAS A LITTLE OLD MAN WITH A BEARD!
GET WHO?
HE'S ALL ALONE! LET'S GET HIM!
SWISH!
LATER
GOLLY! I WONDER WHERE THAT POOR LITTLE OLD MAN WENT? HE COULD BE IN DANGER!
I'M GOING TO GET A DRINK AND...
GASP! IT'S THE LITTLE OLD MAN! HOW DID YOU GET IN THERE, SIR?
SOB! ME BUL-BUL!...ME HIDE FROM BARBARIANS!
4

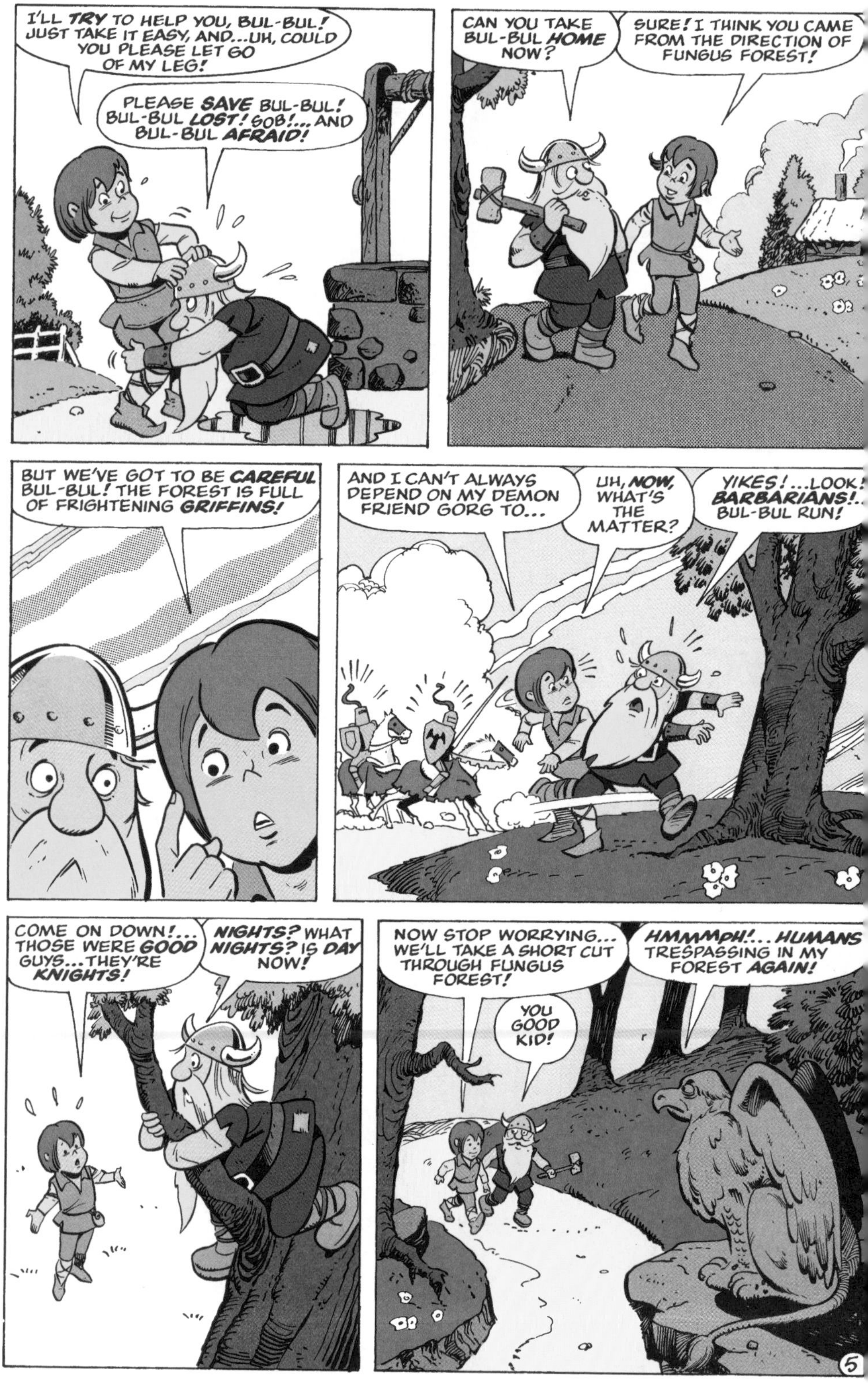
I'LL TRY TO HELP YOU, BUL-BUL! JUST TAKE IT EASY, AND...UH, COULD YOU PLEASE LET GO OF MY LEG!
PLEASE SAVE BUL-BUL! BUL-BUL LOST! SOB!... AND BUL-BUL AFRAID!
CAN YOU TAKE BUL-BUL HOME NOW?
SURE! I THINK YOU CAME FROM THE DIRECTION OF FUNGUS FOREST!
BUT WE'VE GOT TO BE CAREFUL BUL-BUL! THE FOREST IS FULL OF FRIGHTENING GRIFFINS!
AND I CAN'T ALWAYS DEPEND ON MY DEMON FRIEND GORG TO...
UH, NOW, WHAT'S THE MATTER?
YIKES! ...LOOK! BARBARIANS!.. BUL-BUL RUN!
COME ON DOWN!... THOSE WERE GOOD GUYS...THEY'RE KNIGHTS!
NIGHTS? WHAT NIGHTS? IS DAY NOW!
NOW STOP WORRYING... WE'LL TAKE A SHORT CUT THROUGH FUNGUS FOREST!
YOU GOOD KID!
HMMMPH!... HUMANS TRESPASSING IN MY FOREST AGAIN!
5

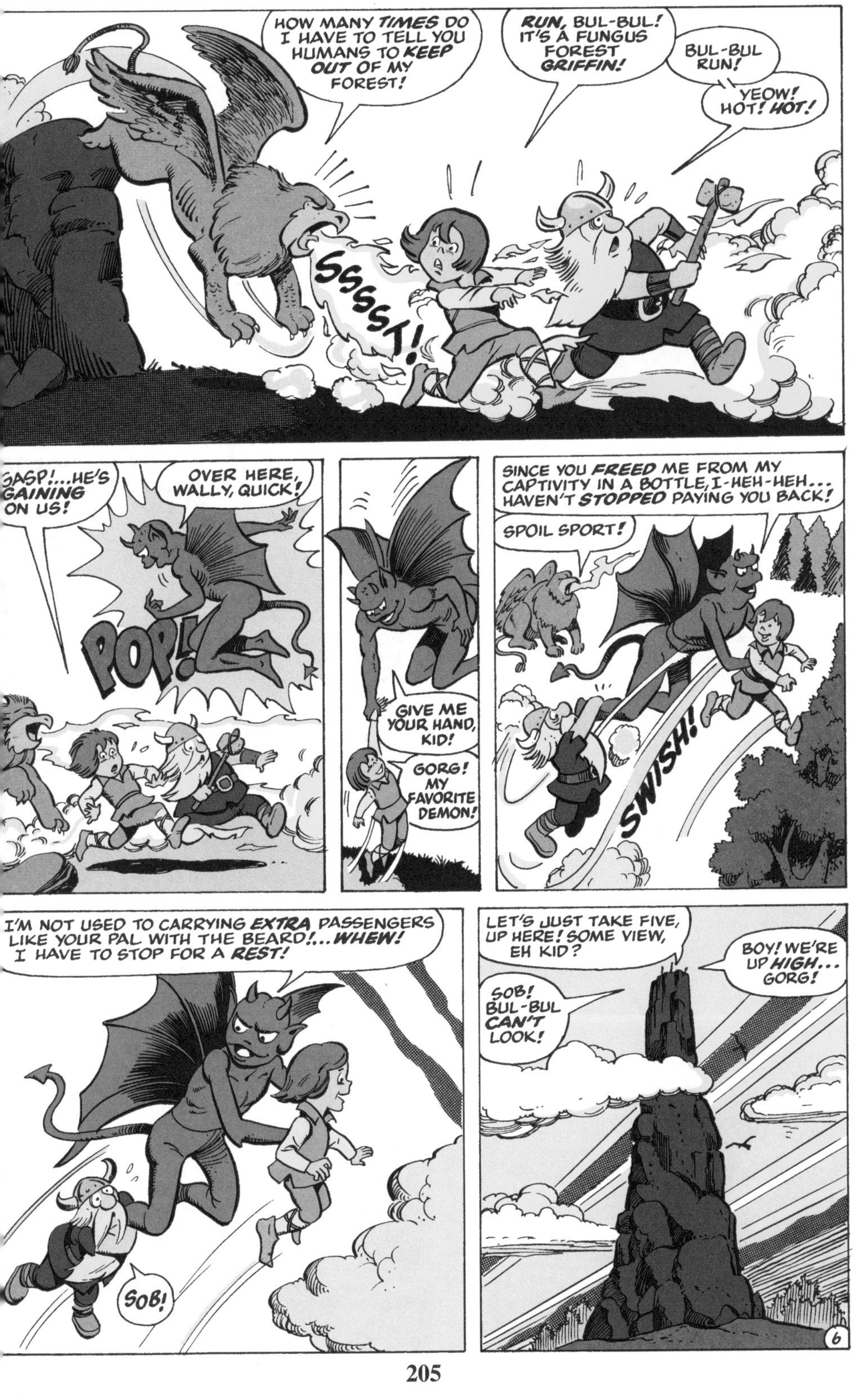
HOW MANY TIMES DO I HAVE TO TELL YOU HUMANS TO KEEP OUT OF MY FOREST!
RUN, BUL-BUL! IT'S A FUNGUS FOREST GRIFFIN!
BUL-BUL RUN!
YEOW! HOT! HOT!
SSSSST!
GASP!...HE'S GAINING ON US!
OVER HERE, WALLY, QUICK!
POP!
GIVE ME YOUR HAND, KID!
GORG! MY FAVORITE DEMON!
SINCE YOU FREED ME FROM MY CAPTIVITY IN A BOTTLE, I-HEH-HEH... HAVEN'T STOPPED PAYING YOU BACK!
SPOIL SPORT!
SWISH!
I'M NOT USED TO CARRYING EXTRA PASSENGERS LIKE YOUR PAL WITH THE BEARD!...WHEW! I HAVE TO STOP FOR A REST!
SOB!
LET'S JUST TAKE FIVE, UP HERE! SOME VIEW, EH KID?
BOY! WE'RE UP HIGH... GORG!
SOB! BUL-BUL CAN'T LOOK!
6

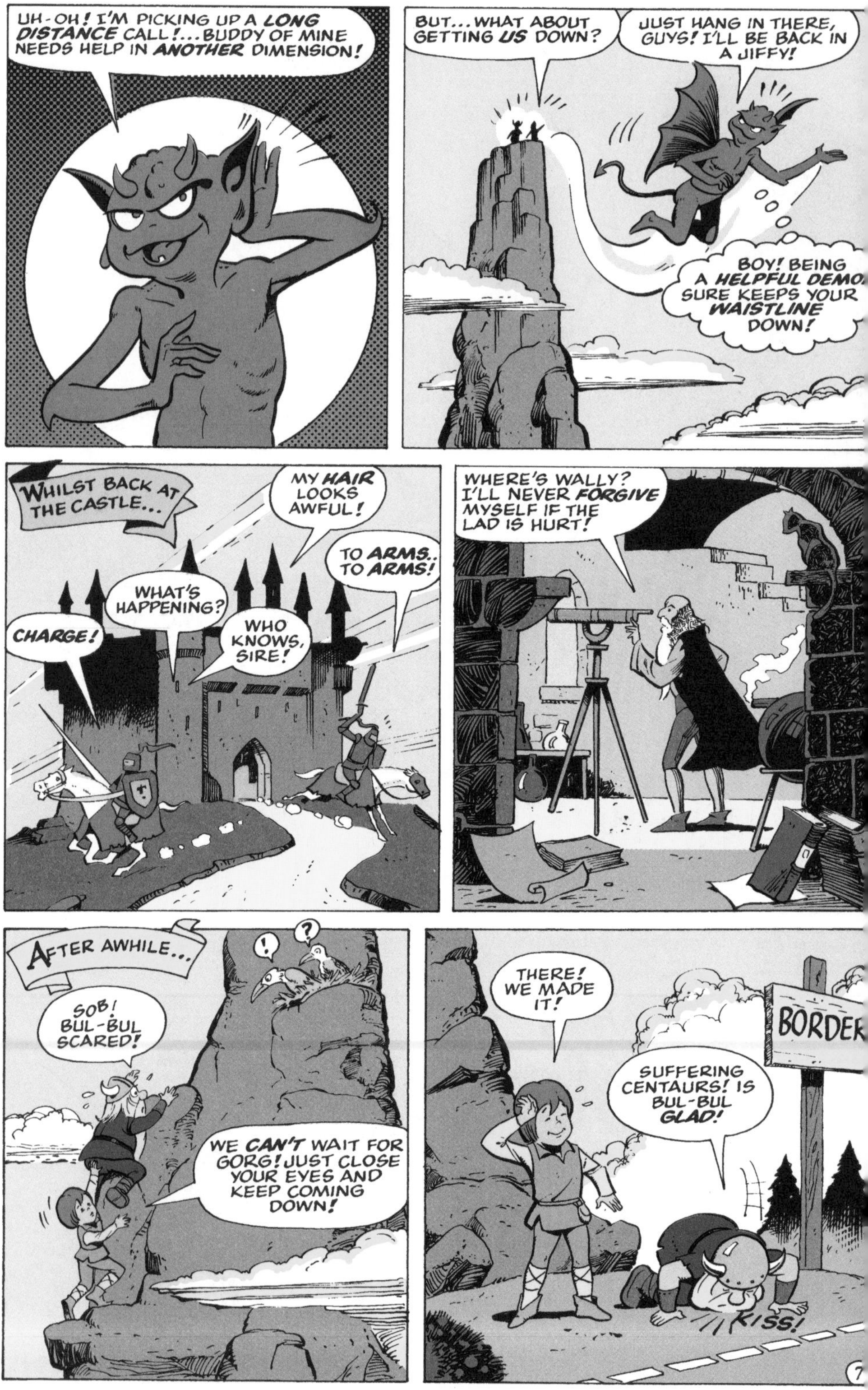
UH-OH! I'M PICKING UP A LONG DISTANCE CALL!... BUDDY OF MINE NEEDS HELP IN ANOTHER DIMENSION!
BUT... WHAT ABOUT GETTING US DOWN?
JUST HANG IN THERE, GUYS! I'LL BE BACK IN A JIFFY!
BOY! BEING A HELPFUL DEMO
SURE KEEPS YOUR WAISTLINE DOWN!
WHILST BACK AT THE CASTLE...
MY HAIR LOOKS AWFUL!
TO ARMS.. TO ARMS!
WHAT'S HAPPENING?
CHARGE!
WHO KNOWS, SIRE!
WHERE'S WALLY? I'LL NEVER FORGIVE MYSELF IF THE LAD IS HURT!
AFTER AWHILE...
!
?
SOB! BUL-BUL SCARED!
WE CAN'T WAIT FOR GORG! JUST CLOSE YOUR EYES AND KEEP COMING DOWN!
THERE! WE MADE IT!
BORDER
SUFFERING CENTAURS! IS BUL-BUL GLAD!
KISS!
7

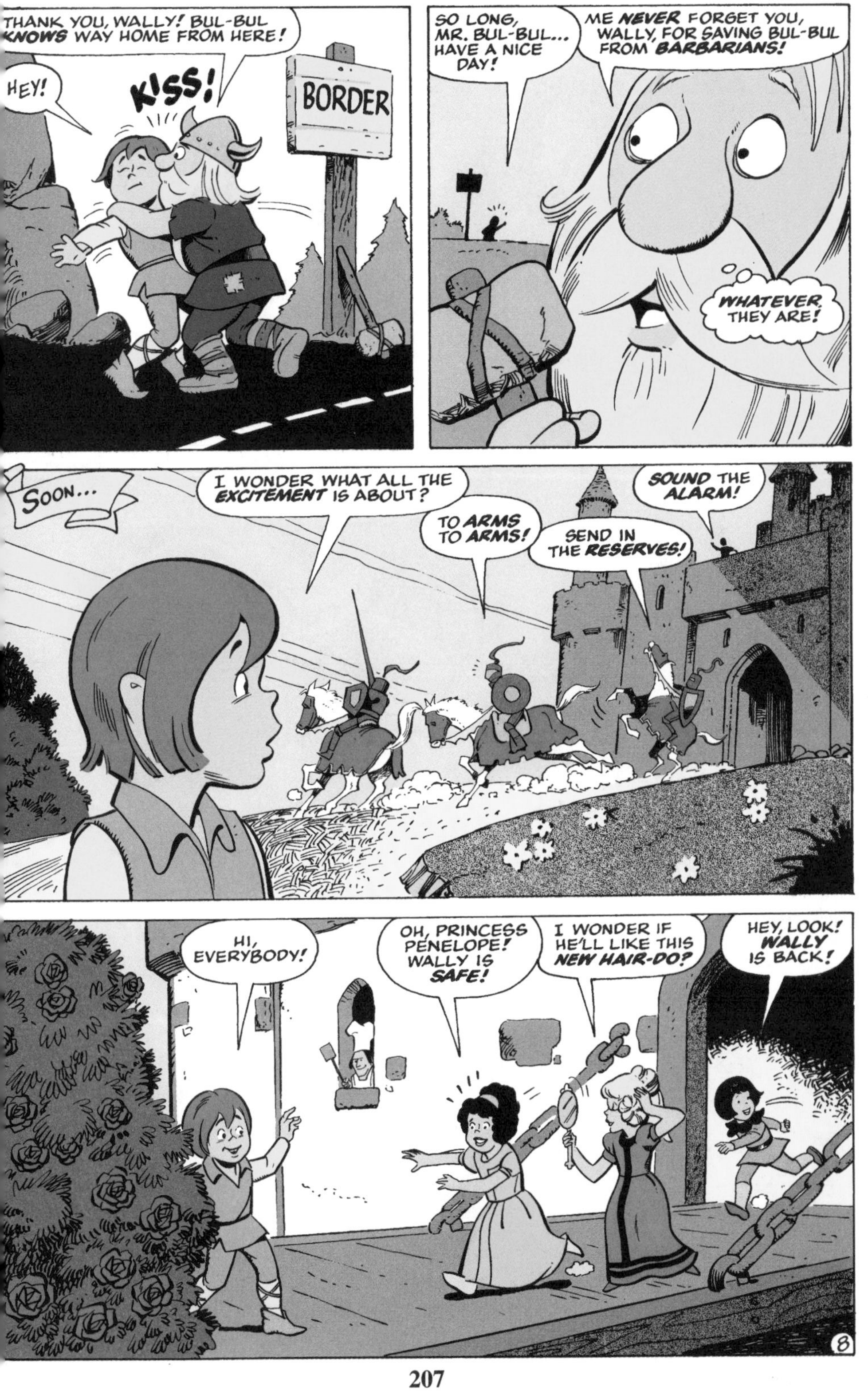

THANK YOU, WALLY! BUL-BUL KNOWS WAY HOME FROM HERE!
HEY!
KISS!
BORDER
SO LONG, MR. BUL-BUL... HAVE A NICE DAY!
ME NEVER FORGET YOU, WALLY, FOR SAVING BUL-BUL FROM BARBARIANS!
WHATEVER THEY ARE!
SOON...
I WONDER WHAT ALL THE EXCITEMENT IS ABOUT?
TO ARMS TO ARMS!
SEND IN THE RESERVES!
SOUND THE ALARM!
HI, EVERYBODY!
OH, PRINCESS PENELOPE! WALLY IS SAFE!
I WONDER IF HE'LL LIKE THIS NEW HAIR-DO?
HEY, LOOK! WALLY IS BACK!
8

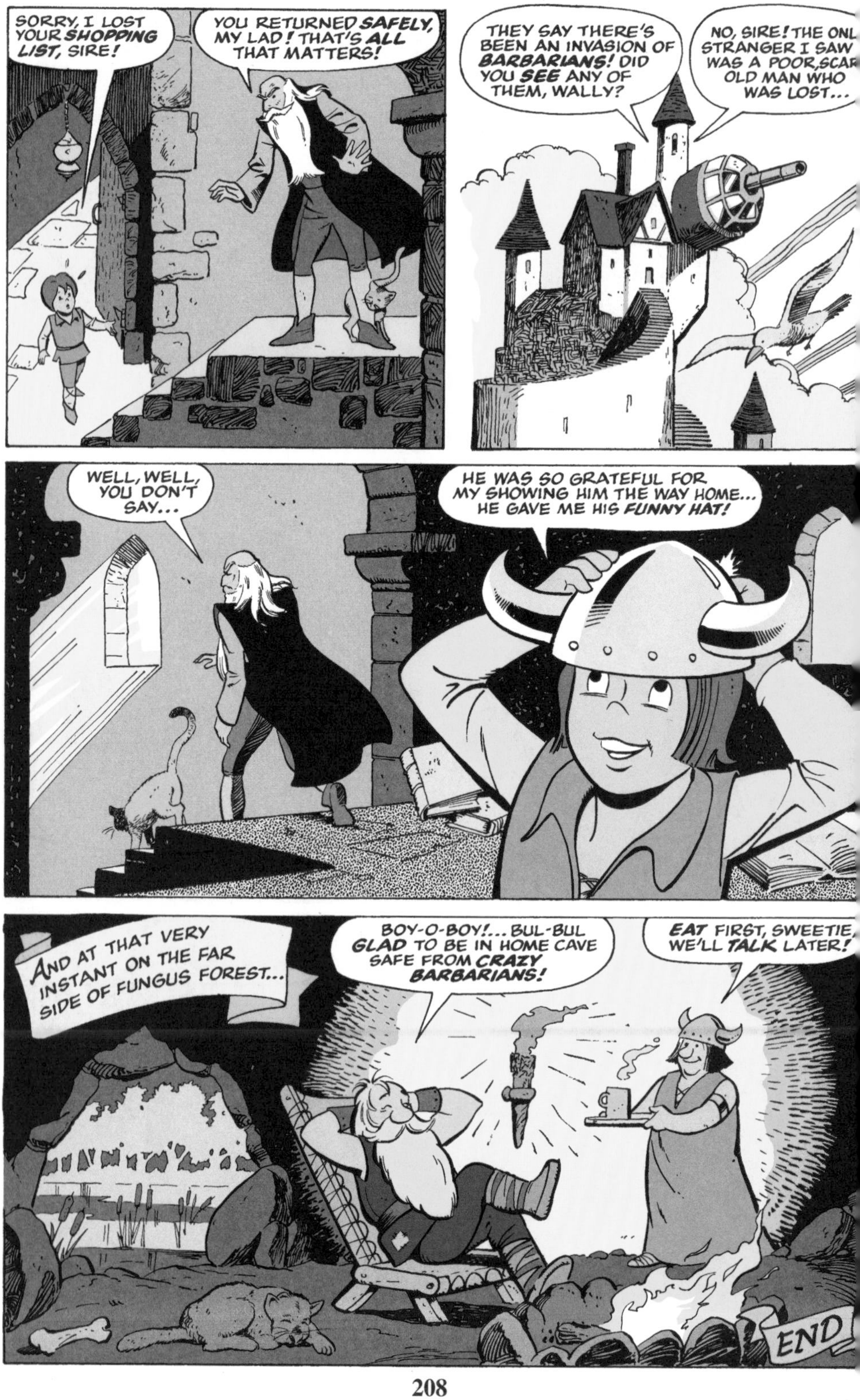
SORRY, I LOST YOUR SHOPPING LIST, SIRE!
YOU RETURNED SAFELY, MY LAD! THAT'S ALL THAT MATTERS!
THEY SAY THERE'S BEEN AN INVASION OF BARBARIANS! DID YOU SEE ANY OF THEM, WALLY?
NO, SIRE! THE ONL STRANGER I SAW WAS A POOR, SCAR OLD MAN WHO WAS LOST...
WELL, WELL, YOU DON'T SAY...
HE WAS SO GRATEFUL FOR MY SHOWING HIM THE WAY HOME... HE GAVE ME HIS FUNNY HAT!
AND AT THAT VERY INSTANT ON THE FAR SIDE OF FUNGUS FOREST...
BOY-O-BOY!... BUL-BUL GLAD TO BE IN HOME CAVE SAFE FROM CRAZY BARBARIANS!
EAT FIRST, SWEETIE, WE'LL TALK LATER!
END